CRIMINAL ANNALS;

OR,

The New Newgate Calendar;

EMBRACING THE

LIVES AND ACTIONS

OF THE

MOST NOTORIOUS CHARACTERS

WHO HAVE OFFENDED AGAINST THE LAWS OF THEIR COUNTRY,

From the Earliest Period to the Present Time.

By JAMES ROBERTSON, Esq.

" VICE IS A MONSTER OF SUCH HIDEOUS MIEN,
THAT, TO BE HATED, NEEDS BUT TO BE SEEN."—POPE.

EMBELLISHED WITH THIRTY-THREE ENGRAVINGS.

LONDON:

R. MACDONALD, 30, GREAT SUTTON STREET,
CLERKENWELL.

R. MACDONALD,
Printer.
GREAT SUTTON STREET, CLERKENWELL.

LIST OF ILLUSTRATIONS.

CLAUDE DU VALL.

HANGED FOR VARIOUS ROBBERIES.

This noted highwayman was born at Damfont, in Normandy. His father was a miller; and his mother, the daughter of a tailor. He was brought up in the Catholic faith, and received a tolerably good education. But, though his father was careful to train up his son in the religion of his ancestors, he was utterly without religion himself. He talked more of good cheer than of the church; of sumptuous feasts than of ardent faith; of good wine than of good works. One time old Du Vall was seized with a severe illness, and strong hopes were entertained that he would die a natural death. In this extreme necessity, a ghostly father visited him with his *Corpus Domini*, informing him, that having heard of his dangerous situation, he had brought his Saviour to comfort him in his last moments. Old Du Vall drawing aside the curtains, and beholding a goodly fat friar, with the host in his hand, " I know now," said he, " that it is our Saviour, because he comes to me in the same manner that he went to Jerusalem,—it is an *ass* that carries him."

Du Vall's parents were soon exempted from the trouble and expense of rearing their son. At the age of thirteen, we find him at Rouen, the principal city of Normandy, in the character of a stable boy. Here he fortunately found return horses going to Paris: upon one of

1   B

these he was permitted to ride, on condition of assisting to dress them at night. His expences were likewise defrayed by some English travellers who were going to the same place.

Arrived at Paris, he remained at the same inn where the Englishmen put up, and subsisted for a while, by running on messages, and performing the meanest offices. He continued in this humble station until the restoration of Charles II., when multitudes from the continent resorted to England. In the character of a footman to a person of quality, Du Vall also repaired to England. The universal joy which seized the nation upon that event contaminated the morals of all: riot, dissipation, and every species of profligacy, abounded. The young French footman entered keenly into these amusements. His funds, however, being soon exhausted, he deemed it no great crime for a Frenchman to exact contributions from the English; in other words, to rob on the highway. In a short time he became so great an adept in his new employment, that he had the honour of being first named in an advertisement issued for the apprehending of some notorious robbers.

One day, Du Vall and some others met a knight and his lady travelling along in their coach. The lady, upon seeing that they were in danger of being attacked, and remembering probably that—

" Music hath charms to soothe the savage breast!"

immediately took up a flageolet, and commenced playing, which she did very dexterously. Du Vall taking the hint, pulled one out of his pocket, and began to play, and in this posture approached the coach. " Sir," said he to the knight, " your lady performs excellently, and I make no doubt she dances well; will you step out of the coach, and let me have the honour to dance a courant with her upon the heath?" " I dare not deny any thing, sir," replied the knight readily, " to a gentleman of your quality and good behaviour; you seem a man of generosity, and your request is perfectly reasonable." Immediately the footman opened the door, and the knight came out. Du Vall leaped lightly off his horse, and handed the lady down. It was surprising to see how gracefully he danced upon the grass; scarcely a dancing-master in London but would have been proud to have shown such agility in a pair of pumps, as Du Vall evinced in a pair of French riding-boots. As soon as the dance was over, he handed the lady to the coach; but, just as the knight was stepping in, " Sir," said he, " you forgot to pay the music." His worship replied, that he never forgot such things, and instantly putting his hand under the seat of the coach, pulled out one hundred pounds in a bag, which he delivered to Du Vall, who received it with a very good grace, and courteously answered, " Sir, you are liberal, and shall have no cause to regret your generosity; this hundred pounds, given so handsomely, is better than ten times the sum taken by force. Your noble behaviour has excused you the other three hundred pounds which you have in the coach with you." After this, he gave him his word that he might pass undisturbed if he met any other of his crew, and then wished them a good journey.

At another time, Du Vall and some of his associates met a coach upon Blackheath, full of ladies, and a child with them. One of the gang rode up to the coach, and in a rude manner robbed the ladies of their watches and rings, and even seized a silver sucking-bottle of the child's. The infant cried bitterly for its bottle, and the ladies earnestly entreated he would only return that article to the child, which he barbarously refused. Du Vall went forward to discover what detained his accomplice, and, the ladies renewing their entreaties to him, he instantly threatened to shoot his companion, unless he returned that article, saying, " Sirrah, can't you behave like a gentleman, and raise a contribution without stripping people? but, perhaps, you have occasion for the sucking-bottle, for, by your actions, one would imagine you were hardly weaned." This smart reproof had the desired effect, and Du Vall in a courteous manner took his leave of the ladies.

An extraordinary scheme of his for committing a robbery is, perhaps, worth introducing here. Arriving one evening at the Crown Inn, in Beaconsfield, where he intended to pass the night, his attention was arrested by hearing singing and dancing and sounds of great mirth above stairs. He instantly inquired the reason of it, and found that there was a wake or fair kept there that day, at which were present most of the young men and maids for several miles about. This he thought might possibly turn to his advantage; so he immediately called for a pint of wine, and, while sipping it, entered into conversation with an old farmer, from whom he learnt that he had just been receiving £100, which he had tied up in a bag in his coat pocket. Du Vall was very attentive to all this; and no sooner did he hear of the farmer's money than he made up his mind that it should ere long change hands. The farmer wishing to go up-stairs to see the fun, Du Vall offered to accompany him; and they entered, to all appearance very innocently, Du Vall making an apology to the company, and telling them that he hoped they were not intruding, when they were pressed to come in, and join the revelry.

His business was now more to watch the old farmer's bag of money, than to mind the diversion of the young people; and after considering some time for a way to execute his design in the most dexterous manner he observed a chimney with a large funnel, which he thought would favour his project. Having contrived the whole affair, he went out and communicated it to the ostler, who consented, for a reward of two guineas, to assist him. He was to dress up a great mastiff in a cow-hide, which he had in the stable, placing the horns directly on the forehead, and then, by the help of a ladder and rope, to let him down the chimney. All this he performed, while the company were merry in the chamber. Du Vall returned from the yard; the dog came down the chimney, howling as he descended, and pushing among them in the most frightful manner. All was now confusion; the music was silenced, and the pipe and the fiddle trodden to pieces; the tables overthrown, and the drink spilt; whilst the company were screaming and crowding down stairs as fast as they were able, every one striving to be foremost, as they supposed the Devil would or must inevitably take the hindmost. While they were in this condition, the supposed Devil made his way through them all, and got into the stable, where the ostler instantly uncased him; so that when the company came to examine the matter, as they could neither hear nor see more of him, they concluded he had vanished.

Now was Du Vall's time to take care of the farmer's hundred pounds, which he very easily obtained by diving into his pocket. As soon as he had got the money, he took horse, and spared neither whip nor spur till he came to London, where he thought himself safe. As soon as things were a little in order again at the inn, there was a dismal outcry for the money; all the suspicious persons were searched, and the house was examined from top to bottom, to no purpose. What could they suppose after this, but that the Devil had taken it away? It passed in this manner, and was looked upon as a judgment inflicted by permission of Providence on the farmer for his covetousness; the farmer being in reality a miserable wretch, who made it his business to get money by all the methods he could, whether lawful or otherwise.

One day Du Vall met with Roper, master of the hounds to Charles II., who was hunting in Windsor Forest; and, taking the advantage of a thicket, demanded his money, or he would instantly take his life. Roper, without hesitation, gave him his purse, containing at least fifty guineas: in return for which Du Vall bound him neck and heels, tied his horse to a tree beside him, and rode across the country.

It was a considerable time before the huntsmen discovered their master. The Squire being at length released, made all possible haste to Windsor, unwilling to venture himself into any more thickets for that day, whatever might be the fortune of the hunt. Entering the town, he was accosted by Sir Stephen Fox, who inquired if he had had any sport. "Sport!" replied Roper, in a great passion, "yes, sir, I have had sport enough from a villain who made me pay full dear for it; he bound me neck and heels, contrary to my desire, and then took fifty guineas from me to pay him for his labour, which I had much rather he had omitted."

England now became too contracted a sphere for the talents of our adventurer; and, in consequence of a proclamation issued for his detection, and his notoriety in the kingdom, Du Vall retired to his native country. At Paris he lived in a very extravagant style, and carried on war with rich travellers and fair ladies, and proudly boasted that he was equally successful with both; but his warfare with the latter was infinitely more agreeable, though much less profitable, than with the former.

There is one adventure of Du Vall at Paris, which we shall lay before our readers. There was in that city a learned Jesuit, confessor to the French king, who had rendered himself eminent both by his politics and avarice. His thirst for money was insatiable, and increased with his riches. Du Vall devised the following plan to obtain a share of the immense wealth of this avaricious father.

To facilitate his admittance into the Jesuit's company, he dressed himself as a scholar, and, waiting a favourable opportunity, went up to him very confidently, and addressed him as follows: "May it please your reverence, I am a poor scholar, who have been several years travelling over strange countries, principally to serve mine own country, for whose advantage I am determined to apply my knowledge, if I may be favoured with the patronage of a man so eminent as yourself." "And what may this knowledge of your's be?" replied the father, very much pleased. "If you will communicate any thing to me that may be beneficial to France, I assure you, no proper encouragement shall be wanting on my side." Du Vall, upon this, growing bolder, proceeded, "Sir, I have spent most of my time in the study of alchemy, or the transmutation of metals, and have profited so much at Rome and Venice, from great men learned in that science, that I can change several metals into gold, by the help of a philosophical powder, which I can prepare very speedily."

The father confessor was more elevated with this communication than with all the discoveries he had obtained in the way of his profession, and his knowledge even of his royal penitent's most private secrets gave him less delight than the prospect of immense riches which now burst upon his avaricious mind. "Friend," said he, "such a thing as this will be serviceable to the whole state, and particularly grateful to the king, who, as his affairs go at present, stands in great need of such a curious invention. But you must let me see some proof of your skill, before I credit what you say, so far as to communicate it to his majesty, who will sufficiently reward you, if what you promise be demonstrated." Upon this, the confessor conducted Du Vall to his house, and furnished him with money to erect a laboratory, and to purchase such materials as were requisite, in order to proceed in this invaluable operation, charging him to keep the secret from every living soul. Utensils being fixed, and every thing in readiness, the Jesuit came to witness the wonderful operation. Du Vall took several metals and minerals of the baser sort, and put them in a crucible, his reverence viewing every one as he put them in. Our alchymist had prepared a hollow tube, into which he conveyed several sprigs of real gold; with this seeming stick he stirred the operation, which, with its heat, melted the gold, and the tube at the same time, so that it sank imperceptibly into the vessel. When the excessive fire had consumed all the different materials he had put in, the gold remained pure, to the quantity of an ounce and a half. This the Jesuit ordered to be examined, and, having ascertained that it was actually pure gold, he became devoted to Du Vall, and, blinded with the prospect of future advantage, credited every thing the impostor said, furnishing him with whatever he demanded, in hopes of being made master of this extraordinary secret. Thus were our alchymist and Jesuit, according to the old saying, "as great as two pickpockets." Du Vall was a professed robber; and what is a court favourite but a picker of other peoples' pockets? So that here were two sharpers endeavouring to out-wit one another. The confessor was as candid as Du Vall could wish; he showed him all his treasures, and several rich jewels which he had received from the king; hoping, by these means, to incline him to discover his wonderful secrets with more alacrity. In short, he

became so importunate, that Du Vall was apprehensive of too minute
an inquiry, if he denied the request any longer : he therefore appointed
a day when the whole was to be disclosed. In the mean time, he took
an opportunity of stealing into the chamber where the riches were deposited, and where his reverence generally slept after dinner ; finding him
in deep repose, he gently bound him, then took his keys, and unhoarded
as much of his wealth as he could carry off unsuspected ; after which, he
quickly took leave of him and France.

Du Vall had several ways of getting money besides those already mentioned, particularly by gaming, at which he was so expert that few men
in his age were able to play with him ; no man living could slip a card
more dexterously than he, nor better understood all the advantages that
could be taken of an adversary, yet, to appearance, no one played fairer.
He would frequently carry off £10, £20, £30, or even £100 at a sitting,
and had the pleasure commonly to hear it all attributed to his good
fortune ; so that few were disheartened by their losses from playing with
him a second or third time.

But what he was most celebrated for, was his conquests among the
ladies, which were almost incredible. He was a handsome man, and
had abundance of that sort of wit which is most apt to take with the fair
sex. Every agreeable woman he saw he was dying for, so that he was ten
thousand times a martyr to love. "Those eyes of yours, madam, have
undone me !" "I am captivated with that good-natured smile !" "O, that
I could by any means in the world recommend myself to your ladyship's
notice !" "What a poor, silly, loving fool am I !" These and a thousand such expressions, full of flames, darts, racks, tortures, death, eyes,
cheeks, &c., were much more familiar to him than his prayers ; and he
had the same fortune in the field of love as Marlborough had in that of
war—namely, Never to lay siege but he took the place.

Many stories might be related of our adventurer's gallantry ; suffice it
to say, perhaps no man ever experienced more amply the favours of the
fair sex than the handsome and fascinating Du Vall.

There is no certain account how long Du Vall followed his vicious
courses in England, after his coming from France, before his detection
and falling into the hands of justice. All we know is, that he was taken,
drunk, at the Hole-in-the-Wall, Chandos Street, Covent Garden, committed to Newgate, arraigned, convicted, condemned, and on Friday, the
21st of January, 1669-70, executed at Tyburn, in the 27th year of his
age.

Troops of ladies, and those not of the meanest degree, visited him in
prison, and interceded for his pardon ; and not a few accompanied him to
the gallows, under vizors, with eyes suffused with tears ; and his
actions and death were celebrated by the immortal author of Hu-
dibras. After he had hanged a convenient time, he was cut down,
and, by persons well dressed, conveyed into a mourning coach. In
this he was carried to the Tangier Tavern, St. Giles, where he lay in state
all night. The room was hung with black, the hearse covered with
escutcheons, eight wax tapers were burning, and as many "tall gentle
men" attended with long cloaks. All was profound silence ; and the

ceremony would have lasted much longer, had not the judges sent to interrupt the pageantry.

As they were undressing him, in order to his lying in state, one of his friends put his hand into his pocket, and found therein the following nonsense, written in a very fair hand :—

" I should be very ungrateful to you, fair English ladies, should I not acknowledge the obligations you have laid me under. I could not have hoped that a person of my birth, nation, education, and condition, could have had charms enough to captivate you all; though the contrary has appeared, by your firm attachment to my interest, which you have not abandoned even in my last distress. You have visited me in prison, and even accompanied me to an ignominious death.

" From the experience of your former loves, I am confident that many among you would be glad to receive me to your arms even from the gallows.

" How mightily and how generously have you rewarded my former services! shall I ever forget the universal consternation that appeared in your faces when I was taken, your visits to me in Newgate, your shrieks and swoonings when I was condemned, and your zealous intercession and importunity for my pardon ? You could not have erected fairer pillars of honour and respect to me, had I been a Hercules.

" It has been the misfortune of several English gentlemen to die at this place, in the time of the late usurpation, upon the most honourable occasion that ever presented itself; yet none of these, as I could ever learn, received so many marks of your esteem as myself: how much the greater therefore is my obligation !

" It does not, however, grieve me, that your intercession for me proved ineffectual; for now I shall die with a healthful body, and, I hope, a prepared mind. My confessor has shown me the evil of my ways, and wrought in me a true repentance; whereas, had you prevailed for my life, I must in gratitude have devoted it to your services, which would certainly have made it very short; for had you been sound, I should have died of a consumption !"

His funeral was attended by numerous persons bearing flambeaux, amidst a numerous train of mourners (most of them ladies); and his interment took place at St. Paul's, Covent Garden. A white marble stone was laid over him, with his arms and the following epitaph engraved thereon :

> " Here lies Du Vall ! Reader, if male thou art,
> Look to thy purse ;—if female, to thy heart.
> Much havoc hath been made of both; for all
> Men he made stand, and women he made fall.
> The second conqueror of the Norman race,
> Knights to his arms did yield, and ladies to his face.
> Old Tyburn's glory ! England's bravest thief !
> Du Vall the ladies' joy ! Du Vall, the ladies' grief !"

MATTHEW HENDERSON.

EXECUTED FOR THE MURDER OF HIS MISTRESS, LADY DALRYMPLE.

This offender was born of honest parents, at North Berwick in Scotland, where he was educated in the liberal manner customary in that country.

Sir Hugh Dalrymple, a member of the British parliament, took Henderson into his service when fourteen years of age, and brought him to London with him. Before he was nineteen years old he married one of his master's maids ; but Sir Hugh, who had a great regard for him, did not dismiss him, though he was greatly chagrined at the circumstance.

Some few days before the commission of the murder, Sir Hugh having occasion to go out of town for a month, summoned Henderson to assist in dressing him ; and while he was thus employed, Sir Hugh's lady going into the room, he casually trod on her toe. She said not a word on the occasion ; but looked at him with a degree of rage that made him extremely uneasy. When Sir Hugh had taken his leave, she demanded of Henderson why he had trod on her toe ; in answer to which he made many apologies, and ascribed the circumstance to mere accident ; but she gave him a blow on the ear, and declared that she would dismiss him from her service. Offended by the insult which he conceived had been offered him, he determined to obtain a deep revenge ; and seeking an opportunity, during the absence of his master from London, he proceeded to put his intention in execution by murdering his mistress.

For this offence he was brought to trial at the Old Bailey, on the 22d April, 1746, when he pleaded guilty, and was sentenced to be hanged on the following Monday. On the night before his execution he made a confession of his crime, from which the following particulars are taken :—On the evening of the 25th March, all the other servants having quitted the house, he proceeded to his bed-room. He had pulled off his shoes, and tied up his hair, when suddenly the thought came into his head, that he would kill his mistress. On which he went into the kitchen, and having furnished himself with a cleaver, retired again to his bed-chamber, where he remained more than a quarter of an hour, deliberating whether he should or should not commit the murder. His heart relented when he remembered how kind his mistress had always been to him ; but then he thought there was no one in the house who could hear him, and he determined upon committing the foul deed. Impelled by a feeling he could not control, he rushed up stairs as far as the first landing-place : but, smitten by his conscience, he descended ; sat some time on his bed ; then again he felt determined, and ascended a part of the stairs, but again came down, incapable for the present of carrying his dreadful purpose into execution. Once more he mustered spirits to go up as far as the first window ; when hearing the watchman crying the midnight hour, he tripped down a few steps: once again he advanced, and had now reached the door, by which only he was separated from the object upon which he was about to commit the foul crime, of which in the end he was guilty. Had that door been locked, all might have been well; but no, the latch turned easily in his hand, and he stood within a yard of his victim. Still he could not kill her, and he was about to retire, when, to use his own words, he " felt the devil at work, and was driven onwards to his fate." He entered the room again, and could distinctly hear her respirations; he opened the curtains softly, and fancied he could perceive the outline of her figure. If he had had a light, he was convinced he never could have killed her. He however, at length, urged by an irresistible impulse, raised the cleaver; and so much did he hesitate, even now, that he made as many as thirteen or fourteen motions with it in the air before he brought himself to strike her,—but then he let the instrument fall with terrible force on her head. On receiving the blow, the unhappy lady attempted to rise, but he prevented her by repeating his blows with fearful effect, until at last she sank exhausted on the floor, and death put a period to her sufferings. The only words which she uttered were, " O Lord, what is this?" He could hear, when she expired, the rattling in her throat, at which he was so terrified that he immediately quitted the room, and threw the cleaver into the privy.

The murder thus perpetrated, he resolved to add to it the crime of robbery; and going back to the room, he stole some money, jewels, and other valuable effects, which he carried to the lodgings of a female of his acquaintance, put them in a box, and immediately went back. On his return he found he had shut himself out; but the maid returning soon afterwards, unlocked the door, and they went in. The maid observing blood on the floor below stairs, suspected that some mischief had happened; on which she ran up stairs, and finding her lady lying in the manner above described, she came down weeping.

As soon as it was daylight, Henderson went to the nephew of Sir Hugh Dalrymple, and informed that gentleman of the misfortune that had happened; on which the maid was taken into custody on suspicion, and carried before a magistrate, who, from her answers, had a strong idea that the fact was committed by Henderson. He was immediately apprehended by a constable, with whom he went very cheerfully; and on being brought before the magistrate to be examined, he at first stoutly denied any participation in the guilt, but, upon being closely questioned, he made so many contradictions and mis-statements in his story, that his guilt became evident, and he at last confessed that he alone had transacted the murderous business. He was accordingly committed to Newgate, tried, and convicted.

After conviction he was attended by a minister of the Presbyterian persuasion. His behaviour was very penitent and contrite during his imprisonment; and at the place of execution he made a speech, advising servants to be obedient to their masters, and to behave with submission, instead of harbouring sentiments of revenge.

His sentence was carried out in its terms; and the body was afterwards hung in chains, in the Edgeware Road.

JOHN YOUNG.

EXECUTED FOR FORGERY.

THERE has seldom occurred a more extraordinary case than that of Serjeant-major and Paymaster John Young, the subject of the present article. The methods he took to avoid his fate, and the desperate resistance he made to prevent his sentence being carried into execution, are, we believe, unparalleled in criminal annals.

John Young was born of a Protestant family at Belfast, in Ireland, and received a liberal education. At the usual time of life he was apprenticed to a linen-draper residing in the town in which he was born; and when he had served about three years, his master died; on which, the widow declining business, he engaged as clerk to a wholesale dealer, whose goods were principally sent to the London market and Chester fair. He remained with this employer till he arrived at manhood; when he absconded, in consequence of one of his master's servant-maids proving with child by him. He intended to settle in Dublin, but in his way to that city he met with a recruiting party belonging to the 4th regiment of Foot, who urged him to drink till he became intoxicated, and then prevailed upon him to enlist.

Young, being handsome in person, and accomplished in manners, was soon distinguished by his officers, who upon the first vacancy promoted him to be a serjeant. He marched from Tournay to join his regiment at Ghent, in Flanders, and arrived but a few days preceding that on which the terrible battle of Fontenoy was fought. His behaviour in that action was greatly commended by his officers, who, upon the return of the regiment to Ghent, conferred upon him many marks of particular respect, and appointed him paymaster to the company to which he belonged.

The regiment in which Young was a serjeant was one of those which were ordered into Scotland for the purpose of suppressing the rebellion, that broke out soon after the battle of Fontenoy; but, as a considerable loss of men had been sustained, he was ordered to go upon the recruiting service to Chester, Manchester, Liverpool, and other places.

The recruits engaged by Young were paid the bounty-money without the least deduction, and he would not encourage them to spend any part of it in an extravagant or useless manner. In the space of four months he raised one hundred and fifty men; and it is presumed that the strict integrity of his conduct greatly promoted his success. Upon joining his regiment in Scotland, his officers advanced him to the post of serjeant-major, as a reward for his services. At the battle of Falkirk he put several of the rebels to death with his halbert, and behaved in other respects with remarkable intrepidity.

Upon the command of the army being assumed by the Duke of Cumberland, the regiment to which Young belonged was ordered to march to the North. On account of the singular bravery they displayed at the battle of Culloden, and the great loss of men, this regiment was not ordered back to Flanders, but permitted to remain in Scotland.

Upon tranquillity being re-established in the Highlands, the 4th regiment was ordered to perform duty in Edinburgh Castle, and Young was again despatched upon a recruiting expedition. He enlisted a considerable number of men at Bristol, and on his return to Scotland his officers complimented him with a handsome present. He was then sent to obtain recruits in Yorkshire; and while at Sheffield, in that county, he engaged in a criminal intercourse with the wife of an innkeeper, who, when he was preparing to depart, secreted property to a considerable amount, and followed her lover to Scotland. In a short time the innkeeper came to Edinburgh in search of his wife, and complained in passionate terms of the cruel and treacherous treatment he had received. The nature of his connexion with this woman being made public, Young appeared to be greatly disconcerted whenever he met with persons to whom he supposed the matter had been communicated; but, in justice to his character, it must be observed, that, so far from encouraging the woman to rob her husband, he was entirely ignorant of every thing relating to the matter till her husband's arrival in Edinburgh.

Notwithstanding the above affair, Young was still held in much esteem by his officers; and in a short time the regiment was ordered to proceed to the North, and remained in the royal barracks at Inverness for about twelve months.

Young being both serjeant-major and paymaster, many notes on the Bank of Scotland necessarily came into his possession. While looking over some of these notes in the guard-room, a man named Parker, whom he had enlisted in England, observed, that if he had a few tools, he could engrave a plate for counterfeiting the notes on the Edinburgh Bank. Young seemed to give but little attention to what the other said; but on the following day took him to an ale-house, and requested an explanation as to the manner of executing the scheme he had suggested. Parker informed him, that, besides engraving an exact resemblance of the letters and figures, he could form a machine for printing such notes, as should not be known from those of the Scotch bank. In short, Young hired a private apartment for Parker, and supplied him with every implement necessary for carrying the iniquitous plan into effect; and, in a short time, some counterfeit notes were produced, bearing a near resemblance to the real ones; and upwards of six months elapsed before the fraud was detected.

Orders being issued for the regiment to march to England, Young determined to procure cash for as many notes as possible previous to his departure from Inverness, knowing that in the southern parts the forgery would be liable to immediate detection. With this view, he applied to Mr. Gordon, who was concerned in a stocking-manufactory at Aberdeen, and prevailed upon him to give 60l. in cash for notes expressing to be of the same value.

On his journey from Inverness, Mr. Gordon parted with several of the notes at different places; but, upon reaching Aberdeen, an advertisement in the newspapers convinced him that he had been deceived. In consequence of this Mr. Gordon wrote to the sheriff of Inverness, who immediately took Young into custody, and found in his possession three hundred notes, and the copper-plate from which they had been printed.

Parker was admitted an evidence for the crown, and Young was removed to Edinburgh for trial before the high court of justiciary. After a trial that lasted a whole day, Young was pronounced guilty, and sentenced to suffer death.

While this malefactor was under confinement, he would not consent to be visited by the clergy, though several, from motives of humanity, were desirous of using their endeavours to prepare him for eternity. He was informed by his fellow prisoners, that if he could procrastinate his execution beyond the appointed time, his life would of necessity be preserved; for that the crown law of Scotland declared, that condemned prisoners should be executed between two and four o'clock on the day expressed. Being ignorant of the law, the unhappy man was amused by this story; and, hoping to escape punishment, he secured the strong iron door of the room in which he was confined in such a manner, that when the gaoler came in order to conduct him to the place of execution, he could not gain admittance.

Upwards of fifty carpenters, smiths, masons, and other artificers were employed to open a passage, but they all declined undertaking a business which they deemed to be impracticable; and they were unanimously of opinion, that an aperture could not be made in the wall without endangering the whole fabric.

Matters being thus circumstanced, the lord-provost and the rest of the magistrates assembled at the prison, and, after a long debate, it was determined to form an opening to the room by breaking through the floor of that immediately above. The opening being made, the prisoner leaped up, and, seizing a musket from one of the city guards, declared, with an oath, that if any man attempted to molest him he would dash out his brains. Six of the soldiers, however, suddenly descended, and one of them received a terrible blow from the prisoner; but he was, immediately after, secured by the other five, and executed in the Grass Market at Edinburgh, on the 19th of December, 1748.

JOHN SHEPPARD.

EXECUTED FOR HOUSE-BREAKING.

THE case of this malefactor having been more the subject of conversation than that of almost any other who ever underwent the sentence of the law, and his adventures being in themselves very remarkable, we shall be the more particular in our account of him.

John Sheppard was born in Spitalfields, in the year 1702. His father, who was a carpenter, bore the character of an honest man ; yet he had another son, named Thomas, who, as well as Jack, turned out a thief. The father dying while the boys were very young, they were left to the care of their mother ; who placed Jack at a school in Bishopsgate Street, where he remained two years, and was then put apprentice to a cane-chair-maker in Houndsditch. His master dying when he had been only a short time with him, he was placed with another person of the same trade ; but here he was so ill-treated that he remained only a short time, when he was taken into the protection of Mr. Kneebone, a woollen-draper in the Strand, who had some knowledge of his father. At length, Mr. Kneebone put him apprentice to a carpenter in Wych Street. He behaved with decency in this place for about four years ; when, frequenting the Black Lion alehouse in Drury Lane, he became acquainted with some abandoned women, among whom the principal was Elizabeth Lyon, otherwise called Edgworth Bess, from the town of Edgworth,

     c

where she was born. While he continued to work as a carpenter, he often committed robberies in the hous s where he was employed, stealing tankards, spoons, and other articles, which he carried to Edgworth Bess; and not being suspected of having committed these robberies, he at length resolved to commence housebreaker. Exclusive of Edgworth Bess, he was acquainted with a woman named Maggot, who persuaded him to rob the house of Mr. Bains, a piece-broker in White Horse Yard; and Jack having brought away a piece of fustian from thence, (which he deposited in his trunk), went afterwards at midnight, and taking the bars out of the cellar-window, entered, and stole goods and money to the amount of twenty-two pounds, which he carried to Maggot. As Sheppard did not go home that night nor the following day, his master suspected that he had made bad connections, and, searching his trunk, found the piece of fustian that had been stolen; but Sheppard, hearing of this, broke open his master's house in the night, and carried off the fustian, lest it should be brought in evidence against him.

Sheppard's master sending intelligence to Mr. Bains of what had happened, the latter looked over his goods, and missing such a piece of fustian as had been described to him, suspected that Sheppard must have been the robber, and determined to have him taken into custody; but Jack, hearing of the affair, went to him, and threatened a prosecution for scandal, alleging that he had received the piece of fustian from his mother, who had bought it for him in Spitalfields. The mother, with a view to screen her son, declared that what he had asserted was true, though she could not point out the place where she had made the purchase. Though this story was not credited, Mr. Bains did not take any farther steps in the affair.

Sheppard's master seemed willing to think well of him, and he continued some time longer in the family; but, after associating himself with the worst of company, and frequently staying out the whole night, his master and he quarreled, and the headstrong youth totally absconded in the last year of his apprenticeship, and became connected with a set of villains of Jonathan Wild's gang.

Jack now worked as a journeyman carpenter, with a view to the easier commission of robbery; and being employed to assist in repairing the house of a gentleman in May Fair, he took an opportunity of carrying off a sum of money, a quantity of plate, some gold rings, and four suits of clothes. Not long after this, Edgworth Bess was apprehended, and lodged in the Round-house of the parish of St. Giles, where Sheppard went to visit her; but the beadle refusing to admit him, he knocked him down, broke open the door, and carried her off in triumph; an exploit which acquired him a high degree of credit among his companions.

In the month of August, 1723, Thomas Sheppard, the brother of Jack, was indicted at the Old Bailey, for two petty offences, and being convicted, was burnt in the hand. Soon after his discharge, he prevailed on Jack to lend him forty shillings, and take him as a partner in his robberies. The first act they committed in concert was the robbing a public-house in Southwark, whence they carried off some money and wearing apparel; but Jack permitted his brother to reap the whole advantage of this booty. Not long after this, the brothers, in conjunction with Edgworth Bess, broke open the shop of Mrs. Cook, a linen-draper in Clare-market, and carried off goods to the value of fifty-five pounds; and in less than a fortnight afterwards stole some articles from the house of Mr. Phillips in Drury-Lane. Tom Sheppard going to sell some of the goods stolen at Mrs. Cook's, was apprehended and committed to Newgate, when, in the hope of being admitted an evidence, he impeached his brother and Edgworth Bess; but they were for some time sought for in vain.

At length James Sikes, otherwise called Hell and Fury, one of Sheppard's companions, meeting with him in St. Giles's, enticed him into a public-house, in the hope of receiving a reward for apprehending him; and while they were drinking, Sikes sent for a constable, who took Jack into custody, and carried him before a magistrate, who, after a short examination, sent him to St. Giles's Round-house: but he broke through the roof of that place, and made his escape in the night.

Within a short time after this, as Sheppard and an associate, named Benson, were crossing Leicester-fields, the latter endeavoured to pick a gentleman's pocket of his watch, but failing in the attempt, the gentleman called out " A pickpocket," on which Sheppard was taken, and lodged in St. Ann's Round-house, where he was visited by Edgworth Bess, who was detained on suspicion of being one of his accomplices. On the following day they were carried before a magistrate, and some persons appearing who charged them with felonies, they were committed to the New Prison; where, as they passed for husband and wife, they were permitted to lodge together, in a room known by the name of New-gate Ward. Being here visited by several of his acquaintance (Blueskin among the number), and provided by them with implements necessary for their escape, Jack proceeded to effect this object with that alacrity and energy which always characterized his operations, and which we are therefore led to lament was not devoted to nobler or more useful actions. The removal of his fetters by means of a file was the work of only a few minutes, and he then, with the assistance of his companion, made preparations for flight. Their first obstacle was the heavy cross bars which defended the aperture for admitting air and light to the cell; but this difficulty was quickly removed by the use of the file. There was then another point of a more dangerous character to overcome, namely, their descent into the yard. The window by which they hoped to effect this was twenty-five feet in height, and the only means of reaching the earth was by the employment of their blankets as ropes; but these would not allow them to touch the ground, for they found they would have a considerable distance to drop after they should arrive at the extreme end of their cord. Bess, however, let herself down by means of this rope, and arrived in perfect safety, and Jack immediately followed. They found some consolation at being at least outside the gaol, although they had yet to climb the walls of the yard, which were surmounted with a strong *chevaux de frise* of iron, and were twenty-two feet in height; but, passing round until they arrived at the great gates, our adventurous pair were enabled, by means of the locks and bolts, to descend, and they stood once again on the open ground outside the gaol. Bess having now re-assumed her clothes, of which she had divested herself in order that they might not impede her in her escape, she and her paramour, once more enjoying the free air of liberty, marched into town.

Our hero's fame was, as may be supposed, greatly increased among the lower orders of people by this exploit; and all the thieves of St. Giles's were soon anxious to become his " palls." Among the rest, one Charles Grace, a cooper, begged that he would take him as an associate in his robberies, alleging as a reason for this request, that the girl he kept was so extravagant, that he could not support her on the profits of his own thefts. Sheppard did not hesitate to make this new connection; but at the same time said, that he did not admit of the partnership with a view to any advantage to himself, but that **Grace** might reap the profits of their depredations. Sheppard and Grace having made acquaintance with Anthony Lamb, an apprentice to a mathematical instrument maker near St. Clement's church, it was agreed to rob a gentleman who lodged with Lamb's master; and at two o'clock in the morning, Lamb let in the other villains, who stole money and effects to a large amount. They left the door open, and Lamb went to bed, to prevent suspicion; but, notwithstanding this, his master did suspect him, and had him taken into custody. He confessed the whole affair before a magistrate, and being committed to Newgate, he was tried, convicted, and received sentence of transportation. Our hero meanwhile escaped, and, joining with Blueskin, committed a number of daring robberies, and sometimes disposed of the stolen goods to a fellow named William Field. Jack used to say, that Field wanted courage to commit a robbery, though he was as great a villain as ever existed.

Sheppard and Blueskin hired a stable near the Horse-Ferry, Westminster, in which they deposited their stolen goods, till they could dispose of them to the best advantage. In this place they had put the woollen cloth stolen from Mr. Kneebone; and Sheppard and Blueskin having applied to Field to look at these goods, and procure a customer for them, he promised to do so. Nor was he worse than his word; for in the night he broke open their warehouse, and stole the ill-gotten property, and then gave information against them to Jonathan Wild, in consequence of which they were apprehended. Blueskin was tried and convicted for this robbery, and suffered death; and Sheppard having also been secured, he too was sentenced to death. On Monday the 30th August, 1724, a warrant was sent for his execution, with other convicts; but here neither his ingenuity nor his courage forsook him any more than on any previous occasion. In the old gaol of Newgate there was, within the lodge, a hatch, with large iron spikes, which hatch opened into a dark passage, whence there were a few steps into the condemned hold. The prisoners were permitted to come down to this hatch to speak with their friends, but any very close communication was prevented by the watchfulness of the gaolers. The visits of Edgeworth Bess to her paramour were not unattended with advantage to the latter, for she managed, whilst engaged in conversation, to supply him with the necessary implements for assisting him to escape. At subsequent visits Jack managed to approach the wicket, and by constant filing rendered one of the spikes so insecure that it might readily be wrenched off. On the evening on which the warrant for his execution arrived, he was visited by Mrs. Maggot (who was a very powerful woman) and Bess; he broke off the spike whilst the keepers were drinking in the lodge, and thrusting his head and shoulders through the aperture, the woman pulled him down, and smuggled him through the outer room into the street.

On the day after his escape he went to a public-house in Spitalfields, whence he sent for an old acquaintance, one Page, a butcher in Clare-market, and advised with him how to render his escape effectual for his future preservation. After deliberating on the matter, they agreed to go to Warnden in Northamptonshire, where Page had some relations; and they had no sooner resolved than they made the journey. But Page's relations treating him with indifference, they returned to London, after being absent only about a week.

On the night after their return, as they were walking up Fleet-street together, they saw a watchmaker's shop open, and only a boy attending: having passed the shop, they turned back, and Sheppard driving his hand through the window, stole three watches, with which they made their escape.

Some of Sheppard's old acquaintance informing him that strict search was making after them, he and Page retired to Finchley, in hopes of lying there concealed till the diligence of the jail-keepers should relax; but the keepers of Newgate having received intelligence of their retreat, took Sheppard into custody, and conveyed him back to his old lodgings.

Such steps were now taken as it was thought would be effectual to prevent his future escape. He was put into a strong room called the Castle, handcuffed, loaded with a heavy pair of irons, and chained to a staple fixed in the floor. The curiosity of the public having been greatly excited by his former escape, he was visited by great numbers of people of all ranks, and scarce any one left him without making him a present in money; though he would more gladly have received a file, a hammer, or a chissel; but the utmost care was taken that none of his visitors should furnish him with such implements.

Notwithstanding this disadvantageous situation, he was continually employing his thoughts on the means of another escape. On the 14th of October the sessions began at the Old Bailey, and the keepers being much engaged in attending the court, he thought they would have little time to visit him, and therefore that the present juncture would be the most favourable to carry his plan into execution. About two o'clock in the afternoon of the following day, one of the keepers carried him his dinner, and having carefully examined his irons, and finding them fast, he left him for the day. Some days before this, he had found a small nail in the room, with which he could at pleasure unlock the padlock that fastened the chain to the staple in the floor; and, in his own account of this transaction, he says, that he was frequently about the room, and had several times slept on the barracks when the keepers imagined he had not been out of the chair. The keeper had not left him more than an hour when he began his operations, by taking off his hand-cuffs, and opening the padlock that fastened his chain to the staple. The circumstances, however, attending this escape, and the difficulties which he had to surmount in effecting it, have been so graphically described, and with such strict adherence to the real facts, by Mr. Ainsworth, in his romance founded on the adventures of this daring offender, that we cannot do better than present our readers with the following extract from that popular and interesting work:—

" His first object was to free himself from his handcuffs. This he accomplished by holding the chain that connected them firmly between his teeth ; and, squeezing his fingers as closely together as possible, he succeeded in drawing his wrists through the manacles. He then twisted the heavy gyves round and round, and partly by main strength, partly by a dexterous and well-applied jerk, snapped asunder the central link, by which they were attached to the padlock. Taking off his stockings, he then drew up the basils as far as he was able, and tied the fragments of the broken chains to his legs, to prevent them from clanking, and impeding his future exertions. Upon a former attempt to make his way up the chimney, he had been impeded by an iron bar which was fixed across it at a height of a few feet. To remove this obstacle, it was necessary to make an extensive breach in the wall. With the broken links of the chain, which served him in lieu of more efficient implements, he commenced operations just above the chimney-piece, and soon contrived to pick a hole in the plaster. He found the wall, as he suspected, solidly constructed of brick and stone ; and, with the slight and inadequate tools which he possessed, it was a work of infinite skill and labour to get out a single brick. That done, however, he was well aware the rest would be comparatively easy ; and as he threw the brick to the ground, he exclaimed triumphantly, " The first step is taken—the main difficulty is overcome."

" Animated by this trifling success, he proceeded with fresh ardour, and the rapidity of his progress was proclaimed by the heap of bricks, stones, and mortar, which before long covered the floor. At the expiration of an hour, by dint of unremitting exertion, he made so large a breach in the chimney that he could stand upright in it. He was now within a foot of the bar, and introducing himself into the hole, he speedily worked his way to it. Regardless of the risk he ran by some heavy stones dropping on his head or feet,—regardless also of the noise made by the falling rubbish, and of the imminent risk to which he was consequently exposed of being interrupted by some of the gaolers, should the sound reach their ears, he continued to pull down large masses of the wall, which he flung upon the floor of the cell. Having worked thus for another quarter of an hour, without being sensible of fatigue, though he was half stifled by the clouds of dust which his exertions raised, he had made a hole about three feet wide and six high, and uncovered the iron bar. Grasping it firmly with both hands, he quickly wrenched it from the stones in which it was mortised, and leapt to the ground. On examination it proved to be a flat bar of iron, nearly a yard in length, and more than an inch square. ' A capital instrument for my purpose,' thought Jack, shouldering it, ' and worth all the trouble I have had in procuring it.' While he was thus musing, he thought he heard the lock tried. A chill ran through his frame, and, grasping the heavy weapon with which chance had provided him, he prepared to strike down the first person who should enter his cell. After listening attentively for a short time without drawing breath, he became convinced that his apprehensions were groundless, and, greatly relieved, sat down upon the chair to rest himself and prepare for future efforts.

" Acquainted with every part of the gaol, Jack well knew that his only chance of effecting an escape must be by the roof. To reach it would be a most difficult undertaking. Still it was possible, and the difficulty was only a fresh incitement. The mere enumeration of the obstacles which existed would have deterred any spirit less daring than Sheppard's from even hazarding the attempt. Independently of other risks, and the chance of breaking his neck in the descent, he was aware that to reach the leads he should have to break open six of the strongest doors of the prison. Armed, however, with the implement he had so fortunately obtained, he did not despair of success. ' My name will not only be remembered as that of a robber,' he mused, ' but it shall be remembered as that of a bold one ; and this night's achievement, if it does nothing else, shall prevent me from being classed with the common herd of depredators.' Roused by this reflection, he grasped the iron bar, which, when he sat down, he had laid upon his knees, and stepped quickly across the room. In doing so, he had to clamber up the immense heap of bricks and rubbish which now littered the floor, amounting almost to a cart-load, and reaching up nearly to the chimney-piece ; and having once more got into the chimney, he climbed to a level with the ward above, and recommenced operations as vigorously as before. He was now aided with a powerful implement, with which he soon contrived to make a hole in the wall.

" The ward which Jack was endeavouring to break was called the Red-room, from the circumstance of its walls having once been painted in that colour ; all traces of which, however, had long since disappeared. Like the Castle, which it resembled in all respects, except that it was destitute even of a barrack bedstead, the Red-room was reserved for state prisoners, and had not been occupied since the year 1716, when the gaol was crowded by the Preston rebels. Having made a hole in the wall sufficiently large enough to pass through, Jack first tossed the bar into the room, and then crept after it. As soon as he had gained his feet, he glanced round the bare black walls of the cell, and, oppressed by the misty close atmosphere, exclaimed, ' I will let a little fresh air into this dungeon : they say it has not been opened for eight years, but I won't be eight minutes in getting out.' In stepping across the room, some sharp point in the floor pierced his foot, and stooping to examine it, he found that the wound had been inflicted by a long rusty nail, which projected from the boards. Totally disregarding the pain, he picked up the nail, and reserved it for future use. Nor was he long in making it avail-

able.   On examining the door, he found it secured by a large rusty lock,
which he endeavoured to pick with the nail he had just acquired ; but all
his efforts proving ineffectual, he removed the plate that covered it with
the bar, and with his fingers contrived to draw back the bolt.

" Opening the door, he then stepped into a dark narrow passage,
leading, as he was well aware, to the Chapel.   On the left there were
doors communicating with the King's Bench Ward, and the Stone
Ward, two large holds on the master debtors' side.   But Jack was too
well versed in the geography of the place to attempt either of them.
Indeed, if he had been ignorant of it, the sound of voices, which he
could faintly distinguish, would have served as a caution to him.
Hurrying on, his progress was soon checked by a strong door, several
inches in thickness, and nearly as wide as the passage.   Running his
hand carefully over it in search of the lock, he perceived, to his dismay,
that it was fastened on the other side.   After several vain attempts to
burst it open, he resolved, as a last alternative, to break through the
wall in the part nearest the lock.   This was a much more serious task
than he anticipated.   The wall was of considerable thickness, and built
altogether of stone ; and the noise he was compelled to make in using
the heavy bar, which brought sparks with every splinter he struck off,
was so great, that he feared it must be heard by the prisoners on the
debtors' side.   Heedless, however, of the consequences, he pursued his
task.   Half an hour's labour, during which he was obliged more than
once to pause to regain breath, sufficed to make a hole wide enough to
allow a passage for his arm up to the elbow.   In this way he was able to
force back a ponderous bolt from its socket ; and, to his unspeakable
delight, found that the door instantly yielded.   Once more cheered by
daylight, he hastened forward and entered the Chapel.

" Situated at the upper part of the south-east angle of the gaol, the
Chapel of Old Newgate was divided on the north side into three grated
compartments, or pens, as they were termed, allotted to the common
debtors and felons.   In the north-west angle there was a small pen for
female offenders ; and on the south, a more commodious inclosure appropriated to the master debtors and strangers.   Immediately beneath the
pulpit stood a large circular pen, where malefactors under sentence of
death sat to hear the condemned sermon delivered to them, and where
they formed a public spectacle to the crowds which curiosity generally
attracted on those occasions.   To return : Jack had got into one of the
pens at the north side of the chapel.   The inclosure by which it was
surrounded was about twelve feet high ; the under part being composed
of oaken planks, the upper part of a strong iron grating, surmounted by
sharp iron spikes.   In the middle there was a gate : it was locked.   But
Jack speedily burst it open with the iron bar.   Clearing the few impedi-
ments in his way, he soon reached the condemned pew, where it had
once been his fate to sit ; and extending himself on the seat, endeavoured
to snatch a moment's repose.   It was denied him, for as he closed his
eyes—though but for an instant—the whole scene of his former visit to
the place rose before him.   There he sat as before, with the heavy fetters
on his limbs, and beside him his three companions, who had since

expiated their offences on the gibbet. The chapel was again crowded with visitors, and every eye fixed upon him. So perfect was the illusion, that he could almost fancy he heard the solemn voice of the Ordinary warning him that his race was nearly run, and imploring him to prepare for eternity. From this perturbed state he was roused by the thoughts of his present position, and fancying he heard approaching voices, he started up. On one side of the chapel there was a large grated window, but, as it looked upon the interior of the gaol, Jack preferred following the course he had originally decided upon, to making any attempt in this quarter. Accordingly he proceeded to a gate which stood upon the south, and guarded the passage communicating with the leads. It was grated, and crested with spikes, like that he had just burst open ; and thinking it a needless waste of time to force it, he broke off one of the spikes, which he carried with him for further purposes, and then climbed over it. A short flight of steps brought him to a dark passage, into which he plunged. Here he found another strong door, making the fifth he had encountered. Well aware that the doors in this passage were much stronger than those in the entry he had just quitted, he was neither surprised nor dismayed to find it fastened by a lock of unusual size. After repeatedly trying to remove the plate, which was so firmly screwed down that it resisted all his efforts, and vainly attempting to pick it with his spike and nail, after an hour's ineffectual labour, he wrenched off the box by means of the iron bar, and the door, as he laughingly expressed it, ' was his humble servant.'

" But this difficulty was only overcome to be succeeded by one still greater. Hastening along the passage, he came to the sixth door. For this he was prepared : but he was not prepared for the almost insurmountable difficulties which it presented. Running his hand hastily over it, he was startled to find it one complicated mass of bolts and bars. It seemed as if all the precautions previously taken were here accumulated. Any one less courageous than himself would have abandoned the attempt from the conviction of its utter hopelessness ; but though it might for a moment damp his ardour, it could not deter him. Once again he passed his hand over its surface, and carefully noted all the obstacles. There was a lock, apparently more than a foot wide, strongly plated, and girded to the door with thick iron hoops. Below it a prodigiously large bolt was shot into the socket, and, in order to keep it there, was fastened by a hasp, and further protected by an immense padlock. Besides this, the door was crossed and recrossed by iron bars, clenched by broad-headed nails. An iron fillet secured the socket of the bolt and the box of the lock to the main post of the door-way. Nothing disheartened by this survey, Jack set to work upon the lock, which he attacked with all his implements ; now attempting to pick it with the nail, now to wrench it off with the bar,—but all without effect. He not only failed in making any impression, but the difficulties seemed to increase ; for after an hour's toil he had broken the nail, and slightly bent the iron bar. Completely overcome by fatigue, with strained muscles and bruised hands, streaming with perspiration, and with lips so parched that he would gladly have parted with a treasure, if he had possessed it, for a draught of water, he sunk against the wall, and while in this state was seized with a sudden and strange alarm. He fancied that the turn-keys had discovered his flight, and were in pursuit of him—that they had climbed up the chimney—entered the bed-rooms—tracked him from door to door, and were now only detained by the gate, which he had left unbroken in the chapel. So strongly was he impressed with this idea, that grasping the iron bar with both hands he dashed it furiously against the door, making the passage echo with the blows. By degrees his fears vanished, and, hearing nothing, he grew calmer. His spirits revived, and encouraging himself with the idea that the present impediment, though the greatest, was the last, he set himself seriously to consider how it might best be overcome. On reflection, it occurred to him that he might perhaps be able to loosen the iron fillet—a notion no sooner conceived than executed. With incredible labour, and by the aid of both spike and nail, he succeeded in getting the point of the bar beneath the fillet. Exerting all his energies, and using the bar as a lever, he forced off the iron band, which was full seven feet high, seven inches wide, and two inches thick, and which brought with it, in its fall, the box of the lock, and the socket of the bolt, leaving no further hindrance. Overjoyed beyond measure at having vanquished this apparently insurmountable obstacle, Jack darted through the door.

Ascending a short flight of steps, Jack found at the summit a door, which, being bolted on the inside, he speedily opened. The fresh air, which blew in his face, greatly revived him. He had now reached what were called the Lower Leads—a flat, covering a part of the prison conti-guous to the gateway, and surrounded on all sides by walls about fourteen feet high. On the north stood the battlements of one of the towers of the gate. On this side a flight of wooden steps, protected by a hand-rail, led to a door opening upon the summit of the prison. This door was crested with spikes, and guarded on the right by a bristling semicircle of similar weapons. Hastily ascending the steps, Jack found the door, as he antici-pated, locked. He could easily have forced it, but he preferred a more expeditious mode of reaching the roof, which suggested itself to him. Mounting the door he had last opened, he placed his hands on the wall above, and quickly drew himself up. Just as he had got on the roof of the prison, St. Sepulchre's clock struck eight. It was instantly answered by the deep note of St. Paul's; and the concert was prolonged by other neighbouring churches. Jack had been thus six hours in accomplishing his arduous task.

" Though nearly dark, there was still light enough left to enable him to discern surrounding objects. Through the gloom he distinctly perceived the dome of St. Paul's, hanging like a black cloud in the air ; and, nearer to him, he remarked the golden ball on the summit of the College of Physicians, compared by Garth to a 'gilded pill.' Other towers and spires—St. Martin's, on Ludgate-hill, and Christ Church, in Newgate-street—were also distinguishable. As he gazed down into the courts of the prison, he could not help shuddering, lest a false step might precipitate him below. To prevent the recurrence of any such escape as that just described, it was deemed expedient, in more recent times, to keep a watchman at the top of Newgate. Not many years ago, two men employed in this duty quarreled during the night, and in the morning their bodies were found stretched upon the pavement of the yard below. Proceeding along the wall, Jack reached the southern tower, over the battlements of which he clambered, and crossing it, dropped upon the roof of the gate. He then scaled the northern tower, and made his way to the summit of that part of the prison which fronted Giltspur-street. Arrived at the extremity of the building, he found that it overlooked the flat roof of a house, which, as far as he could judge in the darkness, lay at a depth of about twenty feet below.

" Not choosing to hazard so great a fall, Jack turned to examine the building, to see whether any more favourable point of descent presented itself, but could discover nothing but steep walls, without a single available projection. Finding it impossible to descend on any side, without incurring serious risk, Jack resolved to return for his blanket, by the help of which he felt certain of accomplishing a safe landing on the roof of the house in Giltspur-street. Accordingly he began to retrace his steps, and pursuing the course he had recently taken, scaling the two towers, and passing along the walls of the prison, he descended by means of the door upon the Lower Leads. Before he re-entered the prison he hesitated, from a doubt whether he was not fearfully increasing his risk of capture; but, convinced that he had no other alternative, he went on. During all this time he had never quitted the iron bar, and he now grasped it with the firm determination of selling his life dearly if he met with any opposition. A few seconds sufficed to clear the passages through which it had previously cost him more than two hours to force his way. The floor was strewn with screws, nails, fragments of wood and stone, and across the passage lay the heavy fillet. He did not disturb any of the litter, but left it as a mark of his prowess. He was now at the entrance of the chapel, and striking the door over which he had previously climbed a violent blow with the bar, it flew open. To vault over the pews was the work of a moment; and having gained the entry leading to the Red Room, he passed through the first door, his progress being only impeded by the pile of broken stones which he himself had raised. Listening at one of the doors leading to the master-debtors' side, he heard a loud voice chanting a Bacchanalian melody; and the boisterous laughter that accompanied the song, convinced him that no suspicion was entertained in that quarter. Entering the Red Room, he crept through the hole in the wall, descended the chimney, and arrived once more in his old place of captivity. How different were his present feelings, compared with those he had experienced on quitting it! Then, though full of confidence, he half doubted his power of accomplishing his designs. Now he had achieved them, and felt assured of success. The vast heap of rubbish on the floor had been so materially increased by the bricks and plaster thrown down on his attack upon the wall of the Red Room, that it was with some difficulty that he could find the blanket, which was almost buried beneath the pile. He next searched for his stockings and shoes, and, when found, put them on. He now prepared to return to the roof, and throwing the blanket over his left arm, and shouldering the iron bar, he again clambered up the chimney, regained the Red Room, hurried along the first passage, crossed the chapel, threaded the entry to the Lower Leads, and in less than three minutes after quitting the Castle, had reached the northern extremity of the prison. Previously to his descent, he had left the nail and spike on the wall, and with these he fastened the blanket to the coping stone. This done, he let himself carefully down by it, and having only a few feet to drop, alighted in safety.

" Having now got fairly out of Newgate for a second time, with a heart throbbing with exultation, he hastened to make good his escape. To his great joy, he found a small garret door in the roof of the opposite house open; he entered it, crossed the room, in which there was only a small truckle-bed, over which he stumbled, opened another door, and gained the stair-head. As he was about to descend, his chains slightly rattled. ' O lud! what's that?' cried a female voice from an adjoining room. ' Only the dog,' replied the rough tones of a man, and all was again silent. Securing the chain in the best way he could, Jack then hurried down two pair of stairs, and had nearly reached the lobby, when a door suddenly opened, and two persons appeared, one of whom held a light. Retreating as quickly as he could, Jack opened the first door he came to, entered a room, and, searching in the dark for some place of concealment, fortunately discovered a screen, behind which he crept."

Having lain down here for about two hours, he once more proceeded down stairs, and saw a gentleman take leave of the family and quit the house, lighted by the servant; and as soon as the maid returned, he resolved to venture at all hazards. In stealing down the stairs he stumbled against a chamber door, but instantly recovering himself, he got into the street.

By this time it was after twelve o'clock, and passing by the watch-house of St. Sepulchre, he bid the watchmen good-morrow, and going up Holborn, he turned down Gray's-Inn-Lane, and about two in the morning got into the fields near Tottenham-Court, where he took shelter in a place that had been a cow-house, and slept soundly about three hours. His fetters being still on, his legs were greatly bruised and swelled, and he dreaded the approach of day-light, lest he should be discovered. He had now above forty shillings in his possession, but was afraid to send to any person for assistance. At seven in the morning it began to rain hard, and continued to do so all day, so that no person appeared in the fields; and during this melancholy day he would, to use his own expression, " have given his right hand for a hammer, a chissel, and a punch." Night coming on, and being pressed by hunger, he ventured to a little chandler's shop in Tottenham Court Road, where he got a supply of bread, cheese, small-beer, and some other necessaries, hiding his irons with a long great coat. He asked the woman of the house for a hammer; but she had no such utensil; on which he retired to the cow-house, where he slept that night, and remained all the next day. At night he went again to the chandler's shop, supplied himself with provisions, and returned to his hiding-place. At six the next morning, which was Sunday, he began to beat the basils of his fetters with a stone, in order to bring them to an oval form, to slip his heels through. In the afternoon the master of the cow-house coming thither, and seeing his irons, said, " For God's sake, who are you?" Sheppard said, he was an unfortunate young fellow, who having had a bastard-child sworn to him, and not being able to give security to the parish for its support, he had been sent to Bridewell, from whence he had made his escape. The man said, if that was all it did not much signify, but he did not care how soon he was gone, for he did not like his looks. Soon after he was gone, Sheppard saw a journeyman shoemaker, to whom he told the same story of the bastard-child, and offered him twenty shillings if he would procure a smith's hammer and a punch. The poor man, tempted by the reward, procured them accordingly, and assisted him in getting rid of his irons, which work was completed by five o'clock in the evening.

When night came on, our adventurer tied a handkerchief about his head, tore his woollen cap in several places, and likewise his coat and stockings, so as to have the appearance of a beggar ; and in this condition he went to a cellar near Charing-Cross, where he supped on roasted veal, and listened to the conversation of the company, all of whom were talking of the escape of Sheppard. On the Monday he sheltered himself at a public-house of little trade, in Rupert-street ; and conversing with the landlady about Sheppard, he told her it was impossible for him to get out of the kingdom, and the keepers would certainly have him again in a few days ; on which the woman wished that a curse might fall on those who should betray him. Remaining in this place till evening, he went into the Haymarket, where a crowd of people were surrounding two ballad-singers, and listening to a song made on his adventures and escape.

On the next day he hired a garret in Newport-market, and soon afterwards, dressing himself like a porter, he went to Blackfriars, to the house of Mr. Applebee, printer of the dying-speeches, and delivered a letter, in which he ridiculed the printer, and the ordinary of Newgate, and inclosed a letter for one of the keepers of the gaol.

Some nights after this, he broke open the shop of Mr. Rawlins, a pawnbroker in Drury-Lane, where he stole a sword, a suit of wearing apparel, some snuff-boxes, rings, watches, and other effects to a considerable amount. Determining to make the appearance of a gentleman among his old acquaintance in Drury-Lane and Clare-Market, he dressed himself in a suit of black and a tie-wig, wore a ruffled shirt, a silver-hilted sword, a diamond ring, and gold watch ; though he knew that diligent search was making after him at that very time. On the 31st of October he dined with two women at a public-house in Newgate-street, and about four in the afternoon they all passed under Newgate in a hackney coach, having first drawn up the blinds. Going in the evening to a public-house in Maypole Alley, Clare-market, Sheppard sent for his mother, and treated her with brandy, when the poor woman dropped on her knees, and begged he would immediately quit the kingdom ; which he promised to do, but he had no intention of keeping his word. Being now grown valiant through an excess of liquor, he wandered from one alehouse and gin-shop to another till near twelve o'clock at night, when he was apprehended in consequence of the information of an alehouse boy who knew him. When taken into custody he was quite senseless, from the quantity and variety of liquors he had drank, and was conveyed to Newgate in a coach, without being capable of making the least resistance, though he had two pistols then in his possession.

His fame was now so much increased by his exploits that he was visited by great numbers of people, and some of them of the highest quality. He endeavoured to divert them by a recital of the particulars of many robberies in which he had been concerned; and when any noblemen came to see him, he never failed to beg that they would intercede with the king for his pardon, to which he thought that his singular dexterity gave him some pretensions.

Having been already convicted, he was carried to the bar of the Court of King's Bench on the 10th of November; and the record of his conviction being read, and an affidavit made that he was the same John Sheppard mentioned in the record, sentence of death was passed on him by Mr. Justice Powis, and a rule of court made for his execution on the Monday following. He regularly attended the prayers in the chapel; but though he behaved with decency there, he affected mirth before he went thither, and endeavoured to prevent any degree of seriousness among the other prisoners on their return. Even when the day of execution arrived, Sheppard did not appear to have given over all expectations of eluding justice; for having been furnished with a penknife, he put it in his pocket, with a view, when the melancholy procession came opposite Little Turnstile, to have cut the cord that bound his arms, and throwing himself out of the cart, among the crowd, to have run through the narrow passage, where the sheriff's officers could not follow on horseback; and he had no doubt but he should make his escape, by the assistance of the mob. It is not impossible but that this scheme might have succeeded; but before Sheppard left the press-yard, one Watson, an officer, searching his pockets, found the knife, and in wresting it from him was so cut with it, as to occasion a great effusion of blood. He had yet a farther scheme for his escape even after execution; for he desired his acquaintance to put him into a warm bed as soon as he should be cut down, and try to open a vein, which he had been told would restore him to life.

He behaved with great decency at the place of execution, and confessed the having committed two robberies, for which he had been tried and acquitted. He was executed at Tyburn on the 16th of November, 1714, in the 23d year of his age. He died with difficulty, and was much pitied by the surrounding multitude. When he was cut down, his body was delivered to his friends, who carried it to a public-house in Long-Acre, whence it was removed in the evening, and buried in the churchyard of St. Martin-in-the-Fields.

It is astonishing to think how much Sheppard and his adventures engaged the attention of the public. For a considerable time there was scarcely a subject of conversation but himself. There were several different histories of his life; and a variety of prints were published, representing his escapes from the condemned hold, and from the castle in Newgate. There were likewise several other prints of his person; the best of which was a mezzotinto, from an original painting of Sir James Thornhill, which gave rise to the following ingenious lines :—

> Thornhill, 'tis thine to gild with fame
> Th' obscure, and raise the humble name;
> To make the form elude the grave,
> And Sheppard from oblivion save.
>
> Though life in vain the wretch implores,
> And exile on the farthest shores,
> Thy pencil brings a kind reprieve,
> And bids the dying robber live.
>
> This piece to latest time shall stand,
> And show the wonders of thy hand.
> Thus former masters graced their name,
> And gave egregious robbers fame.
>
> Apelles Alexander drew;
> Cæsar is to Aurelius due;
> Cromwell in Lely's works doth shine;
> And Sheppard, Thornhill, lives in thine.

It was even thought proper to represent Sheppard's actions on the stage. A pantomime entertainment was contrived, in which the scenes were painted from the place of action. It bore the name of " Harlequin Sheppard : a night-scene, in grotesque characters," and was represented at the Theatre-Royal Drury-Lane.

Another piece was printed, but never acted at the Theatres. It was a farce of three acts, called, " The Prison Breaker ; or the Adventures of John Sheppard." After being neglected some time, a number of songs and catches were intermixed with it ; and having received the name of " The Quaker's Opera," it was exhibited at Bartholomew Fair.

Of the more recent interest which these adventures have excited, through the popular work before alluded to, it is unnecessary to say any thing : they have been the conversation of every circle of society, have formed the subject of ballads in the street, and of representation in almost every theatre in the kingdom.

JOSEPH BLAKE, *otherwise* BLUESKIN.

HANGED FOR BURGLARY.

This offender was a native of London. He was sent to school by his parents for the space of six years; but made little progress in learning, having a very early propensity to acts of dishonesty. While at school, he made an acquaintance with William Blewit, who afterwards entered into Jonathan Wild's gang, and became one of the most notorious villains of the age. No sooner had Blake left school than he commenced pickpocket, and before he was fifteen years of age had been in all the prisons for felons in London. He afterwards turned street-robber, and joined with Oaky, Levee, and many other villains who acted under the directions of Jonathan Wild. They were at length taken into custody, and Blake being admitted an evidence against his companions, they were convicted.

In consequence of these convictions, Blake claimed his liberty, and part of the reward allowed by government; but the court informed him, that he had no right to either, because he was not a voluntary evidence, since, so far from having surrendered, he had made an obstinate resistance, and was much wounded before he was taken; and therefore he must find security for his good behaviour, or be transported.

Not being able to give the requisite security, he was lodged in Wood-Street Compter, where he remained a considerable time, during which Jonathan Wild allowed him three shillings and sixpence a week. At length he prevailed on two gardeners to be his bail; but the court at the Old Bailey hesitating to take their security, they went before Sir John Fryer, who took their recognizance for Blake's good behaviour for seven years.

Blake had no sooner obtained his liberty than he was concerned in several robberies with Jack Sheppard, and particularly that for which two brothers, Brightwell, were tried. The footpad robberies and burglaries they committed were very numerous; but the fact for which Blake suffered was the robbery of Mr. Kneebone, as will appear by the following account.

At the Old Bailey sessions, in October, 1724, Joseph Blake, otherwise Blueskin, was indicted for breaking and entering the dwelling-house of William Kneebone, and stealing 108 yards of woollen cloth, value £36, and other goods. The prosecutor swore, that the bars of his cellar-window were cut, and that the cellar-door, which had been bolted and padlocked, was broke open. He acquainted Jonathan Wild with what had happened, who went to Blake's lodgings, with two other persons; but Blake refusing to open the door, it was broken open by Quilt Arnold, one of Wild's men. On this Blake drew a penknife, and swore he would kill the first man that entered; in answer to which Arnold said, " Then I am the first man, and Mr. Wild is not far behind; and if you don't deliver your penknife immediately, I will chop your arm off." Hereupon the prisoner dropped the knife; and Wild entering, he was taken into custody.

As the parties were conveying Blake to Newgate, they passed by the house of the prosecutor; on which Wild said to the prisoner, "There's the ken." The latter replied, "Say no more of that, Mr. Wild: I know I am a dead man; but what I fear is, that 1 shall afterwards be carried to Surgeon's-Hall, and anatomized." To which Wild replied, "No, I'll take care to prevent that, for I'll give you a coffin."

William Field, who was evidence on the trial, swore that the robbery was committed by Blake, Sheppard, and himself: and the jury brought in a verdict of guilty.

As soon as the verdict was given, Blake addressed the court in the following terms: " On Wednesday morning last, Jonathan Wild said to Simon Jacobs (who was then a prisoner, and afterwards transported), I believe you will not bring £40 this time: I wish Joe (meaning me) was in your case; but I'll do my endeavour to bring you off as a single felon. Then turning to me, he said, I believe you must die—I'll send you a good book or two, and provide you a coffin, and you shall not be anatomized."

Wild was to have been an evidence against this malefactor; but, going to visit him in the bail-dock previous to his trial, Blake suddenly drew a clasped penknife, with which he cut Jonathan's throat, which prevented his giving evidence; but, as the knife was blunt, the wound, though dangerous, did not prove mortal.

While under sentence of death, Blake did not show a concern proportioned to his calamitous situation. When asked if he was advised to commit the violence on Wild, he said, No, but that a sudden thought entered his mind, or he would have provided a knife which would have cut off his head at once."

On the nearer approach of death he appeared still less concerned, and it was thought that his mind was chiefly occupied in meditating means of escape; but seeing no prospect of getting away, he took to drinking, which he continued even to the day of his death, for he was observed to be intoxicated even while under the gallows.

He was executed at Tyburn on the 11th November, 1723.

This malefactor appears to have been a thief almost from his cradle: his habits of vice increased with his years, till at length he died, in the most ignominious manner, a victim to the violated laws of his country.

WILLIAM YORK,

AGED TEN YEARS,

CONVICTED OF MURDERING SUSAN MAHEW, AGED FIVE YEARS.

This case is rendered particularly remarkable by the circumstance of the extreme youth of the offender; the unhappy child being, at the time he committed the dreadful crime of which he was convicted, only ten years of age.

He was a pauper in the poor-house belonging to the parish of Eye, in Suffolk; and was committed, on the coroner's inquest, to Ipswich jail, for the murder of Susan Mahew, another child, five years of age, also an inmate of the same house, who had been his bedfellow.

The following is the substance of his confession, taken before a justice of the peace, which was in most respects proved on the trial, with many corroborating circumstances of his guilt:—

He stated, that a trifling quarrel happening between himself and the deceased child, on the 13th May, 1748, about ten o'clock in the morning, he struck her a blow with his open hand, and made her cry. That she going out of the house shortly afterwards to the dunghill opposite the door, he followed her with a hook in his hand, with the intention of killing her; but, before he came up with her, he threw down the hook, and returned into the house for a knife. He then came out again, took hold of the girl's left hand, and cut her wrist all round to the bone, and then threw her down, and cut her to the bone just above the elbow of the same arm. That, after this, he set his foot upon her stomach, and cut her right arm round about to the bone, both on the wrist and above the elbow. That, still thinking she would not die, he took the hook and cut her left thigh to the bone.

His next care was to conceal the murder; for which purpose he ran and filled a pail with water from a ditch hard by, and washing the blood off the child's body, buried it in the dunghill, together with the blood which was spilt upon the child's clothes, and then went and got his breakfast.

When he was examined, he showed very little concern, and appeared easy and cheerful. All he alleged was, that the child fouled the bed in which they lay together; that she was sulky, and that he did not like her.

The boy was found guilty of the dreadful crime with which he was charged, and sentenced to death; but was respited from time to time on account of his tender years, and at length pardoned.

CHAMBERS APPEARING IN THE CHARACTER OF A GHOST.

ARTHUR CHAMBERS.

HANGED FOR ROBBERY.

Arthur Chambers was of low extraction, and destitute of every amiable quality. From his very infancy he was addicted to pilfering; and the circumstances of his parents rendering them unable to support his extravagances, he had recourse to dishonest means. It is even reported, that before he was dressed in boys' clothes, he committed several acts of theft.

The first thing he attempted was to learn, from an experienced master, all those cant words and phrases current among pickpockets, and by which they can distinguish one another. Chambers was soon an adept in this language; and, being well dressed, he was introduced to the better sort of company, and profited by such opportunities to rob his companions.

In a short time he was confined in Bridewell, to answer, with hard labour, for some small offence. Having obtained his liberty, he left town, where he again began to be suspected, and went to Cornwall. His witty and merry turn gained him reception into genteel companies, and he became a remarkable character in the place. Before he left London, he provided himself with a large quantity of counterfeit crowns and half-crowns, which he vended wherever he went. After many had been

3

deceived, strict search was made, and Chambers detected.   For this offence he was committed to jail, where he remained a year and a half.

As he could no longer remain in Cornwall, he returned to London. Upon his arrival, he went to an alehouse, called for a pot of beer, and a slice of bread and cheese.   Having refreshed himself, he entered into conversation with some persons in a neighbouring box.   The conversation turned upon the superior advantages of a country life, but was suddenly directed to the subject of robbery.   Chambers improved the hint, regretted that no better provision was made for suppressing such villainies; for, added he, death was too great a punishment for a person who robbed even the whole world. " But why do I talk thus?" continued he; " if great offenders are suffered, well may the poor and necessitous say, we must live; and where is the harm of taking a few guineas from those who can spare them, and perhaps have robbed others of them.   For my own part, I look upon a dexterous pickpocket as a very useful person, as he only draws from the purses of those who would otherwise spend their money in gaming, or worse.   Look ye, gentlemen, I can pick a pocket as well as any man in Britain; and yet, though I say it, I am as honest as the best Englishman breathing.   Observe that country gentleman passing by the window there; I will engage to rob him of his watch, though it is scarcely five o'clock."

A wager of ten shillings was instantly taken, and Chambers hastened after the gentleman.   He accosted him at the extremity of Long Lane, and, pulling off his hat, asked the gentleman if he could inform him the nearest way to Knave's Acre.   He replied, that he himself wished to know the way to Moorfields, which Chambers pointed out, with his usual eloquence; and, while the gentleman kept his eyes fixed upon the places to which he directed him, took the opportunity of robbing him of his watch.   He hastened back to the ale-house, threw down the watch, and claimed the wager; but, in a short time, went in quest of the gentleman, and returned him his watch, which he thankfully received, and presented him with half-a-crown.

He next exerted his ingenuity upon a plain countryman, newly come to town.   This rustic had got into the company of sharpers, and stood gazing at a marble table.   Our adventurer stepped up, tapped him on the shoulder, inquired what part of the country he came from, and if he was desirous to find a place as a gentleman's servant.   Robin answered, that it was his very errand to town, to find such a place.   Chambers then said, that he could fit him to a hair.   I believe I can afford you myself four pounds a year standing wages, and six shillings a week board wages, and all cast clothes, which are none of the worst.   This was sufficient to make Robin start out of his skin, who had never before had such an offer made him.   Having arranged every thing to his wish, Robin entered upon his new service.   He received Chambers's cloak, threw it over his arm, and followed his master.   Chambers ordered a coach; and Robin being placed behind, they drove off for an inn.   Dinner was ordered: Robin sat down with his master, and took a hearty meal; who meanwhile instructed him in all the tricks of the town, and the necessity of his being always upon his guard.   He informed him also, that the servants of the inn would be requesting him to join in playing cards, and that he was in danger of being imposed upon; therefore, if he had any money about him, it would be proper to give it him, and he could receive it back when necessary. He pulled out his purse, and delivered all that he had, with which Chambers paid for the dinner, and went off, leaving Robin to shift for himself, and to lament the loss of his money and his new master.

The next victim to the avarice of Chambers was an elderly gentleman, who had married a young lady, and retired with her to a country house he had near Huntingdon. Chambers had often cast his eye towards that house, but was disappointed in his designs. It is probable that his intentions were discovered, as the gentleman always kept firearms in his house; and, by moonlight, was often observed sitting behind the curtain of his window, ready to attack any person who should have the temerity to enter his premises. Chambers was acquainted with all these circumstances; and, accordingly, he collected as many clothes as would make up the appearance of a man, places a ladder to the gentleman's window, and, mounting, makes the head of the fictitious man to strike against the window. The old man, alarmed by the noise, instantly fires his pistol, and down tumbles the bundle of rags.

Meanwhile Chambers hastens down the ladder, and retires to his companions, who were waiting at the back of the house. The gentleman awoke his lady, to inform her of what had happened, and rejoice with him that they had got so completely free of him who was their constant terror. " To prevent, however, any expense or trouble about him, I will now go and dig a hole, and bury him in a corner of the adjoining ground." He accordingly went, and, taking a rope, tied it about the man's neck, dragged him to the intended spot, and interred him. Chambers observing this, places the ladder again to the window, whips up the sash, and went to bed to the lady. Then, assuming the voice and privileges of the husband, he expressed an extreme dread lest the ghost of the slain man might still haunt the house and steal her jewels: he therefore suggested the propriety of concealing them in the adjacent room. The credulous lady, supposing that it was her husband, delivered him the casket, and Chambers, slipping gently down stairs, hastened to his companions with the booty.

When the husband returned, the lady began to talk to him of the safety of her rings and watches, since he had now concealed them. The old man replied that she was certainly dreaming or delirious—that he had taken none of her rings, nor watch, nor jewels. She with equal confidence insisted that he had, and mentioned a certain proof of his having been there. The old man stormed, raged, called up the servants, examined every thing, and, to his great mortification, found that his property had sunk in that one night no less than fifteen hundred pounds. To discover more completely the matter, he went next day, dug up the dead man, and found only a few rags instead of the notorious villain he so much dreaded and detested, and whom he had now still greater reason to detest.

The next adventure of Chambers was directed against the innkeeper of the Greyhound. His wife was rather handsome, but exceedingly facetious; and Chambers being often there, he was inclined to act a similar part to what had been transacted at Huntingdon. He directs his steps thither, and, pretending to have been attacked by three men near the inn, he went in with his clothes all besmeared. The travellers who were in the inn condoled with him on his misfortune, and gave him a change of clothes until his own should be cleaned. To remove the sorrow of the sad disaster, he invited six of his fellow-travellers, with the landlord and his wife, to supper. The glass circulated freely. The wife entertained them with several appropriate songs. Chambers was careful that her glass never remained long empty. In a short time he with pleasure saw all his companions, with the solitary exception of the landlord, sunk in the arms of sleep. He proposed that they should be conveyed to bed, and two or three stout fellows came to perform that office. Chambers was so obliging as to lend his assistance, while he took care that their money and watches should pay for his trouble.

Left alone with the landlord, he proposed that they should have an additional bottle. Another succeeded, before the landlord was in a condition to be conveyed to rest. In aiding the servants with the corpulent innkeeper, he discovered the geography of his bed-room, and, finding the door was directly opposite his own, he retired, not to rest, but to plot and to perfect his villainy.

When he was convinced that the wine had had its complete effects upon the deluded pair, he revisited the bedchamber; waited some time, and extracted what property he could most conveniently carry away; by the dawn of day, dressed himself in the best suit of clothes which his bottle companions could afford, called for the horse of that person whose clothes he now wore, left two guineas with the waiter to pay his bill, gave half-a-crown to the hostler, and rode off for London.

The first enterprise after his arrival was attacking an Italian merchant upon the Exchange. He took him aside, eagerly inquired what goods he had to dispose of, and enters into conversation; one of Chambers's accomplices approaching, joins the conversation. Meanwhile our adventurer found means to extract from his pockets a large purse of gold, and his gold watch; which he delivered to his accomplice. Not satisfied with his first success, and observing a silk handkerchief suspended from his pocket, he walked behind him to seize it, but was detected in the act, and kept fast hold of by the merchant, who cries out, "Thief! thief!" In this dilemma, Chambers's companion runs to the crier, and requests him to give public proclamation, that if any one had lost a purse of gold, upon giving proper information, it would be restored. With the expectation of finding his money again, the merchant lets go his hold, and in the crowd Chambers and his friends retired with their booty.

But Chambers was now resolved to perform an action worthy of his talents. He hired the first floor of a house, and agreed with the landlord for fourteen shillings per week. Having been taken for a man of fortune, both from his appearance and expenses, a mutual confidence was gradually established. When his plot was matured, he one day entered, the apartment of his landlord, with a very pensive and sorrowful look, who anxiously inquired the cause of his great uneasiness. Chambers, with tears in his eyes, informed him, that he had just returned from Hampstead, where he had witnessed the death of a beloved brother, who had left him his sole heir, with an express injunction to convey his remains to Westminster Abbey. He therefore entreated the favour of being allowed to bring his brother's remains at a certain hour to his house, that from thence they might be conveyed to the place of their destination. His request was readily granted.

Chambers went off the next morning, leaving word that the corpse would be there at six o'clock in the evening. At the appointed hour the hearse with six horses arrived at the door. An elegant coffin, with six gilt handles, was carried up stairs, and placed upon the dining-room table, and the horses were conveyed by the men to a stable in the neighbourhood. They informed the landlord that Chambers was detained on business, and would probably sleep that night in the Strand.

This artful rogue was, however, concealed in the coffin, in which air-holes were made, the screw-nails left unfixed, his clothes all on, and only a winding-sheet wrapped above all, and his face disguised with flour. All the family went to bed, except the maid-servant. Chambers arose from his concealment, went down stairs to the kitchen, wrapped in his winding-sheet, and sat down and stared the maid in the face; who, overwhelmed with fear, cried out, " A ghost! a ghost!" and ran up stairs to her master's room. He chid her unreasonable fears, and requested her to return to bed, and compose herself. She obstinately refused, and remained in the room.

In a short time, however, in stalked the stately ghost, took his seat, and conferred a terrible fright upon all three who were present. Retiring from his station when he deemed it convenient, he continued, by the moving of the doors, and the noise raised through the house, to conceal his designs. In the mean time he went down stairs, opened the doors to his accomplices, who assisted in carrying off the plate and every thing which could be removed, not even sparing the utensils of the kitchen. The maid was the first to venture from the room in the morning, and to inform her master and mistress of what had happened, who, more than the night before, chid her credulity in believing that a ghost could rob a house, or carry away any article out of it. The landlord, however, was induced to rise from his bed, move down stairs, and found, to his astonishment and chagrin, that the whole of his plate, and almost the whole of his moveables, were gone, and he had only received in return an empty coffin.

That we may not exhaust the patience of our readers, we shall only add, that Chambers, after continuing his depredations, and being guilty of numerous acts of consummate art and villany, was at last detected, tried, and sentenced to death, and that he finished his singular and vicious career at Tyburn.

AMY HUTCHINSON.

BURNT FOR THE MURDER OF HER HUSBAND.

The Isle of Ely gave birth to this malefactor, who was the daughter of parents rather low in circumstances, but who yet contrived to keep her at school till she was twelve years of age. At sixteen she attracted the attentions of a young man, whose love she returned with equal affection. Her father being apprised of this connexion, strictly charged his daughter to decline it; but there was no arguing against love: the intimacy continued till it became criminal.

The young fellow beginning to grow tired of her, went off to London; and she, determining to be revenged on him for his infidelity, married another suitor, named John Hutchinson, who had formerly been disagreeable to her. The marriage took place immediately; but her first admirer happening to return from London just as the newly-wedded pair were coming out of the church, the bride was greatly affected at the recollection of former scenes, and at reflecting on the irrevocable ceremony which had now passed.

Unable to love the man she had married, and doating to distraction on him she had rejected, she, a few days after her marriage, admitted the latter to his former intimacy with her; a circumstance that gave full scope to the envious tongues of her neighbours.

Hutchinson becoming jealous of his wife, a quarrel ensued; in consequence of which he beat her with great severity: but this producing no alteration in her conduct, he had recourse to drinking, with a view to avoid the pain of reflecting on his situation. In the interim, his wife and the young fellow continued their guilty intercourse uninterrupted; but, considering the life of the husband as a bar to their happiness, it was resolved to remove him by poison. For this purpose the wife purchased a quantity of arsenic; and Mr. Hutchinson being afflicted with an ague, and wishing for something warm to drink, the wife put some arsenic in ale, of which he drank very plentifully; and then she left him, saying she would go and buy something for his dinner.

Meeting her lover, she acquainted him with what had passed; on which he advised her to buy more poison, fearing the first might not be sufficient to operate; but its effects were too fatal, for he died about dinner-time on the same day.

The deceased was buried on the following Sunday, and the next day her former lover renewed his visits; which occasioning the neighbours to talk very freely of the affair, the young widow was taken into custody on suspicion.

The body of the deceased being exhumed, it was discovered that his death had been caused by poison; whereupon the prisoner was tried, convicted, and sentenced to death.

She was strangled and burnt at Ely on the 7th November, 1750, having previously confessed the crime for which she suffered.

"BEHOLD THE HEAD OF A TRAITOR!"

THE EARL OF DERWENTWATER, LORD KÉNMURE, THE EARL OF WINTON, AND OTHERS,

CONCERNED IN

The Rebellion of 1715.

THE circumstances attending the crime of these individuals, intimately connected as they are with the history of this country, must be too generally known to require us to enter into any lengthened detail respecting them. We will, however, give a brief sketch of the origin of the rebellion.

When, in pursuance of the Act of Settlement, King George the First succeeded to the throne of these realms, the Earl of Mar, a Scottish nobleman who had been deeply concerned with Queen Anne's party, was deprived of all the places he held under government; in revenge for which he retired to Scotland, and meditated a scheme to dethrone the king, and overturn the constitution. Being assured of the assistance of a number of the Highlanders, he communicated his plan to some noblemen in Scotland and the north of England, who joined with him

E

in sending an invitation to the Pretender to invade these kingdoms; they also dispatched three men to London, to endeavour to enlist soldiers for the Pretender's service. The names of these men were Robert Whitty, Felix O'Hara, and Joseph Sullivan; and though the business in which they engaged was of the most dangerous nature, yet they continued it for some time; but were at length apprehended, brought to trial, convicted, and executed at Tyburn on the 28th May, 1715.

The Earl of Mar had resolved to keep his proceedings an absolute secret; but it is almost impossible for transactions of this nature to remain so. Information of what had passed having been transmitted to court, the king went to the house on the 20th of July, 1715, and having sent for the Commons, informed both Houses of Parliament, that he had received intelligence of an intention formed by the Pretender to invade his kingdoms; and that he was apprehensive he had but too many abettors in this country. Accordingly, as a preliminary step, the Habeas Corpus act was immediately suspended, and several suspected persons were taken into custody; the militia was raised in different parts of the kingdom; the guards were encamped in Hyde-Park; a number of ships were ordered to guard the coasts, and other steps taken for the public safety.

The Earl of Mar was by this time at the head of three thousand men, with whom he marched from town to town in Scotland, proclaiming the Pretender by the title of James the Third. Some of the soldiers in the castle of Edinburgh having been bribed to assist the Earl of Mar's men in getting over the walls by the aid of rope-ladders, an attempt was made to surprise the castle: but the lord justice clerk was so much on his guard, that this scheme was frustrated, and some of the parties concerned in it suffered death.

Chagrined by this circumstance, and hearing that the French king was just then dead, many of the rebels were for abandoning their enterprise till the arrival of the Pretender. But they were again encouraged by circumstances which took place in another quarter. On the 6th October, 1715, Thomas Foster, Esq., member of parliament for Northumberland, set up the Pretender's standard in that county, and, being joined by several noblemen and gentlemen, they attempted to seize Newcastle, but did not succeed. They were afterwards joined by a body of the Scotch at Kelso, and after marching to different places, they came to Preston in Lancashire.

In the mean time Generals Carpenter and Wills had marched into the North, but finding the rebels gone southward, they went to Preston. This place the rebels attempted to defend against the king's forces, whom they annoyed for some time by firing from the windows of the houses; but the royal troops were at length victorious, after the loss of about 150 men.

It is uncertain how many of the rebels were killed; but the number of prisoners was about 1500, among whom were the Earl of Derwentwater, Lord Widdrington; the Earls of Nithisdale, Winton, and Carnwarth; Viscount Nenmure, and Lord Nairn. The two first noblemen were English peers; the remainder, Scotch. The common soldiers among the rebels were imprisoned at Liverpool, and other places in the neighbourhood; but the above-mentioned noblemen, with other persons above the common rank, to the number of near three hundred men, were brought to London. They arrived at Highgate on the 14th of November, where they were met by a party of the foot-guards, and being tied back to back, and placed two on each horse led by a grenadier, they were in this ignominious manner they were conducted to the metropolis; when the noblemen were committed to the Tower, and the rest to Newgate.

In the mean time a number of the Scotch rebels had marched to Perth, where they proclaimed the Pretender; in consequence of which John Duke of Argyle, who had been commissioned to raise forces, marched against, and came up with them at Sheriffmuir, near Dumblane, on the very day of the other engagement; and the rebellion would have been then crushed, but that some of the duke's troops ran away on the first fire, and got to Stirling, about seven miles from the field of battle: however, the duke obtained a partial victory, by forcing the enemy's lines with his dragoons.

The Earl of Mar retired to Perth on the following day, proposing to cross the Forth, with a view to join the rebels in England; but a fleet lying opposite Edinburgh, prevented this design from being carried into execution.

About this period Sir John M'Kenzie, on the part of the Pretender, having fortified the town of Inverness, Lord Lovat (at this time an adherent of the reigning monarch, but subsequently a friend to the cause of the Stuarts, and for aiding whose rebellion in 1745 he was beheaded) armed his tenants, and drove him from his fortifications; a circumstance of great importance to the royal cause, as a communication was thereby opened between the Highlands and the south of Scotland. The Earl of Seaforth and the Marquis of Huntly now laid down their arms, in consequence of the Earl of Sutherland having also armed his tenants in support of government.

The rebels now went into winter quarters at Perth, and the duke of Argyle at Stirling. The Pretender having landed at Peterhead, with six attendants only, met his friends at Perth on the 22d December, and on the ninth of the following month made a public entry into the palace of Scone (the ancient place of coronation of the Scottish kings), and assuming the dignity of a sovereign prince, issued a proclamation for his coronation, and another for the assembling the states. But this farce continued only for a very short time; for General Cadogan arriving with six thousand Dutch forces to the aid of the Duke of Argyle about the end of January, the latter marched towards Perth, and the rebels fled as soon as they heard of his approach. The Pretender having been encouraged to rebel by France, anticipated succour from the French king; and with this hope he proceeded to Dundee, and from thence to Montrose, where, soon rendered hopeless of receiving any foreign aid, he dismissed his followers. The king's troops pursued, and put many to death; but the Pretender, accompanied by the Earl of Mar, and some of his principal adherents, embarked on board a ship lying at Montrose, put to sea in a dark night, and narrowly escaping the English fleet, landed in France.

The disturbances in the north being thus at an end, both houses of parliament combined to shew their loyalty to their sovereign, and their regard for the public welfare. The unfortunate noblemen who had been secured were committed to the Tower; the House of Commons unanimously agreed to impeach them, and to expel Foster from his seat in their house; and the courts of common law meanwhile proceeded with the trials of less note.

The articles of impeachment having been sent up to them by the Commons, the Lords sat in judgment; Earl Cowper, the lord chancellor, being constituted Lord High Steward. All the peers, except the Earl of Wilton, pleaded guilty to the indictment, but offered various pleas in extenuation of their guilt, in hopes of obtaining mercy. The Earl of Derwentwater suggested that the proceedings of the House of Commons in impeaching him were illegal.

Proclamation being then made, the Lord High Steward proceeded to pass sentence of death upon James Earl of Derwentwater, William Lord Widdrington, William Earl of Nithisdale, Robert Earl of Carnwarth, William Viscount Kenmure, and William Lord Nairn.

His lordship having detailed the circumstances of their impeachment, and answered the argumentative matter contained in their pleas, proceeded to say—

" I must be so just to such of your lordships as profess the religion of the church of Rome, that you had one temptation, and that a great one, to engage in this treason, which the others had not; in that, 'twas evident, success on your part must for ever have established Popery in this kingdom, and that probably you could never expect to have again so fair an opportunity.

" But then, good God ! how must those Protestants be covered with confusion who entered into the same measures, without so much as capitulating for their religion (that ever I could find from any examination I have seen or heard), or so much as requiring, much less obtaining a frail promise, that it should be preserved or even tolerated.

" It is my duty to exhort your lordships thus to think of the aggravations as well as the mitigations (if there be any) of your offences: and if I could have the least hopes, that the prejudices of habit and education would not be too strong for the most earnest and charitable entreaties, I would beg you not to rely any longer on those directors of your consciences, by whose conduct you have very probably been led into this miserable condition; but that your lordships would be assisted by some of those pious and most learned divines of the church of England, who have constantly borne that infallible mark of sincere Christians, universal charity.

" And now, my lords, nothing remains, but that I pronounce upon you (and sorry I am that it falls to my lot to do it) that terrible sentence of the law, which must be the same that is usually given against the meanest offender of the like kind.

" The most ignominious and painful parts of it are usually remitted by the grace of the crown to persons of your quality; but the law, in this case, being deaf to all distinction of persons, requires I should pronounce the sentence, and accordingly it is adjudged by this court—

" That you, James Earl of Derwentwater, William Lord Widdrington, William Earl of Nithisdale, Robert Earl of Carnwarth, William Viscount Kenmure, and William Lord Nairn, and every of you, return to the prison of the Tower from whence you came; from thence you must be drawn to the place of execution; when you come there, you must be hanged by the neck, but not till you be dead, for you must be cut down alive; then your bowels must be taken out, and burnt before your faces; then your heads must be severed from your bodies, and your bodies divided each into four quarters, and these must be at the king's disposal. And God Almighty be merciful to your souls."

After sentence thus passed, the lords were remanded back to the Tower; and on the 18th of February orders were sent to the lieutenant of the Tower and sheriffs for their execution.

Great solicitations were made in favour of them, not only at court, but also in both houses of parliament. The Countess of Nithisdale and Lady Nairn threw themselves at the king's feet, as he passed through the apartments of the palace, and implored his mercy on behalf of their husbands; but their tears and entreaties produced no effect. The Countess of Derwentwater, with her sister, accompanied by the Duchess of Cleveland and Bolton, and several other ladies of the first distinction, was introduced by the Dukes of Richmond and St. Albans into the king's bedchamber, where she invoked his majesty's clemency for her unfortunate consort, but in vain. She afterwards repaired to the lobby of the House of Peers, attended by the ladies of the other condemned lords, and above twenty others of the same quality, and begged the intercession of the house : but no regard was paid to them. Next day petitions were presented to both Houses of Parliament. In the House of Commons a motion for adjournment was made, so as to prevent any further interposition there. In the Upper House, the Duke of Richmond delivered a petition from the Earl of Derwentwater, to whom he was nearly related, but at the same time declared that he himself should oppose his solicitation. The Earl of Derby expressed some compassion for the Earl of Nairn. Petitions from the rest were presented by other lords, moved by pity and humanity. Many of the peers opposed their being received; but it was at length carried by a majority of nine or ten voices, that the same should be received and read. The question was also put, whether the king had power to reprieve in cases of impeachment; which being carried in the affirmative, a motion was made to address his majesty to desire him to grant a reprieve to the lords under sentence; but the movers thereof only obtained this clause, viz. " To reprieve such of the condemned lords as deserve his mercy; and that the time of the respite should be left to his majesty's discretion."

This address having been presented, his majesty replied, " That on this, and on all other occasions, he would do what he thought most consistent with the dignity of his crown, and the safety of his people."

The great parties they had made, as was said, by the means of money, and also the rash expressions too common in the mouths of many of their friends, as if the government did not dare to execute them, contributed not a little to the hastening of their execution; for on the same day the address was presented, the 23d of February, it was resolved in council, that the Earls of Derwentwater and Nithisdale, and the Lord Kenmure, should be beheaded. The Earl of Nithisdale, apprehending he should be included in the warrant, made his escape the evening before, in a woman's riding-hood, which was supposed to have been conveyed to him by his mother on a visit.

On the morning of the 24th February, three detachments of life-guards went from Whitehall to Tower-Hill; and having taken their station round the scaffold, the two lords were brought from the Tower at ten o'clock, and being received by the sheriffs at the bar, were conducted to the Transport-Office on Tower-Hill.

At the expiration of about an hour, the Earl of Derwentwater sent word that he was ready; on which Sir John Fryer, one of the sheriffs, walked before him to the scaffold, and when there, told him he might have what time he pleased to prepare himself for death. His lordship desired to read a paper which he had written, the substance of which was, that he was sorry for having pleaded guilty; that he acknowledged no king but James the Third, for whom he had an inviolable affection, and that these kingdoms would never be happy till the ancient constitution was restored; and he wished his death might contribute to that desirable end. His lordship professed to die a Roman Catholic, and, at the end of his speech, observed, " If that prince, who now governs, had given me life, I should have thought myself obliged never more to take up arms against him." He then read some prayers out of two small books, and kneeled down to try how the block would fit his neck; and having told the executioner that he forgave him, and likewise forgave all his enemies, he directed him to strike when he should repeat the words " Sweet Jesus!" the third time. He then knelt down, and having prepared himself to receive the blow, he said, " Sweet Jesus, receive my spirit! Sweet Jesus, be merciful to me! Sweet Jesus—" and was proceeding in his prayer, when his head was struck off at one blow. The executioner taking it up, exhibited it at the four corners of the scaffold, saying, " Behold the head of a traitor!—God save King George!" The body was immediately wrapped up in black baize, and, being carried to a coach, was delivered to the friends of the deceased.

The scaffold having been cleared, fresh baize put on the block, and saw-dust strewed, so that none of the blood might appear, Lord Kenmure was conducted to the scaffold. His lordship, who was a Protestant, was attended by two clergymen. He declined saying much telling one of them that he had prudential reasons for not delivering his sentiments; which were supposed to arise from his regard to Lord Carnwarth, who was his brother-in-law, and was then interceding for the royal mercy. Lord Kenmure having finished his devotions, declared that he forgave the executioner, to whom he made a present of eight guineas. He was attended by a surgeon, who drew his finger over that part of the neck where the blow was to be struck; and being executed, as Lord Derwentwater had been, his body was delivered to the care of an undertaker.

George Earl of Winton, not having pleaded guilty with the other lords, was brought to trial on the 15th March, when the principal matter urged in his favour was, that he had surrendered at Preston in consequence of a promise from General Wills to grant him his life: in answer to which it was sworn, that no promise of mercy was made, but that the rebels surrendered at discretion. The circumstances of his having left his house with fourteen or fifteen of his servants, well mounted and armed—his joining the Earl of Carnwarth and Lord Kenmure—his proceeding with the rebels through the various stages of their march—and his surrendering with the rest, were circumstances fully proved: notwithstanding which, his council moved in arrest of judgment; but the plea on which this motion was founded being thought insufficient, his peers unanimously found him guilty. The lord high steward then pronounced sentence on him, after having addressed him in forcible terms, in the same manner as he had sentenced the other peers.

Soon after the passing of this sentence the Earl of Winton found means to escape out of the Tower.

In the beginning of April, a commission for trying the rebels met in the Court of Common Pleas, when bills of high treason were found against Mr. Forster, Macintosh, and twenty of their confederates. Forster escaped from Newgate, and reached the continent in safety; the rest pleaded not guilty, and were indulged with time to prepare for their trials. Pitts, the keeper of Newgate, being suspected of having connived at Forster's escape, was tried for his life at the Old Bailey, but acquitted. Notwithstanding this prosecution, which ought to have redoubled the vigilance of the gaolers, Macintosh and several other prisoners broke from Newgate, after having mastered the keeper and turnkey, and disarmed the centinel. The Court proceeded with the trials of those that remained, and a great number were found guilty. Four or five of them suffered the utmost rigour of the law, being hanged, drawn, and quartered at Tyburn.

The judges appointed to try the rebels at Liverpool found a considerable number guilty of high treason. Five were executed at Manchester, six at Wigan, and eleven at Preston: and a thousand prisoners submitted to the king's mercy, and were transported to North America.

———————————

MARY BLANDY.

EXECUTED FOR PARRICIDE

This unhappy young lady was the only daughter of Mr. Francis Blandy, an eminent attorney at Henley-upon-Thames, and town-clerk of that place. Though she had been educated with the utmost tenderness, and every possible care had been taken to impress her mind with sentiments of virtue and religion, yet she was guilty of a crime of the most heinous description—the wilful murder of her father. Her person had nothing in it remarkably engaging; but she was of a sprightly and affable disposition, polite in manners, and engaging in conversation; and was uncommonly distinguished by her good sense. She had read the best authors in the English language, and had a memory remarkably retentive of the knowledge she had acquired. In a word, she excelled most of her sex in those accomplishments which are calculated to grace and dignify the female mind; and, as report had given to her a fortune of no inconsiderable extent, her hand was sought in marriage by many persons whose rank and wealth rendered them fitting to become her partner for life. But among all these visitants none were received with greater pleasure by Mr. and Mrs. Blandy, and their daughter, than those who held commissions in the army. This predilection was evinced in the introduction of the Hon. William Henry Cranston, at that time engaged on the recruiting service for a foot regiment in which he acted as captain.

Miss Blandy was about twenty-six years of age when she became acquainted with Captain Cranstoun, who was then about forty-six. He was the son of Lord Cranstoun, of an ancient Scotch family, which had made great alliances by intermarriages with the nobility of Scotland. Being a younger brother, his uncle Lord Mark Ker procured him a commission in the army, which, with the interest of £1500, was all he had for his support. In the year 1745 he married a Miss Murray, and received a handsome fortune with her; but he was defective in the great article of prudence. His wife was delivered of a son within a year after the marriage; and about this period he received orders to join his regiment in England, and was sent on a recruiting party to Henley, which gave rise to the unhappy connexion which ended so fatally.

It is somewhat extraordinary that a person possessed of so many accomplishments as Miss Blandy, should have formed a *liason* with a man so much older than herself, and who, besides, is represented as being devoid of all personal attractions.

Mr. Blandy, who was acquainted with Lord Mark Ker, was fond of being deemed a man of taste, and so open to flattery, it is hardly to be wondered at, that a man of Cranstoun's artifice ingratiated himself into his favour, and obtained permission to pay his addresses to the daughter. Cranstoun, apprehending that Miss Blandy might discover that he had a wife in Scotland, informed her that he was involved in ч disagreeable law-suit in that country with a young lady who claimed him as a husband; and so sure was he of the interest he had obtained in Miss Blandy's affections, that he had the confidence to ask her if she loved him well enough to wait the issue of the affair. She told him, that if her father and mother approved of her staying for him, she had no objection. This must be allowed to have been a very extraordinary declaration of love, and as extraordinary a reply.

Cranstoun endeavoured to conduct the amour with all possible secrecy; nothwithstanding which, it came to the knowledge of Lord Mark Ker, who wrote to Mr. Blandy, informing him that the captain had a wife and children in Scotland, and conjuring him to preserve his daughter from ruin.

Alarmed by this intelligence, Mr. Blandy informed his daughter of it; but she did not seem equally affected, as Cranstoun's former declaration had prepared her to expect some such news; and when the old gentleman taxed Cranstoun with it, he declared it was only an affair of gallantry, of which he should have no difficulty to free himself.

Mrs. Blandy appears to have been under as great a degree of infatuation as her daughter; for she forbore all farther inquiry, on the captain's bare assurance that the report of his marriage was false. Cranstoun, however, could not be equally easy. He saw the necessity of devising some scheme to get his first marriage annulled, or of bidding adieu to all the gratifications he could promise himself by a second.

After revolving various schemes in his mind, he at length wrote to his wife, requesting her to disown him for a husband. The substance of this letter was, that, having no other way of rising to preferment but in the army, he had but little ground to expect advancement there while it was known he was incumbered with a wife and family; but, could he pass for a single man, he had not the least doubt of being quickly promoted; which would procure him a sufficiency to maintain her, as well as himself, in a genteeler manner than he was now able to do. "All therefore," adds he, " I have to request of you, is, that you will transcribe the inclosed copy of a letter, wherein you disown me for a husband; put your maiden name to it, and send it by the post: all the use I shall make of it will be to procure my advancement, which will necessarily include your own benefit. In full assurance that you will comply with my request, I remain, Your most affectionate husband,— W. H. CRANSTOUN."

Mrs. Cranstoun, ill has she had been treated by her husband, and little hope as she had of more generous usage, was, after repeated letters had passed, induced to give up her claim; and at length sent him the requested paper, signed Murray, which was her maiden name. The villanious captain, being possessed of this letter, made some copies of it, which he sent to his wife's relations, and his own: the consequence of which was, that they withdrew the assistance that they had afforded the lady, which reduced her to an extremity she had never before known. Exclusive of this, he instituted a suit for the dissolution of the marriage; but when Mrs. Cranstoun was heard, and the letters read, the artful contrivance was seen through, the marriage was confirmed, and

Cranstoun was adjudged to pay the expences of the suit. At the next sessions Captain Cranstoun preferred a petition, desiring to be heard by council on new evidence, which, it was pretended, had arisen respecting Miss Murray. This petition after some hesitation was heard; but the issue was, that the marriage was again confirmed, and Cranstoun was obliged to allow his wife a separate maintenance.

Still, however, he paid his addresses to Miss Blandy with the same fervency as before; which coming to the knowledge of Mrs. Cranstoun, she sent her the decree of the court of session, establishing the validity of the marriage. It is reasonable to suppose that this would have convinced Miss Blandy of the erroneous path in which she was treading. On this occasion she consulted her mother; and, Cranstoun having set out for Scotland, the old lady advised her to write to him, to know the truth of the affair. Absurd as this advice was, she wrote to him; but, soon after the receipt of her letter, he returned to Henley, when he had impudence enough to assert that the cause was not finally determined, but would be referred to the House of Lords. Mr. Blandy gave very little credit to this assertion; but his wife assented at once to all he said, and treated him with as much tenderness as if he had been her own child; of which the following circumstance will afford ample proof. Mrs. Blandy and her daughter being on a visit to Mrs. Pocock, of Turville-court, the old lady was taken so ill as to be obliged to continue there for some days. In the height of her disorder, which was a violent fever, she cried, " Let Cranstoun be sent for." He was then with the regiment at Northampton; but, her request being complied with, she no sooner saw him, than she raised herself on the pillow, and hung round his neck, repeatedly exclaiming, " My dear Cranstoun, I am glad you have come; I shall now grow well soon." So extravagant was her fondness, that she insisted on having him as her nurse; and he actually administered her medicines. On the following day she grew better; on which she said, " This I owe to you, my dear Cranstoun; your coming has given me new health and fresh spirits. I was fearful I should die, and you not here to comfort that poor girl. How like death she looks!"

It would be ungenerous to the memory of Mrs. Blandy to suppose that she saw Cranstoun's guilt in its true light of enormity; but certainly she was a most egregious dupe to his artifices.

Mrs. Blandy and her daughter having come to London, the former wanted £40, to discharge a debt she had contracted unknown to her husband; and Cranstoun coming into the room while the mother and daughter were weeping over their distresses, he demanded the reason of their grief; of which being informed, he left them, and soon returning with the requisite sum, he threw it into the old lady's lap. Charmed by this apparent generosity, she burst into tears, and squeezed his hand fervently: on which he embraced her, and said, " Remember, it is a son; therefore do not make yourself uneasy: you do not lay under any obligation to me." Of this debt of forty pounds, ten pounds had been contracted by the ladies while in London, for expences in consequence of their pleasures; and the other thirty, by expensive treats given to Cranstoun at Henley during Mr. Blandy's absence. Soon after this

Mrs. Blandy died; and Cranstoun now complaining of his fear of being arrested for the forty pounds, the young lady borrowed that sum, which she gave him, and made him a present of her watch; so that he was a gainer by his former apparent generosity.

Mr. Blandy began now to shew evident dislike to Captain Cranstoun's visits: but he found means to take leave of the daughter, to whom he complained of the father's ill-treatment, but insinuated that he had a method of conciliating his esteem, and that when he arrived in Scotland he would send her some powders proper for the purpose, on which, to prevent suspicion, he would write " Powders to clean the Scotch pebbles."

It does not appear that the young lady had any idea that the powders he was to send her were of a poisonous nature. She seems rather to have been infatuated by her love; and this is the only excuse that can be made for her subsequent conduct, which appears otherwise totally inconsistent with that good sense for which she was celebrated.

Cranstoun sent her the powders according to promise; and Mr. Blandy being indisposed on the Sunday se'nnight before his death, Susan Gunnel, a maid-servant, made him some water-gruel, into which Miss Blandy conveyed some of the powders, and gave it to her father; and repeating this draught on the following day, he was tormented with the most violent pains in his bowels.

The disorder, which had commenced with symptoms of so dangerous a character, soon increased, and the greatest alarm was felt by the medical attendants of the old gentleman that death would terminate his sufferings. Every effort was made by which it was hoped that his life could be saved; but, at length, when all possibility of his recovery was past, his wretched daughter rushed into his presence, and, in an agony of tears and lamentations, confessed that she was the author of his sufferings, and of his inevitable death. Urged to account for her conduct, which to her father appeared inexplicable, she denied, with the loudest assertions, all guilty intention. She repeated the tale of love, and of the insidious arts employed by Cranstoun, but asserted that she was unaware of the deadly nature of the powders, and that her sole object in administering them was to procure her father's affection for her lover. Death soon terminated the accumulated misery of the wretched parent, and the daughter had scarcely witnessed his demise ere she became an inmate of a gaol.

She was tried on the 3d of March, 1752, before Mr. Baron Legge; and was immediately found guilty, upon her own confession and the evidence of various witnesses. She addressed the jury at great length, repeating the story which has been before related, of her unfortunate love; but all was of no avail,—she was found guilty, and received sentence of death.

After conviction, she behaved with the utmost decency and resignation. She was attended by the Reverend Mr. Swinton, from whose hands she received the sacrament on the day before her execution, declaring that she did not know there was any thing hurtful in the powders she had given her father. The night before her death she spent in devotion; and at nine in the morning of the 6th April, 1752, she left

her apartment, to be conducted to the scaffold, dressed in a black bom-
bazine, and having her arms bound with black ribbons. The clergyman
attended her to the place of execution, to which she walked with the
utmost solemnity of deportment; and, when there, acknowledged her
fault in administering the powders to her father, but declared that, as
she must soon appear before the most awful tribunal, she had no idea of
doing injury, nor any suspicion that the powders were of a poisonous
nature. Having ascended some steps of the ladder, she said, " Gentlemen,
don't hang me high, for the sake of decency." Being desired to go
something higher, she turned about, and expressed her apprehensions
that she should fall. The rope being put round her neck, she pulled her
handkerchief over her face, and was turned off, on holding out a book of
devotions which she had been reading. The crowd of spectators assembled on this occasion was immense; and when she had hung the usual
time, she was cut down, and the body, being put into a hearse, was conveyed to Henley, and interred with her parents, at one o'clock on the
following morning.

It will be now proper to return to Cranstoun, who was the original
contriver of this horrid murder. Having heard of Miss Blandy's
commitment to Oxford gaol, he concealed himself some time in Scotland,
and then escaped to Boulogne in France. Meeting there with Mrs. Ross,
who was distantly related to his family, he acquainted her with his situation, and begged her protection: on which she advised him to change his
name for her maiden name of Dunbar. Some officers in the French
service, who were related to his wife, hearing of his concealment, vowed
revenge if they should meet with him, for his cruelty to the unhappy
woman: on which he fled to Paris; whence he went to Furnes, a town
in Flanders, where Mrs. Ross had provided a lodging for his reception.
He had not been long at Furnes, when he was seized with a severe fit of
illness, which brought him to a degree of reflection to which he had been
long a stranger. At length, he sent for a father belonging to an adjacent
convent, and received absolution from his hands, on declaring himself a
convert to the Romish faith.

Cranstoun died on the 30th of November, 1752; and the fraternity of
monks and friars looked on his conversion as an object of such importance, that solemn mass was sung on the occasion, and the body was
followed to the grave, not only by the ecclesiastics, but by the magistrates of the town.

His papers were then sent to Scotland, to his brother, Lord Cranstoun;
his clothes were sold for the discharge of his debts; and his wife came
into possession of the interest of the £1500 above-mentioned.

ATTACK ON PUERTO VELO BY THE PIRATES.

SIR HENRY MORGAN.

A NOTORIOUS PIRATE.

Sir Henry Morgan, a native of Wales, was descended of a respectable family. His father was a wealthy farmer, but young Morgan had no inclination to that industrious mode of life. Abandoning his father's house, he hastened to a sea-port town, where several vessels were bound for the Isle of Barbadoes. He went into the service of one of these; and, upon his arrival in the island, was sold as a slave. Having obtained his liberty, he went to Jamaica. Finding two pirate vessels ready to go to sea, he went on board one of them, with the intention of becoming a pirate. Having performed several successful voyages, he agreed with some of his companions to unite their wealth and purchase a vessel; which being done, he was unanimously chosen captain.

With this vessel he went to cruise upon the coasts of Campeachy, and, capturing several vessels, returned in triumph to Jamaica. Upon his arrival, one Mansvelt, an old pirate, was equipping a fleet with the intention of landing upon the continent and pillaging the country. The success of Morgan induced Mansvelt to choose him for his vice-admiral. With a fleet of fifteen ships and five hundred men, they set sail from Jamaica, and arrived at the isle of St. Catherine. Here they made a descent, and landed the greater part of their men.

They soon forced the garrison to surrender, and to deliver up all the forts and castles, which they demolished, only reserving one, in which they placed a hundred men, and the slaves they had taken from the

5 F

Spaniards. They then proceeded to an adjoining small island, and having destroyed both islands with fire and sword, and made what arrangements were necessary at the castle which they had garrisoned, they set sail in quest of new spoils. They cruised upon the coasts of Costa Rica, and entered the river Calla with an intention to pillage all the towns upon the coast.

Informed of their arrival and of their former depredations, the governor of Panama collected a force to oppose the pirates. They fled at his approach, and hastened to the isle of St. Catherine, to visit their companions that were left in the garrison. Le Sieur Simon, the governor, had put the large island in a posture of defence, and cultivated the small island with such care, that it was able to afford fresh provisions to the whole fleet. The vicinity of these islands to the Spanish dominions, and the ease with which they could be defended, strongly inclined Mansvelt to retain them in possession.

With this view he returned to Jamaica to send out greater numbers, so that they might be able to defend themselves in case of an attack from the Spaniards. He signified his intentions to the governor of Jamaica upon his return home ; but, afraid of offending the king of England, and of weakening the strength of his own island, the governor declined complying with his wishes. Baffled in his designs, Mansvelt went to Tortuga, to solicit reinforcements from the governor, of that island ; but, before he could effect his purpose, death suddenly put an end to his wicked career.

Meanwhile the governor of the garrison of St. Catharine, receiving no intelligence of his admiral, was greatly anxious concerning the cause of his long absence. The Spanish governor of Costa Rica, apprised of the injury which would accrue to his master by these two islands remaining in the hands of the pirates, equipped a considerable fleet to retake them. But, before proceeding to extremities, he wrote to Le Sieur Simon to inform him, that if he willingly surrendered, he should be amply rewarded, but if he resisted, severely punished. Having no hope of being able to defend the islands against such a superior force, he surrendered them into the hands of their rightful owner. A few days after this, an English vessel arrived from Jamaica with a large supply of men, women, and stores. The Spaniards, seeing the ships from the castle, prevailed upon Le Sieur Simon to go on board to decoy them into the harbour; which he dexterously effected, and they were all made prisoners.

But the active and intrepid mind of Morgan was soon employed in the execution of new plans. He at first equipped one ship, with the intention of collecting as many as he possibly could, to form a strong fleet to carry on his depredations. Being successful in collecting a fleet of twelve sail, with seven hundred men, he rendezvoused in a certain part of the island of Cuba.

This island is situated in twenty to twenty-three degrees north latitude, is one hundred and fifty leagues in length, and about forty in breadth. Its fertility is equal to that of Hispaniola ; it is convenient for commerce, and affords plenty of the hides called hides of Havannah. It is surrounded with a number of small islands, which obtain the general name of Cayos, and are a place of refuge for the pirates, where they hold their councils for concerting their attacks upon the Spaniards. It is plentifully watered with copious streams and pleasant rivers, and many convenient harbours adorn the coasts.

Captain Morgan had only been two months in the south of Cuba, when he called a council of his fleet, to concert measures for attacking some part of the Spanish dominions. Several proposals were agitated; but it was finally resolved to attack the town of El Puerto del Principe.

When arrived in the bay of that place, a Spaniard, who was on board the pirate fleet, swam on shore during the night, and gave intelligence of their designs to the governor and inhabitants of the town, who hastened to conceal their riches, and to muster their whole force to oppose the invaders. Having collected about eight hundred men, cut down trees across the roads to impede the march of the pirates, placed several ambuscades, and taken possession of a pass through which it behoved them to penetrate, the governor, with the remainder of his forces, drew up on an extended plain in the vicinity of the town.

The pirates, finding the passages to the town impenetrable, made a circuit through the woods, escaped several of the ambuscades, and with great difficulty arrived at the plain where the Spaniards were waiting to give them a warm reception. A detachment of horse first attacked them; but Morgan formed his men into a semicircle, and so valiantly and dexterously assailed the Spaniards, that they fled towards the woods for safety; but before they could reach the woods, the greater part fell under the swords of the invaders. After a skirmish of four hours, Morgan and his men entered the town; but the inhabitants, having shut themselves up in their houses, fired upon them from the roofs. Being severely annoyed by the inhabitants in this position, Captain Morgan threatened, " that if they did not surrender willingly, they should soon behold their city in flames, and their wives and children torn to pieces before their eyes." Thus intimidated, they submitted at discretion.

The pirates then proceeded to the most unexampled cruelties; they shut up men, women, and children in the several churches, and pillaged the town; and began to feast and rejoice, while they left their prisoners to starve. Unsatisfied even with this, they tortured them, in order to oblige them to reveal where their money and goods were concealed.

Finding no more to pillage, and provisions becoming scarce, they meditated a departure. With this intention, they intimated to the wretched inhabitants, " that if they did not ransom themselves, they should all be transported to Jamaica, and their city laid in ashes." The Spaniards accordingly sent some of their number to search the woods and country for the required contributions. In a short time they returned, informing Captain Morgan that they had been unsuccessful, but requested the space of fifteen days, in order to obtain the required ransom. To this he consented; but, in a short time, a negro being taken with letters from the governor of St. Jago, requiring the inhabitants to endeavour to gain time from the invaders until he should come to their assistance, Captain Morgan ordered all the spoils to be put on board the ships, and informed the Spaniards, that if they did not on the following day pay the ransom, he would set fire to the city.

The inhabitants replied, that it was totally impossible for them to give such a sum in so short a time, since the messengers whom they had sent were not in the neighbourhood. Morgan knew their intention ; but deeming it unsafe to remain longer in the place, demanded of them four hundred oxen or cows, together with sufficient salt to prepare them, with the additional condition, that they should put them on board his ships. Under this stipulation he retired with his men, taking six of the principal inhabitants as hostages for the performance of the stipulation. The oxen were slain, salted, and put on board with all possible expedition ; the hostages were released ; and Captain Morgan took leave of the place, directing his course to a certain island where he intended to divide his booty.

Arrived at that place, he found he had only fifty thousand pieces of eight in money and goods. This sum being insufficient to pay their debts in Jamaica, the captain proposed that they should attempt new exploits before returning home. The Frenchmen, however, disagreeing with the English, departed, and left Captain Morgan and his countrymen, to the amount of four hundred and sixty, to seek their fortune in their own way. This rupture did not intimidate the heroic captain ; but, labouring to inspire his men with the same spirit, he, with a fleet of nine ships, directed his course towards the continent.

Meanwhile he concealed his intentions from every person in the fleet, only assuring them that, by following his directions, he would certainly enrich them with immense spoils. Arrived upon the coast of Costa Rica, he informed them, that his intention was to attack the town of Puerto Vela by night. To this some objected, on account of the fewness of their numbers ; but the captain replied, " If our number is small, our hearts are great, and the fewer persons we are, the more union, and the better shares of the spoil." Stimulated with the hope of great riches, they unanimously agreed upon the attack.

This place is esteemed the strongest that the king of Spain possesses in the West Indies, except Havannah and Carthagena. There are two castles situated in the entry of the harbour, which are deemed almost impregnable. The garrison consisted of three hundred men, and the town was inhabited by about four hundred families.

Captain Morgan being thoroughly acquainted with the whole coast, and all the approaches to the city, arrived in the dusk of the evening at a place about ten leagues west of the town. He proceeded up the river to another harbour called Puerto Pontia, and came to anchor. Leaving the vessels with a few men, he went with the rest in the boats and canoes, and reaching the shore about midnight, marched to the first watch of the city. An Englishman, who had been prisoner in the town, was their guide ; and he was commanded, with some others, either to take or slay the sentinel. They seized him before he could give the alarm, bound his hands, and brought him to Captain Morgan, who asked him, " how matters went in the city, and what force they had," with many other questions, threatening him with instant death if he refused to declare the truth. He then advanced towards the city, with the sentinel walking before; and when he arrived at the first castle, he surrounded it with his men. He now commanded the sentinel to accost those within the walls, and inform them, that if they did not surrender, they would all be cut to pieces without the least mercy. But, regardless of their threatenings, they instantly began to fire, which gave the alarm to the whole city. The pirates, however, took the castle, and having shut up the officers and men in one room, blew up the castle with all its inhabitants. Pursuing their victory, they attacked the city. The governor not being able to rally, the citizens fled to one of the castles, and from thence fired upon the pirates. The assault continued from the dawn of morning until noon; and victory remained in suspense, until a troop of those who had taken the other castle, came to meet their captain with loud shouts of victory. This inspired the captain with new resolution to exert every effort to take this castle also. He was the more stimulated to this, as the principal inhabitants with their riches, and all the plate belonging to the different churches, were in that fort.

With this view, he caused ten or twelve ladders to be constructed with all expedition; and having brought a number of the religious men and women from the cloisters, he commanded these to be placed before the walls. The governor of the castle was, however, deaf to their cries and entreaties to surrender and save their lives and his own. That brave commander declared, that he would never surrender the castle, and, continuing to fire upon the besiegers, many of the holy brothers and sisters were slain before the ladders could be fastened on the wall. This, however, being at length effected, the pirates ascended in vast numbers, carrying in their hands fire-balls and earthen pots full of powder, which they kindled at the top of the walls, and threw among the Spaniards.

Unable any longer to defend the castle, the garrison threw down their arms, and surrendered. But the brave governor would not submit, and not only slew many of the invaders, but even some of his own men, because they would not continue to repel the enemy. Unable to take him prisoner, the pirates were constrained to put him to death, for, notwithstanding the entreaties of his wife and daughter, he remained inflexible, declaring, " that he would rather die as a valiant soldier, than be hanged as a coward." Having taken the castle, they placed all the wounded by themselves, leaving them to perish of their wounds, the men and women in separate apartments, with a strong guard upon them, and gave themselves up to all manner of debauchery and riotous excess. They next proceeded to torture the prisoners, to constrain them to inform them where they had deposited their money and goods.

Meanwhile, intelligence of these disasters, and of the taking of the city, was conveyed to the president of Panama, who immediately endeavoured to raise such a force as might expel the pirates. The unhealthiness of the climate, their own debaucheries, and the sword, having greatly lessened the number of his men, Captain Morgan gave orders to carry on board all their spoils, and to prepare to sail to another port. While these preparations were advancing, he required the inhabitants to pay 100,000 pieces of eight as the ransom of their city, or he threatened to reduce it to ashes.

In this unhappy dilemma, two messengers were dispatched to the president of Panama, to inform him of their misfortunes, and to solicit his assistance. Having collected an army, he marched towards Puerto Vela. But Morgan stationing an hundred of his men in a narrow pass through which it was necessary they should come, the Spaniards were instantly put to flight, and the president returned home with the remainder of his forces. Thus abandoned to their cruel fate, the wretched inhabitants collected the sum demanded; and Captain Morgan having victualled his fleet, and taken several of the best guns from the castle, sailed for the island of Cuba, to divide his spoils. These he found to amount to 250,000 pieces of eight, with a large quantity of cloth, linen, silks, and other goods. With this immense wealth they sailed for Jamaica, and, arriving there, gave loose to their usual riot and excess.

After having lavished the wealth which they had acquired, Morgan gave orders to his fleet to rendezvous at Cow Island. Rendered famous by his recent adventures, many other pirates now joined him, and he saw himself at the head of a more powerful fleet than he had ever commanded.

Leaving Cow Island, Captain Morgan now set sail for the island of Savona, with a fleet of fifteen ships, and a full complement of men. He proceeded on his voyage until he arrived at the port of Ocoa. Here he landed some of his men, and sent them into the woods to seek water and fresh provisions. They returned with several beasts which they had slain; but the Spaniards, dissatisfied with their conduct, laid a snare to entrap them in their second attempt to hunt in their territories. They ordered three or four hundred men from Santo Domingo to hunt in all the adjacent woods, and emptied them of animals. The pirates, returning in a few days to the hunting, could find none, which induced them to venture farther into the woods. Watching all their motions, the Spaniards collected a herd of cows, and committed the care of them to two or three men. The pirates slew several of them; but the moment they were about to carry them off, the Spaniards fell upon them with desperate fury, and constrained them to retreat to their ships; but, during their retreat, they frequently fired upon their pursuers, so that they fled in their turn. Enraged at this attack, Captain Morgan next day landed two hundred men, and ranged the woods; but finding no enemy, he set fire to the scattered cottages of the peasants, and returned to his ships.

Having waited, with no small degree of impatience, for the ships that had not arrived, he at length sailed for the island of Savona. Arrived at this place, he was still disappointed at the remainder of his fleet not joining him; and while he, with great impatience, waited for them, he sent some of his men to fetch provisions. The Spaniards, however, were now so vigilant, and so well prepared to defend themselves and their property, that they were constrained to return empty-handed.

Despairing of the arrival of his other ships, Captain Morgan made a review of those which were present, and found his forces amounted to five hundred men, provided with eight ships. With this small number he was unable to pursue his original plan, and, by advice of a Frenchman who had been at the taking of Maracaibo, he resolved to sack that place a second time.

After watering at the island of Cuba, they arrived at the sea of Maracaibo, and, after some hot actions in taking possession of the forts at the entrance, they reached the city in small boats and canoes. The inhabitants deserted the city at their approach; and, after taking what property they could find, and exercising unheard-of cruelties and tortures upon the prisoners they found in the neighbourhood, Captain Morgan resolved to sail for Gibraltar, and run the hazard of a battle. Some of the principal prisoners he took with him, and sent others to Gibraltar, to tell the inhabitants of the barbarous cruelty they had seen exercised towards their townsmen, and to assure them, that unless they surrendered to Morgan, they would share the same fate. Notwithstanding a show of resistance at first, every person in the city, with the exception of an idiot, fled when the pirates approached, taking with them their riches and gunpowder, and destroying the guns of the fortress. This solitary individual who had remained in the city, notwithstanding it was evident to Morgan and his associates that he was an idiot, they tortured with unparalleled cruelty, to force him to discover to them the retreat of the inhabitants; of this he knew nothing, yet he died under their ferocious hands. Detachments were sent to scour the country round in search of the fugitives, whom, when they found, they treated with the most barbarous inhumanity. One of these was headed by Morgan himself, who directed his search against the governor; but the latter retired to a high mountain, and completely foiled Morgan and his army. The heavy rains, and want of ammunition, at length reduced the pirates to great distress; and if the Spaniards had not been so dismayed, they would, at this time, have found their invaders an easy prey.

Morgan returned to Gibraltar with a great many prisoners, who negotiated a ransom to save the city from being burnt. He then returned to Maracaibo, where he was informed that a Spanish fleet, consisting of several large vessels, lay at the entrance of the strait, to prevent his escape; which struck his men and himself with great consternation. He assumed a fictitious courage, and sent a letter to the admiral, demanding a very high ransom to prevent the town of Maracaibo from being committed to the flames. This, however, met with no gracious reception, and the Spanish admiral would listen to nothing but the surrender of all the prisoners, hostages, and property. In this dilemma, Morgan assembled his men, and asked them, whether they would give up what they had acquired with such toil and danger, or fight their way through the enemy? To the latter proposition they unanimously agreed.

Despair sharpened their invention and courage. They set about immediately to prepare a fire-ship, with which they intended to destroy the Spanish admiral's vessel, and considerably strengthened their other vessels. Captain Morgan sailed with his fleet, and attacked the enemy early in the morning: the fire-ship grappled with the largest vessel, and soon destroyed her; the other two fled towards the castle at the entrance, where one of them was sunk by her own crew, and the other surrendered to the pirates. Elated with this signal victory, the pirates immediately landed, hoping to find the castle surrender at their appearance. In this however, they were, disappointed, for they met with a most spirited resistance, and were at last obliged to fly to their ships.

Morgan again sailed for Maracaibo, where he repaired the large ship he had taken, and hoisted his own flag on board of it He again sent to the Spanish admiral, demanding a ransom for the city of Maracaibo; to which that brave officer would not listen, but threatened vengeance on the pirates. The inhabitants, however, offered the sum of 20,000 pieces of eight, besides 500 beeves to victual his fleet, if he would spare the town, and free the Spaniards he had made prisoners. To this last clause, however, he would not agree; he feared the Spanish admiral might destroy his fleet with the guns of the castle in passing through the strait; and, for this purpose, he wished to retain the prisoners, to hold out a bribe to the admiral. He sent some of them to the castle, to inform the governor, that unless they were permitted to pass the castle unmolested, he would hang every prisoner in his power. The admiral would not listen to the solicitations of these unfortunate prisoners, but accused them of cowardice, and returned for answer, that he would oppose the passage of the pirates by every means in his power.

This resolution made Morgan pause a while before he decided what was to be done. In the first place, they divided their plunder, which amounted to 250,000 pieces of eight, besides an immense quantity of merchandise and slaves. Morgan then harangued his men, and took counsel what steps they were to follow, in order to get past the castle. A stratagem was at length agreed upon, in which they succeeded. During the day time they sent on shore their boats loaded with men, as if they intended to attack the castle by land. The canoes were hid from the castle for some time by the trees on the banks, but in a short while returned, with the appearance of only two or three men in them, to deceive the enemy, while they were all lying in the bottom of the boats. The Spaniards, expecting the *forces that had been landed* would attack the castle at night, removed all their heavy guns to the land side, and left that which commanded the sea without any, by which the pirates passed unmolested during the night.

When the Spaniards perceived that they were about to escape, they transported their guns to the other side of the castle, and commenced a dreadful fire upon the pirates; but they effected their escape without much loss or damage. Captain Morgan now sent a canoe to the castle with some of the prisoners, and fired seven guns as a farewell salute.

In this voyage they were suddenly overtaken with a great tempest; were constrained to cast anchor, and again to put to sea; and were alternately harassed with the dread of being overwhelmed in the deep, or cast upon shore and murdered by the Spaniards or Indians. Fortunately, however, for Morgan and his crew, the tempest was calmed, and they arrived safe at Jamaica.

Not long after their arrival there, their excesses emptied their coffers, and constrained them to seek for new spoils. Having collected his men at Port Caullion, he held a council to deliberate upon their next adventure. Meanwhile it was found necessary to send four ships and one boat, with four hundred men, to the continent, to pillage some coast towns for provisions, and to search the woods for wild beasts. These vessels were for some days becalmed in the mouth of the river Cow, which informed the Spaniards of their arrival, and gave them time to hide their money and goods, and to prepare for their own defence. Here they seized a ship richly laden, and landed in defiance of all the resistance of the Spaniards, whom they pursued into the woods, and, by torture, constrained many of them to deliver up their money and property. Dissatisfied with all they had received, upon their departure, they demanded four thousand bushels of maize as a ransom for the town.

The return of these ships, and their great success, was the cause of exultation to Morgan and his men. Having equally divided the spoil, they directed their course towards Cape Tiburon; the fleet consisting of thirty-seven sail, with two thousand men, besides marines and boys. The captain divided his fleet into two squadrons, and gave the second squadron to a vice-admiral. He then summoned a council of all his captains, and, besides other directions, enjoined them to carry on hostilities with the Spaniards, as the enemies of the English nation.

From Cape Tiburon, Morgan sailed for St. Catharine's, then in the possession of the Spaniards; landed a thousand men, and advanced to the governor's residence: but he found that the garrison had retired to the adjacent small island, and fortified themselves in the strongest manner. Upon their approach, they received such a warm reception, that they were under the necessity of lying all night upon the ground, destitute of every kind of provisions. But a flag of truce being hoisted, a capitulation took place, and it was finally agreed to surrender the island to Morgan and his crew. Having become masters of the island, they hastened to satiate their hungry appetites, and to indulge in all manner of riot and excess. After some time, they pillaged the store-houses of powder and other stores, carried on board the principal guns, destroyed the remainder, and directed their attack upon the castle of Chagre.

This castle is situated at the entrance of the river, upon a high mountain, and surrounded with wooden pallisadoes. On the land side it has four bastions, and is wholly inaccessible by sea. Unintimidated by these obstacles, the pirates made an attack, but were repulsed with some loss. In the action one of the pirates was wounded with an arrow, which he instantly pulled out, wrapped in cotton, and discharged it from his musket. The arrow fell upon a house thatched with palm-leaves, and the cotton being kindled by the powder, set the house on fire, which communicated to a large quantity of powder, that blew up and caused a dreadful conflagration. While the Spaniards were labouring to extinguish the flames, the pirates set fire to the pallisadoes, and in a short time entered the place. The governor was slain, and the greater part of his men chose rather to leap into the sea, than await the tortures of these cruel pirates.

Having garrisoned the place, and seized all the vessels, he next directed his course towards Panama, at the head of 1200 men; but, too confident in the smiles of fortune, he took too small a stock of provisions with him. In their march they suffered much from famine, but in the space of nine days he beheld Panama.

On the morning of the 10th, Captain Morgan arranged his men; but, by the advice of one of his guides, he did not take the direct road to the city, and therefore escaped some of the ambuscades that were laid for him. The governor of Panama came out to meet him with two squadrons, four regiments, and a number of wild bulls driven by the Indians. Their number and hostile appearance almost intimidated the pirates; but, despairing of all mercy from the hands of those whom they had so often offended, the latter resolved to give them battle. They were first attacked by a party of horse; but, these being routed, the foot soon followed their example, and victory declared upon the side of the pirates. The greater part were either slain or taken prisoners. Among the prisoners was a Spanish captain, who informed Morgan concerning the strength and position of the town; which inclined him to attack it in another direction.

Morgan and his men were bravely repulsed, and suffered much from the great guns placed in every direction; but, in defiance of every opposition and danger, the pirates, in three hours, carried the town. Thus victorious, they slew all who came in their way, and seized upon all the property of the place. To prevent his men from intoxication, (that the Spaniards might not have an opportunity to fall upon them), Morgan assembled his men, and prohibited them from tasting the wine, assigning as a reason, that the Spaniards had mingled poison with it.

The captain gave secret orders to set fire to the city in different places. His own men being dissatisfied with this measure, he endeavoured to throw the odium upon the Spaniards themselves. After doing incredible harm, the pirates retired from the town, and encamped in the fields. They, however, upon finding themselves safe from a second attack, returned to the city, and conveyed away a large quantity of plate and other valuable articles which the fire had not consumed.

While Morgan continued at Panama, he sent out parties in all directions, who so pillaged the country, that he departed from that place loaded with immense plunder, both in money and goods. About half way to Chagre, they were all searched, beginning with the captain himself, to find whether they had concealed any part of the booty. Several of the company, however, boldly accused the captain of concealing some of the more valuable jewels, as it was impossible that no more than 200 pieces of eight should fall to the share of each man from such an immense spoil.

The captain, finding his authority lessened, endeavoured to escape from St. Catharine's with two or three ships; but the arrival of a new governor in Jamaica put a period to the depredations of Morgan and his associates.

USHER GAHAGAN AND TERENCE CONNOR.

EXECUTED FOR DIMINISHING THE COIN.

How lamentable is the consideration that great geniuses are sometimes lost to common honesty; and how often is human nature degraded by the ignominious conduct of those whose attainments might have rendered them worthy and useful members of society!

Usher Gahagan and Terence Connor were natives of Ireland. The former received his education in Trinity College, Dublin, having been intended for the profession of the law, in which several of his relations had become eminent. He had been instructed by his parents in the Protestant religion; but, falling into company with some priests of the Romish persuasion, they converted him to their faith. This became a serious obstacle to his future advancement in life; for as no gentleman could then be admitted a counsellor at law without taking the oaths of supremacy and abjuration, and as Mr. Gahagan's new faith prevented his complying with these terms, he declined any further prosecution of his legal studies. His parents and other relations were greatly offended with his conduct; and those who had particularly interested themselves in the advancement of his fortune, forbade him to visit them, from indignation at the impropriety of his behaviour.

Thus reduced to an incapacity of supporting himself, he sought to relieve his circumstances by a matrimonial scheme; and having addressed the daughter of a gentleman, he obtained her in marriage, and received a good fortune with her. Being treated, however, with undeserved severity, she was compelled to return to her relations. His conduct having now rendered him obnoxious to his acquaintance in Dublin, he quitted that city, and repaired to London, with a view of supporting himself by his literary abilities. On his arrival in the metropolis, he made connections with some booksellers, for whom he undertook to translate Pope's "Essay on Man" into Latin; but becoming the associate of women of abandoned character, he spent his time in a dissipated manner, and thus threw himself out of employment, which might have afforded him a decent support.

He now formed an acquaintance with an Irishman named Hugh Coffey, with whom he engaged in a plan for the diminution of the coin. At this time Gahagan had a lodger named Connor; and it was agreed to receive him as a partner in their iniquitous scheme. They procured proper tools; and, having collected a sum of money, they filed it, and put it off; and, procuring more, filed that also, and passed it in the same manner.

Having continued this business for some months, during which they had saved a sum of money, they went to the Bank, and got some Portugal pieces, under pretence that they were intended for exportation to Ireland. Thus they got money repeatedly at the Bank; but at length one of the tellers suspecting their business, communicated his suspicion to the governors, who directed him to endeavour to discover who they were, and what was their employment.

In pursuance of this order, he, on their next appearance, invited them to drink a glass of wine at the Crown Tavern, near Cripplegate; to which they readily agreed, and met him after the hours of office.

When the circulation of the glass had sufficiently warmed them, Gahagan, with a degree of weakness that is altogether astonishing, informed the teller that he acquired considerable sums by filing gold, and even proposed that he should become a partner with them. The gentleman seemed to accede to the proposal; and, having learned where they lodged, acquainted the cashiers of the Bank with what had passed.

On the following day Coffey was apprehended; but Gahagan and Connor, being suspicious of the danger of their situation, retired to Chalk Farm, a noted resort on the road from London to Hampstead, where they carried the implements for filing. Coffey having been admitted an evidence, it was not long before the place of their retreat was discovered; on which they were apprehended and lodged in Newgate.

Terence Connor was a native of Ireland, and had likewise received a most liberal education. It is recorded of him, that he was so perfectly well read in Roman history, as to be able to turn to any part of it without the assistance of an index. He was, by birth, heir to a considerable fortune; but his father dying without a proper adjustment of his affairs, some intricate law-suits were the consequence, so that the whole estate was only sufficient to discharge the demands of the rapacious lawyers. Connor being thus reduced in circumstances came to London, and became acquainted with Gahagan and Coffey, as we have already stated.

On their trial, the evidence of Coffey was positive; and being supported by collateral proofs, the jury could not hesitate to find them guilty, and they received sentence of death.

After conviction, the behaviour of these unhappy men was strictly suited to their circumstances: they were extremely devout, and apparently resigned to their fate.

Gahagan, as we have already stated, was an excellent scholar. He was the editor of "Brindley's edition of the Classics;" and he translated Pope's "Essay on Criticism" into Latin verse, "The Temple of Fame," and "The Messiah," when in prison; which he dedicated to the Duke of Newcastle, then prime minister, with the hope of obtaining pardon.

These two criminals were executed on the 28th of February, 1749.

THE GERMAN PRINCESS INVEIGLES THE YOUNG LAWYER.

THE GERMAN PRINCESS,

A NOTORIOUS IMPOSTOR AND SWINDLER, HANGED FOR ROBBERY.

This remarkable female character, though denominated a German Princess, for a reason which will be mentioned hereafter, was a native of Canterbury, and her father was a chorister of that cathedral. At an early age she took delight in reading those novels that were then fashionable, such as, " Parismus and Parismenus," " Don Bellianis of Greece," " Amadis de Gaul," " Cassandra and Cleopatra," &c. till, in a little time, she really believed, what she wished, that she was a princess.

In her marriage, however, she lost sight of her exalted conceptions, uniting herself to a journeyman shoemaker, by whom she had two children, who both died in their infancy. The industrious shoemaker soon became unable to support her extravagance, so that she at last left him, to seek her fortune elsewhere.

A woman of her figure, beauty, and address, was not long before she procured another husband. She went to Dover, and married a surgeon of that place. But her former marriage being discovered, she was apprehended, and tried at Maidstone for having two husbands ; but, by some dexterous manoeuvre, was acquitted.

She now embarked for Holland, and travelled by land to Cologne. Having a considerable sum of money, she took handsome lodgings at a house of entertainment, and cut a dashing figure. As it is customary for the gentry of England to frequent Epsom or Tunbridge Wells in the summer, so it was then customary for those of Germany to frequent the Spa.   Our heroine went thither, and was addressed by an old gentleman, who had a good estate in the vicinity.   With the assistance of her landlady, she managed this affair with great art.   He presented her with several fine jewels, besides a gold chain and costly medal, which had been given him for some gallant action under Count Tilly against the valiant Gustavus Adolphus, of Sweden.   He, at length, began to press matrimony with all the keenness of a young lover, and she, unable to resist the siege any longer, consented to make him happy in three days.   Meanwhile he supplied her with money in great profusion, and requested her to prepare what things she pleased for the wedding. She now deemed it high time to be gone, and, to secure her retreat, acquainted her landlady with her design ; who, having already shared largely in the spoils which our adventurer had received from her doating lover, in hopes of pillaging him a little more, encouraged and aided her flight.   Our heroine requested her to go and provide her a seat in a carriage which took a different road from that of Cologne, as she did not wish that her lover should be able to trace her route.

When our Princess found herself alone, she broke open a chest in which the good woman had deposited all her share of the spoil that she had received from our heroine as well as her own money.   Madam made free with all, and took her passage to Utrecht.   From thence she went to Amsterdam, sold her chain and some jewels, and then passed into Rotterdam, from whence she speedily embarked for England.

Landing at Billingsgate, very early one morning, in the end of March, 1663, she found no house open until she came to the Exchange Tavern, where, in the following manner, she attained the title of a German Princess.   In that tavern she got into the company of some gentlemen, who she perceived were full of money.   These addressing her in a rude manner, she began to cry most bitterly, exclaiming, that it was extremely hard for her to be reduced to this extreme distress, who was once a princess.   Here she repeated the story of her extraction and education, and much about her pretended father, the Lord Henry Vandwolway, a Prince of the Empire, who was independent of every man but his Imperial Majesty.   " Certainly," said she, " any gentleman here present may conceive what a painful situation this must be to me ; brought up under the care of an indulgent father, and in all the luxuries of a court, to be reduced thus low.   But, alas ! what do I say ? Indulgent father ! alas ! was it not his cruelty which banished me, his only daughter, from his dominions, merely for marrying, without his knowledge, a nobleman of the court, whom I loved to excess ? Was it not my father who occasioned my dear lord and husband to be cut off, in the bloom of his age, by falsely accusing him of a design against his person —a deed which his virtuous soul abhorred."   The poignancy of her feelings would not allow her to relate more of her unfortunate history.

The whole company were touched with compassion at the melancholy tale, which she related with so much unaffected simplicity, that they had not a doubt of its authenticity.   Compassionating her unfortunate situation, they requested her acceptance of all the money they had about them, promising to return again with more. They were as good as their promise, and she ever after went by the name of the unfortunate German Princess.

The man who kept the inn, a Mr. King, knowing she had come from the continent, and seeing that she had great riches about her, was now disposed, more than ever, to believe the truth of her story. Nor was Madam backward in informing him, that she had collected all she possessed from the benevolent contributions of neighbouring princes, who knew and pitied her misfortunes. "But not one of them," continued she, " durst let my father know what they had done, or where I was; for he was so much more powerful than any of them, that if he understood that any one favoured me, he would instantly make war upon him."

A Mr. John Carleton, brother-in-law to King, and no doubt receiving his information about her from King, became enamoured of the Princess, and presumed to pay his addresses to her. She appeared highly displeased at first, but, from his importunity, was at last prevailed upon to descend from her station, and receive the hand of a common man. Poor Carleton thought himself the happiest of mortals, in being honoured by a union with such an accomplished and amiable princess, possessed of an ample fortune, though far inferior to what she had a right to expect from her noble birth.

But, during this dream of pleasure, Mr. King received a letter, informing him, that the woman who resided at his house and was married to his brother-in-law was an impostor; that she had already been married to two husbands, and had eloped with all the money she could lay her hands on. The consequence was, a prosecution was instituted against her for polygamy; but, from insufficient evidence, she was again acquitted.

She was now introduced as an actress among the players, and by them supported for some time. The public curiosity being excited by a woman who had made such a figure in the world, the house was crowded, and she received great applause in her dramatic capacity. She generally appeared in characters suited to her habits of life, and in scenes which were rendered familiar to her by former deceptions and intrigues. But what tended chiefly to promote her fame, was a play called "The German Princess," written principally upon her account, in which she spoke the following prologue in such a manner as gained universal applause :—

> I've passed one trial; but it is my fear,
> I shall receive a rigid sentence here :
> You think me a bold cheat, but 'case 'twere so,
> Which of you are not? Now you'd swear I know,
> But do not, lest that you deserve to be
> Censured worse than you can censure me :
> The world's a cheat, and we that move in it,
> In our degrees, do exercise our wit;
> And better 'tis to get a glorious name,
> However got, than live by common fame,

The Princess had too much mercury in her constitution to remain long within the bounds of a theatre, London itself being too limited for her volatile disposition. She did not, however, leave the theatre until she had procured many admirers. Her history being well known, as well as her accomplishments and gallantry, introduced her much into company. She was easy of access; though in company she carried herself with an affected air of indifference.

There were two young beaux in particular, who had more money in their pockets than wit in their heads; and from the scarcity of that commodity in themselves, they the more admired her wit and humour. She encouraged their addresses until she had extracted about three hundred pounds from each of them, and then, observing their funds were nearly exhausted, discarded them both, saying, she was astonished at their impudence in making love to a princess!

Her next lover was an old gentleman about fifty, who saw her, and, though he was acquainted with her history, resolved to be at the expense of some hundreds a year, provided she would consent to live with him. To gain his purpose, he made her several rich presents, which she accepted with seeming reluctance. When they lived together as man and wife, she so accommodated herself to his temper and disposition, that he was constantly making her rich presents, which were always accepted with apparent reluctance, as laying her under so many obligations. In this manner they continued, until her doting lover one evening coming home intoxicated, she thought it a proper opportunity to decamp. As soon as he was asleep, she rifled his pockets, took out his pocket-book, containing a bill for an hundred pounds, and some money. She also stripped him of his watch, and, taking his keys, opened his coffers, and carried off every thing that suited her purpose. She next went and presented the bill, and, as the acceptor knew her, he paid her the money without hesitation.

Having thus fleeced her old lover, she took lodgings under the character of a young lady with a thousand pounds, and whose father was able to give her twice as much, but, disliking a person whom he had provided as a husband for her, she had left her father's house, and did not wish to be discovered by any of her friends. She contrived, at the same time, to have different letters sent her, from time to time, containing an account of all the news concerning her father and lover. These being left carelessly about the room, her landlady read them, and became confirmed in the belief of her story.

This woman had a rich nephew, a young man, whom she introduced to her acquaintance, who soon became enamoured of her, and, to gain her favour, presented her with a gold watch, which she was with some difficulty prevailed upon to accept. Her lover already thought the door of paradise was open to him, and their amour proceeded with all the felicity that young lovers could wish. But, in this season of bliss, a porter knocked at the door, with a letter. Her maid, as previously directed, brought it in to her, which she had no sooner read, than she exclaimed, " I am undone! I am ruined!" and pretended to swoon away. The scent-bottle was employed, and her enraptured lover, was all kindness and attention. When she was a little recovered, she presented the letter, saying, " Sir, since you are already acquainted with most of my concerns, I shall not make a secret of this ; therefore, if you please, read this letter, and know the occasion of my affliction." The young gentleman received it, and read as follows :—

" Dear Madam—I have several times taken my pen in hand, on purpose to write to you, and as often laid it aside again, for fear of giving you more trouble than you already labour under. However, as the affair so immediately concerns you, I cannot in justice hide what I tremble to disclose, but must in duty tell you the worst of news, whatever may be the consequence of my so doing.

" Know, then, that your affectionate and tender brother is dead. I am sensible how dear he was to you, and you to him, yet let me entreat you, for your own sake, to acquiesce in the will of Providence, as much as possible, since our lives are all at His disposal who gave us being. I could use another argument to comfort you, that, with a sister less loving than you, would be of more weight than what I have urged ; but I know your soul is above all mercenary views. I cannot, however, forbear to inform you, that he has left you all he had ; and further, that your father's estate, of £200 per annum, can now devolve upon no other person than yourself, who are now his only child.

" What I am next to acquaint you with, may perhaps be almost as bad as the former particular. Your hated lover has been so importunate with your father, especially since your brother's decease, that the old gentleman resolves, if ever he shall hear of you any more, to marry you to him ; and he makes this the condition of your being again received into his favour, and having your former disobedience, as he calls it, forgiven. While your brother lived, he was every day endeavouring to soften the heart of your father, and we were but last week in hopes he would have consented to let you follow your inclinations, if you would come home to him again ; but now there is no advocate in your cause who can work upon the man's peevish temper ; for, he says, as you are now his sole heir, he ought to be more resolute in the disposal of you in marriage.

" While I am now writing, I am surprised with an account that your father and lover are preparing to come to London, where they say they can find you out. Whether or not this be only a device, I cannot tell, nor can I conceive where they could receive their information, if it be true. However, to prevent the worst, consider whether or not you can cast off your old aversion, and submit to your father's commands ; for, if you cannot, it would be most advisable, in my opinion, to change your residence. I have no more to say in the affair, being unwilling to direct you in such a very nice circumstance. The temper of your own mind will be the best instructor you can apply to ; for your future happiness or misery, during life, depends on your choice. I hope that every thing will turn out for the best. From your sincere friend,   " S. E."

Her lover saw she had good reason to be afflicted, and, while he seemed to feel for her, was no less concerned about his own interest. He advised her immediately to leave her lodgings, and added, that he had very elegant apartments, which were at her service. She accepted his offer; and she and her maid, who was informed of her intentions, and prepared to assist her, immediately set out for the residence of her lover. When introduced to their new apartments, they did not go to bed, as they had resolved to depart next morning, but lay down to rest themselves with their clothes on. When the house was quiet, they broke open a desk, took out a bag with a hundred pounds, two suits of clothes, and every thing valuable that they could carry along with them.

Her numerous and varied adventures would far exceed the limits appropriated to one life in this volume. It is sufficient to observe, rather than her hands should be unemployed, or her avaricious disposition ungratified, she would carry off the most trifling article; that, according to the proverb, " all was fish that came to her net ;" and when a watch, a diamond, or a piece of plate could not be found, a napkin, a pair of sheets, or any article of wearing apparel would suffice.

She one day, along with her pretended maid, went into a mercer's shop in Cheapside, and purchased a piece of silk, of the value of six pounds. She took out her purse to pay the mercer, but, to her surprise, found she had no money except some large pieces of gold, for which she had so high an esteem that she could not think of parting with them. The polite mercer could not think of hurting the feelings of a lady so elegantly dressed, and accordingly dispatched one of his shopmen along with her, to receive his money. They went all three in a coach which was ready to receive them. Arrived at the Royal Exchange, Madam ordered the coachman to stop, when, upon pretence of purchasing some ribbons to suit the silk, her maid carried out the parcel, and went along with her, leaving the shopman in the coach to wait their return. The young man waited till he was impatient and ashamed, and then returned home to relate his misfortunes and loss to his master.

Madam next waited upon a French weaver in Spitalfields, and purchased goods to the amount of forty pounds. He went home with her to carry the goods, and receive his money. She desired him to make out another bill, as part of the goods belonged to her niece, who was then in the next room. With all the ceremony natural to a Frenchman, he sat down to write the account, while she took the silk into the adjacent room to show it to her niece. With the aid of a bottle of wine which Madam had placed before him, the first half hour passed away without much uneasiness. At length his patience being pretty nigh exhausted, he called up the people of the house, and inquired for the lady who came in with him. To his utter confusion and disappointment, they informed him that the lady was gone, and would, they believed, return no more. The Frenchman instantly flew in a violent passion; when, to calm his rage, and convince him that they were not confederates in her villainy, they showed him that the proper entry to her room was by a back stair; adding, that she had only taken the room for a month, for which she had paid them, and that, her time being expired, they knew not where she had gone.

Determined to collect her contributions from householders instead of travellers, she next took lodgings at a tailor's. As it was natural for a generous good-hearted lady to promote the prosperity of the family where she resided, Madam employed the tailor to make up the goods she had procured from the mercer and the weaver. Convinced that he had got an excellent job, as well as a rich lodger, the tailor joyfully sat down to make Madam's dresses. As she acquainted him that upon a specified day she was to have a large party, the tailor called in several journeymen to his aid, and had them all finished by that time. Meanwhile she gave her landlady one pound to purchase what things she deemed necessary, promising to pay her the remainder the following day. The day arrived—the guests appeared—an elegant entertainment was served up, and plenty of wine drank. None were without their due portion. The tailor had his glass served so plentifully, that his wife had to lend him her assistance to his bed-chamber. This answered the designs of our Princess. She and all her company departed one by one, each carrying away a silver tankard, or salt, or knife, or fork, while the maid carried off all the clothes that were not upon their backs. The moment they reached the street, the maid was placed in a coach with the booty, and the rest of the company took different directions, and none of them were discovered. Thus a merry night brought a sorrowful morning to the poor tailor.

Madam being attacked with a fit of mourning, sent her confidential maid to a shop in the New Exchange, where she had purchased a few articles the previous day. The woman of the shop, with all possible expedition, selected the best of her articles, and hastened to her lodgings. Madam was so very much indisposed when the milliner arrived, that she could not look at the things, and desired her to return after dinner, when she doubted not but they should agree as to the price. The obliging milliner was satisfied, and requested liberty to leave her goods until she returned ; a request which was readily granted. At the hour appointed she returned, and inquired if the lady up-stairs was at home. To her great mortification, she was informed that she was gone, they could not tell where, and was not expected to return, as she had conveyed away the most valuable part of her effects. Thus, both her landlady and the milliner were left to regret her absence, and to reflect upon their own easy credulity and loss.

But the adventures of Madam increase in magnitude as they increase in number. Being arrayed in her sable robes, and having taken lodgings in Holborn, she sent for a barrister of Gray's Inn, and informed him, that, by the death of her father, she was sole heir to his fortune, but being married to an extravagant husband, she was resolved to secure her property to herself. Here she poured forth a torrent of tears, and the most grievous lamentations, the more to interest the young barrister in her favour. But while the lawyer was squaring his features to the occasion, and talking of the matter in a learned and eloquent strain, a woman runs up stairs, crying, " O ! madam, we are all undone ! my master is below. He has been asking after you, and swears he will come up, and I am afraid the people of the house will not be able to hinder him, he appears so resolute." " O heavens ! exclaimed madam, " what shall I

do?"   " Why ?" says the lawyer.   " Why," quoth she, " I mean to
you: dear me, what excuse shall I make for your being here?   I dare
not tell him your quality and business, for that would endanger all.
And, on the other hand, he is extremely jealous.   Therefore, good sir,
step into that closet until I can send him away."   Surprised, and at a
loss what to do, the lawyer complies.   The closet is locked, and the
curtains of the bed are drawn ; then she opens the door to the husband,
who was loudly demanding admittance.

The moment he entered, he gave his spouse the most opprobrious
language.   " O mistress abandoned !   I understand you have a man in
the room !   A pretty companion for a poor innocent woman, truly !—
one who is always complaining how hardly I use her.   Where is the villain ?   I will sacrifice him this moment."   On this he made to the closet
door, and burst it open like a fury.   The young lawyer was discovered
blushing with shame, though innocent, and trembling in every limb.
The husband's sword was unsheathed, and death was before the barrister's
eyes.   But madam interposed, and seemed determined rather to die
herself, than suffer the blood of an innocent man to stain her chamber.
A companion of the husband also came to her assistance, and, seizing
the arm of the infuriated man, struggled to wrest the sword from his hand.

But the discernment of the lawyer soon discovered the deception;
and, to exculpate and relieve himself, he candidly related the whole
matter, and the reason for which he was introduced into that place.
But all in vain.   The injured and enraged husband insisted that this was
only a feigned narrative to cover his villainy, and that nothing but his
blood, or an adequate remuneration, would assuage his fury.   The cause
was at last referred to the arbitration of the kind stranger, who had interfered and aided madam in protecting the young lawyer.   Five hundred
pounds was proposed as a proper recompense ; but this was far beyond
the power of the lawyer to command.   It was with no small difficulty
agreed that he should give a hundred pounds, rather than be exposed to the consequences of detection in a situation where he was
unable to vindicate his innocence.   He sent a note to a friend for that
sum, the confederates being careful to examine it before it was sent
away, lest it should have been for a constable instead of a hundred
pounds.   Upon payment of that sum, the lawyer was liberated, and went
off with the bitter reflection, that, instead of receiving a good fee for
writing a deed of settlement, he had paid an hundred pounds for only
a few minutes lodging in a closet—but consoled himself with the hopes
of seeing this amiable widow speedily *exalted* to merited honour.

Not long after this, Madam was apprehended, charged with stealing a
silver tankard at Covent Garden, and sent to Newgate.   At the next
sessions she was tried, and transported to Jamaica.

She had only remained there two years, when she returned to England,
and appeared in the character of a great heiress.   The result of this
artifice was, that she was speedily married to a rich apothecary, whom
she soon robbed of above three hundred pounds, and then left him to
resolve the question, whether the loss of his money or of his wife
was the greatest misfortune ?

Madam next went to lodge in a house where a watchmaker and the landlady, with herself and her faithful maid, composed the whole family. Having established a character for sobriety and probity, she invited her landlady and the watchmaker to the play, and treated them with tickets. They accepted of the invitation; and the maid remained at home, as guardian of the garrison. But, during their absence, she broke open the locks, extracted about two hundred pounds, and made free with about thirty watches; so that the spoil amounted, in all, to six hundred pounds, which she carried to the appointed place of rendezvous. Meanwhile, madam, not satisfied with treating the watchmaker and her good landlady with tickets to the play, took them after it was over to a tavern to partake of some refreshment, whence she seized an opportunity to disappear.

But the time fast approached when she was to receive the just reward of her misdeeds. Mr. Freeman, a brewer, having been robbed of two hundred pounds, a strict search was immediately instituted in every suspected place for the thieves. One Lancaster was the person upon whom the suspicion chiefly rested, and, while searching a house for him, they discovered madam walking in a night-gown. The thief-catcher enters her room, and, seeing two letters upon the table, began to examine their contents. Madam was highly displeased with his indiscreet freedom; but, in the course of the dispute which ensued, examining the features of her countenance, he recognized her ladyship, and took both her and her letters along with him.

When removed to the Old Bailey, she was interrogated whether she was the woman who usually went by the name of Mary Carleton. She answered, " Yes." The court then demanded the reason of her return from banishment before her time. She made many trifling excuses, which detained the court for a few days. But, finding these excuses would not answer her purpose, she pleaded pregnancy. A jury of matrons were appointed to examine her, who gave a verdict against her, and she was sentenced to suffer, according to her previous sentence.

In prison she was visited by many persons from curiosity to see such a remarkable character; and some clergymen attended, to conduct her devotions. She confessed herself to be a Roman Catholic, and sincerely bewailed her criminal conduct; frequently wishing that she could renew her life, in order to spend it in a more honourable and virtuous manner.

On the day of her execution she appeared more cheerful and gay than usual, and, placing the picture of her husband upon her arm, she went to Tyburn with it. She appeared devout, and when she heard St. Sepulchre's bell begin to toll, she uttered several pious ejaculations. To a friend, who rode in the cart with her to the place of execution, she delivered two popish books; and, addressing the multitude, owned that she had been a very vain woman, and hoped that her fate would deter others from the same evil ways; and that, though the world had condemned her, she had much to say for herself. Then, praying God to forgive her, as she did her most inveterate enemies, she was in a few minutes launched into eternity. She died in the thirty-eighth year of her age, and in the same month of the year in which she was born.

WILLIAM SAWYER.

EXECUTED FOR A MURDER COMMITTED IN PORTUGAL.

THE circumstances of this very singular case may be shortly stated as follows :—The prisoner was engaged in the commissariat department of the British army ; and in the month of February, 1814, he went out to Portugal, where he lived in the same house, in the Campo Mayor, at Lisbon, with a friend, Mr. Riccord, who had a female, named Harriet Gaskett, under his protection. An attachment grew up between this unfortunate woman and Sawyer, who, however, had a wife at the time in England ; and his attentions were so apparent, that they excited the jealousy of his brother officer, who appears to have remonstrated both with his friend and mistress, which occasioned much unhappiness.

On the 27th of April they met at dinner, with two or three other officers ; but such was the agitation of their feelings, that Riccord, Harriet, and Sawyer ate nothing. The latter appeared greatly dejected, and, as well as Harriet, withdrew as soon as possible.

In the evening the party heard the report of three pistol-shots ; and, on going into the garden, Harriet and Sawyer were both found lying on the ground. Harriet was quite dead, but Sawyer had not been mortally wounded. On his being removed into the house, he was left in the care of a brother officer, while the others went in search of a physician ; and during their absence he contrived to get a razor, with which he cut his throat in a dreadful manner, but not mortally.

Next day the officers met, and reduced the facts to writing, which the prisoner signed, as well as a paper in the following terms :—

" Having laid violent hands upon myself, in consequence of the death of Harriet, I think it but justice to mankind and the world, being of sound mind, solemnly to attest that her death was occasioned by her having taken part of a phial of laudanum, and ' my ' discharging a pistol at her head, provided for the occasion. I took the residue of the laudanum myself, and discharged two pistols at my head. They failing in their effect, I then retired to the house, and endeavoured to put an end to my life, leaving myself the unfortunate object you now behold me.

(Signed)   " WILLIAM SAWYER."

The above paper was attested by three witnesses. The word " my" was interlined.

The prisoner also signed a declaration, that Harriet Gaskett had consented to leave Mr. Riccord, and live with him, and that Mr. Riccord had told her, on her threatening to quit him, that she might go to the prisoner's hotel. The reason assigned by him for the attempted suicide and murder was, that Harriet declared that she thought Mr. Riccord would shoot himself if she quitted him, and that she therefore would not live ; and he added, that he had shot her at her own request, and not in consequence of any quarrel with her, and had then attempted to kill himself.

When the prisoner was sufficiently recovered, he was removed to

England, where, shortly after his arrival, he was indicted at the Old Bailey, April 7th, 1815, for the murder. His case excited great interest, and the court was filled long before the arrival of the judges.

The facts already stated having been proved, the prisoner was called on for his defence. He put in a written paper, in which he stated that, in consequence of his being unable to articulate, from the wound in his throat, he had committed to paper all he had to say in his defence. The paper then went on to state, that the prisoner had felt the sincerest affection for the unfortunate individual in question, towards whom he had never meditated the slightest injury. He perfectly recollected her having entreated him to shoot her, but had no idea of what passed subsequently, till some time afterwards, when he was told he had signed papers, of the contents of which he had no recollection. He then expressed his acknowledgments for the efforts made by his prosecutors to bring forward Mr. Riccord, who would have been a material witness in his behalf; and had only to lament that these efforts had not been attended with success.

Several persons were called to speak to the general humane character of the prisoner, among whom were General Sir Edward Howard and Colonel Sir William Robe.

A Mrs. Nicholls proved that the deceased had lodged with her from June 1813, to February 1814. She was of a most violent and tyrannical dispoition, and had a pistol, which she kept constantly in her room.

Lord Ellenborough having summed up the case, the jury found the prisoner guilty, but recommended him to mercy.

Mr. Alley and Mr. Curwood on behalf of the prisoner then moved in arrest of judgment, upon two technical points which arose upon the face of the indictment, and judgment was respited until the 12th of May. The court on that day, however, gave their opinion that the grounds of motion were unavailable, and sentence of death was immediately passed.

The prisoner appeared deeply affected throughout the proceedings, and, upon the awful decision and sentence, remained motionless for some time, when at length he faintly requested one of the officers to entreat the court to recommend him to the royal clemency.

After sentence of death was passed upon him, he assumed a sullenness of behaviour; and the only declaration he was heard to make was, " that he would not be executed :" and this being considered to import that he was resolved on self-destruction, his intentions, if such they were, were defeated by the constant attendance of two officers night and day. On Sunday his wife went to the prison for the purpose of taking a farewell: but the unhappy man gave a peremptory order that she should not be admitted, and all that could be urged could not induce him to see her. At eight o'clock the following morning, every necessary arrangement being complete, the fatal signal was given, and the unhappy man was launched into eternity. During the ceremony a profound silence prevailed throughout the populace. He died under evident symptoms of paroxysm, and a quantity of blood gushed from his mouth from the cut in his throat. The body was afterwards taken to Bartholomew's Hospital for dissection.

CAPTAIN JOHN LANCEY.

EXECUTED FOR BURNING HIS SHIP.

CAPTAIN LANCEY was a native of Biddeford, in Devonshire, and was respectably connected. At an early age he exhibited a predilection for a seafaring life; and, having served his apprenticeship, he was employed as mate of a vessel belonging to Mr. Benson, a rich merchant of Biddeford, at that time M.P. for Barnstaple.

Having married a sister of Benson's, Lancey was soon advanced to the command of the vessel; and on his return from a voyage, he was surprised at receiving an order from his employer to refit as soon as possible, Mr. Benson saying that he would insure the vessel for twice her value, and that Lancey should destroy her. The latter hesitated at first to assent to this extraordinary proposition, and for a time the suggestion was not again mentioned; but another opportunity being afforded to Benson, on his brother-in-law dining with him, he plied him with wine, and having pointed out to him the poverty to which his family might be reduced in case of his refusal, by his being dismissed from employment, the unhappy man at length yielded to his persuasions.

A ship was now fitted out, bound for Maryland, and goods to a large amount were shipped on board, but re-landed before the vessel sailed, and a lading of brick-bats taken in by way of ballast. The vessel had not been long at sea before a hole was bored in her side, and a cask of combustible ingredients set on fire with a view to destroy her. The fire no sooner appeared than the captain called to some convicted transports, then in the hold, to inquire if they had fired the vessel; but this appears to have been only a feint to conceal the real design. The boat being hoisted out, all the crew got safely on shore; and then Lancey repaired immediately to Benson to inform him of what had passed. The latter instantly dispatched him to a proctor, before whom he swore that the ship had accidentally taken fire, and that it was impossible to prevent the consequences which followed.

The crime was soon afterwards discovered, however, and Lancey was taken into custody; but, secure in his anticipation of protection from Benson, he did not express much concern at his situation. His employer, in the mean time, perfectly aware of the consequences which would fall upon him, fled to avoid them; and this unhappy dupe being brought to trial, was capitally convicted, and received sentence of death. He subsequently lay in prison for about four months, during which time he pursued his devotional exercises with the utmost regularity and was hanged on the 7th June, 1754, at Execution Dock, in the 27th year of his age.

JONATHAN WILD APPREHENDING THOMAS DUNN.

JONATHAN WILD.

EXECUTED FOR CONNIVING WITH FELONS.

The name of this notorious offender must be familiar to all, and his arts and practices are scarcely less universally known. The power exercised by him over thieves of all classes was so great, that he may be considered as having been their chief and director, at the same time that he did not disdain to become their coadjutor, and a participator in the proceeds of their villainy. The system which he pursued will be sufficiently disclosed in the notice which follows of the various transactions in which he was engaged; it appears to have been founded upon the principle of employing a thief so long as his efforts proved profitable, or until his apprehension should be attended with advantage, and then of terminating his career in the most speedy and efficacious manner by the gallows.

Jonathan Wild was born at Wolverhampton, in Staffordshire, about the year 1682. He was the eldest son of his parents, who at a proper age put him to a day-school, which he continued to attend till he had a sufficient knowledge in reading, writing, and accounts, to qualify him for business. His father intended to bring him up to his own trade; but changed that design, and, at about the age of fifteen, apprenticed him for seven years to a buckle-maker in Birmingham. Upon the expiration of his apprenticeship, he returned to Wolverhampton, where he married a young woman of good character, and gained a tolerable livelihood by following his business as a journeyman.

He had been married about two years, in which time his wife had a son, when he formed the resolution of visiting London, and very soon after deserted his wife and child, and set out for the metropolis, where he got into employment; and maintained himself by his trade. Being of an extravagant disposition, many months had not elapsed, after his his arrival in London, when he was arrested and thrown into Wood-street Compter, where he remained a prisoner for debt upwards of four years. In a pamphlet which he published, and which we shall more particularly mention hereafter, he says, that during his imprisonment " it was impossible but he must, in some measure, be let into the secrets of the criminals there under confinement, and particularly of Mr. Hitchin's management."

During his residence in the Compter, Wild assiduously cultivated the acquaintance of the criminals who were his fellow-prisoners, and attended with singular satisfaction to their accounts of the exploits in which they had been engaged. In this prison was a woman named Mary Milliner, who had long been considered one of the most notorious pickpockets and abandoned prostitutes on the town. After having escaped the punishment due to the various felonies of which she had been guilty, she was put under confinement for debt. An intimacy subsisted between them while they remained in the Compter, and they had no sooner obtained their freedom than they lived under the denomination of man and wife. By their iniquitous practices they soon obtained a sum of money, which enabled them to open a public-house in Cock-alley, facing Cripplegate church.

Milliner being personally acquainted with most of the notorious characters by whom London and its environs were infested, and perfectly conversant as to the manner of their proceedings, she was considered by Wild as a most useful companion; and indeed she very materially contributed towards rendering him one of the most accomplished adepts in the arts of villainy.

Wild industriously penetrated into the secrets of felons of every denomination, who resorted in great numbers to his house in order to dispose of their booties; and they looked upon him with a kind of awe, for, as he was well acquainted with their proceedings, they were conscious their lives were continually in his power.

Wild was at little difficulty to dispose of the articles brought to him by the thieves at something less than their real value; for at this period no law existed for the punishment of receivers of stolen goods; but the evil increasing to so enormous a degree, it was deemed expedient by the legislature to frame a law for its suppression. An act therefore was passed, consigning such as should be convicted of receiving goods, knowing them to have been stolen, to transportation for the space of fourteen years.

Wild's practices were considerably interrupted by the above-mentioned law; to obviate the intention of which, however, he suggested the following plan. He called a meeting of all the thieves whom he knew, and observed to them, that if they carried their booties to such of the pawn-brokers who were known not to be much troubled with the scruples of conscience, they would scarcely advance on the property one fourth of its real value; and that if they were offered to strangers, either for sale, or by way of deposit, it was a chance of ten to one but the parties were rendered amenable to the laws. He observed, that the most industrious thieves were now scarcely able to obtain a livelihood; and that they must either submit to be half starved, or to be in continual danger of Tyburn. He informed them that he had devised a plan for removing the inconveniences under which they laboured, recommending them to follow his advice, and to behave towards him with honour. He then proposed that when they had gained any booty they should deliver it to him, instead of carrying it to the pawnbroker, and he would restore the goods to the owners, by which means greater sums would be raised than by depositing them with the pawnbrokers, while the thieves would be perfectly secure from detection.

This proposal was received with general approbation, and it was resolved to carry it into immediate execution. All the stolen effects were to be given into the possession of Wild, who soon appointed con-venient places wherein they were to be deposited, judging it would not be prudent to have them left at his own house.

The infamous plan being thus concerted, it was the business of Wild to apply to persons who had been robbed, pretending to be greatly con-cerned at their misfortunes, saying, that some suspected property had been stopped by a very honest man, a broker, with whom he was acquainted, and that if their goods happened to be in the hands of his friend, restitution should be made. But he failed not to plead that the broker must be rewarded for his trouble and disinterestedness, and to use every argument in his power for exacting a promise that no disagree-able consequences should ensue to his friend, who had imprudently neglected to apprehend the supposed thieves.

Happy in the prospect of regaining their property without the trouble and expence necessarily attending prosecutions, people gene-rally approved the conduct of Wild, and sometimes rewarded him even with one-half of the real value of the goods restored. Persons who had been robbed, however, were not always satisfied with Wild's declaration; and sometimes they questioned him particularly as to the manner of their goods being discovered. On these occasions he pretended to be offended that his honour should be disputed, saying, that his motive was to afford all the service in his power to the injured party, whose goods he imagined might possibly be those stopped by his friend; but since his good intentions were received in so ungracious a manner, and himself interrogated respecting the robbers, he had nothing further to say on the subject, but must take his leave; adding, that his name was Jonathan Wild, and that he was every day to be found at his house in Cock-alley, Cripplegate. This affectation of resentment seldom failed to possess the people who had been robbed with a more favourable opinion of his principles; and the suspicion of his character being removed, he had an opportunity of advancing in his demands.

Wild received no gratuity from the owners of the stolen goods, but deducted his profit from the money which was to be paid to the broker: thus did he amass considerable sums without danger of prosecution, for his offences came under the description of no law then existing. For several years he preserved a tolerably fair character, so consummate was the art he employed in the management of all his schemes.

Wild's business greatly increasing, and his name becoming exceedingly popular, he altered his mode of proceeding. Instead of applying to persons who had been robbed, he opened an office, to which great numbers resorted, in hopes of recovering their effects. He made a great parade in his business, and assumed a consequence that enabled him more effectually to impose on the public. When persons came to his office, they were informed that they must pay a crown in consideration of receiving his advice. This ceremony being dispatched, he entered in his book the names and places of abode of the parties, with all the particulars which they could communicate respecting the robbery, and the reward that would be given, provided the goods were recovered; they were then desired to call again in a few days, when he hoped he should be able to give them some agreeable intelligence. Upon their calling afterwards to know the success of his inquiries, he informed them he had received some information concerning their goods, but that the agent he had employed to trace them had informed him, that the robbers pretended they could get more money by pawning the property, than by returning it for the proposed reward; saying, however, if he could by any means procure an interview with the villains, he doubted not of being able to settle matters agreeably to the terms already proposed, but at the same time artfully insinuating that the most safe, expeditious, and prudent method would be to make some addition to the reward. When he had thus discovered the utmost sum it was likely the people would give for the recovery of their property, he requested them to call again, and in the mean time caused the goods to be ready for delivery.

He derived considerable advantages from examining the persons who had been robbed; for he thence became acquainted with the particulars which the thieves had omitted to communicate, and was enabled to detect them if they concealed any part of their booty. Being thus in possession of the secrets of all the notorious thieves, they were under the necessity of complying with whatever terms he thought proper to exact; for they were conscious, that by opposing his inclination they should involve themselves in the most imminent danger of being sacrificed to the laws of their country.

Through the infamous practices of this man, articles which had been before considered as of no use but to the owners, now became matters claiming a particular attention from the thieves by whom the metropolis and its environs were infested. Pocket-books, books of account, watches, rings, trinkets, and a variety of articles of but small intrinsic worth, were now esteemed a very profitable booty. Books of account, and other writings, being of great importance to the owners, produced very handsome rewards; and the same may be said of pocket-books, which contained memorandums, and sometimes bank-notes, and other articles on which money could be readily procured.

Wild accumulated money so fast, that he considered himself a man of consequence, and, to support his imaginary dignity, he dressed in laced clothes, and wore a sword. He first exercised his martial instrument on the person of his accomplice and reputed wife, Mary Milliner, who having on some occasion provoked him, he instantly struck at her with it, and cut off one of her ears. This event was the cause of a separation; but, in acknowledgment of the great services she had rendered him, by introducing him to so lucrative a profession, he allowed her a weekly stipend till her death.

In the year 1715 Wild removed from his house in Cock-alley to a Mrs. Seagoe's, in the Old Bailey, where he pursued his business with the usual success, notwithstanding the efforts of Hitchin, his rival in iniquity, to suppress his proceedings. This Hitchin had formerly been city-marshal, and was a man every way as wicked as Wild himself. Before Wild had brought the plan of his office to perfection, he had for some time acted as an assistant to Hitchin. These celebrated co-partners in villainy, under the pretext of reforming the manners of the dissolute part of the public, used to parade the streets from Temple-bar to the Minories, searching houses of ill fame, and apprehending disorderly and suspected persons; but such as complimented them with private douceurs were allowed to practise every species of wickedness with impunity. Hitchin and Wild, however, becoming jealous of each other, an open rupture took place, and they parted, each pursuing the business of thief-taking on his own account. In 1718 the Marshal attacked Wild in a pamphlet, called " The Regulator; or, a Discovery of Thieves, Thief-takers, &c.," which was answered by his antagonist. Hitchin, however, having so greatly debased the respectable post of City Marshal, was at length suspended from his office. In order to repair this loss, he determined upon the affectation of burying his resentment, and again confederating with Wild, who readily accepted the ex-marshal's proposals.

The following account of the mode of proceeding of these worthies for the reformation of the public morals and the promotion of their *private* interests, is taken from the pamphlets above alluded to. Towards dark, they proceeded to Temple-bar, and called in at several brandy-shops and ale-houses between that and Fleet-ditch; some of the masters of these houses complimented the marshal with punch, others with brandy, and some presented him with fine ale, offering their service to their worthy protector. The marshal made them little answer; but gave them to understand, all the service he expected from them was, to give him information of pocket-books, or any goods stolen: " For you women of the town," (addressing himself to some females in one of the shops) " make it a common practice to resign things of this nature to the bullies and rogues of your retinue;—but this shall no longer be borne with. I'll give you my word, both they and you shall be detected, unless you deliver all the pocket-books you meet with to me. What do you think I bought my place for, but to make the most of it? and you are to understand that this is my man (pointing to the buckle-maker) to assist me. And if you at any time for the future refuse to yield up the watches and books you take, either to me or my servant, you may be assured of being all sent to Bridewell, and not one of you shall be permitted to walk the streets. For, notwithstanding I am under suspension (the chief reason of which is the not suppressing the practices of such vermin as you), I have still a power of punishing, and you shall dearly pay for not paying your respects to me." Then he asked them to what part of the town they were rambling, and whether they did not see him? to which they answered, that they saw him at a distance, but he caught hold of them so hastily, that they had no time to address him. "We have been strolling," continued the pickpockets, " over Moorfields, and from thence to the Blue-Boar in pursuit of you; but not finding you as usual, we were under some fears that you were indisposed." The marshal replied, he should have given them a meeting there, but had been employed the whole day with his new man. "You are to be very careful," said he, "not to oblige any person but myself, or servant, with pocket-books; if you presume to do otherwise, you shall swing for it, and we are out every night to observe your motions." These instructions given, the pickpockets left us, making their master a low congée, and promising obedience. This was the progress of the first night with the buckle-maker, whom he told that his staff of authority terrified the ignorant to the extent of his wishes.

Some nights afterwards, walking towards the back part of St. Paul's, the marshal thus addressed the buckle-maker, " I'll show you a brandy-shop that entertains no company but whores and thieves. This is a house for our purpose; and I am informed, that a woman of the town who frequents it has lately robbed a gentleman of his watch and pocket-book: this advice I received from her companion, with whom I have a good understanding. We will go into the house, and if we can find this woman, I will assume a most stern countenance (though at best I look like an infernal), and by continued threats extort a confession, and by that means get possession of the watch and pocket-book; in order to which, do you accost her companion apart," (describing her), " and say, that your master is in a damned ill humour, and swears, if she does not instantly make a discovery where the pocket-book may be found, at farthest by to-morrow, he will certainly send her to the Compter, and thence to the workhouse."

The means being thus concerted to gain the valuable goods, both master and man entered the shop in pursuit of the game, and, according to expectation, they found the person they wanted, with several others; whereupon the marshal, showing an enraged countenance, becoming the design, and Wild being obliged to follow his example, the company said, that the master and man looked as sour as two devils: " Devils," said the marshal, " I'll make some of you devils, if you do not immediately discover the watch and pocket-book I am employed to procure." —" We do not know your meaning, sir," answered some. " Who do you speak to? said others: " we know nothing of it." The marshal replied in a softer tone, " You are ungrateful to the last degree, to deny me this small request, when I was never let into the secret of any thing being taken from a gentleman, but I communicated it to you; and there is so little got at this rate that the devil may trade with you for me."

This speech being over, the marshal gave a nod to his man, who called one of the women to the door, and, telling the story above directed, the female answered, " Unconscionable devil! when he gets five or ten guineas, not to bestow above five or ten shillings upon us unfortunate wretches! but, however, rather than go to the Compter, I'll try what is to be done."

The woman, returning-to the marshal, asked him, what he would give for the delivery of the watch, being seven pounds in value, and the pocket-book having in it several notes and goldsmiths' bills? To whom the marshal answered, a guinea; and told her it was much better to comply, than to go to Newgate, which she must certainly expect upon her refusal.

The woman replied, that the watch was in pawn for forty shillings, and if he did not advance the sum, she should be obliged to strip herself for the redemption, though, when her furbelowed scarf was laid aside, she had nothing underneath but furniture for a paper-mill. After abundance of words, he allowed her thirty shillings for the watch and book, which she accepted. The watch, however, was never returned to the owner.

This infamous coadjutor of Wild, the most detestable villain of the two, having been fined twenty pounds and pilloried for a crime too detestable to be named in these pages, left the latter once more alone to execute his plans of depredation on the public.

Wild's artful behaviour, and the punctuality with which he discharged his engagements, obtained him great confidence among thieves of every description; insomuch that if he caused it to be intimated to them that he was desirous of seeing them, and that they should not be molested, they would attend him with the utmost willingness, without entertaining the most distant apprehension of danger, although conscious that he had informations against them, and that their lives were absolutely in his power: but if they presumed to reject his proposals, or proved otherwise refractory, he would address them to the following effect: " I have given you my word that you shall come and go in safety, and so you shall; but take care of yourself, for if ever you see me again, you see an enemy."

The great influence that Wild obtained over the thieves will not be thought a very extraordinary matter, if it is considered that when he promised to use his endeavours to rescue them from impending fate, he was always desirous, and generally able, to succeed. Such as complied with his measures, he would never interrupt; but, on the contrary, afforded them every encouragement for prosecuting their iniquitious practices; and if apprehended by any other person, he seldom failed of procuring their discharge. His most usual method (in desperate cases, and when matters could not be managed with more ease and expedition) was to procure them to be admitted evidence, under pretext that it was in their power to make discoveries of high importance to the public. When they were in prison he frequently attended them, and communicated to them from his own memorandums such particulars as he judged it would be prudent for them to relate in court. When his accomplices were apprehended, and he was not able to prevent their being brought to trial, he contrived stratagems (in which his invention was amazingly fertile) for keeping the principal witness out of court, so that the delinquents were dismissed in for want of evidence.

Jonathan was ever a most implacable enemy to those thieves who were hardy enough to reject his terms, and dispose of their stolen effects for their own separate advantage. He was industrious to the extreme in his endeavours to surrender them into the hands of justice; and being acquainted with all their usual places of resort, it was scarcely possible for them to escape his vigilance.

By subjecting those who incurred his displeasure to the punishment of the law, he obtained the rewards offered for pursuing them to conviction; greatly extended his ascendancy over the other thieves, who considered him with a kind of awe; and at the same time established his character as a man of great public utility.

It was the practice of Wild to give instructions to the thieves whom he employed as to the manner in which they should conduct themselves; and if they followed his directions, it was seldom that they failed of success. But if they neglected a strict observance of his rules, or were, through inadvertence or ignorance, guilty of any kind of mismanagement or error in the prosecution of the schemes he had suggested, it was understood almost as an absolute certainty that he would procure them convicted at the next sessions, deeming them to be unqualfied for the profession of roguery.

He was frequently asked, how it was possible that he could carry on the business of restoring stolen effects, and not be in league with the robbers; and his replies were always to this purpose:—" My acquaintance among thieves is very extensive, and when I receive information of a robbery, I make inquiry after the suspected parties, and leave word at proper places, that if the goods are left where I appoint, the reward shall be paid, and no questions asked. Surely, no imputation of guilt can fall upon me; for I hold no interviews with the robbers, nor are the goods given into my possession."

A lady of fortune being on a visit in Piccadilly, her servants left her sedan at the door, while they went to refresh themselves at a neighbouring public-house. Upon their return the vehicle was not to be found. In consequence of which the men immediately went to Wild, and having informed him of their loss, and complimented him with the usual fee, they were desired to call again in a few days. Upon their second application, Wild extorted from them a considerable reward, and then directed them to attend the chapel in Lincoln's-Inn-Fields on the following morning during the time of prayers. The men went according to the appointment, and under the Piazzas of the chapel perceived the chair, which upon examination they found to contain the velvet seat, curtains, and other furniture, and had received no kind of damage.

A young gentleman, named Knap, accompanied his mother to Sadler's Wells, on Saturday, March 31st, 1716. On their return they were attacked, about ten at night, near the wall of Gray's-Inn Gardens, by five villains. The young gentleman was immediately knocked down, and his mother, being exceedingly alarmed, called for assistance; upon which a pistol was discharged at her, and she instantly fell down dead. A considerable reward was offered, by proclamation in the Gazette, for the discovery of the perpetrator of this horrid crime; and Wild was remarkably assiduous in his endeavours to apprehend the offenders. From a description given of some of the villains, Wild immediately adjudged the gang to be composed of William White, Thomas Thurland, John Chapman, alias Edward Darvel, Timothy Dun, and Isaac Rag.

On the evening of Sunday, April 8th, Wild received intelligence that some of the above-named men were drinking with their prostitutes at a house kept by John Weatherley, in Newtoner's lane. He went to Weatherley's, accompanied by his man Abraham, and seized White, whom he brought away about midnight in a hackney-coach, and lodged in the Round House.

White being secured, information was given to Wild that a man named James Aires was then at the Bell Inn, Smithfield, in company with a woman of the town. Having an information against Aires, Wild, accompanied by his assistants, repaired to the inn, under the gateway of which they met Thurland, whose person had been mistaken for that of Aires. Thurland was provided with two brace of pistols, but being suddenly seized, he was deprived of all opportunity of making use of them, and taken into custody.

They went on the following night to a house in White-Horse-Alley, Drury-Lane, where they apprehended Chapman, alias Darvel. Soon after the murder of Mrs. Knap, Chapman and others stopped the coach of Thomas Middlethwaite; but that gentleman escaped being robbed by discharging a blunderbuss, and wounding Chapman in the arm, on which the villains retired.

In a short time after this, Wild apprehended Isaac Rag at a house which he frequented in St. Giles's, in consequence of an information charging him with burglary. Being taken before a magistrate, in the course of his examination Rag impeached twenty-two accomplices, charging them with being house-breakers, footpads, and receivers of stolen effects, and in consequence thereof he was admitted an evidence for the crown.

Rag had been convicted of a misdemeanor in January, 1714-15, and sentenced to stand three times in the pillory. He had concealed himself in the dust-hole belonging to the house of Thomas Powell, where, being discovered, he was searched, and a pistol, some matches, and a number of picklock keys were found in his possession. His intention was evidently to commit a burglary, but as he had not entered the house, he was indicted for a misdemeanor in entering the yard with intent to steal. He had also been indicted, in October, 1715, for a burglary in the house of Elizabeth Stanwell on the 24th August, but was acquitted.

White, Thurland, and Chapman, were arraigned on the 18th of May, 1716, at the sessions-house in the Old Bailey, on an indictment for assaulting John Knap, gent. putting him in fear, and taking from him a hat and wig, on the 31st of March, 1716. They were also indicted for the murder of Mary Knap, widow: White, by discharging a pistol loaded with powder and bullets, and thereby giving her a wound of which she immediately died. They were also indicted for assaulting robbing John Gough. White was a fourth time indicted by James Russel for a burglary in the house of Henry Cross. These three offenders were executed at Tyburn, the 8th of June, 1716.

Wild was indefatigable in his endeavours to apprehend Timothy Dun, who had hitherto escaped the hands of justice by removing to a new lodging, where he concealed himself in the most cautious manner. Wild, however, did not despair of discovering this offender, who, he supposed, must either perish through want of the necessaries of life, or obtain the means of subsistence by returning to his felonious practices; and so confident was he of success, that he made a wager of ten guineas that he would have him in custody before the expiration of an appointed time.

Dun's confinement at length became exceedingly irksome, and he sent his wife to make enquiries of Wild, to ascertain whether he was still in danger of being apprehended. Upon her departure Wild ordered one of his people to follow her home. She took water at Blackfriars, and landed at the Falcon, but suspecting the man was employed to trace her, she again took water, and crossed to Whitefriars. Observing that she was still followed, she ordered the waterman to proceed to Lambeth, and having landed there, it being nearly dark, she imagined she had escaped the observation of Wild's man, and therefore walked immediately home. The man traced her to Maid-lane, near the Bankside, Southwark, and perceiving her enter a house, he marked the wall with chalk, and then returned to his employer with an account of the discovery he had made.

Wild, accompanied by a fellow named Abraham (a Jew, who acted the part he had done to the worthless marshal), one Riddlesden, and another man, went on the following morning to the house where the woman had been seen to enter. Dun hearing a noise, and thence suspecting that he was discovered, got through a back-window on the second floor upon the roof of the pantry, the bottom of which was about eight feet from the ground. Abraham discharged a pistol, and wounded Dun in the arm; in consequence of which he fell from the pantry into the yard; after his fall Riddlesden discharged a pistol, and wounded him in the face with small shot. Dun was secured, and carried to Newgate, and being tried at the ensuing sessions, he was soon after executed at Tyburn.

At this time Wild had quitted his apartments at Mrs. Seagoe's, and hired a house adjoining to the Cooper's Arms, on the opposite side of the Old Bailey. The unexampled villainies of this man were now become an object of so much consequence as to excite the particular attention of the legislature. In the year 1718 an act was passed, making every person guilty of a capital offence, who should accept a reward in consequence of restoring stolen effects without prosecuting the thief.

It was the general opinion, that the above law would effectually suppress the iniquitous practices of Wild; but, after some interruption to his proceedings, he devised means for evading the law, which were for several years attended with success.

He now declined the custom of receiving money from the persons who applied to him; but, upon the second or third time of calling, informed them, that all he had been able to learn respecting their business was, that if a sum of money was left at an appointed place, their property would be restored the same day. Sometimes, as the person robbed was returning from Wild's house, he was accosted in the street by a man who delivered the stolen effects, at the same time producing a note expressing the sum that was to be paid for them. In cases wherein he supposed danger was to be apprehended, he advised people to advertise, that whoever would bring the stolen goods to Jonathan Wild should be rewarded, and no questions asked them. In the two first instances it could not be proved that he either saw the thief, received the goods, or accepted of a reward, and in the latter case he acted agreeably to the directions of the injured party, and there appeared no reason to criminate him as being in confederacy with the felons. When he was asked what would satisfy him for his trouble, he told the persons who had recovered the property, that what he had done was without any interested view, but merely from a principle of doing good; that therefore he made no claim; that if he accepted a present, he should not consider it as being his due, but as an instance of generosity, which he should acknowledge accordingly.

Our adventurer's business increased exceedingly, and he opened an office in Newtoner's-lane, to the management of which he appointed his man Abraham. This Israelite proved a remarkably industrious and faithful servant to Jonathan, who entrusted him with matters of the greatest importance.

By too strict an application to business, Wild so much impaired his health, that he judged it prudent to retire to the country for a short time. He therefore hired a lodging at Dulwich, leaving both his offices under the direction of Abraham.

A lady had her pocket picked of bank notes to the amount of seven thousand pounds. She related the particulars of her robbery to Abraham, who in a few days apprehended three pickpockets, and conducted them to Jonathan's lodgings at Dulwich. Upon their delivering up all the notes, Wild dismissed them. When the lady applied to Abraham, he restored the property, and she generously made him a present of four hundred pounds, which he delivered to his employer.

Wild's business would not permit him to remain long at Dulwich; and being under great inconvenience from want of Abraham's assistance, he did not keep open his office in Newtoner's-lane more than three months.

About a week after the return of Wild from Dulwich, a mercer in Lombard-street ordered a porter to carry to a particular inn a box containing goods to the amount of two hundred pounds. In his way the porter was observed by three thieves, one of whom, being more genteelly dressed than his companions, accosted the man in the following manner:

" If you are willing to earn sixpence, my friend, step to the tavern at the end of the street, and ask for the roquelaure I left at the bar; but, lest the waiter should scruple giving it to you, take my gold watch as a token. Pitch your burden upon this bulk, and I will take care of it till your return; but be sure you make haste." The man went to the tavern, and having delivered his message, was informed that the thing he inquired for had not been left there; upon which the porter said, " Since you scruple to trust me, look at this gold watch, which the gentleman gave me to produce as a token." What was called a gold watch being examined, proved to be only pewter lacquered. In consequence of this discovery, the porter hastened back to where he had left the box, but neither that nor the sharpers were to be found.

The porter was, with reason, apprehensive that he should incur his master's displeasure if he related what had happened; and, in order to excuse his folly, he determined upon the following stratagem: he rolled himself in the mud, and then went home, saying he had been knocked down, and robbed of his goods.

The proprietor of the goods applied to Wild, and related to him the story he had been told by his servant. Wild told him that he had been deceived as to the manner in which the trunk was lost, and that he should be convinced of it, if he would send for his servant. A messenger was dispatched for the porter; and, upon his arrival, Abraham conducted him into a room separated from the office only by a slight partition, " Your master," said Abraham, " has just been here concerning the box you lost; and he desired that you might be sent for, in order to communicate the particulars of the robbery. What kind of people were the thieves? and in what manner did they take the box away?" In reply the man said, " Why, two or three fellows knocked me down, and then carried off the box." Hereupon Abraham told him, that " if they knocked him down, there was but little chance of the property being recovered, since that offence rendered them liable to be hanged. But (continued he) let me prevail on you to speak the truth; for, if you persist in a refusal, be assured we shall discover it by some other means. Pray, do you recollect nothing about a token? Were you not to fetch a roquelaure from a tavern? and did you not produce a gold watch as a token to induce the waiter to deliver it?"—Astonished at Abraham's words, the porter declared " he believed he was a witch," and immediately acknowledged in what manner he had lost the box.

One of the villains concerned in the above transaction lived in the house formerly inhabited by Wild, in Cock-Alley, near Cripplegate. To this place Jonathan and Abraham repaired; and when they were at the door, they overheard a dispute between the man and his wife, during which the former declared that he would set out for Holland the next day. Upon this they forced open the door; and Wild, saying he was under the necessity of preventing his intended voyage, took him into custody, and conducted him to the Compter.

On the following day the goods being returned to the owner, Wild received a handsome reward; and he contrived to procure the discharge of the thief.

On the 23d or 24th of January, 1718-19, Margaret Dodwell and Alice Wright went to Wild's house, and desired to have a private interview with him. Observing one of the women to be with child, he imagined she might want a father to her expected issue; for it was part of his business to procure persons to stand in the place of the real fathers of children born in consequence of illicit commerce. Being shown into another room, Dodwell spoke in the following manner: " I do not come, Mr. Wild, to inform you that I have met with any loss, but that I wish to find something. If you will follow my advice, you may acquire a thousand pounds, or perhaps many thousands." Jonathan here expressed the utmost willingness to engage in an enterprise so highly lucrative, and the woman proceeded thus: " My plan is this: you must procure two or three stout resolute fellows who will undertake to rob a house in Wormwood-street, near Bishopsgate. This house is kept by a cane-chair maker, named John Cook, who has a lodger, an ancient maiden lady, immensely rich, and who keeps her money in a box in her apartment: she is now gone into the country to fetch more. One of the men must find an opportunity of getting into the shop in the evening, and conceal himself in a saw-pit there: he may let his companions in when the family are retired to rest. But it will be particularly necessary to secure two stout apprentices and a boy, who lie in the garret. I wish, however, that no murder may be committed." Upon this Wright said, " Phoo! phoo! when people engage in matters of this sort, they must manage as well as they can, and so as to provide for their own safety." Dodwell now resumed her discourse to Jonathan: " The boys secured, no kind of difficulty will attend getting possession of the old lady's money, she being from home, and her room under that where the boys sleep. In the room facing that of the old lady, Cooke and his wife lie. He is a man of remarkable courage; great caution therefore must be observed respecting him; and, indeed, I think it would be as well to knock him on the head, for then his drawers may be rifled, and he is never without money. A woman and a child lie under the room belonging to the old lady, but I hope no violence will be offered to them."

Having heard the above proposal, Wild took the women into custody, and lodged them in Newgate. It is not to be supposed that his conduct in this affair proceeded from a principle of virtue or justice, but that he declined engaging in the iniquitous scheme from an apprehension that their design was to draw him into a snare.

Dodwell had lived five months in Mr. Cooke's house, and though she paid no rent, he was too generous to turn her out, or in any manner to oppress her. Wild prosecuted Dodwell and Wright for a misdemeanor, and being found guilty, they were sentenced each to suffer six months imprisonment.

Wild had inserted in his book a gold watch, a quantity of fine lace, and other property of considerable value, John Butler had stolen from a house at Newington-Green; but Butler, instead of coming to account as usual, had declined his felonious practices, and lived on the produce of his booty. Being informed that he lodged at a public-house in Bishopsgate-street, Wild went to the house early one morning, when

Butler, hearing him ascending the stairs, jumped out of the window of his room, and climbing over the wall of the yard got into the street. Wild broke open the door of the room; but was exceedingly disappointed and mortified to find that the man of whom he was in pursuit had escaped. In the mean time Butler ran into a house, the door of which stood open, and descending to the kitchen, where some women were washing, told them he was pursued by a bailiff, and they advised him to conceal himself in the coal-hole.

Jonathan coming out of the ale-house, and seeing a shop on the opposite side of the way open, he inquired of the master, who was a dyer, whether a man had not taken refuge in his house. The dyer answered in the negative, saying, he had not left his shop more than a minute since it had been opened. Wild requested leave to search the house, and the dyer readily complied. Wild asked the women, if they knew whether a man had taken shelter in the house; which they at first denied, but on his informing them that the man he sought was a thief, they said he would find him in the coal-hole.

Having procured a candle, Wild and his attendants searched the place without effect; they then examined every part of the house with no better success. They observed, that the villain must have escaped into the street; on which the dyer said, that it could not be the case; that if he had entered, he must still be in the house, for he had not quitted the shop, and it was impossible that a man could pass into the street without his knowledge; and he advised Wild to search the cellar again. They now all went into the cellar, and after some time spent in searching, the dyer turned up a large vessel, used in his business, and Butler appeared. Wild asked him in what manner he had disposed of the goods he had stolen from Newington-Green, and, upbraiding him as being guilty of ingratitude, declared that he should certainly be hanged.

Butler, however, knowing the means by which an accommodation might be effected, directed Wild to go to his lodgings, and look behind the head of his bed, where he would find what would recompense him for his time and trouble. Wild went to the place, and found what perfectly satisfied him; but as Butler had been apprehended in a public manner, the other was under a necessity of taking him before a magistrate, who committed him for trial. He was tried the ensuing sessions at the Old Bailey; but, by the artful management of Wild, instead of being condemned to die, he was only sentenced to transportation.

Being at an inn in Smithfield, Wild observed a large trunk in the yard, and imagining that it contained property of value, he hastened home, and instructed one of the thieves he employed to carry it off. The man he employed in this matter was named Jeremiah Rann, who was reckoned one of the most dexterous thieves in London. Having dressed himself so as exactly to resemble a porter, he carried away the trunk without being observed.

Mr. Jarvis, a whip-maker by trade, and the proprietor of the trunk, had no sooner discovered his loss, than he applied to Wild, who returned him the goods in consideration of receiving ten guineas. Some time after, a disagreement took place between Jonathan and Rann, and the former apprehended the latter, who was tried and condemned to death. The day preceding that on which Rann was executed, he sent for Mr. Jarvis, and related to him all the particulars of the trunk. Mr. Jarvis threatened Wild with a prosecution; but all apprehensions on that score were soon dissipated by the death of Mr. Jarvis.

Wild being much embarrassed as to the disposal of the property that was not claimed by the respective proprietors, revolved in his mind a variety of schemes; but at length he determined upon purchasing a sloop, in order to transport the goods to Holland and Flanders, and gave the command of the vessel to a notorious thief, named Roger Johnson.

Ostend was the port where this vessel principally traded; but when the goods were not disposed of there, Johnson went to Bruges, Ghent, Brussels, and other places. He brought home lace, wine, brandy, &c.; and these commodities were landed in the night, without adding any thing to the business of the revenue officers. This trade was continued for about two years, when five pieces of lace being lost, Johnson deducted the value of them from the mate's pay. Violently irritated by this conduct, the mate lodged an information against Johnson for running a great quantity of various kinds of goods. In consequence of this the vessel was exchequered, Johnson cast in damages to the amount of 700*l.*, and the commercial proceedings were entirely ruined.

A disagreement had for some time subsisted between Johnson and Thomas Edwards, who kept a house for thieves in Long-lane, concerning the division of some booty. Meeting one day in the Strand, they charged each other with felony, and were both taken into custody. Wild bailed Johnson, and Edwards was not prosecuted. The latter had no sooner recovered his liberty, than he gave information against Wild, whose private warehouses being searched, a great quantity of stolen goods was there found. Wild arrested Edwards in the name of Johnson, to whom he pretended the goods belonged, and he was taken to the Marshalsea, but the next day he procured bail. Edwards determined to wreak his revenge upon Johnson, and for some time industriously sought for him in vain; but meeting him accidentally in Whitechapel-road, he gave him into the custody of a peace-officer, who conducted him to an adjacent ale-house. Johnson sent for Wild, who immediately attended, accompanied by his man Quilt Arnold. Wild promoted a riot, during which Johnson availed himself of an opportunity of effecting an escape.

Information being laid against Wild for the rescue of Johnson, he judged it prudent to abscond, and remained concealed for three weeks; at the end of which time, supposing all danger to be over, he returned to his house. Learning that Wild had returned, Mr. Jones, the high constable of Holborn division, went to his house in the Old Bailey, on the 15th of February, 1725, and apprehended him and Quilt Arnold, and took them before Sir John Fryer, who committed them to Newgate, on a charge of having assisted in the escape of Johnson.

On Wednesday the 24th of the same month, Wild moved to be either admitted to bail, discharged, or brought to trial that sessions. On the following Friday, a warrant of detainer was produced against him in the court. The information of Mr. Jones was also read, setting forth that two persons would be produced to accuse the prisoner of capital offences. The men alluded to in the above affidavit were John Follard and Thomas Butler, who had been convicted; but it being deemed expedient to grant them a pardon on condition of their appearing in support of a prosecution against Wild, they pleaded to the same, and were remanded to Newgate till the next sessions.

On Saturday, May 15th, 1725, Jonathan Wild was indicted for privately stealing, in the house of Catharine Stretham, in the parish of St. Andrew, Holborn, fifty yards of lace, the property of the said Catharine, on the 22d of January, 1724-5. He was a second time indicted for feloniously receiving of the said Catharine, on the 10th of March, ten guineas on account and under pretence of restoring the said lace without apprehending and prosecuting the felon who stole the property.

Previous to his trial, Wild distributed among the jurymen, and other persons who were walking on the leads before the court a great number of printed papers, under the title of " A List of Persons discovered, apprehended, and convicted of several Robberies on the Highway, and also for Burglary and House-breaking, and also for returning from Transportation, by Jonathan Wild." This list contained the names of thirty-five for robbing on the highway, twenty-two for house-breaking, and ten for returning from transportation. To the list was annexed the following *Nota Bene.*

" Several others have been also convicted for the like crimes, but, remembering not the persons' names who had been robbed, I omit the criminals' names.

" Please to observe, that several others have been also convicted for shop-lifting, picking of pockets, &c. by the female sex, which are capital crimes, and which are too tedious to be inserted here, and the prosecutors not willing of being exposed.

" In regard thereof, to the numbers above convicted, some that have yet escaped justice are endeavouring to take away the life of the said

" JONATHAN WILD."

The prisoner being put to the bar, he requested that the witnesses might be examined apart, which was complied with.

The trial then commenced, and the first witness called was Henry Kelly, who deposed, that by the prisoner's directions he went, in company with Margaret Murphy, to the prosecutor's shop under pretence of buying some lace; that he stole a tin box, and gave it to Murphy in order to deliver it to Wild, who waited in the street for the purpose of receiving their booty, and rescuing them if they should be taken into custody; that they returned together to Wild's house, where the box being opened was found to contain eleven pieces of lace; that Wild said, he could afford no more than five guineas, as he should not be able to get more than ten guineas for returning the goods to the owner; that he received, as his share, three guineas and a crown, and that Murphy had what remained of the five guineas.

The prisoner's counsel contended, that he could not be legally convicted because the indictment expressed that *he stole* the lace *in* the house, whereas it had been proved in evidence that he was at a considerable distance outside when the fact was committed. They allowed that he might be liable to conviction as an accessary before the fact, or for receiving the property, knowing it to be stolen; but conceived that he could not be deemed guilty of a capital felony, unless the indictment declared (as the act directs) that he did *assist, command,* or *hire.*

Lord Raymond presided when Wild was tried; and in summing up the evidence his Lordship observed, that the guilt of the prisoner was a point beyond all dispute; but that as a similar case was not to be found in the law books, it became his duty to act with great caution. He was not perfectly satisfied that the construction urged by the counsel for the crown could be put upon the indictment; and as the life of a fellow-creature was at stake, he recommended the prisoner to the mercy of the jury, who brought in their verdict *Not Guilty.*

Wild was then arraigned on the second indictment, for an offence committed during his confinement in Newgate.

Mrs. Stretham, having repeated the evidence which she had before given, went on to state, that on the evening of the robbery she went to the house of the prisoner in order to employ him in recovering the goods, but that not finding him at home, she advertised them, offering a reward of fifteen guineas for their return, and promising that no questions should be asked. The advertisement proved ineffectual, and therefore she again went to the house of the prisoner, and seeing him, by his desire she gave an account of the transaction and of the appearance of the thieves. He promised to inquire after her property, and desired her to call again in a few days. She did so, and at this second visit he informed her that he had gained some information respecting her goods, and expected more; and a man who was present said that he thought that Kelly, who had been tried for passing plated shillings, was the offender. The witness again went to the prisoner on the day on which he was apprehended, and said that she would give twenty-five guineas rather than not have her lace back; on which he told her not to be in too great a hurry, for that the people who had stolen the lace were out of town, and that he should soon cause a disagreement between them, by which he should secure the property on more easy terms. On the 10th of March she received a message, that if she would go to the prisoner in Newgate, and take ten guineas with her, her lace would be returned to her. She went to him accordingly, and a porter being called, he gave her a letter, saying it was addressed to the person to whom he was directed to apply for the lace, and the porter would accompany her to carry the box home. She declined going herself, and then the prisoner desired her to give the money to the porter, who would go for her and fetch the goods, but said that he could not go without it, for that the people who had the lace would not give it up without being paid. She gave the money, and the man went away, but in a short time returned with a box sealed up, but not the box which she had lost. On opening it, she found that it contained all her lace except one piece. She asked the prisoner what satisfaction he expected, when he answered " Not a farthing; I have no interested views in matters of this kind, but act from a principle of serving people under misfortune. I hope I shall soon be able to recover the other piece of lace, and return you the ten guineas, and perhaps cause the thief to be apprehended. For the service I can render you I shall only expect your prayers. I have many enemies, and know not what will be the consequence of this imprisonment."

The judge was of opinion that the case of the prisoner was clearly within the meaning of the act; for it was plain that he had maintained a secret correspondence with felons, and received money for restoring stolen goods to the owners, which money was divided between him and the felons, whom he did not prosecute.

The jury pronounced him guilty, and he was sentenced to be executed at Tyburn, on Monday the 24th of May, 1725.

Wild, when he was under sentence of death, frequently declared that he thought the service he had rendered the public in returning stolen goods to the owners, and apprehending felons, was so great as justly to entitle him to the royal mercy. He said, that had he considered his case as being desperate, he should have taken timely measures for inducing some powerful friends at Wolverhampton to intercede in his favour; and that he thought it not unreasonable to entertain hopes of obtaining a pardon through the interest of some of the dukes, earls, and other persons of high distinction, who had recovered their property through his means. It was observed to him, that he had trained up a great number of thieves, and must be conscious, that he had not enforced the execution of the law from any principle of virtue, but had sacrificed the lives of a great number of his accomplices, in order to provide for his own safety, and to gratify his desire of revenge against those who had incurred his displeasure.

He was observed to be in an unsettled state of mind, and being asked whether he knew the cause thereof, he said, he attributed his disorder to the wounds he had received in apprehending felons, and particularly mentioned two fractures of his skull, and his throat being cut by Blueskin.

He declined attending divine service in the chapel, excusing himself on account of his infirmities, and saying, that there were many people highly exasperated against him, and therefore he could not expect but that his devotions would be interrupted by their insulting behaviour. He said he had fasted four days, which had greatly increased his weakness. He asked the ordinary the meaning of the words, " Cursed is every one that hangeth on a tree;" and what was the state of the soul immediately after its departure from the body? He was advised to direct his attention to matters of more importance, and sincerely repent of the crimes he had committed.

By his desire the ordinary administered the sacrament to him, and during the ceremony he appeared to be somewhat attentive and devout. The evening preceding the day on which he suffered, he inquired of the ordinary, whether self-murder could be deemed a crime, since many of the Greeks and Romans, who had put a period to their own lives, were so honourably mentioned by historians. He was informed, that the most wise and learned heathens accounted those guilty of the greatest cowardice, who had not fortitude sufficient to maintain themselves in the station to which they had been appointed by the providence of Heaven; and that the Christian doctrine condemned the practice of suicide in the most express terms.

He pretended to be convinced that self-murder was a most impious crime; but, about two in the morning, he endeavoured to put an end to his life by taking laudanum: however, on account of the largeness of the dose, and his having fasted for a considerable time, no other effect was produced than drowsiness, or a kind of stupefaction. The situation of Wild being observed by two of his fellow-prisoners, they advised him to rouse his spirits, that he might be able to attend to the devotional exercises; and taking him by the arms, they obliged him to walk, which he could not have done alone, being much afflicted with the gout. The exercise revived him a little, but he presently became exceedingly pale, then grew very faint; a profuse sweating ensued, and soon afterwards his stomach discharged the greatest part of the laudanum. Though he was somewhat recovered, he was nearly in a state of insensibility, and in this situation he was put into the cart, and conveyed to Tyburn.

In his way to the place of execution, the populace treated this offender with remarkable severity, incessantly pelting him with stones, dirt, &c., and execrating him as the most consummate villain that had ever disgraced human nature.

Upon his arrival at Tyburn, he appeared to be much recovered from the effects of the laudanum; and the executioner informed him that a reasonable time would be allowed him for preparing himself for the important change that he must soon experience. He continued sitting some time in the cart; but the populace were at length so enraged at the indulgence shewn him, that they outrageously called to the executioner to perform the duties of his office, violently threatening him with instant death if he presumed any longer to delay. He judged it prudent to comply with their demands, and when he began to prepare for the execution, the popular clamour ceased.

About two o'clock the following morning, the remains of Wild were interred in St. Pancras church-yard; but a few nights afterwards they were taken up (for the use of the surgeons, it was supposed.) At midnight a hearse and six was waiting at the end of Fig-lane, where the coffin was found the next day.

Wild had, by the woman he married at Wolverhampton, a son about nineteen years old, who came to London a short time before the execution of his father. He was a youth of so ungovernable a disposition, that it was judged prudent to confine him while his father was conveyed to Tyburn, lest he should create a tumult, and prove the cause of mischief among the populace. Soon after the death of his father, he accepted a sum of money to become a servant in one of our plantations.

Besides the woman to whom he was married at Wolverhampton, five others lived with him under the pretended sanction of matrimony: the first was Mary Milliner; the second, Judith Nun, by whom he had a daughter; the third, Sarah Grigson, alias Perrin; the fourth, Elizabeth Man, who cohabited with him above five years; the fifth, whose real name is uncertain, married again some time after the death of Wild.

History cannot furnish another instance of such complicated villainy as was shewn in the character of Jonathan Wild, who possessed abilities, which, had they been properly cultivated, and directed into a right course, would have rendered him a respectable and useful member of society; but it is to be lamented, that the profligate turn of his mind readily disposed him to adopt the maxims of the abandoned people with whom he became acquainted.

During his apprenticeship Wild was observed to be fond of reading; but, as his finances would not admit of his buying books, his studies were confined to such as casually fell in his way, and they unfortunately happened to contain those abominable doctrines to which thousands have owed the ruin of both their bodies and souls. In short, at an early period of life he imbibed the principles of Deism, or rather of Atheism; and the sentiments he thus early contracted, he strictly adhered to till the period of his dissolution.

Wild trained up and instructed his dependents in the practice of villainy, and when they became the objects of his displeasure, he laboured with as much assiduity to procure their deaths. Thus his temporal and private interest sought gratification at the expence of every religious and moral obligation. We must conceive it to be impossible for a man acknowledging the existence of an Almighty Being to employ his attention upon devising the means of corrupting his fellow-creatures and cutting them off " even in the blossom of their sins;" but the Atheist having nothing after this world either to hope or fear, is only careful to secure himself from detection, and the success of one iniquitous scheme naturally induces him to engage in others, and the latter actions are generally attended with circumstances of more aggravated guilt than the former.

The adventures of Wild are of a nature to attract great attention, from the multiplicity and variety of the offences of which he was guilty. It has been hinted, that his career of crime being suffered to continue so long was in some degree attributable to the services which he had performed for the government in arresting and gaining information against the disaffected during the troubles which characterised the early part of the reign of George I.; but, whatever may have been the cause of his being so long unmolested, it cannot be doubted that the fact of his long impunity tended much to the demoralisation of society. The existing generation cannot but congratulate itself upon the improvements which have been made in our laws, and the admirable effects which they have produced, as well as the exceedingly active vigilance of the police, by whom crime, instead of being supported and fostered, is checked and prevented.

THE " NO POPERY " RIOTS.

THE RIOTS OF LONDON,

BEGINNING ON THE 2ND JUNE, 1780, AND TERMINATING WITH THE EXECUTION OF THE RIOTERS.

THE history of London, from its earliest epoch, exhibits no event of a more calamitous nature, or more pregnant with mischief, than the riots of 1780. A commotion so daring, and so rapid in its progress, was perhaps never before known. The sovereignty of the king, the safety of the subject, and the security of property, rested on laws which were unsupported; the magistrates were confessedly intimidated; and all good and loyal citizens were seized with a terror and panic which were alone dispelled, and tranquillity restored, by the instrumentality of a military force.

The origin of the riot is ascribed to the passing of an act of parliament, about two years previously, for "relieving his majesty's subjects of the Catholic Religion from certain penalties and disabilities imposed upon them during the reign of William III." A petition to parliament was framed for its repeal, and a general meeting of a body of people forming the Protestant Association, headed by Lord George Gordon, was held on the 29th May, at the Coachmakers Hall, Noble Street, Aldersgate-street. At this meeting the noble lord moved the following resolutions :—

" Whereas no hall in London can contain forty thousand persons,

" Resolved,—That this association do meet on Friday next in St. George's-fields, at ten o'clock in the morning, to consider the most pru-

8

dent and respectful manner of attending their petition, which will be presented the same day to the House of Commons.

" Resolved,—For the sake of good order and regularity, that this association, in coming to the ground, do separate themselves into four divisions, *viz.* the London division, the Westminster division, the Southwark division, and the Scotch division.

" Resolved,—That the London division do take place of the ground towards Southwark ; the Westminster division second ; the Southwark division third ; and the Scotch division upon the left, all wearing blue cockades, to distinguish themselves from the Papists, and those who approve of the late act in favour of popery.

" Resolved,—That the magistrates of London, Westminster, and Southwark, are requested to attend ; that their presence may overawe and control any riotous or evil-minded persons, who may wish to disturb the legal and peaceable deportment of his majesty's subjects."

His lordship having intimated that he would not present the petition unless twenty thousand persons attended the meeting, and the resolutions having been published and placarded through the streets, on the day appointed a vast concourse of people from all parts of the city and its environs assembled in St. George's-fields. The main body took their route over London Bridge, marching in order, six or eight in a rank, through the City towards Westminster, accompanied by flags bearing the words " No Popery." At Charing-Cross, the mob was increased by additional numbers on foot, on horseback, and in various vehicles, so that by the time the different parties met together, all the avenues to both Houses of Parliament were entirely filled with the crowd. The rabble now took possession of all the passages leading to the House of Commons, from the outer doors to the very entrance for the members ; which latter they twice attempted to force open ; and a like attempt was made at the House of Lords, but without success in either instance. In the mean time, Lord George Gordon came into the House of Commons with an unembarrassed countenance, and a blue cockade in his hat, after " riding in the whirlwind and directing the storm ;" but finding it gave offence, he took it out and put it in his pocket ; not however before Captain Herbert, of the navy, one of the members, threatened to pull it out ; while Colonel Murray, another member, declared that if the mob broke into the house, he (looking at Lord George) should instantly be the victim.

The petition having been presented, the populace separated into parties, and proceeded to demolish the Catholic chapels, in Duke-street, Lincoln's Inn Fields, and Warwick-street, Golden-square ; and all the furniture, ornaments, and altars of both chapels were committed to the flames. After various other outrages, the prison of Newgate was attacked. They demanded from the keeper, Mr. Ackerman, the release of their confined associates : he refused to comply ; yet, dreading the consequence, he went to the sheriffs to know their pleasure. On his return he found his house in flames ; and the jail itself was soon in a similar situation. The doors and entrances were broken open with crowbars and sledge hammers ; and it is scarcely to be credited with what rapidity this strong prison was destroyed. The public office in Bow-street, and Sir John Fielding's house, adjoining, were presently destroyed, and all their furniture and effects, books, papers, &c. committed to the flames. Justice Coxe's house in Great Queen-street, Lincoln's Inn Fields, was similarly treated; and the two prisons at Clerkenwell set open, and the prisoners liberated. The King's Bench Prison, with some houses adjoining, a tavern, and the New Bridewell, were also set on fire, and almost entirely consumed.

The mob now appeared to consider themselves as superior to all authority; they declared their resolution to burn all the remaining public prisons; and demolish the Bank, the Temple, Gray's Inn, Lincoln's Inn, the Mansion House, the royal palaces, and the arsenal at Woolwich. The attempt upon the Bank of England was actually made twice in the course of one day; but both attacks were but feebly conducted, and the rioters easily repulsed, several of them falling by the fire of the military, and many others being severely wounded.

To form an adequate idea of the distress of the inhabitants in every part of the city would be impossible. Six-and-thirty fires were to be seen blazing in the metropolis during the night.

At length the continued arrival of fresh troops, from all parts of the country, within fifty or sixty miles of the metropolis, intimidated the rabble; and soon after the disturbances were quelled.

The Royal Exchange, the public buildings, the squares, and the principal streets, were all occupied by troops; the shops were closed; while immense volumes of dense smoke were still rising from the ruins of consumed edifices.

During the riots, many persons, terrified by the alarming outrages of the mob, fled from London, and took refuge in places at a considerable distance from town. The following extract from a letter written at this time by Dr. Johnson to Mrs. Thrale, who was one of those who had fled in alarm on the outbreak of the insurrection may perhaps, prove interesting:—

" The king said in council ' That the magistrates had not done their duty, but that he would do his own;' and a proclamation was published directing us to keep our servants within doors, as the peace was now to be preserved by force.

" The soldiers were sent out to different parts, and the town is now quiet. They are stationed so as to be everywhere within call; there is no longer any body of rioters, and the individuals are hunted to their holes, and led to prison. Lord George Gordon was last night sent to the Tower.

" Several chapels have been destroyed, and several inoffensive Papists have been plundered: but the high sport was to burn the gaols. This was a good rabble trick. The debtors and criminals were set at liberty; but of the criminals, as has always happened, many are already retaken; and two pirates have surrendered themselves, and it is expected they will be pardoned.

" Government now acts with its proper force; and we are all now again under the protection of the king and the law. I thought it would be agreeable to you to have my testimony to the public security; and that you would sleep more quietly when I told you that you were safe.

" There has been, indeed, an universal panic, from which the king was the first that recovered. Without the concurrence or assistance of his ministers, or even the assistance of the civil magistrates, he put the soldiers in motion, and saved the town from calamities such as a rabble's government must naturally produce.

" The public has escaped a very heavy calamity. The rioters attempted the Bank on Wednesday night, but in no great numbers ; Jack Wilkes headed the party that drove them away. It is agreed, that if they had seized the Bank, on Tuesday, at the height of the panic, when no resistance had been prepared, they might have carried away whatever they had found."

The number of persons killed in this dreadful riot is variously stated. Many persons, strangers to the attempt, were destroyed by the necessarily indiscriminate fire of the soldiers and militia ; and although it is impossible to calculate the precise number who lost their lives, from the circumstance of many being carried off by their friends, it is believed to have been about 500.

Lord George Gordon, the leader and instigator of these riots, was subsequently tried in the Court of King's Bench, and by some good fortune escaped conviction. There was little doubt that he was occasionally subject to aberrations of intellect. His death took place some years afterwards in the King's Bench Prison. He had been indicted for a libel on Marie Antoinette, the late unfortunate French queen, and the Count d'Ademar, one of the ministers of state, and having been convicted, fled from punishment, but was afterwards apprehended in Birmingham, attired in the garb of a Jew, with a long beard, &c., where he had undergone circumcision, and had embraced the religion of the unbelievers. He died professing the same faith.

Many of the rioters were apprehended, and having been recognized, were convicted, and suffered death in most instances opposite the places in which the scenes were enacted, in which they were proved to have taken a part. Among them were many women and boys, but there was not one individual of respectability or character. They were all of the lowest class, whose only object was plunder.

Among the rioters, to sum up the account of their infamy and wretchedness, was Jack Ketch himself. This miscreant, whose real name was Edward Dennis, was convicted of pulling down the house of Mr. Boggis, of New Turnstile. The keeper of Tothill-fields Bridewell would not suffer Jack Ketch to go amongst the other prisoners, lest they should tear him to pieces. In order that he might hang up his brother rioters, he was granted a pardon.

BLACKBEARD SHOOTING HANDS IN THE KNEE.

CAPTAIN TEACH, *alias* BLACKBEARD,

A NOTORIOUS PIRATE, KILLED WHILST BEING CAPTURED.

EDWARD TEACH was a native of Bristol. Having gone to Jamaica, he frequently sailed from that port, as one of the crew of a privateer during the French war. In these excursions he gave frequent proofs of his boldness and personal courage; but he never attained any promotion, until Captain Benjamin Hornigold, a pirate, offered him the command of a prize which he had taken.

In the spring of 1717, Hornigold and Teach sailed from Providence for America, and in their way captured a small vessel with a hundred and twenty barrels of flour, which they put on board their own vessels. They seized, also, two other vessels — from the one taking only a few gallons of wine; but from the other, which had a rich cargo on board, they obtained booty to a considerable amount. After clearing upon the coast of Virginia they again put to sea, and in a few days fell in with a large French Guinea-man, bound to Martinico, which they captured; and Teach, seeing she was a better vessel than his own, took the command of her, with part of his former crew, determined to part company from Hornigold, and cruize alone. Hornigold, with the other two vessels, immediately returned to the Isle of Providence, where, on the arrival of Captain Rogers, the new governor, he surrendered himself to the king's mercy, pursuant to the terms of a proclamation.

K

Teach now mounted 40 guns aboard of this Guinea-man, and named her "The Queen Anne's Revenge." Cruising near the island of St. Vincent, he took a large ship called the "Great Allen," and having plundered her of what he thought fit, and put her crew ashore on the island, he burnt the ship.

A few days after this, he fell in with the "Scarborough" man-of-war, which engaged him several hours; but finding the pirate well manned, and rather too strong for her, she gave over the engagement, and returned to Barbadoes, the place of her station. Teach immediately made sail for Spanish America.

In his way thither he met with a pirate sloop of 10 guns, commanded by Major Bonnet, who was lately a gentleman of good estate and reputation in the island of Barbadoes, and who readily accepted Teach's offer to join him. But Teach, finding that Bonnet knew nothing of a maritime life, with the consent of the crew, put in one Richards to be captain of Bonnet's sloop, and received the major on board his own ship, telling him, that as he had not been used to the fatigues and cares of such a post, it would be better for him to decline it and live at his ease in such a ship as his, where he would not be obliged to perform any duty, but might follow the bent of his own inclination.

At Turniff, 10 leagues from the bay of Honduras, the pirates took in fresh water; and while they were at anchor there they discovered a sloop coming in, whereupon Richards, in the "Revenge," slipped his cable, and ran out to meet her. Upon seeing the black flag hoisted, the vessel instantly struck, and came to under the stern of Teach the commodore. This proved to be the "Adventure," from Jamaica. They took the captain and his men on board the large ship, and sent some of their own people, under the command of Israel Hands, master of Teach's ship, to man the sloop for the piratical service.

On the 9th of April they weighed from Turniff, having lain there for about a week, and sailed to the bay, where they found a ship and four sloops. Three of the latter belonged to Jonathan Bernard, of Jamaica, and the other to Captain James; the ship was of Boston, and called the Protestant Cæsar, Captain Wyer commander. Teach hoisted his black colours and fired a gun, upon which Captain Wyer and all his men left the ship, and got ashore in their boat. Teach's quarter-master and eight of his crew took possession of Wyer's ship, and Richards secured all the sloops, one of which they burnt out of spite to the owner. The "Protestant Cæsar" they also plundered and burnt, because she belonged to Boston, where some men had lately been hung for piracy; but the three sloops belonging to Bernard they let go.

From hence they sailed to Turkhill, and then to the Grand Caimans, a small island about 30 leagues westward of Jamaica. Here they took a small turtler, and so sailed to the Havannah, from thence to the Bahama islands and from thence to Carolina, taking a brigantine and two sloops in their way. They lay on the Carolina coast, off the bar of Charlestown, for five or six days. Here they took a ship as she was coming out, bound for London, commanded by Robert Clarke, with some passengers on board for England; the next day they took a vessel coming out of Charlestown, and also two pinks coming into Charlestown, and a brigantine with fourteen negroes on board. All this being done in the face of the town, struck great terror into the whole province of Carolina, which had just before been visited by Vane, another notorious pirate. Meanwhile there were eight sail in the harbour, none of which durst put put to sea, it being next to impossible to escape him; the inward-bound vessels were also afraid to enter, so that the trade of the place was completely stopped, and the inhabitants were in despair. Their calamity was greatly augmented from the circumstance, that a long and desperate war with the natives had just been terminated when they were infested by these robbers.

Teach having detained all the persons taken in these ships as prisoners, and being greatly in want of medicines, resolved to demand a chest of the governor of the province. Accordingly Richards, the captain of the " Revenge " sloop, and two or three more pirates, were sent along with Mr. Marks, one of the prisoners they had taken from Clarke's ship, to make their demands, which they did in a most insolent and daring manner,—Richards informing the governor that unless their demand was granted, and he and his companions permitted to return in safety, every prisoner on board the captured ships should be instantly slain, and every vessel burnt. During the time that Mr. Marks was negotiating with the governor, Richards and his associates walked the streets at pleasure, while indignation flashed from every eye against them, as being the robbers of their property, and the terror of their country.` Though the affront thus offered the government was great and most audacious, yet, to preserve so many men, their demands were acceded to, and a chest was sent on board, valued at between three and four hundred pounds.

Teach, as soon as he had received the medicines and his brother rogues, let go the ships and prisoners, after having first plundered them of specie to the amount of £1500 sterling, besides provisions.

From the bar of Charlestown they sailed to North Carolina,—Captain Teach in the ship he called the man of war, Captain Richards and Captain Hands in the two sloops, and another sloop serving as a tender. Teach began now to think of breaking up the company, and securing the money and the best of the effects to himself and a few of his companions for whom he entertained the greatest friendship, and of cheating the rest. Accordingly, under pretence of running into Topsail inlet to clean, he grounded his ship; and then (as if it had been done by accident) he ordered Hands's sloop to come to his assistance, to get him off again : which he endeavouring to do, ran the sloop on shore near the other, and so they were both lost. This done, Teach goes into the tender sloop with forty men, leaving the " Revenge " there. After this he left seventeen of his crew upon a sandy island, where there was neither bird, beast, nor herb for their subsistence, and they must inevitably have perished had not Major Bonnet received intelligence of their miserable situation, and sent a long-boat for them. After this barbarous deed, Teach with the remainder of his crew, consisting of about twenty persons, went and surrendered to the governor of North Carolina, retaining all the property which had been acquired by his fleet.

This temporary suspension of the depredations of Blackbeard (for so he was now called) did not proceed from a conviction of his former errors or a determination to reform, but only to wait and prepare for a more favourable opportunity to play the same game over again, which he soon after effected with greater security to himself, and with a much better prospect of success, having by this time cultivated a good under-standing with Charles Eden, Esq., the governor.

Through the instrumentality of his kind friend the governor, he ob-tained a legal right to the great ship called " The Queen Anne's Revenge;" for which purpose a court of vice-admiralty was held at Bath Town, where, though Teach had never had any commission in his life, and the sloop belonged to English merchants, and had been taken in time of peace, she was condemned as being a prize taken from the Spaniards.

Before he again embarked on his nefarious exploits, he married a young lady about sixteen years of age, the governor himself performing the ceremony — it being customary there for the marriage ceremony to be performed by a magistrate. This, it was reported, was his *four-teenth* wife, about a dozen of whom were still living. His behaviour to this woman was brutal beyond all comparison even among his own dissolute and abandoned companions.

In 1719 Blackbeard again put to sea upon another piratical expe-dition, shaping his course towards the Bermudas. He met with two or three English vessels in his way, but he took from them nothing but provisions, stores, and other necessaries for his present accommodation. Drawing near the island, he fell in with two French ships, one loaded with sugar and cocoa, and the other light, both bound to Martinico. The ship that had no lading he allowed to proceed on her voyage, having first put the crew of the other ship aboard of her; he then carried home his prize and her cargo to North Carolina, where the governor and the pirates shared their plunder.

When Teach arrived with his prize, he and four of his men went before the governor and made affidavit that they found the French ship at sea without a soul aboard of her; whereupon a court was called, and the vessel condemned. The governor received sixty hogsheads of sugar for his share of the booty, his secretary twenty, and the remainder was divided amongst Teach and his companions.

" Suspicion ever haunts the guilty mind !"

The truth of this axiom was now fully exemplified in the case of Teach and his companions, with respect to their ill-gotten prize. The ship still remained, and it was possible that some one might come into the river who should recognize her, and thereby discover their villainy. To obviate this, Teach, under pretence that she was leaky, and might pos-sibly sink, and stop up the mouth of the inlet or cove where she lay, obtained an order from the governor to tow her out into the river, and set her on fire. This was accordingly done, and when burnt to the water's edge her bottom was sunk, and with it all their fears of its ever rising up in judgment against them.

Blackbeard now being in friendship with the governor of the province, passed several months in the river, giving and receiving visits from the planters, and trading with the vessels which came to the river, sometimes fairly and sometimes in his own way. When he chose to appear the honest man, he made fair purchases on equal barter; but when this did not suit his necessities or his humour, he would rob at pleasure, and leave them to seek redress from the governor; and, the better to cover his intrigues with his excellency, he would sometimes outbrave him to his face, exhibiting towards him a share of that contempt and insolence which he so liberally bestowed upon the rest of the inhabitants of the province.

But there are limits to human forbearance. The captains of the vessels who frequented the river, and had been so often harassed and plundered by Blackbeard, secretly consulted with some of the planters what measures to pursue, in order to banish such an infamous miscreant from their coasts, and to bring him to deserved punishment. Convinced from long experience that the governor himself, to whom it belonged, would give no redress they represented the matter to the governor of Virginia, and entreated that an armed force might be sent from the men-of-war lying there, either to take or destroy the pirates who infested their coast.

Upon this representation, the governor of Virginia consulted with the captains of the two men-of-war as to the best measures to be adopted. It was resolved that the governor should hire two small vessels, which could pursue Blackbeard into all the inlets and creeks; that they should be manned from the men-of-war, and the command given to Lieutenant Maynard, an experienced and resolute officer. When all was ready for their departure, the governor issued a proclamation, offering a great reward to any who, within a year, should take or destroy any pirate.

Upon the 17th of November, 1719, Maynard left James's river in quest of Blackbeard, and on the evening of the 21st came in sight of the pirate. The expedition had been fitted out with all possible expedition and secrecy, no boat being permitted to pass that might convey any intelligence, while care was taken to discover where the pirates were lurking. His excellency the governor of Bermudas, and his secretary, however, having obtained information of the intended expedition, the latter wrote a letter to Blackbeard, intimating, " that he had sent him four of his men, who were all he could meet with in or about town, and so bidding him to be upon his guard." These men were sent from Bath-town to a place where Blackbeard lay, about the distance of twenty-leagues.

The hardened and infatuated pirate, having been often disconcerted with false intelligence, was the less attentive to this information; nor was he convinced of its accuracy, until he saw the sloops sent to apprehend him. Though he had then only twenty men on board, he prepared to give battle. Lieutenant Maynard arrived with his sloops in the evening, and anchored, as he could not venture under cloud of night to go into the place where Blackbeard lay. The latter spent the night in drinking with the master of a trading-vessel, with the same indifference as if no danger had been near. Nay, such was the desperate wickedness of this villain, that it is reported, that, during the carousals of that night, one of his men asking him, " that in case any thing should happen to him during the engagement with the two sloops that were waiting to attack him in the morning, whether his wife knew where he had buried his money ;" he impiously replied, " that nobody but himself and the devil knew where it was, and the longest liver should take all."

In the morning Maynard weighed, and sent his boat to sound, which coming near, the pirate opened her fire. Maynard then hoisted royal colours, and made directly towards Blackbeard with every sail and oar. In a little time the pirate ran aground, and so also did the king's vessel. Maynard lightened his vessel of the ballast and water, and made towards Blackbeard. Upon this he hailed him in his own rude style, " D—— you for villains, who are you? and from whence come you?" The lieutenant answered, " You may see from our colours we are no pirates." Blackbeard bid him send his boat on board, that he might see who he was. But Maynard replied, " I cannot spare my boat, but I will come on board of you as soon as I can with my sloop." Upon this Blackbeard took a glass of liquor, and drank to him, saying, " I'll give no quarters, nor take any from you." Maynard replied, " he expected no quarters from him, nor should he give him any."

During this dialogue, the pirate's ship floated, and the sloops were rowing with all expedition towards him. As she came near, the pirate fired a broadside, charged with all manner of small shot, which killed or wounded twenty men. Blackbeard's ship in a little after fell broadside to the shore; one of the sloops called " The Ranger" also fell astern. But Maynard, finding that his own sloop had the way, and would soon be on board of Teach, ordered all his men down, while himself and the man at the helm, whom he commanded to lie concealed, were the only persons who remained on deck. He, at the same time, desired them to take their pistols, cutlasses, and swords, and be ready for action upon his call; and for the greater expedition, two ladders were placed in the hatchway. When the king's sloop boarded, the pirate's case-boxes, filled with powder, small-shot, slugs, and pieces of lead and iron, with a lighted match in the mouth of them, were thrown into Maynard's sloop. Fortunately, however, the men being in the hold, they did small injury on the present occasion, though they are usually very destructive. Blackbeard seeing few or no hands on deck, cried to his men, that they were all knocked on the head, except three or four; " and therefore," says he, " let's jump on board, and cut to pieces those that are alive."

Upon this, during the smoke occasioned by one of these case-boxes, Blackbeard, with fourteen of his men, entered, and were not perceived untill the smoke was dispelled. The signal was given to Maynard's men, who rushed up in an instant. Blackbeard and the lieutenant exchanged shots, and the pirate was wounded; they then engaged sword in hand, until the sword of the latter broke; but, fortunately, one of his men at that instant gave Blackbeard a terrible wound in the neck and throat. The most desperate and bloody conflict ensued—

Maynard with twelve men, and Blackbeard with fourteen. The sea was dyed with blood all around the vessel, and uncommon bravery was displayed upon both sides. Though the pirate was wounded by the first shot from Maynard, yet he fought with desperate valour, though he had received twenty cuts, and five more shot; at length, when cocking his pistol, he fell down dead. By this time eight of his men had fallen, and the rest being wounded, cried out for quarter, which was granted, as the ringleader was slain. The other sloop also attacked the men who remained in the pirate vessels, until they also cried out for quarter. Such was the desperation of Blackbeard, that, having small hope of escaping, he had placed a negro with a match at the gunpowder-door, to blow up the ship the moment that he should have been boarded by the king's men, in order to involve the whole in general ruin. That destructive broadside at the commencement of the action, which at first appeared so unlucky, was, however, the means of their preservation from the intended destruction.

Maynard severed the pirate's head from his body, suspended it upon his bowsprit-end, and sailed to Bath-town, to obtain medical aid for his wounded men. In the pirate sloop several letters and papers were found, which Blackbeard would certainly have destroyed previous to the engagement, had he not determined to blow her up upon his being taken, and which disclosed the whole villainy between the honourable governor of Bermudas, his honest secretary, and the notorious pirate, who had now suffered the just reward of his crimes.

As soon as Maynard returned to Bath-town, he secured the sixty hogsheads of sugar in the possession of the governor, and the twenty in that of his secretary, their share of the plunder from the condemned ship.

After his men were healed at Bath-town, the lieutenant proceeded to Virginia, with the head of Blackbeard still suspended on his bowsprit-end as a trophy of his victory, to the great joy of all the inhabitants. The prisoners were tried, condemned, and executed; and thus all the crew of that infernal miscreant Blackbeard were destroyed, except two. One of these was taken out of a trading-vessel only the day before the engagement, in which he received no less than seventy wounds, of all which he was cured. The other was Israel Hands, who was the master of the "Queen Anne's Revenge;" he was taken at Bath-town, being wounded in one of Blackbeard's savage humours. One night Blackbeard, drinking in his cabin with Hands, the pilot, and another man, without any pretence took a small pair of pistols, and cocked them under the table; which being perceived by the man, he went on deck, leaving the captain, Hands, and the pilot together. When his pistols were prepared, Blackbeard extinguished the candle, crossed his arms, and fired at his company. The one pistol did no execution, but the other wounded Hands in the knee. Being asked the meaning of this, he answered with an imprecation, "that if he did not now and then kill one of them, they would forget who he was." Hands was tried and condemned, but as he was about to be executed, a vessel arrived with a proclamation prolonging the time of his Majesty's pardon, which Hands pleading, he was saved from a violent and shameful death.

Among a body of desperadoes, like pirates and robbers, it invariably happens that he who goes the greatest length of wickedness is looked upon by the rest with a kind of awe or reverence, as though he were a hero, and therefore entitled to command respect ; and such a one, if he have but courage to enforce obedience, will eventually be a great man amongst them.   Thus it was with Teach, some of whose tricks and frolics were as extravagant as if he aimed at making his men believe that he were a devil incarnate.   The following, perhaps, is a fair sample of these wild freaks.   Being one day at sea, and a little flushed with drink, " Come," says he, " let's make a hell of our own, and try how long we can bear it !"   The idea was seized on with avidity by his companions, and he presently found plenty of volunteers.   Accordingly he and a few of the most daring of them descended into the hold of the vessel, and, after closing the hatches, set fire to a quantity of brimstone and other combustibles, and continued there till they were nearly suffocated, and some of the men began to cry out for air, when he opened the hatches, not a little pleased at having held out the longest.

We shall close the narrative of this extraordinary man's life by an account of the cause why he was denominated Blackbeard.

Plutarch and other historians have noticed that several great men among the Romans took their surnames from certain odd marks in their countenances ; thus Cicero obtained his from the mark of a vetch on his nose : and this habit of giving a soubriquet or nickname indicative of some peculiarity or deformity in a person's character or figure prevails with us even in the present day.   So our hero, Captain Teach, acquired the cognomen of BLACKBEARD, from that large quantity of hair, which, like a frightful meteor, covered nearly his whole face, and terrified America more than any comet that ever appeared there.   This beard, which was black, and came up nearly to his eyes, he suffered to grow to an extravagant length; and he was accustomed to twist it with ribbons, in tails, after the manner of a Ramilies wig, and turn them about his ears. In time of action he wore a sling over his shoulders with three brace of pistols in it.   To add to his wild appearance, he stuck lighted matches under his hat, which appearing on both sides of his face and his eyes, naturally fierce and wild, made him such a figure that the human imagination cannot form a conception of a fury more terrible and alarming; and if he had the appearance and look of a fury, his actions fully corresponded with the character.

THE REV. THOMAS HUNTER,

EXECUTED FOR THE MURDER OF HIS TWO PUPILS.

THIS atrocious offender was born in the county of Fife, and was the son of a rich farmer, who sent him to the university of St. Andrew for education, where he was admitted to the degree of Master of Arts, and prosecuted his studies with no small degree of success.

It was usual at this time for young clergymen, previous to their taking orders, to act as tutor or chaplain in a gentleman's or nobleman's family. Young Hunter accordingly, on leaving college, obtained a situation of this nature in the house of Mr. Gordon, a wealthy and eminent merchant, and one of the baillies (or aldermen) of Edinburgh, where he lived about two years.

The family consisted of Mr. and Mrs. Gordon, their two sons and daughter, and a young woman who attended Mrs. Gordon, besides the usual menial servants. To the care of Hunter was committed the education of the two sons; and for a considerable time he discharged his duty in a manner highly satisfactory to the parents, who considered him a youth of superior genius and great goodness of heart.

The attention of Hunter was attracted by the comeliness of the lady's maid, and a connexion of a criminal nature soon commenced between them, the accidental discovery of which by the three children was ultimately the cause of the murder of two of them.

The lovers had remained so long undetected, that they grew daily less cautious; and one day, when Mr. and Mrs. Gordon were on a visit, Hunter and the girl met in the chamber as usual; but having incautiously left the door unfastened, the children found their way into the room, and saw sufficient to excite surprise in their innocent minds, and subsequently disclosed to their parents such particulars as left no doubt of what had taken place. The maid-servant was immediately discharged; but the chaplain, who had always been considered of a mild and amiable disposition, was allowed to retain his situation, after making a suitable apology for his crime, attributing it to the thoughtlessness of youth, and promising never to offend in the same way again.

From this period, however, Hunter conceived an inveterate hatred for all the children, on whom he determined in his own mind to wreak the most diabolical vengeance by murdering them. Chance for some time prevented him from carrying his horrid purpose into effect, but he at last found an opportunity of executing it as far as regarded the two boys.

When the weather was fine, it was his custom to walk in the fields with his pupils for an hour before dinner, and in these excursions the young lady generally attended her brothers; but at the time when the murder was committed she was prevented accompanying them, Mr. and Mrs. G. having received an invitation to dine with a friend in the city.

By this circumstance Hunter's intention of murdering all the three children was frustrated; but he still persevered in his intention of destroying the boys while they were yet in his power. With this view he took them into the fields as usual, and sat down as if to repose himself on the grass; and whilst his young companions were busily engaged in hunting butter-flies, and gathering wild flowers, which grew round them in abundance, he was preparing the knife to put a period to their lives. His knife being sharpened, he called the lads to him, and having reprimanded them for acquainting their father and mother of the scene to which they had been witnesses, he said that he would immediately put them to death. Terri-fied by this threat, the children ran from him; but he immediately fol-lowed, and brought them back. He then placed his knee on the body of the one, while he cut the throat of the other with his penknife; and then treated the second in the same manner.

The deed, it will be observed, was perpetrated in open day, and it would have been somewhat remarkable if, within a half a mile only of the chief city of Scotland, no human eye had been witness to the horrible atrocity. It happened that a gentleman walking on the Castle hill of Edinburgh had a tolerable view of what passed, and calling some people near him, ran with them to the spot where the children were lying dead; but by this time the murderer had advanced towards a river, with the intention of drowning himself. Those who were in pursuit, came up with him just as he reached the brink of the river, and secured him.

The prisoner was in a few days brought to trial under an old Scottish law, which prescribed that a murderer found with the blood of his victim on his clothes should be prosecuted in the sheriff's court and exe-cuted within three days. The frightful nature of his crime rendered it scarcely uncharitable to pursue a law so rigorous to the very letter. A jury being impanelled, the prisoner was brought to trial, and pleaded guilty; adding, that he only lamented not having murdered Mr. Gor-don's daughter as well as his sons.

The sheriff passed sentence of death on the culprit, which was to the effect, " that on the following day he should be executed on a gibbet erected for that purpose on the spot where he had committed the mur-ders; but that, previous to his execution, his right hand should be cut off with a hatchet, near the wrist; that then he should be drawn up to the gibbet by a rope, and, when he was dead, hung in chains between Edinburgh and Leith, the knife with which he committed the murder being stuck through his hand, which should be advanced over his head, and fixed therewith to the top of the gibbet."

This sentence, barbarous as it may now appear, was fully carried into effect on the 22d August, 1700; and, horrible to state, he who in life had professed to be a preacher of the gospel, on the scaffold declared himself to be an atheist. He closed his life with the following shocking declara-tion: " There is no God—I do not believe there is any—or if there is, I hold him in defiance!"

The body was at first suspended in chains according to the precise terms of his sentence, but was soon afterwards removed to the skirts of a small village near Edinburgh, named Broughton, at the request of Mr. Gordon; who stated that its hanging on the side of the highway through which he frequently passed, tended to re-excite his grief for the occasion that had at first given rise to it.

JOHN SIMPSON,

EXECUTED FOR HOUSE-BREAKING.

THIS man was not so much distinguished by any particular circumstances attending the crime of which he was convicted, as by the atrocities of his former life.

The following particulars are principally drawn from his own declaration while under sentence of death. During a great part of the war in the reign of King William, he was with the army in Flanders, where he used to take frequent opportunities of robbing the tents of the officers. When the army lay before Mons, and his majesty commanded in person, Simpson was one of those who were selected to guard the royal tent. One evening when the king, accompanied by the Earl (afterwards Duke) of Marlborough and Lord Cutts, went out to take a view of the situation of the army, Simpson, with a degree of impudence peculiar to himself, went into his majesty's tent, and stole about a thousand pounds. It was some days before the money was missed, and when the robbery was discovered, Simpson escaped all suspicion. He said he had committed more robberies than he could possibly recollect, having been a highwayman as well as a housebreaker.

His robberies in Flanders, as well as in England, had been very numerous ; and he affirmed that the gates of the city of Ghent had been twice shut up within a fortnight to prevent his escape, and that, when he was taken, his arms, legs, back, and neck were secured with irons ; in which condition he was carried through the streets, that he might be seen by the people.

Simpson and two of his companions used frequently to stop and rob the Roman Catholics at five o'clock in the morning, as they were going to mass. He repeatedly broke into the churches of Brussels, Mechlin, and Antwerp, and stole the silver plate from the altar.

Having killed one of his companions in a quarrel, he was apprehended, tried, and condemned by a court martial, and sentenced to be executed on the following day. During the night, however, he found means to escape, and took refuge in the church of St. Peter, in Ghent, where the army then lay. Being thus in a place of sanctuary, he applied to the priests, who made interest with Prince Eugene ; and their joint intercession with King William, who arrived in the city about four days afterwards, obtained his full pardon, and he was permitted immediately to rejoin the army.

It is but reasonable to think that the obligations he was under to these priests would have inspired him with sentiments of gratitude ; but this was so far from being the case, that, in a few days after he had obtained his pardon, he broke into the church, and robbed it of plate to the value of £1200. He was apprehended on suspicion of this sacrilege ; for as a crime of this kind is seldom committed by the natives of the country, it was at once conjectured to have been perpetrated by some of the soldiers; and information being received that two Jews had embarked in a boat on the Scheldt for Middleburgh on the day succeeding the robbery, and that Simpson had been seen in company with these Jews, suspicion was immediately fixed on him; but as there was no proof that he had sold any plate to these men, he was discharged.

The army being ordered to England, and the regiment reduced, in consequence of the peace of Reswyck in 1697, Simpson received his discharge, along with many others among whom were some of those who had been concerned in his depredations in Flanders. These worthies immediately united, and carried on their depredations on the roads near London, Simpson being chosen as the leader of the gang, and dignified by the title of Captain. When they were unsuccessful on the highway, they had recourse to housebreaking; and they continued these practices for about three years, during which period several of Simpson's companions were executed.

At length Simpson himself was taken; and being indicted for breaking open the dwelling-house of Elizabeth Gawden, and stealing two feather-beds and other articles, he pleaded guilty, and received sentence of death. He declared that he had never murdered any person in consequence of his robberies; but that he had killed four or five men in private quarrels. He was executed at Tyburn on the 20th July, 1700, having first declared that his real name was John Holliday, and that he had broken out of Newgate about the Christmas preceding his last apprehension.

The fate of this malefactor presents a striking lesson of caution to those of his own rank, whether out of or in the army. The former will see that in this instance, as in every other, the paths of vice sooner or later lead to destruction: the latter will, we trust, be taught to learn obedience to their superiors; for had this offender been properly impressed with a sense of that duty, the robbing of his king could never have entered into his imagination. The crime of sacrilege, of which he was repeatedly guilty, has been held in universal abhorrence by all civilized nations, and is justly punished in the severest manner. Many years have now elapsed since his offences brought him to a deplorable end; but it is to be hoped, that distance of time will not weaken the impression, since what was worthy of regard, and proper to enforce serious ideas, at the beginning of the last century, cannot be less so at the present moment.

MURDER OF GALLY AND CHATER BY SMUGGLERS.

BENJAMIN TAPNER, JOHN CORBY, JOHN HAMMOND, WILLIAM CARTER, RICHARD MILLS THE ELDER, RICHARD MILLS THE YOUNGER, WILLIAM JACKSON, AND OTHERS.

EXECUTED FOR MURDER.

WE do not recollect ever to have heard of a case exhibiting greater brutality on the part of the murderers towards their victim than this. The offenders were all smugglers, and the unfortunate objects of their crime were a custom-house officer and a shoemaker, named William Galley and Daniel Chater. It would appear that a daring and very extensive robbery having been committed at the custom-house at Poole, Galley and Chater were sent to Stanstead, in Sussex, to give some information to Major Battine, a magistrate, in reference to the circumstance. They did not, however, return to their homes, and on inquiry, it turned out that they had been brutally murdered. The body of Galley was traced, by means of bloodhounds, to have been buried, while that of Chater was discovered at a distance of six miles, in a well in Harris's Wood, near Leigh, in Lady Holt's Park, covered up with a quanity of stones, wooden railings, and earth.

At a special commission held at Chichester, on the 16th of January 1749, the prisoners Benjamin Tapner, John Corby, John Hammond,

William Carter, Richard Mills the elder, and Richard Mills the younger, were indicted for the murder of Daniel Chater—the three first as principals, and the others as accessories before the fact ; and William Jackson and William Carter were indicted for the murder of William Galley.

From the evidence adduced, the circumstances of this most horrid murder were clearly proved. It appeared that the two murdered persons, having passed Havant on their road to Stanstead, went to the New Inn, Leigh, where they met one Austin, and his brother and brother-in-law, of whom they asked the road, and who conducted them to Rowland's castle, where, they said, they might obtain better information.   They went into the White Hart ; and Mrs. Payne, the landlady, suspecting the object of their mission, sent for the prisoners Jackson and Carter ; and they were soon after joined by some others of the gang.   After they had been all sitting together, Carter called Chater out, and demanded to know where Diamond (one of those suspected of the robbery) was ? Chater replied that he was in custody, and that he was going against his will to give evidence against him.   Galley, following them into the yard, was knocked down by Carter, on his calling Chater away, and they then returned in-doors.   The smugglers now pretended to be sorry for what had occurred, asked Galley to drink some rum, and persisted in plying him and Chater with liquor until they were both intoxicated. They were then persuaded to lie down and sleep ; and a letter to Major Battine, of which they were the bearers, was taken from them, read, and destroyed.

One John Royce, a smuggler, now came in, and Jackson and Carter told him the contents of the letter, and said that they had got the old rogue, the shoemaker of Fording-bridge, who was going to inform against John Diamond the shepherd, then in custody at Chichester.   Here William Steele proposed to take them to a well about two hundred yards from the house, and to murder and throw them in ; but this was rejected ; and after several propositions had been made as to the mode in which they should be disposed of, the scene of cruelty was commenced by Jackson, who, putting on his spurs, jumped on the bed where they lay, and spurred their foreheads, and then whipped them ; so that they both got up bleeding.   The smugglers then took them out of the house ; and Mills swore he would shoot any one who followed or said any thing of what had occurred.

Meanwhile the rest put Galley and Chater on one horse, tied their legs under the horse's belly, and then tied the legs of both together. They now set forward, with the exception of Royce, who had no horse ; and they had not gone above two hundred yards, before Jackson called out, " Whip 'em, cut 'em, slash 'em, d—n ! " upon which all began to whip, except Steele, who led the horse, the roads being very bad.   They whipped them for half a mile, till they came to Woodash, where they fell off, with their heads under the horse's belly, and their legs, which were tied, appeared over the horse's back.   Their tormentors soon set them upright again, and continued whipping them over the head, face, shoulders, &c., till they came to Dean, upwards of half a mile farther ;

and here they both fell again as before, with their heads under the horse's belly, which were struck at every step by the horse's hoofs.

Upon placing them again on the saddle, the villains found them so weak that they could not sit; upon which they separated them, and put Galley before Steele, and Chater before little Sam; and then whipped Galley so severely, that, the lashes coming upon Steele, at his desire they desisted. They then went to Harris's well, and threatened to throw Galley in; but when he desired that they should put an end to his misery at once, "No," said Jackson, "if that's the case, we have something more to say to you;" and they thereupon put him on the horse again, and whipped him over the Downs until he was so weak that he fell off. They next laid him across the horse, and little Sam getting up behind him, subjected him to such cruelty as made him groan with the most excruciating torments, and he fell off again. Being again put up astride, Richards got up behind him; but the poor man soon cried out, "I fall, I fall," and Richards pushed him with force, saying " Fall, and be d—d!" The unhappy man then turned over and expired; and they threw the body over the horse, and carried it off with them to the house of one Scardefield, who kept the Red Lion, at Rake. The landlord remarking the condition of Chater, and Galley's body, the fellows told him that they had been engaged with some officers, had lost their tea, and that some of them were wounded, if not dead. This was sufficient, and Jackson and Carter carried Chater down to the house of the elder Mills, where they chained him up in a turf-house. Their companions, in the mean time, drank gin and brandy at Scardefield's, and it being now nearly dark, they borrowed spades, and a candle and lantern, and making him assist them in digging a hole, they buried the body of the murdered officer. They then separated; but on the Thursday they met again with some more of their associates, including the prisoners Richard Mills, and his two sons Richard and John, Thomas Stringer, Cobby, Tapner, and Hammond, for the purpose of deliberating what should be done with their prisoner. It was soon unanimously resolved that he must be destroyed, and it was detemined that they should take him to Harris's well and throw him in, as it was considered that' that death would be most likely to cause him the greatest pain.

During this time the wretched man was in a state of the utmost horror and misery, being visited occasionally by all his tormentors, who abused him, and beat him violently. At last, when this determination had been arrived at, they all went, and Tapner pulling out a clasp-knife, ordered him on his knees, swearing that he would be his butcher; but being dissuaded from this, as being opposed to their plan to prolong the miseries of their prisoner, he contented himself with slashing the knife across his eyes, almost cutting them out, and completely severing the gristle of his nose. They then placed him upon a horse, and all set out together for Harris's well, except Mills and his sons, they having no horses ready, and saying, in excuse, " that there were enough without them to murder one man." All the way Tapner whipped him till the blood came; and then swore that if he blooded the saddle, he would torture him the more. When they were come within a hundred yards of the well, Jackson and

Carter stopped, saying to Tapner, Cobby, Stringer, Steele, and Hammond, " Go on, and do your duty on Chater, as we have our's upon Galley." It was in the dead of the night that they brought their victim to the well, which was nearly thirty feet deep, but dry, and paled close round; and Tapner having fastened a noose round his neck, they bade him get over the pales.   He was going through a broken place; but though he was covered with blood and fainting with the anguish of his wounds, they forced him to climb up, having the rope about his neck.   They then tied one end of the cord to the pales, and pushed him over the brink; but the rope being short, he hung no farther within it than his thighs, and leaning against the edge, he hung above a quarter of an hour and was not strangled.   They then untied him, and hearing him groan, they determined to go to one William Comleah's, a gardener, to borrow a rope and ladder, saying they wanted to relieve one of their companions who had fallen into Harris's well.   He said they might take them; but they could not manage the ladder in their confusion, it being a long one. They then returned to the well; and still hearing him groan, and fearful that the sound might lead to a discovery, the place being near the road, threw upon him some of the rails and gate-posts fixed about the well, as well as some great stones; and then finding him silent, they left him. Their next consultation was how to dispose of their horses; they killed Galley's, which was grey, and taking his hide off, cut it into small pieces, and hid them so as to prevent any discovery; but a bay horse that Chater had ridden on got from them.

This being the evidence produced, the jury, after being out of court about a quarter of an hour, brought in a verdict of guilty against all the prisoners : whereupon the judge pronounced sentence on the convicts in a most pathetic address, representing the enormity of their crime, and exhorting them to make immediate preparation for the awful fate that awaited them.

They were hanged at Chichester on the 18th of January, 1749, amidst such a concourse of spectators as is seldom seen on the occasion of a puhlic execution.   Carter was hung in chains near Rake, in Sussex; Tapner, on Rook's Hill, near Chichester; and Cobby and Hammond, at Cesley Isle, on the beach, where they sometimes landed the smuggled goods, and where they could be seen at a great distance east and west.

JOHN SMITH,

EXECUTED FOR MURDER.

At the Kent Assizes for December, 1822, John Smith, a pensioner of Greenwich Hospital, was indicted for the wilful murder of Catherine Smith, a woman with whom he had for some time previously cohabited. The prisoner, a fine robust old man, nearly six feet high, entered the court with a firm and steady step, although nearly eighty years of age.

The following is a digested abstract of the evidence for the prosecution. On the morning of the 4th of October, about half past five o'clock, the prisoner went into a public-house called the Cricketers, sat down near the bar, and called for a pot of porter. Immediately afterwards, addressing himself to the landlord, he said, " Hawkins, have you seen my woman this morning ?" He replied in the negative ; upon which the prisoner said, " If you see her go past, call her in." About ten minutes before six, the deceased came into the public-house, in company with another Greenwich pensioner. The deceased called for two glasses of gin. The landlord drew a glass of gin, and set it before her on the bar ; when she said, " You know I take it with peppermint." The landlord was turning round to get the peppermint-bottle, when in an instant the prisoner, who was sitting close to the deceased, rose up and stabbed her with a knife in the right breast. Before this not a word had passed between the prisoner and the deceased. The deceased immediately exclaimed, " You have killed me ! you have killed me !"

The unfortunate woman was urged by the landlord to run to the infirmary immediately. She went out, but before she got the distance of forty paces she dropped down dead. The prisoner was immediately seized by the landlord, who said to him, " You wicked old man, how could you do so rash an act !" He replied, " She has been with that fellow all night."

The prisoner was afterwards searched, and the knife was found upon him, stained with blood; and being asked whether that was the instrument with which he committed the murder, he said it was, and owned that he did it. The point of the instrument, which was a common pocket-knife, upon being examined, appeared as if it had been recently sharpened.

The prisoner, in his defence, entered into a long statement of quarrels between him and the deceased, which, he said, had irritated him and made him unhappy. She had come from London to live with him and take care of him, he being old and infirm ; they had lived together for about fifteen months : but, a short time before this transaction, she was greatly altered in her behaviour towards him. He had, through friends of his own, procured her a situation as helper in one of the wards of the hospital ; she became cold and unkind to him, and at last he discovered that she kept company with Levett, another Greenwich pensioner. On the morning of the 4th of October he went to the Cricketers public-house to get some beer; while he was there, he was cutting a piece of stick-liquorice with his knife, when the deceased and her companion came into the house and stood close to him; he had been drinking the night before; the appearance of the deceased with her paramour affected him very much, and the deceased having trod upon his corns, he in a moment of rage committed the fatal act, but not knowing what he did, and certainly not intending to kill the unfortunate woman. Under such circumstances he hoped a merciful view of his case would be taken.

The judge, having summed up the evidence, left it to the jury, who immediately returned a verdict of " Guilty," and the prisoner was ordered for execution on the following Monday. He retired from the bar with the same firm step and demeanour with which he had entered the court.

At twelve o'clock on Monday, the 23d of December, the dreadful sentence of the law was carried into effect on Penenden Heath. He appeared to be very penitent and resigned, and partook of the sacrament a short time before he left the gaol. At the place of execution he addressed the people, who were assembled in great crowds, and said, " that women were the cause of his downfall." He prayed aloud and very fervently until the drop fell, frequently ejaculating, with a clear and audible voice, " Lord have mercy upon me! Christ have mercy upon me!" and with these words upon his lips he was launched into eternity.

After hanging the usual time, the body was taken to Greenwich College, where it lay one day for public view, and was afterwards dissected and anatomized in the Hospital.

Previous to his execution, this man exhibited one of the most remarkable instances of mental abstraction that perhaps had ever been manifested under the awful circumstances of deliberate murder. He sent for a gentleman of Maidstone, who, attending the summons, received from the prisoner a vehement injunction to make public what he called a history of his life. The surprise of the gentleman may be conceived, when, on examining the paper, he discovered it to be a concise narrative of the place of the prisoner's birth, his propensities, and, finally, his motives for committing the murder, described in doggrel verse. Although the production of an illiterate man, it is truly astonishing that the mind of a man nearly fourscore years old could, by any possibility, under circumstances so peculiarly awful, for a moment be so abstracted from his situation as to admit of so extraordinary a production. The levity of the concluding lines is not the least striking part of this extraordinary effusion. The original has been followed literatim et verbatim.

> In the County of Wicklow I was born
> But now in Maidstone die in scorn
> I once was counted a roving blade
> But to my misfortune had no trade
> Women was always my downfall
> But still I liked and loved them all
> A hundred I have had in my time
> When I was young and in my prime

Women was always my delight
But when I got old they did me slight
A woman from London to me came
She said with You I would fain remain
If you will be constant I'll be true
I never want no man but you—
And on her own Bible a Oath did take
That she never would Me forsake
And during the time that I had Life
She would always prove a loving Wife
And by that Means we did agree
To live together she and Me—
But soon her vows and Oath did break
And to another man did take
Which she fetch'd home with her to lay
And that proved her own destiny
So as Jack Smith lay on his bed
This notion strongly run in his Head
Then he got up with that intent
To find her out was fully bent
Swearing if he found out her Oath she'd broke
He'd stick a knife into her throat
Then to the Cricketers he did go
To see if he could find it out or no
Not long been there before she come in
With this same fellow to fetch some Gin
Then with A Knife himself brought in
Immediately stab'd her under the Chin.
And in five minutes she was no more
But there laid in her purple gore
Now to conclude and end my song
They are both dead dead and gone
They are both gone I do declare
Gone they are but God knows where !

CHARLES DREW,

EXECUTED FOR THE MURDER OF HIS FATHER.

THE only circumstance of peculiarity attending this case—and it is one indeed, we are happy to say, not a little singular—is, that the malefactor was the son of the man whom he murdered. The father, who was possessed of considerable property at Long Melford in Suffolk, discarded his son on account of his connexion with a woman named Elizabeth Boyer. The latter, angered at the contempt exhibited for her, urged her paramour, as well for revenge as for the accession to their means which would be produced by the old man's death, to commit the foul deed which cost him his life. He was apprehended at the instance of a relation, a Mr. Timothy Drew, and, being convicted, was executed on the 9th April, 1740, at St. Edmund's Bury, in the 25th year of his age.

This case so nearly resembles the celebrated story of George Barnwell, that the following anecdote in reference to the tragedy of that name may not be misplaced here. It is related in reference to Mr. Ross, formerly a tragedian of considerable celebrity.

"A gentleman, much dejected in his looks, called one day on Ross, when stricken with years, and told him that his father, a wealthy citizen in London, lay at the point of death, and begged that he might see him, or he could not die in peace of mind. Curious as this request appeared from a stranger, and in such extremity, the actor hesitated; but being much pressed by his visitor, he agreed to accompany him. Arrived at the house of the sick man, Mr. Ross was announced, and soon admitted into his chamber. The dying penitent, now threescore years and ten, casting his languid eyes upon Ross, said, 'Can it be you who raised my fortune—who saved my life? Then were you young, like myself; ay, and amiable amid the direst misfortunes. I determined to amend my life, and avoid your fate.' Here nature in the struggle with death became overpowered, and as the sick man's head fell upon his pillow, he faintly ejaculated, 'O Barnwell! Barnwell!' We may conceive the astonishment of the player, whom age had long incapacitated from representing the unfortunate 'London Apprentice.' The feeble man, renewing his efforts to gratify a dying desire, again opened his eyes, and continued: 'Mr. Ross, some forty years ago, like George Barnwell, I wronged my master, to supply the unbounded extravagance of a Millwood. I took her to see your performance, which so shocked me that I silently vowed to break the connexion then by my side, and return to the paths of virtue. I kept my resolution, and replaced the money I had stolen before my villainy was detected. I bore up against the upbraidings of my deluder, and found a Maria in my master's daughter. We married. I soon succeeded to her father's business, and the young man who brought you here was the first pledge of our love. I have more children, or I would have shown my gratitude to you by a larger sum than I have bequeathed you; but take a thousand pounds affixed to your name. At the dying man's signal, old Ross left the room, overwhelmed by his feelings."

WILLIAM GREGG,

EXECUTED FOR HIGH TREASON IN ASSISTING THE QUEEN'S ENEMIES.

THE treason of which this offender was convicted was that of " adhering to the Queen's enemies, and giving them aid, without the realm," which was made a capital offence by the statute of Edward III.

It appears that Gregg was a native of Montrose, in Scotland; and having received such instruction as the grammar-schools of the place afforded, he completed his education at Aberdeen university, where he pursued those studies which were calculated to fit him for the profession of the church, for which he was intended. London, however, held forth so many attractions to his youthful eye, that the wishes of his relatives were soon overruled; and having visited that city, with good introductions, he was, after some time, appointed secretary to the ambassador at the court of Sweden. But while performing the duties of his office, he was guilty of so many and such great excesses, that he was at length compelled to retire, and London once more became his residence. His good fortune placed him in a situation alike honourable and profitable, but his dishonest and traitorous conduct in his employment was such as to cost him his life, and to involve his employers in political difficulties of no ordinary kind. Having been engaged by Mr. Secretary Harley, minister of the reigning sovereign, Queen Anne, to write dispatches, he took advantage of the knowledge which he thus gained, and voluntarily opened a communication with the enemies of his country. England, it will be remembered, was at this time in a situation of no ordinary difficulty; and the position of her Majesty's ministers, harassed as they were by the opposition of their political antagonists, was rendered even more difficult by the disclosures of their traitorous servant.

We shall take the advantage afforded us by Bishop Burnet's History, of laying before our readers a more authentic account of this transaction than is given by any other channel of information to which we have access. He says, " At this time two discoveries were made, very unlucky for Mr. Harley: Tallard wrote often to Chamillard, but he sent the letters open to the secretary's office, to be perused and sealed up, and so be conveyed by the way of Holland. These were opened, upon some suspicion of them; in which, as he offered his services to the courts of France and St. Germain's, so he gave an account of all transactions here. In one of these he sent a copy of the letter that the Queen was to write in her own hand to the Emperor; and he marked what parts were drawn up by the secretary, and what additions were made to it by the lord treasurer. This was the letter by which the Queen pressed the sending Prince Eugene into Spain; and this, if not intercepted, would have been at Versailles many days before it would reach Vienna.

" He who sent this wrote, that by this they might see what service he could do them, if well encouraged. All this was sent over to the Duke of

Marlborough ; and, upon search, it was found to be written by one Gregg, a clerk, whom Harley had not only entertained, but had taken into a particular confidence, without inquiring into the former parts of his life; for he was a vicious and necessitous person, who had been secretary to the Queen's envoy in Denmark, but was dismissed by him for his ill qualities. Harley had made use of him to get him intelligence, and he came to trust him with the perusal and sealing up of the letters which the French prisoners, here in England, sent over to France ; and by that means he got into the method of sending intelligence thither. He, when seized on, either upon remorse or hopes of pardon, confessed all, and signed his confession : upon that he was tried, and, pleading guilty, was condemned as a traitor, for corresponding with the Queen's enemies.

" At the same time Valiere and Bara, whom Harley had employed as his spies to go often over to Calais, under the pretence of bringing him intelligence, were informed against, as spies employed by France to get intelligence from England, who carried over many letters to Calais and Boulogne, and, as was believed, gave such information of our trade and convoys, that by their means we had many great losses at sea. They were often complained of upon suspicion, but they were always protected by Harley ; yet the presumptions against them were so violent, that they were at last seized on, and brought up as prisoners. "

The Whigs took such advantage of this circumstance, that Mr. Harley was obliged to resign ; and his enemies were inclined to carry matters still further, being resolved, if possible, to find out evidence enough to affect his life. With this view, the House of Lords ordered a committee to examine Gregg and the other prisoners, who were very assiduous in the discharge of their commission, as will appear by the following account, written by the same author :—

" The Lords who were appointed to examine Gregg could not find out much by him : he had but newly begun his design of betraying secrets, and he had no associates with him in it. He told them, that all the papers of state lay so carelessly about the office, that every one belonging to it, even the door-keepers, might have read them all. Harley's custom was to come to the office late on post-nights, and, after he had given his orders, and wrote his letters, he usually went away, and left all to be copied out when he was gone. By that means he came to see every thing, in particular the Queen's letter to the Emperor. He said, he knew the design on Toulon in May last, but he did not discover it ; for he had not entered on his ill practices till October. This was all he could say.

" By the examination of Valiere and Bara, and of many others who lived about Dover and were employed by them, a discovery was made of a constant intercourse they were in with Calais, under Harley's protection. They often went over with boats full of wool, and brought back brandy, though both the import and export were severely prohibited. They, and those who belonged to the boats carried over by them, were well treated on the French side at the governor's house, or at the commissary's : they were kept there till their letters were sent to Paris, and till returns could be brought back, and were all the while upon free cost. The order that was constantly given them was, that if an English or Dutch ship came up with them, they should cast their letters into the sea, but that they should not do it when French ships came up with them ; so that they were looked on by all on that coast as the spies of France. They used to get what information they could, both of merchant-ships and of the ships of war that lay in the Downs, and upon that they usually went over ; and it generally happened that soon after some of those ships were taken. These men, as they were Papists, so they behaved themselves insolently, and boasted much of their power and credit.

" Complaints had been often made of them, but they were always protected ; nor did it appear that they ever brought any information of importance to Harley but once, when, according to what they swore, they told him that Fourbin was gone from Dunkirk, to lie in wait for the Russian fleet, which proved to be true ; he both went to watch for them, and he took the greater part of the fleet. Yet, though this was the single piece of intelligence that they ever brought, Harley took so little notice of it, that he gave no advertisement to the Admiralty concerning it. This particular excepted, they only brought over common news, and the Paris Gazetteer. These examinations lasted for some weeks ; when they were ended, a full report was made of them to the House of Lords, and they ordered the whole report, with all the examinations, to be laid before the Queen."

Upon the conviction of Gregg, both houses of parliament petitioned the Queen that he might he executed ; and on the 28th April, 1708, he was accordingly hanged, at Tyburn.

While on the scaffold, he delivered a paper to the sheriffs of London and Middlesex, in which he acknowledged the justice of his sentence, declared his sincere repentance of all his sins, particularly that lately committed against the Queen, whose forgiveness he devoutly implored. He also expressed his wish to make all possible reparation for the injuries he had done ; and testified the perfect innocence of Mr. Secretary Harley, whom he declared to have been no party to his proceedings. He professed that he died a member of the Protestant church ; and declared that the want of money to supply his extravagances had tempted him to commit the fatal crime which cost him his life.

It is a remarkable circumstance in the life of this offender, that while he was corresponding with the enemy, and taking measures to subvert the government, he had no predilection in favour of the Pretender. On the contrary, he declared, while he was under sentence of death, that " he never thought he had any right to the throne of these realms."

PHILIP ROACH,

THIS fellow was a native of Ireland, and first mate on board a West-Indiaman, which sailed to and from Barbadoes.   Having become acquainted with a fisherman named Neale, who hinted that large sums of money might be acquired by insuring ships and then causing them to be sunk, to defraud the insurers, he was wicked enough to listen to this horrid idea ; and, being recommended to a gentleman who had a ship bound to Cape Breton, he got a station on board, next in command to the captain, by whom he was entrusted with the management of the vessel.

On the voyage, it would appear, he would have abstained from carrying out his diabolical plan ; but having brought some Irishmen on board with him, they persisted in their original design, and in demanding that the vessel should be seized.   Accordingly, one night, when the captain and most of the crew were asleep, Roach gave orders to two of the seamen to furl the sails ; which being immediately done, the poor fellows no sooner descended on the deck, than Roach and his associates murdered them, and threw them overboard.   At this instant a man and a boy at the yard-arm, observing what had passed, and dreading a similar fate, hurried towards the top-mast head, when one of the Irishmen, named Cullen, followed them, and, seizing the boy, threw him into the sea.   The man, thinking to effect at least a present escape, descended on the main-deck ; but he was instantly butchered, and committed to the deep.   The sailors now hurried up from below with all possible expedition, but were seized and murdered as they came on deck, and afterwards thrown into the sea.

The murderers now determined to commence pirates, and Roach was chosen captain.   They had intended to sail up the Gulf of St. Lawrence ; but as they were within a few days voyage of the Bristol Channel, and found themselves short of provisions, they put into Portsmouth ; and, giving the vessel a fictitious name, they painted her afresh, and sailed for Rotterdam.   At this city they disposed of their cargo, and took in a fresh one ; and being unknown, an English gentleman, named Annesley shipped considerable property on board, and took his passage with them for London ; whom they threw overboard after they had been only one day at sea.   When the ship arrived in the river Thames, Mr. Annesley's friends made inquiry after him in consequence of his having sent letters to England describing the ship in which he proposed to embark ; but Roach denied any knowledge of the gentleman, and even disclaimed his own name.   Notwithstanding his confident assertions, it was conjectured who he was ; and a letter which he sent to his wife being stopped, he was taken into custody, and carried before the secretary of state for examination.   While there, having denied that he was the person he was taken to be, his intercepted letter was shown to him ; on which he instantly confessed his crimes, and was committed to take his trial.   He was subsequently hanged, at Execution Dock, on the 5th of August, 1723.

A FLEET MARRIAGE.

THE REV. JOHN GRIERSON AND THE REV. MR. WILKINSON.

TRANSPORTED FOR UNLAWFULLY PERFORMING THE MARRIAGE CEREMONY.

AMONG the singular customs of our forefathers, arising in a great measure from their indifference to decorum, one of the most remarkable was matrimony solemnized, we were going to say, but the fittest word would be "performed," by the parsons in the Fleet prison. These clerical functionaries were disreputable and dissolute men, mostly prisoners for debt, who, to the great injury of public morals, dared to insult the dignity of their holy profession by marrying in the precincts of the Fleet prison, at a minute's notice, any persons who might present themselves for that purpose. No questions were asked, no stipulations made, except as to the amount of the fee for the service, or the quantity of liquor to be drunk on the occasion. It not unfrequently happened, indeed, that the clergyman, the clerk, the bridegroom, and the bride, were drunk at the very time the ceremony was performed. These disgraceful members of the sacred calling had their " plyers," or " barkers," who, if they caught sight of a man and woman walking together along the streets of the neighbourhood, pestered them, as the Jew clothesmen of the present day tease the passer-by in Holywell Street, with solicitations, not easily to be shaken off, as to whether they wanted a clergyman to marry them.

11   M

Mr. Burn, a gentleman who has recently published a curious work on the Fleet Registers, says, he had in his possession an engraving (published about 1747) of " A Fleet Wedding between a brisk young Sailor and a Landlady's daughter at Redriff." " The print," he adds, " represents the old Fleet market and prison, with the sailor, landlady, and daughter just stepping from a hackney-coach, while two Fleet parsons in canonicals are contending for the job. The following verses are in the margin:

" Scarce had the coach discharged its trusty fare,
But gaping crowds surround the amorous pair;
The busy Plyers make a mighty stir,
And whispering cry, ' D'ye want the Parson, Sir?
Pray step this way—just to the Pen in Hand,
The Doctor's ready there at your command:'
' This way,' another cries, ' Sir, I declare,
The true and ancient Register is here:

" Th' alarmed Parsons quickly hear the din,
And haste with soothing words t' invite 'em in:
In this confusion jostled to and fro,
Th' enamour'd couple know not where to go;
Till, slow advancing from the coach's side,
Th' experienced matron came, (an artful guide);
She led the way without regarding either,
And the first Parson spliced 'em both together."

One of the most notorious of these scandalous officials was a man of the name of George Keith, a Scotch minister, who, being in desperate circumstances, set up a marriage-office in May-Fair, and subsequently in the Fleet, and carried on the same trade which has since been practised in front of the Blacksmith's anvil at Gretna Green. This man's wedding business was so extensive and so scandalous, that the Bishop of London found it necessary to excommunicate him. It has been said of this person and " *his journeyman*," that one morning, during the Whitsun holidays, they united a greater number of couples than had been married at any ten churches within the bills of mortality. Keith lived till he was eighty-nine years of age, and died in 1735. The Rev. D. Gaynham, another infamous functionary, was familiarly called the Bishop of Hell.

" Many of the early Fleet weddings," observes Mr. Burn, " were *really* performed at the chapel of the Fleet; but, as the practice extended, it was found more convenient to have other places, within the Rules of the Fleet, (added to which, the Warden was forbidden, by act of parliament, to suffer them,) and thereupon many of the Fleet parsons and tavern-keepers in the neighbourhood fitted up a room in their respective 'odgings or houses as a chapel! The parsons took the fees, allowing a portion to the plyers, &c.; and the tavern-keepers *kept a parson on the establishment*, at a weekly salary of twenty shillings! Most of the taverns near the Fleet kept their own registers, in which (as well as in their own books) the parsons entered the weddings." Some of these scandalous members of the highest of all professions were in the habit of hanging signs out of their windows with the words " WEDDINGS PERFORMED CHEAP HERE."

Keith, of whom we have already spoken, seems to have been a bare-faced profligate; but there is something exceedingly affecting in the stings of conscience and forlorn compunction of one Walter Wyatt, a Fleet parson, in one of whose pocket-books of 1716 are the following secret outpourings of remorse :—

" Give to every man is due, and learn ye way of Truth."

" This advice cannot be taken by those that are concerned in ye Fleet marriages; not so much as ye Priest can do ye thing y^t it is just and right there, unless he designs to starve. For by lying, bullying, and swearing, to extort money from silly and unwary people, you advance your business and get y^e pelf, which always wastes like snow on a sunshiny day."

" The fear of the Lord is the beginning of wisdom. The marrying in the Fleet is the beginning of eternal woe."

" If a clerk or plyer tells a lye, you must vouch it to be as true as y$_e$ Gospel, and if disputed, you must affirm with an oath to y^e truth of a downright damnable falsehood.—Virtus laudatur & alget."[*]

" May God forgive me what is past, and give me grace to forsake such a wicked place, where truth and virtue can't have place unless you are resolved to starve."

But this very man, whose sense of his own disgrace was so deep and apparently so contrite, was one of the most notorious, active, and money-making of all the Fleet parsons. His practice was chiefly in taverns, and he has been known to earn nearly sixty pounds in less than a month.

With such facilities for marriage, and such unprincipled ministers, it may easily be imagined that iniquitous schemes of all sorts were perpetrated under the name of Fleet weddings. The parsons were ready, for a bribe, to make false entries in their registers, to ante-date weddings, to give fictitious certificates, and to marry persons who would declare only the initials of their names. Thus, if a spinster or widow in debt desired to cheat her creditors by pretending to have been married before the debt was contracted, she had only to present herself at one of the marriage-houses in the Fleet, and, upon payment of a small additional fee to the clergyman, a man could instantly be found on the spot to act as bride-groom for a few shillings, and the worthless chaplain could find a blank place in his Register for any year desired, so that there was no difficulty in making the necessary record. They would also, for a consideration, obliterate any given entry. The sham bridegrooms, under different names, were married over and over again, with the full knowledge of the clerical practitioners. If, in other instances, a libertine desired to pos-

---

[*] " On Saturday last a Fleet parson was convicted before Sir. Richard Brocas (on the information of a plyer for weddings there), of forty-three oaths for which a warrant was granted to levy 4l. 6s. on the goods of the said parson; but, upon application to his worship, he was pleased to remit 1s. per oath; upon which the plyer swore he would swear no more against any man upon the like occasion, finding he could get nothing by it."—*Grub Street Journal*, *20th July*, 1732.

sess himself of any young and unsuspecting woman, who would not yield without being married, nothing was easier than to get the service performed at the Fleet without even the specification of names; so that the poor girl might with impunity be shaken off at pleasure. Or if a parent found it necessary to legitimatise his natural children, a Fleet parson could be procured to give a marriage-certificate of any required date. In fact, all manner of people presented themselves for marriage at the unholy dens in the Fleet taverns: runaway sons and daughters of peers,—Irish adventurers and foolish rich widows,—clodhoppers and ladies from St. Giles's,—footmen and decayed beauties,—soldiers and servant-girls,—boys in their teens and old women of seventy,—discarded mistresses, "given away" by their former admirers to pitiable and sordid bridegrooms,—night-wanderers and intoxicated apprentices,— men and women having already wives and husbands,—young heiresses conveyed thither by force, and compelled *in terrorem* to be brides,— and common labourers and female paupers dragged by parish-officers to the profane altar, stained by the relics of drunken orgies, and reeking with the fumes of liquor and tobacco! Nay, it sometimes happened that the "contracting parties" would send from houses of vile repute for a Fleet parson, who could readily be found to attend even in such places and under such circumstances, and there unite the couple in matrimony!

Of what were called the "Parish Weddings" it is impossible to speak in terms of sufficient reprobation. Many of the churchwardens and overseers of that day were in the frequent practice of "getting up" marriages in order to throw their paupers on neighbouring parishes. For example, in the *Daily Post* of the 4th July, 1741, is the following paragraph:—

"On Saturday last the churchwardens of a certain parish in the city, in order to remove a load from their own shoulders, gave forty shillings, and paid the expence of a Fleet marriage, to a miserable blind youth, known by the name of Ambrose Tally, who plays on the violin in Moorfields, in order to make a settlement of the wife and future family in Shoreditch parish. To secure their point, they sent a parish-officer to see the ceremony performed. One cannot but admire the ungenerous proceeding of this city parish, as well as their unjustifiable abetting and encouraging an irregularity so much and so justly complained of, as these Fleet matches. Invited and uninvited were a great number of poor wretches, in order to spend the bride's fortune."

In the *Grub Street Journal* for 1735, is the following letter, faithfully describing, says Mr. Burn, the treachery and low habits of the Fleet parsons:—

"SIR,—There is a very great evil in this town, and of dangerous consequence to our sex, that has never been suppressed, to the great prejudice and ruin of many hundreds of young people every year, which I beg some of your learned heads to consider of, and consult of proper ways and means to prevent for the future. I mean the ruinous marriages that are practised in the liberty of the Fleet and thereabouts, by a set of drunken, swearing parsons, with their myrmidons, that wear black coats, and pretend to be clerks and registers to the Fleet. These ministers of wickedness ply about Ludgate-hill, pulling and forcing people to some peddling ale-house or a brandy-shop to be married, even on a Sunday stopping them as they go to church, and almost tearing their clothes off their backs. To confirm the truth of these facts, I will give you a case or two which lately happened.

" Since Midsummer last a young lady of birth and fortune was deluded and forced from her friends, and, by the assistance of a wry-necked swearing parson, married to an atheistical wretch, whose life is a continued practice of all manner of vice and debauchery. And since the ruin of my relation, another lady of my acquaintance had like to have been trepanned in the following manner. This lady had appointed to meet a gentlewoman at the Old Playhouse in Drury-lane, but extraordinary business prevented her coming. Being alone when the play was done, she bade a boy call a coach for the city. One dressed like a gentleman helps her into it, and jumps in after her. ' Madam,' says he, ' this coach was called for me, but since the weather is so bad, and there is no other, I beg leave to bear you company. I am going into the city, and will set you down wherever you please.' The lady begged to be excused ; but he bade the coachman drive on. Being come to Ludgate-hill, he told her his sister, who waited his coming but five doors up the court, would go with her in two minutes. He went, and returned with his pretended sister, who asked her to step in one minute, and she would wait upon her in the coach. Deluded with the assurance of having his sister's company, the poor lady foolishly followed her into the house, when instantly the sister vanished, and a tawny fellow in a black coat and black wig appeared. ' Madam, you are come in good time ; the Doctor was just a-going.'—' The Doctor !' says she, horribly frightened, fearing it was a madhouse : ' what has the Doctor to do with me !'— ' To marry you to that gentleman. The Doctor has waited for you these three hours, and will be paid by you or that gentleman before you go !'—' That gentleman,' says she, recovering herself, ' is worthy a better fortune than mine,' and begged hard to be gone. But Doctor Wryneck swore she should be married, or, if she would not, he would still have his fee, and register the marriage from that night. The lady, finding she could not escape without money or a pledge, told them, she liked the gentleman so well, she would certainly meet him to-morrow night, and gave them a ring as a pledge, which, says she, ' was my mother's gift on her death-bed, enjoining that if ever I married it should be my wedding-ring.' By which cunning contrivance she was delivered from the black Doctor and his tawny crew. Some time after this I went with this lady and her brother in a coach to Ludgate-hill in the day-time, to see the manner of their picking up people to be married. As soon as our coach stopped near Fleet Bridge, up comes one of the myrmidons. ' Madam,' says he, ' you want a parson?'—' Who are you ?'—says I.—' I am the clerk and register of the Fleet.'—' Show me the chapel.' At which comes a second, desiring me to go along with him. Says he, ' That fellow will carry you to a peddling alehouse.' Says a third, ' Go with me ; he will carry you to a brandy-shop.' In the interim comes the Doctor.

' Madam,' says he, ' I'll do your job for you presently !'—' Well, gentlemen,' says I, ' since you can't agree, and I can't be married quietly, I'll
put it off 'till another time :' so we drove away.   Learned sirs, I write
this in regard to the honour and safety of my own sex ; and if for ou.
sakes you will be so good as to publish it, correcting the errors of a
woman's pen, you will oblige our whole sex, and none more than, Sir,
your constant reader and admirer,   VIRTUOUS."

Such were a few of the iniquities practised by the ministers of the
Fleet.   Similar transactions were carried on at the Chapel in May Fair,
the Mint in the Borough, the Savoy, and other places about London;
until the public scandal became so great, especially in consequence oi
the marriage at the Fleet of the Hon. Henry Fox with Georgiana Caroline, eldest daughter of the Duke of Richmond, that at length—not,
however, without much and zealous opposition—a Marriage Bill was
passed, enacting that any person solemnising matrimony without the
previous publication of banns, or a licence, or in any other place than
a church or lawful public chapel without a *special* licence, should, on
conviction, be adjudged *guilty of felony*, and be transported for fourteen
years, and that all such marriages *should be void*.   This act took effect
from the 25th of March, 1754.

Upon the passing of this law, Keith, the parson who has already been
alluded to, published a pamphlet, entitled " *Observations on the Act
for Preventing Clandestine Marriages ;*" to which he prefixed his portrait.   The following passages are highly characteristic of the man :—

" ' Happy is the wooing that is not long a-doing,' is an old proverb,
and a very true one ; but we shall have no occasion for it after the 25th
day of March next, when we are commanded to read it backwards, and
from that period (fatal indeed to Old England !) we must date the declen-
sion of the numbers of the inhabitants of England."—" As I have married
many thousands, and consequently have on these occasions seen the
humour of the lower class of people, I have often asked the married pair
how long they had been acquainted : they would reply, some more, some
less, but the generality did not exceed the acquaintance of a week, some
only of a day, half a day," &c.—" Another inconveniency which will
arise from this act will be, that the expence of being married will be so
great, that few of the lower class of people can afford it ; for I have often
heard a Fleet-parson say, that many have come to be married when
they have had but half-a-crown in their pockets, and sixpence to buy
a pot of beer, and for which they have pawned some of their clothes."—
" I remember once on a time, I was at a public-house at Radcliff, which
then was full of sailors and their girls : there was fiddling, piping, jigging,
and eating ; at length, one of the tars starts up, and says, ' D—n ye,
Jack, I'll be married just now ; I will have my partner, and . . . . . .
The joke took, and in less than two hours ten couple set out for the
Fleet.   I staid their return.   They returned in coaches, five women in
each coach ; the tars, some running before, others riding on the coach-
box, and others behind.   The cavalcade being over, the couples went up
into an upper room, where they concluded the evening with great jollity.
The next time I went that way I called on the landlord, and asked him

concerning this marriage adventure.   He at first stared at me, but recollecting, he said, those things were so frequent that he hardly took any notice of them ; for, added he, it is a common thing when a fleet comes in, to have two or three hundred marriages in a week's time among the sailors."   He humorously concludes, " If the present Act in the form it now stands should (which I am sure is impossible) be of service to my country, I shall then have the satisfaction of having been the occasion of it, because the compilers thereof have done it with a pure design of suppressing my *Chapel*, which makes me the most celebrated man in this kingdom, though not the greatest."

In a letter to George Montagu, Esq. from Horace Walpole, is the following notice of Keith :—

" I shall only tell you a *bon mot* of Keith's, the marriage-broker, and conclude : ' G—d d—n the Bishops !' said he—' I beg Miss Montagu's pardon—so they will hinder my marrying.   Well, let 'em, but I'll be revenged : I'll buy two or three acres of ground, and by G—d I'll under-bury them all.' "

The passing of the Marriage Act put a stop to the marriages at May Fair ; but the day before the Act came into operation (Lady-day, 1754) sixty-one couple were married there.

It would exceed the limits of this brief sketch were we to give the *official* history of the different scandalous ministers who thus disgraced themselves, and impiously trifled with one of our most sacred institutions. That some of these wretched adventurers were merely pretended clergymen is certain ; but it cannot be denied that many of them were actually in holy orders.

Of this latter class were Grierson and Wilkinson, the subjects of our present notice; who, notwithstanding the heavy penalty imposed by the statute, were not to be deterred from continuing the dangerous and unlawful traffic in which they had been engaged.   Wilkinson, who was the brother of a celebrated comedian of the day, it would appear, was the owner of a chapel in the Savoy, and Grierson was his assistant ; and their proceedings having at length become too notorious to be passed over, proceedings were instituted against them.   Grierson was first apprehended, and his employer sought safety in flight ; but supposing that he could not be deemed guilty of any offence, as he had not actually performed the marriage ceremony, a duty which he left to his journeyman, he returned to his former haunts.   It was not long before he was secured, however ; and having been convicted with Grierson, they were shipped off as convicts together to the colonies, in the year 1757.

WILLIAM TILLY, JOHN CROSSWELL, GEORGE HARD-WICK, JAMES HAYDEN, JOHN HAWDEN, SIMON JACOBS, JOHN SOLOMONS, JOHN PHILLIPS, AND JOHN HENLEY.

CONVICTED OF A CONSPIRACY.

THIS most extraordinary conspiracy to procure the liberation of a prisoner occurred on the 4th of April, 1795.

It appears that a fellow named Isdwell, a Jew, stood charged with a forgery on the Stamp-Office, and for security was committed to the custody of the keeper of the New Prison, Clerkenwell. On the day in question, he persuaded two of the turnkeys that an aunt of his, who was very rich, then lay at the point of death, and that he had been informed that, could she see him before she died, she would give him one thousand pounds.

He proposed, therefore, that if they would let him out, and accompany him to the place, he would give them fifty guineas each for their trouble; and suggested that the matter might be effected without the knowledge of the keeper of the prison or any other person, they having the keys of it at night, and the time required being very short. To this proposal the turnkeys agreed; and accordingly, about one o'clock in the morning, the gates were opened, and Isdwell, with his irons on, was conducted in a hackney-coach by one of them, armed with a blunderbuss, to the house in Artillery-lane, Bishopsgate-street, where, inquiring for the sick lady, they were ushered up stairs.

Isdwell entered the room first, on which several fellows rushed forth, and attempted to keep the turnkey out; but, not succeeding, they put the candles out, wrested the blunderbuss out of his hand, and discharged it at him. At this instant Isdwell was endeavouring to make his escape out of the window, but he received the whole charge in his body, and fell dead on the spot. A desperate conflict then took place, in the course of which the jailor was very severely beaten; but some persons being attracted to the spot by the uproar, the officer was rescued, and the prisoners were apprehended, and lodged in safe custody.

The prisoners were tried for the murder of their companion (to which their offence in reality amounted, his death having been caused by them in executing an unlawful deed) on the 21st April; but the prosecution failed in consequence of the absence of any proof to establish the fact distinctly, the occurrence having happened in the dark. They were, however, detained to be tried for the conspiracy to procure the liberation of the deceased Isdwell, of which they were convicted, and received sentence of transportation.

GOVERNOR WALL,

EXECUTED FOR MURDER.

MR. WALL, or, as he has been more commonly called, Governor Wall, was descended from a good family in Ireland, and entered into the army at an early age. He was of a severe and rather unaccommodating temper; nor was he much liked among the officers.

Mr. Wall was lieutenant-governor of Senegambia, but acted as chief, the first appointment being vacant. His emoluments were very considerable, as, besides his military appointments, he was Superintendent of Trade to the colony. This office he held but for a short time—not more than two years; during which he committed the crime for which he suffered, by ordering Benjamin Armstrong to receive eight hundred lashes, on the 10th of July, 1782, of which he died in five days afterwards.

As soon as the account of the murder reached the Board of Admiralty, a reward was offered for his apprehension; but he evaded justice by living on the Continent, sometimes in France, and sometimes in Italy, but mostly in France, under an assumed name, where he was admitted into good society.

It is most extraordinary that a species of fatality appears almost invariably to attend persons who have been guilty of offences like that of Mr. Wall. A gnawing desire to return to London constantly preyed on the mind of that gentleman; and at length in the year 1797, having first written to a confidential friend to procure him lodgings, he once more appeared in the metropolis. His presence was quickly notified to his relations, who constantly urged the imprudence of this step, and the importance of his again retiring beyond the reach of the laws of England; but all remonstrances proved vain, and he continued to reside in his lodgings at Lambeth, scarcely exhibiting any desire to conceal his name, character, or situation. He soon afterwards removed to new apartments in Upper Thornhaugh-street, Bedford-square; and from this time he seems to have contemplated surrendering himself to the Government, in order that he might take his trial for the offence imputed to him. His mind appeared ill at ease, but he was evidently incapable of coming to any firm determination upon a point of so much importance to his interests and those of his family. It was not until the year 1801 that he at length summoned up courage to do that which he now looked upon as his duty to his country, and then he wrote to the Government in terms singularly indicative of his disposition, saying that " he was ready to give himself up," but not immediately tendering his person to custody.

A communication of this character was not to be overlooked by a minister of state; and although it was very possible, that in case of his continued silence no steps would have been taken to procure the apprehension of Mr. Wall, orders were now given that he should be secured. At this period he was still living in Upper Thornhaugh-street, and there he was apprehended by the officers, who had received instructions from the office of the Secretary of State for the Home Department.

On the 20th of January, 1802, about twenty years after the commission of the crime with which he stood charged, Mr. Wall was indicted at the Old Bailey, and his trial came on before the Chief Baron of the Exchequer, Mr. Justice Rook, and Mr. Justice Lawrence.

Upon the case being called on, the prisoner informed the Court that he was deaf, and requested to be permitted to sit near his counsel; but the Lord Chief Baron informed him, that such an application could not be acceded to, for that there was a situation appointed for persons placed in his condition, and that any distinction would be invidious. The case then proceeded. It was proved by the witnesses, that Armstrong was far from being undutiful in his behaviour; that he was, however, tied to the gun-carriage; and black men, brought there for the purpose—not the drummers, who in the ordinary course of things would have had to flog him, supposing him to have deserved flogging, but black men were directed to inflict the punishment ordered. Each man took his turn, and gave the unhappy sufferer twenty-five lashes, until he had received the number of eight hundred; and the instrument with which the punishment was inflicted was not a cat-o'-nine tails, which is usually employed, but a piece of rope of a greater thickness, which was much more severe than the cat. During the whole time this inhuman punishment was being inflicted, the prisoner stood by, and with a degree of cruelty almost unparalleled urged the executioners to " cut him to the heart and liver," and, in answer to the poor wretch's cries for mercy, he was proved to have declared that " the sick season coming on, with the punishment, would do for him." At the conclusion of the flogging, the miserable being was conducted to the hospital, and there, at the expiration of five days, he died, declaring that he had been punished without trial.

The defence set up was, that the deceased had been guilty of mutiny, and that the punishment was not so severe as was reported, but the deceased was suffered to drink strong spirits when in the hospital. Several witnesses were called on the part of the prisoner, particularly Mrs. Lacy, widow of the captain who succeeded Mr. Wall, and Mary Falkner, who not only agreed with him in the outrageous conduct of the men, and the violent language they used, but both positively swore that Lewis, the first witness against the prisoner, was not the orderly serjeant on that day.—John Falkner, Peter Williams, and some others who were present, were also examined, and their testimony was in full corroboration of the account given by the prisoner, and so far went to his justification; but in many material points it was in direct contradiction to the evidence which had been given by the witnesses for the Crown.

The jury, after being out of court some time, pronounced a verdict of " guilty." The Recorder then proceeded to pass sentence of death upon the prisoner; that he be executed the following morning, and that his body be afterwards delivered to be anatomized according to the statute. Mr. Wall seemed sensibly affected by the sentence, but said nothing more than to request the court would allow him a little time to prepare himself for death. On the 21st of January a respite was sent from Lord Pelham's office, deferring his execution until the 25th, and on the 24th he was further respited till the 28th. During the time of his confinement previous to trial, he occupied the apartment which had been formerly the residence of Mr. Ridgway, the bookseller. His wife lived with him for the last fortnight. Although he was allowed two hours a-day, from twelve to two, to walk in the yard, he did not once embrace this indulgence; and during his whole confinement he never went out of his room, except into the lobby to consult his counsel. He lived well, and was at times very facetious, easy in his manners, and pleasant in conversation; but during the night he frequently sat up in his bed and sang psalms, overheard by his fellow-prisoner. He had not many visitors, and his only attendant was a prisoner, who was appointed for that purpose by the turnkey.

After trial he did not return to his old apartment, but was conducted to a cell; and he was so far favoured as not to have irons put on, but a person was employed as a guard to watch him during the night to prevent his doing violence to himself. On his return from court on the day of trial, his bed was brought to him in the cell, on which he threw himself in an agony of mind, saying it was his intention not to rise until they called him on the fatal morning.

The sheriffs were particularly pointed and precise in their orders, with respect to confining him to the usual diet of bread and water, preparatory to the awful event, and this order was scrupulously fulfilled. The prisoner, during a part of the night, slept, owing to fatigue and perturbation of mind. The next morning his wife applied, but was refused admittance without an order from one of the sheriffs. She applied to Mr. Sheriff Cox, who attended her to the prison.

From the time of the first respite until twelve o'clock on Wednesday night, he did not cease to entertain hopes of his safety. The interest made to save him was very great. The whole of Wednesday it occupied the great law officers; the judges met at the chancellor's in the afternoon, and the conference which then took place lasted upwards of three hours.

All hopes were, however, vain; and at a little after four o'clock, on Thursday the 28th, the scaffold began to be erected by torch-light.

The prisoner had an affecting interview with his wife the night before, from whom he was painfully separated about eleven o'clock. Mrs. Wall then reluctantly departed, overwhelmed with grief, and bathed with tears; while the unfortunate husband declared that he could now with Christian fortitude submit to his unhappy fate.

During the greater part of the night he slept but little; but about four o'clock in the morning his sleep was observed to become sound, and, according to the best recollection of his attendant, he continued in this sleep rather more than an hour; so that he could not have heard the fatal machine in its passage to the Debtors'-door. His voice preserved its usual strength and tone to the end; and, though very particular in his questions respecting the machinery in every part, yet he spoke of his approaching execution and death with perfect calmness. At half after six in the morning, his prison attendant going to his cell, was asked by him " whether the noise he heard was not that of erecting his scaffold?" but he was humanely answered in the negative.

The ordinary, Dr. Ford, soon after entered, when the prisoner devoutly joined him for some time in prayer. They then passed on to an ante-room, when Wall asked " whether it was a fine morning?" On being answered in the affirmative, he said, " The time hangs heavily : I am anxious for the close of this scene." One of the officers then proceeded to bind his arms with a cord, for which he extended them out firmly ; but recollecting himself, he said, " I beg your pardon a moment;" and putting his hand in his pocket, he drew out two white handkerchiefs, one of which he bound over his temples so as nearly to conceal his eyes, over which he placed a white cap, and then put on a round hat ; the other handkerchief he kept between his hands. He then observed, " The cord cuts me ; but it's no matter :" on which Dr. Ford desired it to be loosened, for which the prisoner bowed and thanked him.

As the clock struck eight, the door was thrown open, and Sheriff Cox and his officers appeared. Wall approaching him, said, " I attend you, sir ;" and the procession to the scaffold, over the Debtors' door, immediately succeeded. He had no sooner ascended it, accompanied by the Ordinary, than three successive shouts from an innumerable populace, the brutal effusion of one common sentiment, evidently deprived him of the small portion of fortitude which he had summoned up. He bowed his head under the extreme pressure of ignominy, and the hangman put the halter over it. This done, Mr. Wall stooped forward and spoke to the ordinary, who, no doubt at his request, pulled the cap over the lower part of the face, when in an instant, without waiting for any signal, the platform dropped.

From the knot of the rope turning round to the back of the neck, and his legs not being pulled, as was his particular request, he was suspended in convulsive agony for more than a quarter of an hour. After hanging a full hour, his body was cut down, put into a cart, and immediately conveyed to a building in Cow-cross-street to be dissected. He was dressed in a mixed coloured loose coat, with a black collar, swansdown waistcoat, blue pantaloons, and white silk stockings. He appeared a miserable and emaciated object, never having quitted the bed of his cell from the day of condemnation till the morning of his execution.

The body of the unfortunate man was not exposed to public view, as was usual in such cases. Mr. Belfour, secretary to the Surgeons' Company, had applied to Lord Kenyon to know whether such an exposure was necessary ; and finding that the forms of dissection only were required, the body, after those forms had been complied with, was consigned to the relations of the unhappy man, upon their paying fifty guineas to the Philanthropic Society.

CAPTAIN BLIGH SEIZED BY THE MUTINEERS.

THE MUTINY OF THE BOUNTY.

The case of the mutineers of the Bounty has always attracted considerable attention. The Bounty was an armed vessel, commanded by Capt. Bligh, which quitted England in the autumn of 1788, for the purpose of making discoveries, and of trading among the Southern Islands. Having visited the Friendly and the Otaheitan Islands in the South Pacific Ocean, in the month of April, 1789, she set sail on her way back to England. On the 27th of that month they lost sight of land; and up to that time there had been nothing in the conduct of the crew or petty officers which could induce a supposition that any disorder was likely to take place. We cannot, however, give a more interesting account of the mutiny than by extracting from Captain Bligh's own narrative, which runs as follows :—

" Hitherto the voyage had advanced in a course of uninterrupted prosperity, and had been attended with circumstances equally pleasing and satisfactory. But a very different scene was now to be disclosed; a conspiracy had been formed, which was to render all our past labour productive only of misery and distress; and it had been concerted with so much secrecy and circumspection, that no one circumstance escaped to betray the impending calamity.

" On the night of Monday (April 27) the watch was set as usual. Just before sunrise on Tuesday morning, while I was yet asleep, Mr. Christian, with the master at-arms, gunner's mate, and Thomas Burkitt, seaman, came into my cabin, and seizing me, tied my hands with a cord behind my back; threatening me with instant death if I spoke or made the least noise. I nevertheless called out as loud as I could, in hopes of assistance; but the officers not of their party were already secured by sentinels at their doors. At my own cabin door were three men, besides the four within; all except Christian had musquets and bayonets; he had only a cutlass. I was dragged out of bed, and forced on deck in my shirt; suffering great pain in the mean time from the tightness with which my hands were tied. On demanding the reason of such violence, the only answer was abuse for not holding my tongue. The master, the gunner, surgeon, master's mate, and Nelson the gardener, were kept confined below, and the fore hatchway was guarded by sentinels. The boatswain and carpenter, and also the clerk, were allowed to come on deck, where they saw me standing abaft the mizen-mast, with my hands tied behind my back, under a guard, with Christian at their head. The boatswain was then ordered to hoist out the launch, accompanied by a threat, if he did it not instantly, *to take care of himself.*

" The boat being hoisted out, Mr. Hayward and Mr. Hallet, two of the midshipmen, and Mr. Samuel, the clerk, were ordered into it. I demanded the intention of giving this order, and endeavoured to persuade the people near me not to persist in such acts of violence; but it was to no effect; for the constant answer was, " Hold your tongue, or you are dead this moment."

" The master had by this time sent, requesting that he might come on deck, which was permitted; but he was soon ordered back again to his cabin. My exertions to turn the tide of affairs were continued, when Christian, changing the cutlass he held for a bayonet, and holding me by the cord about my hands with a strong gripe, threatened me with immediate death if I would not be quiet; and the villains around me had their pieces cocked and bayonets fixed.

" Certain individuals were called on to get into the boat, and were hurried over the ship's side; whence I concluded, that along with them I was to be set adrift. Another effort to bring about a change produced nothing but menaces of having my brains blown out.

" The boatswain and those seamen who were to be put into the boat, were allowed to collect twine, canvass, lines, sails, cordage, an eight-and-twenty gallon cask of water; and Mr. Samuel got 150 pounds of bread, with a small quantity of rum and wine, also a quadrant and compass; but he was prohibited, on pain of death, to touch any map or astronomical book, and any instrument, or any of my surveys and drawings.

" The mutineers having thus forced those of the seamen whom they wished to get rid of into the boat, Christian directed a dram to be served to each of his crew. I then unhappily saw that nothing could be done to recover the ship. The officers were next called on deck, and forced over the ship's side into the boat, while I was kept apart from every one abaft the mizen-mast. Christian, armed with a bayonet, held the cord fastening my hands, and the guard around me stood with their pieces cocked; but on my daring the ungrateful wretches to fire, they uncocked them. Isaac Martin, one of them, I saw, had an inclination to assist me; and as he fed me with shaddock, my lips being quite parched, we explained each other's sentiments by looks. But this was observed, and he was removed. He then got into the boat, attempting to leave the ship; however, he was compelled to return. Some others were also kept contrary to their inclination.

" It appeared to me, that Christian was some time in doubt whether he should keep the carpenter or his mates. At length he determined on the latter, and the carpenter was ordered into the boat. He was permitted, though not without opposition, to take his tool chest.

Mr. Samuel secured my journals and commission, with some important ship papers: this he did with great resolution, though strictly watched. He attempted to save the time-keeper, and a box with my surveys, drawings, and remarks for fifteen years past, which were very numerous, when he was hurried away with—" Damn your eyes, you are well off to get what you have."

" Much altercation took place among the mutinous crew during the transaction of this affair. Some swore, " I'll be d—d if he does not find his way home, if he gets any thing with him," meaning me; and when the carpenter's chest was carrying away, " D—n my eyes, he will have a vessel built in a month;" while others ridiculed the helpless situation of the boat, which was very deep in the water, and had so little room for those that were in her. As for Christian, he seemed as if meditating destruction on himself and every one else.

" I asked for arms, but the mutineers laughed at me, and said I was well acquainted with the people among whom I was going; four cutlasses, however, were thrown into the boat, after we were veered astern.

" The officers and men being in the boat, they only waited for me, of which the master-at-arms informed Christian, who then said, " Come, Captain Bligh, your officers and men are now in the boat, and you must go with them; if you attempt to make the least resistance, you will instantly be put to death;" and without further ceremony, I was forced over the side by a tribe of armed ruffians, when they untied my hands. Being in the boat, we were veered astern by a rope. A few pieces of pork were thrown to us, also the four cutlasses. The armourer and carpenter then called out to me to remember that they had no hand in the transaction. After having been kept some time to make sport for these unfeeling wretches, and having undergone much ridicule, we were at length cast adrift in the open ocean.

" Eighteen persons were with me in the boat,—the master, acting surgeon, botanist, gunner, boatswain, carpenter, master, and quarter-master's mate, two quarter-masters, the sail-maker, two cooks, my clerk, the butcher, and a boy. There remained on board Fletcher Christian, the master's mate; Peter Haywood, Edward Young, George Stewart, midshipmen; the master-at-arms, gunner's mate, boatswain's mate, gardener, armourer, carpenter's mate, carpenter's crew, and fourteen seamen, being altogether the most able men of the ship's company.

" Having little or no wind, we rowed pretty fast towards the island of

Tofoa, which bore north-east about ten leagues distant. The ship while in sight steered west-north-west, but this I considered only as a feint, for when we were sent away, " Huzza for Otaheite !" was frequently heard among the mutineers.

" Christian, the chief of them, was of a respectable family in the north of England. This was the third voyage he had made with me. Not-withstanding the roughness with which I was treated, the remembrance of past kindness produced some remorse in him. While they were forcing me out of the ship, I asked him whether this was a proper return for the many instances he had experienced of my friendship? He ap-peared disturbed at the question, and answered with much emotion, " That—Captain Bligh—that is the thing—I am in hell—I am in hell." His abilities to take charge of the third watch, as I had so divided the ship's company, were fully equal to the task.

" Haywood was also of a respectable family in the north of England, and a young man of abilities, as well as Christian. These two had been objects of my particular regard and attention, and I had taken great pains to instruct them, having entertained hopes that, as professional men, they would have become a credit to their country. Young was well recommended ; and Stewart was of creditable parents in the Ork-neys, at which place, on the return of the Resolution from the South Seas in 1780, we received so many civilities, that in consideration of these alone I should gladly have taken him with me: but he had always borne a good character.

" When I had time to reflect, an inward satisfaction prevented the depression of my spirits. Yet, a few hours before, my situation had been peculiarly flattering : I had a ship in the most perfect order, stored with every necessary, both for health and service; the object of the voyage was attained, and two-thirds of it now completed; the remaining part had every prospect of success.

" It will naturally be asked, what could be the cause of such a revolt? In answer, I can only conjecture that the mutineers had flattered them-selves with the hope of a happier life among the Otaheitans than they could possibly enjoy in England ; which, joined to some female connec-tions, most probably occasioned the whole transaction.

" The women of Otaheite are handsome, mild, and cheerful in manners and conversation ; possess great sensibility, and have sufficient deli-cacy to make them be admired and beloved. The chiefs were so much attached to our people, that they rather encouraged their stay than otherwise, and even made them promises of large possessions. Under these and many other concomitant circumstances, it ought barely to be a subject of surprise, that a set of sailors, most of them void of con-nections, should be led away, where they had the power of fixing them-selves in the midst of plenty, in one of the finest islands in the world, where there is no necessity to labour, and where the allurements of dissipation are beyond any conception that can be formed of it. The utmost, however, that a commander could have expected, was desertions, such as have already happened more or less in the South Seas, and not an act of open mutiny.

" But the secrecy of this mutiny surpasses belief. Thirteen of the party who were now with me had always lived forward among the seamen; yet neither they, nor the messmates of Christian, Stewart, Heywood, and Young, had ever observed any circumstance to excite suspicion of what was plotting; and it is not wonderful that I fell a sacrifice to it, my mind being entirely free from suspicion. Perhaps, had marines been on board, a sentinel at my cabin-door might have prevented it; for I constantly slept with the door open, that the officer of the watch might have access to me on all occasions. If the mutiny had been occasioned by any grievances, either real or imaginary, I must have discovered symptoms of discontent, which would have put me on my guard; but it was far otherwise. With Christian, in particular, I was on the most friendly terms; that very day he was engaged to dine with me; and the preceding night he excused himself from supping with me on pretence of indisposition, for which I felt concerned, having no suspicion of his honour or integrity."

Captain Bligh, on taking muster of the remains of his crew left to him, found that he had in his boat the boatswain, the carpenter, the gunner, the surgeon's-mate, two midshipmen, and one master's-mate, with Mr. Nelson the botanist, and a few inferior officers. After a short consultation, it was deemed expedient to put back to the Friendly Islands; and having reached the coast of one of them, they landed, in hopes of improving their stock of provisions. For several days they continued unmolested; but at length, on the 30th of April, they were attacked by the natives with such violence, that one man was killed, and several wounded. They were, therefore, compelled immediately to sheer off; and it became now the subject of inquiry and deliberation what should be their next place of destination. Otaheite was proposed, as it was supposed that the natives would be friendly to them; but the apprehension of falling in with the Bounty determined them against this course; and with one assent they made up their minds to shape their course to Timor, a settlement belonging to the Dutch.

To effect this enterprize they were compelled to calculate the distance, with a view to the apportionment of their provisions; and having discovered that it was near four thousand miles, they agreed that their rations should not exceed an ounce of bread and a gill of water a day for each man. Upon this scanty allowance they subsisted without any other nourishment until the 6th of June, when they made the coast of New Holland, and collected a few shell-fish; and with this small relief they held on their way to Timor, which they reached on the 12th, after being forty-six days in a crazy open boat, so confined in its dimensions as to prevent any of them lying down for repose, and without the least awning to protect them from the rain, which fell almost incessantly for forty days; a heavy sea and squally weather augmenting their misery during a considerable part of the time.

On their reaching Timor, they received every assistance from the governor; and having remained until the 20th of August to recruit their strength, they procured a vessel, in which they took their passage to Batavia. They reached that port on the 2nd of October, and from thence they immediately embarked for the Cape of Good Hope. Captain Bligh quitted the Cape in the month of December, and having reached England, he communicated the particulars of the mutiny to the Admiralty, and his majesty's ship the Pandora was immediately dispatched in search of the mutineers.

It was not until the 25th of April 1792, that dispatches were received from Captain Edwards, stating, that on the Pandora appearing off Otaheite, two men swam from the shore, and solicited to be taken on board. They proved to be two of the Bounty's mutineers, and gave intelligence where fourteen of their companions were concealed on the island. A part of the Pandora's crew were sent in search of them; and after some resistance they were taken and brought prisoners on board.

It then turned out that Christian had taken upon himself the command of the Bounty immediately on the captain's having quitted her, and that his crew consisted of twenty-five men. When the Pandora arrived, Christian, with the other nine mutineers, had previously sailed in the Bounty to some remote island, and every exertion to discover their retreat proved ineffectual. On her return home, the Pandora struck upon a reef of rocks in Endeavour Straits. Her crew escaped from their perilous situation to an island in the Straits, except thirty-three men, and three of the Bounty's people, who perished by the boat oversetting. Captain Edwards was reduced to the necessity of sending one of his officers and some seamen in a small boat to Timor, which they were fourteen days in reaching, and where a vessel was procured, which proceeded to the assistance of the remainder of the crew.

So much had the mutineers of the Bounty conformed to the custom and manners of Otaheite, that when the two men of Christian's crew swam off to the Pandora, they were so tattooed, and exhibited so many other characteristic marks, that, on being first received on board, the Pandora's people took them for natives of the island. The names of these metamorphosed mutineers were Peter Heywood, a midshipman, and Joseph Coleman, the armourer; the latter of whom, Captain Bligh observes, " was detained by Christian contrary to his inclination."

On the 12th of September a court-martial was held on board the Duke, in Portsmouth harbour, on Joseph Coleman, Charles Norman, Thomas Mackintosh, Peter Heywood, Isaac Morris, John Millward, William Muspratt, Thomas Birkett, Thomas Ellison, and Michael Burn. The evidence for the prosecution being closed on Friday the 14th, the Court indulged the prisoners till Monday to give in their defence; and on Tuesday took the whole into their consideration, when they passed sentence of death on Heywood, Morris, Millward, Muspratt, Birkett, and Ellison, the two first of whom the Court recommended to mercy. Coleman, Norman, Mackintosh, and Burn were acquitted, and discharged.

On the 29th of October, Millward, Birkett, and Ellison were executed on board the Brunswick. Heywood and Morris were pardoned, in compliance with the recommendation of the Court.

We shall conclude our narrative with an account of the accidental discovery of the remainder of the crew, many years afterwards, on what was supposed to have been an uninhabited island.

About the commencement of the year 1815, the following letter was received by Vice-admiral Dixon from Sir Thomas Staines, of his majesty's ship Briton :—

"BRITON, *Valparaiso, Oct.* 18*th*, 1814.

"SIR,—I have the honour to inform you, that on my passage from the Marquesas Island to this port, on the morning of the 17th of September, I fell in with an island where none is laid down in the Admiralty or other charts, according to the several chronometers of the Briton and Tagus. I therefore hove-to until day-light, and then closed to ascertain whether it was inhabited, which I soon discovered it to be; and, to my great astonishment, found that every individual on the island (forty in number) spoke very good English. They prove to be the descendants of the deluded crew of the Bounty, which proceeded from Otaheite to the above mentioned island, where the ship was burnt.

"Christian appears to have been the leader, and the sole cause, of the mutiny in that ship. A venerable old man, named John Adams,* is the only surviving Englishman of those who last quitted Otaheite in her; and whose exemplary conduct, and fatherly care of the whole little colony, could not but command admiration. The pious manner in which all those born in the island have been reared, the correct sense of religion which has been instilled into their young minds by this old man, has given him the pre-eminence over the whole of them, to whom they look up as the father of the whole, and one family.

"A son of Christian's was the first born on the island, now about twenty-five years of age, named Thursday October Christian. The elder Christian fell a sacrifice to the jealousy of an Otaheitean man, within three or four years after their arrival on the island. They were accompanied thither by six Otaheitean men and twelve women: the former were all swept away by desperate contentions between them and the Englishmen, and five of the latter have died at different periods; leaving at present only one man and seven women of the original settlers.

"The island must undoubtedly be that called Pitcairn's, although erroneously laid down in the charts. We had the meridian sun close to it, which gave us 25° 4' S. latitude, and 130° 25' W. longitude, by the chronometers of the Briton and Tagus. It is abundant in yams, plantains, hogs, goats, and fowls; but affords no shelter for a ship or vesssel of any description; neither could a ship water there without great difficulty.

"I cannot refrain from offering my opinion, that it is well worthy the attention of our laudable religious societies, particularly that for propagating the Christian religion, the whole of the inhabitants speaking the Otaheitean tongue as well as English.

"During the whole of the time they have been on the island, only one ship has ever communicated with them, which took place about six years since by an American ship called the Topaz, of Boston, Mayhew Folger, master.

* There was no such name in the list of the Bounty's crew; he must, therefore, have assumed it instead of his real nameAlexander Smith.

" The island is completely iron-bound with rocky shores, and landing in boats is at all times difficult, although safe to approach within a short distance in a ship.   " T. STAINES."

As the real position of the island was ascertained to be so far distant from that in which it was usually laid down in the charts, and as the captains of the Briton and Tagus considered it uninhabited, they were not a little surprised, on approaching its shores, to behold plantations regularly laid out, and huts or houses more neatly constructed than those on the Marquesas Islands. When about two miles from the shore, some natives were observed bringing down their canoes on their shoulders, dashing through a heavy surf, and paddling off to the ships ; but their astonishment was unbounded on hearing one of them, on approaching the ship, call out in the English language, " Won't you heave us a rope, now ?"

The first man who got on board the Briton soon proved who they were. His name, he said, was Thursday October Christian, the first born on the Island. He was then about five-and-twenty years of age ; his hair deep black ; his countenance open and interesting, of a brownish cast, but free from that mixture of a reddish tint which prevails on the Pacific islands. His dress was a piece of cloth round his loins, and a straw hat, ornamented with the black feathers of the domestic fowl. " With a great share of good-humour," says Captain Pipon, " we were glad to trace in his benevolent countenance all the features of an honest English face." " I must confess," he continues, " I could not survey this interesting person without feelings of tenderness and compassion." His companion was named George Young, a fine youth of seventeen or eighteen years of age.

If the astonishment of the captains was great on hearing their first salutation in English, their surprise and interest were not a little increased on Sir Thomas Staines taking the youths below, and setting before them something to eat, when one of them rose up, and placing his hands together in a posture of devotion, distinctly repeated, and in a pleasing tone and manner, " For what we are going to receive, the Lord make us truly thankful." They expressed great surprise on seeing a cow on board the Briton, and were in doubt whether she was a great goat, or a horned sow.

The two captains of his majesty's ships accompanied these young men on shore. With some difficulty, and a good wetting, and with the assistance of their conductors, they accomplished a landing through the surf ; and were soon after met by John Adams, a man between fifty and sixty years of age, who conducted them to his house. His wife accompanied him, a very old lady, blind with age. He was at first alarmed, lest the visit was to apprehend him ; but, on being told that they were perfectly ignorant of his existence, he was relieved from his anxiety. Being once assured that the visit was of a peaceable nature, it is impossible to describe the joy these poor people manifested on seeing those whom they were pleased to consider as their countrymen. Yams, cocoa-nuts, and other fruits, with fine fresh eggs, were laid before them ; and the old man would have dressed a hog for his visitors, but time would not allow them to partake of his intended feast.

This interesting new colony, it seemed, now consisted of about forty-six persons, mostly grown-up young people, besides a number of infants. The young men, all born on the island, were very athletic, and of the finest forms; their countenances open and pleasing, indicating much benevolence and goodness of heart: but the young women were objects of particular admiration, tall, robust, and beautifully formed, their faces beaming with smiles, and unruffled good humour, but wearing a degree of modesty and bashfulness, that would do honour to the most virtuous nation on earth; their teeth, like ivory, were regular and beautiful, without a single exception; and all of them, both male and female, had the most marked English features. The clothing of the young females consisted of a piece of fine linen, reaching from the waist to the knees, and generally a sort of mantle thrown loosely over the shoulders, and hanging as low as the ancles; but this covering appeared to be intended chiefly as a protection against the sun and the weather, as it was frequently laid aside, and then the upper part of the body was entirely exposed—and it is not possible to conceive more beautiful forms than they exhibited. They sometimes wreath caps or bonnets for the head, in the most tasty manner, to protect the face from the rays of the sun; and though, as Captain Pipon observes, they have only had the instruction of their Otaheitean mothers, " our dress-makers in London would be delighted with the simplicity, and yet elegant taste, of these untaught females." Their native modesty, assisted by a proper sense of religion and morality instilled into their youthful minds by John Adams, had hitherto preserved these interesting people perfectly chaste, and free from all kinds of debauchery. Adams assured the visitors, that, since Christian's death, there had not been a single instance of any young woman proving unchaste, nor any attempt at seduction on the part of the men. They all labour, while they are young, in the cultivation of the ground; and when possessed of a sufficient quantity of cleared land and of stock to maintain a family, they are allowed to marry, but always with the consent of Adams, who unites them by a sort of marriage-ceremony of his own.

The greatest harmony prevailed in this little society; their own quarrels (and these rarely happened) being, according to their own expression, *quarrels of the mouth:* they are honest in their dealings, which consists of bartering different articles for mutual accommodation.

Their habitations were extremely neat. The little village of Pitcairn formed a square, the houses at the upper end of which were occupied by the patriarch John Adams and his family, consisting of his old blind wife, three daughters from fifteen to eighteen years of age, and a boy of eleven, with a daughter of his wife by a former husband, and a son-in-law. On the opposite side was the dwelling of Thursday October Christian; and in the centre, a smooth verdant lawn, on which the poultry were let loose, fenced in so as to prevent the intrusion of the domestic quadrupeds.

Their agricultural implements were made by themselves from the iron supplied by the Bounty, which, with great labour, they had beat out into spades, hatchets, &c.

JOHN PRICE,

COMMONLY CALLED JACK KETCH, EXECUTED FOR MURDER.

ALTHOUGH the circumstances attending the crime of this malefactor do not present any features of general interest, the fact of his having filled the office of public executioner, and of his suffering on that very scaffold on which he had exercised the functions of his revolting office, render the case not a little remarkable.

He was born of decent parents, in the parish of St. Martin's-in-the-Fields, London; and his father, who was in the service of his country, having been blown up at the demolition of Tangiers, he was put apprentice to a rag-merchant. His master dying, he went to sea, and served with credit on board different ships in the navy for the space of eighteen years; but was at length paid off and discharged from further service.

The office of public executioner becoming vacant, it was given to him, and, but for his extravagance, he might have long continued in it. On returning from an execution, however, he was arrested for debt, which he discharged, in part, with the wages he had that day earned, and the remainder with the produce of three suits of clothes, which he had taken from the bodies of the executed men. But he was soon afterwards lodged in the Marshalsea prison for other debts, and there he remained for want of bail; in consequence of which one William Marvel was appointed in his stead. He continued some time longer in the Marshalsea, when he and a fellow-prisoner broke a hole in the wall, through which they made their escape. It was not long after this that Price committed the offence for which he was executed. He was indicted on the 20th April, 1718, for the murder of Elizabeth, the wife of William White, on the 13th of the preceding month.

In the course of the evidence it appeared that Price met the deceased near ten at night in Moorfields, and attempted to ravish her; but the poor woman (who was the wife of a watchman, and sold gingerbread in the streets) doing all in her power to resist his villainous attack, he beat her so cruelly that streams of blood issued from her eyes and mouth, one of her arms was broken, some of her teeth were knocked out, her head was bruised in a most dreadful manner, and one of her eyes was forced from the socket. Some persons, hearing the cries of the unhappy creature, repaired to the spot, took Price into custody, and lodged him in the watch-house; and the woman, being attended by a surgeon and nurse, was unable to speak, but she answered the nurse by signs, and in that manner described what had happened to her. She died, after having languished four days. The prisoner, on his trial, denied that he was guilty of the murder; but he was found guilty, and sentenced to death. He then gave himself up to the use of intoxicating liquors, and continued obstinately to deny his guilt until the day of execution, when, at length, he admitted the justice of his punishment, but said that he was in a state of intoxication when he committed the crime for which he suffered. He was executed on the 21st May, 1718, at Bunhill-row, and was afterwards hung in chains at Holloway.

MICHAEL VAN-BERGHEN, CATHARINE VAN-BERGHEN, AND GERARD DROMELIUS,

HANGED FOR ROBBERY AND MURDER.

THE subjects of this narrative were natives of Holland; but having settled in England, Michael Van-Berghen and his wife kept a public-house near East-Smithfield, and Dromelius acted as their servant.

A country gentleman named Norris, who lodged at an inn near Aldgate, went into the house of Van-Berghen about eight o'clock in the evening, and continued to drink there till about eleven. Finding himself rather intoxicated, he desired the maid-servant to call a coach to carry him home. As she was going to do so, her mistress whispered her, to return in a little time, and say that a coach was not to be procured. These directions being observed, Norris, on the maid's return, resolved to go without a coach, and accordingly took his leave of the family; but he had not gone far before he discovered that he had been robbed of his purse; whereupon he returned, and charged Van-Berghen and his wife with the robbery. This they positively denied, and threatened to turn him out of the house; but he refused to go, and resolutely went into a room where the cloth was laid for supper. Dromelius now entered the room, and treating Mr. Norris in a very cavalier manner, the latter resented the insult, till a perfect quarrel ensued. Van-Berghen seized a poker, with which he fractured Mr. Norris's skull, and Dromelius stabbed him in different parts of the body, Mrs. Van-Berghen being present.

Mr. Norris being dead, his body was stripped of his coat, waistcoat, hat, wig, &c.; and then Van-Berghen and Dromelius carried the body, and threw it into a ditch which communicated with the Thames; and in the mean time Mrs. Van-Berghen washed the blood of the deceased from the floor of the room. The clothes which had been stripped from the deceased were put up in a hamper, and committed to the care of Dromelius, who took a boat, and carried them over to Rotherhithe, where he employed the waterman to carry the hamper to lodgings which he had taken, and in which he proposed to remain until he could find a favourable opportunity of embarking for Holland.

On the following morning at low water the body was found. Several of the neighbours endeavoured to trace the blood to the place where the murder might have been committed; but though they could not succeed in this, some of them, who were up at a very early hour, recollected that they had seen Van-Berghen and Dromelius coming almost from the spot where the body was found, and remarked that a light had been carried backwards and forwards in Van-Berghen's house.

Hereupon the house was searched; but no discovery was made, except that a little blood was found behind the door of a room which appeared to have been lately mopped. Enquiry was made after Dromelius; but Van-Berghen and his wife would give no other account than that he had left their service; on which they were taken into custody, with the

servant maid, who was a principal evidence against them. At this juncture appeared the waterman who had carried Dromelius to Rotherhithe,
and who knowing him well, he likewise was soon taken into custody.

On the trial, all the circumstances appeared so striking that the jury
did not hesitate to find all the three prisoners guilty, and accordingly
they received sentence of death. They were tried by a jury of half
Englishmen and half foreigners.

After condemnation, and a short time before the day of execution,
Dromelius pretended to make a confession, and assured the ordinary of
Newgate that the murder was committed by himself, and was preceded
and followed by these circumstances: That Mr. Norris being very much
in liquor, and desirous of going to his inn, Mr. Van-Berghen directed
him to attend him thither: that soon after they left the house, Norris
went into a broken building to ease himself; where using opprobrious
language to Dromelius, and attempting to draw his sword, he wrested it
from his hand, and stabbed him with it in several places; that this being
done, Norris groaned very much; and Dromelius hearing a watchman
coming, and fearing a discovery, drew a knife, cut his throat, and thereby
put an end to his life. This story was altogether improbable; for if Mr.
Norris had been killed in the manner above mentioned, some blood would
have been found on the spot, and there would have been holes in his
clothes from the stabbing; neither of which was the case. Still however,
Dromelius persisted in his declaration, with a view to save the life of his
mistress, with whom he was supposed to have had a criminal connection;
indeed, he confessed that he had been too familiar with her.

At the place of execution Mr. and Mrs. Van-Berghen were attended
by some divines of their own country, as well as English clergymen.
Mr. Van-Berghen, unable to speak intelligibly in English, conversed in
Latin; a circumstance from which it may be inferred that he had been
educated in a style superior to the rank in life which he had lately held.
He said the murder was not committed in his house, and that he knew
no more of it than that Dromelius came to him while he lay in bed,
informed him that he had wounded a gentleman, and begged him to aid
his escape; but that when he knew Mr. Norris was murdered, he offered
money to some persons to pursue the murderer: but of this circumstance he brought no proof on his trial.

Mrs. Van-Berghen also solemnly declared that she knew nothing
of the murder till after it was perpetrated, which was not in their house;
that Dromelius coming into the chamber, and saying he had murdered
the gentleman, she went for the hamper to hold the bloody clothes, and
assisted Dromelius in his escape,—a circumstance which she said would
not be deemed criminal in her country. Here, however, she was in error,
for in Holland, accessaries either before or after the fact are accounted as
principals.

The criminals were all executed near the Hartshorn Brewhouse, East
Smithfield, the nearest convenient spot to the place where the murder
was committed, on the 10th July, 1700. The bodies of the men were
afterwards hung in chains between Bow and Mile-End, but that of the
woman was buried.

EUGENE ARAM CONCEALING THE BODY OF CLARKE.

EUGENE ARAM,

EXECUTED FOR MURDER, FOURTEEN YEARS AFTER ITS COMMISSION.

THE trial of Eugene Aram is probably one of the most remarkable on the records of guilt. He was a man of extraordinary endowments, and of good education; so that no one could have suspected him of having committed the horrid crime of murder; but his offence, though long concealed, was at length, and in a most singular manner, discovered.

Eugene Aram was born in a village called Netherdale, in Yorkshire, in the year 1704, of an ancient family, one of his ancestors having served the office of high sheriff for that county in the reign of Edward the Third. The vicissitudes of fortune had, however, reduced them; as we find the father of Eugene, a poor but honest man, by profession a gardener; in which humble walk in life he was, nevertheless, greatly respected. The sweat of his brow alone, we must conclude, was sufficient both to rear and educate his offspring. From the high erudition of the unfortunate subject under consideration, he may be truly called a prodigy. On the very slender stock of learning which he received in a day-school, he built a fabric which, it has been said, would have been worthy the shoulders of our literary Atlas, Dr. Johnson.

During the infancy of Aram, his parents removed to another village, called Shelton, near Newby, in the same county; and, when about six years of age, his father, who had laid by a small sum from his weekly labour, made a purchase of a little cottage in Bondgate, near Rippon. When he was about thirteen or fourteen years of age, he went to his father at Newby, and attended him in the family there, till the death of Sir Edward Blackett. It was in the house of this gentleman, to whom his father was first gardener, that his propensity for literature first appeared. He was, indeed, always of a solitary disposition, and uncommonly fond of retirement and books; and here he enjoyed all the advantages of leisure and privacy. He applied himself at first chiefly to mathematical studies, in which he made a considerable proficiency.

At about sixteen years of age, he was sent to London, to the house of Mr. Christopher Blackett, whom he served for some time in the capacity of book-keeper. After continuing here a year or more, he was taken ill with the small-pox, under which distemper he suffered most severely. He afterwards returned into Yorkshire, in consequence of an invitation from his father, and there continued to prosecute his studies; but he found in polite literature much greater charms than in the mathematics, which occasioned him now chiefly to apply himself to poetry, history, and antiquities. After this he was invited to Netherdale, where he engaged in a school, and married. But this marriage proved an unhappy connexion; for to the misconduct of his wife he afterwards attributed the misfortunes that befell him. In the meanwhile, having perceived his deficiency in the learned languages, he applied himself to the grammatical study of the Latin and Greek tongues; after which he read, with great avidity and diligence, all the Latin classics, historians, and poets. He then went through the Greek Testament; and, lastly, ventured upon Hesiod, Homer, Theocritus, together with all the Greek tragedians.

In 1734, William Norton, Esq., a gentleman who had a friendship for Aram, invited him to Knaresborough. Here he acquired the Hebrew, and read the Pentateuch in that language. In 1744, he returned to London, and served the Rev. Mr. Plainblanc, in Piccadilly, as usher in Latin and writing; and with this gentleman's assistance he acquired a knowledge of the French language. He was afterwards employed as an usher and tutor in various parts of England; during which time he became acquainted with heraldry and botany. He also ventured upon Chaldee and Arabic, the former of which he found easy from its affinity to the Hebrew. He then investigated the Celtic, as far as possible, in all its dialects; and having begun to form collections, and make comparisons between the Celtic, English, Latin, Greek, and Hebrew, and found a great affinity between them, he resolved to proceed through all these languages, and to form a comparative lexicon.

But, amid these learned labours and inquiries, it appears that Aram committed a crime which could not naturally have been expected from a man of so studious a turn. On the 8th of February, 1745, he, in conjunction with a man named Richard Houseman, murdered Daniel Clarke, a shoemaker, at Knaresborough. This unfortunate man, having lately married a woman of good family, circulated a report that his wife was entitled to a considerable fortune, which he should soon receive. Hereupon Aram and Richard Houseman, conceiving hopes of making advantage of the circumstance, persuaded Clarke to make an ostentatious show of his own riches, to induce his wife's relations to give him that fortune of which he had boasted. There was sagacity, if not honesty, in this advice; for the world in general are more free to assist persons in affluence than those in distress.

Clarke was easily induced to comply with a hint so agreeable to his own desires; on which he borrowed, and bought on credit, a large quantity of silver plate, with jewels, watches, rings, &c. He told the persons of whom he purchased, that a merchant in London had sent him an order to buy such plate for exportation; and no doubt was entertained of his credit, till his sudden disappearance in February, 1745, when it was imagined that he was gone abroad, or at least to London, to dispose of his ill-acquired property.

When Clarke was possessed of these goods, Aram and Houseman determined to murder him, in order to share the booty; and, on the night of the 8th of February, 1745, they persuaded Clarke to walk with them in the fields, in order to consult with them on the proper method to dispose of the effects. They walked into a field, at a small distance from the town, well known by the name of Saint Robert's Cave. When they came into this field, Aram and Clarke went over a hedge towards the cave; and when they had got within six or seven yards of it, Houseman, by the light of the moon, saw Aram strike Clarke several times, and at length beheld him fall, but never saw him afterwards. This was the state of the affair, if Houseman's testimony on the trial might be credited.

On the murderers dividing the treasure, Houseman concealed his share in his garden for a twelvemonth, and then took it to Scotland, where he sold it; but Aram, after the lapse of about a month, set off to London, sold his share to a Jew, and then engaged himself as an usher at an academy in Piccadilly. After this he was usher at other schools in different parts of the kingdom; but, as he did not correspond with his friends in Yorkshire, it was presumed that he was dead.

Thus had nearly fourteen years passed on without the smallest clue being found to account for the sudden exit of Clarke; when, in the year 1758, a labourer was employed to dig for stone to supply a lime-kiln, at a place called Thistle Hill, near Knaresborough; and having dug about two feet deep, he found the bones of a human body, which appeared to have been buried double. This incident immediately became the subject of general curiosity and inquiry. Some hints had been formerly thrown out by Aram's wife, that Clarke was murdered; and it was well remembered that his disappearance was very sudden.

This occasioned Aram's wife to be sent for, as was also the coroner; and from Mrs. Clarke's evidence the following facts were adduced. That on the morning of February 8th, 1744-5, as early as two o'clock, Aram, Clarke, and Houseman came to Aram's house, and went up stairs, where they remained for about an hour. They then went out together, and Clarke being the last, she observed that he had a sack or wallet on his back. About four, Houseman and Aram returned, but without their companion, Clarke. "Where is Clarke?" she inquired; but her husband only returned an angry look in reply, and desired her to go to bed, which she refused, and told him, " she feared he had been doing some-thing wrong." Aram then went down stairs with the candle, and she, being desirous to know what they were doing, followed them, and from the top of the stairs heard Houseman say, " She's coming ;—if she does, she'll tell." " What can she tell, poor simple thing?" replied Aram ; " she knows nothing. I'll hold the door to prevent her coming." " It's of no use, something must be done," returned Houseman ; " if she don't split now, she will some other time." " No, no, foolish," her husband said ; " we'll coax her a little till her passion is off, and then"———" What !" said Houseman, sullenly.—" Shoot her," whispered Aram, " shoot her !" Mrs. Aram, hearing this discourse, became very much alarmed, but remained quiet. At seven o'clock the same morning they both left the house, and she, immediately their backs were turned went down stairs, and observed that there had been a fire below, and all the ashes taken out of the grate. She then examined the dunghill, and per-ceived ashes of a different kind lying upon it, and turning them over, found several pieces of linen and woollen cloth very nearly burnt, which had the appearance of wearing apparel. When she returned into the house, she found a handkerchief that she had lent to Houseman the night before, and a round spot of blood on it about the size of a shil-ling. Houseman returned soon afterwards, and she charged him with having done some dreadful thing to Clarke ; but he pretended total ignorance, and added, " she was a fool, and knew not what she said." From these circumstances she fully and conscientiously believed that Daniel Clarke was murdered by Houseman and Eugene Aram, on the 8th of February, 1744-5.

Several other witnesses were examined, all affirming that Houseman and Eugene Aram were the last persons seen with Clarke, especially on the night of the 7th of February, the time after which he was missing. Upon hearing these testimonies, Houseman, who was present, was observed to become very restless, discovering all the signs of guilt, such as trembling, turning pale, and faltering in his speech. Few men guilty of the crime of murder have the strength of heart and self-command to conceal it : by some circumstance or other, the truth will out ; a look, a dream, and not unfrequently, as in this case, their own unfaithful tongue, is the involuntary agent that brings at last the blackened culprit to that punishment which unerringly awaits the man that sheds his brother's blood. Accordingly, upon the skeleton being produced, Houseman taking up one of the bones, dropped this unguarded expres-sion : " This is no more Daniel Clarke's bone than it is mine?" " What?" remarked the coroner instantly—" what? How can you be so sure that that is not Daniel Clarke's bone ?" " Because I can produce a witness," replied Houseman, in evident confusion—" because I can produce a witness, who saw Daniel Clarke on the road two days after he was missing at Knaresborough." This witness was instantly summoned, and stated that he had never seen Clarke after the 8th of February ; a friend, however, had told him (and this only had he mentioned at first) that he met some one very like Clarke ; but, it being a snowy day, and the person having the cape of his great coat up, he could not say with the least degree of certainty who he was. This explanation, so far from proving satisfactory, increased the suspicion against Houseman; and accordingly a warrant was issued against him, and he was apprehended and brought before William Thornton, Esq., who, examining him, elicited a full acknowledgment of the fact of his having been with Clarke on the night in question, on account of some money (twenty pounds) that he had lent him, and which he wanted at the time very pressingly. He further stated, that Clarke begged him to accept the value in goods, to which proposition he assented, and was necessarily therefore several times to and fro between Clarke's house and his own, in order to remove the goods from one to the other. When he had finished, he left Clarke at Aram's house with another man, whom he had never seen before. Aram and Clarke immediately afterwards followed him out of the house of the former, and the stranger was with them. They then went in the direction of the market-place, which the light of the moon enabled him to see, and he lost sight of them. He disavowed most solemnly that he came back to Aram's house that morning with Aram and Clarke, as was asserted by Mrs. Aram; nor was he with Aram, but with Clarke, at the house of the former on that night, whither he only went to see Clarke in order to obtain from him the note.

Being then asked if he would sign his examination, he said he would rather waive it for the present, for he might have something to add, and therefore desired to have time to consider it. The magistrate then committed him to York castle, when, expressing a wish to explain more fully, he was again brought before Mr. Thornton, and in his presence made the following confession:—That Daniel Clarke was murdered by Eugene Aram, late of Knaresborough, a schoolmaster, and, as he believed, on Friday the 8th of February, 1744-5; for that Eugene Aram and Daniel Clarke were together at Aram's house early that morning, and that he (Houseman) left the house and went up the street a little before, and they called to him, desiring he would go a short way with them; that he accordingly went with them to a place called St. Robert's cave, near Grimble bridge, where the two former stopped, and there he saw Aram strike Clarke several times over the breast and head, and saw him fall as if he were dead; upon which he came away and left them. But whether Aram used any weapon or not to kill Clarke, he could not tell; nor did he know what he did with the body afterwards, but believed that Aram left it at the mouth of the cave; for that seeing Aram do this, lest he might share the same fate, he made the best of his way to the Bridge-end, where, looking back, he saw Aram coming from the cave-side (which is in a private rock adjoining the river), and could discern a bundle in his hand, but did not know what it was: upon this he hastened away to the town, without either joining Aram or seeing him again till the next day, and from that time he had never had discourse with him. He stated, however, afterwards, that Clarke's body was buried in St. Robert's cave, and that he was sure it was there, but desired it might remain till such time as Aram was taken. He added further, that Clarke's head lay to the right, in the turn at the entrance of the cave.

Persons were instantly sent to examine St. Robert's cave, when, agreeably to Houseman's confession, the skeleton of a human body (the head lying as he had described) was found. A warrant was instantly issued to apprehend Eugene Aram, who was discovered to be living at Lynd in the capacity of usher at a school. He confessed before the magistrate that he was well acquainted with Clarke, and, to the best of his remembrance, about or before the 8th of February, 1744-5, but utterly denied any participation in the frauds which Clarke stood charged with at the time of his disappearance. He also declared that he knew nothing of the murder, and that the statements made by his wife were without exception false: he, however, declined to sign his examination, on the same plea preferred by Houseman, that he might recollect himself better, and lest any thing should be omitted which might afterwards occur to him. On being conducted to the castle, he desired to return, and acknowledged that he was at his own house when Houseman and Clarke came to him with some plate, of which Clarke had defrauded his neighbours. He could not but observe that the former was very diligent in assisting—in fact, it was altogether Houseman's business; and there was no truth whatever in the statement that he came there to sign a note or instrument. All the property which Clarke had possessed himself of, amounting to a considerable value, was concealed under flax at Houseman's house with the intention of disposing of it little by little to prevent any suspicion of his being concerned in the robbery. The plate was beaten flat in St. Robert's cave. At four o'clock in the morning, they, thinking that it was too late to enable Clarke to leave with safety, agreed that he should stay there till the next night, and he accordingly remained there all the following day. In order then the better to effect his escape, they both went down to the cave, Houseman only entering, while he watched without, lest any person should surprise them. On a sudden he heard a noise, and Houseman appeared at the mouth of the cave, and told him that Clarke was gone. He had a bag with him, containing plate, which he said he had purchased of Clarke, money being much more portable than such cumbersome articles. They then went to Houseman's house, and concealed the property there, he fully believing that Clarke had escaped. He never heard any thing of Clarke subsequently, and was as much surprised to hear there was a suspicion of his being murdered, as that he (Eugene Aram) should be considered to be the murderer. Notwithstanding this surprise, however, his examination having been signed, he was committed with his companion to York castle, there to await the assizes.

On the 3d of August, 1759, they were both brought to the bar. Houseman was arraigned on the former indictment, acquitted, and admitted evidence against Aram, who was thereupon arraigned. Houseman was then called, and deposed to the same effect as has already appeared in his own confession. Several witnesses were called, who gave evidence as to finding several kinds of goods buried in Aram's garden, Aram's knowledge of the fact of Clarke's possessing two hundred pounds, and to show that they both had been seen together on the evening of the 7th of February. After which the skull was produced in court; on the left side there was a fracture, from the nature of which it was impossible to have been done but by the stroke of some blunt instrument. The skull was beaten inwards, and could not be replaced but from within. The surgeon gave it as his opinion, that no such breach could proceed from natural decay; that it was not a recent fracture made by the spade or axe by which it might have been dug up, but seemed to be of some years' standing.

Eugene Aram's defence, which he read, was marked with an undoubted manifestation of very considerable powers; it was learned and argumentative, and in some pasages glowing and eloquent. He thus addressed the court :—

" My Lord,—I know not whether it is of right or through some indulgence of your lordship that I am allowed the liberty at this bar, and at this time, to attempt a defence, incapable and uninstructed as I am to speak; since, while I see so many eyes upon me, so numerous and awful a concourse fixed with attention, and filled with I know not what expectancy, I labour not with guilt, my lord, but with perplexity; for having never seen a court but this, being wholly unacquainted with law, the customs of the bar, and all judiciary proceedings, I fear I shall be so little capable of speaking with propriety in this place, that it exceeds my hope if I shall be able to speak at all.

" I have heard, my lord, the indictment read, wherein I find myself charged with the highest crime, with an enormity I am altogether incapable of—a fact, to the commission of which there goes far more insensibility of heart, more profligacy of morals, than ever fell to my lot; and nothing possibly could have admitted a presumption of this nature, but a depravity not inferior to that imputed to me. However, as I stand indicted at your lordship's bar, and have heard what is called evidence adduced in support of such a charge, I very humbly solicit your lordship's patience, and beg the hearing of this respectable audience, while I, single and unskilful, destitute of friends and unassisted by counsel, say something, perhaps like argument, in my defence. I shall consume but little of your lordship's time : what I have to say will be short; and this brevity, probably, will be the best part of it: however, it is offered with all possible regard and the greatest submission to your lordship's consideration, and that of this honourable court.

" First, my lord, the whole tenor of my conduct in life contradicts every particular of the indictment; yet had I never said this, did not my present circumstances extort it from me, and seem to make it necessary. Permit me here, my lord, to call upon malignity itself, so long and cruelly busied in this prosecution, to charge upon me any immorality of which prejudice was not the author. No, my lord, I concerted no schemes of fraud, projected no violence, injured no man's person or property. My days were honestly laborious, my nights intensely studious; and I humbly conceive my notice of this, especially at this time, will not be thought impertinent or unseasonable, but, at least, deserving some attention; because, my lord, that any person, after a temperate use of life, a series of thinking and acting regularly, and without one single deviation from sobriety, should plunge into the very depth of profligacy precipitately and at once, is altogether improbable and unprecedented, and absolutely inconsistent with the course of things.   Mankind is never corrupted at once.   Villainy is always progressive, and declines from right, step by step, till every regard for probity is lost, and every sense of moral obligation totally perishes.

" Again, my lord, a suspicion of this kind, which nothing but malevolence could entertain and ignorance propagate, is violently opposed by my very situation at that time with respect to health ; for, but a little space before, I had been confined to my bed, and suffered under a very long and severe disorder, and was not able, for half a year together, so much as to walk.   The distemper had left me indeed, yet slowly, and in part—but so macerated, so enfeebled, that I was reduced to crutches; and so far from being well about the time I am charged with this fact, I have never, to this day, perfectly recovered.   Could then a person in this condition take any thing into his head so unlikely, so extravagant? —I, past the vigour of my age, feeble and valetudinary, with no inducement to engage, no ability to accomplish, no weapon wherewith to perpetrate such a deed, without interest, without power, without motive, without means.   Besides, it must needs occur to every one, that an action of this atrocious nature is never heard of, but when its springs are laid open.   It appears that it was to support some indolence, or supply some luxury ; to satisfy some avarice, or oblige some malice ; to prevent some real or some imaginary want : yet I lay not under the influence of these.   Surely, my lord, I may, consistently with both truth and modesty, affirm thus much ; and none who have any veracity and know me, will ever question this.

" In the second place, the disappearance of Clarke is suggested as an argument of his being dead ; but the uncertainty of such an inference from that, and the fallibility of all conclusions of such a sort from such a circumstance, are too obvious and too notorious to require instances; yet, superseding many, permit me to produce a very recent one, and that afforded by this Castle.

" In June 1757, William Thompson, for all the vigilance of this place, in open daylight and double-ironed, made his escape, and, notwithstanding an immediate inquiry set on foot, the strictest search, and all advertisement, was never heard of since.   If, then, Thompson got off unseen, through all these difficulties, how very easy it was for Clarke, when none of them opposed him !   But what would be thought of a prosecution commenced against any one seen last with Thompson ?

" Permit me next, my lord, to observe a little upon the bones which have been discovered.   It is said (which perhaps is saying very far) that these are the skeleton of a man.   It is possible, indeed, it may ; but is there any certain known criterion which incontestably distinguishes the sex in human bones ?   Let it be considered, my lord, whether the ascertaining of this point ought not to precede any attempt to identify them ?

" The place of their depositum, too, claims much more attention than is commonly bestowed upon it ; for, of all places in the world, none could have mentioned any one wherein there was a greater certainty of finding human bones than a hermitage, except he should point out a churchyard; hermitages, in time past, being not only places of religious retirement, but of burial too: and it has scarce or never been heard of, but that every cell now known contains or contained these relics of humanity, some mutilated, some entire. I do not inform, but give me leave to remind your lordship, that here sat solitary Sanctity, and here the hermit or the anchoress hoped to secure that repose for their bones when dead which they here enjoyed when living.

" All the while, my lord, I am sensible this is known to your lordship, and many in this court, better than to me; but it seems necessary to my case that others, who have not at all perhaps adverted to things of this nature, and may have concern in my trial, should be made acquainted with it. Suffer me then, my lord, to produce a few of many evidences that these cells were used as repositories of the dead, and to enumerate a few cases in which human bones have been found, as it happened in this in question; lest, to some, that accident might seem extraordinary, and consequently occasion prejudice.

" 1. The bones, as was supposed, of the Saxon saint Dubritius were discovered buried in his cell at Guy's Cliff, near Warwick; as appears from the authority of Sir William Dugdale.

" 2. The bones thought to be those of the anchoress Rosia were but lately discovered in a cell at Royston,—entire, fair, and undecayed, though they must have lain interred for several centuries; as is proved by Dr. Stukely.

" 3. But my own county—nay, almost this neighbourhood—supplies another instance; for in January, 1747, were found, by Mr. Stovin, accompanied by a reverend gentleman, the bones, in part, of some recluse, in the cell at Lindholm, near Hatfield. They were believed to be those of William Lindholm, a hermit, who had long made this cave his habitation.

" 4. In February, 1744, part of Woburn Abbey being pulled down, a large portion of a corpse appeared, even with the flesh on, and which bore cutting with a knife; though it is certain this had lain above two hundred years, and how much longer is doubtful; for this abbey was founded in 1145, and disolved in 1538 or 1539.

" What would have been said, what believed, if this had been an accident to the bones in question?

" Farther, my lord:—it is not yet out of living memory, that at a little distance from Knaresborough, in a field, part of the manor of the worthy and patriotic baronet who does that borough the honour to represent it in parliament, were found, in digging for gravel, not one human skeleton only, but five or six, deposited side by side, with each an urn placed at its head, as your lordship knows was usual in ancient interments.

" About the same time, and in another field, almost close to this borough, was discovered also, in searching for gravel, another human skeleton; but the piety of the same worthy gentleman ordered both pits to be filled up again, commendably unwilling to disturb the dead.

" Is the invention of these bones forgotten, then, or industriously concealed, that the discovery of those in question may appear the more singular and extraordinary? whereas, in fact, there is nothing extraordinary in it. My lord, almost every place conceals such remains. In fields, in hills, in highway sides, in commons, lie frequent and unsuspected bones; and our present allotments for rest for the departed are but of some centuries.

"Another particular seems not to claim a little of your lordship's notice, and that of the gentlemen of the jury; which is, that perhaps no example occurs of more than one skeleton being found in one cell: and in the cell in question was found but one; agreeable, in this, to the peculiarity of every other known cell in Britain. Not the invention of one skeleton, but of two, would have appeared suspicious and uncommon. But it seems another skeleton has been discovered by some labourer, which was full as confidently averred to be Clarke's as this. My lord, must some of the living, if it promotes some interest, be made answerable for all the bones that earth has concealed and chance exposed? And might not a place where bones lay be mentioned by a person by chance, as well as found by a labourer by chance? Or is it more criminal accidentally to name where bones lie, than accidentally to find where they lie?

"Here, too, is a human skull produced which is fractured. But was this the cause, or was it the consequence, of death? Was it owing to violence, or was it the effect of natural decay? If it was violence, was that violence before or after death? My lord, in May 1732, the remains of William, lord archbishop of this province, were taken up, by permission, in this cathedral, and the bones of the skull were found broken; yet certainly he died by no violence offered to him alive that could occasion that fracture there.

"Let it be considered, my lord, that, upon the dissolution of religious houses and the commencement of the Reformation, the ravages of those times affected both the living and the dead. In search after imaginary treasures, coffins were broken up, graves and vaults dug open, monuments ransacked, and shrines demolished; and it ceased about the beginning of the reign of Queen Elizabeth. I entreat your lordship, suffer not the violence, the depredations, and the iniquities of those times, to be imputed to this.

"Moreover, what gentleman here is ignorant that Knaresborough had a castle, which, though now a ruin, was once considerable both for its strength and garrison? All know it was vigorously besieged by the arms of the Parliament; at which siege, in sallies, conflicts, flights, pursuits, many fell, in all the places round it—and, where they fell, were buried—for every place, my lord, is burial-earth in war; and many, questionless, of these rest yet unknown, whose bones futurity shall discover.

"I hope, with all imaginable submission, that what has been said will not be thought impertinent to this indictment; and that it will be far from the wisdom, the learning, and the integrity of this place, to impute to the living what zeal in its fury may have done—what nature may have taken off, and piety interred—or what war alone may have destroyed, alone deposited.

"As to the circumstances that have been raked together, I have nothing to observe, but that all circumstances whatever are precarious, and have been but too frequently found lamentably fallible; even the strongest have failed. They may rise to the utmost degree of probability, yet they are but probability still. Why need I name to your lordship the two Harrisons, recorded by Dr. Howel, who both suffered upon circumstances because of the sudden disappearance of their lodger, who was in credit, had contracted debts, borrowed money, and went off unseen, and returned a great many years after their execution? Why name the intricate affair of Jacques de Moulin, under King Charles II., related by a gentleman who was counsel for the crown? And why the unhappy Coleman, who suffered innocently, though convicted upon positive evidence; and whose children perished for want, because the world uncharitably believed the father guilty? Why mention the perjury of Smith, incautiously admitted king's evidence, who, to screen himself, unjustly accused Faircloth and Loveday of the murder of Dun; the first of whom, in 1749, was executed at Winchester; and Loveday was about to suffer at Reading, had not Smith been proved perjured, to the satisfaction of the court, by the governor of Gosport Hospital?

" Now, my lord, having endeavoured to show that the whole of this process is altogether repugnant to every part of my life; that it is inconsistent with my condition of health about that time; that no rational inference can be drawn that a person is dead who suddenly disappears; that hermitages are the constant depositaries of the bones of a recluse; that the proofs of this are well authenticated; that the revolutions in religion, or the fortunes of war, have mangled or buried the dead;— the conclusion remains, perhaps, no less reasonable than impatiently wished for. I, at last, after a year's confinement, equal to either fortune, put myself upon the justice, the candour, and the humanity of your lordship; and upon yours, my countrymen, gentlemen of the jury."

The delivery of this address created a very considerable impression in court; but the learned judge having calmly and with great perspicuity summed up the evidence, the jury, with little hesitation, returned a verdict of Guilty. Sentence of death was then passed upon the prisoner, who received the intimation of his fate with becoming resignation.

On the morning after his condemnation, he confessed the justice of his sentence to the two clergymen who attended him, and acknowledged that he had murdered Clarke. He told them, also, that he suspected Clarke of having an unlawful commerce with his wife; and that at the time of the murder he felt persuaded he was acting right, but since he had thought otherwise.

It was generally believed, as he promised to make a more ample confession on the day he was executed of every thing prior to the murder, that the whole would have been disclosed; but he put an end to any farther discovery, by an attempt upon his own life. When he was called from his bed to have his chains taken off, he refused, alleging that he was very weak. On moving him, it was found that he had inflicted a severe wound upon his arm, from which the blood was flowing copiously. He had concealed a razor in the condemned hold some time before. By proper and prompt applications he was brought to himself, and, though weak from loss of blood, conducted to Tyburn at York, where, being asked if he had anything to say, he answered, " No." He was then executed, and his body conveyed to Knaresborough Forest, and hung in chains, pursuant to his sentence.

Two papers were, after his execution, found upon the table in his cell. One was in the form of a letter addressed to a former companion, and was in the following terms :—

" MY DEAR FRIEND,—Before this reaches you, I shall be no more a living man in this world, though at present in perfect bodily health : but who can describe the horrors of mind which I suffer at this instant! Guilt—the guilt of blood shed without any provocation, without any cause but that of filthy lucre—pierces my conscience with wounds that give the most poignant pain ! 'Tis true, the consciousness of my horrid guilt has given me frequent interruptions in the midst of my business or pleasures ; but yet I have found means to stifle its clamours, and contrived a momentary remedy for the disturbance it gave me, by applying to the bottle or the bowl, or diversions, or company, or business ; sometimes one, sometimes the other, as opportunity offered : but now all these, and all other amusements, are at an end, and I am left forlorn, helpless, and destitute of every comfort ; for I have nothing now in view but the certain destruction both of my soul and body.　My conscience will now no longer suffer itself to be hoodwinked or browbeat ; it has now got the mastery ; it is my accuser, judge, and executioner ; and the sentence it pronounceth against me is more dreadful than that I heard from the bench, which only condemned my body to the pains of death, which are soon over ; but conscience tells me plainly that she will summon me before another tribunal, where I shall have neither power nor means to stifle the evidence she will there bring against me ; and that the sentence which will then be pronounced will not only be irreversible, but will condemn my soul to torments that will know no end.

" Oh ! had I but hearkened to the advice which dear-bought experience has enabled me to give, I should not now have been plunged into that dreadful gulf of despair which I find it impossible to extricate myself from ; and therefore my soul is filled with horror inconceivable.　I see both God and man my enemies, and in a few hours shall be exposed a public spectacle for the world to gaze at.　Can you conceive any condition more horrible than mine?　O, no ! it cannot be ! I am determined, therefore, to put a short end to trouble I am no longer able to bear, and prevent the executioner, by doing his business with my own hand, and shall by this means at least prevent the shame and disgrace of a public exposure, and leave the care of my soul in the hands of Eternal Mercy. Wishing you all health, happiness, and prosperity, I am, to the last moment of my life, yours, with the sincerest regard, EUGENE ARAM."

WHITNEY ROBBING OLD HULL THE MISER

EDWARD WHITNEY,

EXECUTED FOR HIGHWAY ROBBERY.

THIS notorious malefactor was born at Stevenage in Hertfordshire, and served an apprenticeship to a butcher. He served his time, it appears, very faithfully; but he was not long his own master before he took to the irregular courses that brought destruction upon him, and branded his name with infamy.

He often confessed that he was disappointed in his first attempt to steal. He and his master went to Romford to purchase calves; and there was an excellent one that they would fain have had in their possession, but the owner and they could not agree about the price. As the owner of the calf kept an alehouse, they went in to taste his ale. While they were enjoying themselves, but lamenting the loss of the calf, Whitney whispered to his master, that it would be foolish in them to give money for the calf, when they might have it for nothing. The good butcher understood his meaning, and entered into his plan.

Unfortunately for their scheme, a fellow who travelled the country with a bear, had put up at the house where the butchers were drinking. The landlord had no place to put the bear in, without removing the calf to another house, which was accordingly done. The butchers continued carousing until it was dark; then having cheerfully paid their reckoning, in the hope that the calf would reimburse them, they left the house, and lurked about the fields until all was quiet. Approaching the place where they had seen the calf put up, Whitney was sent in to fetch it out.

The bear was resting her wearied limbs, when Whitney took hold of her, and was astonished to find the hair of the calf had suddenly grown to such a length. Bruin rose upon all-fours, opining, we suppose, that it was her master about to show her in his usual manner. But she no sooner discovered that it was a stranger who thus rudely assailed her, than she seized him with her fore-paws, and hugged him most lovingly to her bosom. The master, surprised that he was so long in bringing out the calf, began to chide him for his delay. Whitney cried out, that he could not get away himself, and he believed that the devil had hold of him. " If it is the old boy," replied the master, " bring him out, as I should like to see what kind of an animal he is." His importunities at length brought the butcher to his assistance, when they discovered their mistake, and with no small difficulty disentangled Whitney from the fraternal hug of Bruin; which having done, they proceeded home without their prey, determined to attempt stealing calves no more.

Our young adventurer now abandoned the business of buying and slaying animals, and took the George Inn, at Cheshunt. In order to make the most of it, he entertained all sorts of people, whether good or bad; but disappointment attended him in this as well as his former employment, and he was constrained to shut up his house.

He now went up to London, where he lived in the most irregular manner, giving himself wholly up to villainy. After practising the usual tricks of sharpers for some time, he at length took to the highway. He was one day standing at the door of a mercer's shop, when two young ladies, apparently of fashion, passed by, elegantly dressed, one of whom inquired if he had any silks of the newest patterns. Whitney replied, that he had none at present, but should soon have some home from the weaver. He then requested their address, that the goods, when they came to hand, might be sent to them. They were rather at a loss; one of them, however, answered, that they were only lately come to town, and did not remember the name of their street. They added, that, as it was not far off, if he would accompany them, they would show him their habitation.

This was just what he wanted; therefore, going into the shop, as if to leave orders, he hastened along with the ladies—they supposing he was the silk-mercer; and he, that they were actually ladies of fortune, whom he might have an opportunity of robbing, either presently or at some future period. Upon their arrival he was introduced into an elegant parlour, and a collation placed upon the table, with some excellent wine, of which he was requested to partake. He was soon left alone with one of the ladies, and discovering his mistake, was resolved to have some more sport at the expense of a silk-mercer, since he had been taken for one.

Whitney went to a mercer in the neighbourhood, and mentioning the name of a lady of quality said he had been sent by her to request that he would send one of his men with several pieces of his best silks, as the lady wanted to purchase some. The shopkeeper readily consented, and one of the apprentices was dispatched along with him. To deceive the young man, and render it impossible for him to discover the place where he should stop, he conducted him through several streets and lanes, until he at last halted at a house which had an entry into another street. Here he took the parcel, and desired the lad to stand at the door while he went in to show the ladies the silks. Taking the parcel, he went in, and inquired for some person who he was certain was not there. He then requested liberty to pass through to the next street, which would shorten his way. This being granted, he left the mercer's man to wait his return.

Having thus fortunately succeeded, and being able to fulfil his promise of giving one of the ladies a silk dress, he hastened to their abode, where they divided the spoil; and for some days he remained there, indulging in all manner of riot and excess.

He resolved, however, that nobody but himself should enjoy the fruits of his industry ; and since he could not have the profit of his cheat, it would be a piece of honesty in him, he thought, to restore the mercer's goods again. To this end he wrote a letter, informing the shopkeeper where the women lived ; who, getting a warrant and a constable, went and found the silks in their custody. They were frightened enough, it may well be supposed, to find themselves apprehended for having in their possession what they thought had been given by the right owner. But all their excuses were in vain; they were hurried before a magistrate, and committed to Tothill-fields Bridewell.

Whitney one day met a gentleman on Bagshot Heath, whom he commanded to stand and deliver ; on which the other remarked, " It is well you spoke first, sir, for I was about to make a similar demand." " Why then, you are a gentleman thief ?" cried Whitney. " Yes," said the stranger, " but I have had very bad success to-day, for I have been riding up and down all this morning without meeting with any prize." Whitney, upon this, wished him better luck, and took his leave.

At night Whitney and this gentleman happened to put up at the same inn, when the latter narrated to some other travellers by what a stratagem he had escaped being robbed on the road. Whitney had so altered his habit and speech, that the gentleman did not know him again ; so that he heard all the story without being taken notice of. Among other things, he overheard him tell one of the company that he had saved £100 by his contrivance. The person to whom he whispered this was going the same way the next morning, and said he had also a considerable sum about him, and, if he pleased, should be glad to travel with him for security. This was agreed on ; and when morning came, our travellers set out, and Whitney followed about a quarter of an hour after. At a convenient place Whitney having got before them, bid them stand ; and the gentleman whom he had met before not knowing him (he having disguised himself after another manner), briskly cried out, " We were just going to say the same to you, sir." " Were you so ?" quoth Whitney ; " and are you of my profession then ?" " Yes," said they both. " If you are," replied Whitney, " I suppose you remember the old proverb, ' Two of a trade can never agree ;' so that you mustn't expect any favour on that score. But, to be plain with you, gentlemen, I know you very well, and must have your hundred pounds, sir,—and

your considerable sum," turning first to one, and then to the other,—
" otherwise I shall be so bold as to send a brace of bullets through each of
your heads.   You, Monsieur Highwayman, should have kept your
secret a little longer, and not have boasted so soon of having outwitted
a thief.   There is now nothing for you but to deliver or die !"   These
words put them in a sad consternation : they were very unwilling to lose
their money, but more unwilling to lose their lives ; of two evils, therefore, they preferred the least.   The one produced his hundred pounds
first, and then the other his considerable sum, which was much more.

At another time he met with an old miser, named Hull, on Hounslow
Heath.   He could hardly have met with a wretch more in love with
money, and consequently more unwilling to part with it.   The old fellow trembled at every joint, and using the most piteous tones and
humiliating complaints, said, he was a very poor man and had a very
large family, and he would be hard-hearted indeed who would take his
money.   He added, besides, a great deal concerning the illegality of
such an action, and how dangerous it was to pursue such evil courses.
Whitney who knew him well, cried out in a violent passion, " Sir, you
pretend to teach morality to an honester man than yourself.   Is it not
more generous to take a man's money from him bravely, than to grind
him to death by exacting eight or ten per cent under cover of serving
him ?   You make a prey of all mankind : necessity in an honest man is
often the means of his falling into your hands, and you are sure to be the
means of undoing him.   I am a man of more honour than to show any
compassion to one whom I esteem an enemy to the whole species.   For
once, at least, I shall oblige you to lend me what you have without
interest or bond, so make no words !"   Old Hull, upon this, reluctantly
pulled out eighteen pounds, telling him at the same time that he should
some day see him ride up Holborn Hill backwards.   Whitney was
retiring when he heard these words, but, returning, he drew Hull off his
horse, and putting him on again with his face toward the tail, and tying
his legs, " Now," said he, " you old rogue, let's see what figure a man
makes when he rides backwards, and let me have the pleasure at least
of seeing you first in that posture ;" so giving the horse a whip, the
animal proceeded at a desperate pace until it came to Hounslow Town,
where the people untied him, after they had enjoyed themselves at
his expence.

Our dexterous butcher came once to Doncaster, in Yorkshire, where
he put up at the Red Lion Inn, and made a very great figure, having a
pretty round sum in his possession.   While he resided there, he was informed that the landlord of the house was reputed rich ; but that he
was withal so covetous, that he would do nothing to help a relation or
neighbour in distress ; and so very sharp in his business, that it was next to
impossible for any one to impose on him in the least particular.   Nothing
could be so pleasing to such a man as Whitney as outwitting one who
was esteemed able to outwit all the world ; in consequence of which he
resolved to attempt this master-stroke of invention, as he supposed it
must be, if he succeeded.   He therefore gave out, that he had a good
estate, that he travelled about the country merely for his pleasure, and

that he had his money remitted to him as his rents came in; continuing to pay for every thing he had, till, supposing his host to be sufficiently satisfied that he was really what he pretended, he one day took an opportunity of telling him that his money ran short, till he could have returns. "O, my dear sir," says my landlord, "you need not give yourself the least uneasiness about such an affair as this. Every thing I have is at your service, and I shall think myself honoured if you will please to make use of me as a friend." Whitney returned the compliment with many thanks and expressions of esteem, eating and drinking from day to day at the good man's table, his horse also all the while being fed plentifully with the best corn and hay. The better to colour the matter, too, and to prove that he really came out of curiosity to see the country, there was seldom a day passed but that he rode out to some of the neighbouring villages, sometimes getting the innkeeper, sometimes other gentlemen in the town, to bear him company, they being all proud of the honour. It happened, that while he remained there, there was a fair, according to the annual custom. Upon the fair-day, in the morning, a small box, carefully sealed, and very weighty, came directed to him. He opened it, and took out a letter, which he read; and then locked it up, and gave it to his landlady, desiring her to keep it in her custody for the present, because it would be safer than in his own hands; and ordering the landlord, at the same time, to write out his bill, that he might pay him next morning. As soon as he had done this, he went out to the fair. In the afternoon he returned in a great hurry, and desired his horse might be dressed and saddled, he having a mind to show him in the fair, and, if he could, to exchange him for one which he had seen, and which he thought was the finest he had ever fixed his eyes on. "I will have him," says he, "if possible, whether the owner will buy mine or no, and though he cost me forty guineas." He then asked for his landlady, that he might have his box, but was told she was gone to the fair; upon which he swore like a madman, and said he supposed she had locked up what he gave her, and taken the keys with her. "If she has," said he, "I had rather have given ten guineas; for I have no money at all, but what is in your possession." Inquiry was made, and it was found to be as he said, which put him into a still greater passion, though it was what he desired, and even expected, the whole comedy having been invented for the sake of this single scene. The landlord quickly had notice of our gentleman's anger, and the occasion of it; upon which he repairs to him, and begs him to be easy, offering to lend him the sum he wanted till his wife came home. Whitney seemed to resent it highly, that he must be obliged to borrow money when he had got so much of his own. However, as there was no other way, he condescended, with much reluctance, to accept the proposal, adding, that he desired an account of all he was indebted as soon as possible, for it was not his custom to run hands over head! Having received forty guineas, the sum he pretended to want, he mounts his horse, and rides towards the fair; but, instead of dealing there for another horse, he spurred through the crowd as fast as he could conveniently, and made the best of his way to London. At night the people of the inn sat up very late for his coming home, nor did they suspect any thing the first or second night, when they saw nothing of him, he having been out before a day or two together in his progress round the country, which they concluded was the case now. But at the end of two or three days the landlord was a little uneasy; and after he had waited a week to no purpose, he resolved to break open the box, in order to examine it. With this view he goes to the magistrate of the place, procures his warrant for so doing, and a constable, with proper witnesses to be present. We need not tell the reader he was cheated, for every one will naturally conclude so; nor need we say, he was ready to hang himself, when he found only sand and stones covered over: his character may give an idea of his temper at this time. But Whitney did not care for his landlord's passion, so long as he got off safe with the money.

This was, however, the last of his adventures in the country; for, not long after his arrival in town, he was apprehended in Whitefriars, upon the information of a notorious woman called Mother Cozens, who kept a house of ill fame in Milford Lane, over against St. Clement's Church. The magistrate who took the information, committed him to Newgate, where he remained till the next sessions at the Old Bailey.

After his conviction, Sir Samuel Lawrence, recorder of London, made an excellent speech before he passed sentence of death on him and the other malefactors, setting forth the nature of their several offences in very strong expressions, and addressing himself to Whitney in particular, whom he exhorted to a sincere repentance, as it was impossible for him to hope for any reprieve after such a course of villainies as he had practised; vindicating the justice of the law, and urging the certainty of a Providence, which pursues such as him, and at last takes vengeance on them for their crimes.

On Wednesday, the 19th of December, 1694, Whitney was carried to the place of execution, at Porter's Block, near Smithfield; where, having spent a few moments in private devotion, he was turned off, being about thirty-four years of age.

ROBERT AND DANIEL PERREAU,

EXECUTED FOR FORGERY.

THE circumstances attending the case of these prisoners, who were twin brothers, and so much alike that it was with difficulty they could be distinguished apart, are of a very extraordinary nature. Robert Perreau was a surgeon of some eminence, in Golden Square, where he possessed a good practice; while his brother kept an elegant mansion in Harley Street, Cavendish Square, living with a Mrs. Margaret Caroline Rudd, who passed as his wife.

At the sessions held at the Old Bailey in June 1775, Robert Perreau was indicted for forging a bond for the payment of £7500 in the name of William Adair, Esq. (a great government contractor), and also for feloniously uttering and publishing the said bond, knowing it to be forged, with intent to defraud Messrs. Robert and Henry Drummond, bankers.

From the evidence which was adduced it appeared, that on the 10th of March, 1775, the prisoner (Robert Perreau), whose character up to that time had been considered unimpeachable, went to the house of Messrs. Drummond, and seeing Mr. Henry Drummond, one of the partners, said, that he had been making purchase of an estate in Norfolk or Suffolk, for which he was to give £12,000, but that he had not sufficient cash to pay the whole purchase-money; that he had a bond, however, which Mr. Adair had given to his brother Daniel, for £7500, upon which he desired to raise a sum of £5000, out of which he was willing to pay £1400, which he had already borrowed of the firm.

Mr. Drummond, on the production of the bond, had no sooner looked at the signature than he doubted its authenticity, and very politely asked the prisoner if he had seen Mr. Adair sign it. The latter said he had not, but that he had no doubt it was authentic, from the nature of the connexion that subsisted between Mrs. Rudd (who was known to live with Daniel) and that gentleman; a suggestion having previously been thrown out that she was his natural daughter. Mr. Drummond, however, declined advancing any money without the sanction of his brother, and desired Perreau to leave the bond, saying, that it should either be returned on the next day or the money produced. The prisoner made no scruple to obey this suggestion, and retired, promising to call again the next day.

In the interim Mr. Drummond examined the bond with greater attention; and Mr. Stephens, secretary to the Admiralty, happening to call, his opinion was demanded, when, comparing the signature to the bond with letters which he had lately received from Mr. Adair, he was firmly convinced that it was forged. When Perreau came on the following day, Mr. Drummond spoke more freely than he had done before, and told him that he imagined he had been imposed on; but begged, that, to remove all doubt, he would go with him to Mr. Adair, and get that gentleman to acknowledge the validity of the bond, on which the money would be advanced. This was immediately acceded to; and on Mr. Adair seeing the document, he at once declared that the signature was a forgery. The prisoner smiled incredulously, and said that he jested; but Mr. Adair remarked that it was no jesting matter, and that it lay on him to clear up the affair. On this he went away, requesting to have the bond, in order to make the necessary inquiries—a request which was refused; and persons being set to watch him, it was found that, immediately on his arrival at his house, he and his brother and Mrs. Rudd got into a coach, carrying with them all the valuables which they could collect, with a design to make their escape. They were, however, stopped, and taken into custody; and being conveyed to Sir John Fielding, at Bow-street, they there underwent an examination, and upon the evidence adduced were committed to prison. Other charges were subsequently brought against them by Sir Thomas Frankland, from whom they had obtained two sums of £5000 and £4000 on similar forged bonds, as well as £4000, which they had paid when the amount became due; and by Dr. Brooke, who alleged that they had obtained from him £1500, in bonds of the Ayr bank, upon the security of a forged bond for £2100. Mrs. Rudd was then admitted as evidence for the crown. Her deposition was, that she was the daughter of a nobleman in Scotland; that, when young, she married an officer in the army named Rudd, against the consent of her friends; that her fortune was considerable; that, on a disagreement with her husband, they resolved to part; that she made a reserve of money, jewels, and effects, to the amount of £13,000, all of which she gave to Daniel Perreau, whom she said she loved with the tenderness of a wife; that she had three children by him; that he had returned her kindness in every respect till lately, when, having been unfortunate in gaming, he had become uneasy, peevish, and much altered to her; that he cruelly constrained her to sign the bond now in question, by holding a knife to her throat, and swearing that he would murder her if she did not comply; that, being struck with remorse, she had acquainted Mr. Adair with what she had done; and that she was now willing to declare every transaction with which she was acquainted, whenever she should be called upon by law so to do.

Upon the cross-examination of Mr. Drummond, however, he swore that Mrs. Rudd, on being first apprehended, took the whole on herself, and acknowledged that she had forged the bonds; that she begged them " for God's sake to have mercy on an innocent man," and that she said no injury was intended to any person, and that all would be paid; and that she acknowledged delivering the bond to the prisoner. They then entertained an opinion that the prisoner was her dupe; and Mr. Robert Drummond having expressed a notion that she could not have forged a handwriting so dissimilar from that of a woman as Mr. Adair's, she immediately, in order to satisfy them of the truth of what she said, wrote the name " William Adair " on a paper exactly like the signature which appeared attached to the bond.

Mr. Watson, a money-scrivener, also deposed, that he had filled up the bonds at the desire of one of the brothers, and in pursuance of instructions received from him; but he hesitated to fix on either, on account of their great personal resemblance; and being pressed to make a positive declaration, he fixed on Daniel as his employer.

The case of the prosecution being concluded, the prisoner entered upon his defence. In a long and ingenious speech, which he addressed to the jury, he strove hard to prove that he was the victim of the artifices of Mrs. Rudd. He said, that she was constantly conversing about the influence she had over Mr. Adair; that Mr. Adair had, by his interest with the king, obtained the promise of a baronetage for Daniel Perreau, and was about procuring him a seat in parliament; and that Mr. Adair had promised to open a bank, and take the brothers Perreau into partnership with him. That the prisoner received many letters signed "William Adair," which he had no doubt came from that gentleman, in which were promises of giving them a considerable part of his fortune during his life; and that he was to allow Daniel Perreau £2400 a year for his household expenses, and £600 a year for Mrs. Rudd's pin-money. That Mr. Daniel Perreau purchased a house in Harley-street for £4000, which money Mr William Adair was to give them. That when Daniel Perreau was pressed by the person of whom he bought the house for the money, the prisoner understood that they applied to Mr. William Adair, and that his answer was, that he had lent the king £70,000, and had purchased a house in Pall Mall at £7000, in which to carry on the banking business, and therefore could not spare the £4000 at that time. He declared that all attempts at personal communication with Mr. Adair was strenuously opposed by Mrs. Rudd as being likely to destroy the effect of her exertions on his behalf; and contended that his conduct throughout the whole transaction with Mr. Drummond showed that he was innocent of any guilty intention, and that he firmly believed that he was acting honestly and justly. He then called the following witnesses.

George Kinder deposed that Mrs. Perreau (the only name by which he knew Mrs. Rudd) told him, "that she was a near relation of Mr. James Adair; that he looked upon her as his child, had promised to make her fortune, and with that view had recommended her to Mr. William Adair, a near relation and intimate friend of his, who had promised to set her husband and the prisoner up in the banking business." He also deposed, that she said that Mr. Daniel Perreau was to be made a baronet, and described how she would act when she became a lady. The witness further deposed that Mrs. Rudd, often pretended that Mr. William Adair had called to see her, but that he never had seen that gentleman on any visit.

John Moody, a livery-servant of Daniel Perreau, deposed, that his mistress wrote two very different hands; in one of which she wrote letters to his master as from Mr. William Adair, and in the other the ordinary business of the family. That the letters written in the name of William Adair were pretended to have been left in his master's absence; that his mistress ordered him to give them to his master, and pretend that Mr. Adair had been with his mistress for a longer or shorter time, as circumstances required. This witness likewise proved that the hand at the bottom of the bond and that of his mistress's fictitious writing were precisely the same; that she used different pens, ink, and paper, in writing her common and fictitious letters; and that she sometimes gave the witness half-a-crown when he had delivered a letter to her satisfaction. He said, he had seen her go two or three times to Mr. J. Adair's, but never to William's; and that Mr. J. Adair once visited his mistress on her lying-in.

Susannah Perreau (the prisoner's sister) deposed to her having seen a note delivered to Daniel Perreau by Mrs. Rudd for £19,000, drawn as by William Adair on Mr. Croft, the banker, in favour of Daniel Perreau.

Elizabeth Perkins swore, that a week before the forgery was discovered her mistress gave her a letter to bring back to her in a quarter of an hour, and say it was brought by Mr. Coverley, who had been servant to Daniel Perreau; that she gave her mistress this letter, and her master instantly broke the seal.

Daniel Perreau swore, that the purport of this letter was, " that Mr. Adair desired her to apply to his brother, the prisoner, to procure him £5000 upon his (Adair's) bond, in the same manner as he had done before; that Mr. Adair was unwilling to have it appear that the money was raised for him, and therefore desired him to have the bond lodged with some confidential friend, who would not require an assignment of it; that his brother, on being made acquainted with his request, showed a vast deal of reluctance, and said it was very unpleasant work; but undertook it with a view of obliging Mr. William Adair.

The counsel for the prosecution demanding " if he did not disclaim all knowledge of the affair before Mr. Adair," he said, he denied ever having seen the bond before, nor had he a perfect knowledge of it till he saw it in the hands of Mr. Adair.

John Leigh, clerk to Sir John Fielding, swore to the prisoner's coming voluntarily to the office before his apprehension, and giving information that a forgery had been committed. Mr. Leigh was asked if Mrs. Rudd " ever charged the prisoner with any knowledge of the transaction till the justices were hearing evidence to prove her confession of the fact;" and he answered, that he did not recollect that circumstance, but that on her first examination she did not accuse the prisoner.

Mr. Perreau now called several persons of rank to his character. Lady Lyttleton being asked if she thought him capable of such a crime answered, that she " supposed she could have done it as soon herself. Sir John Moore, Sir John Chapman, General Rebow, Captain Ellis, Captain Burgoyne, and other gentlemen, spoke most highly to the character of the prisoner. The jury, however, found him guilty.

It will be unnecessary now to give anything more than a succinct account of the trial of Daniel Perreau, which immediately followed that of his brother. He was indicted for forging and counterfeiting a bond, in the name of William Adair, for £3300, to defraud the said William Adair, and for uttering the same, knowing it to be forged, to defraud Thomas Brooke, doctor of physic. Mr. Scrooke Ogilvie, clerk to Mr. William Adair, proved the forgery; and Dr. Brooke swore to the uttering of the bond.

The defence set up by the prisoner was, that Mrs. Rudd had given the bond to him as a true one; and he asserted in the most solemn manner, that he had no intention to defraud any man. Like his brother, he called several witnesses to show the artifices of which Mrs. Rudd had been guilty; and many persons proved the great respectability of his character.

The jury, however, returned a verdict of Guilty, and both prisoners were sentenced to death; but the execution did not take place until January 1776, in consequence of the proceedings which were subsequently taken against Mrs. Rudd.

After conviction the behaviour of the brothers was, in every respect, proper for their unhappy situation. Great interest was made to obtain a pardon for them, particularly for Robert, in whose favour seventy-eight bankers and merchants of London signed a petition to the king; the newspapers were filled with paragraphs, evidently written by disinterested persons, in favour of men whom they thought dupes to the designs of an artful woman: but all was of no avail.

On the day of execution the brothers were favoured with a mourning-coach, in which to be conveyed to the scaffold; and their conduct throughout was of the most exemplary description. After the customary devotions were concluded, they crossed hands, and joining the four together, in that manner were launched into eternity. They had not hung more than half a minute when their hands dropped asunder, and they appeared to die without pain.

Each of them delivered a paper to the Ordinary of Newgate, which asserted their innocence, ascribing the blame of the whole transaction to the artifices of Mrs. Rudd; and, indeed, thousands of people gave credit to their assertions, and many thought Robert wholly innocent.

They were executed at Tyburn on the 17th of January, 1776.

On the Sunday following, the bodies were carried from the house of Robert, in Golden-square, and, after the usual solemnities, deposited in the vault of St. Martin's Church. A mob of thirty thousand persons attended the execution, and an equal number appeared at the funeral; but nothing occurred to disturb the solemnity of either scene.

On the 8th December, 1775, Mrs. Margaret Caroline Rudd was arraigned on an indictment for feloniously forging a bond purporting to be signed by William Adair, and feloniously uttering and publishing the same.

The principal witnesses were the wife of Robert Perreau, and John Moody, the servant to Daniel Perreau. The first endeavoured to prove that the bond was published, the latter that it was forged. Sir Thomas Frankland proved having lent money on it.

The prisoner, on being called on for her defence, in a short speech declared that she was innocent, and concluded with leaving her case in the hands of the jury, who almost immediately declared her Not guilty.

As soon as the verdict was returned, she quitted the court, and retired to the house of a friend at the west end of the town.

PETER LE MAITRE,

CONVICTED OF ROBBING THE ASHMOLEAN MUSEUM AT OXFORD.

WHEN Lord Thurlow was chancellor of England, some villains broke into his house in Great Ormond-street, and stole the great seal of England, which was never recovered, nor were the thieves known. We have heard also of a valuable diamond being stolen from the late Duke of Cumberland, when, pressing into the theatre in the Haymarket to see the bubble of the bottle conjuror. It is also a fact, that the Duke of Beaufort was robbed of his diamond order of St. George as he went to Court on a royal birthday. But we have now to tell of a museum being plundered of its most curious medals.

Peter Le Maitre, the thief, was a French teacher at Oxford; and, being supposed to be a man of industry and good morals, he was indulged with free admission to the Ashmolean Museum. Thither he frequently went, and appeared very studious over the rare books and other valuable articles there deposited. He was frequently left alone to his researches. At one of such times he stole two medals; at another, he secreted himself until the doors were locked for the night, and when all had retired he came from his lurking-place, broke open the cabinet where the medals were locked up, and possessed himself of its contents; he then wrenched a bar from the window, and made his escape unsuspected.

The college was thrown into the utmost consternation on finding their Museum thus plundered. Several persons were suspected, but least of all Le Maitre, until it was discovered that he had privately left the city in a post-chaise and four, and that he had pledged two of the stolen medals to pay the post-boys. This left little doubt that he was the ungrateful thief. He was advertised and described, and by this means apprehended in Ireland.

He was conveyed back to Oxford, in order to take his trial; and it appeared that two of the stolen medals vere found in a bureau in his lodgings, of which he had the use; and two more were traced to the persons to whom he had sold them.

He had little to offer in extenuation of his crime, and on the clearest evidence he was found guilty, on the 7th March, 1777. He paid the penalty of his offence by five years' hard labour at ballast-heaving on the river Thames.

Whether the ungrateful depredation of Le Maitre stimulated others to the commission of similar crimes we know not, but it is certain that soon afterwards Magdalen College Chapel, Oxford, was broken open by two thieves, who stole from the altar a pair of large silver candlesticks and a silver dish, with which they escaped undetected.

LORD FERRERS SHOOTING HIS STEWARD

LAURENCE EARL FERRERS,

EXECUTED FOR MURDER.

LAURENCE, Earl Ferrers, was a man of singular and most unhappy disposition. Descended of an ancient and noble family, he was doomed to expiate a crime, of which he had been guilty, at Tyburn.

It would appear that the royal blood of the Plantagenets flowed in his veins. The earl gained his title in the following manner. The second baronet of the family, Sir Henry Shirley, married a daughter of the celebrated Earl of Essex, who was beheaded in the reign of Queen Elizabeth; and his son, Sir Robert Shirley, died in the Tower, where he was confined during the Protectorate, for his attachment to the cause of the Stuarts. Upon the Restoration, the second son of Sir Robert succeeded to the title and estates; and Charles, anxious to cement the bonds which attached his friends to him, summoned him to the Upper House of Parliament by the title of Lord Ferrers of Chartley, as the descendant of one of the co-heiresses of the Earl of Essex; the title, which had existed since the reign of Edward III., having been in abeyance since the death of that unfortunate nobleman. In the year 1711, Robert Lord Ferrers was created by Queen Anne Viscount Tamworth and Earl Ferrers. It appears that although the estates of the family were very great, they were vastly diminished by the provision which the Earl thought proper to make for his numerous progeny, consisting of fifteen sons and twelve daughters, born to him by his two wives. At the death of the first earl, his title descended to his second son; but he dying without issue, it went successively to the ninth son, who was childless, and to the tenth, who was the father of Laurence, the subject of the present sketch.

This nobleman was united, in the year 1752, to the youngest daughter of Sir William Meredith. Although his general conduct when sober was not such as to be remarkable, yet his faculties were so much impaired by drink, that when under the influence of intoxication he acted with all the wildness and brutality of a madman. For a time his wife perceived nothing which induced her to repent the step she had taken in being united to him; but he subsequently behaved to her with such unwarrantable cruelty, that she was compelled to quit his protection, and, rejoining her father's family, to apply to Parliament for redress. An act was in consequence passed, allowing her a separate maintenance, to be raised out of her husband's estate; and trustees being appointed, the unfortunate Mr. Johnson (who afterwards fell a sacrifice to the ungovernable passions of Lord Ferrers), having been bred up in the family from his youth, and being distinguished for the regular manner in which he kept his accounts, and his fidelity as a steward, was proposed as receiver of the rents for her use. He at first declined the office; but subsequently, at the desire of the Earl himself, he consented to act, and continued in this employment for a considerable time.

His lordship at this time lived at Stanton, a seat about two miles from Ashby de la Zouch, in Leicestershire; and his family consisted of Mrs. Clifford, a lady who lived with him, and her four natural daughters, besides five men-servants, exclusive of an old man and a boy, and three maids.

Mr. Johnson lived at the house belonging to a farm which he held under his lordship, called the Lount, about half a mile distant from Stanton. It appears that it was his custom to visit his noble master occasionally, to settle the accounts which were placed under his care; but his lordship gradually conceived a dislike for him, grounded upon the prejudice raised in his mind on account of his being the receiver of the countess's portion, and charged him with having combined with the trustees to prevent his receiving a coal contract. From this time he spoke of him in opprobrious terms, and said he had conspired with his enemies to injure him, and that he was a villain; and with these sentiments he gave him warning to quit an advantageous farm which he held under his lordship. Finding, however, that the trustees under the act of separation had already granted him a lease of it, it having been promised to him by the earl or his relations, he was disappointed, and probably from that time he meditated a more cruel revenge.

The circumstances immediately attending the transaction, which terminated in the death of Johnson, were as follow:—

On Sunday the 13th of January, 1760, my lord went to the Lount, and, after some discourse with Mr. Johnson, ordered him to come to him at Stanton on the Friday following, the 18th, at three o'clock in the afternoon. His lordship's usual dinner-hour was two o'clock; and soon after that meal. On the Friday, he went to Mrs. Clifford, who was in the still-house, and desired her to take the children for a walk. She accordingly prepared herself and her daughters, and with the permission of the earl went to her father's, at a short distance, being directed to return at half-past five. The men-servants were next dispatched on errands by their master, who was thus left in the house with the three females only. In a short time afterwards Mr. Johnson came according to his appointment, and was admitted by one of the maid-servants, named Elizabeth Burgeland. He proceeded at once to his lordship's apartment, but was desired to wait in the still-house; and then, after the expiration of about ten minutes, the earl calling him into his own room, went in with him and locked the door. Being thus together, the earl required him first to settle an account; and then charging him with the villainy which he attributed to him, ordered him to kneel down. The unfortunate man went down on one knee; upon which the earl, in a tone of voice loud enough to be heard by the maid-servants without, cried, " Down on your other knee; declare that you have acted against Lord Ferrers; your time is come—you must die:" and then suddenly drawing a pistol from his pocket, which was loaded, he presented it, and immediately fired. The ball entered the body of the unfortunate man ; but he rose up, and entreated that no farther violence might be done him; and the female servants at that time coming to the door, being alarmed by the report, his lordship quitted the room. A messenger was immediately despatched for Mr. Kirkland, a surgeon, who lived at Ashby de la Zouch ; and Johnson being put to bed, his lordship went to him, and asked him how he felt? He answered that he was dying, and desired that his family might be sent for. Miss Johnson soon after arrived, and Lord Ferrers immediately followed her into the room where her father lay. He then pulled down the clothes, and applied a pledget, dipped in arquebusade water, to the wound, and soon after left him.

From this time it appears that his lordship applied himself to his favourite amusement, drinking, until he became exceedingly violent (for at the time of the commission of the murder he is reported to have been sober) ; and on the arrival of Mr. Kirkland he told him that he had shot Johnson, but believed he was more frightened than hurt ; that he had intended to shoot him dead, for that he was a villain and deserved to die ; " but, " said he, " now I have spared his life, I desire you would do what you can for him." His lordship at the same time desired that he would not suffer him to be seized, and declared, that if any one should attempt it, he would shoot him. Mr. Kirkland, who wisely determined to say whatever might keep Lord Ferrers from any further outrage, told him, that he should not be seized, and directly went to the wounded man.

The patient complained of a violent pain in his bowels ; and Mr. Kirkland preparing to search the wound, my lord informed him of the direction of it, by showing him how he held the pistol when he fired it. Mr. Kirkland found the ball had lodged in the body; at which his lordship expressed great surprise, declaring he had tried the pistol a few days before, and that it then carried a ball through a deal board near an inch and a half thick. Mr. Kirkland then went down stairs to prepare some dressings, and my lord soon after left the room. From this time, in proportion as the liquor which he continued to drink took effect, his passions became more tumultuous, and the transient fit of compassion, mixed with fear for himself, which had excited him, gave way to starts of rage and the predominance of malice. He went up into the room where Johnson was dying, and pulled him by the wig, calling him villain, and threatening to shoot him through the head; and, the last time he went to him, he was with great difficulty prevented from tearing the clothes off the bed, that he might strike him.

A proposal was made to him in the evening by Mrs. Clifford, that Mr. Johnson should be removed to his own house; but he replied, " He shall not be removed; I will keep him here to plague the villain." He afterwards spoke to Miss Johnson about her father, and told her that if he died, he would take care of her and of the family, provided they did not prosecute.

When his lordship went to bed, which was between eleven and twelve, he told Mr. Kirkland that he knew he could, if he would, set the affair in such a light as to prevent his being seized, desiring that he might see him before he went away in the morning, and declaring that he would rise at any hour.

Mr. Kirkland, however, was very solicitous to get Mr. Johnson removed; and, as soon as the earl was gone, he set about carrying his object into effect. He in consequence went to Lount, and having fitted up an easy chair with poles, by way of a sedan, and procured a guard, he returned about two o'clock, and carried Mr. Johnson to his house, where he expired about nine o'clock on the following morning.

The neighbours now began to take measures to secure the murderer, and a few of them having armed themselves, set out for Stanton. As they entered the yard, they saw his lordship, partly undressed, going towards the stable, as if to take out a horse. One of them, named Springthorpe, then advancing towards his lordship with a pistol in his hand, required him to surrender; but the latter putting his hand towards his pocket, his assailant, imagining that he was feeling for some weapon of offence, stopped short and allowed him to escape into the house. A great concourse of people by this time had come to the spot, and they cried out loudly that the earl should come forth. Two hours elapsed, however, before anything was seen of him, and then he came to the garret window, and called out, " How is Johnson?" He was answered that he was dead; but he said it was a lie, and desired that the people should disperse; afterwards he gave orders that they should be let in and be furnished with victuals and drink; and finally he went away from the window swearing that no man should take him. The mob still remained on the spot; and in about two hours the earl was descried by a collier, named Curtis, walking on the bowling-green, armed with a blunderbuss, a brace of pistols, and a dagger. Curtis, however, so far from being intimidated by his bold appearance, walked up to him; and his lordship, struck with the resolution he displayed, immediately surrendered himself, and gave up his arms, but directly afterwards declared that he had killed the villain, and gloried in the act. He was instantly conveyed in custody to a public-house at Ashby, kept by a man named Kinsey; and a coroner's jury having brought in a verdict of wilful murder against him, he was on the following Monday committed to the custody of the keeper of the jail at Leicester. Being entitled, however, by his rank to be tried before his peers, he was in about a fortnight afterwards conveyed to London, in his landau, drawn by six horses, under a strong guard; and being carried before the House of Lords, he was committed to the custody of the Black Rod, and ordered to the Tower, where he arrived at about six o'clock in the evening of the 14th February. He is reported to have behaved, during the whole journey and at his commitment, with great calmness and propriety. He was confined in the Round Tower, near the drawbridge; two wardens were constantly in the room with him, and one at the door; two sentinels were posted at the bottom of the stairs, and one upon the drawbridge, with their bayonets fixed; and from this time the gates were ordered to be shut an hour sooner than usual.

During his confinement he was moderate both in eating and drinking; his breakfast was a half-pint basin of tea, with a small spoonful of brandy in it, and a muffin; with his dinner he generally drank a pint of wine and a pint of water, and another pint of each with his supper. In general his behaviour was decent and quiet, except that he would sometimes suddenly start, tear open his waistcoat, and use other gestures, which showed that his mind was disturbed.

Mrs. Clifford and the four young ladies, who had come up with him from Leicestershire, took a lodging in Tower-street, and for some time a servant was continually passing with letters between them: but afterwards this correspondence was permitted only once a day.

Mrs. Clifford came three times to the Tower to see him, but was not admitted; but his children were suffered to be with him some time.

On the 16th of April, having been a prisoner in the Tower two months and two days, he was brought to his trial, which continued till the 18th, before the House of Lords, assembled for that purpose; Lord Henley, keeper of the great seal, having been created lord high steward upon the occasion.

The murder was easily proved to have been committed in the manner we have described; and his lordship then proceeded to enter upon his defence.

He called several witnesses, the object of whose testimony was to show that he was not of sound mind; but none of them proved such an insanity as made him not accountable for his conduct. His lordship managed his defence himself, in such a manner as showed an uncommon understanding. He mentioned the fact of his being reduced to the necessity of attempting to prove himself a lunatic, that he might not be deemed a murderer, with the most delicate and affecting sensibility; and when he found that this plea could not avail him, he confessed that he made it only to gratify his friends; that he was always averse to it himself; and that it had prevented what he had proposed, and what perhaps might have taken off the malignity at least of the accusation.

The peers having in the usual form delivered their verdict of Guilty, his lordship received sentence to be hanged on Monday the 21st of April, and then to be anatomized; but, in consideration of his rank, the execution of the sentence was respited till Monday the 5th of May.

During this interval he made a will, by which he left one thousand three hundred pounds to Mr. Johnson's children, one thousand pounds to each of his four natural daughters, and sixty pounds a year to Mrs. Clifford for her life. But this disposition of his property being made after his conviction, was not valid; although, it was said, the same or nearly the same provision was afterwards made for the parties named.

In the mean time a scaffold was erected under the gallows at Tyburn, and part of it, about a yard square, was raised about eighteen inches above the rest of the floor, with a contrivance to sink down upon a signal given, in accordance with the plan now invariably adopted; the whole being covered with black baize.

On the morning of the 5th May, at about nine o'clock, his lordship's body was demanded of the keeper of the Tower by the sheriffs of London and Middlesex. His lordship being informed of it, sent a message to the sheriffs requesting that he might be permitted to be conveyed to the scaffold in his own landau, in preference to the mourning-coach which was provided for him. This being granted, his landau, drawn by six horses, immediately drew up, and he entered it, accompanied by Mr. Humphries, the chaplain of the Tower, who had been admitted to him on that morning for the first time. On the carriage reaching the outer gate, the earl was delivered up to the sheriffs. Mr. Sheriff Vaillant entered the vehicle with him, expressing his concern at having so melancholy a duty to perform; but his lordship said, " he was much obliged to him, and took it kindly that he accompanied him." The earl was attired in a white suit, richly embroidered with silver; and when he put it on, he said, " This is the suit in which I was married, and in which I will die." The procession being now formed, moved slowly forward: the landau was preceded by a considerable body of horse grenadiers, and by a carriage containing Mr. Sheriff Errington, and his under-sheriff, Mr. Jackson, and was followed by the carriage of Mr. Sheriff Vaillant, containing Mr. Nichols, his under-sheriff, a mourning-coach and six, containing some of his lordship's friends, a hearse and six for the conveyance of his body to Surgeon's Hall after execution, and another body of military. The pace at which they proceeded, in consequence of the density of the mob, was so slow, that his lordship was two hours and three quarters in his landau; but during that time he appeared perfectly easy and composed, though he often expressed his anxiety to have the whole affair over; " that the apparatus of death, and the passing through such crowds, were worse than death itself;" and " that he supposed so large a mob had been collected because the people had never seen a lord hanged before." He told the sheriff, that " he had written to the king to beg that he might suffer where his ancestor, the Earl of Essex, had been executed; and that he was in the greater hopes of obtaining that favour, as he had the honour of quartering part of the same arms, and of being allied to his majesty; but that he had refused, and he thought it hard that he must die at the place appointed for the execution of common felons."

Mr. Humphries took occasion to observe, that the world would naturally be very inquisitive concerning the religion his lordship professed, and asked him if he chose to say any thing upon that subject. His lordship, answered that he did not think himself accountable to the world for his sentiments on religion; but that he had always believed in and adored one God, the maker of all things; that whatever his notions were, he had never propagated them, or endeavoured to gain any person over to his persuasions; that all countries and nations had a form of religion, by which the people were governed; that he looked upon any one who disturbed them in it as an enemy to society; and that he blamed very much my Lord Bolingbroke for permitting his sentiments on religion to be published to the world. That he never could believe what some sectaries teach, that faith alone will save mankind; so that if a man, just before he dies, should only say " I believe," *that* alone will save him.

As to the crime for which he suffered, he declared " that he was under particular circumstances—that he had met with so many crosses and vexations, he scarce knew what he did;" and he most solemnly protested " that he had not the least malice against Mr. Johnson."

When his lordship had got to that part of Holborn which is near Drury-lane, he said " he was thirsty, and should be glad of a glass of wine and water;" upon which the sheriffs represented to him, that a stop for that purpose would necessarily draw a great crowd about him, which might possibly disturb and incommode him, yet, if his lordship still desired it, it should be done; he most readily answered, " That's true—I say no more—let us by no means stop."

When they approached near the place of execution, his lordship, pointing to Mrs. Clifford, told the sheriff " that there was a person waiting in a coach near there, for whom he had a very sincere regard, and of whom he should be glad to take his leave before he died." The sheriff answered, that " if his lordship insisted upon it, it should be so; but that he wished his lordship, for his own sake, would decline it, lest the sight of a person for whom he had such a regard should unman him, and disarm him of the fortitude he possessed." His lordship, without the least hesitation, replied, " Sir, if you think I am wrong, I submit:" and upon the sheriff telling his lordship that if he had anything to deliver to the individual referred to, or to any one else, he would faithfully do it, his lordship delivered to him a pocket-book, in which were a bank-note and a ring, and a purse with some guineas, which were afterwards handed over to the unhappy woman.

The landau being now advanced to the place of execution, his lordship alighted from it, and ascended the scaffold with the same composure and fortitude of mind he had exhibited from the time he left the Tower. Soon after he had mounted the scaffold, Mr. Humphries asked his lordship if he chose to say prayers, which he declined; but, upon his asking him, " if he chose to join with him in the Lord's Prayer," he readily answered " he would, for he always thought it a very fine prayer;" upon which they knelt down together upon two cushions, covered with black baize ; and his lordship, with an audible voice, very devoutly repeated the Lord's Prayer, and afterwards, with great energy, ejaculated, " O God, forgive me all my errors—pardon all my sins !"

His lordship, then rising, took his leave of the sheriff and the chaplain ; and, after thanking them for their many civilities, presented his watch to Mr. Sheriff Vaillant, of which he desired his acceptance ; and requested that his body might be buried at Breden or Stanton, in Leicestershire.

The executioner now proceeded to do his duty, to which his lordship, with great resignation, submitted. His neckcloth being taken off, a white cap, which he had brought in his pocket, being put upon his head, his arms secured by a black sash, and the cord put round his neck, he advanced by three steps to the elevated part of the scaffold, and, standing under the cross-beam which went over it, which was also covered with black baize, he asked the executioner " Am I right ?" Then the cap was drawn over his face, and, upon a signal given by the sheriff (for his lordship, upon being before asked, declined to give one himself), that part upon which he stood instantly sunk down from beneath his feet, and he was launched into eternity, May the 5th, 1760.

From the time of his lordship's ascending the scaffold, until his execution, was about eight minutes ; during which his countenance did not change, nor his tongue falter.

The accustomed time of one hour being passed, the coffin was raised up, with the greatest decency, to receive the body, and, being deposited in the hearse, was conveyed by the sheriffs, with the same procession, to Surgeons' Hall, to undergo the remainder of the sentence. A large incision was then made from the neck to the bottom of the breast, and another across the throat ; the lower part of the belly was laid open, and the bowels taken away. It was afterwards publicly exposed to view in a room up one pair of stairs at the Hall ; and on the evening of Thursday, the 8th of May, it was delivered to his friends for interment.

The following verse is said to have been found in his apartment :—

" In doubt I lived, in doubt I die,
Yet stand prepared the vast abyss to try,
And, undismay'd, expect eternity."

CHRISTOPHER LAYER, ESQ.

EXECUTED FOR HIGH TREASON.

MR. LAYER was a barrister, of considerable standing and reputation, at the time when he was convicted and executed on a charge of being the projector of a scheme for the destruction of the king, and the subversion of the government, with a view to the elevation of the Pretender to the throne of England.

Numerous were the plots which had been laid for the same purpose, and frequent were the proceedings which had been had upon complaints laid before the various courts of criminal justice in the kingdom, since the year 1715, when the rebellion first broke out; but the plan laid by Mr. Layer was one of those which gained the greatest degree of notoriety. This infatuated man had received a liberal education, and was a member of the society of the Inner Temple; but being impressed with the possibility of the success of a scheme for the dethronement of the existing monarch, and the elevation of the Pretender to the rank to which it was contended that he was entitled, he made a journey to Rome, in order to confer with that prince upon the propriety of putting his design into execution, promising that he would effect so secret a revolution in England, that no person in authority should be apprised of the scheme until it had been actually completed. Having procured the concurrence of the prince, he instantly returned to London, and proceeded to the completion of his preparations. His plan was to hire an assassin to murder the king on his return from Kensington; and, this being done, the other parties engaged in the plot were to seize the guards; and the Prince of Wales and his children, and the great officers of state, were to be secured and confined during the confusion that such an event would naturally produce.

Mr. Layer having settled a correspondence with several Roman Catholics, nonjurors, and other persons disaffected to the government, he engaged a small number of disbanded soldiers, who were to be the principal actors in the intended tragedy. A meeting of the whole of the partisans having, however, been held at Stratford, they talked so loudly of the plot, that their designs were suspected, and information was conveyed to the authorities; upon which Layer was taken into custody under a secretary of state's warrant, and conveyed to the house of a king's messenger for security. His chambers being searched, papers were found, the contents of which sufficiently indicated his intentions, and witnesses as to repeated declarations on his part, in reference to the rebellion, having been discovered in the persons of two women who were living under his protection, it was determined that a prosecution should be instantly commenced against him. But it was not until he had nearly given his jailors the slip, that this determination was carried into execution with effect; for it appears that the prisoner, conceiving the practicability of an escape from the room where he was confined, through an ale-house which was situated at the back of the messenger's house, resolved to make an attempt to procure his liberty. He therefore formed a rope of his blanket, and, dropping from the window of his apartment, he fell into the yard below, unscathed; but, in his descent, he overset a bottle-rack, and from the noise which was caused the family of the house was disturbed. Mr. Layer managed, nevertheless, to gain the street in the confusion which prevailed; but being instantly pursued by officers, he was traced to have taken a boat at the Horse-ferry, Westminster, from thence to St. George's Fields; and he was at length overtaken at Newington Butts. On the following day he was committed to Newgate; and a grand jury of the county of Essex having found a true bill against him for high treason, his trial came on before Chief Justice Pratt and the other judges of the Court of King's Bench, in the month of January 1723, when, after an inquiry which lasted sixteen hours, he was found guilty, and sentenced to death in the customary manner.

As he had some important affairs to settle, from the nature of his profession, the court did not order his execution till more than two months after he had been condemned; and the king repeatedly reprieved him, to prevent his clients being sufferers by his affairs being left in a state of confusion.

After conviction Mr. Layer was committed to the Tower; and at length the sheriffs of London and Middlesex received a warrant to execute the sentence of the law. He was carried to Tyburn on a sledge, on the 15th March 1723, to be hanged, being dressed in a suit of black, full trimmed, and wearing a tie-wig. At the place of execution he was assisted in his devotions by a nonjuring clergyman; and when these were ended, he spoke to the surrounding multitude, declaring that he deemed King James (so he called the Pretender) his lawful sovereign. He said that King George was a usurper, and that damnation would be the fate of those who supported his government. He insisted that the nation would never be in a state of peace till the pretender was restored, and therefore advised the people to take up arms in his behalf. He professed himself willing to die for the cause, and expressed great hopes that Providence would eventually support the right heir to the throne. His body having been suspended during the accustomed time, it was quartered, and the head was afterwards exposed on Temple Bar.

Among others concerned in this strange scheme was Lord Grey, an ancient nobleman of the Roman Catholic religion, who died a prisoner in the Tower before the necessary legal proceedings against him could take place.

JOHN CARR,

EXECUTED FOR FORGERY.

THIS offender was born of respectable parents, who gave him a good education, in the north of Ireland. He went to Dublin at the age of sixteen, where he soon afterwards entered into business as a wine-merchant; but, being uncontrolled, he fell into bad habits and company, and was compelled to give up his trade. An associate inviting him to join him at Kilkenny, he proceeded thither by coach; among the passengers by which was a lady, the elegance of whose appearance and manners impressed him with an idea that shew as of rank. He determined, if possible, to profit by the opportunity afforded him, and become better acquainted with her; he accordingly on arriving at the inn, prevailed on the company to remain the next day at Kilkenny, and view the Duke of Ormond's seat and the curiosities of the town. This proposal being acceded to, the evening was spent in the utmost harmony and good-humour; and the fair stranger even then conceived an idea of making a conquest of Mr. Carr, supposing from his appearance that he was a man of distinction. It was now " diamond cut diamond." In the morning the fair incognita dressed herself to great advantage, not forgetting the ornament of jewels, which she wore in abundance; so that when she entered the room, Carr was astonished at her appearance. She found the influence she had over him, and resolved to afford him an early opportunity of speaking his sentiments; and while the company were walking in the gallery of the Duke of Ormond's palace, an occasion presented itself, which was not lost by either party. The lady at first affected displeasure at so explicit a declaration; but, soon assuming a more affable deportment, she told him she was an Englishwoman of rank; that his person was not disagreeable to her; and that, if he was a man of fortune, and the consent of her relations could be obtained, she should not be averse to listening to his addresses. She further said, that she was going to spend part of the summer at Mallow, where his company would be agreeable; and he followed her to that place, contrary to the advice of his friend, who had formed a very unfavourable opinion of the lady's character.

He remained with her, until the end of the season induced them to return to Dublin; and then a trip to England was proposed, preparatory to the final steps being taken to complete the nuptial arrangements. The gallantry and wits of the gentleman were sorely tested to procure the requisite funds for the trip; but he at length succeeded in obtaining such a sum as he and the lady deemed sufficient. The passage only remained to be secured; and the too credulous sharper was employed in obtaining it, when in his absence, the lady shipped all the effects on board a vessel bound for Amsterdam, and, having dressed herself in man's apparel, embarked and sailed, leaving Carr to regret his credulity.

Thus reduced to want, he went to London, where he enlisted as a foot-soldier, and was discharged after several years' service. He subsequently entered as a marine, but soon afterwards came to London again, and opened a shop in Hog-lane, St. Giles's. He now married a girl who he thought had money; but soon discovering her poverty, he abandoned her, and removed to Short's Gardens, where he entered into partnership with a cork-cutter. Having obtained the promise of support from his partners' customers, he set up on his own account, and was tolerably successful, though his passion for gambling prevented his retaining any part of the produce of his business. His new companions at the gaming-table, having an eye to their own profit, offered to procure him a wife of fortune, though they knew he had a wife living, and actually contrived to introduce him to a young lady of property, with whom a marriage would probably have taken place, but that one of them, struck with remorse of conscience, developed the affair to her father, and frustrated the whole scheme. Being now again thrown upon his own resources, he engaged himself as porter to a merchant; but while in this condition, his master having entrusted him with a check of sixty pounds, he got it cashed, and spent the money in the lowest debauchery. He afterwards again entered as a marine, and in course of time was advanced to the rank of sergeant.

The vessel in which he sailed was of considerable power; and having taken a merchant-ship richly laden, and soon afterwards several smaller vessels, the prize-money amounted to a considerable sum. This gave Carr an idea that very great advantages might be obtained by privateer-ing. Having procured a discharge, he entered on board a privateer, and was made master-at-arms. In a few days the privateer took two French ships, one of which they carried to Bristol, and the other into the harbour of Poole. Refitting their ships, they sailed again, and in two days took a French privateer, and gave chase to three others, which they found to have been English vessels belonging to Falmouth, which had been captured by a French privateer. These they retook, and carried into Falmouth; in their passage to which place they made a prize of a valuable French ship, the produce of which contributed to enrich the crew. On their next trip, they saw a ship in full chase of them, on which they prepared for a vigorous defence; and an action soon after taking place, many hands were lost by the French, who at length at-tempted to sheer off, but were taken after a chase of some leagues.

The commander of the English privateer, being desperately wounded in the engagement, died in a few days; on which Carr courted his widow, and a marriage would have taken place, but that she was seized with a violent fever, which deprived her of life—but not before she had be-queathed him all she was possessed of. Having disposed of her effects, he repaired to London, where he commenced smuggler: but his ill-gotten goods being seized on by the officers of the revenue, he took to the still more dangerous practice of forging seamen's wills, and gained money thus for some time; but, being apprehended, he was brought to trial at the Old Bailey, convicted, and was sentenced to die. He was hanged at Tyburn on the 16th of November, 1750.

FOOTE READING HIS SATIRICAL PIECE TO THE DUCHESS.

THE COUNTESS OF BRISTOL, OTHERWISE THE DUCHESS OF KINGSTON,

CONVICTED OF BIGAMY.

THIS celebrated lady was the daughter of Colonel Chudleigh, the descendant of an ancient family in the county of Devon. Her father dying while she was yet young, her mother was left in possession only of a small estate with which to bring her up, and to fit her for that grade of society in which from her birth she was entitled to move. Being possessed, however, of excellent qualities, she improved the connexion which she had among persons of fashion, with a view to the future success in life of her daughter. The latter, meanwhile, as she advanced in years, improved in beauty; and, upon her attaining the age of eighteen, was distinguished as well for the loveliness of her person as for the wit and brilliancy of her conversation. Her education had not been neglected: despite the small fortune possessed by her mother, no means were omitted by which her mind might be improved; and an opportunity was about this time afforded for the display of her accomplishments. The father of George the Third held his court at Leicester-house; and Mr. Pulteney, who then blazed as a meteor on the opposition benches in the House of Commons, was honoured with the particular regard of his Royal Highness. Miss Chudleigh had been introduced to Mr. Pulteney.

16   O

He had admired her for the beauties of her mind and of her person; and, his sympathies being excited in her behalf, he obtained for her, at the age of eighteen, the appointment of maid of honour to the Princess of Wales.   His efforts, however, did not stop here: he also endeavoured to improve the cultivation of her understanding by instruction; and to him Miss Chudleigh read, and with him, when separated by distance, she corresponded.

The station to which Miss Chudleigh had been advanced, combined with her numerous personal attractions, produced her many admirers; some with titles, and others in the expectation of them.   Among the former was the Duke of Hamilton, whom Miss Gunning had afterwards the good fortune to obtain for a consort.   The duke was passionately attached to Miss Chudleigh, and pressed his suit with such ardour as to obtain a solemn engagement on her part, that, on his return from a tour for which he was preparing, she would become his wife.   There were reasons why this event should not immediately take place; but that the engagement would be fulfilled at the specified time was considered by both parties as a moral certainty.   A mutual pledge was given and accepted: the duke commenced his proposed tour; and the parting condition was, that he should write by every opportunity, and that Miss Chudleigh of course should answer his epistles.   Thus the arrangement of fortune seemed to have united a pair who possibly might have experienced much happiness, for between the duke and Miss Chudleigh there was a strong similarity of disposition; but fate had not destined them for each other.

Miss Chudleigh had an aunt, whose name was Hanmer.   At her house the Hon. Mr. Hervey, son of the Earl of Bristol, and a captain in the royal navy, was a visitor.   To this gentleman Mrs. Hanmer became so exceedingly partial, that she favoured views which he entertained towards her niece, and engaged her efforts to effect, if possible a matrimonial connexion.   There were two difficulties which would have been insurmountable, had they not been opposed by the fertile genius of a female: Miss Chudleigh disliked Captain Hervey, and she was betrothed to the Duke of Hamilton.

No exertions which could possibly be made were spared to render this latter alliance nugatory; and the wits of this woman were exerted to the utmost to favour the object which she had in view.   The letters of his grace were intercepted by Mrs. Hanmer; and his supposed silence giving offence to her niece, she worked so successfully on her pride as to induce her to abandon all thoughts of her lover, whose passion she had cherished with delight.   A conduct the reverse of that imputed to the duke was observed by Captain Hervey: he was all that assiduity could dictate or attention perform.   He had daily access to Miss Chudleigh; and each interview was artfully improved by the aunt to the promotion of her own views.   The letters of his grace of Hamilton, which regularly arrived, were as regularly suppressed; until, piqued beyond endurance, Miss Chudleigh was prevailed on to accept the hand of Captain Hervey, and by a private marriage to insure the participation of his future honours and fortune.   The ceremony was performed in a private chapel adjoining the country mansion of Mr. Merrill, at Lainston, near Winchester, in Hampshire.

The union of Miss Chudleigh with Captain Hervey proved to her the origin of every subsequent unhappiness. The connubial rites were attended with unhappy consequences; and from the night following the day on which the marriage was solemnized, she resolved never to have any further connexion with her husband. To prevail on him not to claim her as his wife required all the art of which she was mistress; and the best dissuasive was the loss of her situation as maid of honour, should the marriage become publicly known. The circumstances of Captain Hervey were not in a flourishing condition, and were ill calculated to enable him to ride with a high hand over his wife; the fear of lossing the emoluments of her office, therefore, operated most powerfully to induce him to obey the injunctions which she imposed upon him in this respect. His conduct even now, however, exhibited a strong desire to act with a degree of harshness most unusual so soon after marriage; and the consequence was, that any feelings of respect which his wife might have fancied she entertained for him were soon dispelled. Her own expression subsequently was, that " her misery commenced with the arrival of Captain Hervey in England, and the greatest joy she experienced was on the intelligence of his departure."

To mere outward observers, her marriage being unknown, Miss Chudleigh, or Mrs. Hervey—a maid in appearance, a wife in disguise—seemed placed in a most enviable condition. The attractive centre of the circle in which she moved, the invigorating spirit and life of the society around her, she was universally admired. Her royal mistress smiled upon her; the friendship of many was at her call; the admiration of none could be withheld from her: but, amidst all her fancied happiness, she wanted that peace of mind which was so necessary to support her against the conflicts which arose in her own breast. Nor was her own heart, that inward monitor, the only source of her trouble. Her husband, quieted for a time, grew obstreperous as he saw the jewel admired by all, which was, he felt, entitled only to his love; and feeling that he possessed the right to her entire consideration, he resolved to assert its power. In the mean time every art which she possessed had been put into operation to soothe him to continued silence; but her further endeavours being unsuccessful, she was compelled to grant his request, and to attend an interview which he appointed, at his own house, and to which he enforced obedience by threatening an instant and full disclosure in case of her non-compliance. The meeting was strictly private, all persons being sent from the house with the exception of a black servant; and on Mrs. Hervey's entrance to the apartment in which her husband was seated, his first care was to prevent all intrusion by locking the door. This meeting, like all others between her and her husband, was unfortunate in its effects: the fruit of it was the birth of a boy, whose existence it will be readily supposed she had much difficulty in concealing. Her removal to Brompton for a change of air became requisite during the term of her confinement; and she returned to Leicester-house, perfectly recovered from her indisposition; but the infant soon sinking in the arms of death, left only the tale of its existence to be related.

In the mean time, the sum of her unhappiness had been completed by the return of the Duke of Hamilton. His grace had no sooner arrived in England, than he hastened to pay his adoration at the feet of his idol, and to learn the cause of her silence, when his letters had been regularly dispatched to her. An interview which took place soon set the character of Mrs. Hanmer in its true light; but while Miss Chudleigh was convinced of the imposition which had been practised upon her, she was unable to accept the proffered hand of her illustrious suitor, or to explain the reason for her apparently ungracious rejection of his addresses. The Duke, flighty as he was in other respects, in his love for Miss Chudleigh had at least been sincere; and the strange request on her part that he would not again intrude his visits upon her, raised emotions in his mind which can hardly be described. The rejection of his grace was followed by that of several other persons of distinction; and the mother of Miss Chudleigh, who was quite unaware of her private marriage with Captain Hervey, could not conceal her regret and anger at the supposed folly of her daughter.

It was impossible that these circumstances could long remain concealed from the society in which Miss Chudleigh moved; and, in order to relieve herself from the embarrassments by which she was surrounded, she determined to travel on the Continent—trusting that time would eradicate the impression of her fickleness which she left behind her, and that change of scene would remove the pain which every day spent in the theatre of her former operations could not fail to sink deeper into her heart. Germany was the place selected by her for her travels, and she, in turn, visited the chief cities of its principalities. Possessed as she was of introductions of the highest class, she was gratified by obtaining the acquaintance of many crowned heads. Frederic of Prussia conversed and corresponded with her. In the Electress of Saxony she found a friend whose affection for her continued to the latest period of life. The Electress was a woman of sense, honour, virtue, and religion; and her letters were replete with kindness. While her hand distributed presents to Miss Chudleigh out of the treasury of abundance, her heart was interested for her happiness. This she afterwards evinced during her prosecution; for at that time a letter from the Electress contained the following passage:—" You have long experienced my love;—my revenue, my protection, my every thing, you may command. Come then, my dear life, to an asylum of peace. Quit a country where, if you are bequeathed a cloak, some pretender may start up, and ruin you by law to prove it not your property. Let me have you at Dresden."

On her return from the continent, Miss Chudleigh ran over the career of pleasure, enlivened the court circles, and each year became more ingratiated with the mistress whom she served. She was the leader of fashion, played whist with Lord Chesterfield, and revelled with Lady Harrington and Miss Ashe. She was a constant visitant at all public places, and in 1742 appeared at a masked ball in the character of Iphigenia.

Reflection, however, put off for the day, too frequently intruded, an unwelcome visitor, at night. Captain Hervey, like a perturbed spirit, was eternally crossing the path trodden by his wife. If in the rooms at Bath, he was sure to be there. At a rout, ridotto, or ball, this destroyer of her peace embittered every pleasure, and even menaced her with an intimation that he would disclose the marriage to the princess.

Miss Chudleigh, now persuaded of the folly and danger of any longer concealment from her royal mistress, determined that the design, which her husband had formed from a malicious feeling, should be carried out by herself from a principle of rectitude; and she, in consequence, communicated to the princess the whole of the circumstances attending her unhappy union. The recital was one which could excite no feeling of disrespect or of anger; and her royal mistress pitied her, and continued her patronage up to the hour of her death.

At length a stratagem was either suggested, or it occurred to Miss Chudleigh, at once to deprive Captain Hervey of the power to claim her as his wife. The clergyman who had married them was dead. The register-book was in careless hands. A handsome compliment was paid for the inspection; and while the person, in whose custody it was, listened to an amusing story, Miss Chudleigh tore out the register. Thus imagining the business accomplished, she for a time bade defiance to her husband; whose taste for the softer sex having subsided, from some unaccountable cause, afforded Miss Chudleigh a cessation of inquietude.

A change in the circumstances of the captain, however, effected an alteration in the feelings of his wife. His father having died, he succeeded to the title of the Earl of Bristol, and his accession to nobility was accompanied by an increase of fortune. Miss Chudleigh saw that by assuming the title of Countess of Bristol she would probably command increased respect, and would obtain greater power; and, with a degree of unparalleled blindness, she went to the house of Mr. Merrill, the clergyman in whose chapel she had been married, to restore those proofs of her union which she had previously taken such pains to destroy. Her ostensible reason was a jaunt out of town; her real design was to procure, if possible, the insertion of her marriage with Captain Hervey in the book which she had formerly mutilated. With this view she dealt out promises with a liberal hand. The officiating clerk, who was a person of various avocations, was to be promoted to the extent of his wishes. The book was managed by the lady to her content, and she returned to London, secretly exulting in the excellence and success of her machination. While this was going on, however, her better fate influenced in her favour the heart of a man who was the exemplar of amiability—this was the Duke of Kingston: but, re-married as it were by her own stratagem, the participation of ducal honours became legally impossible. The chains of wedlock, which the lady had been so industrious in assuming or putting off, as seemed most suitable to her views, now became galling in the extreme. Every advice was taken, every means tried, by which her liberation might be obtained; but all the efforts which were made proved useless, and it was found to be necessary to acquiesce in that which could not be opposed successfully or pass unnoticed. The duke's passion, meanwhile, became more ardent and sincere; and, finding the apparent impossibility of a marriage taking place, he for a series of years cohabited with Miss Chudleigh, although with such external observances of decorum, that their intimacy was neither generally remarked nor known.

The disagreeable nature of these proceedings on their part was, however, felt by both parties, and efforts were again made by means of which a marriage might be solemnized. The Earl of Bristol was sounded; and it was found that, grown weary of a union with a woman whom he now disliked, and whom he never met, he was not unwilling to accept the proposals held out; but, upon his learning the design with which a divorce was sought, he declared that he would never consent to it, for that his countess's vanity should not be flattered by her being raised to the rank of a duchess. The negotiations were thus for a time stopped; but afterwards, there being a lady with whom he conceived that he could make an advantageous match, he listened to the suggestions which were made to him with more complacency, and at length declared that he was ready to adopt any proceedings which should have for their effect the annihilation of the ties by which he was bound to Miss Chudleigh. The civilians were consulted: a jactitation suit was instituted; but the evidence by which the marriage could have been proved was kept back, and the Earl of Bristol failing, as it was intended he should fail, in substantiating the marriage, a decree was made, declaring the claim to be null and unsupported. Legal opinions now only remained to be taken as to the effect of this decree, and the lawyers of the Ecclesiastical Courts, highly tenacious of the rights and jurisdiction of ther own judges, declared their opinion to be that the sentence could not be disturbed by the interference of any extrinsic power. In the conviction, therefore, of the most perfect safety, the marriage of the Duke of Kingston with Miss Chudleigh was publicly solemnized. The wedding favours were worn by persons of the highest distinction in the kingdom; and, during the life-time of his grace, no attempt was made to dispute the legality of the proceedings. For a few years the duchess figured in the world of gaiety without apprehension or control. She was raised to the pinnacle of fortune, and enjoyed that which the whole of her latter life had been directed to accomplish—the parade of title, but without that honour which integrity of character can alone secure. She was checked in her career of pleasure, however, by the death of her duke. The fortune which his grace possessed, it appears, was not entailed; and it was at his option, therefore, to bequeath it to the duchess or to the heirs of his family, as seemed best to his inclination. His will, excluding from every benefit an elder, and preferring a younger nephew as the heir in tail, gave rise to the prosecution of the duchess, which ended in the beggary of her prosecutor and her own exile. The demise of the Duke of Kingston was neither sudden nor unexpected. Being attacked with a paralytic affection, he lingered but a short time, which was employed by the duchess in journeying his grace from town to town, under the false idea of prolonging his life by change of air and situation. At last, when real danger seemed to threaten, even in the opinion of the duchess, she dispatched one of her swiftest-footed messengers to her solicitor, Mr. Field, of the Temple, requiring his immediate attendance. He obeyed the summons; and, on his arrival at the house, the duchess imparted her wishes, which were, that he would procure the duke to execute, and be himself a subscribing witness to a will more to the taste of the duchess than that which had been executed. The duke had bequeathed the income of his estates to his relict during her life, expressly under the condition of her continuing in a state of widowhood. Perfectly satisfied, however, as the duchess seemed with the inclinations of her dearest lord, she did not relish the Temple of Hymen being shut against her. Earnestly therefore did she press Mr. Field to have a will immediately executed, which would leave her at liberty to give her hand to the conqueror of her heart; and, in her anxiety to have this restraint shaken off, she had nearly deprived herself of every benefit derivable from the demise of the duke. When Mr. Field was introduced to his grace, his intellects were perceptibly affected; and, although he knew the friends who approached him, a transient knowledge of their persons was the only indication of the continuance of his mental powers which he exhibited. Mr. Field very properly remonstrated against the impropriety of introducing a will for execution to a man in such a state; but this occasioned a severe reprehension from the duchess, who reminded him that his business was only to obey the instructions of his employers. Feeling for his professional character, however, he positively refused either to tender the will or to be in any manner concerned in endeavouring to procure its execution; and with this refusal he quitted the house, the duchess beholding him with an indignant eye as the annoyer of her scheme, when in fact, by not complying with it, he was rendering her an essential service; for had the will she proposed been executed, it would most undoubtedly have been set aside, and the heirs would consequently have excluded the relict from every thing, except that to which the right of dower entitled her; and the marriage being invalidated, she would in this, as in other respects, have been ruined by her own stratagem. Soon after the frustration of this attempt the Duke of Kingston expired.

No sooner were the funeral rites performed than the duchess adjusted her affairs, and embarked for the continent, proposing Rome for her temporary residence. Ganganelli at that time filled the papal chair. From the moderation of his principles, the tolerant spirit which he on every occasion displayed, and the marked attention he bestowed on the English, he acquired the title of the Protestant Pope; and to such a character the Duchess was a welcome visitor. Ganganelli treated her with the utmost civility—as a sovereign prince, he gave her many privileges—and she was lodged in the palace of one of the cardinals. Her vanity being thus gratified, her grace, in return, treated the Romans with a public spectacle. She had built an elegant pleasure-yacht; a gentleman who had served in the navy was its commander; and under his orders the vessel, at considerable trouble and expense, was conveyed up the Tiber. The sight of an English yacht in this river was one of so unusual a character that it attracted crowds of admirers.

But while all seemed happiness and pleasure, proceedings were con-

cocting in London, which promised effectually to put a stop to any
momentary sensations of bliss which the duchess might entertain.
Mrs. Cradock, who, in the capacity of a domestic, had witnessed the
marriage which had been solemnized between her grace and the Earl of
Bristol, found herself so reduced in circumstances that she was compelled
to apply to Mr. Field for assistance. Her request was rejected; and,
notwithstanding her assurance that she was perfectly well aware of all the
circumstances attending the duchess's marriage, and that she should not
hesitate to disclose all she knew in a quarter where she would be liberally
paid—namely, to the disappointed relations of the Duke of Kingston—
she was set at defiance. Thus refused, starvation staring her in the face,
and stung by the ingratitude of the duchess's solicitor, she immediately
set about the work of ruin which she contemplated. The Duke of Kingston had borne a marked dislike to one of his nephews, Mr. Evelyn
Meadows, one of the sons of his sister, Lady Frances Pierpoint. This
gentleman being excluded from the presumptive heirship, joyfully received the intelligence that a method of revenging himself against the
duchess was presented to him. He saw Mrs. Cradock; learned from her
the particulars of the statement which she would be able to make upon
oath; and, being perfectly satisfied of its truth, he preferred a bill of indictment against the Duchess of Kingston for bigamy, which was duly
returned a true bill. Notice was immediately given to Mr. Field of the
proceedings, and advices were forthwith sent to the duchess to appear
and plead to the indictment, to prevent a judgment of outlawry.

The duchess's immediate return to England being thus required, she
set about making the necessary preparations for her journey; and as
money was one of the commodities requisite to enable her to commence
her homeward march, she proceeded to the house of Mr. Jenkins, the
banker in Rome, in whose hands she had placed security for the advance
of all such sums as she might require. The opposition of her enemies,
however, had already commenced; they had adopted a line of policy
exactly suited to the lady with whom they had to deal. Mr. Jenkins
was out, and could not be found. She apprised him, by letter, of her
intended journey, and her consequent want of money; but still he
avoided seeing her. Suspecting the trick, her grace was not to be trifled
with; and finding all her efforts fail, she took a pair of pistols in her
pocket, and driving to Mr. Jenkins's house, once again demanded to be
admitted. The customary answer, that Mr. Jenkins was out, was given;
but the duchess declared that she was determined to wait until she saw
him, even if it should not be until a day, month, or year, had elapsed;
and she took her seat on the steps of the door, which she kept open with
the muzzle of one of her pistols, apparently determined to remain there.
She knew that business would compel his return, if he were not already
in-doors; and at length, Mr. Jenkins, finding further opposition useless,
appeared. The nature of her business was soon explained. The conversation was not of the mildest kind. Money was demanded, not
asked. A little prevarication ensued; but the production of a pistol
served as the most powerful mode of reasoning; and the necessary sum
being instantly obtained, the duchess quitted Rome. Her journey was

retarded before she reached the Alps; a violent fever seemed to seize on her vitals; but she recovered, to the astonishment of her attendants. An abscess then formed in her side, which rendering it impossible for her to endure the motion of the carriage, a kind of litter was provided, in which she slowly travelled. In this situation nature was relieved by the breaking of the abscess; and, after a painfully tedious journey, the duchess reached Calais. At that place she made a pause; and there it was that her apprehension got the better of her reason. In idea she was fettered and incarcerated in the worst cell of the worst prison in London. She was totally ignorant of the bailable nature of her offence, and therefore expected the utmost that can be imagined. Colonel West, a brother of the late Lord Delaware, whom the duchess had known in England, became her principal associate; but he was not lawyer enough to satisfy her doubts. By the means of former connexions, and through a benevolence in his own nature, the Earl of Mansfield had a private meeting with the duchess; and the venerable peer conducted himself in a manner which did honour to his heart and character.

Her spirits being soothed by the interview, the duchess embarked for Dover, landed, drove post to Kingston-house, and found friends displaying both zeal and alacrity in her cause. The first measure taken was to have the duchess bailed. This was done before Lord Mansfield; the Duke of Newcastle, Lord Mountstuart, Mr. Glover, and other characters of rank attending.

The duchess had through life distinguished herself as a most eccentric character. Her turn of mind was original, and many of her actions were unaccountable. She had already in a manner invited disgrace, and she now neglected the means of preventing it. Mrs. Cradock, the only existing evidence against her, again solicited a maintenance for the remaining years of her life; and voluntarily offered, in case a stipend should be settled on her, to retire to her native village, and never more intrude. The offer was rejected by the duchess, who would only consent to allow her twenty pounds a year, and on condition of her sequestering herself in some place near the Peak of Derbyshire. This the duchess considered as a most liberal offer; and she expressed her astonishment that it should be rejected.

Under the assurances of her lawyers, the duchess was as quiet as that troublesome monitor, her own heart, would permit her to be; and, when reconciled in some measure to the encounter which she was about to meet, her repose was most painfully disturbed by an adversary who appeared in a new and most unexpected quarter. This was the celebrated Foote, the actor, who, having mixed in the first circles of fashion, was perfectly acquainted with the leading transactions of the duchess's life, and had resolved to turn that knowledge to his own advantage. As in the opinion of Mandeville private vices are public benefits, so Foote deemed the crimes and vices of individuals lawful game for his wit. On this principle he proceeded with the Duchess of Kingston; and he wrote a piece, founded on her life, called " The Trip to Calais." The scenes were humorous; the character of the duchess admirably drawn; and the effect of the performance of the farce on the stage would have been that which was most congenial to the tastes of the scandal-mongers of the day—namely, to make the duchess ashamed of herself. The real object of Mr. Foote, however, was of a nature more likely to prove advantageous to himself—it was to obtain money to secure the suppression of the piece; and with this view he contrived to have it communicated to her grace, that the Haymarket Theatre would open with an entertainment in which she was taken off to the life. Alarmed at this, she sent for Foote, who attended with the piece in his pocket; but, having been desired to read it, he had not gone far before the character of Lady Kitty Crocodile being introduced, the duchess could no longer control her anger, but, rising in a violent rage, she exclaimed, " Why, this is scandalous; what a wretch you have made me." Mr. Foote assured her that the character was not intended to " caricature " her ;—even in his serious moments being unable to control his desire to pun—for he left her to infer that it was a true picture. The duchess, having taken a few turns about the room, became more composed, and requested that the piece might be left for her perusal, engaging that it should be returned by the ensuing evening. The actor readily complied, and retired; but the lady being left to consider her own portrait, was so displeased with the likeness, that she determined, if possible, to prevent its exposure on the stage. The artist had no objection to sell his work, and she was inclined to become the purchaser ; but, on the former being questioned as to the sum which he should expect for suppressing the piece, he proportioned his expectations to what he deemed the duchess's power of gratifying them, and demanded two thousand guineas, besides a sum to be paid as compensation for the loss of the scenes which had been painted for the farce, and which were not applicable to any other purpose. The magnitude of the demand, as well it might, staggered the duchess; and having intimated her extreme astonishment at so exorbitant a proposition, she expressed a wish that the sum might be fixed within the bounds of moderation and reason. The actor was positive; concluding, that as his was the only article in the market, he might name his own price : but the result was, that by demanding too much, he lost all. A cheque for fourteen hundred pounds was offered ; the amount was increased to sixteen hundred pounds, and a draft on Messrs. Drummond's was actually signed ; but the obstinacy of the actor was so great, that he refused to abate one guinea from his original demand. The circumstance might at any other time have passed among the indifferent events of the day, and as wholly undeserving of the public notice ; but those long connected with the duchess, and in habits of intimacy, felt the attack made on her as directed by a ruffian hand, at a moment when she was least able to make resistance. His grace the Duke of Newcastle was consulted. The chamberlain of the household (the Earl of Hertford) was apprised of the circumstance ; and his prohibitory interference was earnestly solicited. He sent for the manuscript copy of " The Trip to Calais," perused, and censured it.

But, besides these and other powerful aids, the duchess called in professional advice. The sages of the robe were consulted, and their opinions were, that the piece was a malicious libel ; and that, should it be represented, a short-hand writer ought to be employed to attend on the night of representation, to minute each offensive passage, as a groundwork of a prosecution. This advice was followed, and Foote was intimidated. He denied having made a demand of two hundred guineas; but the Rev. Mr. Foster contradicted him in an affidavit. Thus defeated in point of fact, Foote found himself baffled also in point of design. The chamberlain would not permit the piece to be represented.

Foote now had recourse to another expedient. He caused it to be intimated "that it was in his power to publish, if not to perform it; but, were his expenses reimbursed (and the sum which her grace had formerly offered would do the business), he would desist." This being communicated to the duchess, she in this, as in too many cases, asked the opinion of her friends, with a secret determination to follow her own. Foote, finding that she began to yield, pressed his desire incessantly; and she had actually provided bills to the amount of one thousand six hundred pounds, which she would have given him, but for the Rev. Mr. Jackson, who, being asked his opinion of the demand, returned this answer: "Instead of complying with it, your grace should obtain complete evidence of the menace and demand, and then consult your counsel whether a prosecution will not lie for endeavouring to extort money by threats. Your grace must remember the attack on the first Duke of Marlborough by a stranger, who had formed a design either on his purse or his interest, and endeavoured to menace him into a compliance." This answer struck the Earl of Peterborough and Mr. Foster very forcibly, as in perfect coincidence with their own opinions. Mr. Jackson was then solicited to wait on Mr. Foote; Mr. Foster, the chaplain of the duchess, professing himself to be too far advanced in years to enter into the field of literary combat. Mr. Jackson consented to be the champion on the following condition—that the duchess would give her honour never to retract her determination, nor to let Foote extort from her a single guinea. Her grace subscribing to this condition, Mr. Jackson waited on Mr. Foote at his house in Suffolk-street, and intimated to him the resolution to which the duchess had come. The actor, however, still wished to have matters compromised; and to this end he addressed a letter to the duchess, which began with stating "that a member of the privy council and a friend of her grace (by whom he meant the Duke of Newcastle) had conversed with him on the subject of the dispute between them; and that, for himself, he was ready to have everything adjusted." This letter afforded the duchess a triumph. Every line contained a concession; and, contrary to the advice of her friends, she insisted upon the publication of the whole correspondence.

This circumstance for a time served to turn the current of attention into a new channel. But, while the public notice was withdrawn from her grace, she felt the necessity which existed to adopt some course to meet the impending danger. An opportunity presented itself which remained only to be embraced to secure her object. It became the subject of a discussion in the House of Lords, whether the trial of her grace should not be conducted in Westminster Hall; and the expense which would necessarily be incurred by the country was by many urged as being a burden which ought not to rest upon the public purse. Lord Mansfield, privately desiring to save the duchess from the disgrace and ignominy of a public trial, strove to avail himself of this objection in her favour; and so great had become the differences of opinion entertained upon the subject, that the withdrawal of the prosecution altogether would have been a matter which would have been considered desirable rather than improper. Here then was the critical moment at which the duchess might have determined her future fate. A hint was privately conveyed to her that the sum of ten thousand pounds would satisfy every expectation, and put an end to the prosecution; and doubts being expressed of the sincerity of the proposal, the offer was made in distinct terms. The duchess was entreated by her friends to accept the proposition which was made, and so at once to relieve herself and them from all fear of the consequences which might result to her; but, through a fatal mistaken confidence, either in the legal construction of her case or in her own machinations, she refused to accede to the offers which were held out. Resting assured of her acquittal, she resisted every attempt at dissuasion from her purpose of going to trial; and assumed an air of indifference about the business, which but ill accorded with the doubtful nature of her position. She talked of the absolute necessity of setting out for Rome; affected to have some material business to settle with the Pope; and, in consequence, took every means, and urged every argument in her power, to procure the speedy termination of the proceedings—as if the regular course of justice had not been swift enough to overtake her. In the midst of her confidence, however, she did not abandon her manœuvring; but, at the very moment when she was petitioning for a speedy trial, she was engaged in a scheme to get rid of the principal witness against her. Mrs. Cradock, to whom before she had refused a trifling remuneration, might now have demanded thousands as the price of her evidence. A negotiation was carried on through the medium of a relation of her's, who was a letter-carrier, which had for its object her removal from England; and an interview was arranged to take place between her and the duchess, at which the latter was to appear disguised, and was to reveal herself only after some conversation, the object of which was, that terms might be proposed. But her grace was duped: for having changed her clothes to those of a man, she waited at the appointed hour and place without seeing either Mrs. Cradock or the person who had promised to effect the meeting; and she afterwards learned that every particular of this business was communicated to the prosecutors, who had instructed the letter-carrier to pretend an acquiescence in the scheme.

Thus baffled in a project which had a plausible appearance of success, the only method left was the best possible arrangement of matters preparatory to the trial. On the 15th of April, 1766, the business came on in Westminster-hall. The queen was present, accompanied by the prince of Wales, the princess royal, and others of the royal family. Many foreign ambassadors also attended, as well as several of the nobility.

Proclamation being made for silence, the lord high steward mentioned to the prisoner the fatal consequences attending the crime of which she stood indicted, signifying that, however alarming and awful her present circumstances, she might derive great consolation from considering that she was to be tried by the most liberal, candid, and august assembly in the universe.

The duchess then read a paper, setting forth that she was guiltless of the offence alleged against her, and that the agitation of her mind arose, not from the consciousness of guilt, but from the painful circumstance of being called before so awful a tribunal on a criminal accusation. She begged, therefore, that if she was deficient in the observance of any ceremonial points, her failure might not be understood as proceeding from wilful disrespect, but should be attributed to the unfortunate peculiarity of her situation. It was added, that she had travelled from Rome in so dangerous a state of health that it was necessary for her to be conveyed in a litter; and that she was perfectly satisfied that she would have a fair trial, since the determination respecting her cause, on which materially depended her honour and fortune, would proceed from the most unprejudiced and august assembly in the world.

The lord high steward then desired the lady to give attention while she was arraigned on an indictment for bigamy; and proclamation for silence having been again made, the duchess (who had been permitted to sit) arose, and read a paper, representing to the Court that she was advised by her counsel to plead the sentence of the Ecclesiastical Court in the year 1769 as a bar to her being tried on the present indictment. The lord high steward informed her that she must plead to the indictment; in consequence of which she was arraigned.

Four days were occupied in arguments of counsel respecting the admission or rejection of the sentence of the Spiritual Court; but the peers having decided that it could not be admitted, the trial proceeded. The first witness examined was

Anne Cradock, whose testimony was as follows:—I have known her grace the Duchess of Kingston ever since the year 1742, at which time she came on a visit to the house of Mr. Merrill, at Lainston, in Hampshire, during the Winchester races. At that time I lived in the service of Mrs. Hanmer, Miss Chudleigh's aunt, who was then on a visit at Mr. Merrill's, where Mr. Hervey and Miss Chudleigh first met, and soon conceived a mutual attachment for each other. They were privately married one evening at about eleven o'clock in Lainston church, in the presence of Mr. Mountney, Mrs. Hanmer, the Rev. Mr. Ames, the rector who performed the ceremony, and myself. I was ordered out of the church, to entice Mr. Merrill's servant out of the way. I saw the bride and bridegroom put to bed together, and Mrs. Hanmer obliged them to rise again; they went to bed together the following night. In a few days Mr. Harvey was under the necessity of going to Portsmouth in order to join Sir John Danvers' fleet, in which he was then a lieutenant; and being ordered to call him at five o'clock in the morning, I went into the bedchamber at the appointed hour, and found him and his lady sleeping in bed together. I was unwilling to disturb them, as I thought that the delay of an hour or two would make no difference, but they afterwards parted. My husband, to whom I was not then married,

17   S

accompanied Mr. Hervey in the capacity of servant. When Mr. Hervey returned from the Mediterranean, he and his lady lived together, and I then thought that she was pregnant. Some months after, Mr. Hervey went again to sea, and during his absence I was informed that the lady was brought to bed ; and I was afterwards confirmed in the information by the lady herself, who said that she had a little boy at nurse, whose features greatly resembled those of Mr. Hervey.

In answer to questions put by the Duke of Grafton, the witness said that she had never seen the child ; that it was dark when the marriage took place in the church, and that Mr. Mountney carried a wax light attached to the crown of his hat. Upon being asked by the Earl of Hilsborough whether she had not received a letter containing some offer to induce her to appear now as a witness, she admitted that Mr. Fossard of Piccadilly had written to her, offering her a sinecure place on condition of her coming forward to give evidence against her grace, and stating that she might, if she pleased, exhibit the letter to the Earl of Bristol. The cross-examination of the witness on this point was continued during the remainder of the sitting of their lordships ; and on the following day (the 20th of April) it was resumed, the Earls of Derby, Hillsborough, and Buckinghamshire questioning her with considerable acumen. She at length confessed that pecuniary offers had been made to her to induce her to appear, and that she had acceded to the terms proposed.

Mrs. Sophia Pettiplace was examined as to the facts deposed to by Mrs. Cradock ; but she was able to afford no positive information upon the subject. She lived with her grace at the time of the supposed marriage, but was not present at the ceremony, and only believed that the duchess had mentioned the circumstance to her.

Cæsar Hawkins, Esq., deposed that he had been acquainted with the duchess several years, he believed not less than thirty. He had heard of a marriage between Mr. Hervey and the lady at the bar, which circumstance was afterwards mentioned to him by both parties, previous to Mr. Hervey's last going to sea. By the desire of her grace, he was in the room when the issue of the marriage was born, and once saw the child. He was sent for by Mr. Hervey soon after his return from sea, and desired by him to wait upon the lady with proposals for procuring a divorce, which he accordingly did, when her grace declared herself absolutely determined against listening to such terms ; and he knew that many messages passed on the subject. Her grace some time after informed him, at his own house, that she had instituted a jactitation suit against Mr. Hervey in Doctors' Commons. On another visit she appeared very grave, and, desiring him to retire into another apartment, said she was exceedingly unhappy, in consequence of an oath, which she had long dreaded, having been tendered to her at Doctors' Commons to disavow her marriage, which she would not do for ten thousand worlds. Upon another visit, a short time after, she informed him that a sentence had passed in her favour at Doctors' Commons, which would be irrevocable unless Mr. Hervey pursued certain measures within a limited time, which she did not apprehend he would do. Hereupon he inquired how she got over the oath; and her reply was, that the circumstance of her marriage was so blended with falsities, that she could easily reconcile the matter to her conscience; since the ceremony was a business of so scrambling and shabby a nature, that she could as safely swear she was *not* as that she *was* married.

Judith Phillips, being called, swore that she was the widow of the Rev. Mr. Ames; that she remembered when her late husband performed the marriage ceremony between Mr. Hervey and the prisoner; that she was not present, but derived her information from her husband; that some time after the marriage the lady desired her to prevail upon her husband to grant a certificate, which she said she believed her husband would not refuse; that, Mr. Merrill, who accompanied the lady, advised her to consult his attorney from Worcester; that, in compliance with the attorney's advice, a register-book was purchased, and the marriage inserted therein, with some late burials in the parish. The book was here produced, and the witness swore to the writing of her late husband.

The writing of the Rev. Mr. Ames was also proved by the Rev. Mr. Inchin and the Rev. Mr. Dennis; and the entry of a caveat to the duke's will was proved by a clerk from Doctors' Commons. The book in which the marriage of the Duke of Kingston with the lady at the bar was registered on the 8th of March, 1769, was produced by the Rev. Mr. Trebeck, of St. Margaret's, Westminster; and the Rev. Mr. Samuel Harpur, of the British Museum, swore that he performed the marriage ceremony between the parties on the day mentioned in the books produced by Mr. Trebeck.

On Monday, the 22d of April, after the attorney-general had declared the evidence on behalf of the prosecution to be concluded, the lord high steward called upon the prisoner for her defence, which she read; and the following are the most material arguments it contained to invalidate the evidence adduced for the prosecution. She appealed to the Searcher of all hearts, that she never considered herself as legally married to Mr. Hervey. She said, that she considered herself as a single woman, and as such was addressed by the late Duke of Kingston; and that, influenced by a legitimate attachment to his grace, she instituted a suit in the Ecclesiastical Court, when her supposed marriage with Mr. Hervey was declared null and void; but, anxious for every conscientious as well as legal sanction, she submitted an authentic statement of her case to the Archbishop of Canterbury, who, in the most decisive and unreserved manner, declared that she was at liberty to marry, and afterwards granted, and delivered to Dr. Collier, a special licence for her marriage with the late Duke of Kingston. She said, that on her marriage she experienced every mark of gracious esteem from their majesties, and her late royal mistress, the Princess Dowager of Wales, and was publicly recognized as Duchess of Kingston. Under such reputable sanctions and virtuous motives for the conduct she pursued, strengthened by a decision that had been esteemed conclusive and irrevocable for the space of seven centuries, if their lordships should deem her guilty on any rigid principle of law, she hoped, nay, she was conscious, they would attribute her failure as proceeding from a mistaken judgment and erroneous advice, and would not censure her for intentional guilt. She bestowed the highest encomiums on the deceased duke, and solemnly assured the Court that she had in no one instance abused her ascendancy over him; and that so far from endeavouring to engross his possessions, she had declared herself amply provided for by that fortune for life which he was extremely anxious to bequeath to her in perpetuity. As to the neglect of the duke's eldest nephew, she said, it was entirely the consequence of his disrespectful behaviour to her; and she was not dissatisfied at a preference to another nephew, whose respect and attention to her had been such as the duke judged to be her due on her advancement to the honour of being the wife of his grace.

The lord high steward then desired Mr. Wallace to proceed with the evidence on behalf of the duchess. The advocate stated the nature of the evidence he meant to produce to prove that Anne Cradock had asserted to different people that she had no recollection of the marriage between Mr. Hervey and the lady at the bar; and that she placed a reliance on a promise of having a provision made for her in consequence of the evidence she was to give on the present trial. To invalidate the depositions of Judith Philips, he ordered the clerk to read a letter, wherein she supplicated her grace to exert her influence to prevent her husband's discharge from the duke's service; and observed, that Mrs. Philips had, on the preceding day, sworn that her husband was not dismissed, but voluntarily quitted his station in the household of his grace.

Mr. Wallace called Mr. Berkley, Lord Bristol's attorney, who said, his lordship told him he was desirous of obtaining a divorce, and directed him to Anne Cradock, saying, she was the only person then living who was present at his marriage; and that a short time previous to the commencement of the jactitation suit, he waited upon Anne Cradock, who informed him that her memory was bad, and she could remember nothing perfectly in relation to the marriage, which must have been a long time before.

Anne Pritchard deposed, that about three months before she had been informed by Mrs. Cradock that she expected to be provided for soon after the trial, and that she expected to be able to procure a place in the Custom-house for one of her relations.

This being the whole of the evidence to be produced on behalf of her grace, the lord high steward addressed their lordships, saying, that the evidence on both sides having been heard, it now became their lordships' duty to proceed to the consideration of the case; that the importance and solemnity of the occasion required that they should severally pronounce their opinions in the absence of the prisoner at the bar, and that it was for the junior baron to speak first.

The prisoner having then been removed, their lordships declared that they found her guilty of the offence imputed to her.

Proclamation was then made, that the usher of the black rod should replace the prisoner at the bar; and, immediately on her appearing, the lord high steward informed her, that the lords had maturely considered the evidence adduced against her, as well as the testimony of the witnesses who had been called on her behalf, and that they had pronounced her guilty of the felony for which she was indicted. He then inquired whether she had anything to say why judgment should not be pronounced against her?

The duchess immediately handed in a paper containing the words, " I plead the privilege of the peerage," which was read by the clerk at the table.

The lord high steward then informed her grace, that the lords had considered the plea, and agreed to allow it, adding, " Madam, you will be discharged on paying the usual fees."

The duchess during the trial appeared to be perfectly collected ; but on sentence being pronounced she fainted, and was carried out of court.

This solemnity was concluded on the 22nd of April, 1776 ; but the prosecutors still had a plan in embryo to confine the person of the Countess of Bristol (for to this rank she was now again reduced) to the kingdom, and to deprive her of her personal property. A writ of *ne exeat regno* was actually in the course of preparation ; but private notice being conveyed to her of this circumstance, she was advised immediately to quit the country. In order to conceal her flight, she caused her carriage to be driven publicly through the streets, and invited a large party to dine at her house ; but, without waiting to apologise to her guests, she drove to Dover in a post-chaise, and there entering a boat with Mr. Harvey, the captain of her yacht, she accompanied him to Calais. Circumstances of which she had been advised, and which had occurred during the period of her absence from Rome, rendered her immediate presence in that city necessary ; and, proceeding thither without loss of time, she found that a Spanish friar, whom she had left in charge of her palace and furniture, had found means to convert her property into money, and, after having seduced a young English girl who had also been left in charge of her palace, had absconded. Having obtained the whole of her plate from the public bank where she had deposited it, she returned to Calais ; which place she adopted for her residence in consequence of the expeditious communication between it and London, that she might be afforded the earliest intelligence of the proceedings of her opponents. Their business was now to set aside, if possible, the will of the Duke of Kingston. There was no probability of their success in this attempt, but sufficient doubt existed in the mind of the countess to keep all her apprehensions alive.

The will of his grace of Kingston, however, received every confirmation which the courts of justice could give ; and the object of the countess now was to dissipate rather than expend the income of his estates. A house which she had purchased at Calais was not sufficient for her purpose ; a mansion at Montmartre, near Paris, was fixed on, and the purchase of it negotiated in as short a time as the duchess could desire. There were a few obstacles, however, to its enjoyment, which were not considered until the purchase was completed. The house was in so ruinous a condition as to be in momentary danger of falling. The land was more like the field of the slothful than the vineyard of the industrious ; and these evils were not perceived by the countess till she was in possession of it. A lawsuit with the owner of the estates was the consequence ; and the countess went to St. Petersburgh, and there turned brandy distiller, and returned to Paris before it was concluded. The possession of such a place, however, was not sufficient for the countess; she proceeded to make a purchase of another house, built upon a scale of infinite grandeur. The brother of the existing French king was the owner of a domains suited in every respect for the residence of a person of such nobility, and the countess determined to become its mistress. It was called the terroriry of St. Assise, and was situated at a pleasant distance from Paris, abounding in game of all descriptions, and rich in all the luxuriant embellishments of nature. The mansion was of a size which rendered it fit for the occupation of a king; it contained three hundred beds. The value of such an estate was too considerable to be expected in one payment; she therefore agreed to discharge the whole of the sum demanded, which was fifty-five thousand pounds, by instalments. The purchase on the part of the countess was a good one. It afforded not only game, but rabbits in plenty; and finding them of superior quality and flavour, her ladyship, during the first week of her possession, had as many killed and sold as brought her three hundred guineas. At St. Petersburgh she had been a distiller of brandy; and now at Paris she turned rabbit-merchant.

Such was her situation, when one day, while she was at dinner, she received the intelligence that judgment respecting the house near Paris had been awarded against her. The sudden communication of the news produced an agitation of her whole frame. She flew into a violent passion, and burst an internal blood-vessel. But she appeared to have surmounted even this, until a few days afterwards, when preparing to rise from her bed, a servant who had long been with her endeavoured to dissuade her from her purpose. The countess said, "I am not very well, but I will rise;" and on a remonstrance being attempted, she said, "At your peril disobey me; I will get up and walk about the room; ring for the secretary to assist me." She was obeyed, dressed, and the secretary entered the chamber. The countess then walked about, complained of thirst, and said, "I could drink a glass of my fine Madeira, and eat a slice of toasted bread. I shall be quite well afterwards; but let it be a large glass of wine." The attendant reluctantly brought, and the countess drank the wine. She then said, "I am perfectly recovered; I knew the Madeira would do me good. My heart feels oddly. I will have another glass." The servant here observed that such a quantity of wine in the morning might intoxicate rather than benefit. The countess persisted in her orders, and the second glass of Madeira being produced, she drank that also, and pronounced herself to be charmingly indeed. She then walked a little about the room, and afterwards said, "I will lie down on the couch; I can sleep, and after that I shall be entirely recovered." She seated herself on the couch, a female having hold of each hand. In this situation she soon appeared to have fallen into a sound sleep, until the women felt her hands colder than ordinary, and she was found to have expired. She died August 26th, 1796.

JONATHAN BRADFORD DISCOVERED AT THE BED SIDE OF MR. HAYES

JONATHAN BRADFORD,

EXECUTED FOR A MURDER WHICH HE DID NOT COMMIT.

JONATHAN BRADFORD kept an inn in Oxfordshire, on the London road to Oxford, and bore an unexceptionable character. In the year 1736, Mr. Hayes, a gentleman of fortune, being on his way to Oxford on a visit to a relation, put up at Bradford's, where he joined company with two gentlemen, with whom he supped, and, in conversation, unguardedly mentioned that he had about him a large sum of money. In due time they retired to their respective chambers—the gentlemen, to a two-bedded room, leaving, as is customary with many, a candle burning in the chimney-corner. Some hours after they were in bed, one of the gentlemen being awake, thought he heard a deep groan in the adjoining chamber; and this being repeated, he softly awakened his friend. They listened together; and the groans increasing, as of one dying, they both instantly arose, and proceeded silently to the door of the next chamber, from whence they heard the groans; and, the door being ajar, saw a light in the room. They entered; but it is impossible to paint their consternation, on perceiving a person weltering in his blood in the bed, and a man standing over him, with a dark lanthorn in one hand, and a knife in the other. The man seemed as stupified as themselves, but his terror carried with it all the terror of guilt. The gentlemen soon discovered that the person was the stranger with whom they had supped, and that

17

the man who was standing over him was their host. They immediately seized Bradford, disarmed him of his knife, and charged him with being the murderer. He assumed by this time the air of innocence, positively denied the crime, and asserted that he came there with the same humane intention as themselves; for that, hearing a noise, which was succeeded by a groaning, he got out of bed, struck a light, armed himself with a knife for his defence, and had but that minute entered the room before them. These assertions were of little avail; he was kept in close custody till the morning, and then taken before a justice of the peace.

At the next assizes Bradford was brought to trial. Nothing could be stronger than the evidence of the two gentlemen: they testified to the finding of Mr. Hayes murdered in his bed—Bradford at the side of the body with a light and a knife—and that knife, and the hand that held it, bloody! They further stated, that, on their entering the room, he betrayed all the signs of a guilty man, and that a few moments preceding they had heard the groans of the deceased.

Bradford's defence on his trial was the same as before. He had heard a noise; he suspected some villainy transacting; he struck a light; he snatched a knife (the only weapon near him) to defend himself; and the terrors he discovered were merely the terrors of humanity, the natural effect, on innocence as well as guilt, of beholding such a horrid scene.

This defence, however, was considered weak, when contrasted with the several powerful circumstances against him. Never was circumstantial evidence more strong; and the jury found him guilty, even without going out of the box. Bradford was executed shortly afterwards, still declaring he was not the murderer, nor privy to the murder of Mr. Hayes; but he died disbelieved by all.

Yet were his assertions not untrue! The murder was actually committed by Mr. Hayes's footman; who, immediately on stabbing his master, rifled his breeches of his money, gold watch, and snuff-box, and escaped to his own room; which could have been, from the very circumstances, scarcely two seconds before Bradford's entering the unfortunate gentleman's chamber. The world owes this knowledge to a remorse of conscience in the footman (eighteen months after the execution of Bradford) on a bed of sickness; it was a death-bed repentance, and by that death the law lost its victim.

It is much to be wished that this account could close here; but it cannot. Bradford, though innocent, and not privy to the murder, was, nevertheless, a murderer in design. He had heard, as well as the footman, what Mr. Hayes had declared at supper, as to his having a large sum of money about him, and he went to the chamber with the same diabolical intention as the servant. He was struck with amazement—he could not believe his senses; and in turning back the bedclothes, to assure himself of the fact, he, in his agitation, dropped his knife on the bleeding body, by which both his hand and the knife became bloody. These circumstances Bradford acknowledged to the clergyman who attended him after his sentence.

JOHN AYLIFFE,

EXECUTED FOR FORGERY.

THE following case is extraordinary only for the duplicity and excess of meanness exhibited by the wretched subject of it, in his application to Mr. Fox (afterwards the first Lord Holland) to save his life, at the moment he was defending himself elsewhere at the. expense of that gentleman's character. He was executed at Tyburn, in 1759, and his fate attracted much of the public attention. The following account is chiefly compiled from the statements published in the Annual Register for that year.

The parents of Ayliffe were upper servants in the family of Gerard Smith, Esq. He was in early life placed at Harrow school, and qualified to become a teacher at the free school of Lyneham, with a salary of ten pounds a year. While in that situation he married the daughter of a clergyman at Twickenham, with a fortune of £500, against the consent of her relatives.

He spent his wife's fortune extravagantly; and, about two years after his marriage, he was taken into the family of Mrs. Horner, mother of Lady Ilchester, as house-steward, and subsequently employed as an agent for the management of her estates. This lady probably recommended him to Mr. Fox, who procured for him the post of commissary of the musters. He then built himself a house at Blandford Forum in Dorsetshire, and filled it with pictures and costly furniture. By this extravagance, and his abortive projects to gain money, he dissipated his income, though it was very considerable, and involved himself deeply in debt. Thus pressed for money, he had recourse to several fraudulent contrivances to relieve himself. He forged a promise of presentation to the rectory of Brinkworth, in the hand-writing of Mr. Fox, adding the names of two persons as subscribing witnesses. By means of this paper, he prevailed on a clergyman to become his security in borrowing money, and also to engage to marry a certain young woman. It happened that the marriage had not taken place when Ayliffe's affairs became desperate; but his failure ruined the unfortunate clergyman, who died broken-hearted. After his death the following paper was found in his pocket.

" July 29, 1759, wrote the following letter to John Ayliffe Satan, Esq.

" SIR,—I am surprised you can write to me, after you have robbed and most barbarously murdered me. Oh! Brinkworth!

" Yours, T. E———d."

In April 1759, Ayliffe committed the forgery for which he suffered. Mrs. Horner, to whom he had been steward, at her death left her property chiefly to Mr. Fox, and requested that gentleman to make some provision for Ayliffe. Accordingly, Mr. Fox executed the lease of an estate in Wiltshire to him for his life and the lives of his wife and son,

reserving a rent of only thirty-five pounds, which was much below the
real annual value of the property. Ayliffe, some time after, borrowed
money on the security of this lease; and, to make it appear more valuable, copied it on a fresh skin of parchment, altering the reserved rent
from thirty-five to five pounds. To this copy he forged the name of
Mr. Fox, and of the witnesses who had subscribed the real lease. To
conceal this transaction from the knowledge of Mr. Fox, he proposed to
the person from whom he borrowed the money an oath of secrecy. This
was not agreed to, and he was obliged to be satisfied with a promise that
Mr. Fox should not be told of the mortgage. But the interest of the
money not being regularly paid, the mortgagee felt himself no longer
bound to keep the secret; and accordingly applied to Mr. Fox to pay
off the mortgage. This Mr. Fox declined doing; and, in the course of
the affair, the amount of the reserved rent was mentioned; the deed was
produced, and the fraud became manifest. In the meantime, about a
month after Ayliffe had forged the lease, he was arrested for sums
amounting to £1100, and thrown into the Fleet prison. During his
confinement there, he produced a deed of gift from Mrs. Horner to
himself of £420 in money. Mrs. Horner had died towards the close of
the year 1757; and Ayliffe alleged that she, being unwilling to let Lady
Ilchester and her relations know how she had disposed of this property,
directed him not to mention the donation till after her death. He said
he had since concealed the circumstance from Mr. Fox, lest it should
hurt his interest with that gentleman.

, Soon after this claim was set up, the forgery of the lease was found
out, and a prosecution instituted against Ayliffe. In the meantime he
affected to represent Mr. Fox's proceedings as being instituted with no
other view than to extort from him a renunciation of the deed of gift
which he professed to have received from Mrs. Horner. So far did he
persist in this diabolical accusation, that at the very time he was sup-
plicating Mr. Fox he wrote thus to the Secretary of State:—

" Mr. Fox is now pleased to disown the signing or setting his hand to
the lease, alleging it not to be original, though he acknowledged his
having signed the same lease, so mortgaged as aforesaid, to several
persons; and for this your petitioner is convicted and sentenced to
death."

At the same time that he sent the above accusation against Mr. Fox,
he forwarded the following letter to that gentleman:—

" HONOURED SIR,—The faults I have been guilty of shock my very
soul, and particularly those, sir, towards you, for which I heartily ask
God's and your pardon. The sentence I have had pronounced against
me fills me with horror, such surely as never was felt by any mortal.
What can I say? Oh, my good God! that I could think of anything I
could do to induce you to have mercy on me, and prevail on you, good
sir, to intercede for my life. I would do anything in the whole world,
and submit to anything for my life, either at home or abroad. For
God's sake, good sir, have compassion on your unhappy and unfortunate servant,   " JOHN AYLIFFE.

" Press Yard, Newgate, Oct. 28th, 1759."

Two days before he sent these letters he was tried and convicted at the Old Bailey Sessions, and received the usual sentence.

Mr. Fox, throughout the whole affair, had treated his ungrateful servant with much kindness and generosity, procuring for him every convenience which his situation would admit, sending him money, and paying the rent of his apartment in prison. A proof of the excessive depravity of this man is further evinced in a letter he wrote to Mr. Pitt, who had ever been the political antagonist of Mr. Fox. In this he stated, that it was in his power to make some disclosures relative to the conduct of the latter as a minister of state so much to his disadvantage, that the knowledge of them would leave him entirely at the mercy of Mr. Pitt. This application proved worse than fruitless, as that gentleman was the last person in the world who would have adopted so mean a mode of undermining a rival. He forwarded Ayliffe's letter to Mr. Fox, who, in justice to his own character, left the unfortunate man to his fate.

Finding his artifices as ineffectual as they were wicked, Ayliffe wrote again to Mr. Fox, offering to make a full confession of his guilt. In reply, that gentleman told him, that, although he pitied him, and forgave him, he was not to expect any advantage from his disclosures; and that he could only advise him to make his peace with God. The culprit, finding his hopes of mercy were at an end, confessed that the deed of gift from Mrs. Horner was a fraud; that he had prepared it ready for signing, and slipped it in among some leases which Mrs. Horner executed without reading.

Ayliffe seems to have been very unprepared for death, possibly flattering himself with the hope of a pardon. He was in the utmost agonies during the greater part of the night previous to his execution, but slept about two hours towards the approach of morning. His agitation of mind had induced a fever, which producing an intolerable thirst, he endeavoured to allay it by drinking large and repeated draughts of water.

On his way to the place of execution his violent agitation seemed to have subsided; and at the fatal tree he behaved with decency and composure. Some persons present called out " A reprieve !" but he paid no regard to what was said; and his hopes, respecting this life, appeared now to have vanished.

Ayliffe suffered the penalty of the law, at Tyburn, November 19th, 1759, being about thirty-six years of age.

After execution his body was put into a hearse, and conveyed into Hertfordshire for interment, agreeably to his own request.

MORGAN PHILLIPS,

EXECUTED FOR MURDER AND ARSON.

THE inhabitants of Narbeth, a small village in the county of Pembroke, were, in the middle of one night in the month of March, 1779, alarmed with the appearance of fire bursting from a farm-house near the turnpike. Before they could render assistance the house was nearly burnt to the ground, and the family were missing. On examining the ruins, the remains of the owner, Mr. Thomas, an old and respectable farmer, were found on a bench in a leaning posture, but so much burnt that it was impossible to determine whether he had been first murdered, or had perished by the flames.

Proceeding in the search, the next unhappy victim found was his niece, a fine young woman of about thirty years of age, whose body lay across the feet of a half-burnt bedstead, with a thigh broken, and an arm missing. Among the ruins of another room was discovered the body of a labouring man, much burnt, but with a large wound on the back of his head, from which much blood had issued ; and Mrs. Thomas's servant-woman, who was exceedingly robust, was also found dead at the entrance of one of the rooms, with several deep wounds in her head, and her hair clotted with blood. Her body was not so much burned as the others; and near her was discovered a large kitchen spit, half bent, with which it was conjectured she had opposed the murderers, for there could now be no doubt that the horrid scene which presented itself was the work of some person who, for the sake of plundering the house, had massacred its inhabitants and then fired the premises, in order to conceal the bloody crime. So horrible a deed excited universal indignation, and every means was taken to discover the perpetrators of it.

A man named John Morris, a lazy, worthless character, who had been already in custody upon other charges, was apprehended on suspicion of being concerned in the affair ; but he effectually put an end to all hopes of eliciting any information from him by throwing himself into a coal-pit, in spite of the efforts of the constables, in whose care he was, to restrain him, where his mangled remains were afterwards found. At length suspicion fell on Morgan Phillips ; and he, finding the general belief to be that he was guilty of this most horrible crime, at length confessed that he and Morris had been its perpetrators ; that they had broken into the house of the farmer, and, having murdered the family, from whom they met with considerable resistance, they had carried off all the valuable property which they could find, and had then set fire to the farm to prevent discovery.

The prisoner being put upon his trial at Haverfordwest, his confession was read to him, and assented to as being true ; and its leading points being corroborated by other witnesses, he was found guilty, and suffered death at the same place on the 5th of April, 1779.

EMMET AT THE HEAD OF HIS PARTIZANS IN THOMAS STREET.

ROBERT EMMET,

EXECUTED FOR HIGH TREASON.

THIS enthusiast was the son of Dr. Emmet, a man of good family, and possessed of considerable wealth; but who, having imbibed opinions favourable to republicanism, took care to instil them into his children. His eldest son was implicated in the Irish rebellion of 1798, and escaped with his life upon the terms offered to Arthur O'Connor, Dr. M'Nevin, and others, and accepted by them; and, like them, he became an exile in a foreign land.

The hero of the present sketch was intended for the Irish bar, and received a most liberal education. In Trinity College he became conspicuous, not only for his abilities, but for his display of eloquence in the "Historical Debating Society," a school which matured the talents of Bushe, Burrows, and several other members of the Irish bar. Young Emmet, however, wanted discretion; and having too often avowed his political principles, a prosecution was threatened; to avoid which he precipitately fled to France, where his republican opinions became confirmed.

In 1803 he returned to Dublin, not being then more than twenty-four years of age, and found himself in possession of three thousand five hundred pounds, left him by his father, then recently deceased. With this money, and the talents and connexions which he possessed, he might easily have established his own independence; but the sober business of

18   T

life had no attractions for him; he aspired to greater fame, and resolved to attempt the separation of his country from England.

Wild and extravagant as the scheme was, he entered seriously upon it, and easily found abettors among those who had escaped the angry vengeance of 1798. Having procured several associates, he took a house in Patrick-street, and converted it into a rebel depôt for powder, guns, swords, pikes, &c. In the purchase and preparation of these he expended upwards of a thousand pounds; but, before the plan of insurrection was ripe, the powder in the magazine through accident ignited, and the whole depôt was blown into the air. Such, however, was the fidelity of Emmet's partisans, that no discovery took place, further than that caused by the explosion; and the government, who ordered the guns to be brought to the Castle, remained ignorant of the purpose for which those destructive implements were provided.

A mind so sanguine as that of Emmet was not to be damped by an accidental disappointment: he collected his partisans, took another house in a lane in Thomas-street, and again commenced preparations for a popular rebellion. The ramifications of treason were easily extended through Ireland, where the discontent of the Catholics induced them to join in any extravagant scheme which promised them redress of grievances. Emmet had correspondents in every county; and the 23d of July, 1803, was the day appointed for a general rising, the signal of which was to be an attack upon Dublin.

The plan of surprising the metropolis was admirably adapted for its sanguinary purpose; but fortunately several disappointments took place, and Emmet was unable to proceed as he intended. In the confusion of such a moment the rebels deceived one another; and several hundred men, who came in from the country, returned home, being told that the *rising* was postponed, while those who remained were crowded into the depôt, and impeded the preparations. It was too late, however, to retract, or alter the intended movement, as Emmet expected the whole country to rise on that night. He therefore made the desperate attempt, and, with eighty followers, sallied out, at nine o'clock, into Thomas-street, and made towards the Castle, which he intended to surprise.

The experience of a few minutes showed him his madness and folly; for he quickly found himself without authority, in the midst of a ruffianly mob, who would neither obey nor accompany him, but who soon convinced him, that, though cowardly, they were brutal and sanguinary. When he had arrived at the market-house, his followers had diminished to eighteen; and as he was now convinced of his rashness, he prevented the discharge of a rocket which was to be the signal for the outposts to commence hostilities. This act saved the lives of hundreds; for the Wexford men, to the number of three hundred, had assembled on the Coal-quay, and other large bodies had met in the barley-fields behind Mountjoy-square; all of whom, in consequence, escaped uninjured, and were prevented from inflicting injury on others.

The rebel band in Thomas-street, meanwhile, largely increased in numbers; but, being without a leader, they remained confused and inactive. At this moment, however, an act of atrocity was perpetrated, sufficiently serious to exhibit the nature of the design. The coach of the lamented Lord Kilwarden, chief-justice of the Court of King's Bench, containing his lordship, and his nephew and niece (the Rev. Mr. Wolfe, and Miss Wolfe), drove up, and was instantly surrounded. Much confusion prevailed, and his lordship received a deadly stab, from the hand of an assassin, which eventually deprived him of life; his nephew was dragged from the vehicle, and ill-treated; but Miss Wolfe was borne to an opposite house in the arms of a lusty rebel, apparently more humane than his comrades.

The precise particulars of the murder of Lord Kilwarden are not known, and have always been the subject of controversy. By some it is alleged, that it was the unpremeditated act of a ferocious rabble; by others, that he was mistaken for another person; but there is another account, which admits the mistake in the first instance, but subjoins other particulars, which appear sufficiently probable. It is related, that in the year 1795, when his lordship was attorney-general, a number of young men, between the ages of fifteen and twenty years, were indicted for high treason, who upon the day appointed for their trial appeared at the bar wearing shirts with tuckers and open collars, in the manner usual with boys. When the chief-justice of the King's Bench appeared in court to proceed with their trial, he remarked, " Well, Mr. Attorney, I suppose you are ready to go on with the trial of these tuckered traitors?" The attorney-general was quite prepared to proceed at once; but, disgusted with the remark which had been made, he said, " No, my lord, I am not ready;" and he added, in a lower tone to the prisoners' counsel, " If I have any power to save the lives of these boys, whose extreme youth I did not before observe, that man shall never have the gratification of passing sentence upon one of these *tuckered* traitors." He performed his promise, and soon afterwards procured pardons for them all, upon condition of their going abroad. One of them, however, refused to accept the pardon upon the condition imposed; and being obstinate, he was tried, convicted, and executed. After his death, it is said that his relatives, readily listening to every misrepresentation which flattered their resentment, became persuaded that the attorney-general had selected him alone to suffer the utmost severity of the laws. One of these, a person named Shannon, was an insurgent of the 23rd July; and when Lord Kilwarden, hearing the popular cry of vengeance, exclaimed from his carriage, " It is I, Kilwarden, chief-justice of the King's Bench," Shannon immediately cried out, " Then you are the man I want," and instantly plunged a pike into his lordship's body.

Whatever may be the truth or falsehood of this story, his lordship's death, there is no doubt, was the effect of the violence of the mob on this occasion; and it appears, that the fatal wound had scarcely been given, when a party of military reaching the spot, the people were put to flight, and his lordship's body rescued from further violence, and conveyed to Werburgh-street.

Major Swan soon after arrived, and, in his fury at the attack upon so good a man, exclaimed indignantly, that every rebel taken with arms in his hands ought to be instantly hanged; when his lordship, who still lived, turned round, and impressively exhorted him " to let no man suffer but by the laws of his country." In a few minutes after, this great and good man expired.

For a few hours the rebels continued to skirmish with the military, and several men were killed. By morning, however, all appearance of rebellion had vanished, and large rewards were offered for the apprehension of the leader, Robert Emmet, who had fled to the Wicklow mountains, where a considerable rising had been projected, and succeeded in preventing the intended movement. " Defeated in our first grand attempt," said he, " all further endeavours must be futile : our friends are dispirited ; and our only hope is now in patience. The justice of our cause must one day triumph ; and let us not indiscreetly protract the period by any premature endeavours to accelerate it. No doubt, I could, in forty-eight hours, wrap the whole kingdom in the flames of rebellion ; but as I have no ambition beyond the good of my country, I best study her interest, and the interest of freedom, by declining to elevate my name upon the ruin of thousands, and afford our tyrants an apology to draw another chain around unhappy Ireland. In revolts, the first blow decides the contest : we have aimed one ; and missing the mark, let us retire unobserved, and leave the enemy ignorant of the hand which was raised for their destruction. Impenetrable secresy surrounds all our measures : the loss we have sustained is inconsiderable ; and, unacquainted with their own danger, and the extent of our resources, the tyrants of Ireland will relapse into false security, and afford us, perhaps sooner than we imagine, another opportunity to attack the hydra of oppression. Let me therefore, my friends, advise you to act with that prudence which becomes men engaged in the grandest of all causes —the liberation of their country. Be cautious, be silent ; and do not afford our enemies any ground for either tyranny or suspicion ; but, above all, never forget that you are *United Irishmen*—sworn to promote the liberty of your country by all the means in your power."

This unfortunate young man was every way an enthusiast ; for his love was as extravagant as his patriotism. It appears that soon after his return from France he visited at the house of Curran, the celebrated Irish barrister, and became attached to that gentleman's youngest daughter. Their affection was mutual, but unknown to Mr. Curran. Upon the failure of the insurrection, Emmet might easily have effected his departure from the kingdom, had he attended solely to his safety ; but, in the same spirit of romantic enthusiasm which distinguished his short career, he could not submit to leave the country to which he could never more return, without making an effort to have one final interview with the object of his unfortunate attachment, in order to receive her personal forgiveness for what he now considered as the deepest injury. With a view of obtaining this last gratification, he selected a place of concealment midway between Mr. Curran's country-house and Dublin ; but before the meeting took place he was arrested. On his person were found some papers, which showed that he corresponded with Mr. Curran's family, in consequence of which that gentleman's house was searched, and the letters there found were produced in evidence against him,

His trial came on, at the Sessions-House, Green-street, Dublin, September 19th, 1803, before Lord Norbury; and the evidence being conclusive, his conviction followed. When called upon in the usual way, before sentence was passed, he addressed the Court as follows:—

" I am asked if I have anything to say why sentence of death should not be pronounced upon me. Were I to suffer only death, after being adjudged guilty, I should bow in silence; but a man in my situation has not only to combat with the difficulties of fortune, but also the difficulties of prejudice: the sentence of the law, which delivers over his body to the executioner, consigns his character to obloquy. The man dies, but his memory lives; and that mine may not forfeit all claim to the respect of my countrymen, I use this occasion to vindicate myself from some of the charges advanced against me.

" I am charged with being an emissary of France. 'Tis false: I am no emissary—I did not wish to deliver up my country to a foreign power, and, least of all, to France. No; never did I entertain the idea of establishing French power in Ireland—God forbid! On the contrary, it is evident from the introductory paragraph of the Address of the Provisional Government, that every hazard attending an independent effort was deemed preferable to the more fatal risk of introducing a French army into the country. Small would be our claims to patriotism and to sense, and palpable our affectation of the love of liberty, if we were to encourage the profanation of our shores by a people who are slaves themselves, and the unprincipled and abandoned instruments of imposing slavery on others. If such an inference be drawn from any part of the proclamation of the Provisional Government, it calumniates their views, and is not warranted by the fact. How could they speak of freedom to their countrymen?—how assume such an exalted motive, and meditate the introduction of a power which has been the enemy of freedom in every part of the globe? Reviewing the conduct of France to other countries, could we expect better towards us? No! Let not, then, any man attaint my memory by believing that I could have hoped for freedom through the aid of France, and betrayed the sacred cause of liberty by committing it to the power of her most determined foe: had I done so, I had not deserved to live; and dying with such a weight upon my character, I had merited the honest execration of that country which gave me birth, and to which I would have given freedom.

" Had I been in Switzerland, I would have fought against the French —in the dignity of freedom, I would have expired on the threshold of that country, and they should have entered it only by passing over my lifeless corpse. Is it, then, to be supposed, that I would be slow to make the same sacrifice to my native land? Am I, who lived but to be of service to my country, and who would subject myself to the bondage of the grave to give her independence—am I to be loaded with the foul and grievous calumny of being an emissary of France? My lords, it may be part of the system of angry justice to bow a man's mind by humiliation to meet the ignominy of the scaffold; but worse to me than the scaffold's shame or the scaffold's terrors would be the imputation of having been the agent of French despotism and ambition: and while I have breath, I will call upon my countrymen not to believe me guilty of so foul a crime against their liberties and their happiness.

" Though you, my lord, sit there a judge, and I stand here a culprit, yet you are but a man, and I am an other; I have a rigththerefore to vindicate my character and motives from the aspersions of calumny; and as a man to whom fame is dearer than life, I will make the last use of that life in rescuing my name and my memory from the afflicting imputation of having been an emissary of France, or seeking her inter- ference in the regulation of our internal affairs.

" Did I live to see a French army approach this country, I would meet it on the shore with a torch in one hand and a sword in the other— I would receive them with all the destruction of war! I would animate my countrymen to immolate them in their very boats; and before our native soil should be polluted by a foreign foe, if they succeeded in land- ing, I would burn every blade of grass before them, raze every house, contend to the last for every inch of ground; and the last spot on which the hope of freedom should desert me, that spot I would make my grave. What I cannot do, I leave a legacy to my country, because I feel con- scious that my death were unprofitable, and all hope of liberty extinct, the moment a French army obtained a footing in this land. God forbid that I should see my country under the hands of a foreign power.

" My lamp of life is nearly expired—my race is finished; the grave opens to receive me, and I sink into its bosom. All I request, then, at parting from the world, is the charity of its silence. Let no man write my epitaph; for as no man, who knows my motives, dare vindicate them, let not prejudice or ignorance asperse them; let them and me repose in obscurity and peace, and my tomb remain uninscribed, till other times and other men can do justice to my character."

Judgment was then passed on him in the usual form, and he was ordered for execution. On his return to Newgate he drew up a state- ment of the insurrection, and the cause of its failure, which he requested might be sent to his brother, Thomas Addis, who was then at Paris.

The unfortunate young man, on the night before his execution, wrote to Mr. Curran and his son Robert, excusing himself for his conduct towards Miss Curran; and the firmness and regularity of the original hand-writing afford an affecting proof of the little influence which the approaching event exerted over his frame. The same enthusiasm which allured him to his destruction enabled him to support its utmost rigour. He met his fate with unostentatious fortitude; and although few could ever think of justifying his projects or regretting their failure, yet his youth, his talents, and the great respectability of his connexions, and the evident delusion of which he was the victim, have excited more general sympathy for his unfortunate end, and more forbearance towards his memory, than is usually extended to the errors or sufferings of poli- tical offenders.

Moore, the celebrated Irish bard, has lamented his fate in the follow- ing melody :—

" Oh! breathe not his name—let it sleep in the shade,
    Where cold and unhonour'd his relics are laid!

Sad, silent, and dark, be the tears that we shed,
As the night-dew that falls on the grass o'er his head.

But the night-dew that falls, though in silence it weeps,
Shall brighten with verdure the grave where he sleeps;
And the tear that we shed, though in secret it rolls,
Shall long keep his memory green in our souls."

Several of Emmet's deluded followers met the fate of the leader, and by their ignominious deaths taught their countrymen the folly and madness of attempting to separate Ireland from this kingdom by violent means.

The following pathetic history of Miss Curran, after the death of her lover, is extracted from Washington Irving's " Sketch Book," in which it appears under the title of " The Broken Heart." It is rather long, but its beauty will amply repay the trouble of its perusal :—

" Every one must recollect the tragical story of young E———, the Irish patriot; it was too touching to be soon forgotten. During the troubles in Ireland, he was tried, condemned, and executed, on a charge of treason. His fate made a deep impression on public sympathy. He was so young—so intelligent—so generous—so brave—so everything that we are apt to like in a young man. His conduct under trial, too, was so lofty and intrepid! The noble indignation with which he repelled the charge of treason against his country—the eloquent vindication of his name—and his pathetic appeal to posterity, in the hopeless hour of condemnation—all these entered deeply into every generous bosom, and even his enemies lamented the stern policy that dictated his execution.

" But there was one heart, whose anguish it would be impossible to describe. In happier days and fairer fortunes, he had won the affections of a beautiful and interesting girl, the daughter of a late celebrated Irish barrister. She loved him with the disinterested fervour of a woman's first and early love. When every worldly maxim arrayed itself against him; when blasted in fortune, and disgrace and danger darkened around his name, she loved him the more ardently for his very sufferings. If, then, his fate could awaken the sympathy even of his foes, what must have been the agony of her whose soul was occupied by his image! Let those tell who have had the portals of the tomb suddenly closed between them and the being they most loved on earth—who have sat at its threshold, as one shut out in the cold and lonely world, from whence all that was most lovely and loving had departed.

" But then the horrors of such a grave! so frightful, so dishonoured! There was nothing for memory to dwell on, that could soothe the pang of separation—none of those tender, though melancholy circumstances, that endear the parting scene—nothing to melt sorrow into those blessed tears, sent, like the dews of heaven, to revive the heart in the parching hour of anguish.

" To render her widowed situation more desolate, she had incurred her father's displeasure by her unfortunate attachment, and was an exile from the paternal roof. But could the sympathy and kind offices of friends have reached a spirit so shocked and riven by horror she would have experienced no want of consolation; for the Irish are a people of quick and generous sensibilities. The most delicate and cherishing attentions were paid her by families of wealth and distinction. She was led into society, and they tried by all kinds of occupation and amusement to dissipate her grief, and wean her from the tragical story of her lover. But it was all in vain. There are some strokes of calamity that scathe and scorch the soul—that penetrate to the vital seat of happiness, and blast it, never again to put forth bud or blossom. She never objected to frequent the haunts of pleasure, but she was as much alone there as in the depth of solitude. She walked about in a sad reverie, apparently unconscious of the world around her. She carried with her an inward woe, that mocked all the blandishments of friendship, and ' heeded not the song of the charmer, charm he never so wisely.'

"The person who told me her story had seen her at a masquerade. There can be no exhibition of far-gone wretchedness more striking and painful than to meet it in such a scene. To find it wandering like a spectre, lonely and joyless, where all around is gay—to see it dressed out in the trappings of mirth, and looking so wan and woe-begone, as if it had tried in vain to cheat the poor heart into a momentary forgetfulness of sorrow. After strolling through the splendid rooms and giddy crowd with an utter air of abstraction, she sat herself down on the steps of an orchestra, and looking about some time with a vacant air, that showed her insensibility of the garish scene, she began, with the capriciousness of a sickly heart, to warble a little plaintive air. She had an exquisite voice; but on this occasion it was so simple, so touching, it breathed forth such a soul of wretchedness, that she drew a crowd mute and silent around her, and melted every one into tears.

"The story of one so true and tender could not but excite great interest in a country remarkable for enthusiasm. It completely won the heart of a brave officer, who paid his addresses to her, and thought that one so true to the dead could not but prove affectionate to the living. She declined his attentions, for her thoughts were irrecoverably engrossed by the memory of her former lover. He, however, persisted in his suit. He solicited not her tenderness, but her esteem. He was assisted by her conviction of his worth, and her sense of her own destitute and dependent situation—for she was existing on the kindness of her friends. In a word, he at length succeeded in gaining her hand, though with the solemn assurance that her heart was unalterably another's.

"He took her with him to Sicily, hoping that a change of scene might wear out the remembrance of early woes. She was an amiable and exemplary wife, and made an effort to be a happy one; but nothing could cure the silent and devouring melancholy that had entered into her very soul. She wasted away in a slow, but hopeless decline; and at length sunk into the grave, the victim of a broken heart."

JOHN HATFIELD,

EXECUTED FOR FORGERY.

THIS man was the son of poor parents who lived at Mortram, near Longdale, in Cheshire, where he was born in the year 1759. Having by some means procured the situation of rider or traveller to a linen-draper in the north of England, he became acquainted, in the course of his travels, with a young woman under the guardianship of a respectable farmer, but who was in reality the natural daughter of Lord Robert Manners. The secret of her birth was not generally known, but it was communicated to our hero, with an intimation that upon her marriage, provided it should be with the consent of her father, a dowry of £1000 would be paid. He therefore lost no time in securing the good-will of the young lady; and having then obtained the consent of her noble father, he was married to her, and received from his lordship the sum of £1500. The money, however, was soon spent in the gaieties of London, and he was compelled to retreat with his wife into the country, where he continued until the year 1782. He then again visited the metropolis, having deserted his wife and three children, and, in spite of his fallen fortunes, proceeded to live in a style of considerable extravagance, boasting of his near connexion with the Rutland family, and of his estates in the country. In the course of his residence in London his unhappy wife died, and our hero was almost immediately afterwards conveyed to the King's Bench for a debt of £160. By means of an imposture he succeeded in obtaining the payment of this debt by the Duke of Rutland, and his consequent discharge, and he was again thrown upon the town to live by his wits.

In the year 1785 the Duke of Rutland was appointed lord-lieutenant of Ireland; and directly after his arrival in Dublin, Hatfield followed him. Taking up his abode at an hotel in College-green, he acquainted the landlord with his pretended connexion with the viceroy, and declared that he was only prevented from proceeding at once to the Castle by the circumstance of his carriage, and horses, and servants, not having yet arrived. A month was passed by the lodger in a pretended state of disappointment at the non-appearance of his equipage; and at the expiration of that period the landlord took the liberty of presenting his bill, which amounted to upwards of £60. Mr. Hatfield was in nowise confused, but said, that although, fortunately, his agent was then in Ireland holding a public situation, he was at that time on a visit in the country, from which he would not return for three days. The landlord was satisfied; but on the fourth day he again made his appearance, and was now directed to a gentleman at the Castle, to whom he forthwith proceeded with his account. The answer was of a nature most unsatisfactory to his wishes; for the supposed agent very frankly told him, that he was the dupe of an impostor; and the only consolation he received was the information, that others had suffered as well as himself.

His guest was now no longer welcome at his table ; but, being under the necessity of driving him from his own house, he provided him with other lodgings in the Marshalsea, to which he was conveyed by virtue of a writ issued at his instance. On his entering the gaol, Hatfield whispered the keeper and his wife, " to be sure and keep it a profound secret, that he was a relation to the viceroy, as it might not be agreeable to his Excellency that it should be known that he was in prison." These people, astonished at the discovery, which they then made for the first time, conducted him to the best apartment, had a table provided, and continued to furnish him with all the necessary commodities for his support during the ensuing three weeks. In the meantime, however, he had again petitioned the Duke for fresh supplies ; and his Grace, being apprehensive that he might continue his impositions in Dublin, released him on condition of his quitting Ireland ; and, in order to be assured that this stipulation was obeyed, he sent a servant to see him on board the next vessel sailing for Holyhead.

He now visited Scarborough, and there practised similar impositions ; but his frauds being discovered, he was arrested and lodged in gaol, where he continued for a period of eight years and a half. At the expiration of that time, a Miss Nation, of Devonshire, paid his debts, and procured his liberation ; and, furthermore, bestowed her hand on him in marriage. He then had the good fortune to obtain admission into a respectable firm at Tiverton as partner, and continued to live during about three years in apparent respectability ; but then, having put up as a candidate for the borough of Queenborough, his real character was discovered, and he was made a bankrupt. He now retired, leaving his second wife and two children behind him ; and nothing more was heard of him until the year 1802, when he drove up in a carriage to the Queen's Head Inn, at Keswick, and assumed the name of Colonel the Hon. Alexander Augustus Hope, brother of the Earl of Hopetoun, and member for Linlithgow. Unfortunately some evil genius directed his steps to the once happy cottage of poor Mary, the only daughter of Mr. and Mrs. Robinson, an old couple, who kept a small public-house at the side of the beautiful lake of Buttermere, in Cumberland, and who, by their industry, had amassed a small property ; and poor Mary of Buttermere, whose charms have since become so celebrated from Wordsworth's sweet poem in which they are described, was doomed to become the victim of his villainous schemes. During a short stay at Buttermere, he contrived to wheedle himself into the good graces of poor Mary. But he was not to be satisfied with the possession of a country girl, when higher game was in view. On his first arrival at Keswick, he had become acquainted with an Irish gentleman named Murphy, a member of the then existing Irish House of Commons, who with his family, and accompanied by a young lady, possessed of a considerable fortune, and no less personal attractions, was on a tour through the justly admired lakes of Cumberland. The affable condescension with which his advances were received, induced him to suppose that his address and manners were not displeasing to the young lady or her guardian, and he resolved to improve the opportunity which presented itself. Quitting the society of the gentle Mary therefore, he returned to Keswick, and, ere long, had so far ingratiated himself with the young lady as to obtain a promise of her hand in marriage. Being known only by his assumed title, he was urged to write to Lord Hopetoun, to acquaint him with the intended union, and he promised instantly to comply with a request which appeared so reasonable. Writing letters therefore, which by virtue of his pretended rank of M.P. he franked, he dispatched them; and, until answers were received, he proposed various trips to while away the time. The preparations for the marriage, however, occupied the time and attention of the young lady to too great a degree to permit her quitting Keswick, and Hatfield seized the opportunity to continue his courtship to the Beauty of Buttermere. In this manner some weeks elapsed without any communication being received from the Earl of Hopetoun, and the frequent and prolonged absences of the supposed colonel excited some surprise among his Irish friends.

At length, on the 1st October 1802, a letter was received by Mr. Murphy from Hatfield, dated Buttermere, in which a request was contained, that a draft inclosed, purporting to be drawn by Col. Hope on Mr. Crampt, a banker in Liverpool, might be cashed; and that gentleman, still having no good reason to doubt the integrity of his correspondent, immediately transmitted to him £30, the amount of the check. On the 4th of the same month, however, Wood, the landlord of the Queen's Head, where the whole party had been stopping, brought over intelligence from the village of Lorton, in Buttermere, that Colonel Hope had been married on the previous day to Mary Robinson. On inquiry it turned out that this was perfectly true, and that the marriage having taken place, the bride and bridegroom had gone to Scotland to spend the honeymoon. It being now obvious that the latter, whoever he might be, had acted most dishonourably towards his ward, Mr. Murphy determined to write to Lord Hopetoun, for the purpose of ascertaining how far he was entitled to the name and rank which he had assumed. Circumstances soon transpired, which induced a belief that he had no pretensions to the character which he had taken, and a warrant was issued for his apprehension. In the mean time he had proceeded with his bride as far as Longtown, on their wedding trip; but on reaching that spot he pretended surprise at not meeting some friends whom, he said, he had expected, and returned to Buttermere. He was there charged with having assumed a fictitious name, but he flatly denied the truth of the allegation; but the warrant being brought, by which he was alleged to have forged several franks as M.P. for Linlithgow, he was committed to the care of a constable. He, however, found means to make his escape from this custody; and having with great boldness passed through several towns where his person was known, he was at length apprehended within sixteen miles of Swansea, and committed to Brecon gaol. Before the magistrates he declared that his name was Tudor Henry; but, his person being identified, he was sent to London to be examined. He was then transmitted to Cumberland, where he was charged with forging several franks, and also the bill for which he had obtained cash at Keswick, and committed for trial; the charge for bigamy, which also stood against him, not being preferred.

He was tried at the ensuing Carlisle assizes before Sir A. Thompson, when the jury found him guilty, and he was sentenced to death.

A notion very generally prevailed that he would escape capital punishment, and the arrival of the mail was daily expected with the greatest impatience. No pardon arriving, however, Saturday, 3rd September 1803, was at last fixed upon for his execution.

The gallows was erected on the preceding night, between twelve and three o'clock, in an island formed by the river Eden, on the north of the town, between the two bridges. From the hour when the jury found him guilty, he behaved with the utmost serenity and cheerfulness. He received the visits of all who wished to see him, and talked upon the topics of the day with the greatest interest or indifference. He could scarcely ever be brought to speak of his own case; and when he did, he neither blamed the verdict, nor made any confession of his guilt. He said that he had no intention to defraud those whose names he forged; but was never heard to say that he was to die unjustly. The alarming nature of the crime of forgery, in a commercial country, had taught him from the beginning to entertain no hope of mercy.

By ten o'clock in the morning of September 3rd, his irons were struck off; and he then appeared as usual. A little after, two clergymen attended, and prayed with him. He afterwards wrote several letters, and at three o'clock ate a hearty dinner with the gaoler. Having afterwards drunk two glasses of wine, and partaken of some coffee, he set out for the scaffold. He was pinioned in the turnkey's lodge, where he sent for the executioner, and gave him some silver. When he came to the gallows, he asked whether that " was the tree he was to die on?" On being answered in the affirmative, he exclaimed, " Oh! a happy sight, I see it with pleasure."

On his being turned off, great apprehensions were entertained that it would be necessary to tie him up a second time. The noose slipped twice, and he fell down above eighteen inches, his feet at last almost touching the ground; but his excessive weight, which occasioned this accident, speedily relieved him from pain. He expired in a moment, and without any struggle.

He was cut down after he had hung about an hour. On the preceding Wednesday he had had a carpenter to take the measure for his coffin, and he ordered it to be a strong one, plain and neat, requesting that, after he was taken down, he might be put into it immediately, with the apparel he might have on, and carried to the churchyard of Burgh-on-Sands to be interred. The parishioners of Burgh, however, objected to his being laid there, and the body was consequently conveyed in the hearse to St. Mary's, Carlisle, where it was interred in a distant corner of the churchyard, far from the other tombs. No priest attended, and the coffin was lowered without any religious service. Notwithstanding his various and complicated enormities, his untimely end excited considerable commisseration. His manners were extremely polished and insinuating, and he was possessed of qualities which might have rendered him an ornament of society.

INTRODUCTION OF A STRANGER TO THE WALTHAM BLACKS.

THE WALTHAM BLACKS.

THE actions of these offenders became so much the object of public notice, that it was deemed necessary to frame a particular act of parliament in order to bring them to justice. They were accustomed to go in great numbers, with their faces blacked, into the parks of the nobility and gentry, and shoot and steal deer, &c.; and at length they murdered the Bishop of Winchester's gamekeeper, on Waltham Chace. From the circumstances of this being the principal scene of their depredations, and from their blacking their faces, they obtained the name of the *Waltham Blacks.*

The offence of deer stealing was formerly only a misdemeanor at common law; but, to put down offenders of this description, an act of parliament was passed in the year 1723, by which it was made felony, punishable with death, for any persons whatever, armed with offensive weapons, and having their faces blacked, or being otherwise disguised, to appear in any forest, chace, park, or grounds inclosed wherein deer are kept, or in any warren where hares or coneys are kept, or in any high road, heath, or down, and unlawfully to hunt, kill, or steal any red or fallow deer, &c. &c.

The following extract from a letter written by a gentleman who had fallen in with some of this black fraternity, will form a fitting introduction to a more particular history of them.

" Dear Sir—You must have heard of the ' Waltham Blacks,' a set of whimsical merry fellows, that are so mad as to run the greatest hazards for a haunch of venison, or spending a merry evening. For my part, I took the stories of them for fables, until experience taught me to the contrary by the following adventure.

" My horse being lamed with a stone in his foot, I was under the necessity of putting up at a small ale-house, with a stable and a yard behind it. The man received me very civilly; but when I inquired if he could accommodate me all night, he answered that he had no room. I requested him to put something to my horse's foot, and I would sit up all night. He was silent. The good wife was more rude, and insisted upon her husband bringing my horse out instantly; but, putting a crown into her hand, and promising another in the morning, she became more accommodating. She then told me, that there was a small bed up stairs, upon which she would lay a pair of clean sheets, and added, that she supposed I was more of a gentleman than to take any notice of what I saw passing there. This created in me much uneasiness: I concluded that I had fallen into a den of highwaymen; and that I should not only be robbed, but have my throat cut. Necessity, however, constrained me to submit.

" It was now dark, and I heard three or four men dismount from their horses, lead them into the yard; and, as they were coming into the room, I heard the landlord say, ' Indeed, brother, you need not be uneasy; I am positive the gentleman is a man of honour.' Another said, ' What good could our death do to a stranger? The gentleman will be happy of our company. Hang fear! I'll lead the way.' So said, so done; in came five, so effectually disguised, that, unless it were in the same disguise, I should not be able to distinguish any one of them. Down they sat, and their captain accosted me with great civility, and requested me to honour them with my company at supper. Supposing that my landlord would not permit either a robbery or a murder in his house, I gradually became composed.

" About ten, I heard the noise of a number of horses arriving, and the feet of men stamping in an upper room. In a little time the landlord came to inform me that supper was upon the table. Upon this we all went up stairs, and the captain, with a ridiculous kind of ceremony, introduced me to a man more disguised than the rest, sitting at the head of the table; at the same time adding, that he hoped I should have no objection to pay my respects to Prince Oronooko, King of the Blacks. Then I began to perceive what kind of persons they were, and was astonished that the hurry and agitation I was in had prevented me from discovering sooner.

" The supper consisted of eighteen dishes of venison in various shapes —roasted, boiled, with broth, hashed collops, pastries, umble pies, and a large haunch in the centre, larded. The table we sat at was large, and twenty-one sat down to supper. Each had a bottle of claret, and the man and woman of the house sat at the lower end of the table. A few of them had good musical voices, and the evening was spent with as great jollity as by the rakes at King's Arms, or the city apprentices at

Sadlers' Wells. About two, the company broke up, all of them assuring me, that, upon any Thursday evening, they would be happy to see me at supper.

" They also did me the honour to inform me of the rules by which their society was regulated. The Black Prince informed me, that their government was monarchical, and that, when they went upon any expedition, he had an absolute command. But in time of peace, and at table, he condescends to live familiarly with his subjects, as friends. That no person was admitted into their association until he was twice drunk, that they might be perfectly acquainted with his temper. When it is agreed that a brother is to be admitted, he must provide himself with a good horse, a brace of pistols, and a gun to lie on the saddle-bow. Then he is sworn upon the horns over the chimney, and, having a new name conferred upon him, he is entered upon the roll, and constituted a member.

" In the morning I presented my landlady with the second crown, and prosecuted my journey with no small degree of amazement. Nor, I suppose, sir, can all your rambling about London produce any thing similar. I am yours, &c."

We shall now present our readers with a short sketch of the lives of a few who were members of this fraternity, and who suffered the effects of their folly and criminality. The first we shall mention is Richard Parvin, who kept a public-house in Portsmouth—a dull, slow man, who always denied his being concerned with these people, though the evidence was undeniably clear against him. It was proved that he was in the forest, when the actions charged against the rest were committed; but he said, that he had a maid who left his service, and that, in search of her, he was led across the forest, and, calling at the house of Mr. Parford, who kept an ale-house in the forest, he might have supposed that he was one of that band. He said, that if his finances had enabled him to bring witnesses from Berkshire, he could have proved his innocence; but the Mayor of Portsmouth, upon his being apprehended, had seized upon all his substance, and that his family was not only in distress, but he was destitute of the means necessary to evince his complete innocence. He persisted in maintaining his innocence to the last.

Edward Elliot, a boy about seventeen, was the next who received sentence of death with Parvin. The boy declared, that about a year before he was apprehended, he met with thirty or forty men in the county of Surrey, who dragging him along, the chief of them told him that he enlisted him into the service of the King of the Blacks; therefore he commanded me to disguise my face, and obey whatever he chose to order, else I should be turned into a beast, constrained to carry their burdens, and live, like a horse, upon grass and water. He also mentioned some of their witchcraft arts, that he had seen them practise. Two men had offended them, and refused to take their oath; they blindfolded and buried them, in holes dug in the earth, up to the chin, then ran towards them barking, as if they had been dogs; and when they had terrified them in this ridiculous manner, they took them out, and desired them, for the future, to beware how they offended any of the black nation, lest they should not escape so easily. He mentioned likewise, that carters had often been constrained to go out of their way to carry their venison, and that they were afraid so much as to complain.

Elliot gave the following account of the crime for which he suffered. He said, that one morning six of these men came to him, and advised him to go to Farnham-Holt, and said that he need not fear, because there were persons of fortune concerned with them, who would protect him against all harm. He admitted, however, that he did consent to go, but trembled all the way, and was scarcely arrived at the Holt, when the deer was killed. That the keepers found him separated from the rest, sauntering after a fawn, which he intended as a present to a young woman at Guildford, and that the keepers bound him, and went in search of his associates. The keepers were six in number, and the blacks seven, and they commenced in great fury with quarter-staves. The keepers, unwilling to have blood shed, admonished them to retire. They not only refused, but Marshal, one of them, fired and killed one of the keepers. The keepers then fired, and, wounding some of the blacks, three fled, and two, Marshal and Kingshel, were taken. Meanwhile Elliot lay all the time in the most inexpressible agony, well knowing, whatever blood was spilt that he should be accountable for along with the rest. The keepers returned, and carried him with them, and his fetters were never off until the morning of his execution. He conducted himself soberly, and with much concern and penitence.   5

Robert Kingshel was about twenty-six years of age. He lived in the house with his parents and brother, whose business he was taught by them. They were at all pains to restrain him from bad company; but the night before that unhappy accident happened, when all the family were in bed, Barber came, knocked softly at the window of his chamber, when he arose, and rode behind him to the Holt, calling upon their accomplices by the way. He said, that it was eight in the morning before they were attacked by the keepers; that the latter desired them to retire, but they refused, unless Elliot, who was bound, should be set at liberty, and restored to them; and that this being refused, the fight ensued. From the moment that he was apprehended, he laid aside all thoughts of a pardon, and was anxiously concerned to prepare for his awful fate.

Henry Marshal, the unfortunate person by whom the murder was committed, seemed to have the least sense of his crime. In the judgments of Heaven, he was deprived of the use of his reason and speech shortly after the commission of the murder, and remained so until the day before his death. Then a clergyman waited upon him, and represented the nature of the horrible crime which he had committed; but he treated his admonitions with neglect, saying, " Sure he might stand upon his own defence, and was not bound to run away, and leave his companions in danger." Such was the language he employed only a few hours before his death. He only regretted his sin inasmuch as it had brought punishment upon him; and he in no respect considered it as heinous, either in the sight of God, or meriting the punishment awarded him. In this manner the vicious reason themselves into the legality of taking away the life of a fellow-creature, merely because, in the exercise of his duty, he endeavours to arrest their criminal career, and bring them to deserved punishment.

There were also two brothers, John and Edward Pink. These were accounted honest and industrious persons before this crime, in which they were detected. They, however, acknowledged that they had been concerned in the crime for which they suffered. That they met Parvin's maid upon the road, the woman mentioned in that man's narrative (and whom Parvin said he was in pursuit of when he was in the forest—and it certainly is a strong circumstance in support of the innocence of Parvin); that they put a dagger into her hand, and forced her to cut the throat of a deer; that she wore it afterwards, and rode upon a horse with pistols over the saddle. That in this dress they carried her to Parford's house upon the forest, where they dined upon a haunch of venison, feasted sumptuously, and sent out two of their companions to slay more deer, not in the King's Forest, but in Waltham Chace. One of these persons they called their King, and the other Lyon. None of the brothers objected any thing against the evidence produced on the trial. They, however, could scarcely be persuaded that the crime for which they suffered merited death. They said, that deer were wild beasts, and that the poor as well as the rich might lawfully use them.

James Ansel, the seventh person of this band who suffered, was the most notorious offender. He had no settled employment, but lived by his vices, and indulged in all manner of wickedness during many years. In London, Portsmouth, Guildford, and many other towns, he had long been employed in robbing, housebreaking, and every species of depredation. In uniting himself with the black band, he descended in the scale of vice. But, as his offences were more numerous, and more heinous, except in the instance of the murder, he entertained no hope of life after his apprehension, and behaved himself in a corresponding manner; but, as informing upon other persons would not obtain him a pardon, he obstinately refused to give any information, though he admitted that he knew of twenty who were notorious offenders in the same respect. When accused of his former robberies, he did not deny them, and said that he knew he would have been indicted at the assizes, but that there were many circumstances which would have rendered it difficult, if not impossible, for any prosecutor to have proved him guilty.

It is rather a singular fact, that though many of these fellows appeared bold and daring before their apprehension, yet, partly with sickness, and partly through the fear of death, none of them was able to stand or speak at the place of execution, except Ansel. Nay, it was actually believed by many who were present, that some of them were dead before they were thrown off.

It was not this example which deterred the young fellows of that part of the country from acting a similar part. But, by the vigilance of the keepers, and the severity of the laws, the whole nation of the blacks was extirpated, and those country rakes were constrained to vent their profligate dispositions in less dangerous employments.

WILLIAM SHAW,

CONVICTED OF THE MURDER OF HIS DAUGHTER, WHO, IT WAS AFTER-
WARDS DISCOVERED, HAD KILLED HERSELF.

THERE are many curious and interesting cases on record, of persons
having been convicted on circumstantial evidence, whose innocence has
been subsequently demonstrated; and the following may be placed
amongst the most curious of these.   Poor Shaw was, in all probability,
an austere father, and his daughter as probably a wilful and vindictive
child; but they should not be considered less the objects of pity on that
account.

William Shaw was an upholsterer at Edinburgh, in the year 1721.
He had a daughter, Catharine Shaw, who lived with him.   She encouraged the addresses of John Lawson, a jeweller, to whom her father
declared the most insuperable objections, alleging him to be a profligate
young man, addicted to every kind of dissipation.   He was forbidden
the house; but the daughter continuing to see him clandestinely, the
father, on the discovery, kept her strictly confined.

The father had, for some time, pressed his daughter to receive the
addresses of a son of Alexander Robertson, a friend and neighbour;
and one evening, being very urgent thereon, she peremptorily refused,
declaring that she preferred death to being young Robertson's wife.
The father grew enraged, and the daughter more positive; so that the
most passionate expressions arose on both sides, and the words *barbarity,
cruelty*, and *death*, were frequently pronounced by the daughter!   At
length he left her, locking the door after him.

The greater part of the buildings in Edinburgh are formed on the plan
of the chambers in our inns of court, so that many families inhabit rooms
on the same floor, having all one common staircase.   William Shaw
dwelt in one of these, and a single partition only divided his room from
that of James Morrison, a watch-case maker.   This man had indis-
tinctly overheard the conversation and quarrel between Catharine Shaw
and her father, but was particularly struck with the repetition of the
above words, she having pronounced them loudly and emphatically.   For
some little time after the father was gone out, all was silent, but presently Morrison heard several groans from the daughter.   Alarmed, he
ran to some of his neighbours under the same roof.   These, entering
Morrison's room, and listening attentively, not only heard the groans,
but distinctly heard Catharine Shaw faintly exclaim, "Cruel father,
thou art the cause of my *death!*"   Struck with this, they flew to the
door of Shaw's apartment; they knocked—no answer was given.   The
knocking was repeated—still no answer.   Suspicions had before arisen
against the father— they were now confirmed: a constable was procured,
an entrance forced, and Catharine was found weltering in her blood, and
the fatal knife by her side!   She was alive, but speechless; but, on being
questioned as to owing her death to her father, she was just able to make
a motion with her head, apparently in the affirmative, and expired.

Just at this critical moment William Shaw returns, and enters the room. All eyes are on him! He sees his neighbours and a constable in his apartment, and seems much disordered thereat; but, at the sight of his daughter, he turns pale, trembles, and is ready to sink. The first surprise and the succeeding horror leave little doubt of his guilt in the minds of the beholders; and even that little is done away on the constable discovering that his shirt is bloody.

He was instantly hurried before a magistrate, and, upon the depositions of all the parties, committed to prison on suspicion. He was shortly afterwards brought to trial, when, in his defence, he acknowledged the having confined his daughter, to prevent her intercourse with Lawson; that he had frequently insisted on her marrying Robertson; and that he had quarelled with her on the subject the evening she was found murdered, as the witness Morrison had deposed: but he averred, that he left his daughter unharmed and untouched; and that the blood found upon his shirt was there in consequence of his having bled himself some days before, and the bandage becoming untied. These assertions did not weigh a feather with the jury, when opposed to the strong circumstantial evidence of the daughter's expressions, of ' barbarity, cruelty, death,'—and of ' cruel father, thou art the cause of my death,' —together with that apparently affirmative motion with her head, and the blood so seemingly providentially discovered on the father's shirt.

On these several concurring circumstances was William Shaw found guilty, executed, and hung in chains, at Leith Walk, November, 1721.

There was not a person in Edinburgh who did not believe the father guilty, notwithstanding his last words were, " I am innocent of my daughter's death." But in August, 1722, as a man, who had become possessor of the late William Shaw's apartments, was rummaging by chance in the chamber where Catharine Shaw died, he perceived a paper which had fallen into a cavity on one side of the chimney. It was folded as a letter, and, on opening it, was found to contain the following:—" Barbarous father, your cruelty in having put it out of my power ever to join my fate to that of the only man I could love, and tyrannically insisting upon my marrying one whom I always hated, has made me form a resolution to put an end to an existence which is become a burthen to me. I doubt not I shall find mercy in another world; for sure no benevolent being can require that I should any longer live in torment to myself in this! My death I lay to your charge: when you read this, consider yourself as the inhuman wretch that plunged the murderous knife into the bosom of the unhappy—CATHARINE SHAW."

This letter being shown, the hand-writing was recognised and avowed to be Catharine Shaw's by many of her relations and friends. It became the public talk; and the magistracy of Edinburgh, on a scrutiny, being convinced of its authenticity, ordered the body of William Shaw to be taken from the gibbet, and given to his family for interment; and, as the only reparation to his memory and the honour of his surviving relations, they caused a pair of colours to be waved over his grave, in token of his innocence.

MARIA THERESA PHIPOE

(KNOWN ALSO BY THE NAME OF MARY BENSON),

EXECUTED FOR MURDER.

THIS abandoned woman was remarkable for her masculine behaviour and daring disposition, as will be fully shown in detailing the particulars of her very interesting trial.

Two years only previous to her committing the horrid murder for which she suffered, she was convicted of forcibly taking from Mr. John Cortois, a promissory note of hand for £2000. The manner in which she extorted this property is highly characteristic of the ferocity of her nature. She then kept a house and a servant, for the purpose of receiving visits from the other sex. Among other dupes to her artifice, was Mr. John Cortois, whom she seized soon after he sat down in her house, and, knowing that he possessed considerable property, bound him, with the assistance of the other desperate female, acting as her servant, to his chair with a cord, and with horrid imprecations threatened, and even attempted to cut his throat, unless he gave her his note for £2000. In a state of terror he signed the written instrument. This done, the ferocious female thought she might negotiate the note with more safety if he was killed, calling to mind Satan's proverb, that " Dead men tell no tales." For this diabolical purpose she again attempted to murder him, and ordered him instantly to prepare for death, either by swallowing arsenic, by a pistol, or by stabbing with a knife, which she brandished over his head. At length the terrified gentleman became desperate in his turn, and attempted to escape. Mrs. Phipoe seized him, and from her masculine gripe it was only with the utmost exertion that he extricated himself, not without having several of his fingers badly cut in the struggle.

For this most atrocious offence she was indicted and tried. The infamous accomplice acting as her servant was admitted evidence for the prosecution, and she, as well as Mr. Cortois, swore to the facts above mentioned.

She was found guilty; but her counsel moved for an arrest of judgment upon a point of law, and upon argument it was determined, that, great as were the aggravations accompanying the commission of the crime, it did not amount to felony.

She was therefore indicted for the assault, found guilty, and sentenced, on the 23d of May, 1795, to twelve months imprisonment in Newgate; at the expiration of which term she was discharged.

So great was her propensity to vice, that a very few months elapsed before she committed the murder for which she was executed. The following are the shocking particulars of the horrid transaction :—

She was indicted by the different names already given, for that she, the said prisoner, not having the fear of God before her eyes, but being moved by the instigation of the devil, did, in Garden-street, in the parish of St. George's in the East, with malice aforethought, on the body of Mary Cox, commit the foul crime of murder.

It appeared in evidence that the deceased was acquainted with the prisoner, and that she had called at her lodgings that morning. Soon after the mistress of the house heard a scuffle and a groaning; she called two neighbours, and, going to the prisoner's door, which was locked, asked what was the matter? The prisoner replied, the woman was only in a fit, and that she was getting better. She then opened the door a little, when the witness saw she was bloody. Two persons went for a doctor, and a third pushing open the door, saw the deceased bleeding upon the ground. She ran down stairs, crying Murder! and, to her great terror, was followed by the wounded woman, who laid hold of her. Mrs. Benson came down after the deceased had got in the kitchen, where she was when the surgeon and beadles came; she was unable to speak, but yet made herself understood by one of the beadles, that she had been thus wounded by the woman up stairs. He went up to the prisoner, who was sitting on the bed, and said to her, "For God Almighty's sake, what have you done to the woman below?" She answered, "I don't know; I believe the devil and passion bewitched me." There was part of a finger and a case knife lying upon the table; he said, "Is this the knife you did the woman's business with?" she answered, "Yes;"—"Is this your finger?"—"Yes."—"Did the woman below cut it off?"—"Yes;" but this the deceased denied, upon his afterwards questioning her with it.

The surgeon described the deceased to have received five stabs upon the throat and neck, besides several wounds in different parts of the body, and agreed with the surgeon who afterwards attended her in the hospital, that those wounds were undoubtedly the cause of her death.

The day after, the deceased made a declaration before a magistrate, wherein she stated, that she had purchased of the prisoner a gold watch and other articles, for which she paid eleven pounds, and then asked for a china coffee-cup, which stood upon the chimney-piece, into the bargain. The prisoner bid her take one; but, while doing so, stabbed her in the neck, and afterwards had her under her hands more than an hour, she calling murder all the time, till at last she got her upon the bed, when she said she would kill her outright, that she might not tell her own story.

The prisoner, in her defence, said, that the deceased wanted to purchase only part of the things which she wanted to dispose of, and, upon her refusing to divide them, she became angry, and said that she only wanted the money to go to London to be Cortois's mistress again: the prisoner replied, that it was a lie, for she never had been Cortois's mistress; the deceased retorted, that it had been proved so at the Old Bailey. She said that was a lie; and from this they both proceeded to very abusive language, and much violence. There were two knives lying on the table; the deceased took up one, and making a violent blow at the prisoner, cut off one of her fingers. In the heat of her passion, full of pain, and streaming with blood, she stabbed her; but solemnly declared, that she had no recollection of what passed afterwards, until she found herself in her own room, covered with blood. This, she said, was the truth. The deceased, if alive, must confess she had been most in fault, and that which affected her the most was, that she had done her any injury.

The landlady where the deceased lived, and another person to whom she was well known, proved that she had great respect for the prisoner, and had often heard her declare she believed the prisoner had the same for her.

Mr. Baron Perryn, who tried the prisoner, then addressed the jury as follows :—

" Gentlemen,—This is a charge against the prisoner at the bar, Maria Theresa Phipoe, otherwise Mary Benson, for the wilful murder of Mary Cox, by stabbing her in different parts of the body, and giving her several mortal wounds, of which she died ; you have heard the evidence on both sides, both on the part of the prosecution, and also on the part of the prisoner, at considerable length ; and all that will be necessary for me, in the discharge of my duty, will be to recapitulate that evidence ; and if I mistake in any point, I request the counsel on both sides will correct me. [Here the learned judge summed up the evidence on both sides, and then added,] Gentlemen, this is the evidence : it is a very suspicious circumstance against the prisoner, that she should send out her landlady at that particular time to buy brandy and bread, and when she returned, to prevent her bringing it up stairs, saying that it would not be wanted for some time ; that is a presumption that she was occupied about something which interested her at the time. With respect to the understanding of the prisoner, the witnesses have all sworn, who speak to that point, that she was in her proper senses. You have heard the defence which she has made. Now, to be sure, if she had given the same account to the beadles, which she has done in court to-day, it would have operated very much in her favour : if this latter account was true, what could be the meaning of concealing the knife in her bosom, and giving it up with so much reluctance.

" It was stated by the deceased, and by several witnesses, that she had locked the door, and for some time denied admission to her neighbours. If she had been attacked, as she alleged, and was so remarkably subject to passion, why did she obstruct the means of preventing her passion from producing any mischief. Her threatening to kill the deceased outright, that she might not be able to tell her own story, was a very unfavourable circumstance to her. There does not appear to be any colour for her barbarous treatment of the deceased, who had always regarded her with affection ; and all the evidence which the prisoner has produced in her behalf does not appear to me to diminish the enormity of the charges against her. But it is for you to pronounce on the case, as it appears to your judgments and consciences : if, from all the circumstances, you are of opinion that she has intentionally and maliciously committed the crime charged against her, you must find her guilty ; but if it appears to you that the deceased was the aggressor, and drew her fate upon herself, you will of course pronounce a verdict of acquittal."

The jury retired for twenty minutes, and returned with a verdict of " Guilty."

Proclamation being made in the usual form, Mr. Baron Perryn immediately proceeded to pass sentence, that she should be executed on the Monday following, and her body afterwards dissected and anatomized, according to the statute. When the judge came to this part of the sentence, the prisoner said, " You may speak out—I am not afraid ;" and when he had finished with the usual words, " The Lord have mercy on your soul," she said, " I do not place very great dependence on *your* mercy."

The prisoner appeared, both before and after the examination of the witnesses, much concerned about her property, and said, she had not received back all the money that lay about the room when the officers entered it ; and on the two notes being produced in court, she said they were not her's, for the property she required was all in gold.

However improper her conduct was before, she now behaved with due decorum, being attended by a Roman Catholic priest.

She left a guinea for the most deserving debtor in the gaol, and gave the same sum to the executioner.

After hanging an hour in the view of a great number of spectators, one third of whom were females, the body was cut down, and delivered to the surgeons for dissection.

In her last moments she confessed the justice of her sentence, but denied having cut off her own finger, saying, it was done in the scuffle with the woman she murdered. She also denied to the last having poisoned a young woman some years since, who had left her a legacy of one thousand pounds. She owned to having been guilty of many enormities, and attributed her frequent gusts of passion to the use of laudanum.

Her body was publicly exhibited in a place built for the purpose in the Old Bailey.

RICHARD THORNHILL, ESQ.,

Mr. Thornhill and Sir Cholmondeley Deering having dined together, on the 7th of April, 1711, in company with several other gentlemen, at the Toy at Hampton Court, a quarrel arose, during which Sir Cholmondeley struck Mr. Thornhill. A scuffle ensuing, the wainscot of the room broke down, and Thornhill falling, the other stamped on him, and beat out some of his teeth. The company now interposed, and Sir Cholmondeley, convinced that he had acted improperly, declared that he was willing to ask pardon; but Mr. Thornhill said, that asking pardon was not a proper retaliation for the injury that he had received; adding, "Sir Cholmondeley, you know where to find me." Soon after this the company broke up, and the parties went home in different coaches, without any farther steps being taken towards their reconciliation.

On the next day, the following letter was written by Mr. Thornhill:—
"April 8th, 1711.

"Sir,—I shall be able to go abroad to-morrow morning, and desire you will give me a meeting with your sword and pistols, which I insist on. The worthy gentleman who brings you this will concert with you the time and place. I think Tothill Fields will do well; Hyde Park will not, at this time of year, being full of company. "I am your humble servant,   "RICHARD THORNHILL."

On the 9th of April, Sir Cholmondeley went to the lodgings of Mr. Thornhill, and the servant showed him into the dining-room. He ascended with a brace of pistols in his hands; and soon afterwards, Mr. Thornhill coming to him, asked him if he would drink tea, but he declined. A hackney-coach was then sent for, and the gentlemen rode to Tothill Fields, where, unattended by seconds, they proceeded to fight their duel. They fired their pistols almost at the same moment, and Sir Cholmondeley, being mortally wounded, fell to the ground.

On the 18th of May, Mr. Thornhill was indicted at the Old Bailey for murder; and the facts having been proved, the accused called several witnesses to show how ill he had been used by Sir Cholmondeley; that he had languished some time of the wounds he had received, during which he could take no other sustenance than liquids, and that his life was in imminent danger. Several persons of distinction swore that Mr. Thornhill was of a peaceable disposition, and that, on the contrary, the deceased was of a remarkably quarrelsome temper. It was also deposed that Sir Cholmondeley, being asked if he came by his hurt through unfair usage, replied, "No: poor Thornhill! I am sorry for him; this misfortune was my own fault, and of my own seeking. I heartily forgive him, and desire you all to take notice of it, that it may be of some service to him, and that one misfortune may not occasion another."

The jury acquitted Mr. Thornhill of the murder, but found him guilty of manslaughter; in consequence of which he was burnt in the hand.

THE COUNTESS OF CROMARTIE SUING FOR HER HUSBAND'S PARDON.

THE EARL OF KILMARNOCK AND LORD BALMERINO,

BEHEADED FOR HIGH TREASON.

HAVING given a history of the principal offenders who were executed for being concerned in the rebellion of 1715, our readers will naturally expect an account of those who suffered for the share they had in the subsequent insurrection of 1745; in which we shall be as particular as the limits of our plan will allow.

Great Britain being at war with France, and having an army in Flanders, the French thought, that by making a descent in the north of Scotland, and fomenting a rebellion there, they should oblige the court of London to withdraw its troops from Flanders, which would enable the French to act with more effect against the allied army.

In the summer of 1745, the French fitted out a ship at Port Lazare, on board of which were about fifty Irish and Scotch papists; and this vessel being joined off Belleisle by a French man of war, having the Pretender on board, they sailed together to coast the southern parts of England, and make good a landing among the Western Isles of Scotland. Captain Brett, in an English ship of war, falling in with them off the Land's-End, disabled one of the French vessels, so that she was obliged to return to France; but the other, in which was the young Pretender, prosecuted her voyage towards the north of Scotland, and arrived at the Isle of Sky, opposite to Lochaber, in the county of

20   x

Inverness, about the end of the month of July. The people being disembarked, the Pretender took up his residence with a papist named Macdonald, and continued with him about three weeks. Some of the Scottish clans, to the number of about two thousand men, then joining him, he erected a standard, with the motto " *Tandem Triumphans* " (at length triumphant).

The rebels now marched towards Fort William, where the Pretender published a manifesto, which his father had signed at Rome, containing abundant promises to such as would adhere to his cause; two of which were, the dissolution of the union of the two kingdoms, and the payment of the national debt. This circumstance induced many of the ignorant country people to flock to his standard, till at length his undisciplined rabble began to assume the appearance of an army, which struck terror into the well-affected wherever it came.

These transactions, however, had not passed so secretly, but that the governor of Fort William informed the Lord Justice Clerk of Edinburgh of all he could learn of the affair; on which the latter dispatched an express to the north, ordering the assistance of all officers civil and military: and this express arrived about the time that the Pretender erected his standard. The governor of Fort William having received these orders, dispatched two companies of the first regiment of foot to oppose the rebels; but many of the unhappy men fell a sacrifice to their martial ardour, and several of the officers were made prisoners; though on giving their parole of honour they were afterwards released.

In the interim the Lord Justice Clerk ordered Sir John Cope, commander in chief of the forces in the south of Scotland, to march against the rebels; but in making the circuit of the immense mountains of Argyleshire, the two armies failed to meet; on which Sir John went to Inverness, to refresh his troops after the fatigue of the march.

The armies having thus casually missed each other, the rebels proceeded to Perth. Having taken possession of that place, the Pretender issued his orders for all persons who held public money to pay it into the hands of his secretary. During the Pretender's stay at Perth, several noblemen and gentlemen joined him, particularly Lord George Murray, brother to the Duke of Athol, and a person who assumed the title of Duke of Perth. These new adherents bringing with them their tenants and dependents, the rebel troops began to assume an air of consequence, and the Pretender was proclaimed at the market-cross of Perth.

In the mean time General Cope sent from Inverness an express to Aberdeen, for the transport-vessels in that harbour to be ready to receive his troops; and embarking on the 18th of September, he disembarked them at Dunbar. During these transactions General Guest, who commanded the castle of Edinburgh, gave the magistrates of that city several pieces of cannon for the defence of the place; and Colonel James Gardiner repaired from Stirling to Edinburgh with two regiments of dragoons; but, learning that General Cope had landed at Dunbar, which is 27 miles east of Edinburgh, he proceeded to effect a junction with that general.

The Pretender and his adherents now marched to Dumblain, where in a council of war it was determined to cross the Forth at Stirling;

but one of the arches of the bridge having been destroyed by General Blakeney, the rebels were compelled to ford the river at a place three miles to the westward. This being done, they marched towards Callington, four miles from Edinburgh. Some volunteers of that city were dispatched to prevent their proceeding farther; but the rebels wheeling southwards, encamped that night at a village called Duddingston, and on the following day the Pretender proceeded through the Royal Park, and took possession of Holyrood-House.

The money in the bank of Edinburgh, and the records in the public offices, were now removed to the castle for security, and the gates of the city were kept fast during the whole day. But five hundred of the rebels having concealed themselves in the suburbs, took an opportunity, at four o'clock the next morning, to follow a coach which was going in, and seizing the gate called the Netherbow, they maintained their ground while the body reached the centre of the city, and formed themselves in the Parliament Close. Thus possessed of the capital, they seized 2000 stand of arms, and on the following day marched to oppose the royal army under the command of General Cope.

The two armies being within sight of each other near Preston Pans on the evening of the 20th, Colonel Gardiner earnestly recommended it to the general to attack them during the night; but, deaf to this advice, he kept the men under arms till morning, though they were already greatly harassed. · At five in the morning the rebels made a furious attack on the royal army, and threw them into unspeakable confusion, the two regiments of dragoons falling back on the foot. Colonel Gardiner, with five hundred foot, behaved with uncommon valour, and covered the retreat of those who fled; but the colonel receiving a mortal wound, the rebels made prisoners of the rest of the king's troops. The loss thus sustained by the royal army was 300 killed, 450 wounded, 520 taken prisoners—total, 1270; while the rebels lost only 50 men in all.

Flushed with this victory, the rebels returned in high spirits to Edinburgh, which was only seven miles distant from the place of action. They now sent foraging parties through the country, with orders to seize all the horses and waggons they could find; and in the interim a party of the insurgents attempted to throw up an intrenchment on the Castle Hill. Hereupon the governor, compelled to oppose the assailants, yet anxious for the safety of the inhabitants, sent a messenger in the night to intimate to those who lived near the Castle Hill, that they would do well to remove out of danger.

As soon as it was daylight, the battery of the rebels was destroyed by a discharge of cannon from the half-moon, and thirty of them killed, with three of the inhabitants who had rashly ventured near the spot.

The city being greatly deficient in provisions, a gentleman ordered above fifty fine bullocks to be driven into the city, under a pretence that they were for the use of the rebels; and the persons who drove them leaving them on the Castle Hill, the governor and five hundred men sallied forth, and drove them it at the gate, while the rebels played their artillery with unremitting fury.

While the rebels continued in Edinburgh, which was about seven weeks, some noblemen and their adherents joined them; so that their army amounted to almost 10,000 men. They now levied large contributions, not only in Edinburgh, but through the adjacent country; and those who furnished them received receipts signed " CHARLES, *Prince Regent.*" Some ships from France now arrived in the Forth, laden with ammunition; and a person who attended the Pretender was dignified with the title of Ambassador from his Most Christian Majesty.

General Wade having the command of some forces which had reached Yorkshire, and some Dutch troops that were sent to augment them, he marched to Newcastle, with a view to deter the rebels from entering the southern part of the kingdom. The celebrated prelate, Dr. Herring, archbishop of York, distinguished himself gloriously on this interesting occasion. Joining with the high-sheriff to assemble the freeholders, the archbishop preached an animated sermon to them; and then the several parties agreed to assist each other in support of their civil and religious rights. Many people in Yorkshire were prevented from engaging in the rebellion by this spirited and well-timed conduct.

The Lord President Forbes, and the Earl of Loudon, acted in a manner equally zealous in Scotland. Having collected a number of the loyal Highlanders into a body, many others who would have joined the rebels were thereby deterred; and this proceeding proved of the most essential service in the suppression of the rebellion.

The rebels quitting Edinburgh in the beginning of November, marched to Dalkeith, where they encamped; and a report was circulated that they proposed to make an attack on Berwick; but this proved to be only a contrivance to conceal their real designs. In the mean time more than a thousand rebels deserted, in consequence of General Wade's publishing a pardon to such as would return to their duty as good subjects within a limited time. Still, however the rebels had above 8000 men able to bear arms; yet General Wade would have marched to attack them, but that his soldiers were many of them ill, owing to the severity of the season and the fatigues they had undergone.

The rebels advanced to Carlisle on the 9th of November, and demanded that the garrison should surrender: which was refused for some days; but a scarcity of provisions rendering longer resistance useless, the governor delivered up the city, into which the rebels entered, and the Pretender was proclaimed.

The surrender of Carlisle being made known to General Wade, he marched from Newcastle with such of his troops as were in any condition to move; and the first division reached Hexham in the afternoon of the 17th November, the second arriving at the same place about midnight: but the General found it expedient to return to Newcastle with the third, who were unable to bear the fatigue of prosecuting the march. The inhabitants of Newcastle subscribed to purchase flannel waistcoats for those distressed men, and furnished them with the best accommodations in their power.

About this period King George II. arriving in London, from a visit to his German dominions, both houses of parliament immediately assembled, and a bill was passed for suspending the Habeas Corpus act for six months. The apprehension and commitment of many suspected persons in both kingdoms followed; but it did not appear to stop the progress of the rebellion; for the insurgents had by this time reached Manchester, where they raised a regiment consisting chiefly of Roman Catholics.

The whole kingdom was now in a ferment, and every loyal subject was anxious for his personal security. The Duke of Cumberland being in Flanders, it was judged advisable to send for him to take the command of the king's forces. About the time he arrived in London, the rebels had advanced as far as Derby: but his royal highness lost no time in travelling into Staffordshire, where he collected all the force he could, to stop their farther inroads into the kingdom. The Duke expected a junction of the forces under General Wade, who had marched from Newcastle to Darlington, and, taking a westward course, had stationed his troops near Wetherby. The rebels having advice of this motion, it was proposed by some of them to march into North Wales; but others opposed this, on the presumption that they should then be surrounded by the royal army, and compelled to surrender themselves prisoners at discretion, as they would have no opportunity of retreating to Scotland.

The rebels, while at Derby, held frequent councils respecting their proceedings. The inhabitants of the place remarked that the principal men among them seemed very low in spirits; and this dejection increased when they heard that an English man of war had taken a ship bound from France for their use, laden with arms and money.

General Wade having reviewed his troops at Wetherby on the 5th December, marched to join the Duke of Cumberland in Staffordshire; so that the rebels were compelled to retreat northwards, hoping for supplies to arrive from France.

At this time they received the agreeable news that John Lord Drummond had defeated the Highlanders commanded by the Earl of Loudon, and had arrived at Perth with 3000 men. This somewhat encouraged them; and having raised what money they could at Derby, they proceeded to Manchester; in their way to which they damaged the highways, and destroyed the bridges, to retard the progress of the king's troops. They were now in possession of fifteen pieces of cannon, some of which they brought from Carlisle, and others from Edinburgh; but most of these were useless, for want of engineers to work them.

The Pretender reaching Manchester on the 9th December, his soldiers were treated very contemptuously by some people of the town; on which Mr. Murray, secretary to the young adventurer, issued an order for the payment of £2500 on pain of military execution. The rebels now proceeded by the way of Preston and Lancaster to Kendal, at which last place they halted one night; but some of the inhabitants fired guns from their windows, so exasperated were they against them.

In the interim the king's troops, under the command of the Duke of Cumberland and Sir John Ligonier, arrived near Litchfield, where orders were issued to distress the rebels to the utmost. Sir John commanded the fort; but the Duke put himself at the head of the dragoons, with a view of coming up with the rebels, and in the hope of meeting General Wade near Kendal or Lancaster. Mr. Wade having held a council of war at Ferrybridge, it was determined to march northward; but on the arrival of the army at Wakefield, intelligence was brought that the rebels had retired; on which Mr. Wade dispatched the dragoons, under the command of General Oglethorpe, to join his royal highness, while himself retreated to Newcastle with the infantry.

Though the season was severe, and the roads inexpressibly bad, Mr. Oglethorpe, by means of forced marches, conducted his troops 100 miles in three days, and joined the Duke of Cumberland at Lancaster on the 14th December. Here the dragoons were reviewed by his royal highness; and on the following day they marched to Kendal, in the hope of overtaking the rebels: but the latter retreated on hearing of their advance.

His royal highness overtaking the rebels at Clifton on the 18th, dislodged them from that place after a sharp encounter. While the royal army was engaged with the rear of the rebels, the main body of the latter retired to Carlisle, where, being still greatly pressed by the royal troops, they left only 500 of their Lancashire troops in garrison, and on the following day pursued their route for Scotland, in three divisions. Several of them were drowned in crossing the River Esk; and the Duke arrived at Carlisle, and summoned it to surrender, the day after they had quitted it. Some hesitation was at first made; but the Duke sending to Whitehaven for some artillery, offers of capitulation were made by the rebels. On this his royal highness returned an answer, importing that their submission must be unconditional, for that he could not make terms with rebels; whereupon they all surrendered; and, being taken into the cathedral, were there handcuffed, and conveyed to different prisons. This service being performed; and information being received that the French had an intention of invading England, the Duke of Cumberland went to London, to give his advice as a privy counsellor, in consequence of an express demanding his attendance. Lord Loudon so exerted himself while the rebels were gone into England, that he prevented many parties of Highlanders from joining them. A thousand men were raised at Edinburgh, and a like number at Glasgow; on which the Pretender ordered the people of Glasgow to pay £30,000 on pain of military execution; and with this order they were obliged to comply.

Three bodies of the rebels from Carlisle, meeting near Glasgow on the last day of the year 1745, marched to Stirling, which they summoned to surrender. The town being indefensible, the magistrates threw open the gates; and a summons was sent to General Blakeney, to surrender the castle: but this he absolutely refused, saying, that he would defend it to the utmost extremity. On this the rebels began to besiege it; but receiving intelligence that General Hawley had marched to Linlithgow, they abandoned the siege, and met the army under the general's command near Falkirk.

General Hawley drew up his troops to the best possible advantage on the 17th of January, and an engagement ensued; but many of the soldiers could not fire their muskets, owing to some snow and rain which fell at the time. The dragoons, who had given way at Preston Pans, now again retreated; and if General Huske had not rallied a square battalion of infantry, the rebels would have surrounded the king's troops. Many officers fell in this action; and at length victory declaring for the rebels, the royal army retreated to Linlithgow, and thence to Edinburgh.

On the following day the rebels buried their dead; and then marching back to Stirling, again summoned General Blakeney to surrender; but his answer was, that " he would be buried under the ruins of the castle, sooner than yield it into their hands!" On this they began a second siege; but having only seven pieces of cannon, their efforts were very feeble, while many of them were destroyed by the guns from the castle; on which they raised the siege soon afterwards.

The king's officers, who had been made prisoners at Preston-Pans, were sent to Perth; but the inhabitants of that place rising while the Pretender was at Stirling, rescued the prisoners, and conducting them to Edinburgh, they were very serviceable in the operations of the ensuing campaign.

A general apprehension for the public safety now prevailed throughout Scotland; and a minute narrative of the state of affairs being from time to time transmitted to London, it was resolved to take such steps as might effectually crush the rebellion.

Hereupon the Duke of Cumberland set out for Scotland, and arrived at Edinburgh on the thirtieth of January, to the great joy of all the loyal subjects; and taking the command of the army, immediately marched in pursuit of the rebels. The army was in three divisions: and his royal highness halted the first night at Linlithgow; while General Mordaunt marched towards Falkirk, to secure the roads and bridges.

On the following day the rebels blew up the church of St. Ninian's, containing their magazine of powder; and then crossed the Forth above Stirling, in great confusion. On this General Mordaunt pursued them at the head of the dragoons and Argyleshire men, but discontinued the pursuit on his arrival at Stirling. When his royal highness reached Stirling, he went to the castle, and expressed his approbation of General Blakeney's conduct, in terms highly honourable to that commander.

The rebels proceeding northwards, Lord John Drummond, and Lord Lewis Gordon joined them with some auxiliary forces; but such a distraction now prevailed in their councils, and they were so apprehensive of failure in their grand attempt, that they were almost reduced to despair.

In the mean time the expedition undertaken by the Duke of Cumberland was conducted with equal diligence and success. It was but about a week from his leaving London till he saw the rebels flying before him; while the loyal Scots hailed him as one sent from heaven to their relief. The rebels were now much disheartened; but, in order to keep up the spirits of their party, they propagated a report that some troops from France were to be landed to assist them; and that they should be able to harass the king's troops by removing the seat of war to the Highlands. Their designs being penetrated by the Duke of Cumberland and his generals, the royal army marched to Perth, where a great number of volunteers joined them, and thence to Aberdeen; the king's troops sustaining the rigours of the season with a spirit that did them honour. Several towns between Aberdeen and Inverness being in possession of the rebels, particularly Strathbogie, the Generals Mordaunt and Bland forced them from that place, where there were more than a thousand of them, under the command of Colonel Roy Stewart, who had come from France with the young Pretender. At this time a ship arrived from France, with some cash for the rebels, who circulated a report that the sum was very large; though this was far from being the truth.

His royal highness marched from Aberdeen on the 8th April, and encamped near Culloden, where Lord Albemarle joined him; and on the following day the combined army passed the river Spey, without any material loss. While they passed this river the rebels were within view, but they retired hastily towards Elgin, and were pursued by Kingston's light horse, and the Highlanders of Argyleshire, but not in time to effect any important service. The king's troops arriving at Nairn on the 15th of the month, the rebels intended to have surprised them; but their plan was rendered abortive by the sagacious conduct of the Duke of Cumberland, who reviewed his troops on this day; but the rebels came to a resolution to engage on the following. His royal highness drew up his forces in order of battle on the morning of the 16th, but the rebels not appearing in sight, the army marched by defiles, and continued this motion till between twelve and one o'clock, when they saw the rebels; and then the army formed in three lines, being flanked by the dragoons, and supported by the artillery. The following is the conqueror's account of the battle of Culloden, which we extract from the London Gazette :—

" On Tuesday the 15th of April the rebels burnt Fort Augustus, which convinced us of their resolution to stand an engagement with the king's troops. We gave our men a day's halt at Nairn, and on the 16th marched from thence, between four and five, in four columns. The three lines of foot (reckoning the reserve for one) were broken into three from the right, which made the three columns equal, and each of five battalions. The artillery and baggage followed the first column upon the right, and the cavalry made the fourth column on the left. After we had marched about eight miles, our advanced guard, composed of about forty of Kingston's, and the Highlanders, led by the quartermaster-general, perceived the rebels at some distance making a motion towards us on the left; upon which we immediately formed, but, finding the rebels were still a good way from us, we put ourselves again upon our march in our former posture, and continued it to within a mile of them, where we formed in the same order as before. After reconnoitring their situation, we found them posted behind some old walls and huts, in a line with Culloden House. As we thought our right entirely secure, General Hawley and General Bland went to the left with two regiments of dragoons, to endeavour to fall upon the right flank of the rebels; and Kingston's horse was ordered to the reserve. The ten pieces of cannon were disposed, two in each of the intervals of the first line; and all our highlanders (except 140, which were upon the left with General Hawley, and who behaved extremely well) were left to guard the baggage. When we had advanced within 500 yards of the rebels, we found the morass upon our right was ended, which left our right flank quite uncovered to them; his royal highness thereupon immediately ordered Kingston's horse from the reserve, and a little squadron of about sixty of Cobham's, which had been patrolling, to cover our flank. We spent about half an hour after that, trying which should gain the flank of the other; and his royal highness having sent Lord Bury forward within a hundred yards of the rebels, to reconnoitre something that appeared like a battery to us, they thereupon began firing their cannon, which was extremely ill-pointed and ill-served; ours answered them, which began their confusion. They then came running on, in their wild manner; and upon the right, where his royal highness had placed himself, imagining the greatest push would be there, they came down three several times within a yard of our men, firing their pistols, and brandishing their swords; but the Royals and Pulteney's hardly took their firelocks from their shoulders, so that after those first attempts they made off, and the little squadrons on our right were sent to pursue them. General Hawley had, by the help of our highlanders, beat down two little stone walls, and came in upon the right flank of their second line. As their whole body came down to attack at once, their right somewhat outflanked Burrel's regiment, which was our left; and the greatest part of the little loss we sustained was there; but Bligh's and Simpel's giving a fire upon those who had outflanked Burrel's, soon repulsed them; and Burrel's regiment, and the left of Monro's, fairly beat them with their bayonets. There was scarce a soldier or officer of Burrel's, and of that part of Monro's which engaged, who did not kill one or two men each with their bayonets and spontoons (the officers' half-pikes). The cavalry, which had charged from the right and left, met in the centre, except two squadrons of dragoons, which we missed, and they were gone in pursuit of the runaways. Lord Ancram was ordered to pursue with the horse as far as he could; and did it with so good effect that a very considerable number was killed in the pursuit. As we were on our march to Inverness, and were nearly arrived there, Major-General Bland sent the annexed papers, which he received from the French officers and soldiers surrendering themselves prisoners to his royal highness. Major-General Bland had also made great slaughter, and took about fifty French officers and soldiers prisoners in his pursuit. By the best calculation that can be made, it is thought the rebels lost 2000 men upon the field of battle and in the pursuit. We have here 122 French and 326 rebel prisoners. Lieutenant-Colonel Howard killed an officer, who appeared to be Lord Strathallan, by the seal and different commissions from the Pretender found in his pocket. It is said Lord Perth, Lords Nairn, Lochiel, Keppock, and Appin Stuart, are also killed. All their artillery and ammunition were taken, as well as the Pretender's and all their baggage. There were also twelve colours taken. The Pretender's son, it is said, lay at Lord Lovat's house at Aird the night after the action. Lord Sutherland's and Lord Reay's people continue to exert themselves, and have taken upwards of one hundred rebels; and there is great reason to believe Lord Cromartie and his sons are also taken. The killed, wounded, and missing, of the king's troops, amount to about 300. The French officers will be all sent to Carlisle, till his Majesty's pleasure shall be known. The rebels, by their own accounts, make their loss greater by 2000 men than we have stated it. Four of their principal ladies are in custody, viz. Lady Ogilvie, Lady Kinloch, Lady Gordon, and the Laird of M'Intosh's wife. Major Grant, the governor of Inverness, is retaken; and Generals Hawley, Lord Albemarle, Huske, and Bland, have orders to inquire into the reasons for his surrendering of Fort George."

The young Pretender escaped to the house of Lord Lovat, where he was disguised in the dress of a woman, to prevent his falling into the hands of the king's troops. After quitting the house of Lord Lovat, he repaired to the Isle of Sky, where he lodged in holes of the rocks, and supported the calls of nature with the utmost difficulty. At length, after numberless hazards and imminent escapes, for the space of four months, a French frigate arrived off the western islands of Scotland, in which he embarked, and was safely landed in France.

Soon after this decisive battle of Culloden, the Earls of KILMARNOCK and CROMARTIE, and Lord BALMERINO, with many other rebel chiefs, were taken into custody, on a charge of having given advice and assistance to the Pretender.

Lord Kilmarnock, who was distinguished by the comeliness of his appearance, was brought up in the profession of the Presbyterian faith; but his lordship had married a lady who was strongly attached to Jacobitie principles, and who made repeated efforts to convert him to her political sentiments: he resisted all her arguments, however, till within a few months of the landing of the Pretender, when, having applied to the ministry for a place under government, and his suit being rejected, he determined to join him.

Lord Cromartie derived his descent from a family which had a kind of hereditary attachment to the house of Stuart. James II. had advanced his grandfather to the dignity of an earldom, for supporting him in his unjustifiable views against the rights and privileges of his subjects.

Lord Balmerino, as well as the Earl of Cromartie, was a non-juror. He was the youngest son of the preceding Lord Balmerino, and had succeeded to the title but just before the battle of Culloden. He had been concerned in the rebellion in 1715, but received a pardon through the intercession of his friends.

The Lords Kilmarnock, Cromartie, and Balmerino were, on the 28th July, 1746, brought up to answer for their crimes before the House of Peers assembled in Westminster-Hall. The two former pleaded Guilty; but Lord Balmerino pleaded Not guilty; on which he was put on his trial, and convicted on the fullest evidence.

When the unfortunate noblemen were carried up to receive sentence,

Cromartie and Kilmarnock most humbly besought the peers to make interest with the king in their favour; but Balmerino scorned to ask such a favour, and smiled at his approaching fate. Great interest being exerted to save the earls, it was hinted to Balmerino, that his friends ought to exert themselves in his behalf; to which, with great magnanimity, he only replied, " I am very indifferent about my own fate; but had the two noble Lords been my friends, they would have squeezed my name in among theirs."

The Countess of Cromartie, who had a very large family of young children, was incessant in her applications for the pardon of her husband; to obtain which she took a very plausible method. She procured herself to be introduced to the Princess of Wales, attended by her children in mourning; and urged her suit in the most suppliant terms. The Princess had at that time several children. Such an argument could scarcely fail to move; and a pardon was granted to Lord Cromartie, on the condition that he should never reside north of the River Trent. This condition was literally complied with; and his lordship died in Soho-square in the year 1766.

Orders being given for the execution of Lords Kilmarnock and Balmerino on the 18th of August, 1746, a scaffold was erected on Tower-hill, and the coffins were placed on it while the sheriffs went to the Tower to demand the bodies of these devoted victims to public justice. When the sufferers were brought out of the Tower, Kilmarnock cried out, " God save King George!" but Balmerino, still true to his former principles, exclaimed, " God save King James!" The way to the place of execution was lined by soldiers of the foot-guards, and parties of the horse and grenadier guards closed the procession to the fatal spot, where they had no sooner arrived than the noblemen were conducted to different apartments, appropriated to the purposes of their private devotions. Lord Kilmarnock was attended by Dr. Foster, an eminent dissenting minister, who had frequently visited him during his confinement; and a clergyman of the established church attended Lord Balmerino. On his way to the place of execution, the spectators asking " Which is Lord Balmerino?" he cheerfully replied, " I am Lord Balmerino, gentlemen, at your service."

The unfortunate sufferers having taken a final leave of each other, Lord Kilmarnock and his friends joined in prayer with Dr. Foster; after which his lordship drank a glass of wine, and ate a biscuit. He then applied to one of the sheriffs, requesting that the sentence of the law might be first executed on Lord Balmerino: but this, he was told, could not be complied with, as his name stood first in the warrant of execution. Hereupon he took leave of his friends; said he should not address the people on the occasion; and having desired Dr. Foster to attend him to the last fatal moment, ascended the steps of the scaffold. So extreme was his penitence, so pungent his sorrow, that the surrounding multitude no sooner saw him, than they burst into tears. On the sight of the coffin, block, and hatchet, he turned about to a friend, and said " This is terrible!" He then kneeled down, and prayed devoutly: and the whole of his conduct so affected the executioner that he fainted, but was recovered by the help of a glass of wine. The man then entreated his lordship's pardon; when the latter bade him re-assume his courage, and told him that when he had finished his devotions, he would drop his handkerchief as a signal for the stroke. His lordship's friends now assisted him in preparing for the dreadful fate that awaited him; but a considerable time elapsed in tucking his hair, which was very long, under a night-cap. During this dreadful interval he seemed agitated with a thousand fears; his body was convulsed by the horrors of his mind; and when he knelt down to the block, he laid his hands over it— a circumstance that again intimidated the executioner, who desired him to remove his hands, which was accordingly done: but now it was discovered that his waistcoat was in the way; on which he arose, and being assisted by his servant in taking it off, he again kneeled down. After a short time spent in prayer, he dropped his handkerchief; and his head, except a small piece of skin, was severed at one stroke. The head being received in a cloth of red baize, was put into the coffin with the body, and conveyed to the Tower.

During great part of this solemn interval Lord Balmerino exercised himself in devotion, and then conversed with his friends with an astonishing degree of ease and fortitude. Every one present wept but himself; who seemed possessed with a conscious integrity of mind that supported him in this arduous trial. Saw-dust being strewed over the scaffold, to hide the blood, the under-sheriff attended Lord Balmerino, when the latter, preventing what he was going to say, asked if Lord Kilmarnock had suffered; and put some questions respecting the executioner. His questions being answered, he said to his friends, " Gentlemen, I shall detain you no longer;" and having taken his leave of them with an air of great unconcern, walked to the scaffold in so intrepid a manner as to astonish all the spectators. Going up to the executioner, he took the axe from his hand, and having attentively regarded it, clapped him on the shoulder, as an encouragement not to be fearful in the discharge of his office. Then going to the extremity of the scaffold, he inquired for the hearse, and desired that it might be drawn nearer; which was readily complied with. Having thrown his coat, waistcoat, and neckcloth on his coffin, he put on a flannel waistcoat, and taking out of his pocket a plaid night-cap, he put it on his head, saying, he died a Scotchman. Having fitted his neck to the block, he spoke a short time to the executioner, and then addressed the spectators as follows: " Perhaps some may think my behaviour too bold; but remember, I now declare it is the effect of confidence in God, and a good conscience; and I should dissemble if I exhibited any signs of fear." Having placed his head on the block, he stretched out his arms, and prayed in the following words: " O Lord, reward my friends, forgive my enemies, and receive my soul." This said, he gave the signal for the stroke; but the executioner was so affected by the magnanimity of his behaviour, that he struck him three times before the head parted from the body. It was received in a piece of red baize, as Lord Kilmarnock's had been; and a hearse having conveyed the deceased to the Tower, he was interred in the same grave with the Marquis of Tullibardine, who had died during his imprisonment.

LORD LOVAT THREATENING TO HANG LORD SALTOUN

LORD LOVAT.

BEHEADED FOR HIGH TREASON.

THIS lord, who in 1715 had been a supporter of the house of Hanover, in 1745 changed sides, and became a friend of the party which he had before opposed. He was a man of uncommon abilities and refined education; but he seems to have wanted goodness of heart and steadiness of principle. The duplicity of his conduct was very great; for while he affected an attachment to the reigning family, he held a correspondence with the Pretender, who sent him a patent of-creation to a dukedom. Indeed, the advice of this crafty old peer chiefly contributed to the commencement and continuance of the rebellion. He professed the Roman Catholic religion, and was more than eighty years of age at the time of his death.

His career in life began in 1692, when he was appointed a captain in Lord Tullibardine's regiment, but he resigned his commission in order to prosecute his claim to be the Chief of the Frasers; in order to effect which he laid a scheme to get possession of the heiress of Lovat, who was about to be married to a son of Lord Saltoun. He took some of his dependents to the house of that nobleman, and, having caused a gibbet to be erected, swore he would hang the father and son, except all pretensions to the young lady were resigned. This was complied with through terror, and even the contract of marriage was given up. He now

intended to have seized the young lady's person; but her mother, a
widow lady, having secreted her, he was determined on revenge.
He went to the house of the mother, and, taking a clergyman with
him, and being attended by several armed ruffians, he compelled
the old lady to marry one of the persons who came with him.   This
being done, he cut off her stays with his dirk, and obliged her to go to
bed; and he and his associates waited the consummation of this forced
marriage.   For this breach of the peace he was indicted, but fled from
justice.   He was, nevertheless, tried for a rape, and for treason in opposing
the laws with an armed force; and sentence of outlawry was passed
against him.   Going to France in 1698, he turned Papist, by which he
acquired the good opinion of the abdicated king, James II., who employed him to raise recruits in Scotland; but he revealed the substance
of his commission to the British ministry: which circumstance being
discovered by some Scotch Catholics, an account of it was transmitted to
France; so that on his next visit to that country, in the year 1702, he
was lodged in the Bastile, where he continued some years; but at length
obtaining his liberty, he went to St. Omer's, where he entered into the
order of Jesuits.

Returning to Scotland on the demise of Queen Anne, he succeeded to
the title of Lovat, to which a good fortune was annexed.   In the
following year, when the Pretender landed in Scotland, he for a while
abetted his cause; but finding his interest decline, he raised a regiment
in opposition to him.   This latter part of his conduct coming to the
knowledge of king George I., Lovat was sent for to court, where he
was highly caressed.   At the time we are now writing of, when he
was supporting the rebellion of 1745 with men and money, the Lord
President Forbes wrote to him, and conjured him in the most earnest
manner to take a decisive and vigorous part in behalf of government;
and Lovat answered him in such a manner, as seemed to imply an
assent to all he urged, though at this very time the men he had sent
to assist the rebels were commanded by his own son.   He was apprehended in his own house, some days after the battle of Culloden, by a
party of dragoons; but being so infirm that he could not walk, he was
carried in a horse-litter to Inverness, whence he was sent in a landau
to Edinburgh, under the escort of a party of dragoons.   He petitioned
the Duke of Cumberland for mercy; and hoping to work upon his
feelings, recapitulated his former services—the favours that he had
received from the duke's grandfather, king George I., and dwelt much
upon his access to court, saying, " he had carried him to whom he now
sued for life in his arms when a baby, and held him up while his
grandfather fondled him."   Having been lodged one night in the castle,
he was conveyed to London, and committed to the Tower, only two
days before Kilmarnock and Balmerino suffered the dreadful sentence
of the law.   On the 9th of March, 1747, he was taken from the Tower
to Westminster Hall for trial; and the evidence adduced clearly proving
his guilt, he was fully convicted.   He was next day brought up for
judgment, and sentence of death was pronounced.

After conviction Lord Lovat behaved with uncommon cheerfulness, appearing by no means intimidated at the fate that awaited him. His friends advising him to apply for the royal mercy, he declined it, saying, that the remnant of his life was not worth asking for. He was always cheerful in company; entertained his friends with stories, and applied many passages of the Greek and Roman history to his own case.

On the arrival of the warrant for his execution, Lord Lovat read it, and pressing the gentleman who brought it to drink a bottle of wine with him, entertained him with such a number of stories as astonished his visitor, that his lordship should have such spirits on so solemn an occasion. The major of the Tower inquiring after his health one morning, he said, " I am well, sir; I am preparing myself for a place where hardly any majors go, and but few lieutenant-generals." Having procured a pillow to be placed at the foot of his bed, he frequently kneeled on it, to try how he should act his part at the fatal block; and, after some practice, thought himself sufficiently perfect to behave with propriety. The day before his death he spent with his friends, conversing cheerfully both on public and private affairs. He told the barber who shaved him to be cautious not to cut his throat, as it might baulk many persons of the expected sight on the following day. Having eaten a hearty supper, he desired that some veal might be roasted, that he might have some of it minced for his breakfast, being a dish of which he was extremely fond. He then smoked his pipe, and retired to rest. Waking about three in the morning, he employed some time in devotion, and then reposing himself till five o'clock, he arose, and drank a glass of wine and water, as he was accustomed to do every morning. He then employed himself about two hours in reading, which he could do without spectacles, notwithstanding he was 80 years of age, for he had lived a life of temperance, and his eye-sight was uncommonly good. He now conversed in his customary manner, exhibiting no sign of apprehension; and at eight o'clock sent his wig to the barber; and also desired the warder to purchase a purse, in which to put the money that he intended for the executioner; and he particularly desired that it might be a good one, lest the man should refuse it.

The coffin, with his name and age, and decorated with ornaments proper to his rank, having been placed on the scaffold, Mr. Sheriff Alsop went to the gate of the Tower at eleven o'clock, to demand the body; of which Lord Lovat being informed, he requested a few minutes for his private devotions; and then returned cheerfully, and said, " Gentlemen, I am ready." Having descended one pair of stairs, General Williamson requested him to repose himself a few minutes in his apartment. Complying with this invitation, he staid about five minutes, behaved with the utmost politeness to the company, and having drank a glass of wine, got into the governor's coach, which conveyed him to the gate of the Tower, where he was received by the sheriffs. Being conducted to a house near the scaffold, he told the sheriff, he might give the word of command when he pleased; " for," added he, " I have been long in the army, and know what it is to obey." While his lordship was going up the steps to the scaffold, assisted by two warders, he looked round, and seeing so great a concourse of people, " God save us!"

said he, " why should there be such a bustle about taking off an old grey head, that cannot get up three steps without three bodies to help it."

Turning about, and observing one of his friends dejected, he clapped him on the shoulder, saying, " Cheer up thy heart, man; I'm not afraid, why shouldst thou be so?" As soon as he came upon the scaffold, he asked for the executioner, and presented him with the purse containing the ten guineas; and then desiring to see the axe, he felt the edge, and said, " he believed it would do." Soon after he rose from the chair which was placed for him, and looked at the inscription on his coffin; on sitting down again, he repeated from Horace,

> " Dulce et decorum est pro patria mori;"

and afterwards from Ovid,

> " Nam genus et proavos, et quæ non fecimus ipsi,
> Vix ea nostra voco."

After a few minutes spent in devotion, he dropped his handkerchief, which was the preconcerted signal, and the executioner at one blow severed his head from his body, which was received in a cloth of red baize, and put into the coffin with the body, and conveyed to the Tower in a hearse.

Immense crowds of spectators were on scaffolds on Tower-hill, to behold the final exit of this extraordinary man: but some of them paid dear for their curiosity; for, before he was brought out of the Tower, one of the scaffolds broke down, by which several persons were killed on the spot, and a great number had their bones broken, and were otherwise terribly bruised. Thus was this man, whose life had been a scene of tyranny and perfidious duplicity, an occasion of injuring many others almost in the moment of his death.

Lord Lovat was beheaded on the 9th of April, 1747.

———

The following lines upon the execution of these noblemen are said to have been repeated with great energy by Dr. Johnson, although there appears to be no ground for supposing that they were the Doctor's own composition. They first appeared in the Gentleman's Magazine.

> " Pitied by gentle minds, Kilmarnock died;
> The brave, Balmerino, were on thy side;
> Ratcliffe, unhappy in his crimes of youth,
> Steady in what he still mistook for truth,
> Beheld his death so decently unmoved,
> The soft lamented, and the brave approved.
> But Lovat's end indifferently we view,
> True to no king, to no religion true:
> No fair forgets the ruin he has done;
> No child laments the tyrant of his son;
> No Tory pities, thinking what he was;
> Nor Whig compassions, for he left the cause;
> The brave regret not—for he was not brave;
> The honest mourn not—knowing him a knave."

FRANCIS TOWNLEY, JAMES DAWSON, AND OTHERS,

EXECUTED FOR HIGH TREASON.

These prisoners were parties to the same plot, and all of them held rank in the Pretender's army.

Colonel Townley was the son of — Townley, Esq., of Townley Hall, Lancashire, and being educated in the rigid principles of popery, went abroad early in life, and entering into the service of France, distinguished himself in the military line, particularly at the siege of Philipsbourg. Coming to England in 1742, he associated chiefly with those of the Catholic religion; and it was thought that he induced many of them to take an active part in the rebellion. When the Pretender came to Manchester, Townley offered his services; which being accepted, he was commissioned to raise a regiment, which he soon completed; but being made a prisoner at Carlisle, he was conducted to London, tried and executed.

JAMES DAWSON, a native of Lancashire, was genteelly born, and liberally educated at St. John's College in Cambridge. After leaving the university, he repaired to Manchester, where the Pretender gave him a captain's commission. Dawson had paid his addresses to a young lady, to whom he was to have been married immediately after his enlargement, if the solicitations that were made for his pardon had been attended with the desired effect. The circumstances of his love, and the melancholy that was produced by his death, are so admirably touched in the following ballad of Shenstone, that Dawson's story will probably be remembered and regretted when that of the rest of the rebels will be forgotten. That man must have lost all feeling who can read this beautiful ballad, equally remarkable for its elegance, its simplicity, and its truth, and remain unaffected.

JEMMY DAWSON. A BALLAD.

COME, listen to my mournful tale,
  Ye tender hearts and lovers dear;
Nor will you scorn to heave a sigh,
  Nor will you blush to shed a tear.

And thou, dear Kitty, peerless maid,
  Do thou a pensive ear incline;
For thou canst weep at ev'ry woe,
  And pity every plaint, but mine.

Young Dawson was a gallant youth,
  A brighter never trod the plain;

And well he loved one charming maid,
　　And dearly was he loved again.

One tender maid, she loved him dear;
　　Of gentle blood the damsel came,
And faultless was her beauteous form,
　　And spotless was her virgin fame.

But curse on party's hateful strife,
　　That led the faithful youth astray,
The day the rebel clans appear'd:
　　Oh, had he never seen that day!

Their colours and their sash he wore,
　　And in their fatal dress was found;
And now he must that death endure,
　　Which gives the brave the keenest wound.

How pale was then his true-love's cheek,
　　When Jemmy's sentence reach'd her ear!
For never yet did Alpine snows
　　So pale, nor yet so chill, appear.

Yet might sweet mercy find a place
　　And bring relief to Jemmy's woes,
O George, without a pray'r for thee
　　My orisons should never close.

The gracious prince that gives him life,
　　Would crown a never-dying flame;
And every tender babe I bore
　　Should learn to lisp the giver's name.

But though, dear youth, thou shouldst be dragg'd
　　To yonder ignominious tree,
Thou shalt not want a faithful friend
　　To share thy bitter fate with thee.

O, then the mourning coach was call'd;
　　The sledge moved slowly on before;
Though borne in a triumphal car,
　　She had not loved her fav'rite more

She follow'd him, prepar'd to view
　　The terrible behest of law;
And the last scene of Jemmy's woes
　　With calm and stedfast eye she saw.

Distorted was that blooming face,
　　Which she had fondly loved so long;

And stifled was that tuneful breath,
　　Which in her praise had sweetly sung:

And sever'd was that beauteous neck,
　　Round which her arms had fondly closed;
And mangled was that beauteous breast,
　　On which her love-sick head reposed:

And ravish'd was that constant heart,
　　She did to every heart prefer;
For though it could his king forget,
　　'Twas true and loyal still to her.

Amidst those unrelenting flames
　　She bore this constant heart to see;
But when 'twas moulder'd into dust,
　　Yet, yet, she cry'd, I'll follow thee.

My death, my death can only shew
　　The pure and lasting love I bore;
Accept, O Heav'n, of woes like ours,
　　And let us, let us weep no more.

The dismal scene was o'er and past,
　　The lover's mournful hearse retired;
The maid drew back her languid head,
　　And, sighing forth his name, expired.

Though justice ever must prevail,
　　The tear my Kitty sheds is due;
For seldom shall we hear a tale
　　So sad, so tender, and so true.

These offenders were hanged on Kennington Common. They had not hung above five minutes when Townley was cut down, being yet alive; and his body being placed on the block, the executioner chopped off his head with a cleaver. His heart and bowels were then taken out, and thrown into the fire; and the other parties being severally treated in the same manner, the executioner cried out, "God save King George!"

The bodies were quartered, and delivered to the keepers of the New Gaol, who buried them. The heads of some of the parties were sent to Carlisle and Manchester, where they were exposed; but those of Townley and another were fixed on Temple Bar.

———————

It would be useless to attempt to enumerate the other persons whose crimes and misfortunes at this time consigned them to the gibbet; but some account of the escape of the Pretender may not be uninteresting. It would appear that the battle of Culloden having decided the fate of his cause, where the Pretender had his horse shot under him by one of

the king's troopers as he was endeavouring to rally his soldiers, he
retired to the house of a factor of Lord Lovat, at about ten miles from
Inverness, where he met with that lord, and supped with him. After
supper he started on his journey to Fort Augustus, and next day went
on to Invergarry. A boy whom he found there caught him a salmon,
and he dined, and afterwards waited for some of his troops, who had
promised to meet him there. Being disappointed, however, in his object,
he proceeded to Lockharcaige, and arrived there on the 18th of April,
at about two in the morning, and slept; but at five he set out on foot,
and travelled through the Glen of Morar, where he arrived at four the
next morning. He reached Arrashag in twelve hours after, and was
there joined by Captain O'Neil on the 27th, who informed him that his
cause was hopeless, and recommended him, therefore, to sail at once for
France. One Donald M'Leod was engaged to hire a ship, and on the
28th the Chevalier went on board an eight-oared boat, in company with
Sullivan and O'Neil, ordering the people who belonged to the boat to
make the best haste they could to Stornaway, where it was proposed
they should take ship. The night proving very tempestuous, they all
begged of him to go back, which he would not do; but, to keep up the
spirits of the people, he sang them a Highland song. The weather
growing worse and worse, about seven in the morning of the 29th they
were driven on shore on a point of land called Rushness, in the island
of Benbecula, where, when they got on shore, the Pretender helped to
make a fire to warm the crew, who were almost starved to death with
cold. On the 30th, at six in the evening, they set sail again for Stornoway; but, meeting with another storm, were obliged to put into the island
of Scalpa, in the Harris, where they all went on shore to a farmer's
house, passing for merchants that were shipwrecked in their voyage to
the Orkneys; the Pretender and Sullivan going by the name of Sinclair,
the latter passing for the father, and the former for his son. They
thought proper to send from thence to Stornoway, with instructions to
freight a ship for the Orkneys; and on the 3rd of May they received a
message that a ship was ready. On the 4th they set out for that place,
where they arrived on the 5th about noon; but meeting with their messenger, Donald M'Leod, they found that he had got into company, and
told a friend of his for whom he had hired the ship; upon which there
were two hundred people in arms at Stornoway, upon a report that the
Pretender was landed with 500 men, and was coming to burn the town;
so that they were obliged to lie all night upon the moor, with no other
refreshment than biscuit and brandy. On the 6th they resolved to go
in the eight-oared boat to the Orkneys; but the crew refused to venture,
so that they were obliged to steer south along the coast-side, where
they met with two English ships; and this compelled them to put into
a desert island, where they remained till the 10th, without any provision
but some salt fish they found upon the place. About ten in the morning of that day they embarked for the Harris, and at break of day on
the 11th they were chased by an English vessel, but made their escape
among the rocks. About four in the afternoon they arrived on the
island of Benbecula, where they remained till the 14th, and then they

set out for the mountain of Currada, in South Uist, where they staid till the militia of the Isle of Skye came to the island of Irasky. They now sailed for the island of Uia, where they remained three nights, till, having intelligence that the militia were coming towards Benbecula, they immediately got into their boat, and sailed for Lochbusdale. Being met, however, by some ships of war, they were obliged to return to Lochagnart, and at night sailed for Lochbusdale; upon arriving at which place they staid eight days on a rock, making a tent of the sail of the boat. They found themselves here in a most dreadful situation; for, having intelligence that Captain Scott had landed at Kilbride, they were obliged to separate, and the Pretender and O'Neil went to the mountains, where they remained all night, and soon after were informed that General Campbell was at Bernary; so that now they had forces very near on both sides of them, and were absolutely at a loss which way to move. In their road they met with a young lady, one Miss M'Donald, to whom Captain O'Neil proposed assisting the Pretender to make his escape, which at first she refused; but, upon his offering to put on women's clothes, she consented, and desired them to go to the mountain of Currada till she sent for them. They accordingly staid there two days; but hearing nothing from the young lady, the Pretender concluded she would not keep her word, and therefore resolved to send Captain O'Neil to General Campbell, to let him know he was willing to surrender to him; but about five o'clock in the evening a message came from the young lady, desiring them to meet her at Rushness. Being afraid to pass by the Ford, because of the militia, they luckily found a boat, which carried them to the other side of Uia, where they remained part of the next day, afraid of being seen by the country people. In the evening they set out for Rushness, and arrived there at twelve at night. However not finding the young lady, and being alarmed by a boat full of militia, they were obliged to retire two miles back, where the Pretender remained on a moor till O'Neil went to the young lady, and prevailed upon her to come to the place appointed at night-fall of the next day. About an hour after, they had an account of General Campbell's arrival at Benbecula, which obliged them to move to another part of the island, where, as the day broke, they discovered four sail close on the shore, making directly up to the place where they were; so that there was nothing left for them but to throw themselves among the heath. When the wherries were gone, they resolved to go to Clanronald's house; but when they were within a mile of it, they heard that General Campbell was there, which forced them to retreat again. The young Pretender having at length, with the assistance of Captain O'Neil, found Miss M'Donald in a cottage near the place appointed, it was there determined that he should put on women's clothes, and pass for her waiting-maid. This being done, he took leave of Sullivan and O'Neil with great regret, who departed to shift for themselves, leaving him and his new mistress in the cottage, where they continued some days, during which she cured him of the itch. Upon intelligence that General Campbell was gone further into the country, they removed to her cousin's, and spent the night in preparing for their departure to the Isle of Skye: and they set out the next morning for that place, with only one man-servant, named M'Lean, and two rowers. During their voyage they were pursued by a small vessel; but a thick fog rising, they arrived safe at midnight in that island, and landed at the foot of a rock, where the lady and her maid waited while her man M'Lean went to see if Sir Alexander M'Donald was at home. M'Lean found his way thither, but lost it in returning; and his mistress and her maid, after in vain expecting him the whole night, were obliged in the morning to leave the rock, and go in the boat up the creek to some distance, to avoid the militia which guarded the coast. They went on shore again about ten o'clock, and, attended by the rowers, inquired the way to Sir Alexander's. When they had gone about two miles, they met M'Lean; and he told his lady, that Sir Alexander was with the Duke of Cumberland, but his lady was at home, and would do them all the service she could. They then immediately discharged their boat, and went directly to the house, where they remained two days, being always in her ladyship's chamber, except at night, to prevent a discovery. But a party of the M'Leods, having intelligence that some strangers were arrived at Sir Alexander's, and knowing his lady to be well affected to the Pretender, came thither, and demanding to see the new-comers, were introduced to Miss's chamber, where she sat with her new maid. The latter, hearing the militia were at the door, had the presence of mind to get up and open it, which occasioned his being the less noticed; and after they had narrowly searched the chests, they withdrew. The inquiry, however, alarmed the young lady, and the next day she sent her apparent maid to a steward of Sir Alexander's; but hearing that his being in the island was known, he removed to Macdonald's, at Kingsborough, ten miles distant, where he remained but one day; for, on receiving intelligence that it was rumoured that he was disguised in a woman's habit, Macdonald furnished him with a suit of his own clothes, and he went in a boat to M'Leod's at Raza. No prospect of escaping to France, however, presented itself there, and he returned to the Isle of Skye, being thirty miles, with no attendant but a ferryman, M'Leod assuring him that the elder Laird of Mackinnon would there render him all the service in his power. On his reaching M'Kinnon's, the old man instantly knew him, and advised him to go to Lochaber; and he accordingly proceeded thither in a vessel procured for that purpose. M'Donald, at the head of 100 resolute Highlanders, then appeared to assist him, and after roving about with them from place to place, he at length removed to Badenoch. He was there very much harassed by the King's troops, and losing many of his men in the skirmishes which daily took place, they were at length obliged to disperse; and the Pretender, with Lochiel of Borrisdale and some others, skulked about in Moidart. Here they received information that two French privateers were at anchor in Locknanaugh, in one of which, *L'Heureux*, this unfortunate prince eventually embarked, with twenty-three gentlemen, and 107 soldiers, and soon after arrived safely in France.

LEVI WEIL, ASHER WEIL, JACOB LAZARUS, AND SOLOMON PORTER,

EXECUTED FOR THE MURDER OF JOHN SLOW.

THIS daring violation of the law, which long roused the public in-dignation against the whole Jewish people, happened in the house of Mrs. Hutchings, in the King's-road, Chelsea, who was a farmer's widow, left by her husband in good circumstances, and with three children, two boys and a girl.

On a Saturday evening, just as the Jewish Sabbath was ended, a nume-rous gang of Jews assembled in Chelsea Fields; and having lurked about there until ten o'clock, went at that hour to the house of Mrs. Hutchings, and demanded admittance. The family had all retired to rest, with the exception of Mrs. Hutchings and her two female servants, who, being alarmed by the unseasonable request of the applicants, proceeded in a body to know their business. The door was no sooner opened, however, than a number of fellows—all of whom had the appearance of Jews—rushed in, and seizing the terrified females, threat-ened them with instant death in the event of their offering any resistance. Mrs. Hutchings, being a woman of considerable muscular strength, for a time opposed them; but her antagonists having soon overpowered her, they tied her petticoats over her head, and proceeded to secure the servants. The girls having been tied back to back, five of the fellows proceeded to ransack the house, while the remainder of the gang re-mained below to guard the prisoners. Having visited the rooms occupied by the children of Mrs. Hutchings in turn, the ruffians proceeded to the apartment in which two men, employed as labourers on the farm, named John Slow and William Stone, were lying undisturbed by the outcry which had been raised below. It was soon determined that these men were likely to prove mischievous, and that they must be murdered; and Levi Weil, a Jewish physician, who was one of the party, and the most sanguinary villain of the gang, aimed a blow at the breast of Stone, intended for his death, but which only stunned him. Slow started up, and the villains cried " Shoot him! shoot him!" a pistol was instantly fired at him, and he fell, exclaiming, " Lord have mercy on me! I am murdered!"

They dragged the wounded man out of the room to the head of the stairs; but in the mean time Stone, recovering his senses, jumped out of bed, and escaped to the roof of the house, through the window. The thieves now descended and plundered the house of all the plate they could discover; but finding no money, they went to Mrs. Hutchings, and threatened to murder her if she did not disclose the place of its concealment. She gave them her watch, and was afterwards compelled to give up a purse containing £65, with which they immediately retired. Mrs. Hutchings now directly set her female servants at liberty, and having gone in search of the men, she found Slow, who declared he was dying, and dropped insensible on the floor. He languished until the following afternoon, and then died of the wounds which he had received.

It was a considerable time before the perpetrators of this most diabolical outrage were discovered; but they were at length given up to justice by one of their accomplices, named Isaacs, who was a German Jew, and who, reduced to the greatest necessity, was tempted by the prospect of reward to impeach his fellows. It then turned out that the gang consisted of eight persons, who were headed by the physician before-mentioned. Dr. Weil had been educated in a superior manner. He had studied physic in the university of Leyden, where he was admitted to the degree of Doctor in that faculty; and then, coming to England, he practised in London, with no inconsiderable degree of success, and was always known by the name of Doctor Weil; but so destitute was he of all principle, and such was the depravity of his heart, that he determined to engage in the dangerous practice of robbery. Having formed his fatal resolution, he wrote to Amsterdam, to some poor Jews, to come to England, and assist him in his intended depredations on the public; and at the same time informed them that in England large sums were to be acquired by the practice of theft.

The inconsiderate men no sooner received Dr. Weil's letter than they procured a passport from the English consul, and, embarking in the Harwich packet-boat, arrived in England.

They lost no time in repairing to London, and immediately attended Dr. Weil. He informed them that his plan was, that they should go out in the day-time, and minutely survey such houses near London as might probably afford a good booty, and then attack them at night.

At the sessions held at the Old Bailey, in the month of December, 1771, Levi Weil, Asher Weil, Marcus Hartagh, Jacob Lazarus, Solomon Porter, and Lazarus Harry, were indicted for the felony and murder above-mentioned, when the two of the name of Weil, with Jacob Lazarus and Solomon Porter, were capitally convicted; while Marcus Hartagh and Lazarus Harry were acquitted for want of evidence.

These men, as was customary in all cases of murder, when it could be made convenient to the Court, were tried on a Friday, and on the following day they were anathematised in the synagogue. As their execution was to take place on the Monday following, one of the rabbis went to them in the press-yard of Newgate, and delivered to each of them a Hebrew-book; but declined attending them to the place of death, nor even prayed with them at the time of his visit.

They were attended to Tyburn, the place of execution, by immense crowds of people, who were anxious to witness the exit of wretches, whose crimes had been so much the object of public notice.

Having prayed together, and sung a hymn in the Hebrew language, they were launched into eternity, December 9, 1771.

After the bodies had hung the customary time, they were conveyed to Surgeons' Hall to be dissected.

GARDELLE KNEELING BY THE BODY OF HIS VICTIM.

THEODORE GARDELLE,

EXECUTED FOR MURDER.

THEODORE GARDELLE was a foreigner, a man of education and talents in the profession of painting. He was born at Geneva, a city famed for having given birth to great men in both the arts and sciences. He chose the miniature style of painting; and having acquired its first rudiments, he went to Paris, where he made great proficiency in the art. He then returned to his native place, and practised his profession for some years with credit and emolument; but, being unhappy in his domestic concerns, he repaired to London, and took lodgings at Mrs. King's, in Leicester Fields, in the year 1760. Some time afterwards, for the benefit of purer air, he removed to Knightsbridge; but, finding that place too far from his business, he returned to his former residence at Mrs. King's, who was the unfortunate subject of his crime.

The circumstances attending the murder were as follow. On Thursday, the 19th of February, 1761, in the morning, the maid got up at about seven o'clock, and was shortly afterwards summoned by Gardelle, who gave her two letters, a snuff-box, and a guinea; and desired her to deliver the letters, one of which was directed to a Mr. Mozier, in the Haymarket, and the other to a person who kept a snuff-shop at the next door, and to bring him from the latter place a pennyworth of snuff.

The girl received the messages, and went to her mistress, telling her what Gardelle had desired her to do; to which her mistress replied, "Nanny, you can't go, for there is nobody to answer at the street-door." The girl being willing to oblige Gardelle, or being for some reason desirous to go out, answered, that Mr. Gardelle would come down and sit in the parlour till she came back. She then went again to Gardelle, and told him what objection her mistress had made, and what she had said to remove it. Gardelle then said he would go down, as she had proposed, and he did so. The girl immediately went on his errand, and left him in the parlour (which was next to Mrs. King's apartment) shutting the street-door after her, and taking the key to let herself in when she returned.

Immediately after the girl was gone out, Mrs. King, hearing the tread of somebody in the next room, called out, " Who is there?" and at the same time opened her chamber door. Gardelle was at a table, very near the door, having just then taken up a book that lay upon it, which happened to be a French grammar. He had some time before drawn Mrs. King's picture, which she wanted to have made very handsome, and had teased him so much about it that the effect was just contrary. It happened, unfortunately, that the first thing she said to him, when she saw it was he whom she had heard walking about in the room, was something reproachful about this picture: Gardelle was provoked at the insult; and, as he spoke English very imperfectly, he, for want of a less improper expression, told her, with some warmth, that she was " an impertinent woman." This threw her into a transport of rage, and she gave him a violent blow with her fist on the breast; so violent that, he said in his confession, he could not have supposed such a blow could have been given by a woman. As soon as the blow was struck, she drew a little back, and at the same instant, he says, he laid his hand on her shoulder and pushed her from him, rather in contempt than anger, or with a design to hurt her; but her foot happening to catch in the floor-cloth, she fell backwards, and her head came with great force against the corner of the bedstead: the blood immediately gushed from her mouth, not in a continued stream, but as if by different strokes of a pump. He instantly ran to her, expressing his concern at the accident; but she pushed him away, and threatened, though in a feeble and interrupted voice, to punish him for what he had done. He was, he says, terrified exceedingly at the thought of being condemned for a criminal act upon her accusation, and again attempted to assist her by raising her up, as the blood still gushed from her mouth in great quantities; but she still exerted all her strength to keep him off, and still cried out, mixing threats with her screams. He then seized an ivory comb with a sharp taper point continued from the back, for adjusting the curls of her air, which lay upon her toilet, and threatened her in his turn, to prevent her crying out; but as she still continued to cry out, though with a voice still fainter and fainter, he struck her with this instrument, probably in her throat, upon which the blood flowed from her mouth in yet greater quantities, and her voice was quite stopped. He then drew the bed-clothes over her, to prevent her blood from spreading on the floor, and to hide it from his sight; and he stood some time motionless by her, and then fell down by her side in a swoon. When he came to himself, he perceived the maid was come in: he therefore went out of the room without examining the body to see if the unhappy wretch was quite dead, and his confusion was then so great that he staggered against the wainscot, and hit his head so as to raise a bump over his eye.

It appears that he subsequently sent the girl away, informing her that he had her mistress's orders to dismiss her, and paid her ten shillings for her wages; and the latter, having been unable to find either her mistress or Gardelle on her first returning to the house, and knowing the former to be a woman of light character, concluded that they must have been in bed together, and that her mistress being ashamed to meet her, determined to get rid of her. Her suspicions were not at all raised therefore, and she went away, informing Gardelle that Mr. Wright, who lodged in the house, but had been out of town, would return that evening with his servant. On her departure, the first thing that Gardelle did was to go into the chamber, to the body, which, upon examination, he found quite dead; he therefore took off the blankets and sheets with which he had covered it, stripped off the shifts, and laid the body quite naked upon the bed. Before this, he said, his linen was not stained; but it was much stained by his removing the body. He then took the two blankets, the sheet, the coverlet, and one of the curtains, and put them into the water-tub in the back wash-house to soak, they being all much stained with blood; her shift he carried up stairs, put it in a bag, and concealed it under his bed; his own shirt, now bloody, he pulled off, and locked up in a drawer of his bureau.

When all this was done, he went and sat down in the parlour, and soon after, it being about nine o'clock, Mr. Wright's servant came in without his master, who had changed his mind, and was gone to a gentleman's house in Castle Street. He went up into his room, the garret, and sat there till about eleven o'clock: he then came down, and, finding Gardelle still in the parlour, asked if Mrs. King was come home; if not, who must sit up for her? Gardelle said, she was not come home, and he would sit up for her.

In the morning, Friday, when Pelsey came down stairs, he again asked if Mrs. King was come home; and Gardelle told him that she had been at home, but was gone again. He then asked how he came by the hurt on his eye; and he said he got it by cutting some wood to light the fire in the morning. Pelsey then went about his master's business, and at night was again let in by Gardelle, who, upon being asked, said he would sit up that night also. The next morning, Saturday, Pelsey again inquired for Mrs. King; and Gardelle, though he had professed to sit up for her but the night before, now told him she was gone to Bath or Bristol.

On Saturday, Mozier, an acquaintance of Gardelle's, who had been also intimate with Mrs. King, and had spent the evening with her the Wednesday before the murder, came by appointment about two or three o'clock, having promised to go with her that evening to the Opera. He was let in by Gardelle, who told him that Mrs. King was gone to Bath or Bristol, as he had told Pelsey. This man, and another acquaintance of Gardelle's, perceiving that he was chagrined, as they thought, and disspirited, seem to have imagined that Mrs. King's absence was the cause, and that if they could get him another girl they should cure him; and having picked up a prostitute in the Haymarket, they brought her that very Saturday to Gardelle, at Mrs. King's. Gardelle apologized for the confusion in which the house appeared, and Mozier (or Muzard, as he was sometimes called) asked her if she would take care of the house: she readily consented; and Gardelle acquiescing, they left her with him. He asked her what her business was; she said she worked plain-work: he then told her he had some shirts to mend, and that he would satisfy her for her trouble if she would mend them.

All this while the body continued as he had left it on Thursday night, nor had he once been into the room since that time. But this night, the woman and Pelsey having retired to their beds, he first conceived a design of concealing or destroying the dead body by parts, and went down to put it into execution; but the woman, whose name was Sarah Walker, getting out of bed and following him, he returned up stairs and went to bed with her. He rose on the Sunday morning between seven and eight, and left Walker in bed, saying it was too soon for her to rise; she fell asleep again, and slept till ten: it is probable that in the mean time he was employed on the body, for when she came down, between ten and eleven, he was but beginning to light the parlour-fire. He had spoken to her the night before to get him a char-woman, and he was now in so much confusion that he did not ask her to stay to breakfast: she went out, therefore, and hired one Pritchard as a char-woman, at 1s. a-day, victuals and drink. In the afternoon she brought Pritchard to the house, and found with Gardelle two or three men and two women. Gardelle went up with her, and stayed by her while she made his bed, and the company all went out together. The char-woman kept house, and about ten o'clock they returned and supped in Gardelle's room. She was then dismissed for the night, and ordered to come the next morning at eight.

The next morning, Monday, the char-woman was ordered to tell Pelsey, the footman, that Walker was a relation of Mrs. King's, who was come to be in the house till Mrs. King returned; but Pelsey knew that she and Gardelle had but one bed; for when he came down on Monday morning, Gardelle's chamber-door stood open, and, looking in, he saw some of her clothes. On Monday night he again inquired after Mrs. King, and Gardelle told him she was at Bath or Bristol, he knew not where; he differed at times in his account of her, but no suspicion of murder was yet entertained. On Tuesday morning, Pelsey, who was going up to his master's room, smelt an offensive smell, and asked Gardelle who was shoving up the sash of the window on the staircase, what it was; Gardelle replied, somebody had put a bone in the fire: the truth, however, was, that while Walker was employed in mending and making some linen in the parlour, he had been burning some of Mrs, King's bones in the garret. At night, Pelsey renewed his inquiries after Mrs. King, and Gardelle answered with seeming impatience, "Me know not of Mrs. King; she give me great deal of trouble, but me shall hear of her Wednesday or Thursday;" yet he still talked of sitting up for her.

On Tuesday night he told Mrs. Walker he would sit up till Mrs. King came home, though he had before told her she was out of town, and desired her to go to bed, to which she consented. As soon as she was in bed, he renewed his horrid employment of cutting the body to pieces, and disposing of it in different places: the bowels he threw down the necessary; and the flesh of the body and limbs, cut to pieces, he scattered about in the cock-loft, where he supposed they would dry without putrefaction. About two o'clock in the morning, however, he was interrupted; for Walker, having waked, and not finding him, went down stairs, and found him standing upon the stairs; he then, at her solicitation, went up with her to bed.

Wednesday passed like the preceding days, and on Thursday he told his female companion that he expected Mrs. King home in the evening, and desired that she would provide herself a lodging, giving her, two of Mrs. King's shifts; and, being thus dismissed, she went away.

Pritchard, the char-woman, still continued in her office, and it was through her that the horrid deed was at length discovered. The water having failed in the cistern on the Tuesday, she had recourse to that in the water-tub in the back kitchen; upon pulling out the spigot, a little water run out, but as there appeared to be more in, she got upon a ledge, and putting her hand in she felt something soft; she then fetched a poker, and pressing down the contents of the tub, she got water in a pail. This circumstance she told Pelsey, and they agreed the first opportunity to see what the things in the water-tub were; yet so languid was their curiosity, and so careless were they of the event, that it was Thursday before this tub was examined: they found in it the blankets, sheets, and coverlet that Gardelle had put in it to soak; and after spreading, shaking, and looking at them, they put them again into the tub; and the next morning when Pelsey came down, he saw the curtain hanging on the banisters of the kitchen-stairs. Upon looking down he saw Gardelle just coming out at the wash-house door, where the tub stood. When Pritchard, the char-woman, came, he asked her if she had been taking any of the clothes out of the tub, and found the sheets had been wrung out. Upon this the first step was taken towards inquiring after the unhappy woman, who had now lain dead more than a week in the house. Pelsey found out the maid whom Gardelle had dismissed, and asked her if she had put any bed-clothes into the water; she said, No, and seemed frightened.

These particulars also came to the knowledge of Mr. Barron, an apothecary in the neighbourhood, who went the same day to Mrs. King's house to enquire of Gardelle where she was. He trembled, and told him, with great confusion, that she was gone to Bath. The next day, therefore, Saturday, he carried the maid before Mr. Fielding, the justice, to make her deposition, and obtained a warrant to take Gardelle into custody. When the warrant was obtained, Mr. Barron, with the constable, and some others, went to the house, where they found Gardelle, and charged him with the murder; he denied it, but soon after dropped down in a swoon. When he recovered, they demanded the key of Mrs. King's chamber; but he said she had got it with her in the country; the constable therefore got in at the window, and opened the door that communicated with the parlour, and they all went in. They found upon the bed a pair of blankets wet, and a pair of sheets that appeared not to have been lain in, and the curtain also which Pelsey and the char-woman had seen first in the water-tub, and then on the banisters, was found put up in its place wet. Upon taking off the clothes, the bed appeared bloody, the blankets also were bloody, and marks of blood appeared in other places; having taken his keys, they went up into his room, where they found the bloody shift and shirt.

The prisoner, with all these tokens of his guilt, was then carried before Sir John Fielding; and, though he stiffly denied the fact, was committed for trial. On the Monday, a carpenter and bricklayer were sent to search the house for the body, and Mr. Barron went with them. In the necessary they found the bowels of a human body; and in the cock-loft they found one of the breasts, some other muscular parts, and some bones. They perceived also that there had been a fire in the garret; and some fragments of bones, half consumed, were found in the grate, so large as to be known to be human. On the Thursday before, Gardelle had carried an oval chip-box to one Perronneau, a painter in enamel, who had employed him in copying, and, pretending it contained colours of great value, desired him to keep it; saying, he was uneasy to leave it at Mrs. King's while she was absent at Bath. Perronneau, when he heard Gardelle was taken up, opened the box, and found in it a gold watch and chain, and a pair of ear-rings, which were known to be Mrs. King's. At the strength of this evidence Gardelle gave way, and confessed the fact. He was sent to the New Prison, where he attempted to destroy himself by taking opium, and by swallowing halfpence to the number of twelve; but although he injured himself considerably in this latter attempt, he did not effect his purpose.

On Thursday, the 2d of April, he was tried at the Old Bailey; and in his defence, he insisted only that he had no malice to the deceased, and that her death was the consequence of the fall. He was convicted, and sentenced to be executed on Saturday the 4th. The account which he wrote in prison, and which is mentioned in this narrative, is dated the 28th of March, though he did not communicate it till after his trial. The night after his condemnation his behaviour was extravagant and outrageous; yet the next morning he was composed and quiet, and said he had slept three or four hours in the night. He declared he had no design to rob Mrs. King, but that he removed some of the things merely to give credit to the story of her journey to Bath.

He was executed on the 4th of April, 1761, amidst the shouts and hisses of an indignant populace, in the Haymarket, near Panton Street, to which he was led by Mrs. King's house, where the cart made a stop, and at which he just gave a look. His body was hung in chains on Hounslow Heath.

. .

ELIZABETH BROWNRIGG,

EXECUTED FOR MURDER.

ELIZABETH BROWNRIGG, when a young woman, lived servant with a merchant in Goodman's Fields, and there it was that she became ac-quainted with James Brownrigg, who had just served his apprenticeship to a painter in the same neighbourhood.

Some time after their marriage they settled at Greenwich, where Brownrigg carried on his trade as a painter about six years, and then came to settle in London. Mrs. Brownrigg had no less than sixteen children in the space of twenty years after her marriage, and three of them were alive at the time she suffered.

She was always considered by her neighbours as a faithful wife and a most affectionate mother; and, in order to be as useful as possible to her family, she learned midwifery. The overseers of the parish of St. Dunstan's in the West made choice of her to deliver such women as were taken in labour in their workhouse, and, notwithstanding many illiberal reflections that were thrown out against her, seems always to have acted in that station with equal skill and humanity.

In 1765, the overseers of Whitefriars precinct bound out a poor girl, Mary Mitchell, as an apprentice to Brownrigg; and, much about the same time, the governors of the Foundling Hospital bound to him another poor girl, whose name was Mary Jones.

The reason why Brownrigg took so many girls was, it seems, that his wife having taken women to lay in privately in her house, found that the girls would not cost her so much money as hired servants, who would be necessary on such occasions. It does not appear that these poor girls were used with any greater cruelty at first than common cor-rection for trifling faults; nor is it to be supposed that their conduct was any worse than that of poor girls in general. They had not, however, been long in their place, when Mrs. Brownrigg discovered such a malicious antipathy to them, that she frequently took Mary Jones, the Foundling girl, and, laying her on the back of two chairs on the kitchen floor, whipped her so long that she was obliged to desist merely from the want of strength.

By such treatment the girl received many injuries in different parts of her body, particularly in her head and shoulders; but, for all that, her inhuman mistress, instead of pitying her, used, when she had done whipping, to throw a pail of water over her. The room in which the girl slept was adjoining the passage, and near to the street-door; and, as she observed that the key was left in when the family went to bed, she resolved to avail herself of that circumstance, and, by running away, escape from the cruelty of her inhuman tormentor.

Accordingly, one morning she slipped out of bed, and getting hold of the key, opened the door in the easiest manner she could, and made her escape into the street, without being discovered.

Being thus at liberty, she was at a loss where to go, as she had no knowledge of any of her relations, nor any home but the Foundling Hospital. She resolved, however, to go to the hospital, and accordingly she asked her way thither of every one whom she met in the street.

As soon as she came to the gate, she was admitted; and having told the steward in what manner she had been used, and at the same time showing her wounds, was admitted till such time as a proper inquiry could be made into her mistress's conduct.

Mary Mitchell was now left alone, and continued to suffer all the afflictions that her inhuman mistress could heap upon her, till she had served one year of her time, and then she also determined to run away. Accordingly, she found means to get out, but the same day she was met in the street by Brownrigg's youngest son, who brought her back to her place of confinement, where she was treated with much greater cruelty than before.

Soon after Mary Mitchell was brought back, Mary Clifford, another poor girl, was bound by the overseers of Whitefriars precinct to Brownrigg, and it was not long before she experienced the same cruelties as had been inflicted on the others. She was for the most trifling offence tied up naked, and beat with a cane, a horsewhip, a hearth-broom, or anything that came in the way, till she was not able to speak, her strength being exhausted by the severity of her punishment.

It was the misfortune of this poor girl, either by bad nursing or natural weakness, not to be able to keep her water; and her mistress, taking notice that the bed was wet, ordered her to lie on a mat in the cellar, in a place that had been used as a coal-hole. This coal-hole was cold and damp; and after she had been some time in it, the mat was taken away, and a sack with some straw put in its room.

While she was confined in this wretched place she had no other sustenance than bread and water, and no other covering than her own clothes, unless it accidentally happened that she laid hold of some rag of an old blanket, which her mistress was sure to take from her as soon as she discovered it, so that, during some very cold nights, she lay almost naked.

One time, when she was almost dead with hunger, she broke open the cupboard, but found nothing in it; and at another time she broke down some boards to get at water. Her mistress, having discovered what she had done—what every one would have done in the same deplorable condition—resolved to punish her in the severest manner that her hellish malice could contrive.

She was first made to strip naked, and kept in that condition a whole day, being every now and then beat severely with the butt-end of a whip. When she had gone through this hellish discipline, a jack-chain was put round her neck, the end of which was fastened to the yard-door, after which the chain was pulled as tight as it possibly could be without choking her; and when she had been tormented a whole day in that manner, she was put down into the coal-hole, with the chain still about her neck, and her hands tied behind her, and was left to spend the night in that manner, without either victuals or drink.

As Brownrigg was, consistently with the articles of their indentures, obliged to find them in clothes, in order to be at as little expense as possible, whenever it was found that any rent happened in their gowns or petticoats, they were stripped almost naked, and in that manner kept for whole days together.

The office of gaoler to the unfortunate innocents was commonly performed by the eldest son of Brownrigg, but sometimes by the apprentice; and the latter declared, that one night, when he went to tie them up, they were stark naked, without a bit of rag to cover any part of their bodies.

In this manner the girls were so often inhumanly beat that their heads and shoulders became like one scab, for the skin broke off as soon as any plaster was applied to the wounds; and yet, for all that, the inhuman mistress continued to whip them in the same barbarous manner as before. At different times they were stripped naked, when Mrs. Brownrigg intended to wreak her vengeance upon them, and their hands were tied to a leaden water-pipe, that ran along the ceiling of the kitchen; but that giving way, Brownrigg, with his own hands, drove a staple into the main beam, through which a cord was drawn, and then they were hung up in the same manner as before.

Sometimes the inhuman woman would lay hold of the girl's cheeks, and pull the skin down with such force that her eyes would be ready to start from their sockets, and blood gushed from them. This severity induced the poor girl, Mary Clifford, to tell her complaint to a Frenchwoman, a lodger in the house, who had come there to lay in; and she having upbraided Mrs. Brownrigg for her cruelty to a helpless orphan, instead of altering her conduct, ran to the girl with a pair of scissors in her hand, and cut her tongue in two different places.

On the 13th of July, in the morning, Mrs. Brownrigg, having for several days threatened the girls, went down to the kitchen, and stripped Mary Clifford naked, and hung her up to the staple: although her head and shoulders were then very sore, and her whole body was covered over with scabs, the relentless tyrant continued to beat her in the most inhuman manner.

When she had whipped her till the blood flowed in great abundance she was let down in presence of the other girl, Mary Mitchell; and though in the most miserable condition that can be imagined, she was ordered to wash herself in a tub filled with cold water.

While she was washing herself, her mistress struck her with the butt end of a whip on her lacerated shoulders; and, lest the tragedy should not have been completed, she was tied up, and used in the same barbarous manner, no less than five times that very day.

Her wounds were now mortal, and in that dismal place she might have paid the debt of nature, and her mistress possibly escaped punishment, had it not been for a strange incident.

The father of Mary Clifford had married a second wife; but as he had been dead some time, she, being a native of Cambridgeshire, went down to reside there. Having some business in London, she came to inquire for the girl, but was denied admittance to her; and Brownrigg threatened that, if she came any more, he would take her before the lord mayor.

Upon that the woman went away; but the wife of Mr. Deacon, a baker, who lived next door to Brownrigg, called her in, and told her she was sure she had often heard girls groan in their house, and doubted not that her daughter-in-law was one. Mrs. Deacon took the woman's direction, and in the mean time told her that nothing should be wanting on her part to make a discovery.

Brownrigg had bought a hog, which he had sent home to fatten; and it being confined under a shed, it was necessary to open a skylight above it, in order to remove the noxious smell. This gave Mr. Deacon's apprentice an opportunity of looking down from one of his master's windows, and he saw the girl, Mary Clifford, lying in a most shocking condition. He called to her several times, but received no answer; and then, in order to attract her notice, he threw down some small pieces of the ceiling.

The poor girl made several attempts to speak, but was unable; and the young man heard her mistress call out to her in an angry tone, " What is the matter with you!" Intelligence of this was instantly sent to the mother-in-law, who went next day, with the overseers and Mr. Deacon's apprentice, to Brownrigg's house. They inquired for Mary Clifford; but Brownrigg swore she was not there, and, in order to deceive them, produced Mary Mitchell.

Deacon's apprentice declared that Mary Mitchell was not the girl whom he had seen in so deplorable a condition; upon which Mr. Grundy, overseer, sent for a constable, who searched the house, though in vain. Mr. Grundy, who, from the whole of his conduct, seems to have been a man of spirit and prudence, took Mary Mitchell along with him to the workhouse, regardless of all Brownrigg's threatenings, who said she was his apprentice, and brought an attorney to intimidate him.

When the people in the workhouse began to strip the girl, it was found that she had no shift on, and the rest of her clothes stuck fast to the wounds she had received. The girl said, that Mary Clifford was in the house; and Mr. Grundy, going back to Brownrigg's, ordered him to produce her immediately.

Brownrigg sent again for his attorney, who did all he could to intimidate Grundy; but he, regardless of what he said, declared that he would answer for his conduct in any court of justice whatever, and therefore told Brownrigg, that unless the girl was instantly produced, he would charge him with murder.

His attorney, well knowing no bail could be taken in such a case, advised Brownrigg to produce her, which he did from a hole under the beaufette, where she had been concealed. The shocking condition in which she appeared cannot be described; her body was like one entire ulcer, ready to mortify.

During the time the inquiry had been making, Mrs. Brownrigg and her son made their escape; but Mr. Grundy took the father with the two girls before Mr. Crosby, the sitting alderman, who committed Brownrigg to prison. and sent the girls to Bartholomew Hospital. Mary

Clifford died within a few days afterwards, and an inquest being taken, a verdict was found of " Wilful Murder against James Brownrigg, his wife, and his son John."

In the mean time a reward was offered by the parish of St. Dunstan's in the West, for apprehending Mrs. Brownrigg and her son; and they were traced from one place to another, till it was found that they had taken their passage in the coach to Dover; but, they not coming to the inn according to agreement, the coach went without them.

They were in such terror that they went over to Wandsworth under feigned names, and took lodgings in the house of Mr. Dunbar, who kept a chandler's shop, where they remained for some time in the most private manner; but one day Dunbar, happening to look over a newspaper, saw such a description of Mrs. Brownrigg and her son, as convinced him that his lodgers were the persons.

Next day, being Sunday, he came to London, and gave notice to Mr. Owen, the churchwarden, who immediately sent Mr. Wiegrave, the constable, and Mr. Deacon, the baker, to recognise them.

When they came to Dunbar's house, they found the mother and son sitting in a room by themselves, and brought them to London in so quiet a manner that no persons in the town knew that they were in the custody of a constable, except the landlord and his wife.

Next sessions they were all three indicted; but the jury found only Mrs. Brownrigg guilty of murder; her husband and her son being ordered to remain in prison, to be tried for a misdemeanor; and accordingly they were afterwards convicted, and sentenced to suffer six months' imprisonment in Newgate.

In the mean time, Mrs. Brownrigg having received sentence of death, was taken to the condemned cell; and to a clergyman who attended her she confessed her guilt, and at the same time acknowledged the justness of her sentence.

On the morning of her execution she was brought into the press-yard, and the last farewell she took of her husband and son was as moving as can be conceived. She fell on her knees, and implored pardon of her Maker in the most earnest manner, begging that God, for Christ's sake, would deliver her from blood-guiltiness.

While they were taking her to the place of execution, the people testified their abhorrence of her in such a manner as is shocking to mention. Undoubtedly their indignation against her crime arose from a principle of compassion to the unfortunate sufferers, who had been the objects of her diabolical cruelty; but some of them went so far as to wish her soul in hell, declaring they doubted not the devil would come and fetch her.

When she was brought to the gallows, she prayed devoutly, and then, being turned off, hung the usual time; after which her body was carried to Surgeons' Hall to be dissected.

She was executed at Tyburn on the 14th of September, 1767.

JOHN SMITH AND ROBERT MAYNE,

EXECUTED FOR MUTINY ON BOARD THE KING GEORGE.

ON the trial of these men, with five more of the crew, it appeared that disputes arose on board the King George, a fine privateer, of 32 guns and 200 men, commanded by Captain Reed, and cruising against the enemies of their country, concerning some prize wine, which was stowed in the hold. Some of the crew insisted on its being hoisted up to be used for the whole ship's company; but as this would have been attended, in their situation, with both difficulty and danger, it was consequently opposed by Captain Reed and his officers. Being thus disappointed, a factious discontented set endeavoured to corrupt the remainder, and soon gained over so formidable a party, that they determined to seize the ship, and turn pirates in the Indian seas. In order to effect this, when off Cape Ortugal, the mutineers demanded the keys of the arm-chests; and, on the refusal of their request, they drove the captain and officers into the cabin, placed a guard at the door, and brought a nine-pounder carriage-gun, loaded with round and grape shot, to fire among the officers; but were prevailed upon to desist by the entreaties of Mr. Gardener, the sailing master.

They then offered the latter the command of the ship, acquainting him with their intention of steering for the East Indies; but, on his refusal, they put him under a guard, and took the ship into their own care, until they had, for want of skill, nearly lost her. They then released Mr. Gardener, and gave him the helm; when he steered into Camarinas, in Spain, where most of the mutineers took to the roads, and made their escape.

Such as were apprehended were brought to trial; and though two more (viz. Thomas Baldwin and Laurence Tiernan) were found guilty, yet Smith and Mayne, who were the ringleaders of the mutiny only were hanged. They suffered at Execution Dock, May 10th, 1762.

They were both Irishmen and Roman Catholics, and were attended by a priest of that religion.

A few years after this affair, a mutiny broke out among the crew of the Namur, of ninety guns. Fifteen were tried, found guilty, and ordered to be hanged; and they were taken for execution on board the Royal Ann, with halters round their necks. While waiting for the fatal gun being fired, however, they were told that his majesty had pardoned fourteen of them, but that one of them must die; and, to determine whom, they were ordered to cast lots. What must have been the feelings of these miserable men at this awful moment! The fatal lot fell upon the second man that drew, Matthew M'Can, who was soon run up to the yard-arm, where the body hung nearly an hour.

The pardoned seamen were turned over to the Grafton and the Sunderland, then under sailing orders for the East Indies.

THE MEETING BETWEEN TURPIN AND KING.

RICHARD TURPIN,

EXECUTED FOR HORSE-STEALING.

THE fame of this notorious offender is perhaps unequalled by that of any of his compeers in guilt—from what cause it were difficult to say; for we find on examining his history, instead of a daring, gallant, and generous spirit, which our legendary narratives would assign to him, he sinks before the withering glance of *truth* into a petty pilferer, a heartless plunderer, and a brutal murderer. Fancy and fiction, however, have done more to secure the reputation of Turpin as a hero and a man of courage, than any pains he ever took to obtain the character for himself. It is almost needless to add, that the story of the ride to York, and the wondrous deeds of the highwayman's steed, " Black Bess," are merely the fabrications of some poetical brain.

Richard Turpin was the son of John Turpin, of Hempstead, in Essex. He was put apprentice to a butcher in Whitechapel, with whom he served his time; during which period he was frequently guilty of misdemeanors, and conducted himself in a loose and disorderly manner.

On the expiration of his apprenticeship he married a young woman named Palmer, and set up in business for himself at Sutton in Essex. Having no credit in the market, and no money in his pocket, he was shortly so reduced as to be tempted to maintain himself by unlawful means; and accordingly he very often used to rob his neighbours of sheep, lambs, and oxen. His proceedings, however, received an unexpected check; for having stolen two oxen belonging to Mr. Giles, of Plaistow, he drove them to his own house; but two of Giles's servants suspecting who was the robber, a warrant was procured for the apprehension of Turpin; who, learning that the officers were in search of him, made his escape from the back-window at the very moment they were entering at the door.

Having retreated to a place of security, he found means to inform his wife where he was concealed; on which she furnished him with money, and he travelled into the hundreds of Essex, where he joined a gang of smugglers, with whom he was for some time successful, till a set of Custom-house officers, by one fortunate stroke, deprived him of all his ill-acquired gains.

Thrown out of this kind of business, he connected himself with a gang of deer-stealers, the principal part of whose depredations were committed in Epping Forest, and the parks in its neighbourhood: but this business not succeeding to the expectation of the robbers, they commenced house-breaking.

Their plan was to fix on houses which they presumed contained valuable property; and, while one of them knocked at the door, the others rushed in, and seized whatever they deemed worthy of notice.

The first attack of this kind was at the house of Mr. Strype, an old man who kept a chandler's shop at Watford, whom they robbed of all the money in his possession, but did not offer him any personal violence.

Turpin acquainted his associates that there was an old woman at Loughton, who was in possession of seven or eight hundred pounds; whereupon they agreed to rob her. When they came to the door, one of them knocked, and the rest forcing their way into the house, tied handkerchiefs over the eyes of the old woman and her maid. This being done, Turpin demanded what money was in the house; and the owner hesitating to tell him, he threatened to set her on the fire if she did not make an immediate discovery. Still, however, she declined to give the desired information; on which the villains actually placed her on the fire, where she sat till the tormenting pains compelled her to discover her hidden treasure; so that the robbers possessed themselves of above £400, and decamped with the booty.

The gang appears to have proceeded with some success; for soon afterwards they robbed the house of a farmer at Barking of above £700, in a most daring manner, and then they determined to attack the house of Mr. Mason, the keeper of Epping Forest. Turpin, it appears, was absent from this expedition, for he was unable to remain with so much money in his pocket as he possessed, and had therefore started to London to spend it in riot and intoxication. His companions, however, were true to their faith, and having obtained a considerable booty, sought him in town, and shared the produce of the robbery with him.

On the 11th January, 1735, Turpin and five of his companions went to the house of Mr. Saunders, a rich farmer at Charlton, in Kent, between seven and eight in the evening, and having knocked at the door, asked if Mr. Saunders was at home. Being answered in the affirmative, they rushed into the house, and found Mr. Saunders with his wife and friends playing at cards in the parlour. They told the company, that they should remain uninjured if they made no disturbance. Having made prize of a silver snuff-box which lay on the table, a part of the gang stood guard over the rest of the company, while the others attended Mr. Saunders through the house, and breaking open his escrutoires and closets took away above £100, exclusive of plate.

During these transactions the servant-maid had run up stairs, barred the door of her room, and called out, " Thieves !" with a view of alarming the neighbourhood; but the robbers broke open the door of her room, secured her, and then robbed the house of all the valuable property they had not before taken. Finding some minced pies, and some bottles of wine, they sat down to regale themselves; and meeting with a bottle of brandy, they compelled each of the company to drink a glass of it.

Mrs. Saunders fainting through terror, they administered some drops in water to her, and recovered her to the use of her senses. Having staid in the house a considerable time, they packed up their booty and departed, having first declared, that if any of the family gave the least alarm within two hours, or advertised the marks of the stolen plate, they would return and murder them at a future time.

Their next attack was on the house of Mr. Sheldon, near Croydon, where they obtained a considerable booty in money and jewels.

They then concerted the robbery of Mr. Lawrence, of Edgware, near Stanmore, in Middlesex, for which place they set out on the 4th of February, and arrived at a public-house in that village about five o'clock in the evening. From this place they went to Mr. Lawrence's house, where they arrived about seven o'clock, just as he had discharged his work-people. Leaving their horses at the outer-gate, they went forwards, and found a boy who had just returned from folding his sheep; they presented a pistol, and threatened instant destruction if he made any noise. They then took off his garters, and tied his hands, and told him to direct them to the door, and when they knocked to answer, and bid the servant open it, in which case they would not hurt him. But when the boy came to the door, he was so terrified that he could not speak; on which one of the gang knocked, and a man-servant, thinking it was one of the neighbours, opened the door; whereupon they all rushed in, armed with pistols.

Having seized Mr. Lawrence and his servant, they threw a cloth over their faces, and taking the boy into another room, demanded what fire-arms were in the house; to which he replied, only an old gun, which they broke in pieces. They then bound Mr. Lawrence and his man, and made them sit by the boy; and Turpin searching the gentleman, took from him a guinea, a Portugal piece, and some silver; but not being satisfied with this booty, they forced him to conduct them up stairs, where they broke open a closet, and stole some money and plate. Being dissatisfied, they threatened to murder Mr. Lawrence if more booty was not forthcoming, and one of them took a kettle of water from the fire, and threw it over him; but it providentially happened not to be sufficiently hot enough to scald him.

In the interim the maid-servant, who was churning butter in the dairy, hearing a noise in the house, apprehended some mischief, and blew out her candle to screen herself; but being found in the course of the search, one of the miscreants compelled her to go up stairs, where he gratified his brutal passion by force. They then robbed the house of all the valuable effects they could find, locked the family in the parlour, threw the key into the garden, and took their ill-gotten plunder to London.

The particulars of this atrocious robbery being represented to the king, a proclamation was issued for the apprehension of the offenders, promising a pardon to any one of them who would impeach his accomplices; and a reward of fifty pounds was offered, to be paid on conviction. This however, had no effect; the robbers continued their depredations as before, and, flushed with the success they had met with, seemed to bid defiance to the laws.

On the 7th of February, six of them assembled at the White Bear, in Drury Lane, where they agreed to rob the house of Mr. Francis, a farmer near Marylebone. They accordingly proceeded forthwith, and having bound all the servants and Mr. Francis in the stable, they rushed into the house, tied Mrs. Francis, her daughter, and the maid-servant, and beat them in a most cruel manner. One of the thieves stood as a sentry while the rest rifled the house, in which they found a silver tankard, a medal of Charles the First, a gold watch, several gold rings, a considerable sum of money, and a variety of valuable linen and other effects, which they conveyed to London.

Hereupon a reward of one hundred pounds was offered for the apprehension of the offenders: in consequence of which two of them were taken into custody, tried, convicted on the evidence of an accomplice, and hanged in chains. The whole gang being now dispersed, Turpin went into the country, to renew his depredations on the public.

On a journey towards Cambridge, he met a man genteelly dressed, and well mounted; and expecting a good booty, he presented a pistol to the supposed gentleman, and demanded his money. The party thus stopped happened to be one King, a famous highwayman, who knew Turpin; and when the latter threatened instant destruction if he did not deliver his money, King burst into a fit of laughter, and said, " What, dog eat dog?—Come, come, brother Turpin; if you don't know me, I know you, and shall be glad of your company."

These brethren in iniquity soon struck the bargain, and immediately entered on business, and committed a number of robberies; till at length they were so well known, that no public-house would receive them as guests. Thus situated, they fixed on a spot between the King's Oak and Loughton Road, on Epping-Forest, where they made a great cave, which was large enough to receive them and their horses.

This cave was inclosed within a sort of thicket of bushes and brambles, through which they could see passengers on the road, while they themselves remained unobserved.

From this station they used to issue, and robbed such a number of persons, that at length the very pedlars who travelled the road carried fire-arms for their defence. While they were in this retreat, Turpin's wife used to supply them with necessaries, and frequently remained in the cave during the night.

Having taken a ride as far as Bungay in Suffolk, they observed two young women receive fourteen pounds for corn, on which Turpin resolved to rob them of the money. King objected, saying it was a pity to rob such pretty girls; but Turpin was obstinate, and obtained the booty.

Upon their return home the following day, they stopped a Mr. Bradley, of London, who was riding in his chariot with his children. The gentleman seeing only one robber, was preparing to make resistance, when King called to Turpin to hold the horses. They took from him his watch, money, and an old mourning ring; but returned the latter, as he declared its intrinsic value was trifling, yet he was unwilling to part with it. Finding that they readily parted with the ring, he asked what he must give for the watch; on which King said to Turpin, " What say ye, Jack? Here seems to be a honest fellow; shall we let him have the watch?" Turpin replied, " Do as you please;" on which King said to the gentleman, " You must pay six guineas for it: we never sell for more, though the watch should be worth six and thirty." The gentleman promised that the money should be left at the Dial, in Birchin lane.

The greatest crime of which Turpin appears to have been guilty was committed soon after this—it was that of murder. The active inquiries which the police of the day were making after him and his companion, obliged them to separate; but Turpin, being less wary than King, continued to inhabit their old dwelling in the forest. The tempting offer of £100 reward induced the servant of a gentleman, named Thompson, and a higgler, to go out in the hope of capturing the highwayman; and Turpin, being unaware of their object, and seeing them approach his cave with a gun, mistook them for poachers. He called to them, telling them that there were no hares in that thicket; upon which the servant exclaimed, " No, but I have found a Turpin," and instantly presenting his gun, called upon him to surrender. Turpin spoke to him in a friendly way, but retreating from him at the same time, seized his own gun, and shot him dead on the spot, when the higgler ran off with the greatest precipitation. The consequence of this most detestable act was, that a great outcry was raised against the highwayman, and he was compelled to quit the place on which he had hitherto relied for his concealment. It was afterwards examined, and there were found in it two shirts, two pairs of stockings, a piece of ham, and part of a bottle of wine. His place of refuge was now in Hertfordshire; and he sent a letter to his wife to meet him at a public-house in the town of Hertford. Going to keep his appointment, he met a butcher, to whom he owed a sum of money. The latter demanded payment, and Dick promised to get the money of his wife, who was in the next room; but while the butcher was hinting to some of his acquaintance that the person present was Turpin, and that they might take him into custody after he had received his debt, the highwayman made his escape through a window, and rode off with great expedition.

He soon found King; but their meeting was unfortunate for the latter, for it ended in his death. Proceeding together towards London in the dusk of the evening, when they came near the Green Man on Epping Forest, they overtook a Mr. Major, who being mounted on a very fine horse, while Turpin's beast was jaded, the latter obliged him to dismount, and exchange. The robbers now pursued their journey towards London; and Mr. Major, going to the Green Man, gave an account of the affair; on which it was conjectured that Turpin was the robber. It was on a Saturday evening that this robbery was committed; and Mr. Major being advised to print handbills immediately, notice was given to the landlord of the Green Man, that such a horse as was lost had been left at the Red Lion in Whitechapel. The landlord going thither, determined to wait till some person came for it; and, about eleven at night, King's brother came to pay for the horse, and take him away, on which he was immediately seized, and conducted into the house. Being asked what right he had to the horse, he said he had bought it; but the landlord, examining a whip which he had in his hand, found a button at the end of the handle half broken off, and the name of Major on the remaining half. Upon this he was given into the custody of a constable; but as it was not supposed that he was the actual robber, he was told that he should have his liberty if he would discover his employer. Hereupon he said that a stout man, in a white duffil coat, was waiting for the horse in Red Lion-street; on which the company going thither, saw King, who drew a pistol, and attempted to fire it, but it flashed in the pan: he then endeavoured to pull out another pistol, but could not, as it got entangled in his pocket. Turpin was at this time watching at a short distance off, and, riding towards the spot, saw his companion seized by some officers who had arrived. King immediately cried out, " Shoot him, or we are taken;" on which Turpin fired, but his shot penetrated the breast of his companion. King called out, " Dick, you have killed me!" and Turpin rode off at full speed.

King lived a week after this affair, and gave information that Turpin might be found at a house near Hackney Marsh; and, on inquiry, it was discovered that Turpin had been there on the night that he rode off, lamenting that he had killed King, who was his most faithful associate.

For a considerable time our hero skulked about the forest, having been deprived of his retreat in the cave since he shot the servant of Mr. Thompson; but a more active search for him having commenced, he determined to make good his retreat into Yorkshire, where he thought that he would be unknown, and might the more readily evade justice. The circumstance which induced him to take this step appears to have been an attempt made by a gentleman's huntsman to secure him by hunting him down with blood-hounds, whom he escaped only by mounting an oak, when he had the satisfaction to see them pass by without noticing him.

Going first, therefore, to Long Sutton, in Lincolnshire, he stole some horses, for which he was taken into custody; but he escaped from the constable as the latter was conducting him before a magistrate, and hastened to Welton, in Yorkshire, where he went by the name of John Palmer, and assumed the character of a gentleman.

He now frequently went into Lincolnshire, where he stole horses, which ne brought into Yorkshire, and there sold or exchanged them. From his being apparently a dealer in horses, he became acquainted with many of the surrounding gentry and farmers, and frequently accompanied them on hunting and shooting expeditions. On one of these occasions he was returning home, when he wantonly shot a cock belonging to his landlord. Mr. Hall, a neighbour who witnessed the act, said, " You have done wrong in shooting your landlord's cock ;" on which Turpin answered, that if he would stay while he loaded his gun, he would shoot him too. Irritated by the insult, Mr. Hall communicated what had occurred to the owner of the cock, whereupon complaint being made to the magistrates, a warrant was granted for the apprehension of the offender ; and on his being taken into custody, he was examined before the magistrates at Beverley, and committed for want of sureties. Inquiries being made, the good opinions which had been formed from his mode of life were soon dissipated, and it was conjectured that, instead of being a horse-dealer, he was a horse-stealer. The magistrates, therefore, proceeded to him, and demanded to know what his business was ; and he answered, that about two years before he had carried on business at Long Sutton as a butcher, but that, having contracted some debts for sheep that proved rotten, he had been compelled to abscond, and to go into Yorkshire to live. The clerk of the peace being commissioned to ascertain the truth of this story, learned that he had never been in business, and that he was suspected to be a horse-stealer, and had been in custody but had escaped, and that there were many informations against him for various offences. He was then committed to York Castle ; and soon afterwards some persons coming from Lincolnshire claimed a mare and a foal which were in his possession, and stated that they had been stolen recently before. His real name and character were soon afterwards discovered by means of the following letter, which he wrote to his brother in Essex.

" York, February 6, 1739.

" DEAR BROTHER,—I am sorry to inform you, that I am now under confinement in York Castle for horse-stealing. If I could procure an evidence from London to give me a character, that would go a great way towards being acquitted. I had not been long in this county before my apprehension, so it would pass off the readier. For heaven's sake, dear brother, do not neglect me ; you well know what I mean when I say, I am yours,   "JOHN PALMER."

The letter was returned to the Post Office unopened, because the postage was not paid ; and Mr. Smith, the schoolmaster, by whom Turpin had been taught to write, knowing the hand, carried the letter to a magistrate, by whom it was broken open, and it was thus discovered that the supposed John Palmer was Dick Turpin. Mr. Smith was in consequence dispatched to Yorkshire, and immediately selected his former pupil from the other prisoners, and subsequently gave evidence at the trial as to his identity.

On the rumour that the noted Turpin was a prisoner in York Castle, persons flocked from all parts of the country to take a view of him, and debates ran high whether he was the real person or not. Among others

who visited him was a young fellow who pretended to know the famous
Turpin.   Having regarded him a considerable time with looks of great
attention, he told the keeper he would bet him a half a guinea that he
was not Turpin; on which the prisoner, whispering the keeper, said,
" Lay him the wager, and I'll go you halves."

When this notorious malefactor was brought to trial, he was convicted
on two indictments, and received sentence of death.   After conviction,
he wrote to his father, imploring him to intercede with a gentleman and
lady of rank, to make interest that his sentence might be remitted, and
that he might be transported; but although the father did what was in
his power, the notoriety of his son's character was such, that no persons
would exert themselves in his favour.

The prisoner meanwhile lived in the most gay and thoughtless manner,
regardless of all considerations of futurity, and affecting to make a jest
of the dreadful fate that awaited him.

Not many days before his execution, he bought a new fustian frock
and a pair of pumps, in order to wear them at the time of his death;
and on the day before that appointed for the termination of his life, he
hired five poor men, at five shillings each, to follow the cart as
mourners.   He gave hatbands and gloves to several persons, and left
a ring and other articles of property to a married woman with whom
he had been acquainted in Lincolnshire.

On the morning of his death he was put into a cart, and, being followed by his mourners, was drawn to the place of execution; in his
way to which he bowed to the spectators with an air of the most astonishing indifference and intrepidity.

When he came to the fatal tree, he ascended the ladder; and, on his
right leg trembling, he stamped it down with an air of assumed courage,
as if he was ashamed to be observed to discover any signs of fear.
Having conversed with the executioner about half an hour, he threw
himself off the ladder, and expired in a few minutes.   Turpin suffered
at York, April 10, 1739.

The spectators of the execution seemed to be much affected at the
fate of this man, who was distinguished by the comeliness of his appearance.   The corpse was brought to the Blue Boar, in Castle-gate,
York, where it remained till the next morning, when it was interred
in the church-yard of St. George's parish, with an inscription on the
coffin bearing the initials of his name, and his age.   The grave was made
remarkably deep, and the people who acted as mourners took such
measures as they thought would secure the body; but about three
o'clock on the following morning some persons were observed in the
churchyard, who carried it off; and the populace, having an intimation
whither it was conveyed, found it in a garden belonging to one of the
surgeons of the city.

Hereupon they took the body, laid it on a board, and carried it
through the streets in a kind of triumphal manner; they then filled the
coffin with unslackened lime, and buried it in the grave where it had
been before deposited.

DAVID BROWN DIGNUM,

CONVICTED OF PRETENDING TO SELL PLACES UNDER GOVERNMENT.

THE case of this offender may be well looked upon as a warning to many of those whose advertisements are daily seen in the newspapers of the present day, offering a premium to any person who will find a situation for the advertiser.

Dignum was indicted on the 5th April, 1777, at the Guildhall, Westminster, for defrauding Mr. John Clarke of the sum of £100. 2s. 10d., which he had obtained from him under pretence of investing him with the office of Clerk of the Minutes in his majesty's custom-house in Dublin. The evidence in the case was very simple. The negotiation was commenced between Mr. Clarke and the prisoner at an early period in the year; and the money having been paid over, the prisoner handed to the prosecutor a stamped paper or warrant, bearing the signature of Lord Weymouth, and countersigned by " Thomas Daw," which he told him would enable him to assume the office which it mentioned. Upon his proceding to do so, however, he was found to have been hoaxed; and, upon inquiry, he discovered that the signatures were to some other instruments. The jury immediately found the prisoner guilty; but the magistrates hesitated a long time on the punishment which should be inflicted on such an offender, and at length sentenced him to work five years on the river Thames.

The prisoner, while in Tothill-fields Bridewell, tried every means in his power to effect his escape, and offered to bribe his attendant in the prison with a bank-note of ten pounds, to favour his escape in a large chest. Upon his conviction, no time was lost in conveying him on board the ballast-lighter. Being possessed of plenty of money, and having high notions of gentility, he went to Woolwich in a post-chaise, with his negro servant behind, expecting that his money would procure every indulgence in his favour, and that his servant would be still admitted to attend him. But in this he was egregiously mistaken; the keepers of the lighter would not permit him to come on board, and Dignum was immediately put to the duty of the wheelbarrow.

On Monday, the 5th of May, Dignum sent a forged draft for £500 for acceptance to Mr. Drummond, banker, at Charing-cross, who, discovering the imposition, carried the bearers before Sir John Fielding, but they were discharged; and it was intended to procure an habeas corpus to remove Dignum to London for examination.

This plan, however, was soon seen through; for, on consideration, it seemed evident that Dignum, by sending the forged draft from on board the lighter, preferred the chance of escape, even though death presented itself on the other side, to his situation; so that no further steps were taken in the affair, and he remained at work for the period to which he was sentenced by the laws of his country.

JAMES HILL, *alias* HIND, *alias* ATKINS, *alias* JOHN THE PAINTER,

EXECUTED FOR FIRING PORTSMOUTH DOCK-YARD.

A MORE dangerous character than the subject of this notice has rarely existed. His offence was aimed at the very safety of the kingdom, and, if successful, and followed up by the operations of his more powerful friends, for whose benefit it eventually appeared that he committed the foul crime of which he was guilty, the most disastrous consequences might have ensued.

Hill, it appears, was a Scotchman by birth, and by trade a painter; from which circumstance he obtained the name by which he was generally known, of " John the Painter." Having gone to America at an early age, and resided there for some years, he imbibed principles adverse to the interests of his own country ; and, transported with party zeal, formed the desperate resolution of committing a most atrocious crime against the welfare of England—namely, the burning of the dock-yards at Portsmouth and Plymouth. At about four o'clock in the afternoon of the 7th of December, 1776, a fire broke out in the round-house of Portsmouth dock, by which the whole of that building was consumed, and from whose ravages the rest of the surrounding ware-houses were with difficulty saved. The fire was at first attributed to accident ; but, on the 5th of January following, three men, who were engaged in the hemp-house, discovered a tin machine, somewhat resem-bling a tea-canister, and near the same spot a wooden-box, containing various kinds of combustibles. This circumstance being communicated to the commissioner of the dock, and circulated among the public, several vague and indefinite suspicions fell upon Hill, who had been lurking about the dock-yard, where he was distinguished by the appella-tion of " John the Painter."

In consequence of advertisements in the newspapers, offering a reward of fifty pounds for apprehending him, he was secured at Odiham, and on the 17th of February was examined at Sir John Fielding's office, Bow-street ; where John Baldwin, who had also exercised the trade of a painter in different parts of America, attended, by the direction of Lord Temple. The prisoner's conversations with Baldwin operated very materially in securing his conviction.

He had told Baldwin, that he had taken a view of most of the dock-yards and fortifications about England, had noted the number of ships in the navy, their weight of metal and number of men, and had been to France two or three times to inform Silas Deane, the American envoy, of his discoveries ; that Deane gave him bills to the amount of £300, and letters of recommendation to a merchant in the city, which he had burned, lest they should lead to a discovery. He informed Baldwin further, that he had instructed a tinman's apprentice at Canter-bury to make him a tin canister, which he carried to Portsmouth, where he hired a lodging at one Mrs. Boxall's, and tried his preparations for setting fire to the dock-yard. After recounting his manner of preparing matches and combustibles, he said that, on the 6th of the preceding December, he got into the hemp-house, and having placed a candle in a wooden box, and a tin canister over it, and sprinkled turpentine over some of the hemp, he proceeded to the rope-house, where he placed a bottle of turpentine, and having laid matches, made of paper daubed over with powdered charcoal and gunpowder diluted with water, and other combustibles, about the place, he returned to his lodgings. These matches were so contrived as to continue burning for twenty-four hours, so that by cutting them into proper lengths he might provide for his escape, knowing the precise time when the fire would reach the combustibles. He had hired lodgings in two other houses, to which he also intended to set fire, that the engines might not be all employed together in quenching the conflagration at the dock. On the 7th he again went to the hemp-house, intending to set it on fire; but he was unable to effect his object, owing to a halfpenny-worth of common house matches that he had bought not being sufficiently dry. This disappointment, he said, rendered him exceedingly uneasy, and he went from the hemp-house to the rope-house, and set fire to the matches he had placed there. His uneasiness was increased because he could not return to his lodgings, where he had left a bundle containing an " Ovid's Metamorphoses," a " Treatise on War and making Fireworks," a " Justin," a pistol, and a French passport, in which his real name was inserted.

When he had set fire to the rope-house he proceeded towards London, deeply regretting his failure in attempting to fire the other building, and was strongly inclined to discharge a pistol into the windows of the house where he had bought the bad matches. He jumped into a cart, and gave the woman who drove it sixpence to induce her to drive quick; and when he had passed the sentinels, he observed that the fire had made such a rapid progress that the elements seemed in a blaze. At about ten o'clock the next morning he arrived at Kingston, and having remained there until dusk, at that time he proceeded on towards London in the stage. Soon after his arrival, he went to the house of the gentleman on whom the bills had been drawn; but having related his story, he was received with distrust, and therefore went away. On his reaching Hammersmith, he wrote back to the merchant, saying that he was going to Bristol; and he added, that " the handy works he meant to perform there would soon be known to the public." Soon after his arrival in Bristol, he set fire to several houses, which were all burning at one time, and the flames were not extinguished until damage to the amount of £15,000 had been caused. He also set fire to some combustibles which he had placed among the oil-barrels on the quay, but in this instance without the effect which he desired.

His trial commenced on the 6th of March, 1777, at Winchester Castle, when witnesses were produced from different parts of the country, who proved the whole of his confession to Baldwin to be true, and gave other evidence of his guilt.

When called upon for his defence, he complained of the reports circulated to his prejudice; and observed, that it was easy for such a man as Baldwin to feign the story he had told, and for a number of witnesses to be collected to give it support. He declared that God alone knew whether he was, or was not, the person who set fire to the dock-yard; and begged it might be attended to how far Baldwin ought to be credited: that if he had art enough, by lies, to extract any thing out of him, his giving it to the knowledge of others was a breach of confidence; and if he would speak falsely to deceive him, he might also impose upon a jury.

The learned judge having delivered his charge to the jury, after a moment's consideration, they returned a verdict of Guilty. The sentence of death was immediately passed upon the prisoner, and he was ordered for execution on the 10th of March following, when he was hanged within sight of the ruins which he had occasioned.

His body for several years hung in chains on Blockhouse Point, on the opposite side of the harbour to the town.

To these particulars we shall add his confession. On the morning after his condemnation he informed the turnkey, of his own accord, that he felt an earnest desire to confess his crime, and to lay the history of his life before the public; so that, by discovering the whole of his unaccountable plots and treasonable practices, he might make some atonement to his injured country for the wrongs he had done it, of which he was now truly sensible.

This request being made known to the Earl of Sandwich, then first Lord of the Admiralty, that nobleman directed Sir John Fielding to send down proper persons to take and attest his confession.

He said, that the diabolical scheme of setting fire to the dock-yards and the shipping originated in his own wicked mind, on the very breaking out of the rebellion in America; and he had no peace until he proceeded to put it in practice. The more he thought of it, the more practicable it appeared; and with this wicked intent he crossed the Atlantic. He had no sooner landed than he proceeded to take surveys of the different dock-yards; and he then went to Paris, and had several conferences with Silas Deane, the rebel minister to the Court of France. Deane was astonished at Hill's proposals, which embraced the destruction of the English dock-yards and shipping; but, finding the projector an enthusiast in the cause of America, and a man of daring spirit, he gradually listened to his schemes, and supplied him with money to enable him to carry them into execution, procured him a French passport, and gave him a letter of credit on a merchant in London. He then confirmed the evidence given against him, and in particular that of the witness Baldwin; and added, that had he been successful in his attempts upon Portsmouth and Plymouth dock-yards, he should have been rewarded with a commission in the American navy

APPLICATION OF THE TORTURE DENOMINATED PICKETING.

GOVERNOR PICTON,

INDICTED FOR APPLYING THE TORTURE TO LOUISA CALDERON, TO EXTORT A CONFESSION.

WHATEVER may have been the opinion of former times respecting the application of torture it cannot but be universally abhorred in the present enlightened age. The following remarks of the French philosopher Voltaire admirably illustrate this, and at the same time serve to introduce the present case.

"All mankind being exposed to the attempts of violence and perfidy," says he, "detest the crimes of which they may possibly be the victims; all desire that the principal offender and his accomplices may be punished; nevertheless, there is a natural compassion in the human heart, which makes all men detest the cruelty of torturing the accused into confession. The law has not condemned them; and yet, though uncertain of the crime, you inflict a punishment more horrible than that which they are to suffer when their guilt is confirmed. 'Possibly thou mayest be innocent; but I will torture thee that I may be satisfied; not that I intend to make thee any recompense for the thousand deaths which I have made thee suffer in lieu of that which is preparing for thee.' Who does not shudder at the idea! St. Augustin opposed such cruelty. The Romans tortured their slaves only; and Quintilian, recollecting that they were men, reproved the Romans for such want of humanity.

Thomas Picton, Esq. was indicted for putting to the torture a female, Louisa Calderon, one of his majesty's subjects in the island of Trinidad in the West Indies, in order to extort confession.

Mr. Garrow stated the case for the prosecution; and, whilst he expressed the strongest desire to bring to condign punishment the perpetrator of an offence so flagrant as that charged upon the defendant, yet much more happy should he be to find that there was no ground upon which the charge could be supported, and that the British character was not stained by the adoption of so cruel a measure. The island of Trinidad, he said, surrendered to Sir Ralph Abercrombie in the year 1797; and he entered into a stipulation, by which he conceded to the inhabitants the continuance of their laws, and appointed a new governor until his Majesty's pleasure should be known, or, in other words, until the king should extend to this new acquisition to his empire all the sacred privileges of the laws of England. He had the authority of the defendant himself for stating, that the system of jurisprudence adopted under the Spanish monarch for his colonial establishments was benignant, and adapted to the protection of the subject, previous to the surrender of this island to the British arms.

In December, 1801, when this crime was perpetrated, Louisa Calderon was of the tender age of ten or eleven years. At that early period she had been induced to live with a person named Pedro Ruiz as his mistress; and although it might appear to them very singular that she should sustain such a situation at that time of life, yet it was a fact, that in that climate women often became mothers at twelve years old, and lived in a state of concubinage, if, from their condition, they could not form a more honourable connexion. While she lived with Ruiz, she was engaged in an intrigue with Carlos Gonzales, the pretended friend of the former, who robbed him of a quantity of dollars. Gonzales was apprehended; and she also, as some suspicion fell upon her in consequence of the affair, was taken into custody. She was taken before the justice, and, in his presence, denied having any concern in the business. The magistrate felt that his powers were at an end; and whether the object of her denial were to protect herself or her friend, was not material. The extent of his authority being thus limited, the officer of justice restored her to General Picton; and he had now to produce, in the handwriting of the defendant, this bloody sentence:— "Inflict the torture upon Louisa Calderon." There was no delay in proceeding to its execution. The girl was informed in the jail, that, if she did not confess, she would be subjected to the torture; that under this process she might probably lose her limbs or her life: but the calamity would be on her own head, for, if she would confess, she would not be required to endure it. While her mind was in the state of agitation this notice produced, her fears were aggravated by the introduction of two or three negresses into her prison, who were to suffer under the same experiment for witchcraft, and as a means of extorting confession. In this situation of alarm and horror, the young woman persisted in her innocence; and a punishment was inflicted, improperly called picketing. That was a military punishment, perfectly distinct in its nature. This was not picketing, but the torture. It was true, the soldier exposed to this did stand with his foot on a picket, or sharp piece of wood; but, in mercy to him, a means of reposing was afforded on the rotundus major, or interior of the arm. Her position might be easily described. The great toe was lodged upon a sharp piece of wood, while the opposite wrist was suspended in a pulley, and the other hand and foot were lashed together. Another time the horrid ceremony was repeated, with this difference, that her feet were changed.

" It appeared to him, that the case, on the part of the prosecution, would be complete when these facts were established in evidence ; but he was to be told, that though the highest authority in this country could not practise this on the humblest individual here, yet that, by the laws of Spain, it could be perpetrated in the island of Trinidad. He would venture to assert, that if it were the acknowledged law of Trinidad, it could be no justification of a British governor. Nothing could vindicate such a person, but the law of imperious necessity, to which all must submit. It was his duty to impress upon the minds of the people of that colony, the great advantages they would derive from the benign influence of British jurisprudence ; and that, in consequence of being received within the pale of this government, torture would be for ever banished from the island. It was not sufficient for him, therefore, to establish this sort of apology ; it was required of him to show, that he complied with the institutions under circumstances of irresistible necessity. This governor ought to have been aware that the torture was not known in England ; and that it never would be, never could be tolerated in this country.

" The trial by rack was utterly unknown to the law of England, though once, when the Dukes of Exeter and Suffolk, and other ministers of Henry VI., had laid a design to introduce the civil law into this kingdom as the rule of government, for a beginning thereof they erected a rack of torture, which was called in derision the Duke of Exeter's daughter, and still remained in the Tower of London, where it was occasionally used as an engine of state, not of law, more than once in the reign of Queen Elizabeth. But when, upon the assassination of Villiers, Duke of Buckingham, by Felton, it was proposed in the Privy Council to put the assassin to the rack, in order to discover his accomplices, the judges, being consulted, declared unanimously, to their own honour, and the honour of the English law, that no such proceeding was allowable by the laws of England.

" But what were they to say to this man, who, so far from having found torture in practice under the former governors, had attached to himself all the infamy of having invented this instrument of cruelty ? Like the Duke of Exeter's daughter, it never had existence until the defendant cursed the island with its production. He had incontestible evidence to show this ingenuity of tyranny in a British governor ; and the moment he produced the sanguinary order, the man was left absolutely without defence. The date of this transaction was removed at some distance. It was directed that a commission should conduct the affairs of the government, and among the persons appointed to this important situation was Colonel Fullarton.   In the exercise of his duties in that situation, he attained the knowledge of these facts; and with this information he thought it incumbent on him to bring this defendant before the jury; and, with the defendant, the victim of this enormity would also be produced."

Lousia Calderon was then called.   She appeared about eighteen years of age, of a very interesting countenance, being a Mulatto or Creole, and of a very genteel appearance.   She was dressed in white, with a turban of white muslin, tied on in the custom of the country.   Her person was slender and graceful.   She spoke English but very indifferently; and was examined by Mr. Adam through the medium of a Spanish interpreter.

She deposed that she resided in the island of Trinidad in the year 1798; and lived in the house of Don Pedro Ruiz, and remembered the robbery.   She and her mother were taken up on suspicion, and brought before Governor Picton, who committed them to prison, under an escort of three soldiers.   She was put into close confinement; and, before she was taken there, the governor said, " If she did not confess who had stolen the money, the hangman would have to deal with her." She was afterwards carried to the room where the torture was prepared.   Her left hand was tied up to the ceiling by a rope, with a pulley; her right hand was tied behind, so that her right foot and hand came in contact, while the extremity of her left foot rested on the wooden spike.   A drawing representing her exact situation, with the negro holding the rope by which she was suspended, was then shown to her; when she gave a shudder, expressive of horror, which nothing but the most painful recollection of her situation could have excited; on which Mr. Garrow expressed his concern that his Lordship was not in a position to witness this accidental, but conclusive, evidence of the fact.

The remainder of the witness's evidence corroborated the statement of Mr. Garrow.   She remained upon the spike three quarters of an hour, and the next day twenty-two minutes.   She swooned away each time before she was taken down, and was then put into irons, called the " grillos," which were long pieces of iron, with two rings for the feet, fastened to the wall, and in this situation she remained during eight months.   The effect produced by the torture was excruciating pain; her wrists and ankles were much swollen, and the former bore the marks of the barbarity employed towards her to the present day.

Don Rafael Shandoz, an alguazil in the island, bore testimony to his having seen the girl immediately after the application of the torture. The apartment in which she was afterwards confined was like a garret, with sloping sides, and the grillos were so placed that, by the lowness of the room, she could by no means raise herself up, during the eight months of her confinement.   There was no advocate appointed to attend on her behalf, and no surgeon to assist her.   No one but a negro, belonging to Ballot, the gaoler, to pull the rope.   The witness had been four or five years in the post of alguazil.   He never knew the torture inflicted in the island until the arrival of the defendant.   There had been before no instrument for the purpose. The first he saw was in the barracks among the soldiers. Before Louisa Calderon, the instrument had been introduced into the gaol perhaps about six months. The first person he saw tortured in Trinidad was by direction of the defendant, who said to the gaoler, " Go and fetch the black man to the picket-guard, and put him to the torture." After the eight months' confinement, both Carlos and Louisa were discharged.

The order for the application of the torture, in the following words —" Applicase la question a Louisa Calderon,"—(Apply the torture to Louisa Calderon)—was then proved to be in the handwriting of the defendant; and the suggestion of the alcade Beggerat, before whom the girl had been examined, that slight torture should be applied, was read.

Don Juan Montes then said, that he had known the island of Trinidad since the year 1793. That the torture was never introduced until after the conquest of the island, and was then practised by order of the defendant. It was first used with the military in 1799, and two years afterwards in the gaol.

Mr. Dallas, for the defendant, rested his defence upon the following statements :—

First,—By the law of Spain, in the present instance, torture was directed; and, being bound to administer that law, he was vindicated in its application.

Secondly,—The order for the torture, if not unlawfully, was not maliciously issued.

Thirdly,—If it were unlawfully, yet, if the order were erroneously or mistakenly issued, it was a complete answer to a criminal charge.

The learned counsel entered at considerable length into these positions, during which he compared the law of Spain, as it prevailed in Trinidad, to the law of England as it subsisted in some of our own islands; and he contended that the conduct of General Picton was gentleness and humanity, compared to what might be practised with impunity under the authority of the British government.

Mr. Gloucester, the attorney-general of his Majesty in the island, was then called, and deposed to the authenticity of several books on the laws of the island, among which were the Elisondo, the Curia Philippica, the Bobadilla, the Colom, and the Recopilacion de Leyes. Various passages in these books were referred to, and translated, for the purpose of showing that torture was not only permitted in certain cases, but in the particular instance before the jury.

Mr. Garrow was then allowed to call a witness to show that, however such a law might at any time have existed, or might still exist, in Spain, it did not prevail in the West Indian colonies of that power.

Lord Ellenborough in summing up, recommended the jury to divest their minds of every feeling which they might have contracted in the course of the present trial, and to throw every part of the case out of their consideration, except that which related to this simple point,--What was the law by which the island of Trinidad was governed at the period of its capture by the British? It was for the consideration of the jury whether the law then subsisting authorised personal torture to be inflicted. By the indulgence of the government of this country, the subsisting law was to continue; the question was, What was that subsisting law? The jury would observe, that it did not necessarily follow, because Trinidad was a colony of Old Spain, that it must therefore, in every part, have the laws of Old Spain. It did not originally form any part of that country, but had been annexed to it; and on what terms, there was no positive evidence. It was therefore for the jury to say, in the absence of all positive proof on the subject, and in the face of so much negative evidence, whether the law of Spain was so fully and completely established in Trinidad as to make torture a part of the law of that island. Without going through the authorities, he thought the jury might take it to be the existing law of Old Spain, that torture might be inflicted. It was too much to say, that a discontinuance of a practice could repeal a law; but they had to determine whether they were convinced that torture had ever been part of the law of Trinidad; and also whether they were convinced that it was part of the law of Trinidad at the time of its capture. If so, they would enter a special verdict; if otherwise, they would find the defendant guilty.

The jury found—There was no such law existing in the island of Trinidad, as that of torture, at the time of the surrender of that island to the British.

Lord Ellenborough.—" Then, gentlemen, General Picton cannot derive protection from a supposed law, after you have found that no such law remained in that island at the surrender of it; and therefore your verdict should be, that he is guilty."

By the direction of Lord Ellenborough they therefore found the defendant " Guilty."

The trial lasted from nine in the morning till seven at night.

Mr. Dallas moved on the 25th of April for a new trial, upon the following grounds:—

First,—The infamous character of the girl, who lived in open prostitution with Pedro Ruiz, and who had been privy to a robbery committed upon her paramour by Carlos Gonzales; and that when a complaint laid against her had been brought before a magistrate, she, refusing to confess, had been ordered to be tortured.

Secondly,—That Governor Picton, who condemned her to this torture, did not proceed from any motives of malice, but from a conviction that the right of torture was sanctioned by the laws of Trinidad; and that he was rooted in this opinion by a reference to the legal written authorities in that island.

Thirdly,— That whatever his conduct might be, it was certainly neither personal malice nor disposition to tyranny, but resulted, if it should prove to be wrong, from a misapprehension of the laws of Trinidad.

Fourthly,—That one of the principal witnesses in this trial, M. Vargass, had brought forward a book, entitled " Recopilacion des Leyes des Indes," expressly compiled for the Spanish colonies, which did not authorise torture, and that the defendant had no opportunity of ever seeing that book; but it had been purchased by the British Institution, at the sale of the Marquis of Lansdowne's library, subsequent to his indictment, and that having consulted it, it appeared that when that code was silent upon criminal cases, recourse was always to be had to the laws of Old Spain, and that those laws sanctioned the torture.

The Court, after some consideration, granted the rule to show cause why a new trial should not be had; and as the second trial, which was eventually allowed, was attended with a different result from that of the first, we think it no more than just to the memory of Governor Picton to conclude our notice of this affair with the following apology for his conduct from a respectable monthly publication:—

" In an evil hour the British Colonel associated with him, in the government of the island, the British naval commander on the station, and Colonel Fullarton. This was, as might have been expected, the origin of disputes and the source of anarchy. It is well known that Fullarton, on his return to England, preferred charges against Picton, which were taken into consideration by the Privy Council, and gave rise to a prosecution that lasted for several years. No pains were spared to sully his character, to ruin his fortunes, and to render him an object of public indignation. A little strumpet, by name Louisa Calderon, who cohabited with a petty tradesman in the capital of Trinidad, let another paramour into his house (of which she had the charge) during his absence, who robbed him, with her knowledge and privity, of all he was worth in the world. The girl was taken before the regular judges of the place; who, in the course of their investigation, ascertained the fact that she was privy to the robbery, and therefore sentenced her, in conformity with the laws of Spain, then prevalent in the island, to undergo the punishment of the *picket* (the same as is adopted in our own regiments of horse); but, as it was necessary that this sentence should receive the governor's confirmation before it could be carried into effect, a paper, stating the necessity of it, was sent to the government-house, and the governor, by his signature, conveyed his assent to the judges. The girl was accordingly picketed, when she acknowledged the facts above stated, and discovered her accomplice. That the life of this girl was forfeited by the laws of every civilized country is a fact that will not admit of dispute; yet clemency was here extended to her, and she was released, having suffered only the punishment above stated; which was so slight, that she walked a considerable distance to the prison, without the least appearance of suffering, immediately after it was inflicted. But what was the return for the lenity of the governor? He was accused by Colonel Fullarton of having put this girl (whom he had never *seen*) to the *torture*, contrary to law; and the caricaturists of England were enlisted in the service of persecution. After a trial which seemed to have no end, after an expense of *seven thousand pounds*, which must have completed his ruin, had not his venerable uncle, General Picton, defrayed the whole costs of the suit, while the expenses of his prosecutor were all paid *by the government*, his honour and justice were established on the firmest basis, and to the perfect satisfaction of every upright mind."

ROBERT ASLETT,

MR. ASLETT had been in the employ of the Bank of England for about five and twenty years, and had conducted himself faithfully and meritoriously until he was induced, unfortunately, to speculate in the funds; when, in dereliction of that duty and fidelity which he owed to his employers, he subtracted immense sums from the property entrusted to his care.

In the year 1799, having gone through the necessary and regular gradations, he was appointed one of the cashiers. It was a part of the business of the Bank to purchase Exchequer bills to supply the exigencies of government, and the purchases were entrusted to the care of Mr. A. Newland; but on account of that gentleman's growing infirmities, he having been fifty-eight years in the service of the Bank, the management was left wholly under the care and direction of Mr. Aslett. The purchases were made of Mr. Goldsmid, by the means of Mr. Templeman, a broker. It was usual to make out a bill in the name of the person from whom they were made, which was delivered to Mr. Aslett, to examine and enter in what is called the Bought-book, and he gave orders to the cashiers to reimburse the broker. The bills were afterwards deposited in a strong chest, kept in Mr. Newland's room; and when they had increased in bulk by subsequent purchases, they were selected by Mr. Aslett, who tied them up in large bundles, and carried them to the parlour, that is to say, the room in which the directors held their meetings, accompanied by one of the clerks, with the original book of entry, when the directors in waiting received the envelope, and deposited it in the strong iron chest, which had three keys, and to which none but the directors had access; and from which it could not be brought forth until the time of payment, unless by consent of at least two of the directors. Therefore it was not possible for them to find their way into the hands of the public or the monied market, unless embezzled for that purpose. On the 26th of February, 1803, Mr. Aslett, according to the practice, made up three envelopes of Exchequer bills, of £1000 each bill; the first containing bills to the amount of £100,000, the second £200,000, and the third £400,000; making in the whole £700,000. These were, or in fact ought to have been, carried into the parlour, and were signed as being received by two of the directors, Messrs. Paget and Smith; but one of the bundles, namely, that containing the £200,000 worth of bills, was withdrawn.

The confidence which the Governor and Company had placed in Mr. Aslett had enabled him to conceal the transaction from the 26th of February to the 9th of April; but on that day, in consequence of an application made by Mr. Bish, the whole was discovered. On the 16th of March, Mr. Aslett went to that gentleman, and requested he would purchase for him £50,000 Consols, to which request no objection was made, provided he deposited the requisite securities. The fluctuation of the market at that time was six per cent., and Aslett, in order to cover any deficit, deposited with Mr. Bish three Exchequer bills, Nos. 341, 1060, and 2694, which he knew had been previously deposited in the Bank. From some circumstances, and from his general knowledge of the whole of the business of the funds, Mr. Bish suspected all was not right, and he accordingly went to the Bank, where an investigation took place, at which Mr. B. Watson, one of the directors, was present. Mr. Newland was sent for, and asked whether any of the Exchequer bills could, by possibility, get into the market again from the Bank? To which he answered in the negative, observing that they were a dormant security. The same question was put to Mr. Aslett, and the same answer given by him. It was found necessary to tell him that the bills in question, which could be proved to have been in the Bank, had found their way into the money-market; and at the same time it was observed, that he had made purchases, to a large amount, of stock with the bills. This was acknowledged by him; but he said he had done so for a friend, named Hosier, residing at the west end of the town; and he declared that they were not Bank property, nor to be found in the Bought-book. The directors, however, were not satisfied on this point, and he was immediately secured. His trial was postponed to July, as it occurred to those employed in the prosecution that the bills in question had been issued with an informality in them, not having the signature of the Auditor of the Exchequer. They were aware of the objections that might be taken, and Parliament not then being sitting, it was thought advisable to postpone the trial, lest it might create an alarm in the money-market. The fact was no sooner known, than a bill was brought into Parliament for remedying those defects, and to render the bills valid.

On Friday, July 8, 1804, Mr. Aslett's trial commenced. Mr. Garrow, on the part of the prosecution, stated the facts above mentioned; but when about to call witnesses to give evidence, Mr. Erskine insisted that the Exchequer bills, which the prisoner stood charged with having stolen, were not good bills till the act of parliament had made them so, and consequently that they were pieces of waste paper when stolen. The Chief Baron Macdonald, Mr. Justice Rooke, and Mr. Justice Lawrence concurred, that the present indictment could not be maintained; and the jury were accordingly desired to acquit the prisoner.

He was afterwards, however, tried on nine other indictments, the evidence being the same, Mr. Garrow having applied to the Court to detain him in custody, it being, he said, the intention of the Bank Directors to issue a civil process against him for £100,000 and upwards, the moneys paid for the bills which he had converted to his own use.

Mr. Kirby at first hesitated to receive the prisoner, understanding he was acquitted; but was peremptorily desired by the Court to take him back.

Mr. Aslett was dressed in a lightish brown coat, his hair being full powdered. He appeared quite collected, but held down his head, never once looking up, except when the application was made to keep him in custody, when he expressed symptoms of great surprise, and looked very stedfastly at the Court.

On Saturday, September 17, Mr. Aslett was again brought to the bar of the Old Bailey, before Baron Chambre and Mr. Justice Le Blanc. The prisoner was attended by four or five gentlemen, who continued in the dock during the whole time of the trial.

Three indictments were read, with two counts in each, charging the prisoner with secreting and embezzling three notes. The first indictment was, for that he, being an officer or servant of the Governor and Company of the Bank of England, had secreted and embezzled a certain piece of paper, partly written and partly printed, purporting to be an Exchequer bill, No. 835, of the value of £500; the second, No. 3694, for one thousand pounds; and the third, No. 6061, for one thousand pounds. One count in each stated them as securities, and the other as effects belonging to the said Governor and Company. There were other counts, diversifying the statement of the property in other forms.

Mr. Garrow stated the case at considerable length to the jury. There was one point, to which he called particular attention, and that was, that the prisoner had been tried before, and acquitted of the offence of purloining Exchequer bills to an immense amount, as it was then proved to the satisfaction of the learned judges on the bench, for whom he entertained the highest respect, that they were not actually such as might in law be termed Exchequer bills, in consequence of their not having been signed as the act directs. The present indictments, however, stated them as papers *purporting* to be Exchequer bills, which they evidently were on the face of them, and subdivided the charge, by stating them at one time as securities, and at another time as effects belonging to the Company. This he had no doubt that the jury would be convinced of upon hearing them read; and it was an important duty which the Bank owed to the public, that they should not suffer so great a delinquent to escape the justice of the country, in consequence of any want of exertion on their part.

Mr. Erskine, on behalf of the prisoner, delivered a most animating address to the jury. He stated, that the former indictments against the gentleman at the bar had been objected to on grounds which were approved of by the learned judges who then sat upon the bench. He was now brought up again to be tried for exactly the same offence, though differently stated; and he thought that the present proceeding was liable to the same objections which were then admitted to be valid by the bench; but he should oppose it on much stronger grounds. He then objected to the legality of Mr. Jenning's signature, in the place of that of Lord Grenville, as auditor of the Exchequer. That the same illegality in a criminal sense existed with respect to all bills issued at that time from the Exchequer, was manifest from the circumstance of the legislature having found it necessary to pass an act expressly for the purpose of making them legal in a civil view; and that act had a most humane proviso, which declared, in plain terms, that the act was to be considered to make the Exchequer bills issued at that time valid only in a civil view, and would not have a retrospective effect as to any criminal offence committed before the passing of the act. The learned gentleman stated, that, as securities, they were nothing in law, for a person, at the time of their being passed, could not recover at law. As to the idea of calling them effects, he considered that, though the legislature had thought proper to pass an act for the protection of that company above all others, by passing what is generally termed the Bank Act, in consequence of the immense magnitude of that concern, yet effects must obviously mean the same as in a case of petty larceny would be considered effects, that is, something intrinsically valuable in themselves, without taking in or mixing in the mind the idea of their professed or avowed value. If that was not the case, a clerk who took away a loose half sheet of paper lying about the office, or a pen that was worn to the stump, came within the limits of the act, and would be liable to a prosecution for felony. If he did not know the highly respectable character which that company supported, and the very great ability by which they were counselled, he should be induced to say that the prosecution of the gentleman at the bar a second time, for exactly the same offence of which he had been before acquitted by law, was vexatious; and he should declare, not only as a lawyer, but as a man, that they were rather inclined to be severe towards the prisoner, than that they should be thought in the least to relax from their duty, or from an idea of justice to the public. The articles stated in the indictments must either be really and *bonâ fide* Exchequer bills, or else they were no securities; they were no effects in law; they were no more than pieces of waste paper, for the embezzlement of which he had never known a prosecution to be sustained at law. The generosity of government, or the justice of the country, could not be called on to pay a single farthing for them; the strings of the national purse were only to be drawn by the consent of the legislature, and at that time there was no such consent obtained. The learned gentleman then quoted several cases, showing that chattels or effects must be something intrinsically valuable in themselves; and said, it was his firm belief that the learned judges at present on the bench would deliver an opinion similar in effect to that which had already been delivered by the learned judges sitting on that bench at the time of Mr. Aslett's former trial: he believed that they would find themselves in the same situation, and instruct the jury to find a verdict for the acquittal of that gentleman without hearing any evidence upon the case, as in his opinion it was not such as could be supported in law.

Mr. Sergeant Best followed on the same side, and the Court determined to reserve the point for consideration. Evidence was then given in proof of the facts stated at the beginning of this article, and the jury returned a verdict of Guilty.

On February 16, 1804, Mr. Aslett was brought to the bar to receive his sentence, when Mr. Baron Hotham addressed him as follows:—

" Robert Aslett, you were tried and convicted in this Court, in the September sessions, 1803, for embezzling effects belonging to the Governor and Company of the Bank of England, you being an officer and servant of that Bank, and, as such, entrusted with their property. It was argued by your counsel, that the bills were not valid or legal bills, having been signed by a person not properly authorized by Lord Grenville, though they had been issued as such.   On this indictment you have been lawfully convicted by a jury of your countrymen ; but judgment has been suspended till the opinion of the twelve judges of England was taken on this important case, in order to ascertain whether these bills were good, according to the statute 15 Geo. II.   Eleven of these judges were of opinion that some of the objections, so ably argued by your counsel, should be sustained ; they have since held various conferences, which produced various different opinions ; and it is now my duty to communicate to you the result of their investigation.   Several points were argued in your favour, upon all of which, however, except one, the judges have given their decision against you.   The only material question for consideration was, whether or not these bills fall within the meaning of the statute 15 Geo. II., and can be denominated effects according to that act.   On this point, indeed, the judges were not unanimous, but the majority are of opinion that they are effects and securities within the true meaning of the act.   The great object of the legislature was to add security and administer protection to the Bank of England. The immense national concerns with which it was and still is entrusted, called upon the legislature for particular provisions in its favour.   These principles of legislation must now be applied to the object under contemplation ; and the view we take of any code of laws must be more comprehensive when it concerns so materially such a large incorporated body, than when it only relates to private individuals.   Considering this law then in the enlarged and liberal view on which it was framed by the legislature (at the same time that all the judges disclaim any wish to strain any part of it where it is so penal), the recollection of the enormous weight of Exchequer bills, in which the public were so deeply and materially concerned, cannot fail to occur to every mind.   That these bills had become the fair and valuable property of the Bank was allowed on all hands ; but still it was argued that they were not such securities as fell within the true meaning of the act of parliament, because they were not of any positive or intrinsic value.   Now, whatever shall be deposited with the Bank was expressly guarded by the words of the act ; and although the bills in question be of no descriptive legal value, yet they carry about them such a consequence at least as makes their preservation of the utmost importance to the Bank.   In that view, therefore, they surely have their value.   They are at least valuable papers, whatever they may be called, and the holders of them have them as such, having paid for them the value which they respectively import. They are therefore to be included in the true meaning of the word securities, which may be in the end available to any person who may be possessed of them."

The conviction was therefore determined to be good, and on the following Monday, 20th February, 1804, this unfortunate man received sentence of death.   This punishment was, however, subsequently commuted to transportation.

PAGE IN DISGUISE ROBBING A TRAVELLER.

WILLIAM PAGE,

EXECUTED FOR HIGHWAY ROBBERY.

WILLIAM PAGE was the son of a respectable farmer at Hampton; and being a lad of promising parts, he was sent to London to be educated, under the care of his cousin, a haberdasher. His early life, by the superstitious believers in old sayings, would be adduced as proof positive of the truth of the adage, that " a man who is born to be hanged will never be drowned;" and, although we cannot put much faith generally in such notions, we cannot help in this instance pointing out some peculiarities in the adventures of our hero, which might have been considered by him as a sufficient indication of his fate. The early chronicler of his life says, that, during the hard frost in the winter of 1739, Page was sliding, with other boys, on the canal in St. James's Park, when the ice broke under him, and he sank; and the ice immediately closing over him, he must have perished, but just at this juncture the ice again broke with another boy near him, and Page arose precisely at the vacancy made by the latter, and was saved, although his companion was drowned. A second instance of the intervention of his good fortune occurred in the summer following this singular escape. Page was then trying to swim with corks in the Thames, when they slipped from under his arms, and he sank; but a waterman got him up, and he soon recovered. On the third occasion, he was going up the river on a party of pleasure, about five years afterwards, with several other young fellows, when the boat overset with them in Chelsea Reach, and every one in it was drowned except Page. But his fourth and last escape from a watery grave was even more miraculous than any of those which preceded it. About eighteen months after that which is last related, he was on a voyage to Scotland. The ship in which he sailed foundered in Yarmouth Roads, and most of the people on board perished; but another vessel, observing their distress, sent out a long boat, by the help of which Page and a few others saved their lives.

To return, however, to the ordinary events of his life. It appears, that his cousin having given him employment in his shop, his vanity prevented him from bestowing that attention on his business to which it was entitled; and his extravagance being checked by his relation, who stopped his pocket-money in order to curb his refined notions, he had recourse to plunder to supply his necessities. Money being repeatedly missed from the till, and all attempts to discover the thief among the servants having failed, suspicion at length rested on our hero; and his guilt having been distinctly proved, he was dismissed from his situation forthwith. An effort which he made to conciliate his relation after this proved ineffectual; and his father, who had learned the nature of his irregularities, having refused to render him any assistance, he at length journeyed to York, and there joined a company of strolling players. His exertions in his new capacity were not unsuccessful; but at length attempting to play Cato while in a state of intoxication, his character in the play and his condition of person were found to agree so badly, that he was compelled to be carried from the stage, and was dismissed from his engagement. He afterwards went to Scarborough, where his necessities compelled him to accept a situation as livery-servant with a gentleman; but his master having been robbed on his way to town, he formed a notion that highway robbery was an easy and profitable mode of living, and determined that so soon as he should have the means of starting in the profession, he would become a " gentleman of the road." Quitting his master at the end of twelve months, he became acquainted with a woman of abandoned character, in conjunction with whom he took lodgings near Charing Cross, and then commenced highwayman. His first expedition was on the Kentish road. Meeting the Canterbury stage near Shooter's-hill, he robbed the pasengers of watches and money to the amount of about thirty pounds; and then riding through great part of Kent, to take an observation of the cross-roads, he returned to London. He now took lodgings near Grosvenor-square, and frequenting the billiard-tables won a little money, which, added to his former stock, prevented his having recourse to the highway again for a considerable time; but at length he met with a gambler who was more expert than himself, and who stripped him of all his money. He then again sought the road as a means of subsistence. His exertions were for some time fruitless; but at length meeting with a handsome booty, he was emboldened by his success; and taking handsome lodgings, he soon gained the friendship of some young men of fashion. His next object was to improve his mind and person; and having gained some knowledge, by dint of impudence and a pleasing exterior, he got introduced into decent society.

By this time he had drawn, from his own observation and for his private use, a most curious map of the roads twenty miles round London; and, driving in a phaeton and pair, he was not suspected for a highwayman.

In his excursions for robbery he used to dress in a laced or embroidered frock, and wear his hair tied behind; but when at a distance from London, he would turn into some unfrequented place, and, having disguised himself in other clothes, would proceed to the main road, and commit a robbery. This done, he hastened back to the carriage, resumed his former dress, and drove to town again. He was frequently cautioned to be on his guard against a highwayman, who might meet and rob him: " No, no," said he, " he cannot do it a second time, unless he robs me of my coat and shirt, for he has taken all my money already."

He had once an escape of a very remarkable kind. Having robbed a gentleman near Putney, some persons came up at the juncture, and pursued him so closely that he was obliged to cross the Thames for his security. In the interim, some haymakers crossing the field where Page's carriage was left, found and carried off his gay apparel; and the persons who had pursued him, meeting them, charged them with being accomplices in the robbery. A report of this affair being soon spread, Page heard of it, and throwing his clothes into a well, he went back almost naked, claimed the carriage as his own, and declared that the men had stripped him, and thrown him into a ditch. All the parties now went before a justice of the peace; and the maker of the carriage appearing, and declaring that it was the property of Mr. Page, the poor haymakers were committed for trial; but obtained their liberty after the next assizes, as Page did not appear to prosecute.

After this, he made no farther use of the phaeton as a disguise for his robberies; but it served him occasionally on parties of pleasure, which he sometimes took with a girl whom he had then in keeping.

Page was passionately fond of play, and his practice this way was occasionally attended with good fortune. One night he went to the masquerade with only ten guineas, but joining a party at cards, he won above five hundred pounds. But this money was no sooner in his possession, than a lady, most magnificently dressed, made some advances to him, on which he put the most favourable construction. After some conversation, she told him that her mother was a widow who would not admit of his visits; but that possibly he might prevail on her attendant, whose husband was a reputable tradesman, to give them admission to her house.

Page, who had repeatedly heard the other address her by the title of " My lady," became very importunate with the good woman to grant this favour; and at length, all parties having agreed, the servants were called. Page handed the lady and her attendant into a coach, on which was the coronet of a viscountess. Two footmen with flambeaux got up behind, and the coachman was ordered to drive home. The " home " which they reached, however, was a brothel; and on the lady quitting him in the morning, he found that she had been dex-terous enough to rob him of his pocket-book and its contents, which no doubt more than compensated her for the favour which she had bestowed upon him.

The road and the gaming-table were now his only means of support; and he found a fitting companion in his proceedings in the person of an old schoolfellow named Darwell, in conjunction with whom, in the course of three years, he committed upwards of three hundred rob-beries.   At length, however, their inquitous proceedings caused an active search to be made for them; and Darwell being apprehended, "peached" upon his companion, and disclosed the places where it was most likely that he would be found.

The consequence was, that Page was apprehended at the Golden Lion, near Hyde Park, when three loaded pistols were found on him, with powder, balls, a wig to disguise himself, and the map of the roads round London which we have already mentioned.

He was sent to Newgate, and an advertisement inserted in the papers, requesting such persons as had been robbed to attend his re-examination; but he denied all that was alleged against him; and, as he was always disguised when he committed any robbery, no person present could identify his person.

He was tried at length on suspicion of robbing Mr. Webb in Belfourd Lane, but acquitted for want of evidence; and after this he was tried at Hertford, but again acquitted for a like reason.

From Hertford he was removed to Maidstone gaol; and being tried at Rochester for robbing Captain Farrington on Blackheath, he was capi-tally convicted, and received sentence of death.   After conviction he acknowledged his guilt, yet exerted himself in the most strenuous man-ner to procure a pardon.   He wrote to a nobleman with this view, and also sent a letter to a gentleman with whom he had lived as a servant, begging his interest that he might be sent to America as a foot soldier; but his endeavours proved fruitless, and he was ordered for execution.

This extraordinary malefactor suffered at Maidstone, on the 6th of April, 1758.

DR. WILLIAM DODD,

EXECUTED FOR FORGERY.

The apprehension of such a man as Dr. Dodd on a charge of forgery was a matter of the greatest surprise among all ranks of people. He stood high in estimation as a divine, a popular preacher, and an elegant scholar. He was the promoter of many public charities; and of some others he may be said to have been the institutor. The Magdalen, for reclaiming young women who have swerved from the path of virtue; the Society for the Relief of Poor Debtors; and that of the Humane Society for the recovery of persons apparently drowned, owe their institution to him. He was patronised by the King, and more immediately by Lord Chesterfield; and his church preferments were lucrative. It appeared, however, that his expences out-ran his income, and for a supply of cash he committed a forgery on his former pupil, the Earl of Chesterfield.

A singular circumstance in the life of Dr. Dodd was his publication, a few years previous to his execution, of a sermon entitled "The Frequency of Capital Punishments inconsistent with justice, sound policy, and religion." This, he says, was intended to have been preached at the Chapel-Royal, at St. James's, but omitted on account of the absence of the court during the author's month of waiting. The following extract will show his opinion on this subject. He says—

"It would be easy to show the injustice of those laws which demand blood for the slightest offences; the superior justice and propriety of inflicting perpetual and laborious servitude; the greater utility thereof to the sufferer, as well as to the state, especially when we have a variety of necessary occupations, peculiarly noxious and prejudicial to the lives of the honest and industrious, and in which they might be employed who had forfeited their lives and their liberties to society."

The method adopted in his forgery is also remarkable. He pretended that the noble lord had urgent occasion to borrow £4000, but did not choose to be his own agent, and begged that the matter might be secretly and expeditiously conducted.

The doctor employed one Lewis Robertson, a broker, to whom he presented a bond, not filled up or signed, that he might find a person who would advance the requisite sum to a young nobleman who had lately come of age. After applying to several persons who refused the business because they were not to be present when the bond was executed, Mr. Robertson, absolutely confiding in the doctor's honour, applied to Messrs. Fletcher and Peach, who agreed to lend the money. Mr. Robertson returned the bond to the doctor, in order to its being executed; and on the following day the doctor produced it as executed and witnessed by himself. Mr. Robertson, knowing that Mr. Fletcher was a man who required all legal observances to be attended to, and that he would therefore object to the bond as bearing the name of one

witness only, put his name under that of Dr. Dodd, and in that state
carried the bond to him, and received from him the sum of £4000 in
return, which he paid over to his employer.

The bond was subsequently produced to the Earl of Chesterfield;
who, immediately on seeing it, disowned it, and expressed himself at a
loss to know by whom such a forgery upon him could have been committed. It was evident, however, that the attesting witnesses must,
if their signatures were genuine, be acquainted with its author; and
Mr. Manly, his lordship's agent, went directly to consult Mr. Fletcher
upon the best course to be taken; and after some deliberation, Mr.
Fletcher, a Mr. Innis, and Mr. Manly proceeded to Guildhall to prefer
an information with regard to the forgery against Dr. Dodd and Mr.
Robertson. Mr. Robertson was without difficulty secured; and then
Fletcher, Innis, and Manly, accompanied by two of the lord mayor's
officers, went to the house of the doctor in Argyle-street, whither he
had recently removed.

They opened the business—the doctor was very much struck and
affected. Manly told him, if he would return the money, it would be
the only means of saving him. He instantly returned six notes of £500
each, making £3000, and drew on his banker for £500; the broker
returned £100, and gave a judgment on his goods for the remaining £400,
which judgment was immediately carried into execution. All this was
done by the doctor in full reliance on the honour of the parties, that the
bond should be returned to him cancelled; but, notwithstanding this
restitution, he was taken before the lord mayor, and charged as above
mentioned. The doctor declared he had no intention to defraud Lord
Chesterfield, or the gentlemen who advanced the money. He hoped
that the satisfaction he had made in returning the money would atone for
his offence. He was pressed, he said, exceedingly for £300, to pay some
bills due to a tradesman. He took this step as a temporary resource,
and would have repaid it in half a year. "My Lord Chesterfield,"
added he, "cannot but have some tenderness for me, as my pupil. I
love him, and he knows it. There is nobody wishes to prosecute. I am
sure my Lord Chesterfield don't want my life—I hope he will shew
clemency to me. Mercy should triumph over justice." Clemency,
however, was denied; and the doctor was committed to the Compter, in
preparation for his trial. On the 19th of February, Dr. Dodd being put
to the bar at the Old Bailey, addressed the court in the following words:—

" My lords,—I am informed that the bill of indictment against me
has been found on the evidence of Mr. Robertson, who was taken out of
Newgate, without any authority or leave from your lordships, for the
purpose of procuring the bill to be found. Mr. Robertson is a subscribing witness to the bond, and, as I conceive, would be swearing to
exculpate himself, if he should be admitted as a witness against me; and
as the bill has been found upon his evidence, which was surreptitiously
obtained, I submit to your lordships that I ought not to be compelled to
plead to this indictment; and upon this question I beg to be heard by
my counsel.

" My lords, I beg leave also further to observe to your lordships, that the gentlemen on the other side of the question are bound over to prosecute Mr. Robertson."

Previous to the arguments of the counsel, an order, which had been surreptitiously obtained from an officer of the court, dated Wednesday, February 19th, and directed to the keeper of Newgate, commanding him to carry Lewis Robertson to Hicks's-hall, in order to his giving evidence before the grand inquest on the present bill of indictment; likewise a resolution of the court, reprobating the said order; and also the recognizance, entered into by Mr. Manly, Mr. Peach, Mr. Innis, and the Right Hon. the Earl of Chesterfield, to prosecute and give evidence against Dr. Dodd and Lewis Robertson for the said forgery, were ordered to be read; and the clerk of the arraigns was directed to inform the court whether the name Lewis Robertson was indorsed as a witness on the back of the indictment, which was answered in the affirmative.

The counsel now proceeded in their arguments for and against the prisoner. Mr. Howarth, one of Dr. Dodd's advocates, contended, that no person ought to be called on to plead or answer to an indictment, if it appears upon the face of that indictment that the evidence upon which the bill was found was not legal, or competent to have been adduced before the grand jury.

Mr. Cooper, counsel on the same side, followed this idea, and hoped that Mr. Dodd might not be called on to plead to the bill of indictment, and that the bill might be quashed. Mr. Buller likewise argued on the same side.

The other counsel employed for the prosecution replied to these arguments with equal ingenuity and professional knowledge. It was now agreed that the trial should proceed, and the question respecting the competency of Robertson's evidence be reserved for the opinion of the twelve judges. The indictment charged him with forging a bond for the payment of £4000, with intent to defraud, &c., and the facts already stated were sworn to by the respective witnesses. When the evidence was gone through, the court called upon the doctor for his defence, when he addressed the Court as follows:—

" My lords, and gentlemen of the jury,—Upon the evidence which has been this day produced against me, I find it very difficult to address your lordships; there is no man in the world who has a deeper sense of the heinous nature of the crime for which I stand indicted than myself. I view it, my lords, in all its extent of malignancy towards a commercial state like ours; but, my lords, I humbly apprehend, though no lawyer, that the moral turpitude and malignancy of the crime always, both in the eye of law and of religion, consists in the intention. I am informed, my lords, that the act of parliament on this head runs perpetually in this stile, *with an intention to defraud.* Such an intention, my lords and gentlemen of the jury, I believe, has not been attempted to be proved upon me, and the consequences that have happened, which have appeared before you, sufficiently prove that a perfect and ample restitution has been made. I leave it, my lords, to you, and the gentlemen of the jury, to consider, that if an unhappy man ever deviates from the law of right, yet if, in the first single moment of reflection, he does all that he can to make a full and perfect amends, what, my lords, and gentlemen of the jury, can God or man desire further?

" My lords, there are a variety of little circumstances, too tedious to trouble you with, with respect to this matter. Were I to give loose to my feelings, I have many things to say, which I am sure you would feel with respect to me ; but, my lords, as it appears on all hands, as it appears, gentlemen of the jury, in every view, that no injury, intentional or real, has been done to any man living, I hope that, therefore, you will consider the case in its true state of clemency. I must observe to your lordships, that though I have met with all candour in this court, yet I have been pursued with excessive cruelty ; I have been prosecuted after the most express engagements, after the most solemn assurances, after the most delusive, soothing arguments of Mr. Manly; I have been prosecuted with a cruelty scarcely to be paralleled. A person avowedly criminal in the same indictment with myself has been brought forth as a capital witness against me ; a fact, I believe, totally unexampled. My lords, oppressed as I am with infamy, loaded as I am with distress, sunk under this cruel prosecution, your lordships and the gentlemen of the jury cannot think life a matter of any value to me. No, my lords, I solemnly protest, that death, of all blessings, would be most pleasant to me after this pain. I have yet, my lords, ties which call upon me—ties which render me desirous even to continue this miserable existence. I have a wife, my lords, who, for twenty-seven years, has lived an unparalleled example of conjugal attachment and fidelity, and whose behaviour during this trying scene would draw tears of approbation, I am sure, even from the most inhuman. My lords, I have creditors, honest men, who will lose much by my death. I hope, for the sake of justice towards them, some mercy will be shewn to me. If, upon the whole, these considerations at all avail with you, my lords, and you gentlemen of the jury—if, upon the most impartial survey of matters, not the slightest intention of injury can appear to any one—and I solemnly declare it was in my power to replace it in three months—of this I assured Mr. Robertson frequently, and had his solemn assurances that no man should be privy to it but Mr. Fletcher and himself—and if no injury was done to any man upon earth, I then hope, I trust, I fully confide myself in the tenderness, humanity, and protection of my country."

The jury retired for about ten minutes, and then returned with a verdict, that " the prisoner was guilty ;" but at the same time presented a petition, humbly recommending the doctor to the royal mercy.

The opinion of the judges was, that he had been legally convicted.

On the last day of the sessions Dr. Dodd was again put to the bar, when the clerk of the arraigns said—

Dr. William Dodd,—You stand convicted of forgery—what have you to say why this court should not give you judgment to die according to law?

Dr. Dodd, in reply, addressed the court as follows :—

" My lords,—I now stand before you a dreadful example of human infirmity. I entered upon public life with the expectations common to young men whose education has been liberal, and whose abilities have been flattered; and when I became a clergyman, I considered myself as not impairing the dignity of the order. I was not an idle, nor, I hope, a useless minister: I taught the truths of Christianity with the zeal of conviction, and the authority of innocence.

" My labours were approved—my pulpit became popular; and I have reason to believe, that of those who heard me, some have been preserved from sin, and some have been reclaimed.—Condescend, my lord, to think, if these considerations aggravate my crime, how much they must embitter my punishment! Being distinguished and elevated by the confidence of mankind, I had too much confidence in myself; and thinking my integrity, what others thought it, established in sincerity, and fortified by religion, I did not consider the danger of vanity, nor suspect the deceitfulness of my own heart. The day of conflict came, in which temptation seized and overwhelmed me! I committed the crime, which I entreat your lordships to believe that my conscience hourly represents to me in its full bulk of mischief and malignity. Many have been overpowered by temptation, who are now among the penitent in heaven! To an act now waiting the decision of vindictive justice, I will now presume to oppose the counter-balance of almost thirty-years (a great part of the life of man) passed in exciting and exercising charity in relieving such distresses as I now feel—in administering those consolations which I now want. I will not otherwise extenuate my offence, than by declaring, what I hope will appear to many, and what many circumstances make probable, that I did not intend finally to defraud: nor will it become me to apportion my own punishment, by alleging that my sufferings have been not much less than my guilt. I have fallen from reputation, which ought to have made me cautious, and from fortune, which ought to have given me content. I am sunk at once into poverty and scorn: my name and my crime fill the ballads in the streets—the sport of the thoughtless, and the triumph of the wicked! It may seem strange, my lord, that, remembering what I have lately been, I should still wish to continue what I am! but contempt of death, how speciously soever it may mingle with heathen virtues, has nothing in it suitable to Christian penitence. Many motives impel me to beg earnestly for life. I feel the natural horror of a violent death, the universal dread of untimely dissolution. I am desirous to recompense the injury I have done to the clergy, to the world, and to religion, and to efface the scandal of my crime by the example of my repentance; but, above all, I wish to die with thoughts more composed, and a calmer preparation. The gloom and confusion of a prison, the anxiety of a trial, the horrors of suspense, and the inevitable vicissitudes of passion, leave not the mind in a due disposition for the holy exercises of prayer and self-examination. Let not a little time be denied me, in which I may, by mediation and contrition prepare myself to stand at the tribunal of Omnipotence, and support the presence of that Judge, who shall distribute to all according to their works, —who will receive and pardon the repenting sinner, and from whom the merciful shall obtain mercy! For these reasons, my lords, amidst shame and misery, I yet wish to live; and most humbly implore, that I may be recommended by your lordships to the clemency of his majesty."

Here he sunk down overcome with mental agony; and some time elapsed before he was sufficiently recovered to hear the dreadful sentence of the law, which the Recorder pronounced upon him, in the following words:—

"Dr. William Dodd,—You have been convicted of the offence of publishing a forged and counterfeit bond, knowing it to be forged and counterfeit; and you have had the advantage which the laws of this country afford to every man in that situation—a fair, an impartial, and an attentive trial. The jury, to whose justice you appealed, have found you guilty; their verdict has undergone the consideration of the learned judges, and they found no ground to impeach the justice of that verdict; you yourself have admitted the justice of it; and now the very painful duty that the necessity of the law imposes upon the court, to pronounce the sentence of that law against you, remains only to be performed. You appear to entertain a very proper sense of the enormity of the offence which you have committed; you appear, too, in a state of contrition of mind, and I doubt not have duly reflected how far the dangerous tendency of the offence you have been guilty of is increased by the influence of example, in being committed by a person of your character, and of the sacred function of which you are a member. These sentiments seem to be your's: I would wish to cultivate such sentiments; but I would not wish to add to the anguish of a person in your situation by dwelling upon it. Your application for mercy must be made elsewhere, it would be cruel in the court to flatter you; there is a power of dispensing mercy, where you may apply. Your own good sense, and the contrition you express, will induce you to lessen the influence of the example, by publishing your hearty and sincere detestation of the offence of which you are convicted; and that you will not attempt to palliate or extenuate, which would indeed add to the degree of influence of a crime of this kind being committed by a person of your character and known abilities; I would therefore warn you against any thing of that kind. Now, having said this, I am obliged to pronounce the sentence of the law, which is—That you, Dr. William Dodd, be carried from hence to the place from whence you came; that from thence you are to be carried to the place of execution, when you are to be hanged by the neck until you are dead." To this Dr. Dodd replied, " Lord Jesus, receive my soul !"

Great exertions were now made to save Dr. Dodd. The newspapers were filled with letters and paragraphs in his favour. Individuals of all ranks exerted themselves in his behalf: parish officers went, in mourning, from house to house, to procure subscriptions to a petition to the king; and this petition, which, with the names, filled twenty-three sheets of parchment, was actually presented. Even the lord-mayor and common-council went in a body to St. James's to solicit mercy for the convict.

As clemency, however, had been denied to the unfortunate Perreaus, it was deemed unadvisable to extend it to Dr. Dodd. This unhappy clergyman was attended to the place of execution, in a mourning coach, by the Rev. Mr. Villette, ordinary of Newgate, and the Rev. Mr. Dobey. Another criminal, named John Harris, was executed at the same time. It is impossible to give an idea of the immense crowds of people that thronged the streets from Newgate to Tyburn.—When the prisoners arrived at the fatal tree, and were placed in the cart, Dr. Dodd exhorted his fellow-sufferer in so generous a manner, as testified that he had not forgot the duty of a clergyman, and was very fervent in the exercise of his own devotions. Just before the parties were turned off, the doctor whispered the executioner. What he said is not ascertained; but it was observed that the man had no sooner driven away the cart, than he ran immediately under the gibbet, and took hold of the doctor's legs, as if to steady the body, and the unhappy man appeared to die without pain.

A paper, of which the following is a copy, had been delivered by Dr. Dodd to Mr. Villette to be read at the place of execution, but was omitted, as it seemed impossible to make all present aware of its contents.

"To the words of dying men regard has always been paid. I am brought hither to suffer death for an act of fraud, of which I confess myself guilty with shame, such as my former state of life naturally produces, and I hope with such sorrow as He, to whom the heart is known, will not disregard. I repent that I have violated the laws by which peace and confidence are established among men; I repent that I have attempted to injure my fellow-creatures; and I repent that I have brought disgrace upon my order, and discredit upon religion: but my offences against God are without number, and can admit only of general confession and general repentance. Grant, Almighty God, for the sake of Jesus Christ, that my repentance, however late, however imperfect, may not be in vain!

"The little good that now remains in my power is to warn others against those temptations by which I have been seduced. I have always sinned against conviction; my principles have never been shaken; I have always considered the Christian religion as a revelation from God, and its divine Author as the Saviour of the world; but the laws of God, though never disowned by me, have often been forgotten. I was led astray from religious strictness by the delusion of show and the delights of voluptuousness. I never knew or attended to the calls of frugality, or the needful minuteness of painful economy. Vanity and pleasure, into which I plunged, required expense disproportionate to my income; expense brought distress upon me; and distress, importunate distress, urged me to temporary fraud.

"For this fraud I am to die; and I die declaring, in the most solemn manner, that, however I have deviated from my own precepts, I have taught others, to the best of my knowledge, and with all sincerity, the true way to eternal happiness. My life, for some few unhappy years past, has been dreadfully erroneous; but my ministry has been always sincere. I have constantly believed; and now I leave the world solemnly avowing my conviction, that there is no other name under Heaven by which we can be saved but only the name of the Lord

Jesus; and I entreat all who are here to join with me in my last petition, that, for the sake of that Lord Jesus Christ, my sins may be forgiven, and my soul received into his everlasting kingdom.

"June 27, 1777."   "WILLIAM DODD."

The body of the Doctor was on the Monday following carried to Cowley, in Buckinghamshire, and deposited in the church there.

During the doctor's confinement in Newgate (a period of several months) he chiefly employed himself in writing various pieces, which show at once his piety and talents. The principal of these were his "Thoughts in Prison," in five parts, from which we cannot doubt but that our readers, in finishing our life of so eminent, yet unfortunate, a man, will be gratified by the insertion of a few short extracts. "I began these thoughts," says the unhappy man, writing in 'Newgate, under date of the 23d of April, 1777, after his condemnation, "merely from the impression in my mind, without plan, purpose, or motive, more than the situation of my soul.

"I continued thence on a thoughtful and regular plan; and I have been enabled wonderfully, in a state which in better days I should have supposed would have destroyed all power of reflection, to bring them nearly to a conclusion. I dedicate them to God, and the reflecting serious among my fellow-creatures; and I bless the Almighty for the ability to go through them amidst the terrors of this dire place (Newgate), and the bitter anguish of my disconsolate mind! The thinking will easily pardon all inaccuracies, as I am neither able nor willing to read over these melancholy lines with a curious or critical eye. They are imperfect, but in the language of the heart; and, had I time and inclination, might, and should be, improved. But——

(Signed)   "W. D."

The unfortunate author's "Thoughts on his Imprisonment" are thus introduced :—

"My friends are gone! harsh on its sullen hinge
Grates the dread door: the massy bolts respond
Tremendous to the surly keeper's touch:
The dire keys clang, with movement dull and slow,
While their behest the ponderous locks perform :
And, fasten'd firm, the object of their care
Is left to solitude—to sorrow left.

"But wherefore fasten'd? Oh! still stronger bonds
Than bolts, or locks, or doors of molten brass,
To solitude and sorrow could consign
His anguish'd soul, and prison him, though free!
For whither should he fly, or where produce
In open day, and to the golden sun,
His hapless head! whence every laurel torn.
On his bald brow sits grinning Infamy :
And all in sportive triumph twines around
The keen, the stinging arrows of Disgrace."

MEETING OF WITCHES.

Witchcraft.

—

MARY BATEMAN, THE YORKSHIRE WITCH,

EXECUTED FOR MURDER.

The insidious arts practised by this woman rendered her a pest to the neighbourhood in which she resided, and she richly deserved the fate which eventually befel her.

She was indicted at York, on the 18th of March, 1809, for the wilful murder of Rebecca Perigo, of Bramley, in the same county, in the month of May in the previous year.

The examination of the witnesses who were called to support the case for the prosecution showed, that Mrs. Bateman resided at Leeds, and was well known at that place, as well as in the surrounding districts, as a " witch," in which capacity she had been frequently employed to work the cure of " evil wishes," and the other imaginary illnesses to which the credulous lower orders at that time supposed themselves liable. Her name had thus become celebrated in the neighbourhood for her success in the arts of divining and witchcraft, and it may be readily concluded that her efforts in her own behalf were no less profitable.

In the spring of 1806 Mrs. Perigo, who lived with her husband at Bramley, a village at a short distance from Leeds, was seized with a

" flacking," or fluttering in her breast, whenever she lay down, and
applying to a quack doctor of the place, he assured her that it was
beyond his cure, for that an " evil wish" had been laid upon her, and
that the arts of sorcery must be resorted to in order to effect her relief.
While in this dilemma, she was visited by her niece, a girl named Stead,
who at that time filled a situation as a household servant at Leeds, and
who had taken advantage of the Whitsuntide holidays to go round to
see her friends.   Stead expressed her sorrow to find her aunt in so terrible a situation, and recommended an immediate appeal to the prisoner,
whose powers she described as fully equal to get rid of any affection of
the kind, whether produced by mortal or diabolical charms.   An application was at once determined on, and Stead was employed to broach
the subject to the diviner.   She, in consequence, paid the prisoner
a visit at her house in Black Dog Yard, near the Bank, at Leeds,
and having acquainted her with the nature of the malady by which her
aunt was affected, was informed by her, that she knew a lady, who lived
at Scarborough, and that if a flannel petticoat, or some article of dress
which was worn next the skin of the patient, was sent to her, she would
at once communicate with her upon the subject.   On the following
Tuesday, William Perigo, the husband of the diseased, proceeded to her
house, and having handed over his wife's flannel petticoat, the prisoner
said that she would write to Miss Blythe, who was the lady to whom she
had alluded, at Scarborough, by the same night's post, and that an
answer would doubtless be returned by that day week, when he was to
call again.   On the day mentioned Perigo was true to his appointment,
and the prisoner produced to him a letter, saying that it had arrived
from Miss Blythe, and that it contained directions as to what was to be
done.   After a great deal of circumlocution and mystery, the letter was
opened and read by the prisoner, and it was found to contain an
order, " that Mary Bateman should go to Perigo's house, at Bramley,
and take with her four guinea notes, which were inclosed, and that
she should sew them into the four corners of the bed, in which the
diseased woman slept, where they were to remain for eighteen months;
that Perigo was to give her four notes of like value, to be returned to
Scarborough ; and that unless all these directions were strictly attended
to, the charm would be useless and would not work."   On the fourth of
August the prisoner went over to Bramley, and having shown the four
notes, proceeded apparently to sew them up in silken bags, which she
delivered over to Mrs. Perigo to be placed in the bed.   The four notes
desired to be returned were then handed to her by Perigo, and she
retired, directing her dupes frequently to send to her house, as letters
might be expected from Miss Blythe.   In about a fortnight another
letter was produced; which contained directions, that two pieces of iron
in the form of horse-shoes should be nailed up at Perigo's door by the
prisoner, but that the nails should not be driven in with a hammer, but
with the back of a pair of pincers, and that the pincers were to be sent to
Scarborough, to remain in the custody of Miss Blythe for the eighteen
months already mentioned in the charm.   The prisoner accordingly
again visited Bramley, and, having nailed up the horse-shoes, received

and carried off the pincers. In October the following letter was received by Perigo, bearing the signature of the supposed Miss Blythe :—

"My dear Friend,—You must go down to Mary Bateman's, at Leeds, on Tuesday next, and carry two guinea notes with you and give her them, and she will give you other two that I have sent to her from Scarborough ; and you must buy me a small cheese about six or eight pounds weight, and it must be of your buying, for it is for a particular use, and it is to be carried down to Mary Bateman's, and she will send it to me by the coach.—This letter is to be burned when you have done reading it."

From this time to the month of March, 1807, a great number of letters were received, demanding the transmission of various articles to Miss Blythe through the medium of the prisoner, the whole of which were to be preserved by her until the expiration of the eighteen months ; and in the course of the same period money to the amount of near seventy pounds was paid over, Perigo, upon each occasion of payment, receiving silk bags, containing what were pretended to be coins or notes of corresponding value, which were to be sewn up in the bed as before. In March, 1807, the following letter arrived :—

"My dear Friends,—I will be obliged to you if you will let me have half-a-dozen of your china, three silver spoons, half-a-pound of tea, two pounds of loaf sugar, and a tea canister to put the tea in, or else it will not do—I durst not drink out of my own china. You must burn this with a candle."

The china, &c., not having been sent, in the month of April Miss Blythe wrote as follows :—

"My dear Friends,—*I will be obliged to you if you will buy me a camp bedstead, bed and bedding, a blanket, a pair of sheets, and a long bolster must come from your house.*—You need not buy the best feathers, common ones will do. I have laid on the floor for three nights, and I cannot lay on my own bed *owing to the planets being so bad concerning your wife,* and I must have one of your buying, or it will not do.—You must bring down the china, the sugar, the caddy, the three silver spoons, and the tea, at the same time when you buy the bed, and pack them up altogether.—My brother's boat will be up in a day or two, and I will order my brother's boatman to call for them all at Mary Bateman's, and you must give Mary Bateman one shilling for the boatman, and I will place it to your account. Your wife must burn this as soon as it is read, or it will not do."

This had the desired effect ; and the prisoner having called upon the Perigos, she accompanied them to the shops of a Mr. Dobbin and a Mr. Musgrave, at Leeds, to purchase the various articles named, which were eventually bought at a cost of sixteen pounds, and sent to Mr. Sutton's, at the Lion and Lamb Inn, Kirkgate, there to await the arrival of the supposed messenger.

At the end of April the following letter arrived :—"My dear Friends, —I am sorry to tell you, you will take an illness in the month of May next, one or both of you, but I think both, but the work of God must have its course.—You will escape the chambers of the grave ; though you seem to be dead, yet you will live. Your wife must take half a pound of honey down from Bramley to Mary Bateman's at Leeds, and it must remain there till you go down yourself, and she will put in such like stuff as I have sent from Scarbro' to her, and she will put it in when you come down; and see her yourself, or it will not do. You must eat pudding for six days, and you must put in such like stuff as I have sent to Mary Bateman from Scarbro', and she will give your wife it; but you must not begin to eat of this pudding while I let you know. If ever you find yourself sickly at any time, you must take each of you a tea-spoonful of this honey. I will remit twenty pounds to you on the 20th day of May, and it will pay a little of what you owe. You must bring this down to Mary Bateman's, and burn it at her house, when you come down next time."

The instructions contained in this letter were complied with, and the prisoner having first mixed a white powder in the honey, handed over six others of the same colour and description to Mrs. Perigo, saying that they must be used in the precise manner mentioned upon them, or they would all be killed. On the 5th of May another letter arrived in the following terms:—

" My dear Friends,—You must begin to eat pudding on the 11th of May, and you must put one of the powders in every day as they are marked, for six days—and you must see it put in yourself every day, or else it will not do. If you find yourself sickly at any time, you must not have no doctor, for it will not do; and you must not let the boy that used to eat with you, eat of that pudding for six days; and you must make only just as much as you can eat yourselves, if there is any left it will not do. You must keep the door fast as much as possible, or you will be overcome by some enemy. Now think on and take my directions, or else it will kill us all. About the 25th of May I will come to Leeds, and send for your wife to Mary Bateman's; your wife will take me by the hand and say, " God bless you that I ever found you out." It has pleased God to send me into the world that I might destroy the works of darkness; I call them the works of darkness, because they are dark to you—now mind what I say, whatever you do. This letter must be burned in straw on the hearth by your wife."

The absurd credulity of Mr. and Mrs. Perigo even yet favoured the horrid designs of the prisoner; and, in obedience to the directions which they received, they began to eat the puddings on the day named. For five days they had no particular flavour, but upon the sixth powder being mixed the pudding was found so nauseous, that the former could only eat one or two mouthfuls, while his wife managed to swallow three or four. They were both directly seized with violent vomiting, and Mrs. Perigo, whose faith appears to have been greater than that of her husband, at once had recourse to the honey. Their sickness continued during the whole day; but although Mrs. Perigo suffered the most intense torments, she positively refused to hear of a doctor's being sent for, lest, as she said, the charm should be broken, by Miss Blythe's directions being opposed. The recovery of the husband from the illness by which he was affected, slowly progressed; but the wife, who persisted in eating the honey, continued daily to lose strength, and at length expired on the 24th of May, her last words being a request to her husband not to be " rash" with Mary Bateman, but to await the coming of the appointed time.

Mr. Chorley, a surgeon, was subsequently called in to see the body; but although he expressed his firm belief that the death of the deceased was caused by her having taken poison, and although that impression was confirmed by the circumstance of a cat dying immediately after it had eaten some of the pudding, no further steps were taken to ascertain the real cause of death, and Perigo even subsequently continued in communication with the prisoner.

Upon his informing her of the death of his wife, she at once declared that it was attributable to her having eaten all the honey at once; and then, in the beginning of June, he received the following letter from Miss Blythe :—

" My dear Friend,—I am sorry to tell you that your wife should touch of those things which I ordered her not, and for that reason it has caused her death; it had liked to have killed me at Scarborough, and Mary Bateman at Leeds, and you and all; and for this reason she will rise from the grave, she will stroke your face with her right hand, and you will lose the use of one side, but I will pray for you.—I would not have you go to no doctor, for it will not do. I would have you to eat and drink what you like, and you will be better. Now, my dear friend, take my directions, do, and it will be better for you.—Pray God bless you. Amen. Amen. You must burn this letter immediately after it is read."

Letters were also subsequently received by him, purporting to be from the same person, in which new demands for clothing, coals, and other articles were made; but at length, in the month of October, 1808, two years having elapsed since the commencement of the charm, he thought that the time had fully arrived when, if any good effects were to be produced from it, they would have been apparent, and that therefore he was entitled to look for his money in the bed. He, in consequence, commenced a search for the little silk bags, in which his notes and money had been, as he supposed, sewn up; but although the bags indeed were in precisely the same positions in which they had been placed by his deceased wife, by some unaccountable conjuration the notes and gold had turned to rotten cabbage-leaves and bad farthings. The darkness, by which the truth had been so long obscured, now passed away, and having communicated with the prisoner by a stratagem, meeting her under pretence of receiving from her a bottle of medicine, which was to cure him from the effects of the puddings which still remained, he caused her to be apprehended. Upon her house being searched, nearly all the property sent to the supposed Miss Blythe was found in her possession, and a bottle containing a liquid mixed with two powders, one of which proved to be oatmeal, and the other arsenic, was found in her pocket when she was taken into custody.

The rest of the evidence against the prisoner went to show that there was no such person as Miss Blythe living at Scarborough, and that all the letters which had been received by Perigo were in her own hand-writing, and had been sent by her to Scarborough to be transmitted back again.   An attempt was also proved to have been made by her to pur-chase some arsenic at the shop of a Mr. Clough, in Kirkgate, in the month of April, 1807; but the most important testimony was that of Mr. Chorley, the surgeon, who distinctly proved that he had analysed what remained of the pudding, and of the contents of the honey pot, and that he found them both to contain a deadly poison, called corrosive subli-mate of mercury, and that the symptoms exhibited by the deceased and her husband were such as would have arisen from the administration of that drug.

The prisoner's defence consisted of a simple denial of the charge; and the learned judge then proceeded to address the jury, recounting the evidence, and observing on the extraordinary credulity of Perigo, which neither the loss of his property, the death of his wife, nor his own severe sufferings, could dispel; and the jury, after conferring for a moment, having found the prisoner guilty, the judge proceeded to pass sentence of death upon her.

The prisoner having intimated that she was pregnant, the judge ordered the sheriff to impannel a jury of matrons.   This order created a general consternation among the ladies; but in about half an hour, twelve married women being impannelled, they were sworn in court, and charged to inquire " whether the prisoner was quick with child?"   The iury of matrons then retired with the prisoner, and, on their return, delivered their verdict, which was, that Mary Bateman is not quick with child.   The execution of course was not respited, and she was remanded back to prison.

Mary Bateman was born of reputable parents at Aisenby, near Thirsk, in the north riding of Yorkshire, in the year 1768; her father, whose name was Harker, carrying on business as a small farmer.   As early as at the age of five years, she exhibited much of that sly knavery which afterwards so extraordinarily distinguished her character; and many were the frauds and falsehoods, of which she was guilty, and for which she was punished.   In the year 1780, she first quitted her father's house, to undertake the duties of a servant in Thirsk; but having been guilty of some peccadilloes, she proceeded to York in 1787.   Before she had been in that city more than twelve months, she was detected in pilfering some trifling articles of property belonging to her mistress, and was compelled to run off to Leeds without waiting either for her wages or her clothes.   For a considerable time she remained without employment or friends; but at length, upon the re-commendation of an acquaintance of her father, she obtained an engagement in the shop of a mantua-maker, in whose service she remained for more than three years.   She then became acquainted with John Bateman, to whom, after a three weeks' courtship, she was married, in the year 1792.

Within two months after her marriage, she was found to have been guilty of many frauds, and she only escaped prosecution by inducing her husband to move frequently from place to place, so as to escape apprehension; and at length poor Bateman, driven almost wild by the tricks of his wife, entered the supplementary militia. Mrs. Bateman was now entirely thrown upon her own resources, and, unable to follow any reputable trade, she in the year 1799 took up her residence in Marsh Lane, near Timble Bridge, Leeds, and proceeded to deal in fortune-telling and the sale of charms. From a long course of iniquity, carried on chiefly through the medium of the most wily arts, she had acquired a manner, and a mode of speech peculiarly adapted to her new profession; and abundance of credulous victims, upon whom she was able to prosecute her schemes, daily presented themselves to her.

Her first daring attempt was upon a Mrs. Greenwood, whom she persuaded that her husband was in a situation of the greatest peril, which would be aggravated by the circumstance being mentioned to him; that he was in danger of being accused of a crime, for which he would be instantly sacrificed, and that so relentless and determined were his prosecutors, that unless four pieces of gold, four pieces of leather, four pieces of blotting-paper, and four brass screws were given to her, to " screw them down," he would be dead before the morning. Mrs. Greenwood, unfortunately for the trick, was not possessed of even one piece of gold, and the proposition of the " witch," that she should steal what she wanted, so startled her, that she had fortitude enough to emancipate herself from the trammels which had been thrown round her.

Her next attempt was upon a poor woman named Stead, upon whose jealous fears she worked so far as to obtain from her nearly the whole of her furniture, under pretence of " screwing down " a woman, with whom she represented that her husband was intimate. Stead was about to enter the army; and Mrs. Bateman easily found means to persuade him, as she had persuaded his wife, of her powers, and obtained from him all the little money which he had obtained as his bounty, under the pretence of " screwing down " his officers to give him promotion. The fascinating and all-powerful Miss Blythe had not yet been discovered, but her operations were now performed through the medium of a Mrs. Moore, whose existence, it may readily be supposed, was as doubtful as that of her subsequent coadjutor.

Terror was the great engine by which this woman carried on her frauds; and as the wife of Stead had still a few articles of furniture and clothing, the last sad wreck of their property, she persuaded her, if something was not done to prevent it, her daughter, who was then only about eight years of age, would, when she attained the age of fourteen, become pregnant of an illegitimate child, and that either she would murder herself, or she would be murdered by her seducer; to prevent which, 17s. was to be placed in Mary Bateman's hands. This money she was to hand over to the invisible Mrs. Moore, who was to reduce the coin to a " silver charm," which charm was to be worn round the girl's arm till the period of danger was past, but which, when the bubble burst, three months after, was cut from the child's arm, and, by a strange transmutation of metal, the silver had turned to pewter.

In the midst of these scenes of fraud in one party and weakness in the other, a relation of Stead's came over to Leeds in a state of pregnancy, and forsaken by her lover. This young woman was a fine subject for the artful Mary Bateman, who soon learned her misfortune, and undertook, on condition that a guinea was given to her for Mrs. Moore, to make the lover marry her. The money was paid, but no lover appeared. It was then found out that he was too strong for the first charm, and that more money and more screws would be necessary to " screw him down" to the altar of Hymen. Still he came not; and the girl finding the money she had fast diminishing, procured a service in a respectable family in Leeds, the master of which being a bachelor, Mary soon contrived to persuade the silly girl that she could by her arts oblige him to marry her. Here a difficulty arose—the unborn child was in the way; but Mary, ever ready to undertake any business, however desperate, engaged to remove the impediment, and for that purpose administered certain medicines to the ill-fated young woman, which produced the desired effect, and abortion ensued. The master, after all, was not to be caught; but the girl's former sweetheart coming over to Leeds married her, though she was, at that time, owing as is supposed to the medicine given to her by Mary Bateman, in a very emaciated state. In speaking of her connexion with this vile woman, she used the following remarkable expressions:—" Had I never known Mary Bateman, my child would now have been in my arms, and I should have been a healthy woman—but it is in eternity, and I am going after it as fast as time and a ruined constitution can carry me." The unhappy girl died soon after, a melancholy instance of the direful effects which too great credulity and weakness of mind may produce.

The artifices and frauds of which she had been hitherto guilty, however, shrink into comparative obscurity, when opposed to the offences which Mrs. Bateman subsequently committed. The case of the unhappy Mrs. Perigo has been already mentioned, and its circumstances detailed; but there is too much reason to believe that she was concerned in producing the death of three persons, a crime of still greater and more cold-blooded cruelty. The Misses Kitchen were Quaker ladies, who carried on the business of linen-drapers near St. Peter's Square, Leeds; and Mrs. Bateman, by representations of her skill in divination and reading the stars, managed so far to ingratiate herself into their good graces as to become their confidante and most intimate adviser. She attended their shop, was a constant visitor at their house, and her interference extended even to the domestic concerns of the family. In the month of September, 1803, the younger Miss Kitchen was attacked with a severe and painful illness, and Bateman possessing the full confidence of the family procured medicines from a person whom she described as a country doctor; but instead of their producing any improvement in the condition of the unhappy patient, in less than a week she died. Her mother lived in Wakefield, and she arrived in time only to receive the last breath of her daughter; but in two days she, as well as the surviving sister, died, and they were all three placed in the same grave. Throughout the whole of these distressing illnesses

Mary Bateman was the sole attendant upon these unhappy women; and after their death she took upon herself the task of rendering them those last melancholy offices, which are usually the duty of the near relations of the deceased. No person was admitted by her to enter the house, under pretence that the deceased persons had been affected by the plague, except those whose presence was necessary in order to the performance of the rites of sepulture; and for many weeks the neighbourhood was shunned, lest the supposed infection might spread. Mrs. Bateman, however, in the midst of all, exhibited the most praiseworthy and disinterested affection for the poor ladies, and, in the face of all danger, hesitated not to minister to their wants, and even after death to take those precautions, in fumigating the house, which were supposed to be necessary. She prepared their meals, and by her hands alone were the medicines administered, which she professed to have been prescribed. Several months had elapsed before any inquiries were made as to the condition in which the deceased persons had died, and then some of their creditors, having determined to ascertain what property they had left behind them, entered the house. To their surprise they discovered that of the furniture and stock, of which the deceased had been known to be possessed, scarce a vestige remained; and the discovery of some articles of property in the house of Bateman, which were known to have belonged to the deceased ladies, but which the former declared had been given to her by them, afforded grounds for a well-founded suspicion that poison was the "plague" of which they had died, although under the circumstances of the case, and after the lapse of so long a time, evidence could not be obtained which could be deemed conclusive upon the subject. The determined cruelty exercised in the case of the Perigos appeared to sanction the suspicions which were entertained; and, after conviction, Mrs. Bateman was minutely questioned upon the subject, but all efforts to induce a confession of this crime, or of that of which she was found guilty, proved unavailing.

It would be useless to follow this wretched woman through the subsequent scenes of her miserable life. Fraud and deceit were the only means by which she was able to carry on the war, and numerous were the impudent and heartless schemes which she put into operation to dupe the unhappy objects of her attacks. Her character was such as to prevent her long pursuing her occupation in one position, and she was repeatedly compelled to change her abode, until she at length took up her residence in Black Dog Lane, where she was apprehended. Her husband at this time had returned from the militia several years, and although he followed the trade to which he had been brought up, there can be little doubt that he shared the proceeds of his wife's villainies.

A few anecdotes upon the subject of the belief in witchcraft in former days, will form an appropriate, and, we trust, not an uninteresting conclusion to the present article.

The reign of James the Sixth of Scotland, and First of England, may be said to have been the witchcraft age of Great Britain. Scotland had always been a sort of fairy land; but it remained for that sagacious prince, at a time when knowledge was beginning to dispel the mists of superstition, to contribute, by his authority and writings, to convert a prejudice of education into an article of religious belief amongst the Scottish people. He wrote and published a "Treatise on Dæmonologie;" the purpose of which was, to "resolve the doubting hearts of many, as to the fearful abounding of those detestable slaves of the Devil, witches or enchanters." The authority of Scripture was perverted, to show, not only the possibility, but certainty, that such "detestable scenes" do exist; and many most detestable stories of evil enchantment were added, to establish their "fearful abounding." The treatise, which is in the form of a dialogue, treats also of the punishment which such crimes deserve; concluding, that "no sex, age, nor rank, should be excused from the punishment of death, according to the law of God, the civil and imperial law, and the municipal law of all Christian nations." In answer to the question, "What to judge of deathe, I pray you!" The answer is, "It is commonlie used to trye, but their is an indifferent thing to be used in every country, according to the law or costume thereof."

Such, in fact, was the cruel and barbarous law of James's native country; and such became the law also of England, when he succeeded to the sceptre of Elizabeth. Many hundreds of unfortunate creatures in both countries became its victims, suffering death ignominiously for an impossible offence: neither sex, nor age, nor rank, as James had sternly enjoined, was spared; and it was the most helpless and inoffensive, such as aged and lone women, who were most exposed to its malignant operation.

There were persons regularly employed in hunting out, and bringing to punishment, those unfortunate beings suspected of witchcraft.

MATTHEW HOPKINS.

Matthew Hopkins, who resided at Manningtree, in Essex, was witchfinder for the associated counties of Essex, Suffolk, Norfolk, and Huntingdonshire. In the years 1644, 1645, and 1646, accompanied by one John Stern, he brought many to the fatal tree as reputed witches. He hanged, in one year, no less than sixty reputed witches of his own county of Essex. The old, the ignorant, and the indigent, such as could neither plead their own cause nor hire an advocate, were the miserable victims of this wretch's credulity, spleen, and avarice. He pretended to be a great critic in *special marks,* such as moles, scorbutic spots, or warts, that frequently grow large and pendulous in old age, but which were absurdly supposed to be teats to suckle imps. His ultimate method of proof was by tying together the thumbs and toes of the suspected person, about whose waist was fastened a cord, the ends of which were held on the banks of the river by two men, in whose power it was to strain or slacken it. Swimming, upon this experiment, was deemed a sufficient proof of guilt; for which king James (who is said to have recommended, if he did not invent it) assigned a ridiculous reason, that, " as some persons had renounced their baptism by water, so the water refuses to receive them." Sometimes those who were accused of diabolical practices were tied neck and heels, and tossed into a pond: if they floated or swam, they were consequently guilty, and were therefore taken out and burned; but if they were innocent, they were *only* drowned. The experiment of swimming was at length tried upon Hopkins himself in his own way, and he was upon the event condemned, and, as it seems, executed as a wizard.

In a letter from Serjeant Widrington to Lord Whitelocke, mention is made of another fellow of the same profession as Hopkins. This fellow received twenty-shillings a-head for every witch he discovered, and thereby obtained rewards amounting to thirty pounds.

In an old print of this execrable character, he is represented with two witches. One of them, named Holt, is supposed to say, " My Impes are, 1. Ilemauzyr; 2. Pyewackett; 3. Pecke in the Crown; 4. Griezell Griediegutt." Four animals attend: Jarmara, a black dog; Sacke and Sugar, a hare; Newes, a ferret; Vinegar Tom, a bull-headed greyhound. This print is in the Pepysian library.

Amongst a number of women (as many as sixteen) whom Hopkins, in the year 1644, accused at Yarmouth, was one, of whom the following account is given. It appears that she used to work for Mr. Moulton (a stocking merchant, and alderman of the town), and upon a certain day went to his house for work; but he being from home, his man refused to let her have any till his master returned; whereupon, being exasperated against the man, she applied herself to the maid, and desired some knitting-work of her; and when she returned the like answer, she went home in great discontent against them both. That night, when she was in bed, she heard a knock at her door, and going to her window, she saw (it being moon-light) a tall black man there; and asked what he would have? He told her that she was discontented because she could not get work; and that he would put her into a way that she should never want anything. On this she let him in, and asked him what he had to say to her? He told her, he must first see her hands; and taking out something like a penknife, he gave one of them a scratch, so that a little blood followed, a scar being still visible when she told the story; then he took some of the blood in a pen, and pulling a book out of his pocket, bid her write her name; and when she said she could not, he said he would guide her hand. When this was done, he bid her now ask what she would have. And when she desired first to be revenged on the man, he promised to give her an account of it next night; and so, leaving her some money, went away. The next night he came to her again, and told her he could do nothing against the man, for he went constantly to church, and said his prayers morning and evening. Then she desired him to revenge her on the maid; and he again promised her an account thereof the next night: but he said the same of the maid, and that therefore he could not hurt her. But she said that there was a young child in the house, which was more easy to be dealt with. Whereupon she desired him to do what he could against it. The next night he came again, and brought with him an image of wax, and told her they must go and bury that in the church-yard, and then the child, which he had put in great pain already, should waste away as that image wasted. Whereupon they went together and buried it. The child, having lain in a languishing condition for about eighteen months, and being very near death, the minister sent this woman with this account to the magistrates, who thereupon sent her to Mr. Moulton's, where, in the same room that the child lay, almost dead, she was examined concerning the particulars aforesaid; all which she confessed, and had no sooner done, than the child, who was three years old, and was thought to be dead or dying, laughed, and began to stir and raise itself up; and from that instant began to recover. The woman was convicted upon her own confession, and executed accordingly.

THE LANCASHIRE WITCHES.

A more melancholy tale does not occur in the annals of necromancy, than that of the Lancashire witches, in 1612. The scene of the story is in Penderbury Forest, four or five miles from Manchester, remarkable for its picturesque and gloomy situation. It had long been of ill repute, as a consecrated haunt of diabolical intercourse, when a country magistrate, Roger Nowel by name, took it into his head that he should perform a great public service by routing out a nest of witches, who had rendered the place a terror to all the neighbouring vulgar. The first persons he seized on were Elizabeth Demdike and Ann Chattox. The former was eighty years of age, and had for some years been blind, and principally subsisted by begging, though she had a miserable hovel on the spot, which she called her own. Anne Chattox was of the same age, and had for some time been threatened with the calamity of blindness. Demdike was held to be so hardened a witch that she had trained all her family to the mystery—namely, Elizabeth Device, her daughter, and James and Alison Device, her great-grandchildren. These, together with John Baldock, and Jane his mother, Alice Natter Catharine Hewitt, and Isabel Roby, were successively apprehended by the diligence of Nowel and one or two neighbouring magistrates, and were all of them by some means induced to make, some a more liberal, and others a more restricted confession of their misdeeds in witchcraft, and were afterwards hurried away to Lancaster Castle, fifty miles off, to prison. Their crimes were said to have universally proceeded from malignity and resentment; and it was reported to have repeatedly happened for poor old Demdike to be led by night from her habitation into the open air, by some member of her family, where she was left alone for an hour to curse her victims, and pursue her unholy incantations, and was then sought and brought back again to her hovel, her curses never failing to produce the desired effect.

The poor wretches had been but a short time in prison, when information was given that a meeting of witches was held, on Good-Friday, at

Malkin's Tower, the habitation of Elizabeth Device, to the number of twenty persons, to consult how, by infernal machinations, to kill one Lovel, an officer, to blow up Lancaster Castle, deliver the prisoners, and to kill another man, of the name of Lister. The last object was effected; the other plans, by some means, which are not related, were prevented.

The prisoners were kept in jail till the summer assizes; but in the mean time the poor blind Demdike died in confinement.

The other prisoners were severally indicted for killing by witchcraft certain persons who were named, and they were all found guilty. The principal witnesses against Elizabeth Device were James Device and Jennet Device, her grandchildren, the latter only nine years of age. When this girl was put into the witness-box, the grandmother, on seeing her, set up so dreadful a yell, intermixed with such horrible curses, that the child declared she could not go on with her evidence unless the prisoner was removed. This was agreed to; and both brother and sister swore, that they had been present when the Devil came to their grandmother in the shape of a black-dog, and asked her what she desired. She said, the death of John Robinson; when the dog told her to make an image of Robinson in clay, and afterwards crumble it into dust, and as fast as the image perished the life of the victim would waste away, and in conclusion the man would die. This testimony was received; and, upon the conviction which followed, ten persons were led to the gallows on the twentieth of August, (Anne Chattox, eighty years of age, among the rest) the day after the trials, which lasted two days, were finished.

The judges who presided on these trials were Sir James Altham and Sir Edward Bromley, barons of the Exchequer.

Guluim, who gives the most simple and interesting account of this melancholy case, conjectures, with much reason, that the old women had played at the game of commerce with the Devil in order to make their simpler neighbours afraid of them, and that they played the game so long, that in an imperfect degree they deceived themselves. But when one of them actually saw her grandchild, of nine years old, placed in the witness-box, with the intention of consigning her to a public and ignominious death, then her reveries of her imagination vanished, and she deeply felt the reality, that while she had been thus imposing on the child in devilish sport, she had been whetting the dagger that was to take her own life. It was then no wonder that she uttered a supernatural yell, and poured curses from her heart.

Such was the first case of the Lancashire Witches. In that which follows, the accusation was clearly traced to be founded on a most villainous conspiracy.

About the year 1634, a boy named Edmund Robinson, whose father, a very poor man, dwelt in Pendle Forest, the scene of the alleged witching, declared, that, while gathering wild-flowers in one of the glades of the forest, he saw two greyhounds, which he supposed to belong to a gentleman in the neighbourhood. Seeing nobody following them, the boy alleged that he proposed to have a course; but, though a hare was started, the dogs refused to run. Young Robinson was about to punish them with a switch, when one Dame Dickenson, a neighbour's wife, started up instead of the one greyhound, and a little boy instead of the other. The witness averred, that Mother Dickenson offered him money to conceal what he had seen, which he refused, saying, " Nay; thou art a witch!" Apparently she was determined he should have full evidence of the truth of what he said, for she pulled out of her pocket a bridle, and shot it over the head of the boy who had so lately represented the other greyhound. He was then directly changed into a horse; Mother Dickenson mounted, and took Robinson before her. They made to a large house or barn, called Hourstown, into which he entered with the others. He there saw six or seven persons pulling at halters, from which, as they pulled them, meat ready-dressed came flying in quantities, together with lumps of butter, porringers of milk, and whatever else might, in his fancy, complete a rustic feast. He declared that, while engaged in the charm, they made such ugly faces and looked so fiendish, that he was frightened.

This story succeeded so well, that the father of the boy took him round to the neighbouring churches, where he placed him standing on a bench after service, and bade him look round and see what he could observe. The device, however clumsy, succeeded; and no less than seventeen persons were apprehended at the boy's selection, and conducted as witches to Lancaster Castle. These seventeen persons were tried at the assizes, and found guilty; but the judge, whose name has unfortunately been lost, unlike Sir James Altham and Sir Edward Bromley, saw something in the case that excited his suspicion, and, though the juries had not hesitated in any one instance, respited the convicts, and sent up a report of the affair to the government. Twenty-two years had not elapsed since the former case in vain. Four of the prisoners were, by the judge's recommendation, sent for to the metropolis, and were examined, first by the king's physician, and then by Charles I. in person. The boy's story was strictly scrutinized, and in the end he confessed that it was all an imposture, in which he had been instructed by his father; and the whole seventeen prisoners received the royal pardon.

THE BORROSTOWNESS WITCHES.

So late as the year 1679, several unfortunate persons were tried and executed at Borrostowness, in Scotland, for witchcraft, four of them being poor widows. The following is a literal copy of the indictment upon which they were arraigned:—

" Annaple Thomsone, widow in Borrostowness, Margaret Pringle, relect of the deceast John Campbell, seivewright there, &c. &c.

" Aye, and ilk ane of you, are indigtted and accused, that whereas, notwithstanding the law of God particularlie sett down in the 20th chapter of Leveticus and the 18th chapter of Deuteronomy, and be the lawes and actes of parliament of this kingdome and constant practis thereof, particularlie to the 27 act 29 parliament Q. Marie, the cryme of witchcraft is declaired to be one horreid, abominable, and capitall cryme, punishable with the pains of death and confiscatiown of move-ables:—nevertheless it is of veritie, that you have comitted and are gwyltie of the said crime of witchcraft, in awa far ye have entered in practicion with the devile, the enemie of your salvatiown, and have renownced our blessed Lord and Savior, and your baptizme, and have given yoursellfes, both soulles and bodies, to the devile, and swyndrie wyth witches, in divers places. And particularlie ye, the said Annaple Thompsóne, had a meeting with the devile the time of your weidow-hood, before you were married to your last husband, in your coming betwixt Linlithgow and Borrostówness, where the devile, in the lykeness of one black man, told you, that you was one poor puddled bodie, and had one lyiff and difficulties to win throu the world; and promesed iff ye wald followe him, and go alongst with him, you should never want, but have one better lyiff; and about fyve wekes thereafter the devile appeared to you, when you was going to the coal-hill, abowt sevin a-clock in the morning. Having renewed his former temtatiown, you did condeshend thereto and declared yourselff content to follow him and become his servant; whereupon the devile   *   *   *   and ye and each persone of you wis at several metting with the devile, in the linkes of Borrostowness, and in the house of you, Bessie Vicker; and ye did eate and drink with the devile, and with one another, and with witches in her howss in the night tyme; and the said Wm. Crow brought the ale, which ye drank, extending about sevin gallons, from the howss of Elizabeth Hamilton; and you, the said Annaple, had another metting about fyve wekes ago, when you wis goeing to the coal-hill of Grange, and he inveitted you to go alongst and drink with him in the Grange farmes; and you, the said Margaret Pringle, have bein one witch this many yeeres by gone, hath renownced your bap-tizme and becum the devile's servant, and promeis to follow him; and the devile took you by the right hand, whereby it was for eight days greivowslie pained, but, having it twitched new again, is immedeatelie became haill; and you, the said Margaret Hamilton has bein the devile's servant these eight or nine years by gone, and he appeared and con-versed with you at the town well of Borrostowness, and several times at your owin howss, and drank several choppens of ale with you.   *   * and the devile gane you ane fyne merk piece of gold, which a lyttle after becam ane skleite stone; and you, the said Margaret Hamilton, relict of James Pullevart, has been ane witch, and the devile's servant, thertie yeres since, hath renounced your baptisme, as said is   *   * *   *   *   *   *   *   *   *   *   *

And ye, and ilk of you, was at a meeting with the devile and other witches, at the croce of Murestain, above Renneil, upon the threttein of October last, where you all danced, and the devile acted the piper, and where you endevored to have destroyed Andrew Mitchell, sone to John Mitchell, elder in dean of Kenneil."

The charges made against the " poor puddled bodies," Annaple Thomsone and her associates, however ludicrous they may seem, were substantiated to the satisfaction of a jury; and for so meeting, and dancing and drinking, and frolicking with his Satanic majesty, who condescended to act the piper, the unfortunate defendants were solemnly condemned " to be taken to the west end of Borrostowness (the ordinary place of execution there), upon Tuesday the 23rd day of December current, betwixt two and four in the afternoon, and there to be wirrid at a steach [that is, like a bull or a badger, by dogs in human shape] till they be dead, and thereafter to have their bodies burned to ashes.

THE WITCHES OF NEW ENGLAND.

The strange and eventful history of the witches of New England is perhaps generally known to the educated and informed; still there must be many who are not aware of all its melancholy details. As a story of witchcraft, without any poetry in it, without anything to amuse the imagination or interest the fancy, it perhaps surpasses every thing upon record. The prosecutions for witchcraft in New England were numerous, and they continued, with little intermission, principally at Salem, during the greater part of the year 1692. The accusations were of the most vulgar and contemptible sort—invisible pinchings and blows, fits, with the blastings and mortality of cattle, and wains stuck fast in the ground, or losing their wheels. A conspicuous feature in nearly the whole of these stories was what they named " the spectral sight," or, in other words, that the profligate accusers first feigned, for the most part, the injuries they received, and next saw the figures and action of the persons who inflicted them, when they were invisible to every one else. Hence the miserable persecutors gained the power of gratifying the wantonness of their malice, by pretending that they suffered by the hand of any one against whom they had an ill will. The persons so charged, though unseen by any one but the accuser, and who in their corporeal presence were at a distance of miles, and doubtless wholly unconscious of the mischief that was hatching against them, were immediately taken up and cast into prison. And, what was more monstrous and incredible, there stood the prisoner on trial for his life, while the witnesses were permitted to swear that his spectre had haunted them, and afflicted them with all manner of injuries!

The first specimen of this sort of accusation was given by one Paris, the minister of a church at Salem, in the end of the year 1691, who had two daughters, one nine years old, the other eleven, who were afflicted with fits and convulsions. The first person fixed on as the mysterious author of these evils was Tituba, a female slave in the family, and she was harassed by her master into a confession of unlawful practices and spells. The girls then fixed on Sarah Good, a female known to be the victim of a morbid melancholy, and Osborne, a poor man who had for a considerable time been bed-ridden, as persons whose spectres had perpetually haunted and tormented them; and Good was, twelve months afterwards, hanged on this accusation.

The next person destined to fall under a similar imputation was one George Burroughs, also a minister of Salem. He had, it seems, buried two wives, both of whom the busy gossips said he had used ill in their life-time, and consequently it was whispered that he had murdered them. He was accustomed foolishly to vaunt that he knew what people said of him in his absence, and this was brought as a proof that he dealt with the devil. Two women who were witnesses against him interrupted their testimony with exclaiming that they saw the ghosts of the murdered wives present (who, they said, had promised them they would come), though no one else in the court saw them; and this was taken in evidence. Burroughs conducted himself in a very injudicious way on his trial; but when he came to be hanged, he made such an impressive speech, accompanied with such fervent protestations of innocence, as melted many of the spectators into tears.

The accusations, founded upon such stories as these, spread with wonderful rapidity. In Salem, many were seized with fits, exhibited frightful contortions of their limbs and features, and became fearful spectacles to the bystanders. When asked to assign the cause of all this, they pretended that they saw some neighbour (some one already solitary and afflicted, and on that account in ill odour with the townspeople) scowling upon, threatening, and tormenting them. Presently persons specially gifted with the " spectral sight," formed a class by themselves, and were sent about at the public expense from place to place, that they might see what no one else could see. The prisons were filled with persons accused, and the utmost horror was entertained, as of a calamity which in such a degree had never before visited that part of the world. It happened, most unfortunately, that Baxter's " Certainty of the World of Spirits" had been published but the year before, and a number of copies had been sent out to New England. There seemed a strange coincidence and sympathy between vital Christianity as therein described, and the fear of the devil which appeared to have " come down unto them with great wrath." Mr. Increase Mather, and Mr. Cotton Mather, his son, two clergymen of the highest reputation in the neighbourhood, by the solemnity and awe with which they treated the subject, and the earnestness and zeal which they displayed, gave a sanction to the lowest superstition and virulence of the ignorant. All the forms of justice were brought forward on this occasion. There was no lack of judges, grand juries and petty juries, and executioners, and still less of prosecutors and witnesses. The first person that was hanged was on the 10th of June, five more on the 19th of July, five on the 19th of August, and eight on the 22nd of September. Multitudes confessed that they were witches; for this appeared the only way for the accused to save their lives. Husbands and children fell down on their knees, and implored their wives and mothers to own their guilt. Many were tortured by being tied neck and heels together, till they confessed whatever was suggested to them. It is remarkable, however, that not one persisted in her confession at the place of execution.

The most interesting incident in this affair was the fate of Giles Cory, and Martha, his wife. The woman was tried on the 9th of September, and hanged on the 22nd. In the interval, on the 16th, the husband was brought up for trial. He said he was not guilty; but being asked how he would be tried, he refused to go through the customary form, and say, " By God and my country." He observed, that of all that had been tried not one had as yet been pronounced Not guilty; and he resolutely refused in that mode to undergo a trial. The judge directed therefore, that, according to the barbarous mode prescribed in the mother country, he should be laid on his back, and pressed to death with weights gradually accumulated on the upper surface of his body, a proceeding which had never before been resorted to by the English in North America. The man persisted in his resolution, and remained mute till he expired.

The whole of this dreadful tragedy, says Mr. Godwin, in his " Lives of the Necromancers," was kept together by a thread. The spectre-seers, for a considerable time, prudently restricted their accusations to persons of ill repute, or otherwise of no consequence in the community. By-and-bye, however, they lost sight of this caution, and pretended they saw the figures of some persons well connected, and of unquestioned honour and reputation, engaged in acts of witchcraft. Immediately the whole fell to pieces in a moment. The leading inhabitants presently saw how unsafe it would be to trust their reputations and their lives to the mercy of these profligate accusers. Of fifty-six bills of indictment that were offered to the grand jury on the 3rd of January, 1693, twenty-six only were found true bills, and thirty thrown out. On the twenty-six bills that were found, three persons only were pronounced guilty by the petty jury, and these three received their pardon from the government. The prisons were thrown open ; fifty confessed witches, together with two hundred persons imprisoned on suspicion, were set at liberty, and no more accusations were heard of. The " afflicted," as they were techni-cally termed, recovered their health ; the " spectral sight" was univer-sally scouted ; and men began to wonder how they could ever have been the victims of so horrible a delusion.

Dr. Cook, in his General and Historical Review of Christianity, gives a melancholy description of the condemnation of a woman for witchcraft by a tribunal at Geneva, about the middle of the seventeenth century. An enumeration of some of the particulars of this case will afford a tolerably correct notion of the horrible cruelty which, in almost all proceedings against witchcraft, was practised in different parts of Europe. The woman was accused of having sent devils into two young women, and of having brought distempers upon several others,—a charge suffi-ciently vague. To substantiate the accusation, the members of the tri-bunal availed themselves of an opinion, that the devil imprinted certain marks upon his chosen disciples, the effect of which was, that no pain could be produced by any application to the parts of the body where these marks were. They sent two surgeons to examine whether such marks could be discovered in the accused ; who reported, not much to the credit of their medical skill and philosophy, that they had found a mark, and that, having thrust a needle into it the length of a finger, she had felt no pain, and that no blood had issued from the wound. Being brought to the bar, the prisoner denied the statement of the surgeons; upon which she was examined by three more, with whom were joined two physicians. It might have been expected that a body of men who had received a liberal education, and who must have had some acquaintance with the nature and construction of the human frame, would have presented a report showing the absurdity of the examination upon which they were employed. This, however, did not occur to them; and they gravely proceeded to thrust sharp instruments into the mark already mentioned, and into others which they thought they had found out; but as the miserable patient gave plain indication that she suffered from their operations, they were staggered, and satisfied themselves with declaring, that there was something extraordinary in the marks, but that they were not perfectly like those commonly to be seen in witches. She was, notwithstanding, doomed to another investigation, the result of which was, that after some barbarous experiments, she felt no pain, and hence it was inferred that the marks were satanical. She had, previously to this last inquiry, been actually put to the rack; but she retained her fortitude and presence of mind, firmly maintaining that she had sent no devils into the persons whom it was alleged she had thus injured. She was again threatened with the torture; and, from dread of undergoing it, made a confession, which it is painful to think was not at once discerned to be the ravings of insanity. Similar proceedings were continued; and the conclusion of the whole was, that she was condemned to be hanged and burned, for giving up herself to the devil, and for bewitching the two girls!

TRIAL OF LADY FOWLIS FOR WITCHCRAFT.

Catherine Ross, Lady Fowlis, was the daughter of Ross of Balnagown, and second wife of the fifteenth Baron of Fowlis. The object of her crimes was to destroy her step-sons, Robert and Hector Monro, with about thirty of their principal kinsmen, in order that her own children might succeed to the possessions of their father, which were considerable, and lay in the counties of Ross, Sutherland, and Inverness. Her brother, George Ross, seems to have been in league with her for the accomplishment of this diabolical purpose; and his wife, the young Lady of Balnagown, was marked out as a victim, whose removal, with that of the rest of the family, might pave the way for his marriage with the wife of Robert Monro, the young laird. Their schemes were brought into active operation in the summer of 1577. Towards the end of that year, four of their accomplices, Agnes Roy, Christian Ross, of Canorth, William M'Gillievoricdam, and Thomas M'Kane More M'Allan M'Evoch, were arraigned in a justice court held in the cathedral kirk of Ross, convicted, and burnt. One of the judges who presided at this trial was Robert Monro, the husband of the principal instigator of the crimes, and father of the family whose lives were practised against. Lady Fowlis, upon the discovery of her wickedness, fled into the county of Caithness. After she had remained there for three quarters of a year, her husband was persuaded to receive her home again, and she seems to have lived unmolested during the rest of the life of the old baron; and even the young laird, for whose destruction she had perseveringly laboured, made no exertion to bring her to justice. His brother

Hector, however, on succeeding him in 1590, procured a commission for the punishment of certain witches and sorcerers, which was understood to be aimed at his step-mother; but before he had time to act upon the power thus granted, she had influence enough to obtain a suspension of the commission; and it was not till July, 1591, that she was brought to trial.   The evidence mainly relied upon was the notoriety of the facts, and the confession of the accomplices; each count of the indictment closed with a reference to the record of the process before the provincial court, with the occasional addition of " as is notour," " as is manifest be the haille countie of Roiss," or words to that effect.   The verdict was favourable to the accused; but Mr. Pitcairn is of opinion, that her escape was owing to her powerful influence.   " The inquest," he says, " bears all the appearance of a selected or packed jury, being very inferior in rank and station of life, contrary to the usual custom." The dittory or indictment is the only part of the proceedings that is preserved; indeed, the reading of it seems to have constituted the whole case of the prosecutor, and the simple denial of the " samin and the haill poyntis thereof," the whole case for the accused; after which the jury retired to consider their verdict.

The first method adopted to compass the deaths of the persons who stood in the way of her ambition was, to form figures to represent the young Laird of Fowlis and the young Lady Balnagown, which were to be shot at with elf-arrows, in conformity with the belief, that if these charmed weapons struck the typical bodies, the wounds would be felt in the real bodies, and produce invisibly the desired effect.   For the performance of the necessary rites, a meeting of three witches took place in the house of Christian Ross, at Canorth; Christian herself being one of them, Lady Fowlis another, and Marjory M'Allester, a hag of peculiar eminence, distinguished also by the name of Loskie Loncart, the third. Having constructed two images of clay, they placed them on the north side of the western chamber, and Loskie, producing two elf-arrows, delivered one to Christian Ross, who stood by with it in her hand, while with the other Lady Fowlis shot twice at the figure of Lady Balnagown, and Loskie three times at that of Robert Monro, without success.   In the mean time the images, not having been properly compacted, crumbled to pieces; and their purpose being thus thwarted for the present, the unhallowed convocation broke up, Loskie having engaged, at the command of Lady Fowlis, to make two other figures.   M'Gillievoricdam seems now to have been taken into their counsels; and, by his advice, an image in butter of the young Laird of Fowlis was placed by the side of the wall in the same western chamber of Canorth, and shot at eight times with an elf-arrow by Loskie, without effect.   This was on the 2nd of July, 1577; and, nothing discouraged by repeated failures, a clay figure of the same person was constructed on the 6th, when the indefatigable Loskie discharged the elf-arrows twelve times, sometimes reaching the image, but never wounding it.   The other two hags stood by, anxiously watching for a successful shot; Christian Ross having provided three quarters of fine linen cloth to be bound about the typical corpse, which was to be interred opposite the gate of the Stank of Fowlis, in order to complete the full representation of every circumstance which they were desirous of producing as its consequence. The main part of the rite, however, consisted in the infliction of a wound; and this not having been accomplished, they desisted from their labour.

The more secret arts of witchcraft having failed to effect the desired ends, Lady Fowlis next had recourse to poison; and numerous were the consultations held to concoct drugs and devise means for administering them. The same assistants figured as the chief agents in this equally abominable work. A stoup full of poisoned ale was first mixed in the barn of Drumnyer; but opportunity not serving for its immediate use, it was kept three nights in the kiln, and the stoup being leaky, the liquor was lost, all but a very small quantity; to prove the strength of which, Lady Fowlis caused her servant lad, Donald Mackay, to swallow it. The three confederates were assembled on this occasion; and as the draught did not kill the boy, but only threw him into a state of stupor, Loskie Loncart was dismissed with an injunction to make " ane pig-full of ranker poysoune." The obedient hag prepared the potion, and sent it to her patroness, by whom it was delivered to her nurse, Mary More, to be conveyed to Angus Leith's house, where the young laird then was, that it might be employed for his destruction.. Night being the time chosen for dispatching her on this errand, she broke the vessel by the way, spilt the liquor, and, wishing probably to ascertain the nature of what had been intrusted to her under such circumstances of mystery, tasted it, and paid the forfeit of her curiosity with her life : and what helps to show the deadly qualities of their preparation, the indictment adds, " the place quhair the said pig brak, the gers that grew upon the samin wes so hirch by (beyond) the natur of other gers, that nather cow nor scheip evir preavit (tasted) thairof." It were endless to detail all the traffickings and messengers kept scouring the country to collect the required quantity of poison. Loskie Loncart was lodged and maintained a whole summer in Christian Ross's house, for the greater convenience of assisting to drug drinks, and devise means of administering them. M'Gillievoricdam was sent to consult the gipsies about the most effectual way of poisoning the young laird. He also purchased a quantity of the powder used to destroy rats, of a merchant in Elgin, and another portion in Tain, and was strictly questioned by Lady Fowlis, whether it would suit best to mix the ingredient with egg, brose, or kail. No fitting opportunity seems to have occurred for administering any of the potions to Robert Monro; but, after three interviews, John M'Farquhar, Lady Balnagown's cook, was prevailed upon by the present of two ells of grey cloth, a shirt, and twelve and fourpence (Scots), to lend them his aid in accomplishing their purpose on his mistress. That young lady being to entertain a party of friends one night at her house at Ardmore, a witch, named Catherine Monday, carried poison thither to M'Farquhar, who poured it on the principal dish, which was kidneys. This woman remained to witness the effects, and afterwards declared that she " skunnerit," or revolted at the sight, which was " the sarest and maist cruell that evir scho saw, seeing the vomit and vexacioun that was on the young Lady Balnagown and her

company." The victim of these horrible practices did not die immediately, but contracted a deadly sickness, " quhairin," says the indictment, " scho remains yet (that is, twelve years after taking the poison)
incurable."

Immediately after the acquittal of Lady Fowlis, her step-son and
prosecutor, the seventeenth Baron of Fowlis, was presented at the bar
on an accusation in some respects similar, of which he also was found
Not guilty, by a jury, the majority of whom had sat on the preceding
trial. In January, 1588-9, this gentleman being taken ill, sent a servant
with his own horse to bring to his assistance Marian M'Ingarrach, who
is characterised as being " ane of the maist notorious and rank wichis
in all this realme," and who, as soon as she entered the house where he
lay sick, gave him three drinks of water from three stones (probably
rude stone cups). After a long consultation, she declared there was no
hope of recovery, unless the principal man of the patient's house should
suffer death for him ; and it was determined, after some discussion, that
this substitute should be George Monro, eldest son of Catharine Monro,
Lady Fowlis. A plan was next devised for transferring the *onus
moriendi*, for the present, to George ; according to which, in the first
place, no person was to have admittance to the house in which Hector
lay, until his half-brother came ; and, on his arrival, the sick man
with his left hand was to take his visitor by the right, and not to
speak until spoken to by him. In conformity with these injunctions,
several friends, who called to inquire for the patient, were excluded,
and messengers were dispatched to George Monro's house, and to
other parts of the country where he was thought to be engaged in
the sports of the chase. Before he could be found, seven expresses had
been sent after him, and five days expired. On the intelligence that
his brother desired earnestly to see him, he repaired to the place, and
was received in the form prescribed by the witch, Hector with his left
hand grasping George's right, and abstaining from speaking until asked
" how he did," to which he replied, " the better that you have come to
visit me," and he uttered not a word more, notwithstanding his urgency
to obtain an interview. The younger Monro having in this manner been
brought fairly within the compass of the witch's spells, she that night
mustered certain of her accomplices, and, having provided spades, repaired to a spot where two lairds' lands met, and, at ' ane after mid-
nycht,' digged a grave of the exact length of Hector Monro, and laid
the turf of it carefully aside. They then came home, and M'Ingarrach
gave her assistants instructions concerning the part that each was to
perform in the remaining ceremonies. The object—namely, the preservation of Hector's life, and the death of George in his stead—being
now openly stated, some of those present objected, that if the latter
should be cut off suddenly, the hue and cry would be raised, and all
their lives would be in danger. They therefore pressed the presiding
witch not to make the sacrifice immediately, but to cause it to follow
after such an interval as might obviate suspicion, which she accordingly
engaged to accomplish, and warranted him to live till the 17th day of
the ensuing April, at least. This being arranged to the satisfaction of

the persons assembled, the sick man was laid in a pair of blankets, and carried out to the place where the grave had been prepared. The party were strictly enjoined to be silent, and only M'Ingarrach, and Christian Neil, Hector's foster-mother, were to utter the necessary incantations. Being come to the spot, their living burden was deposited in the grave, the turf being spread over him, and held down with staves. M'Ingarrach stood by the side of the grave, and Neil, holding a boy, a son of Hector Leith, by the hand, ran the breadth of nine rings, then returned, and demanded, " Which is your choice?" Thereupon the other replied, " Mr. Hector, I choose you to live, and your brother George to die for you." This form of conjuration was twice gone through that night; and, on its completion, the sick man was lifted up, carried home—not one of the company uttering a word further—and replaced in bed.

To the efficacy of this spell was attributed not only the recovery of Hector, but the death of George Monro, though the latter continued in perfect health not only for the time warranted by the witch, but for a year longer. He was taken ill in April, 1590, and died on the 3rd of June following. M'Ingarrach was highly favoured by the gentleman who supposed he owed to her his life. As soon as his health was restored ' be the devilisch moyan foirsaid,' he carried her to the house of his uncle at Kilurmmody, where she was entertained with as much obsequious attention as if she had been his spouse, and obtained such pre-eminence in the country that no one durst offend her, though her ostensible character was only that of keeper to his sheep. Upon the information of Lady Fowlis, the protector of M'Ingarrach was compelled to present her at Aberdeen, where she was examined before the king, and produced the stones out of which she had made the baron drink. These enchanted cups were delivered to the keeping of the justice clerk; but we are not informed as to the fate of the witch herself.

The indictment charged the prisoner that ' ye gat yowr health be the develisch means foirsaid.' And further, it said, ' ye are indicted for art and part of the cruel, odious, and shameful slaughter of the said George Monro, your brother, by the enchantments and witchcrafts used upon him by you and of your devise, by speaking to him within youre bed, taking of him by the right hand, conform to the injunctions given to you by the said Marian Ingarrach, in the said month of January, 1589 yearis; *throw the which inchantmentis he tuke ane deidlie sickness in the moneth of Apryle,* 1589 *yearis, and continewed thairin until the moneth of Junii thairafter, and diceissit in the said moneth of Junii, being the third day of that instant!'*

MICHAEL WHITING,

Michael Whiting lived at Downham, where he occasionally preached, being a Methodist parson ; but as the bounty of those who listened to his pious exhortations was not very large, he endeavoured to add to his resources by keeping a shop, in which he sold bread, meal, &c., and also drugs, being at once a comforter of the soul and body.

Whitney's wife had two brothers, named George and Joseph Langman, both of them under age, and also a sister, aged ten years, who all lived together on a small farm near Downham. To possess himself of the small estate of these youths, Whiting had recourse to a most diabolical plan.

The little sister was sent to his shop for some bread, and, learning from her that the brothers' housekeeper was about going from home for a few days, he affected much kindness, and promised to pay them a visit. He did so, and with unusual liberality brought with him materials for making a pudding or two, observing to the housekeeper, " Catherine, be sure you make the boys a pudding before you go." After doling out a few texts of Scripture, which he had ready on all occasions, and which he applied with about as much judgment as Sancho Panza did his proverbs, he departed, taking with him the little girl, tenderly remarking that her sister would take better care of her than her brothers during the housekeeper's absence.

Catherine made the puddings ; but remarked, during the process, that the dough would not properly adhere, and when she departed she left them in the kneading-trough. The brothers, not suspecting that any mischief was intended, boiled one of the puddings for dinner, and, when properly done, sat down to partake of it ; but before they had swallowed three mouthfuls, they were seized with violent vomitings. Suspecting that the pudding was poisoned, they threw a small piece of it to a sow in the yard ; which she had scarcely swallowed, when the poor animal was taken sick, and after lingering a short time died.

The elder brother, by the application of proper medicine, soon recovered ; but the younger lingered for a long time ere he regained his health. The pudding was now analysed by a professor of chemistry, who found it to contain a large quantity of corrosive sublimate of mercury, and no other poisonous ingredient,—a fact which destroyed the defence set up by Whiting, that he had laid some *nux vomica* for rats, some of which he supposed had got among the meal.

For this offence Whiting was indicted at the Isle of Ely assizes, on Thursday the 5th of March, 1811 ; when, in addition to the above facts, it was proved that, in the event of the Langmans' death, he would come in for their property in right of his wife, as the heiress of her brothers.

The trial lasted till six o'clock in the evening, when the jury retired, and, after a deliberation of ten minutes, found the prisoner Guilty ; and he was immediately sentenced to be hanged.

THE FLASH KEN.

JAMES HARDY VAUX,

TRANSPORTED FOR PRIVATELY STEALING.

The adventures of James Hardy Vaux are not inferior in interest to those of the renowned Lazarillo de Tormes; and, like that celebrated rogue, in order that the public may profit by his example, he has given the world a narrative of his exploits, in which philosophers may read the workings of an unprincipled conscience, the legislator may discover the effects of the existing laws upon the mind of a criminal, and the citizen may learn to detect the frauds by which he is so constantly beset.

James Hardy Vaux was born at Guildford, in the county of Surrey, in the year 1782, where his father, who was a foreigner, lived in the service of a Mr. Sumner, as cook and house-steward. The mother of this unfortunate man was born of highly respectable parents, her father being a Mr. Lowe, a solicitor in London; and her marriage with her husband took place much against the wishes of her friends. In 1785 Mr. Lowe retired from business, and going to live in the country, he took with him his little grandson, whom he treated with parental fondness, sent him to school, and gave him a liberal education, such as to qualify him for his own profession. Mrs. Vaux's first imprudence had partially alienated the affections of her parents, and her subsequent conduct did not tend to restore their good opinion. Young Vaux, therefore, was entirely abandoned to the care of his grandfather and grandmother, and he complains that his natural parents never treated him with anything like a proper affection.

Young Vaux always entertained an ardent passion to enter the army or navy; but as his grandfather would not consent to his entering either of these professions, the desire was abandoned, and after much hesitation he was, at the age of fourteen, bound apprentice to Parker and Co., linen-drapers, at Liverpool.

As this step may be called his first entrance into life, we will let him speak for himself, as his conduct in his first situation clearly indicates his character, while it forcibly reminds youth of the danger they run in yielding to the first incentives to crime.

" The opportunities I had, during my residence in Liverpool, of viewing the daily arrivals and sailings of merchant ships to and from all parts of the world, particularly the Guineamen, which formed a remarkably fine class of vessels, revived the latent desire I had for a seafaring life; and I wanted but little incitement, had the smallest opportunity offered, to take French leave of my masters, and gratify my rambling propensities. For the first month of my probation I behaved extremely well, and by my quickness and assiduity gained the good opinion of my employers, who wrote of me in the most favourable terms to my friends; nor did my expenses exceed my allowance for pocket-money, which was fully adequate to every rational enjoyment.

" Among my fellow-apprentices was a young man named King, some years older than myself, with whom, from a similarity of sentiment, I formed a close intimacy. He was of an excellent disposition, but a great lover of pleasure; and as his servitude was far advanced, and his prospects peculiarly flattering, he was under very little restraint, but gave the reins to his passion for dissipation. His expenses were profuse; but whether he indulged in them at the expense of his probity, I could never ascertain. He soon introduced me to several young men of his own stamp, and I became in a short time as great a rake as the best of them: nor was our conversation confined to our own sex, scarcely a night passing without our visiting one or other of those houses consecrated to the Cyprian goddess, with which the town of Liverpool abounds. In such a course of life, it is not likely that I could submit to limited hours: my companions and I seldom returned home before midnight, and sometimes not until the ensuing morning. Though we took measures to keep this from the ears of our employers, it could not fail to be known in time; and the consequence was a strong, but tender, remonstrance on my imprudence, which much affected me at the moment; but the impression was transitory, and soon effaced. I plunged deeper and deeper into the vortex of folly and dissipation, until I was obliged to have recourse for advice to the Æsculapius of Gilead House. This irregular mode of life had borne hard upon my finances, but I had not, as yet, had recourse to fraud or peculation. I was liberally supplied by my relations on leaving Shropshire, and I had received my first quarterly allowance; but an event which soon followed tempted me to the first breach of confidence and integrity. I had in my youth been passionately fond of cock-fighting, a sport for which the county of Salop has been always famed; and, though so young, I had constantly kept several cocks at walk, unknown to my parents, so that I had acquired a considerable share of experience and knowledge on the subject. One day, when I was sent with some muslins to wait on a lady in the environs of Liverpool, near the canal, I accidentally passed a cock-pit, where a great crowd was assembled, and I understood that a grand main was about to commence. Elated at this pleasing intelligence, I hastened to execute my commission; and returning to the house, entered it, and, leaving my wrapper of goods in the care of the landlady, I went into the pit, and took my seat. The company was, as usual, of a motley description; but there were many genteel persons. I ventured a few trifling bets at first with various success; but at length an opportunity offering, which I considered as next to a certainty, I laid the odds to a large amount, flattering myself that, by this stroke of judgment, I should be enabled to figure away with increased éclat among my gay companions. After I had so done, greater odds were still vociferated; but in a moment the scene was changed! the fallen cock, in the agonies of death, made a desperate effort, and, rising for a moment, cut the throat of his antagonist, who was standing over him in the act of crowing with exultation on his victory! I was soon surrounded by my creditors, to whom I disbursed every shilling I had about me, among which were some pounds I had just received from the lady for goods and for which I had given her a receipt. I was still something deficient, for which I pledged my honour to one of the parties, giving my address, and promising payment on an early day. I now returned home, filled with remorse and shame; but as the first false step of a young person insensibly leads to another, I added to my guilt by concealing the affair from my employers, and directed them to book the articles the lady had selected. I had a degree of false shame about me, which rendered me incapable of confessing the truth and promising amendment, or all might still have been well. In the evening I had recourse to the bottle to drown my chagrin; and I determined to purloin a certain sum every day, in the course of my attendance on retail customers, until I had liquidated my debt of honour! Then I vowed to stop and reform. Delusive idea! how little did I then know my own weakness, or the futility of such resolutions in a young mind! And who, that once begins a career of vice, can say to himself, ' Thus far will I go, and no farther?' After I had discharged my engagement, I found a small sum must be raised for pocket-money and other exigencies, as it would be above two months before I could expect a remittance.

I therefore continued my peculation, and at length my evil genius suggested to me, that I might, by venturing a small sum, become more fortunate at the cock-pit, and repair the loss I had sustained, as miracles don't happen every day, and the odds must win in the long run. Thus I argued with myself; and, fatally for me, I tried the experiment.

" From this moment I never missed a day's fighting at the cock-pit;
and when on business which required my speedy return, I could not
tear myself from the spot, but frequently stayed out several hours, and
afterwards forged a lie to account for my delay. I sometimes came off
a winner; but as I was not then acquainted with the art of hedging, by
which the knowing ones commonly saved themselves, I was sure to be
a loser at every week's end. But I managed matters so well, that my
frequent abstractions from the till were not discovered, however they
might be suspected. The extensive trade of the shop rendered it next
to impossible; and what I abstracted was a trifle compared to the gross
receipts of the day. My continued misconduct became now the subject
of frequent remonstrances on the part of Mr. Parker, the resident
partner; which not having the desired effect, that gentleman wrote
to my friends, informing them in general terms that I had unhappily
formed improper connexions, and that my late levity of conduct rendered me unfit to be continued in their house, and therefore desiring I
might be recalled without delay. Mr. Parker concluded with a remark,
which I shall never forget, and which was peculiarly gratifying to my
grandfather's (perhaps too partial) feelings; after expatiating on my
general capacity for business, he added, ' his smartness of activity are
really wonderful.' This letter produced a speedy answer, in consequence
of which I was directed to hasten my departure. This took place in a
few days, and Mr. Parker gave me a great deal of wholesome advice at
parting; observing, that although it was not in his power to charge me
with any direct criminality, my inconsiderate behaviour, and the continued excesses of my conduct, left but too much room for unfavourable
conjectures.

Having now tasted the vicious cup of pleasure, Vaux found a village
too limited a sphere for his ambition, and resolved to try his fortune in
London. His grandfather, having many friends in his own profession,
gave him letters of introduction, which, on his arrival in the metropolis,
procured him a situation as copying clerk in a solicitor's office. Resolv-
ing to be master of his own conduct, he did not visit the house of his
father, who by this time had tried many businesses, but was unfortunate
in all; but took private lodgings, and for three months conducted himself with great propriety. But, getting acquainted with several young
persons of both sexes, he gradually gave way to dissipation, visited the
theatres, and became irregular in his attendance at the office, in consequence of which he was formally dismissed.

Finding it still necessary to have some employment, he procured,
through one of his dissipated companions, the son of a wealthy citizen,
a situation as clerk in the warehouse of Messrs. Key and Sons, wholesale stationers, in Abchurch Lane, Lombard Street, at a guinea a week.
Here, however, he continued but for a short time; for he could not
endure a confinement in the East End, so far from the resort of his old
acquaintances, who chiefly frequented Covent Garden and the purlieus
of Drury Lane.

" During an abode," says he, " of ten months in London, as I was frequently pushed for money, I availed myself of a genteel appearance

and pretty good address, and, taking advantage of the credulity of several tradesmen in the neighbourhood, I ordered wearing apparel of various kinds, and sometimes other goods, upon credit, without much concern about the day of payment. However, I always took care to procure a bill of parcels with the articles, which precluded any charge of fraud, and left the matter, at the worst, but a debt contracted ; for which, being a minor, I knew I could not be arrested. This was my first deviation from honesty since I left Liverpool. I was also frequently obliged to change my lodgings; and, as payment of my rent would have required ready money, for which I had so many other uses, I commonly decamped under favour of the night, having previously removed my effects by various stratagems.

" On quitting my city employment, I returned to the law, for which I still retained a partiality ; and obtained a more liberal salary than before, in an office equally respectable. But as I now wrote uncommonly fast, I soon quitted the station of a weekly clerk, and obtained writings to copy by the sheet from the law-stationers, by which I could earn considerably more money ; and in this employment I continued to labour diligently for several hours every day, and sometimes half the night.

" When I had a mind to relax from this occupation, and particularly if my finances were at a low ebb, I frequently resorted to the Blue Lion, in Gray's Inn Lane, a house noted for selling fine ale, and crowded every night by a motley assemblage of visitors, among whom were many thieves, sharpers, and other desperate characters, with their doxies. I was introduced to this house (from which hundreds of young persons may date their ruin) by a fellow-clerk, who appeared to have a personal intimacy with most of these obnoxious persons. However, though I listened eagerly to their conversation (part of which was then unintelligible to me), and fancied them people of uncommon spirit, I was not yet sufficiently depraved to cultivate their acquaintance ; but sat with a pipe in my mouth, enveloped in smoke, ruminating, like a philosopher, on the various characters who tread the great stage of life, and felt a sort of secret presentiment that I was myself born to undergo a more than common share of vicissitudes and disappointments."

During this nightly resort to the Blue Lion he became acquainted with a young man named D——, who had been steward on board a king's ship, but who had spent all his money, and had now resolved to go to Portsmouth, in the hope of procuring a situation similar to the one he had left. Vaux, naturally inconstant, determined on accompanying him ; and, having converted most of their clothes into money, they set off on foot, but had not proceeded farther than Kingston, when their cash became exhausted, and they owed a trifle to the mistress of the Eight Bells.

" In this dilemma," says Vaux, " a sudden thought struck me. Calling for pen, ink, and paper, I told my companion I had a scheme in my head for raising a supply, but would not impart it until I had tried its success. I then drew up a sort of memorial to the following effect :—

" ' To the Ladies and Gentlemen of Kingston.—The writer hereof, a young man of respectable family and good education, having, by a series of misfortunes, been reduced to the greatest distress, is now on his way to Portsmouth, in hopes of procuring a situation in the navy; but, being destitute of money for his present support, humbly solicits your charitable assistance towards enabling him to pursue his journey. To a noble mind, the pleasure of doing a good action is its own reward. The smallest donation will be gratefully received, and any lady or gentleman inclined to relieve the writer is earnestly requested to subscribe his or her name hereto.'—

" Having completed this production, I desired my friend to wait patiently for my return, and assured him I doubted not of bringing speedy relief. I now set out on my expedition, and immediately waited on Mr. Mayor, who was a grocer; but in this first essay I was unsuccessful. His worship declared he never encouraged applications of this sort from strangers, and desired me to go about my business. I, however, took the liberty of subscribing his name to my memorial by way of sanction, and gave his charity credit for a donation of five shillings. Young as I was at that time, I well knew that example, in matters of this kind, goes a great way. Having visited a number of genteel houses, with various success, I was on the point of returning, to impart my good luck to my companion, when, coming to a very handsome mansion-house in the suburbs of the town, I thought I ought not to omit calling, and a person at that moment passing by, I inquired whose residence it was, and which was the entrance to the premises. I was informed that it was the residence of Lady W——; that a little further on I should perceive a door in the brick wall, which extended along the road-side; and that if I entered at that door, and proceeded in a straight direction, I should arrive at the servants' hall; but my informer cautioned me to keep close to another wall on my left hand, which divided this avenue from the lawn in front of the mansion, because there was a very large and fierce dog at the upper end, but which, being chained up, could not reach me if I followed the above direction. I thanked this obliging person, and immediately proceeded to the door described, which I entered, and walked cautiously, and not without some fear, by the wall-side, till I perceived, by the lights in the kitchen and out-offices, that I was near the premises.

" It was now very dark, and I was carefully exploring my way, my mind full of apprehensions at the thought of this terrible dog, when, lo! at that instant, to my inexpressible consternation, the ferocious animal made a spring at me, and I gave myself up for dead. However, though he was certainly within a yard of me, he did me no mischief; but my alarm was so great, that, without knowing how or where to fly for refuge, I ran precipitately from the spot; and, when I recovered myself from the fright, found myself in the pleasure-ground, in front of the mansion-house. It appeared that I had, without knowing it, escaped through a door in the wall, which was opened on my left hand at the moment I was alarmed by the dog. I was now more at a loss than ever, for I knew of no way to get out of the pleasure-ground except by the aforesaid door, and fear of the dog prevented my attempting that passage. After wandering about for a few minutes, I approached the mansion, and, going up to one of the parlour windows, which were very large, and on a level with the terrace before the house, I applied my eye to the glass, and discovered, through an aperture in the inside shutters, a numerous and splendid party of ladies and gentlemen at dinner. Having considered a moment, I determined on a very bold step, as I saw no alternative but remaining all night in the open air, exposed to the inclemency of the weather. Taking advantage of a pause in the company's conversation, I tapped with my finger at the window, and immediately the whole party were struck with wonder. In the midst of their surprise I repeated my knock; and then, after several voices exclaiming " Good God! there is certainly somebody at the window," &c. a gentleman rose from the table, and, advancing towards me, opened first the shutters, and then the window itself, which might, in fact, be called a pair of folding-doors; and these being thrown back, I walked in with the most respectful air I could assume, and presented myself to the astonished company. Having bowed twice or thrice, and given time for their alarm to subside, I began to make my speech.

" Apologizing for my presumptuous intrusion, I stated in a concise manner the fright I had endured from the dog, my embarrassment at not being able to find means of egress from the pleasure-ground, and my having consequently taken the liberty of knocking at the window. I then presented my memorial, which was read in turn by most of the company, each of whom surveyed me with evident surprise. Having answered such queries as they thought proper to put to me, I was desired by the lady of the house to withdraw to the kitchen for a short time; and a servant was ordered to attend me thither. The parlour dinner being over, and the dishes brought out, I was desired to fall to; and, being really hungry, I wanted no pressing.

" At length I was summoned to attend the company in the parlour; and her ladyship then expressing her concern for my misfortunes, and her anxious hope that I should speedily find an end to them, presented me with half a guinea. The rest of the party also said many handsome things, and the majority of them contributed to my relief.

" Returning to the Eight Bells, I imparted my adventures to my friend, who was, of course, much pleased at my success; for I had realised between four and five pounds. I found this begging scheme so productive, that I was in no hurry to pursue the Portsmouth speculation; and, as we were both satisfied with our present quarters, it was agreed that we should continue a few days longer in Kingston, in which time I proposed to follow up my success by making a regular circuit among the inhabitants; and I, in fact, determined to levy similar contributions in every town which lay in our route.

" The following day I again sallied forth and met with equal success, visiting not only the houses of private persons, but even the respectable shopkeepers, &c.; and I may here state, once for all, that in the course of this as well as my subsequent speculations of the same nature, I met

with various receptions according to the charitable or churlish dispositions of the people to whom I applied. The donations I commonly
received were from one shilling to five ; sometimes, but rarely, I was
presented with gold, particularly at the seats of the nobility and gentry ;
all which lying within a short distance of the road I travelled, I made a
point of calling at ; and, for my information on this subject, I provided
myself with a comprehensive ' Book of Roads,' in which those objects
are correctly laid down. It was my custom in general to travel on foot,
making short stages, and putting up at a good inn in every town I
entered, where I lived upon the best during my stay, and associated
with London riders and other respectable guests."

On the evening of the second day, however, he was arrested and
carried before the magistrates, charged as a rogue and vagabond. He
referred the magistrates to one of his grandfather's friends in London ;
and the inquiries there satisfying them, he was discharged out of custody on the second day of confinement, and hastened back to town, his
companion having proceeded to Portsmouth.   After spending one
dissipated evening in London, he set out next day to Portsmouth ; and,
notwithstanding the check he had received three days earlier, he
stopped in Kingston, and levied contributions in the usual way on
the charitable inhabitants, avoiding, of course, that part of the town
where he had been before. This practice he continued on the road,
and after the payment of his expenses he still had £15 in his pocket.
On reaching Portsmouth, his fervour for the navy cooled at finding his
friend D—— had procured a situation as merchant's clerk, and he was,
after some time, induced to enter into the service of an attorney. A
short employment was quite sufficient to satisfy his industrious fit, and
he soon quitted Portsmouth in disgust, and proceeded once more
towards the great metropolis. There his good fortune threw before
him an opportunity, which steadiness on his part only required to
render most advantageous. Dining one day at the Saracen's Head,
Snow-Hill, he entered into conversation with a gentleman named Ken-
nedy, a surgeon in the navy, who, pleased with his manner and address,
procured for him an appointment as midshipman on board the Astrea
frigate. Delighted with the prospect of at length entering the navy, he
wrote to his grandfather, who immediately furnished him with £100 to
purchase an outfit. On the voyage he became weary of his position
as a midshipman ; and the captain being in want of a clerk, he tendered
his services, and was accepted. At the conclusion of a long cruise in the
northern latitudes, the vessel made for England ; and on their arrival in
the Thames, Vaux proceeded to London. He there met with a dashing
Cyprian, and, unmindful of the future, he remained with her until all
his money was spent ; and then he found that his vessel had sailed,
carrying with her his clothes, books, and all the little property of which
he was possessed. Now, driven to the greatest distress, he had recourse
to the gaming-table, where for a short time he contrived, by associating
with professed gamblers, to procure a precarious existence. But the
summer approaching, and dupes becoming fewer, he obtained, by application to Messrs. Dalton and Edwards, King's Bench Walk, a

situation as clerk, at one pound a week, with Mr. Dalton, a solicitor, of Bury St. Edmund's. " Upon the whole," says he, " this was one of the most agreeable employments I ever engaged in; and, had I prudently retained it for a few years, there is no doubt I should have met with the most liberal encouragement from my employer.   But my natural inconstancy still prevailed; and I had been but a few weeks at Bury, before I grew tired of the country, and thought of nothing but returning to London, with such spoil as I could obtain from the credulity of the tradesmen in the town.   With this view I bespoke clothes, boots, linen, and other articles at various shops, informing the parties that I should expect credit till the expiration of my quarter, to which, on account of the respectable gentleman I served, they readily consented.   As soon as any of these goods were brought home I immediately packed them up in small portable parcels, which I sent up to London by the coach, consigned to a pawnbroker with whom I was on intimate terms, desiring him to receive and keep them safe until he saw me.   I also coached off, in the same clandestine manner, such of my own apparel &c. as I had in my trunk, in which, to prevent discovery, I deposited stones or bricks to preserve its gravity.   By these means I had nothing to impede my sudden departure, when rendered necessary by the arrival of the expected quarter-day.

" I had now been about two months at Bury, and had no intention of absconding till the expiration of the third; when an accidental event induced me to hasten my departure.   One afternoon Mr. Dalton had written several letters in the office, and, the footman being elsewhere engaged, he requested me to drop them in the post-office in my way home.   I accordingly brought them out in my hand, and happening inadvertently to cast my eye on the superscriptions, I perceived that one was addressed to Mr. Lyne, tailor, Cecil Street, Strand, London. Being curious to know what correspondence Mr. Dalton could have with a tailor, I opened this letter, and found the contents to the following effect:—' Mr. Lyne,—By the waggon which goes from hence on Monday next, and arrives at the Blue Boar in Bishopsgate on Wednesday night, I shall send you a portmanteau corded and sealed, but not locked, containing two coats, sixteen waistcoats, fourteen pair of breeches, and a suit of uniform of the City Light Horse.   Most of these articles are nearly as good as new; but, as they have now become unfashionable, I desire you will dispose of them to the best advantage, on my account, and send me down by the same conveyance two suits made in the present taste,' &c.

" It immediately struck me, that if I took measures accordingly, I might arrive in town time enough to intercept and obtain this trunk from the inn; for which purpose I put this letter in my pocket, and the others in the post-office.   The next day, happening to go into Mr. Dalton's kitchen, I there saw the portmanteau corded up, and directed; and, on questioning the servant in a careless manner about it, he informed me that he was going to carry it to the inn, the following evening, in readiness for the departure of the waggon.   The same afternoon it happened (which was a most fortunate circumstance for me) that Mr. Dalton again begged of me to put some letters in the post-office, which he had not done above twice or thrice since I came into his service. Looking at these letters, I saw, to my surprise, another addressed to Mr. Lyne as before, which, eagerly opening, I found was to mention something Mr. Dalton said he had forgot in his letter of the preceding day. I immediately destroyed this second letter, which, had it come to hand, might have frustrated my design.

" I now prepared matters for eloping, and sent off the remainder of my effects by the coach, as before; but my good fortune produced another windfall, of which I had no expectation. The day before my intended departure, I was walking in the market-place with a young man, who was clerk to another attorney in the town; and, the conversation turning upon watches, my companion observed, that if I wished to purchase one, he would introduce me to a maker of his acquaintance, who would use me well on his account. I took him at his word, and begged he would immediately do so. We were then within a few doors of the shop, into which we entered; and I perceived over the window in large characters, ' Lumley and Gudgeon, watchmakers.' I laughed inwardly at the singularity of the latter name, which I considered ominous of my success in the imposition I meant to put upon him. After a short preliminary conversation, my acquaintance, having business to do, took his leave, and Mr. Gudgeon himself proceeded to show me several watches. I informed him that I wished to have a good one, but my circumstances would not allow me to go to a high price. Mr. Gudgeon assured me it was better to have a good one at once, and recommended me to a very handsome gilt watch, capped and jewelled, and his own make, which he said he could warrant to perform well, and for which he asked me eight guineas. I replied, that as my weekly salary from Mr. Dalton was but one pound, I could not afford to give so much, and began to examine others of a cheaper kind, but still letting him see that I had a strong inclination for the one he had recommended. This induced him to repeat his praises of the latter, and to press me with greater energy to fix upon it. I at length (with a show of much reluctance) suffered myself to be persuaded; but I begged leave to observe, that as I was influenced in every thing by the advice of my good master, Mr. Dalton, I would not venture to make so extensive a purchase without his approbation; that if he would therefore entrust me with the watch, I would consult Mr. Dalton, and give him (Mr. Gudgeon) a decisive answer the next morning: this he declared himself willing to do; on which I took both the watch and my leave together, and returned home.

" The next morning I attended the office as usual, but of course took no notice to Mr. Dalton of the affair in hand. During the space of time I allowed myself for dinner, I again called on Mr. Gudgeon, and told him that I would keep the watch, provided he would receive the payment by instalments, as I could not afford to pay the whole price at once. I therefore proposed to give him on the ensuing Saturday one or two guineas, as I should find most convenient, and to pay him half-a-guinea a week afterwards, until the whole was liquidated. To this he readily agreed, and, having fitted a key to the watch, he begged leave to show me some chains and seals. Of the former he had none but gilt ones: I selected one of the neatest, and a handsome gold seal. I then desired to have a bill of parcels of the whole, observing, that whenever I paid a sum upon account, Mr. Gudgeon could make a memorandum of it at the bottom by way of receipt. Having obtained this, I departed, promising to be punctual in paying my first instalment on the day appointed. This took place on Tuesday, the portmanteau being now on its way to London; and the same evening I quitted my lodgings privately, leaving nothing behind but a trunk, containing brick-bats and stones, and walked by moonlight to a village four miles distant, through which the stage-coach was to pass next morning at seven o'clock. I procured some supper at a decent public-house, and retired to rest, desiring to be called in time for the coach. At the expected hour the stage made its appearance, in which I seated myself, and about eight the same evening arrived at the Blue Boar, just two hours after the waggon, which I perceived standing in the yard."

He received the portmanteau with little difficulty, and having disposed of its contents in various ways, lived upon the produce for five or six weeks, at the termination of which he thought it right to look out for a new situation. He found one in the office of Mr. Preston, solicitor; and, with the imprudence of dishonest persons, entered upon it, though the office was next door to Dalton and Edwards, who had sent him down to Bury St. Edmund's. He was soon recognized by a clerk of Messrs. Dalton and Edwards, and, being called into the parlour by Mr. Preston one morning, he was surprised at seeing his late master, who snatched the watch out of his fob, and promised to restore it to the owner. Vaux was then taken into custody: but a friend of his grandfather having come forward, and indemnified Mr. Dalton for his loss, he was suffered to go at large, on a promise that he would quit London, where he was likely to come to disgrace and infamy, and endeavour to obtain employment in the country.

The country had no charms for him, however, and he set about procuring a situation in some retail shop in town, for the sole purpose of embezzling the receipts. In consequence of an advertisement in a newspaper, he applied to a Mr. Gifford, the keeper of a masquerade warehouse, and there he obtained employment upon a forged representation of his good character. He did not fail at this place in collecting a good booty, and having at length, by means of stealing goods from the shop, and embezzling money which he had received on his master's account, secured about sixty pounds worth of property, he suddenly absconded, and commenced a round of dissipation and gaiety. He had been at large scarcely a fortnight, however, before he was taken into custody at the instance of his late master, and upon his prosecution was committed to the quarter sessions; but there his good fortune aided him, and in consequence of some informality in the proceedings, he was acquitted.

Upon a second appearance at the same bar he was not quite so successful; and it appears that having been detected in the act of picking pockets with a companion named Bromley, they were both secured, and, having been convicted, they were, on the 23rd September, 1800,

sentenced to seven years transportation.   Vaux was sent to Port Jackson in the following May, and there he was assigned to a Mr. Baker, a
store-keeper at Hawkesbury, about twenty-six miles from Paramatta,
who appointed him his clerk.   In consequence of his good conduct
during the ensuing three years, he was promoted to a place in the
secretary's office, in Sydney; but there, conspiring with his fellows in
the commission of various frauds, he was discovered, and sentenced to be
worked in a road-gang.   During two months he continued in Sydney in
this degraded condition, but was then drafted to Castle Hill, a plan-
tation twenty-four miles in the interior; and there, after about ten
months' service, he was appointed clerk to the superintendent of the
works.   Having subsequently served the office of clerk to the magistrates at Paramatta, he at length, on the 10th February, 1807, returned
to England.   There he found a woeful change had taken place, his
father and his grandmother being dead; and all served to remind him of
the sinful course of life he had led, and of his fallen condition.   All his
resolutions against returning to a dishonest mode of living were however
unavailing, and at length he became a professed and a professional thief.
In order the better to carry on his new trade, he associated himself with
some fellows of dissolute habits; but at length meeting with his old friend
Bromley, he resolved to quit his new companions, and to pursue his
avocation with one accomplice only.

   " I generally spent the mornings, that is, from about one to five
o'clock P. M. (which are the fashionable hours for shopping), in visiting
the shops of jewellers, watchmakers, pawnbrokers, &c.   Having conceived hopes that this species of robbery would turn to a good account,
and depending upon my own address and appearance, I determined to
make a circuit of the town, and not to omit a single shop in either of
those branches; and this scheme I actually executed so fully, that I
believe I did not leave ten shops untried in all London, for I made a
point of commencing every day in a certain street, and going regularly
through it on both sides of the way.   My practice was to enter a shop
and request to look at gold seals, chains, brooches, rings, or any other
small articles of value; and, while examining them, and looking the
shopkeeper in the face, I contrived by sleight of hand to conceal two or
three (sometimes more) in the sleeve of my coat, which was purposely
made wide.   On some occasions I purchased a trifling article to save
appearances; at other times I took a card of the shop, promising to call
again; and, as I generally saw the remaining goods returned to the window, or place from whence they were taken, before I left the shop, there
was hardly a probability of my being suspected, or of the property being
missed.   In the course of my career I was never once detected in the
fact, though, on two or three occasions so much suspicion arose, that I
was obliged to exert all my effrontery and to use very high language, in
order, as the cant phrase is, to *bounce* the tradesman *out of it*; and my
fashionable appearance, and affected anger at his insinuations, had
always the effect of convincing him that he was mistaken, and inducing
him to apologise for the affront put upon me.   I have even sometimes
carried away the spoil, notwithstanding what had passed; and I have

often gone a second and a third time to the same shop with as good success as at the first. To prevent accidents, however, I made it a rule never to enter a second shop with any stolen property about me; for, as soon as I quitted the first, I privately conveyed my booty to Bromley, who was attending my motions in the street, and herein I found him eminently useful. By this course of depredation, I acquired on the average about ten pounds a week, though I sometimes neglected shopping for several days together. In the evenings I generally attended one of the theatres, where I mixed with the best company in the boxes, and, at the same time that I enjoyed the amusements of the place, I frequently conveyed pocket-books, snuff-boxes, and other portable articles, from the pockets of their proprietors into my own.

" In the mean time, the manner in which I spent my life, abstracted from the disgraceful means by which I supported myself, was (as I have formerly hinted) perfectly regular and inoffensive. Though I lived by depredation, yet I did not, like the abandoned class of common thieves, waste my money and leisure time in profligate debauchery, but applied myself to the perusal of instructive and amusing books, my stock of which I daily increased. I occupied genteel apartments in a creditable house, the landlord of which understood me to hold a situation under government; and every part of my conduct at home tended to confirm his opinion of my respectability. I was scrupulously exact in paying my rent, as well as the different tradesmen in the neighbourhood with whom I had occasion to deal; nor did I ever suffer any person of loose character to visit me, but studiously concealed from those of my acquaintance my place of residence. I was sometimes, indeed, so imprudent as to resort, for company's sake, to some of those public-houses frequented by thieves and other dissolute characters, the landlord of which is himself commonly an experienced thief, or returned transport. When I had a mind to relax a little, or grew tired of domestication, I disguised my appearance as much as I could, and repaired to a house of this description, sometimes taking my Dulcinea with me, whom I shall shortly introduce to the reader, and whose person and dress I was not a little proud of exhibiting in public. This fondness for flash-houses, as they are termed, is the rock on which most persons who live by depredation unhappily split, and will be found in the sequel to have brought me to my present deplorable condition; for the police-officers, or traps, are in the daily habit of visiting these houses, where they drink with the thieves &c. in the most familiar manner; and, I believe, often obtain secret information by various means from some parties respecting the names, characters, pursuits, &c., of others. By this imprudent conduct I also became personally known to many of the officers, which was productive of great danger to me in the exercise of my vocation; whereas, had I avoided such houses, I might have remained unknown and unsuspected by them for a series of years."

The Dulcinea alluded to above was an unhappy girl of the town, whom he took into keeping, and afterwards married. This poor creature behaved to him in the most exemplary manner, and proved by her conduct that she was worthy of a better fate.

Going one day to a public meeting at the Mermaid Tavern, Hackney, he picked a gentleman's pocket of a silver snuff-box, which he handed to the landlady. The box was missed by the owner, and on Vaux claiming it, he was taken into custody; but such is the glorious uncertainty of the law, that he was acquitted on his trial, contrary to his own expectation.

" The next adventure," says Vaux, " I shall have occasion to relate, more fully confirms the justice of the remark, that the connexions formed by persons during temporary confinement in a gaol commonly lead to further acts of wickedness, and frequently entail on the parties a more severe punishment than that which they have just escaped. This was exactly my unhappy case, and I now come to the most fatal era of my eventful life.

" In the same ward with myself were confined two brothers, very genteel young men, who had been recently cast for death for privately stealing some valuable rings, &c., from the shop of a jeweller, Leadenhall Street. In the course of our frequent conversations on the subject with which we were all three alike most conversant, the brothers informed me that they had, like myself, made a successful tour of the jewellers' shops in London; and on our comparing notes as to the particular persons we had robbed, or attempted to rob, they pointed out about half-a-dozen shops, which, it appeared, I had omitted to visit, arising either from their making no display of their goods, or from their being situated in private streets, where I had no idea of finding any such trades. Though at that time neither they nor myself entertained much hope of my acquittal, it was agreed that, in the event of my being so fortunate as to recover my freedom, I should pay my respects to the several tradesmen I had so overlooked; and I promised, in case I was successful, to make them a pecuniary acknowledgment in return for their information. At the moment of my joyful departure from Newgate, they accordingly furnished me with a list of the shops in question, and gave me full instructions and useful hints for my guidance therein. They particularly pointed out a Mr. Bilger, a goldsmith and jeweller of the first eminence in Piccadilly. This gentleman, they assured me, I should find, in the technical phrase, a *good flat*. A day or two after my release I made the prescribed experiments, and was fortunate enough to succeed pretty well at nearly every shop; but I reserved Mr. Bilger for my final essay, as he was the principal object of consideration, and from whom I expected to obtain the most valuable booty."

He called on Mr. Bilger about five o'clock in the evening, and after introducing himself, and stating that he required a very elegant diamond ring, requested to see his assortment. Mr. Bilger having stated that he had not a single article of that description by him, an appointment was made in an hour's time, when some were to be obtained. At which time our hero was punctual to his appointment; but, rather to his mortification, only three rings were produced for his inspection, Mr. Bilger expressing his regret at not being able to show him any more.

" I proceeded to examine the rings," he says, " one of which was marked sixteen guineas, another nine guineas, and the third six guineas. They were all extremely beautiful; but I affected to consider them as too paltry, telling Mr. Bilger that I wanted one to present to a lady, and that I wished to have a ring of greater value than the whole three put together, as a few guineas would not be an object in the price. Mr. Bilger's son, who was also his partner, now joined us, and was desired by his father to sketch a draught in pencil of some fancy rings, agreeable to the directions I should give him. The three rings I had viewed were now removed to the end of the counter next the window, and I informed the young man that I wished to have something of a cluster, a large brilliant in the centre, surrounded with smaller ones; but repeated my desire, that no expense might be spared to render the article strictly elegant, and worthy a lady's acceptance. The son having sketched a design of several rings on a card, I examined them with attention, and appeared in doubt which to prefer, but desired to see some loose diamonds, in order to form a better idea of the size &c. of each ring described in the drawing. Mr. Bilger, however, declared he had not any by him. It is probable he spoke the truth; or he might have lost such numbers by showing them, as to deter him from exhibiting them in future. Without having made up my mind on the subject, I now requested to see some of his most fashionable brooches or shirt-pins. Mr. Bilger produced a show-glass, containing a variety of articles in pearl, but he had nothing of the kind in diamonds. I took up two or three of the brooches, and immediately *sunk* a very handsome one, marked three guineas, in my coat sleeve. I next purloined a beautiful clasp for a lady's waist, consisting of stones set in gold, which had the brilliancy and appearance of real diamonds, but marked only four guineas. I should have probably gone still deeper, but at this moment a lady, coming in, desired to look at some ear-rings, and the younger Mr. Bilger immediately quitted his father to attend upon her at the other end of the shop. It struck me, that now was my time for a decisive stroke. The card containing the diamond rings, procured from the maker, lying very near the show-glass I was viewing, and many small articles irregularly placed round about them, the candles not throwing much light upon that particular spot, and Mr. Bilger's attention being divided between myself and the lady, to whom he frequently addressed himself, I suddenly took the three rings from the card, and committed them to my sleeve to join the brooch and lady's clasp; but had them so situated that I could in a moment have released and replaced them on the counter, had an inquiry been made for them. I then looked at my watch, and, observing that I was going to the theatre, told Mr. Bilger that I would not trouble him any further, as the articles before me were too tawdry and common to please me, but that I would put the card of draughts in my pocket-book; and if I did not meet with a ring of the kind I wanted before Monday or Tuesday, I would certainly call again and give him final directions. I was then drawing on my gloves, being anxious to quit the shop while I was well; but Mr. Bilger, who seemed delighted with the prospect of my custom, begged so earnestly that I would allow him to show me his brilliant

assortment of gold watches that I could not refuse to gratify him,
though I certainly incurred a great risk by my compliance. I therefore
answered, ' Really, Mr. Bilger, I am loath to give you that unnecessary
trouble, as I have, you may perceive, a very good watch already, in
point of performance, though it cost me a mere trifle—only twenty
guineas; but it answers my purpose as well as a more valuable one.
However, as I may probably, before long, want an elegant watch for
a lady, I don't care if I just run my eye over them.' Mr. Bilger
replied that the greater part of his stock were fancy watches, adapted
for ladies; and he defied all London united to exhibit a finer collection.
He then took from his window a show-glass, containing about thirty
most beautiful watches, some ornamented with pearls or diamonds,
others elegantly enamelled, or chased in the most delicate style. They
were of various prices, from thirty to one hundred guineas; and the
old gentleman rubbing his hands with an air of rapture, exclaimed,
' There they are, sir—a most fashionable assortment of goods; allow
me to recommend them, they're all a-going, sir—all a-going.' I smiled
inwardly at the latter part of this speech, and thought to myself, ' I
wish they were going, with all my heart, along with the diamond rings.'
I answered they were certainly very handsome, but I would defer a
minute inspection of them till my next visit, when I should have more
time to spare. These watches were ranged in exact order, in five
parallel lines; and between each watch was placed a gold seal or other
trinket appertaining to a lady's watch. It was no easy matter, therefore, to take away a single article without its being instantly missed,
unless the economy of the whole had been previously deranged. I
contrived, however, to display a few of the trinkets on pretence of
admiring them, and ventured to secrete one very rich gold seal, marked
six guineas. I then declared I could stay no longer, as I had appointed to meet a party at the theatre; but that I would certainly
call again in a few days, and lay out some money in return for the
trouble I had given. Mr. Bilger expressed his thanks in the most
respectful terms, and waited upon me to the door, where he took leave
of me with a very low *congé, à la mode de France*, of which country he
was a native. I now put the best foot foremost, and having gained a
remote street, turned my head, and perceived Bromley at my heels,
who seized my hand, congratulating me on my success, and compli-
menting me on the address I had shown in this exploit; for he had
witnessed all that passed, and knew that I had succeeded in my object,
by the manner in which I quitted the shop. He informed me that Mr.
Bilger had returned to his counter, and, without attending to the arrangement of the articles thereon, had joined his son, who was still
waiting upon the lady, and that he, Bromley, had finally left them both
engaged with her."

Such was his rapacity, that he renewed his visits to Mr. Bilger's shop;
but the reception he met satisfied him that he was suspected. He,
however, left an order for a splendid ring; and while the jeweller's son,
as Vaux thought, was taking down his directions, he was only writing a
description of his person, and a handbill in a few days was widely circu-

lated among the pawnbrokers, peace-officers, &c. A day or two after Vaux called at Turner's—a pawnbroker, in Brydges Street, Covent Garden—to redeem some articles he had pledged, when he saw such manœuvres in the shop as induced him to make a precipitate retreat, and go into concealment.

At length, " necessity," as he says himself, forced him out ; and, the first night, he stole, from a shop in Ludgate Street, property to the amount of four or five pounds, with which he was so much pleased that he returned for his wife, and took her out to walk. Contrary to her earnest remonstrance, they went to a flash-house near Clare Market, where the landlord betrayed him into the hands of justice, and he was hurried off to the watch-house. Next day he underwent an examination at Bow Street, and was remanded. During the interval between his first and second appearance he had completely metamorphosed his person by cutting his hair and whiskers, and putting on a mean suit of clothes. But all would not do ; he was recognised through his disguise, and fully committed. His trial came on at the Old Bailey, February the 15th, 1809, and, the facts being sworn to, he was found guilty— death. His sentence was afterwards commuted to transportation for life, preparatory to which he was conveyed on board the Retribution hulk at Woolwich.

" I had now," says Vaux, " a new scene of misery to contemplate ; and, of all the shocking scenes I had ever beheld, this was the most distressing. There were confined in this floating dungeon nearly 600 men, most of them double-ironed—and the reader may conceive the horrible effects arising from the continual rattling of chains, the filth and vermin naturally produced by such a crowd of miserable inhabit- ants—the oaths and execrations constantly heard among them—and, above all, from the shocking necessity of associating and communicating more or less with so depraved a set of beings. On arriving on board, we were all immediately stripped, and washed in large tubs of water ; then, after putting on each a suit of coarse slop clothing, we were ironed, and sent below, our own clothes being taken from us, and detained till we could sell or otherwise dispose of them, as no person is exempted from the obligation to wear the ship-dress. On descending the hatch- way, no conception can be formed of the scene which presented itself. I shall not attempt to describe it ; but nothing short of a descent to the infernal regions can be at all worthy of a comparison with it. I soon met with many of my old Botany Bay acquaintances, who were all eager to offer me their friendship and services,—that is, with a view to rob me of what little I had, for in this place there is no other motive or subject for ingenuity. All former friendships or connexions are dis- solved, and a man here will rob his best benefactor, or even messmate, of an article worth one halfpenny. Every morning, at seven o'clock, all the convicts capable of work, or, in fact, all who are capable of getting into the boats, are taken ashore to the Warren, in which the Royal Arsenal and other public buildings are situated, and are there employed at various kinds of labour, some of them very fatiguing ; and, while so employed, each gang of sixteen or twenty men is watched and directed by a fellow called a guard. These guards are most commonly of the lowest class of human beings—wretches devoid of all feeling—ignorant in the extreme—brutal by nature, and rendered tyrannical and cruel by the consciousness of the power they possess: no others, but such as I have described, would hold the situation, their wages being not more than a day-labourer would earn in London. They invariably carry a large and ponderous stick, with which, without the smallest provocation, they will fell an unfortunate convict to the ground, and frequently repeat their blows long after the poor sufferer is insensible. At noon the working party return on board to dinner, and at one again go on shore, where they labour till near sun-set. On returning on board in the evening, all hands are mustered by a roll; and the whole being turned down below, the hatches are put over them, and secured for the night. As to the food, the stipulated ration is very scanty; but of part even of that they are defrauded. Their provisions, being supplied by contractors, and not by government, are of the worst kind, such as would not be considered eatable or wholesome elsewhere; and both the weight and measure are always deficient. The allowance of bread is said to be about twenty ounces per day. Three days in the week they have about four ounces of cheese for dinner, and the other four days a pound of beef. The breakfast is invariably boiled barley, of the coarsest kind imaginable; and of this the pigs of the hulk come in for a third part, because it is so nauseous that nothing but downright hunger will enable a man to eat it. For supper, they have, on banyan days, burgoo, of as good a quality as the barley, and which is similarly disposed of; and on meat days, the water in which the beef was boiled is thickened with barley, and forms a mess called ' smiggins,' of a more detestable nature than either of the two former! The reader may conceive that I do not exaggerate when I state that among the convicts the common price of these several eatables is,—for a day's allowance of beef, one halfpenny;—ditto, of cheese, one halfpenny;—ditto, of bread, three-halfpence; but the cheese is most commonly so bad that they throw it away. It is manufactured, I believe, of skimmed milk, for this particular contract. The beef generally consists of old bulls or cows who have died of age or famine; the least trace of fat is considered a phenomenon, and it is far inferior upon the whole to good horse-flesh. I once saw the prisoners throw the whole day's supply overboard the moment it was hoisted out of the boat, and for this offence they were severely flogged. The friends of these unhappy persons are not allowed to come on board, but must remain alongside during their visit. The prisoners are, it is true, suffered to go into their boat, but a guard is placed within hearing of their conversation; and if a friend or parent has come one hundred miles, they are not allowed above ten minutes' interview; so that, instead of consolation, the visit only excites regret at the parties being so suddenly torn asunder. All letters, too, written by prisoners, must be delivered unsealed to the chief mate for his inspection, before they are sent ashore; and such as he thinks obnoxious are, of course, suppressed. In like manner all letters received from the post-office are opened and scrutinized. If I were to attempt a full description of the miseries endured in these ships, I could fill a volume; but I shall sum up all by stating, that, besides robbery from each other, which is as common as cursing and swearing, I witnessed among the prisoners themselves, during the twelvemonth I remained with them, one deliberate murder, for which the perpetrator was executed at Maidstone, and one suicide; and that unnatural crimes are openly committed."

From the misery of the hulks he was removed, on the 15th of June 1810, for the second time, to Botany Bay. His wife, who had all along manifested the utmost attention, was prevented by a succession of unfortunate circumstances from seeing him previous to his departure; nor does it appear that he knew what became of her afterwards. On the 16th of the following December, the transport arrived at Sydney Cove, where Vaux found that the report of his exploits in London had preceded him. He endeavoured to make interest with the governor, in the hope of being employed as a clerk; but this being his second visit, he was listened to with distrust, and was sent up the country to a settler, who used him with great barbarity. To escape from this tyranny Vaux feigned himself sick, and thus procured his removal to the hospital, from which he was discharged in a month, and appointed overseer to a town gang. He now resolved to lead a correct life, and establish, if possible, a character for himself, seeing, as he says, the necessity of good conduct, from the consequences that invariably attend on an improper one. If we believe him, he adhered firmly to his vows of rectitude; but his notorious character operated against him, and he fell a victim to prejudice and the depravity of a youth, who was a veteran in iniquity. This young villain's name was Edwards. He was servant to Mr. Bent the judge-advocate, from whom he purloined bills and money. Vaux, suspecting his dishonesty, warned him of his danger; but the artful thief accounted for his being so flush of money by the presents he was in the habit of receiving from his master's visitors.

One evening he came running into Vaux's lodgings, and requested of him to keep some articles and parcels which he put into his hand. Vaux at first refused, but was ultimately prevailed on to keep them for a few minutes. Edwards had scarcely departed when he thought he had done wrong, and acquainted his landlord with the transaction. That person desired him to go immediately and deliver the property up to the judge-advocate in a public manner, as the only way left him to escape being implicated with Edwards; and with this advice Vaux resolved to comply, but having stopped first to smoke a pipe, before he had finished it, two officers entered and apprehended him. His conduct was open, and his landlord deposed in his favour; but Edwards accused him, in revenge for giving up the property, of being an accomplice, and he was finally banished to the Coal River, where he continued doing all kind of work for two years, after which he was permitted to return to Sydney, where he was once more placed in the town-gang.

Again he renewed his vows of rectitude, but was unable to obtain any station less degrading than the one in which he was placed. The picture before him was disheartening in the extreme—an exile for life—and compelled to labour at the basest and lowest employment of mankind. A British sailor took compassion on him, and offered, in 1814, to conceal him in his vessel until she should sail, and he embraced the generous proposal; but, after lying close and undiscovered for four days, some one on board gave information, and the unfortunate wretch was dragged ashore, punished with fifty lashes, and sentenced to transportation to the Coal River for one year.

"In a few days," says he in his Memoirs, "I was accordingly embarked with eleven other prisoners, and a second time landed at Newcastle, from whence I had been absent nearly twelve months. On my arrival, it happened that the storekeeper of that settlement was in want of a clerk, and he applying to the commandant for me, I was appointed to that situation, in which I still continue; and having scrupulously adhered to my former vows of rectitude, and used every exertion to render myself serviceable to my employer, and to merit his good opinion as well as that of the commandant, I have had the satisfaction to succeed in these objects; and I am not without hope that, when I am permitted to quit my present service and return to Sydney, my good conduct will be rewarded with a more desirable situation. I have now been upwards of seven years a prisoner, and, knowing the hopeless sentence under which I labour, I shall, I trust, studiously avoid in future every act which may subject me to the censure of my superiors, or entail upon me a repetition of those sufferings I have already too severely experienced. I have thus described (perhaps too minutely for the reader's patience) the various vicissitudes of my past life. Whether the future will be so far diversified as to afford matter worthy of being committed to paper, either to amuse a vacant hour, or to serve as a beacon which may warn others to avoid the rocks on which I have unhappily split, is only known to the great Disposer of events."

The "Memoirs written by himself," from which we have extracted the most interesting passages, here terminate.

We have been the more willing to give the adventures of this notorious villain, as he gives them,—although we confess that we are of opinion that there is some exaggeration in what he states—because, however great may be the depravity, of which he admits he was guilty, his punishments and his miseries convey a moral, most forcibly depicting the danger of such a line of conduct as he adopted. His memoirs were written by himself in the year 1816, and were published in London in about three years afterwards. Of his subsequent career we know little, but we learn by recent accounts received from Sydney, that this hoary old sinner, at the age of fifty-seven, has been convicted and sentenced to an imprisonment of two years duration, upon a charge of indecently assaulting a girl of tender age. Whatever may have been his course of life in later years, however frightful may have been his career of sin in his younger days, we hold that this new offence, of which he has been found guilty, is the crowning crime of the whole; and we regret that the human heart should have arrived at such a degree of profligacy, as to admit the guilt of youth, and to be unable to withstand its temptation, in old age.

TRIAL BY BATTLE.

ABRAHAM THORNTON,

TRIED FOR MURDER.

THIS case is remarkable, not only for the lamentable atrocity of the offence imputed to the unfortunate prisoner, but from the fact also of the brother of the deceased person having lodged an appeal, upon which the prisoner demanded " wager of battle," the consequence of which was the repeal of the old law by which the wager was allowed in former ages, and which, though grown into disuse, still remained in existence.

Thornton was a well-made young man, the son of a respectable builder, and was by trade a bricklayer. He was indicted at the War-wick assizes, in August 1817, for the murder of Mary Ashford, a lovely and interesting girl, whose character was perfectly unsullied up to the time at which she was most barbarously ravished and murdered.

From the evidence adduced it appeared, that the poor girl went to a dance at Tyburn, a few miles from Birmingham, on the evening of the 26th of May 1817, where she met the prisoner, who professed to admire her, and was heard to say, " I will have connexion with her, though it cost me my life." He danced with her, and accompanied her from the room about three o'clock in the morning. At four o'clock she called at a friend's at a place called Erdington, and the offence alleged against the prisoner was committed immediately afterwards. The circumstances proved in evidence were, that the footsteps of a man and woman were traced from the path through a harrowed field, through which her way

lay home to Langley.   The marks were at first regular, but afterwards
exhibited proofs of the persons whose footsteps they represented, running
and struggling; and at length they led to a spot where a distinct impression of a human figure and a large quantity of coagulated blood
were discovered, and on this spot the marks of a man's knees and toes
were also distinguishable.   From thence the man's footsteps only were
seen, and accompanying it blood marks were distinctly traced for a considerable space towards a pit; and it appeared plainly as if a man had
walked along the footway carrying a body, from which the blood
dropped.   At the edge of the pit, the shoes, bonnet, and bundle of the
deceased were found; but only one footstep could be seen there, and
that was a man's.   It was deeply impressed, and seemed to be that of a
man who thrust one foot forward to heave something into the pit; and
the body of the deceased was discovered lying at the bottom.   There
were marks of laceration upon the body; and both her arms had the
marks of hands, as if they had pressed them with violence to the ground.

By his own admission Thornton was with her at four o'clock, and the
marks of the man's shoes in the running corresponded exactly to his.
By his own admission, also, he was intimate with her; and this admission
was made, not before the magistrate, nor till the evident proofs were discovered on his clothes: her clothes, too, afforded most powerful
evidence.   At four in the morning she called at a friend's, Hannah Cox,
and changed her dancing-dress for that in which she had gone from
Birmingham.   The clothes she put on there, and which she had on at
the time of her death, were all over blood and dirt.

The case, therefore, appeared to be, that Thornton having danced with
her during the night, had shown her, perhaps, those attentions which
she might naturally have been pleased with; had afterwards waited for
her on her return from Erdington, and, after forcibly violating her,
had thrown her body into the pit.

The prisoner declined saying anything in his defence, stating that he
would leave every thing to his counsel, who called several witnesses to
the fact of his having returned home at an hour which rendered it very
improbable, if not impossible, that he could have committed the murder,
and have traversed the distance from the fatal spot to the places in
which he was seen, in the very short time that appeared to have elapsed;
but it was acknowledged that there was considerable variation in the
different village-clocks; and the case was involved in so much difficulty,
from the nature of the defence, although the case for the prosecution
appeared unanswerable, that the judge's charge to the jury occupied no
less than two hours.   " It were better," he said in conclusion, " that the
murderer, with all the weight of his crime upon his head, should escape
punishment, than that another person should suffer death without being
guilty;" and this consideration weighed so powerfully with the jury,
that, to the surprise of all who had taken an interest in this awful case,
they returned a verdict of Not Guilty, which the prisoner received with
a smile of silent approbation, and an unsuccessful attempt to conceal
the violent apprehensions by which he had been inwardly agitated.

He was then arraigned *pro formâ* for the rape; but the counsel for the prosecution declined offering evidence on this indictment, and he was accordingly discharged.

Thus ended, for the present, the proceedings on this most brutal and ferocious violation and murder; but the public at large, and more particularly the inhabitants of the neighbourhood in which it had been committed, were far from considering Thornton innocent, and subscriptions to defray the expense of a new prosecution were entered into.

The circumstances of the case having been investigated by the secretary of state, he granted his warrant to the sheriff of Warwick to take the defendant into custody on an appeal of murder, to be prosecuted by William Ashford, the brother and heir-at-law of the deceased. He was in consequence lodged in Warwick gaol, and from thence subsequently removed by a writ of *habeas corpus* to London, the proceedings on the appeal being had in the Court of King's Bench, in Westminster Hall. On the 6th of November the appellant, attended by four counsel, appeared in court, when the proceedings were adjourned to the 17th, by the desire of the prisoner's counsel; and on that day the prisoner demanded trial by *wager of battle*. The revival of this obsolete law gave rise to much argument on both sides; and it was not until the 16th of April 1818, that the decision of the Court was given upon the question. The learned judges gave their opinions seriatim, and the substance of the judgment was, that the law must be administered as it stood, and that therefore the prisoner was entitled to claim trial by battle: but the Court added, that the trial should be granted only " in case the appellant should show cause why the defendant should not depart without day." On the 20th the arguments were resumed by the appellant's counsel; but the defendant was ordered to " be discharged from the appeal, and to be allowed to go forth without bail."

Though the rigid application of the letter of the law thus a second time saved this unfortunate man from punishment, nothing could remove the conviction of his guilt from the public mind. Shunned by all who knew him, his very name became an object of terror, and he soon afterwards attempted to proceed to America; but the sailors of the vessel in which he was about to embark refused to go to sea with a character on board who, according to their fancy, was likely to produce so much ill-luck to the voyage, and he was compelled to conceal himself until another opportunity was afforded him to make good his escape.

The " trial by battle," which in this case was so remarkably claimed, may be thus described:—

When the privilege of *trial by battle* was claimed by the appellee, the judges had to consider whether, under the circumstances, he was entitled to the exercise of such privilege; and his claim thereto having been admitted, they fixed a day and place for the combat, which was conducted with the following solemnities:—

A piece of ground was set out, of sixty feet square, enclosed with lists, and on one side was a court erected for the judges of the Court of Common Pleas, who attended there in their scarlet robes; and also a bar for the learned serjeants at law. When the court was assembled,

proclamation was made for the parties, who were accordingly introduced into the area by the proper officers, each armed with a *baton*, or
staff of an ell long, tipped with horn, and bearing a four-cornered leather
target for defence.   The combatants were bare-headed and bare-footed,
the appellee with his head shaved, the appellant as usual, but both
dressed alike.   The appellee pleaded Not Guilty, and threw down his
glove, and declared he would defend the same by his body; the appellant took up the glove, and replied, that he was ready to make good the
appeal body for body.   And thereupon the appellee taking the Bible
in his right hand, and in his left the right hand of his antagonist, swore
to this effect :—

" Hear this, O man, whom I hold by the hand, who callest thyself [John]
by the name of baptism, that I, who call myself [Thomas], by the name of
baptism, did not feloniously murder thy father [William] by name, nor am
anyway guilty of the said felony.   So help me God and the saints; and this
I will defend against thee by my body, as this Court shall award."

To which the appellant replied, holding the Bible and his antagonist's
hand, in the same manner as the other :—

" Hear this, O man, whom I hold by the hand, who callest thyself [Thomas]
by the name of baptism, that thou art perjured, because that thou feloniously
didst murder my father [William] by name.   So help me God and the
saints; and this I will prove against thee by my body, as this Court shall
award."

Next an oath against sorcery and enchantment was taken by both the
combatants in this or a similar form :—

" Hear this, ye justices, that I have this day neither ate, drank, nor have
upon me neither bone, stone, or grass; or any enchantment, sorcery, or
witchcraft, whereby the law of God may be abased, or the law of the devil
exalted.   So help me God and his saints."

The battle was thus begun, and the combatants were bound to fight
until the stars appeared in the evening.   But if the appellee were so
far vanquished that he could not or would not fight any longer, he was
adjudged to be hanged immediately; and then, as well as if he were
killed in battle, Providence was deemed to have determined in favour
of the truth, and his blood was declared attainted.   But if he killed the
appellant, or could maintain the fight from sun-rising till the stars
appeared in the evening, he was acquitted.   So also, if the appellant
became recreant, and pronounced the word *craven*, he lost his *liberam
legem*, and became infamous; and the appellee recovered his damages,
and was for ever quit, not only of the appeal, but of all indictments
likewise of the same offence.

There were cases where the appellant might counterplead, and oust
the appellee from his trial by battle : these were vehement presumption
or sufficient proof that the appeal was true ; or where the appellant was
under fourteen, or above sixty years of age, or was a woman or a priest,
or a peer, or, lastly, a citizen of London, because the peaceful habits
of the citizens were supposed to unfit them for battle.

It is almost needless to add, that this remnant of barbarity has now
ceased to exist, an act of parliament, the introduction of which was
attributable to the above case, having been passed to abolish it.

THE CATO STREET CONSPIRACY.

ARTHUR THISTLEWOOD, RICHARD TIDD, JAMES INGS, WILLIAM DAVIDSON, AND JOHN THOMAS BRUNT;

EXECUTED FOR HIGH TREASON.

To many of our readers probably the name of Thistlewood will be familiar, as that of a man deeply connected with a plot, generally known as the Cato Street Conspiracy, which aimed at the assassination of the whole of the then ministry, and the consequent overthrow of the government of the country.

It was not until the 24th February, 1820, that the public were made aware of the existence of the infernal machinations of this band of desperadoes, and then only did they learn it through the medium of the public press, which at once announced its existence and its frustration. Ere the morning had passed, however, a proclamation was plentifully distributed throughout the leading thoroughfares of the metropolis, offering a reward of £1000 for the apprehension of the notorious Arthur Thistlewood, on a charge of high treason and murder, and denouncing the heaviest penalties against all who should harbour or conceal him from justice.

It would appear that it had been long known to the government, that a plan was in meditation for the murder of all the members of the administration, and that Thistlewood was one of the originators of and prime movers in the horrid design ; but, in accordance with the system which then existed, of waiting until the crime should be all but matured, in order to secure the conviction of the offenders, they determined to make no effort to crush the scheme until the period should arrive when their own safety should render it necessary. The conspirators meanwhile having weighed various plans and projects for the accomplishment of their object, eventually determined to select the evening of Wednesday the 23rd of February as that on which they would carry out their plot, and it was deemed advisable that this night should be fixed upon, because it became known to them by an announcement in the news-papers, that a cabinet dinner would then be held at the house of Lord Harrowby in Grosvenor-square. Contemptible as the means possessed by the conspirators were to carry their design fully into execution, it is certain, from the confession of one of them, that the first part of their project was planned with so much circumstantial exactness, that the assassination of all the ministers would have been secured. It would appear that it was arranged, that one of the party should proceed to Lord Harrowby's house with a parcel addressed to his lordship, and that when the door opened, his companions should rush in, bind, or, in case of resistance, kill the servants, and occupy all the avenues of the house, while a select band proceeded to the chamber where the ministers were at dinner, and massacred the whole of them indiscriminately. To increase the confusion hand-grenades were prepared, which it was in-tended should be thrown lighted into the several rooms ; and one of the party engaged to bring away the heads of lords Castlereagh and Sid-mouth in a bag which he had provided for that purpose.

Thus far the conspirators might probably have carried their plans into effect ; but of the schemes for a general revolution, which these men, whose number never exceeded thirty, appear to have considered themselves capable of accomplishing, we cannot seriously speak. Among other arrangements the Mansion House, selected as we suppose for its proximity to the Bank, was fixed upon for the " palace of the provisional government."

The place chosen for the final organization of their proceedings, and for collecting their force previous to immediate action, was a half-dilapidated tenement in an obscure street called Cato-street, near the Edgware-road. The premises were composed of a stable, with a loft above, and had been for some time unoccupied. The people in the neighbourhood were ignorant that the stable was let, till the day fixed upon for the perpetration of their atrocious purpose, when several persons, some of whom carried sacks and other packages, were seen to go in and out, carefully locking the door after them.

The information upon which ministers proceeded, in frustrating ·the schemes of the conspirators, was derived from a man named Edwards, who pretended to enter into their views, for the purpose of betraying them.

Thus accurately informed of the intentions of the gang, measures were taken for their apprehension. A strong body of constables and police-officers, supported by a detachment of the Guards, was ordered to proceed to Cato-street, under the direction of Mr. (afterwards Sir

Richard) Birnie, the magistrate. On arriving at the spot they found that the conspirators had taken the precaution to place a sentinel below, and that the only approach to the loft was by passing up a ladder, and through a trap-door so narrow as not to admit more than one at a time. Ruthven led the way, followed by Ellis, Smithers, and others of the Bow-street patrol; and, on the door being opened, they discovered the whole gang, in number between twenty and thirty, hastily arming themselves. There was a carpenter's bench in the room, on which lay a number of cutlasses, bayonets, pistols, sword-belts, and a considerable quantity of ammunition. Ruthven, upon bursting into the loft, announced himself as a peace-officer, and called upon them to lay down their arms. Thistlewood stood near the door with a drawn sword, and Smithers advanced upon him, when the former made a lunge, and the unfortunate officer received the blade in his breast, and almost immediately expired.

About this time the Guards, who had been delayed in consequence of their having entered the street at the wrong end, arrived under the command of Captain (Lord Adolphus) Fitzclarence, and mounted the ladder; but as the conspirators had extinguished the lights, fourteen or fifteen of them succeeded in making their escape, and Thistlewood the chief of the gang, was among the number. A desperate conflict now took place, and at length nine persons were made prisoners; namely Ings, Wilson, Bradburn, Gilchrist, Cooper, Tidd, Monument, Shaw, and Davidson. The whole of them were immediately conveyed to Bow-street, together with a large quantity of arms, consisting of pistols, guns, swords, and pikes, and a large sack full of hand-grenades, besides other ammunition, which had been found in the loft. The same means, by which the conspiracy had been discovered, were now adopted in order to procure the discovery of the hiding-place of Thistlewood, and it was found that instead of his returning to his own lodgings in Stanhope-street, Clare Market, on the apprehension of his fellows, he had gone to an obscure house, No. 8, White-street, Moorfields. On the morning of the 24th February, at nine o'clock, Lavender and others of the Bow-street patrol were dispatched to secure his apprehension; and after planting a guard round the house, so as to prevent the possibility of his escaping, they entered a room on the ground-floor, where they found the object of their inquiry in bed, with his stockings and breeches on. In his pockets were found some ball-cartridges and flints, a black girdle or belt, which he was seen to wear at Cato-street, and a military sash.

On the 15th April, 1829, a special commission having been issued, the prisoners were arraigned at the bar of the Old Bailey on the charge of high treason, and also of murder, in having caused the death of the unfortunate Smithers. There were eleven prisoners—Arthur Thistlewood, William Davidson (a man of colour), James Ings, John Thomas Brunt, Richard Tidd, James Gilchrist, and Charles Cooper; and they all pleaded Not guilty to the charges preferred against them.

Counsel having been assigned to the prisoners, and the necessary forms having been gone through, Thistlewood received an intimation that his case would be taken on Monday morning the 17th of the same month, and the prisoners were remanded to that day.

At the appointed time, accordingly, Arthur Thistlewood was placed at the bar. He looked pale, but evinced his usual firmness. The jury having been sworn, and the indictment read, the attorney-general stated the case at great length, and twenty-five witnesses were examined in support of the prosecution, among whom were several accomplices, whose testimony was satisfactorily corroborated. Some of those who appeared to give evidence had been apprehended on the fatal night in Cato-street, but were now admitted witnesses for the crown. After a trial which occupied the court four days, Thistlewood was found Guilty of high treason. He heard the verdict with his wonted composure, seeming to have anticipated it; for when it was pronounced he appeared quite indifferent to what so fatally concerned him.

The evidence against Tidd, Ings, Davidson, and Brunt, whose trials came on next in succession, differed little from that upon which Thistlewood was convicted, and they were also found Guilty. Their trials being separate, occupied the court six days. On the evening of the tenth day the six remaining prisoners, at the suggestion of their counsel, pleaded Guilty, having been permitted to withdraw their former plea, by which they eventually escaped capital punishment.

On Friday, April the 28th, the eleven prisoners were brought up to receive sentence. When the usual question was put to Thistlewood by the clerk of arraigns, why he should not receive sentence to die, he pulled a paper from his pocket, and read as follows:—

" I am asked, my lord, what I have to say that judgment of death should not be passed upon me according to law. This to me is mockery —for were the reasons I could offer incontrovertible, and were they enforced even by the eloquence of a Cicero, still would the vengeance of my Lords Castlereagh and Sidmouth be satiated only in the purple stream which circulates through a heart more enthusiastically vibrating to every impulse of patriotism and honour than that of any of those privileged traitors to their country, who lord it over the lives and property of the sovereign people with barefaced impunity. The reasons which I have, however, I will now state—not that I entertain the slightest hope from your sense of justice or from your pity. The former is swallowed up in your ambition, or rather by the servility you descend to, to obtain the object of that ambition—the latter I despise. Justice I demand; if I am denied it, your pity is no equivalent. In the first place, I protest against the proceedings upon my trial, which I conceive to be grossly partial, and contrary to the very spirit of justice; but, alas! the judges, who have heretofore been considered the counsel of the accused, are now, without exception, in all cases between the crown and the people, the most implacable enemies of the latter. In every instance, the judges charge the jury to find the subject guilty; nay, in one instance, the jury received a reprimand, and that not in the gentlest terms, for not strictly obeying the imperious mandate from the bench.

" Many people, who are acquainted with the barefaced manner in which I was plundered by my Lord Sidmouth, will, perhaps, imagine that personal motives instigated me to the deed; but I disclaim them. My every principle was for the prosperity of my country; my every feeling, the height of my ambition, was the securing the welfare of my starving brother Englishmen. I keenly felt for their miseries; but when their miseries were laughed at, and when, because they dared to express those miseries, they were cut down by hundreds, inhumanly massacred and trampled upon, when infant babes were sabred in their mothers' arms, nay, when the breast from whence they drew the tide of life was severed from the body which supplied that life, my feelings became too intense, too excessive for endurance, and I resolved on vengeance—I resolved that the lives of the instigators should be the requiem to the souls of the murdered innocents.

" In this mood I met with George Edwards; and if any doubt should remain upon the minds of the public, whether the deed I meditated was virtuous or contrary, the tale I will now relate will convince them, that in attempting to exercise a power which the law had ceased to have, I was only wreaking national vengeance on a set of wretches unworthy of the name or character of men.

" This Edwards, poor and penniless, lived near Picket-street in the Strand, some time ago, without a bed to lie upon, or a chair to sit in. Straw was his resting-place; his only covering a blanket. Owing to his bad character, and his swindling conduct, he was driven from thence by his landlord. It is not my intention to trace him through his immorality; suffice it to say, that he was in every sense of the word a villain of the deepest atrocity. His landlord refused to give him a character. Some short time after this, he called upon his landlord again; but mark the change in his appearance—dressed like a lord, in all the folly of the reigning fashion. He now described himself as the right heir to a German baron, who had been some time dead; that Lords Castlereagh and Sidmouth had acknowledged his claims to the title and property, had interfered in his behalf with the German government, and supplied him with money to support his rank in society. From this period I date his career as a government spy.

" He got himself an introduction to the Spenceans—by what means I am not aware of; and thus he became acquainted with the reformers in general. When I met with Edwards, after the massacre at Manchester, he described himself as very poor; and, after several interviews, he proposed a plan for blowing up the House of Commons. This was not my view. I wished to punish the guilty only, and therefore I declined it. He next proposed that we should attack the ministers at the fête given by the Spanish ambassador. This I resolutely opposed, because the innocent would perish with the guilty: besides, there were ladies invited to the entertainment, and I, who am shortly to ascend the scaffold, shuddered with horror at the idea of that, a sample of which had previously been given by the agents of government at Manchester, and which the ministers of his majesty applauded. Edwards was ever ready at invention; and at length he proposed attacking them at a cabinet dinner, I asked, where were the means to carry his project into effect?

He replied, if I would accede, we should not want for means   He was as good as his word; by him, notwithstanding his apparent penury, the money was provided for purchasing the stores which your lordships have seen produced in court upon my trial.   He, who was never possessed of money to pay for a pint of beer, had always plenty to purchase arms or ammunition.   Amongst the conspirators, he was ever the most active; ever inducing people to join him, up to the last hour ere the undertaking was discovered.

" I had witnesses in court, who could prove they went to Cato-street, by appointment with Edwards, with no other knowledge or motive than that of passing an evening amongst his friends.   I could also have proved, that subsequent to the fatal transaction, when we met in Holborn, he endeavoured to induce two or three of my companions to set fire to houses and buildings in various parts of the metropolis.   I could prove that, subsequent to that again, he endeavoured to induce men to throw hand-grenades into the carriages of the ministers as they passed through the streets; and yet this man—the contriver, the instigator, the entrapper—is secured from justice and from exposure, by those very men who seek vengeance against the victims of his and their villainy.   To the attorney and solicitor general I cannot impute the clearest motives: their object seems to me to have been rather to secure a verdict against me, than to obtain a full and fair exposition of the whole affair since its commencement.   If their object was justice alone, why not bring Edwards as a witness, if not as an accomplice? but no, they knew that by keeping him in the back-ground, my proofs, ay, my incontrovertible proofs, of his being a hired spy, the suggester and promoter, must, according to the rules of court, also be excluded.   Edwards and his accomplices arranged matters in such a manner as that his services might be dispensed with on the trial, and thus were the jury cut off from every chance of ascertaining the real truth.   Adams, Hieden, and Dwyer were the agents of Edwards; and truly he made a most admirable choice, for their invention seems to be inexhaustible.

" With respect to the immorality of our project, I will just observe, that the assassination of a tyrant has always been deemed a meritorious action.   Brutus and Cassius were lauded to the very skies for slaying Cæsar; indeed, when any man, or any set of men, place themselves above the laws of their country, there is no other means of bringing them to justice, than through the arm of a private individual.   If the laws are not strong enough to prevent them from murdering the community, it becomes the duty of every member of that community to rid the country of its oppressors.   High treason was committed against the people at Manchester, but justice was closed against the mutilated, the maimed, and the friends of those who were upon that occasion indiscriminately massacred.   The Prince, by the advice of his ministers, thanked the murderers, still reeking in the gore of their hapless victims.   If one spark of honour, if one spark of independence still glimmered in the breasts of Englishmen, they would have risen to a man.   Insurrection then became a public duty; and the blood of the victims should have been the watch word to vengeance on their murderers.   The banner of independence should have floated in the gale, that brought their wrongs and their sufferings to the metropolis. Such, however, was not the case; Albion is still in the chains of slavery. I quit it without regret: I shall soon be consigned to the grave,—my body will be immured beneath the soil whereon I first drew breath,—my only sorrow is, that that soil should be a theatre for slaves, for cowards, for despots. My motives, I doubt not, will hereafter be justly appreciated. I will now conclude, therefore, by stating, that I shall consider myself as murdered, if I am to be executed on the verdict obtained against me by the refusal of the court to hear my evidence.

" I could have proved Dwyer to be a villain of the blackest dye; for, since my trial, an accomplice of his, named Arnold, has been capitally convicted at this very bar for obtaining money under circumstances of an infamous nature. I seek not pity; I demand but justice. I have not had a fair trial, and upon that ground I protest that judgment ought not to be passed against me."

The Lord Chief Justice, during the reading of this address, more than once interposed, to prevent the prisoner from either seeking to justify assassination, or slandering the characters of witnesses who had appeared to give evidence in that court. The prisoner, however, proceeded to read till he had finished what had been written on the paper in his hand. His manner was rapid and confused; and the mode in which he pronounced several words gave abundant evidence that the paper was not his own composition.

The other prisoners having been separately asked in the same manner proceeded severally to address the court—all, however, nearly to the same purport as Thistlewood—some at considerable length, and others contenting themselves by saying that they were drawn in by Edwards.

The crier of the court now proclaimed silence in the usual manner, while sentence of death was being passed upon the prisoners;—and the Lord Chief Justice then proceeded to address the prisoners severally by their respective names.

After a most admirable and affecting speech, he passed sentence in the usual form upon them, directing that after they should have been hanged, their heads should be severed from their bodies, and their bodies divided into four quarters, which should be at the disposal of his majesty.

The execution of Thistlewood, Ings, Brunt, Davidson, and Tidd, took place on the following Monday, at Newgate. Davidson was the only prisoner who did not reject religious consolation; and Thistlewood, when on the scaffold, turned away from the ordinary with an expression of indifference and contempt.

Thistlewood having been first called upon to ascend the gallows, did so with much alacrity; and he was immediately followed by Tidd, who shook hands with all his companions, except Davidson, who was standing apart from the rest. At the moment he was going out, Ings seized him by the hand, exclaiming with a shout of laughter, " Come, give us your hand; good bye !" but the remark was coldly received by the unfortunate convict, who dropped a tear, at the same time making

some observation with regard to his "wife and daughter." Ings, however, with the most astonishing degree of levity, cried out "Come, my
old cock-o'-wax, keep up your spirits, it will be all over soon." Tidd
appeared to squeeze his hand, and then attempted to run up the steps
to the scaffold. In his haste and agitation he stumbled, but quickly
recovered himself, and, with a species of hysterical action, jumped upon
the stage, and there stamped his feet, as if anxious for the executioner to
perform his dreadful office. He was received by the gazing multitude
with loud cheers, which he acknowledged by repeated bows. While the
executioner was fixing the fatal noose, he appeared to recognise a friend
at an opposite window, and nodded to him with much ease and fami-
liarity of manner. He repeatedly turned round and surveyed the
assembled mob; and catching sight of the coffins, which were ranged
behind the gallows, he smiled upon them with affected indifference and
contempt. While waiting for the completion of the preparations for the
execution of those whom he had left behind him in the press-room, he,
as well as Thistlewood, was observed repeatedly to refresh himself by
sucking an orange. Upon Mr. Cotton's approaching him, he also, like
that prisoner, rejected his proffered services.

Ings was the next who was summoned, and while on the scaffold he
exhibited the same indecent levity of manner which he had shown in the
press-room. He laughed, while he sucked an orange; and on his being
called, he screamed with a sort of mad effort,

"Oh! give me Death or Liberty!"

to which Brunt, who stood near him, rejoined, "Ay, to be sure; it is
better to die free than to live like slaves."

On being earnestly and charitably desired to turn their attention to
more serious subjects, and to recollect the existence of a God, into whose
presence they would soon be ushered, Brunt said, "I know there is a
God;" and Ings, agreeing to this, added, "that he hoped he would be
more merciful to them than they were then."

Just as the hatch was opening to admit him to the steps of the scaffold,
he turned round to Brunt, and, smiling, shook him by the hand, and then
with a loud voice cried out, "Remember me to King George the
Fourth; God bless him, and may he have a long reign!" Then recollecting that he had left off the suit of clothes in which he had been tried,
but which after his conviction he had exchanged for his old slaughtering
jacket, because, as he said, he was resolved that Jack Ketch should have
no coat of his, he desired his wife might have what clothes he had thrown
off. He then said to Mr. Davies, one of the turnkeys, "Well, Mr.
Davies, I am going to find out the great secret." He was again proceeding to sing,

"Oh! give me Death or Liberty!"

when he was called to the platform, upon which he leaped and bounded
in the most frantic manner. Then turning himself round towards Smithfield, and facing the very coffin that was soon to receive his mutilated
body, he raised his pinioned hands as well as he could, and leaning
forward, with savage energy, roared out three distinct cheers to the

people, in a voice of the most frightful and discordant hoarseness. But it was pleasing to remark, that these unnatural yells of desperation, which were evidently nothing more than the ravings of a disordered mind, or the ebullitions of an assumed courage, were not returned by the motley mass of people who heard them.

Davidson was the next summoned; and it is truly gratifying to state the difference that marked the character and conduct of him who had derived his fortitude to face death, and all its awful preparations, from other principles and sources than those from which the others appear to have borrowed their wild determination. He had paid earnest and devoted attention to the consolatory offices bestowed upon him by the ordinary of the jail; and when he was called upon to ascend the scaffold, he did so with a firm and steady step, but with that respectful humiliation which became his situation. He gently bowed to the people before him, and continued fervently praying with Mr. Cotton until the last duty of the executioner was performed.

The last summoned to the fatal platform was Brunt, whose conduct presented nothing particularly worthy of remark. The whole of the necessary arrangements were completed within a very few minutes after he had ascended the drop; and the fatal signal being given, the bolt was withdrawn, and the whole of the men almost instantly died. When their bodies had hung for half an hour, a new character entered upon the scaffold—the person who was to perform that part of the sentence which required the deceased men to be decapitated. He was masked; and, from the ready and skilful manner in which he performed his office, it was supposed by many that he was a surgeon. The heads were exhibited successively at the corners of the stage; and the whole ceremony having now been completed, the bodies were carried into the interior of the jail in the coffins which had been prepared for them.

It will be observed that there were six prisoners remaining, upon whom sentence was not executed. Of these, Gilchrist, who in reality turned out to be no party to the plot, received his majesty's pardon, and the other five were transported for life.

Having thus detailed the circumstances of this most diabolical conspiracy, we shall now give a brief biography of its principal promoters.

Arthur Thistlewood was a native of Horncastle, in Lincolnshire, where he was born in the year 1770. His father was a land steward to a most respectable family in the neighbourhood, and maintained through life an unblemished reputation. The subject of this sketch was, early in life, put to school with a view to his being educated as a land-surveyor; but having exhibited a disinclination for business, at the age of twenty-one, through the instrumentality of his friends, he obtained a lieutenancy in the militia, which he subsequently exchanged for a like commission in a marching regiment. He shortly afterwards married a lady possessed, as he supposed, of a fortune of £10,000; but, upon his proceeding to make inquiries, he found that she was entitled only to a life interest in the money, and that on her decease it would revert to a distant relation. Sixteen months after this marriage, Mrs. Thistlewood died in childbed, and her husband was left without a shilling. He had, how-

ever, retained his commission, and at the commencement of the revolu-
tionary war he accompanied his regiment to the West Indies; but he
soon gave up his rank, and, quitting the army, proceeded to America.
From thence he sailed to France, where he arrived soon after the fall
of the tyrant Robespierre; and there he became fully initiated into all
the feelings and doctrines of the revolutionists. He afterwards entered
the French army, and was present at several battles; and, although a
person of moderate capacity, he obtained a considerable knowledge of
military tactics. He, was, besides a good swordsman, and possessed
undeniable courage. His habitual hatred of oppression, it appears,
involved him in many disputes; and it is but justice to say that most
of these redound to his credit. After the peace of Amiens, he returned
to England, and found himself possessed of a considerable estate, which
accrued to him on the death of a relative; but his evil genius still accompanied him. He sold his property to a person at Durham for
£10,000, who becoming a bankrupt before the money was paid, Thistlewood found himself again reduced to comparative poverty.

His father and brother, both of whom resided in Lincolnshire, now
took a farm and stocked it for him; but, in consequence of the high rent
and taxes, he found himself an annual loser by the speculation, and, in
consequence, abandoned agriculture. Previous to this, however, he
had been married to his second wife, Miss Wilkinson, of Horncastle, a
woman who perfectly coincided in the political opinions of her husband.
Driven from the country, he repaired to London with his wife, and
contracted an acquaintance with the Spenceans. A propensity to
gaming seems to have been the first step to his ruin. In early life he
lost considerable sums at the *hells* of London, and this vicious habit did
not abandon him in his later years.

In London, his constant companions were the Watsons, Evans, and
others of the same character: and the consequence of this connexion
was his apprehension and trial, on a charge of high treason, with Dr.
Watson, and others, from which he escaped by the verdict of the jury.
This might have taught him prudence; but he was scarcely released from
incarceration when he sent a challenge, to fight a duel, to Lord Sidmouth;
the consequence of which was a motion in the Court of King's Bench, and
he was sentenced to six months' imprisonment in Horsham Jail.

Before this last confinement his dress was genteel, and his air that of
a military man; but, after his release from Horsham Jail, his appearance indicated extreme poverty.

Oppressed by want, and instigated by revenge, he forgot the lessons
misfortune should have taught him; and listening to the sanguinary
suggestions of others, he entered but too eagerly into the plot for his connexion with which he was executed. The police watched his movements,
and his every word and action were reported to the secretary of state.
Strange, indeed, was the infatuation he laboured under; and, if we look
upon him as perfectly sane, his conduct must appear unaccountable.

In person Thistlewood was tall and thin; his countenance was dark,
but by no means expressive. He had no family by either of his wives,
but a natural son took leave of him on the day before his execution.

Richard Tidd was born at Grantham, in the year 1773, and was brought up to the trade of a shoemaker. At the age of sixteen years he quitted his master, and went to Nottingham. Having lived there until he reached the age of nineteen, he proceeded to London. Here he appears to have taken considerable interest in the politics of the day; but having, in the year 1803, committed perjury, by swearing himself a freeholder, in order to enable him to vote for Sir Francis Burdett as member for Middlesex, he fled to Scotland to avoid prosecution. Having resided there during five years, he then returned to England, and, after a short stay at Rochester, proceeded once again to the metropolis, where he became a party to the plot for which Colonel Despard and others were executed, but escaped their fate by being temporarily absent from town. During the war he enlisted into more than half the regiments of the crown, but had no sooner received the bounty money, than he deserted. In 1818 he commenced his last residence in London, and he then exhibited violent political feelings. Having become acquainted with Brunt, he was introduced by him to Edwards, and the assumed violence of the latter suiting his feelings well, he eagerly closed with every proposition which he made, however desperate it might be. It is not a little remarkable that he had always an impression on his mind that he should be hanged, and he frequently declared his belief to this effect to his friends. He left a wife and daughter behind him to deplore the truth of his prediction.

James Ings was the son of a respectable tradesman in Hampshire; and being possessed of a considerable property when he came of age, he married a respectable young woman, and entered into business as a butcher, at Portsmouth. Trade growing bad and his property having decreased, some of his tenements were sold, and he came up to London in 1818, with a little ready money, produced by the sale of a house, and opened a butcher's shop at the west end of the town. He could, however, get no business, and in a few months gave up the shop; and, with a few pounds he had left, he opened a coffee-house in Whitechapel. Here he sold, besides coffee, political pamphlets; and having read the different Deistical publications, from being a churchman he became a confirmed Deist.

For some weeks before the Cato-street discovery, Ings was in the utmost distress, quite penniless; and the means of subsistence were actually supplied to him by Edwards. At his instigation, also, he hired a room, in which he lodged, which was sufficiently capacious to contain a very considerable portion of the arms and ammunition of the gang.— He left a wife and four children to deplore his ignominious death.

William Davidson was born in the year 1786, at Kingston in Jamaica, and was the second son of Mr. Attorney-General Davidson, a man of considerable legal knowledge and talent. His mother was a native of the West Indies, and a woman of colour. He was sent to England when very young, for the purpose of receiving an education suitable to his condition of life. After some time he was apprenticed to a respectable attorney at Liverpool, at whose office he remained near three years when he became tired of confinement, and ran away from his master.

He now entered on board a merchantman, and on his first voyage was impressed. He arrived in England about six months afterwards, and wrote to his father's friend a supplicatory letter, and then, at his own particular desire, he was apprenticed to a cabinet-maker in Liverpool.

Davidson, though a man of colour, had a prepossessing person, and was upon the point of marriage with the daughter of a respectable tradesman at Liverpool, when, however, the match was broken off by his friends. He then took a passage on board a West-India merchantman, intending to return to his father; but he was again impressed on the voyage. On his returning to port, he took the first opportunity of running away, and having obtained some money from his friends, he got work as a journeyman at Litchfield. He subsequently paid his addresses to a Miss Salt, who was possessed of about £7000 of her own money; but her friends disapproving of the match, he became unsettled in his mind, and indisposed for business; and although his mother supplied him with £1200 to commence trade on his own account at Birmingham, in the course of twelve months he spent the whole of that sum, and again repaired to London. Here he obtained work, and was eventually married to a Mrs. Lane, a widow with four children, who lived at Walworth, with whose assistance he began trade on his own account. Success, however, did not attend him, and he was compelled to remove to London, and to take a lodging at Mary-le-bone. While here, he appears to have joined the conspirators, into whose plans he entered with great willingness. He left two children of his own by his wife, both of whom were under four years of age.

John Thomas Brunt, was born in Union-street, Oxford-street; where his father carried on business as a tailor. He was for some time employed in the shop of a shoemaker, and subsequently became an excellent workman in that business, and up to the age of twenty-three was the chief support of his mother, his father having died while he was yet young. At that age he married a respectable young woman, named Welch. On the 1st of May 1806, she brought him a boy, who was fourteen years of age on the day his unfortunate father suffered the sentence of the law. Brunt was thirty-eight years of age.

The following particulars with regard to Edwards, whose name so frequently occurs during the preceding narrative, will enable the reader to form a just estimate of his character.

It appears that he had been originally a modeller, and kept a little shop in Fleet-street, where he sold plaster-of-Paris images. His poverty had been always apparent until a few months previous to the Cato-street plot, when there is no doubt he accepted the wages of government, and became a spy. For this office he appears to have been admirably adapted, as he was shrewd, artful, and unprincipled. His former acquaintance with the Spenceans procured him the confidence of some of its deluded members; and through them he got acquainted with Thistlewood and the others, and there is little doubt that the Cato-street plot was "got up" by him, though he found the unfortunate men who became its victims willing instruments in his hands.

IKEY SOLOMON'S ESCAPE.

IKEY *alias* ISAAC SOLOMON,

TRANSPORTED FOR RECEIVING STOLEN GOODS.

THERE are few offenders whose name and character are more universally known than Ikey Solomon's; but there are few also with regard to whom more certain information cannot be obtained. The following brief particulars, we believe, are correct; but the difficulty of procuring positive knowledge upon the subject must prove an excuse for the shortness of our memoir.

Solomon was born in the neighbourhood of Petticoat-lane in the year 1785, of poor parents, who, as their name imports, were of the Jewish persuasion. At an early age young Ikey was compelled to exert himself to procure his own living; for it is a custom which exists among the poorer classes of the Jews, that every child shall be early instructed in habits of industry. At the age of eight years, therefore, he was dispatched into the streets with a supply of oranges and lemons, which constituted his first stock in trade. The profits of his business as a fruiterer were not deemed by the young Jew a sufficient remuneration for his labours, and the profession of a *sham ringer,* as it was technically termed, or of a passer of base coin, was added by him to that which he openly carried on, and his youth served him materially in enabling him to escape detection.

At the age of fourteen years he had acquired considerable knowledge

I I

of the general habits of thieves, and he is reported to have practised picking pockets, when opportunity offered, with great success. As he grew older, however, his person and proceedings became known, and, apprehending that some unpleasant consequences might arise from his carrying on so dangerous a profession, he determined to quit it, and to join a gang engaged in one no less enterprising, but attended with less cause of fear—that of duffing. By this means he obtained a wide connexion, while the sums which he realised amply repaid him for the change which he had made in his mode of life. The business of a fence, or receiver of stolen goods, in which afterwards he became so notorious, appears, even at this early period of his life, to have struck his fancy; and although the extent of his trade was limited, by reason of his want of the necessary capital to carry it on, his purchases being confined to the produce of the robberies of area sneaks and young pick-pockets, he acquired much celebrity amongst his fellows in the same business.

After some time, from some unexplained cause, he quitted this mode of life, and joined a gang of thieves associated at the west end of the town. Always avaricious, he was guilty of unfair play even among his " pals," and the old adage of " honour among thieves " was set at nought by him in his division of the spoil which he obtained in the course of his daily exertions. For this breach of good faith he was expelled the community, and he determined upon making an effort in his own behalf, single-handed. His good fortune now forsook him, and, after a very short practice, he was taken into custody for stealing a " dumby," or pocket-book. This was the first occasion on which he had any reason to fear the consequences of his numerous thefts. In the city, according to his own account, he had been frequently in custody, but had escaped by feeing the officers; but his apprehension having now taken place in " the county," as it is usually denominated, or beyond the city bounds, he knew that he stood little chance of escaping by such means.

For this offence he was tried at the Old Bailey in the year 1807, being then twenty-two years of age; and a conviction having followed, he was sentenced to transportation for life. He was removed to the hulks at Chatham, preparatory to his being sent to one of our penal colonies, but, by good luck, was permitted to remain in England, in the hope that he might reform. His uncle, it appears, was a slop-seller at this port, where he carried on a considerable, and, it was believed, a respectable trade. Through his instrumentality his nephew was retained in his native country; and, after six years, the fortunate Ikey obtained a pardon. A circumstance occurred, however, in reference to this event, which is worthy of notice. Ikey was not the only person of the same name who had been guilty of an offence against the laws of *meum* and *tuum*, and confined on board the same hulk. His equally unfortunate namesake, in the year 1813, by the exercise of influence, succeeded in obtaining a remission of his sentence, and a pardon and order for his discharge were sent down to Chatham. By an error, either of accident or design, but which it was we have no means of deciding, our hero was discharged instead of the person really intended. His surprise and gratitude at this unexpected favour induced him, on his return to London, to proceed to the Home Office to express his thanks for his liberation; but here, to his dismay, he was informed that there was some mistake—that he was not the person intended to be pardoned, and that he must return to his ship. He had prudence enough to do that at once, which he knew he would be compelled to do eventually; but the circumstances operated so much in his favour, that in three months afterwards a genuine pardon in his name was received, which once again sent him to perform his part upon the stage of life.

His first employment was to all appearance an honest one. He was engaged by his uncle at Chatham as a barker, or salesman; and, in the course of a couple of years, he realised a sum of £150, with which he determined to start in business for himself. He therefore proceeded to London, and in a short time we find him possessed of a house and shop in Bell-alley, Winfield-street. He lost no time in renewing his acquaintance with some of his former associates, and he found that many of them, who had escaped the fangs of the police so long, had now become expert thieves, or experienced housebreakers. His old trade of a " fence " appeared to him the most profitable, and, at the same time, the best in every other respect, in which he could embark, and his desire to deal in stolen goods was soon circulated among his connexions. For this business his general knowledge admirably adapted him, and he speedily obtained as much business as his small capital would enable him to get through. As every transaction, however, increased his means, so his sphere of action became more extended, and ere long he was engaged fully in every species of business which came within the usual course of persons engaged in the same profession. Forged notes, or " queer screens," as they were called, afforded him means of speculation, which produced the most profitable results; but the danger of carrying on this branch of his trade, arising from the vigilance of the officers employed by the Bank of England for its suppression, at length determined him to give it up, and to confine his operations to that which he looked upon as a safer game, the purchase and disposal of the produce of the robberies of his friends.

In this line he was probably one of the most successful in London. Every year afforded him new opportunities of extending his connexion, and the profits which he obtained were enormous. His house was looked upon as the universal resort of almost all the thieves of the metropolis; but so cautiously and so cunningly did he manage his transactions, as to render every effort of the police to procure evidence of his guilt unavailing. His purchases were, for the most part, confined to small articles, such as jewellery, plate, &c.; and in his house, under his bed, he had a receptacle for them, closed by a trap-door, so nicely fitted that it escaped every examination which was made. In the space between the flooring and the ceiling of the lower room, there were abundant means to conceal an extent of valuable property which was quite astonishing.

Solomon's trade was now at its height, and he found that one house would be sufficient to contain all his property. He had been married some years before to a person of the same persuasion with himself; but it appears that constancy was not one of the virtues of which he was able to boast. It suggested itself to him, therefore, that while a second house would enable him to secrete a considerable quantity of additional property, he might also hide there from his wife a new object, to whom his affections had united him. With these double views, he took a house in Lower Queen-street, Islington, unknown to his own family, in which he followed out the plan which he had laid down for his guidance. The lady and the valuables were placed in it.

At about this period, however, a very extensive robbery of watches and jewellery took place in Cheapside, in which there is no doubt Solomon participated in the character of receiver. The excitement produced by the occurrence raised considerable alarm in his mind lest he should be discovered and apprehended, and he determined on a trip to Birmingham, in order that the affair might blow over. During his absence from home, his wife discovered his Islington retreat; and her anger, as may be supposed, was not expressed to him in the gentlest or most becoming way upon his return.

This discovery, and the still pending investigation of the circumstances of the robbery in Cheapside, created so much alarm in his mind, that he determined to emigrate to New South Wales, taking with him all his property. His arrangements were commenced; but his wife, whose fears pictured to her the sailing of her husband with her rival, and her own abandonment in England, most strongly opposed the plan. Ikey, however, persisted in carrying out his expressed intention, when his apprehension at his Islington abode effectually prevented the fulfilment of his plans. The charges preferred against him were those of receiving stolen goods, and Ikey was committed to Newgate for trial. Property, it was said, to a very large amount had been seized, amongst which many articles which had been stolen were identified. Whilst awaiting his trial, a plan of escape was concocted, which was completely successful, and which was conducted in the following manner :—

It is a part of the law of the land, that every prisoner who is in custody, no matter what his offence, is entitled to apply to a judge of one of the superior courts, to be admitted to bail. The application is made for a writ of *habeas corpus,* upon which the prisoner is taken from the prison where he is confined, before the judge, in whose presence the matter is to be argued. Solomon's friends determined to adopt this course; and the application being made, the writ was granted, and a certain day was fixed for the argument. The prisoner, in obedience to the writ, was sent in the custody of two officers to Westminster; and as the trio passed Bridge-street, Blackfriars, it was proposed that they should have a coach. The proposition appeared to be anticipated by a man, whose vehicle was near the head of the rank, and his carriage was immediately engaged. The three men entered it, and were driven to Westminster; but when they arrived there, the judge was found to be engaged. An adjournment took place to a neighbouring public-house, and while there, Mrs. Solomon joined the party with one or two friends, and brandy and water was speedily introduced in abundance. The turnkeys were not sparing in their libations, but were interrupted in their orgies by the announcement that the judge was ready. The argument took place—the bail was refused, as it was known it would be—and a second adjournment to the public-house took place. One more glass was swallowed, and Ikey, his wife, and the two turnkeys, once more entered the vehicle. A short ride threw Smart, the head turnkey, into a species of stupor; and in Fleet-street, Mrs. Solomon was so affected by her husband's danger, as to fall into fits. Solomon entreated the under turnkey, who still remained awake, not to take him to prison, until he had set his wife down at a friend's house, and this request, being probably backed by a fee, was granted. The coach, which it is almost needless to say was driven by one of Ikey's relations, proceeded to Petticoat-lane, and there pulling up at a house, the door was suddenly opened. Ikey popped out, ran into a house, the door of which stood open, but was closed immediately after him, through the passage, into a house at the back, and again through an interminable variety of windings, until at length he was lodged in a place of security. The turnkey was almost as stupified as his fellow at this surprising disappearance of his prisoner; and Mrs. Solomon having speedily recovered from her fits, the two jailors were left to find their way back to Newgate, and to tell their tale at their leisure. The turnkeys, it is almost needless to say, had been drugged.

This escape was so admirably conducted, that all traces of Solomon were lost, and, notwithstanding the most strenuous exertions of the police, no tidings of him could be obtained. For two months, it appears, he lay concealed at Highgate, and at the expiration of that time he found means to quit the country in a Danish vessel for Copenhagen, from whence in about three months he proceeded to New York.

Ever active in " turning a penny," he was soon engaged in his old trade in forged notes, which was here carried on to a great extent. He became convinced, however, that he could make money by other means also, and he wrote to his wife, desiring her to send him a quantity of cheap watches, which he had good reason to believe would turn to good account. In this letter, according to his own statement, he charged his wife to send him none but " righteous " (honestly obtained) watches, and not to touch one which had been got " on the cross;" but it appears she did not act up to his advice, for she was found guilty of receiving a watch knowing it to have been stolen, which turned out to be one of those which she was about to ship off to the new world to her husband, to be employed by him in his new speculation. For this offence she was sentenced to be transported for fourteen years; and, in obedience to her sentence, she was conveyed to Van Dieman's Land. Ikey, in his account of this affair, does not scruple to assert, that his wife had in truth been guilty of no offence whatever; and he seeks to confirm his assertion by relating the circumstances under which the watch was obtained. He declares that there were some persons in England who had been so enraged at his escape, as to be determined to revenge themselves upon him by every means in their power. With this view they sought to tamper with one of his relations, then in custody, in order to procure the entrapment of his wife in some supposed illegal transaction. Mrs. Solomon at this time was engaged in the purchase of the watches for her husband, and she consulted some of her friends upon the best means of procuring them. The imprisoned relation about this time was set at liberty to carry out his scheme, and he being applied to, produced and sold to her the very watch for the possession of which eventually she was convicted. How far this is true, as regards the individual referred to, we cannot say; but we believe it to be impossible that villainy so gross as that which he imputes, could be connived at by any person holding a responsible public situation in the police.

Ikey, it seems, upon hearing of his wife's misfortune, found himself the object of suspicion where he was, and he determined that he would follow Mrs. Solomon; and, having assembled the family at Hobart Town, endeavour to alleviate her sufferings. In this place he proposed to strike out some new pursuit for their support; but he never imagined that the laws of England would pursue him in the very place to which he was about to proceed as a refuge from them.

Upon his arrival at Hobart Town, he lived for some time in comparative decency, having opened a general shop, which he conducted with much profit, and having also purchased a public-house, which he let to another person. But he soon found that his dreams of security were not to be realised. An order arrived from England for his apprehension, and he was hurried off by the next vessel sailing for London, to take his trial for the numerous offences with which he was charged. He had just time to transfer his property to his son before he sailed, and at length, on the 27th of June, 1830, he was once more lodged in Newgate, where he was confined in the Transport Yard, which was considered the most secure place in the prison.

At the following Old Bailey sessions he was indicted upon eight different charges, and his trial came on on Friday, the 9th of July 1830. His conduct throughout was remarkable for great firmness, which was increased by his being acquitted on the first and second days upon five of the indictments preferred against him. On the following Monday he was again placed at the bar, and then on the sixth and eighth charges verdicts of Guilty were returned. The verdict on the seventh indictment was one of Not guilty, owing to the absence of a material witness in India.

A point of law was raised as to the propriety of these convictions, and the prisoner was remanded, in order that the matter might be discussed before the superior judges. Solomon was kept in suspense during a period of ten months; but at length, on the 13th of May, 1831, he received an intimation that the opinion of the judges was against him, and sentence of seven years' transportation was passed on each indictment.

Upon this sentence he was conveyed to the hulks, and on the 31st of May, 1831, he once more sailed from Portsmouth. In obedience to an order made upon a petition which he had caused to be presented at the Home Office. he was conveyed to Hobart Town, where his family was, instead of to Sydney; and, upon his arrival at that place, he found his son still carrying on the business which he had commenced. By good conduct, Solomon eventually obtained for himself the rank of overseer of convicts, and we believe that he still retains that situation.

Some anecdotes of the mode in which he conducted his business in London will not be uninteresting, exhibiting as they do the general habits of receivers of stolen goods.

It may be admitted, as an established fact, that no man who does not possess very considerable connexions can attempt to carry on the business of a " fence " with success. An acquaintance and co-partnery with persons residing at the out-ports, and with the itinerant dealers in jewellery, travelling inland, are necessary to enable them to put off the proceeds of their dishonest dealings; for while, by the former, bank notes and other property, the identity of which cannot be destroyed, can be dispatched abroad, by the latter, watches and other articles of trifling value can be distributed among towns and villages in remote districts, from which it is unlikely they will ever find their way to the great mart of London, where they can be recognised. Diamonds, and other valuable stones, may be taken out and re-set according to another fashion, while the settings are destroyed; but in most instances receivers admit no articles into their houses until they are satisfied that they cannot be recognised. In the first of these respects Solomon was amply provided with associates, and he was too good a judge in most cases to permit any possibility of detection to arise. When a large robbery was contemplated, he was always apprised of it, and the place and time were fixed at which he should go and look over its produce. The first thing he said when he met the parties was, " Now I am to offer you a price for these things; first assist in removing all the marks, and then I will talk to you." When the goods consisted of linen or cloth, every means of identification was removed; the head and fag ends being cut off, and occasionally the list and selvage, if they were peculiar. The marks on the soles of boots and shoes were obliterated by hot irons, and those on the linings were as speedily removed by their being cut out, and others placed in their stead. After this, he found no difficulty in vending every species of property which could be converted into apparel, to the numerous ready-made and slop shops, in which trade so many Jews are engaged. Watches of great value, which could find purchasers only in large towns, were either metamorphosed by skilful hands, or sent to the continent. If a watch were valuable for its works more than its case, the interior was soon entombed in another. A boot and shoe-maker, some years since, in Princes-street, Soho, was, in one night, robbed of his stock, value £300; the whole was carried away in sacks in coaches, and the next morning found its way, before twelve o'clock, to the premises of our hero. By threats and offers to one of the coachmen, who who happened to be recognised by a servant in the neighbourhood, as having been at the door the night before, he was induced to give information of the place to which the goods had been conveyed. The shoemaker sent a man to watch the premises, while he went to seek for two officers; the man was in time to see the goods removed to the house of

Solomon. When the shoemaker and the officers arrived, they entered the premises, but Ikey defied them to touch an article, so carefully had the marks been removed. The shoemaker was compelled to admit that he could not swear to them, and at once saw that he stood no chance of procuring the restoration of his goods. Solomon then said that he had purchased them fairly, but, out of mere compassion for his loss, whether the goods had been his or not, he would sell them for the price which he had paid for them. The robbed man was glad to accept of these terms, and it cost him upwards of one hundred pounds to re-stock his shop with his own goods.

Solomon was allowed to be a most ready and superior judge of the intrinsic value of all kinds of property, from a glass bottle to a five hundred guinea chronometer; how it could be disposed of; and what was the value thieves generally estimated it at. He established among the rogues a regular rule of dealing, which is continued to this day, namely, to give a fixed price for all articles of the same denomination. For instance, a piece of linen was in his view a piece of linen, whether fine or coarse; the same with a piece of print, a silver watch, or a gold one: taking the good, as he used to tell the young and inexperienced thief, with the bad *vons*. By this plan he sometimes obtained very valuable watches at a moderate rate. He, however, outbid all his opponents in the purchase of stolen bank-notes; this he was for a long time enabled to do, in consequence of his connexion with Jews in Holland. All stolen bank-notes which come into the hands of those who buy them, are sent to the Continent, to pass in the way of purchases through some regular mercantile house, when they find their way, by remittances to London houses, into the Bank, where they must be paid. The price given by Solomon for large notes, was 15*s.* in the pound; and he calculated that on an average he could send them their circuit of safety for 1*s.* in the pound: thus securing for himself 4*s.* profit on each 20*s.*, that is twenty per cent., and this is now the regular price for stolen notes with the London fences.

At the time of Solomon's apprehension his chief store was in Rosemary-lane, and he was reported to have had goods of the value of £20,000 then collected there. A very great proportion of this property was seized, and Solomon bitterly complained of the manner in which he was deprived of his goods. A great portion of the articles were restored to their owners; but, as late as the year 1832, a considerable amount was sold, which was avowed to have belonged to this notorious offender.

HENRY STANYNOUGHT,

TRIED FOR THE MURDER OF HIS SON.

THIS melancholy case excited, at the time of its occurrence, almost universal sympathy, as well for the unfortunate victim of the attack, as for the miserable parent by whom that attack was made.

Mr. Stanynought was a stationer in a respectable way of business, residing in Connaught-terrace, Edgeware-road. On the morning of Friday, the 4th of September 1835, his shopman was horror-struck at perceiving his master run down stairs in a state of partial nudity, bleeding profusely from a wound which he had inflicted on his breast with a case-knife, which he carried in his hand. Rushing towards Mr. Stanynought, he at once was informed by him of the death of his son by his hands. An instant alarm was given; and the declaration of the wretched father, that he had killed his son, was found to be true. Mr. Stanynought and his son, aged about twelve years, it appears, had retired to rest in the same room on the previous evening; and in the course of the night the former was heard moving about by his servant. The body of the deceased child presented a melancholy spectacle. It was lying with the face towards the bed, and the poor boy had evidently died of suffocation. There was, however, a deep wound across the forehead, which seemed to have been dealt with some blunt instrument. Mr. Stanynought, upon being questioned, at once declared that the dreadful act had been committed by him. He said that he had long meditated the destruction of both his child and himself, and that he had burned charcoal in the room in which they slept on two nights without effect. On the previous evening he had taken laudanum; and in the course of the night he had struck his son with the boot-jack; but, finding his blows ineffectual, he had smothered him with a pillow.

Further inquiry at once elicited the fact that the wretched man was subject to occasional fits of insanity—a malady from which both his father and grandfather had suffered. The apprehension of the same disease displaying itself in his son, appeared to be the sole cause of the dreadful deed which he had committed.

At the coroner's inquest, held on Monday the 7th of September, the circumstances attending the death of the deceased were elicited, with the additional fact of the insanity of the father. Proof of this feature in the case before the coroner's jury, however, was unavailing, and a verdict of " Wilful Murder," was returned.

Between this time and the period of his trial, Mr. Stanynought almost completely recovered from the effects of the wound he had committed upon himself. On Friday, the 25th of September, the wretched man was put upon his trial at the Central Criminal Court, when his insanity being clearly proved, a verdict of acquittal was returned upon that ground.

He was therefore ordered to be detained during his majesty's pleasure, and was subsequently conveyed to a mad-house.

JOHN PEGSWORTH,

EXECUTED FOR MURDER.

THE murder of which this unfortunate man was convicted appears to be entirely unjustified by any of those circumstances, which, in some instances, form a palliative, small though it be, for offences of a similar description.

The object of his crime was Mr. John Holiday Ready, who carried on the business of a tailor and draper, at No. 125, Ratcliffe Highway. It appears that Pegsworth was a man in a decent station of life, occupying a situation as messenger in the tea-department of St. Katherine's Docks; and he at one time also pursued the trade of a tobacconist, in a shop opposite to that of Mr. Ready, No. 69, Ratcliffe Highway, which, however, only a short time before the murder, he had given up. In the course of his residence here, he became indebted to Mr. Ready in the amount of 20s., for a jacket which had been supplied to him for his son; but although he had been frequently pressed to pay the sum which was due, he always declined upon some frivolous ground. At length Ready, determined no longer to wait for his money, summoned his debtor to the Court of Requests; and Mrs. Ready having proved the debt, on the 10th of January, 1837, an order was made on the defendant to pay the amount with costs. On Pegsworth returning home, he expressed himself much exasperated at the conduct of Ready, and said that he would be " the death of him." His wife endeavoured to pacify him, but in vain ; and he went out, vowing vengeance against the man who, he said, had injured him. Proceeding through Ratcliffe Highway, he purchased a large knife, such as would be used in killing a pig, at the shop of a cutler ; and, armed with this formidable weapon, he went direct to the house of Ready. He entered the shop, and calmly and coolly conversed with Mrs. Ready; and her husband having invited him to sit down in the back parlour, he at once advanced towards him. For a few minutes he continued in conversation upon the subject of the debt, when presently he demanded to know whether his creditor intended to proceed upon the judgment which he had obtained? Mr. Ready answered decidedly in the affirmative, upon which he suddenly drew forth his knife, and stabbed the unfortunate man in the right breast. The murdered man exclaimed that he was stabbed, and instantly expired ; while his wife rushed frantically into the street, as soon as she discovered what had occurred, calling loudly for assistance. Several persons instantly ran into the house, and they found Pegsworth in the act of withdrawing the knife from the wound, but making no effort whatever to escape. He was immediately secured, and surgical aid was called in, but it was found that the knife of the assassin had passed through the principal arteries into the lungs, and that the unfortunate Mr. Ready was quite dead.

At a coroner's inquest held on the body of the deceased on Thursday the 12th of January, a verdict of " Wilful Murder" was returned against Pegsworth, and he was fully committed to Newgate for trial. Before his trial Pegsworth confessed that he had been guilty of the act with which he stood charged, but he declared that he was intoxicated, and in a high degree of excitement at the time. He professed the most sincere repentance for his act, and declared his intention to pass the remainder of his short life in prayers for forgiveness.

On Friday the 3d of February, the prisoner was arraigned on the indictment which had been preferred against him at the Central Criminal Court. He immediately confessed himself guilty of the offence imputed to him, and, notwithstanding the humane interference of the learned judge, refused to withdraw that plea.

On Tuesday the 7th of February, the prisoner was brought up to receive sentence, when the recorder addressed to him the following observations: " Let me implore you," said he, " to bethink yourself of the awful situation in which you stand, on the brink of eternity and of the grave, beyond which there is no room for repentance. The legislature, in cases of murder, has, by a recent statute, interposed an increased interval between conviction and condemnation, and between condemnation and the final execution of the dreadful sentence of the law. It has done so in its humanity, and consistently with sound policy ; but it has extended to the murderer a mercy which the murderer has not shown to his victim. The rash hand of the guilty individual who without warning hurries a fellow-creature to another world, cuts off from him the opportunity of approaching his Maker in prayer, or of preparing for that judgment which is painful for the best, and overwhelming for those who are not ready." [Here the prisoner became visibly affected.] " You will be afforded an interval for seeking that mercy at the throne of God which you cannot expect from the laws of man." The learned gentleman then passed the sentence of death upon the prisoner.

On Wednesday the 1st of March the case of the prisoner was reported to his Majesty, and he was ordered for execution on the following Tuesday, the 7th of March.

On that day the sentence was carried into effect; the wretched convict meeting his fate with becoming resignation.

ROBERT SALMON,

CONVICTED OF MANSLAUGHTER BY ADMINISTERING MORISON'S PILLS.

THIS case arose out of the extremely dangerous practice of administering quack medicines. Morison's Vegetable Pills have been for many years an article from the sale of which immense profits have been derived; but it is to be regretted that in more than one instance the life of the patient has been sacrificed by their undue and improper use.

At the Central Criminal Court Sessions, which commenced on Monday the 4th of April, 1836, Mr. Robert Salmon, a medicine-vender in Farringdon-street, was indicted for the manslaughter of Mr. John M'Kenzie, by administering to him certain large and excessive quantities of pills, composed of gamboge, cream of tartar, and other noxious and deleterious ingredients.

The deceased, it appeared, was the master of a vessel, and lived in the neighbourhood of the Commercial-road. He was induced to take some of Morison's pills as a purgative, upon the representations of a Mrs. Lane, a woman who was employed by his wife as a sempstress, and who sold the Hygeian medicines; and subsequently Mr. Salmon's aid having been claimed, on account of his suffering from rheumatism in the knee, he recommended increased and still-increasing doses, until at length the deceased became so ill that his life was placed in jeopardy. Medical aid was now called in, but it was too late, and death soon put an end to his sufferings. A *post-mortem* examination left no doubt that the medicine prescribed by the prisoner had been the cause of this termination of the case, and the present indictment was in consequence preferred.

On the part of the defendant, a great many persons were called from all parts of the kingdom, who stated, that they had taken large quantities of these pills with the very best results, as a means of cure for almost every species of malady to which the human frame is subject. One person stated that he had taken no fewer than twenty thousand of them in two years, and that he had found infinite relief from swallowing them in very large doses.

Mr. Justice Patteson left the case to the jury, who had to decide upon the facts which had been proved; and, after about half an hour's consideration, they found a verdict of " Guilty," with a recommendation to mercy, upon the ground that the defendant was not the compounder, but the vender only of the medicines.

On the following Saturday, the 9th of April, the defendant was brought up to receive judgment. The learned judge having sentenced him to pay a fine of £200, added, " I think it right to caution you, that in the event of your being again found guilty of conduct of a similar description, the character of your offence will be materially altered. I hope that the punishment which is now inflicted on you will deter others from rashly administering medicines, with the nature of which they are unacquainted, in large quantities, as the result may be fatal."

INAUGURATION OF UNIONISTS.

JAMES LOVELACE AND OTHERS, "THE DOR-CHESTER LABOURERS,"

TRANSPORTED FOR ADMINISTERING UNLAWFUL OATHS.

THE case of the "Dorchester labourers" attracted at the time a considerable degree of the public interest, principally from the circumstance that they were indicted and found guilty on a statute which had been generally supposed to have been intended to apply only to offences of a political nature,—a supposition favoured by the title and even the preamble of the act itself, which referred to the suppression of *seditious meetings;* whereas the offence of which these men were convicted was the administration of illegal oaths at meetings held for the purpose of the regulation of wages.

The names of the prisoners were James Lovelace, George Lovelace, Thomas Stanfield, James Hammet, and James Brine; and they were tried at the Dorchester assizes, on the 17th March, 1834. The charges preferred against them will more fully appear from the following summary of the statement by the counsel for the prosecution, and of the facts proved in evidence against them.

Mr. Gambier stated, that the charge against the prisoners was, that on a certain day in December, they, all together, or one of them, administered an unlawful oath to a person of the name of Legg, for the purpose of binding the party to whom it was administered not to disclose any illegal combination which had been formed, and not to inform or give evidence against any person associated with them, and not to reveal any unlawful oath which might be taken. The first part of the charge was, that the purport of the oath was to bind the party to obey the orders of a body of men not lawfully constituted. The indictment was framed on an Act of the 37th George III., cap. 123. The preamble of that act related to seditious meetings; but the enacting part was of a more general nature, including confederacies formed not merely for seditious purposes, but for any illegal purpose whatever; and his lordship would be aware, that there was an authority which had decided that the enacting part of a statute was not restrained by the preamble. One clause of the act related to oaths administered for the purpose of binding a party not to reveal an unlawful combination. The allegation in the indictment was, that the prisoners administered an illegal oath to certain persons, binding them not to disclose an illegal confederacy. He should therefore show that the combination was illegal—that it was the practice of the association to administer oaths, that the members were bound to obey the commands of men not legally constituted, and that they were bound to secrecy. With regard to the form of the oath and the mode of administering it, it was proper he should call his lordship's attention to the 5th section of the act, which provided that any engagement in the nature of an oath should be deemed an oath within the meaning of the act, in whatever form or manner the same should be administered.

The learned counsel then proceeded to state the facts of the case to the jury, and to call his witnesses, from whose evidence it appeared that the prisoners were agricultural labourers, and that on the day stated in the indictment Legg and others were conducted to the house of Thomas Stanfield, at Tollpuddle, and, after waiting a short time, were blindfolded and taken into a room, when certain papers were read over to them while on their knees; and on the bandage being taken from their eyes, they saw the figure of a skeleton, with the words " Remember your end," written over it. They were then sworn to obey the rules and regulations of the society, and not to divulge its secrets or proceedings. They were to pay a shilling on entrance, and a penny a week afterwards, to support the men who were out of work (those who had struck) till their masters raised their wages. The defendants were all present, and Lovelace wore a dress like a surplice.

The general laws of the society were produced and read to the jury, from which it was collected that the society was to be called " The Friendly Society of Agricultural Labourers." Regular officers and periods of meeting were appointed, and the mode of making collections pointed out. The twentieth and twenty-first rules were as follows:—
" That if any master attempts to reduce the wages of his workmen, if they are members of this order, they shall instantly communicate the same to the corresponding secretary, in order that they may receive the support of the grand lodge; and in the mean time they shall use their utmost endeavours to finish the work they may have in hand, if any, and shall assist each other, so that they may all leave the place together, and with as much promptitude as possible."—" That if any

member of this society renders himself obnoxious to his employer solely on account of taking an active part in the affairs of this order, and, if guilty of no violation or insult to his master, shall be discharged from his employment solely in consequence thereof, either before or after the turn-out, then the whole body of men at that place shall instantly leave, and no member of this society shall be allowed to take work at that place until such member be reinstated in his situation."

After the counsel for the defendants had addressed the court and the jury, contending that no offence had been proved, the judge summed up, enforcing on the jury that they must satisfy themselves as to the illegality of the oath which Legg had taken, and which had been administered to other members of the society. The precise formality of the oath, his lordship observed, was not under inquiry; the Act of Parliament referred to an oath fixing an obligation on a party to whom it is administered. To sustain and prove this charge, the jury must be satisfied that the oath administered to Legg was to bind him not to divulge the secrets of the society; if so, it came within the meaning of the act. It was also a question, whether the dress of James Lovelace, which resembled a clergyman's surplice, was not intended to give a degree of solemnity and additional force to the proceedings. The representation of a skeleton seemed also to have been intended to strike awe on the minds of the persons to whom the oath was administered. In taking the oath, if they were satisfied that it was intended as an obligation on the conscience of the person taking it, it clearly came within the meaning of the act. His lordship proceeded to remark on the rules of the society, which spoke of the violation of an obligation, evidently referring to the oath which was administered by the prisoners, and that such violation would be deemed by the society a crime. His lordship also read from a book belonging to the society the names of several persons (the prisoners among others) who had contributed to its funds; leaving the jury to draw their conclusions from these facts, and the whole chain of evidence which had been repeated to them.

The jury, after about five minutes consultation, found all the prisoners " Guilty," and they were sentenced to be transported for seven years.

In pursuance of this sentence the prisoners were subsequently conveyed to New South Wales. This proceeding was looked upon as exceedingly harsh under the circumstances of the case, and loud and repeated remonstrances were made, both in and out of parliament, against it. For a considerable time the government declined to interfere; at length, however, they yielded to the incessant exertions of the friends of the prisoners, and granted a free pardon to them all.

At the commencement of the year 1838, those who had chosen to return to England were landed at Plymouth—some of them having preferred to remain in the colony to which they had been transported. An attempt was made to excite great sympathy in their behalf, and a species of public entry was made by them into London; but the whole affair turned out a failure: the good sense of the people in general was found to have induced a feeling not altogether in accordance with a supposition that these men had been martyrs.

MURDER OF THE MARRS AND WILLIAMSONS.

THE close of the year 1811 was productive of two scenes of blood, which struck horror into all hearts; we allude to the murders of the families of the Marrs and Williamsons, in Ratcliffe Highway, which were accomplished under circumstances of the most frightful atrocity and of the most extraordinary mystery.

Mr. Marr was a linen-draper in a respectable way of business living in Ratcliffe Highway; and his household establishment consisted of himself, his wife and infant child, a shop-boy, and a servant woman. It was his custom to close his shop at about eleven o'clock, when he and his assistant proceeded to dispose of the commodities which had been exposed for sale during the day by placing them on the shelves. On a dark evening at the beginning of the month of December, 1811, he was engaged in the customary manner, his shop being closed, when the servant woman was dispatched to procure some oysters for supper from a neighbouring shop. On her quitting her master's house she left the door a-jar, in order that she might procure a ready access on her return, and she went directly to the house of a person who resided only a few doors off to purchase the fish. She found, however, that they had sold the whole of their stock, and she was therefore compelled to go further; and having purchased the quantity required, and had them opened, she returned immediately to the residence of Mr. Marr. On her reaching the door, she found that it was closed, and she rang the bell. No answer was, however, returned, and she repeated her application to the wire. Still no one came, and a watchman coming up at the moment inquired what she was doing there? She informed him of the errand on which she had been sent, and that she could not obtain an entrance, upon which he pulled the bell with great violence, but his efforts were attended with no better effect than those of the servant girl. Some alarm was now begun to be felt, and the next-door neighbour coming out, to learn the cause of the interference of the constables, three or four persons soon collected, amongst whom a consultation was held as to the best mode of proceeding. Various courses were suggested, a continued application to the knocker and bell being made in the mean time; and at length, no answer being given, it was determined that the wall which divided Mr. Marr's back premises from those of the adjoining house should be scaled, in order that the cause of the silence might be ascertained. The watchman, aided by the strangers who had collected near him, soon made an entrance into Mr. Marr's premises; but on going into the house a sight met his eyes, before which the stoutest heart would have quailed. The murdered remains of Mr. Marr and his shop-boy lay before him in the shop; the body of Mrs. Marr was in the passage, and that of the infant in its cradle, all warm and all steeped in gore.

The watchman, having recovered from the effect of the stupor which this horrid sight had produced in his mind, immediately ran to the

door, and having opened it gave an alarm to those outside of the frightful murders which had been committed.   An apprehension was entertained that the assassins might still be employed in plundering the house,
and instant search was made, but without success ; and it was ascertained
that the murderers, intimidated probably by the girl's ringing the bell,
had escaped from the back window, across some mud which lay in the
back yard, and through a way whose intricacies could have been
threaded only by persons who had previously reconnoitred the
situation.   In the mean time the report of the murders had spread
like wild-fire, and thousands of persons collected round the house, notwithstanding the late hour of the night ; but, although many volunteers
were found, and an instant search was made through the whole of the
surrounding districts, nothing was discovered which could in the re-
motest degree afford a clue to the discovery of the persons implicated
in the diabolical transaction.   A minute examination of the house took
place when daylight afforded an opportunity for it to be done with good
effect, and then a ripping chisel or hook, such as are used by carpenters
and joiners, was found lying near the body of Mr. Marr, and some
marks of blood were discovered on the window through which the murderers had escaped ; but nothing was found which could induce a supposition that any goods or money had been carried off.

Upon an inquest being held, several comparatively unimportant discoveries were made, but no facts were proved which could at all lead
to the discovery of the persons implicated in the foul deed, and after
several adjournments a verdict of " Wilful murder against some person
or persons unknown" was returned.

The horror and dismay produced by the atrocious event which we
have just detailed had not yet subsided ; the exertions of the police to
discover the parties concerned in it had not yet abated ; the earth
which had been thrown over the graves of the unhappy victims was not
yet settled, ere the neighbourhood of Ratcliffe Highway was again the
scene of a crime as horrible as that which still struck terror into the
minds of all persons.

On Thursday night, the 19th December, the neighbourhood of New
Gravel-lane was thrown into a state of the most violent confusion by
loud cries of " Murder !" proceeding from the King's Arms public-
house, situated at No. 81 in that lane.   The recollection of the late
event was still fresh in the minds of all, and crowds of persons instantly
ran to the spot to learn the cause of alarm, rendered doubly appalling
by recent circumstances.   Nor was the sight which met their eyes at
all calculated to allay the apprehensions which had been raised.   A
man almost in a state of nudity was seen descending from the second-
floor window of the house mentioned by means of two sheets tied
together, and exclaiming, with expressions of the most violent agitation
and terror, " They are murdering the people in the house."   On his
reaching the extremity of the line which he was using, he was still eight
feet from the ground ; but he was assisted in his descent by the watchman, who received him into his arms, and he then repeated the alarm
which he had already given.   The greatest horror was felt at what was

supposed to be a repetition of the frightful scene which had been so recently enacted, and a short consultation was held as to the best mode of affording relief to the inmates of the house. It was determined that the most speedy means must be taken; and, in accordance with a resolution which was arrived at, an entry was forced through the cellar flap. A man named Ludgate, a butcher living in Ashwell's Buildings, close by, a Mr. Hawse, and a constable, were the first persons who entered by this means; and almost at the same instant a gentleman named Fox obtained admission through some wooden bars at the side of the house, with a cutlass in his hand. The first object that was seen in the cellar was the body of Mr. Williamson, which lay at the foot of the stairs; and on its being examined, it was found that his throat was dreadfully cut, and that besides his leg was broken, and he had sustained a severe fracture of the skull, while the weapon with which he appeared to have been attacked, an iron crow-bar or maul, was lying at his side. In the parlour, the body of Mrs. Williamson was found with the skull fractured and the throat cut, the blood still issuing from the wound, while at her side lay that of the servant woman, whose head was horribly bruised, and whose throat was cut in a similar manner.

Surgical aid was instantly procured; but, upon the bodies being examined, it was found that the vital spark had fled.

Upon the premises being examined, in which the diabolical murders had been committed, it was found that the under part of the house was used as a skittle-ground, next to the entrance of which was the cellar-door; and from the bloody marks which appeared on both doors, it was obvious that the murderers had attempted to escape by both those means. It was discovered, also, that the villains had eventually effected their exit from the house by means of a back window which looked into an open space belonging to the London Dock Company, from which there was easy access to many different streets branching off in various directions. The wounds on the heads of the unfortunate deceased, it was obvious, had been inflicted by the iron crow-bar which had been found; and from their position, as well as from the inclination in the cuts in the throats of the deceased persons, it appeared that the murderer was left-handed. During the time occupied in the perpetration of the horrid deed, a public-house, almost adjoining that of Mr. Williamson, was filled with people drinking, while only a few doors on the other side there was a rendezvous for seamen, the windows of both of which looked into the open ground into which the murderers must have escaped.

In the course of the following day the most active measures were taken to secure the murderers. Police officers were dispatched in all directions; a reward of £100 was offered by the parish for their apprehension; and the magistrates sat at Shadwell Police-office during the whole day, ready to receive and act upon any information which might be brought to them. On the day succeeding, a coroner's inquest was held upon the bodies of the deceased persons, when Mr. Anderson, constable, and John Turner, the man who had escaped from the window, were examined.

Mr. Anderson deposed, that he was a constable, and knew Mr. and Mrs. Williamson; they were highly respected in the neighbourhood, and for the space of fifteen years kept the King's Arms public-house, which was the resort of foreigners of every description. At eleven o'clock every night they invariably closed their house. On Thursday night, the 19th of December 1811, Mr. Williamson pursued his usual course. Ten minutes before eleven witness called for a pot of beer. During the time Mrs. Williamson was drawing the beer, Mr. Williamson, who was sitting by the fire, said to him, " You are an officer—there has been a fellow listening at my door with a brown coat on; if you should see him, take him into custody, or tell me." He answered, " he certainly would, for his and his own safety," and then retired. Witness lived next door but one to the deceased. Between twenty and thirty minutes after he left the King's Arms, he intended to go for another pot of beer; as soon as he got out of his house he heard a noise, when he saw the lodger lowering himself down into the street by the sheets. He ran into the house for his staff, and proceeded to the spot. The watchman caught the lodger in his arms, when witness and others broke the cellar-flap open, and, having descended, began to look round the cellar. On coming to the staircase, they saw Mr. Williamson lying on his back, with his legs upon the stairs, his head downwards: by his side was an iron instrument, similar to a stonemason's crow, about three feet long, and three quarters of an inch in diameter: it was much stained with blood. Mr. Williamson had received a wound on the head, his throat was dreadfully cut, his right leg was broken by a blow, and his hand severely cut. From these marks of violence witness supposed Mr. Williamson made great resistance, as he was a very powerful man. They then proceeded up into the sitting-room, where they saw Mrs. Williamson lying on her left side; her skull was fractured, and her throat cut and bleeding most profusely. Near to her was the servant woman, lying on her back, with her head under the grate; her skull was more dreadfully fractured than that of her mistress, her throat most inhumanly cut, and none of the bodies were cold. Witness then stated that the premises were afterwards examined, and it was discovered that the murderers had made their escape from a back window looking into a piece of waste ground belonging to the London Dock Company. The sill of the window was stained with blood, and the sash remained thrown up. The distance which the villains had to jump did not exceed eight feet, and the ground beneath was soft clay; so they could sustain no injury even had they fallen. From the waste ground in question there was no difficulty whatever in escaping, as it communicated with several by-streets.

John Turner, the man who escaped from the window, and who was a lodger in the house, deposed as follows:—

" I went to bed about five minutes before eleven o'clock. I had not been in bed more than five or ten minutes before I heard the cry of ' We shall all be murdered!' which I suppose was the cry of the woman-servant. I went down stairs, and saw one of the villains cutting Mrs. Williamson's throat, and rifling her pockets. I immediately ran up stairs, took off the sheets from my bed, fastened them together, and lashed them to the bed-posts. I called to the watchman to give the alarm; I was hanging out of the front window by the sheets; and the watchman received me in his arms, naked as I was. A great mob had then assembled opposite the door; and as soon as I got upon my legs, the door was forced open. I entered, and found the bodies lying as described. There was nobody lodged in the house but myself, except a grand-daughter of Mrs. Williamson. I have lived in the house about eight months, and during that time I have found the family to be the most peaceful people that could keep a public-house. The man whom I saw rifling Mrs. Williamson's pocket, as far as I could see by the light in the room, was about six feet in height, dressed in a genteel style, with a long dark loose coat on. I said nothing to him; but, terrified, I ran up stairs, and made my escape as already mentioned. When I was down stairs, I heard two or three very great sighs; and when I was first alarmed, I heard distinctly the words, ' We shall all be murdered.'" Turner further deposed, that at the time he went to bed Mrs. Williamson was on the stairs, taking up a silver punch-ladle and watch, which were to be raffled for on the following Monday, into her bed-room for security.

Other witnesses were examined, but their testimony differed in no material respect from that of the persons whose evidence we have detailed; and the jury, as in the case of the Marrs, returned a verdict of " Wilful Murder against some person or persons unknown."

After the termination of this necessary inquiry before the coroner, however, the most minute investigation of every circumstance connected with this lamentable affair was carried on by the magistrates of Shadwell. Many persons were taken into custody, but discharged for want of evidence; but an Irishman, named Cornelius Driscoll, was detained on suspicion of being implicated in the horrid deed, on account of a pair of breeches covered with blood being found in his possession.

Of all the persons seized, however, suspicion fell strongest upon a man named John Williams, who cheated justice by committing suicide before his guilt or his innocence could be fully established.

This man was apprehended on suspicion of being concerned in the murders; and, on his examination, John Frederick Ritchen, a Dane, who was also in custody, was sworn as a witness. He stated, that he had lodged at the Pear-Tree public-house, kept by Mr. Vermillee, with the prisoner, for about twelve weeks and three or four days, but knew little of him except in the light of a fellow-lodger. He knew that he was acquainted with two men, a carpenter and a joiner, and about three or four weeks before he had seen them all three drinking together at the bar of the public-house. On the night of the murder of the Marr family Williams was out, and a few minutes before he returned there was a knock at the door, which Mrs. Vermillee opened. The witness had gone down to open the door, but seeing Mrs. Vermillee, he went up to his own room; and, when there, heard her in conversation with a man, whose voice resembled that of one of the two men before mentioned. A few minutes afterwards Williams himself came in. This was almost half-past one o'clock. Three or four days before Williams was taken up, he observed that the large sandy-coloured whiskers, which had before formed a striking feature in his appearance, had been cut off. About eleven o'clock on the day after the murder of the Marr family, the witness went from curiosity to examine the premises, which he entered, and saw the dead bodies. From thence he returned to the Pear Tree, where he found Williams in the back yard, washing out his stockings, but he did not tell him where he had been. He was then questioned respecting his knowledge of the maul, which is a round bar of iron about an inch in diameter, between two and three feet in length, flattened at the end into the shape of a chisel, but not with a cutting edge, being apparently a tool for caulking. He said it resembled one he had seen about the Pear-Tree public-house, but he could not identify it. A pair of blue woollen trowsers, and also a pair of canvass trowsers, were then produced, which had been found between the mattrass and the bed-clothes of the hammock in which the witness slept. The legs of the blue trowsers had evidently been washed, for the purpose of cleaning them from mud, of which the appearance was still visible in the creases, which had not been effectually cleansed. These trowsers were damp at the time of the examination; the canvass trowsers were also damp, but they presented no particular appearance. The witness stated, that both these pairs of trowsers had formerly belonged to a person since gone to sea, and he had since worn them himself.

Mrs. Orr, residing near the Pear Tree, stated, that on the Saturday before Marr's murder, about half-past one o'clock in the morning, she was getting up linen, when she heard a noise about the house, as if a man was attempting to break into the house. She was frightened, and asked, " Who was there?" A voice answered, which she knew to be Williams's, " I am a robber!" She answered, " Whether you are a robber or not, I will let you in, and am glad to see you." Williams entered, seating himself till the watchman was calling the hour of past two o'clock. He then got up from his chair, and asked the landlady if she would have a glass. She assented; but as he would not go for it, she went to the Pear-Tree public house, but could gain no admittance. She returned, when Williams inquired how many rooms there were in her house, and the situation of her back premises. She replied, there were three rooms, and that her back yard communicated with Mrs. Vermillee's house. The watchman came into Mrs. Orr's house, although Williams resisted it for some time, and he told her that he had picked up a chisel by the side of her window. Williams ran out unobserved at this information; soon afterwards he returned. The watchman was going, when Williams stopped him, and desired him to go to the Pear Tree, and get some liquor. The house was then open. While the watchman was gone for the liquor, Williams took up the chisel, and said, " D—n my eyes, where did you get this chisel?" Mrs. Orr did not part with it, and retained the instrument till the Monday following. Hearing that Williams was examined, she went to Mrs. Vermillee's, and showed her the chisel. Mrs. Vermillee looked at it, and compared it with the tools in one Patterson's chest, when it was found to bear the same marks, and declared that it was taken out of her house. Mrs. Orr instantly delivered the chisel to the magistrates of Shadwell-street office, as being a further trace to the villainy. Mrs. Orr said, she knew Williams for eleven weeks ; he frequently nursed her child, and used to joke with her daughter, and once asked her whether she should be frightened if he came in the dead of night to her bedside? The daughter replied, that if it was he who came, she should not be frightened. They both thought him an agreeable young man, of a most insinuating address.

In consequence of the information of this witness, a minute examination of the ripping chisel found at Mr. Marr's took place, and it was found to be marked like that discovered by the watchman at Mrs. Orr's. The husband of Mrs. Vermillee was in custody on suspicion in Newgate, and he was consulted, and expressed his belief that it was taken from the same tool chest as that chisel. The plot now seemed to thicken against the prisoner, and little doubt was entertained of his connexion with the carpenter and joiner, and of their having all been engaged in the perpetration of these most horrid murders, when all further efforts on the part of the police were checked, by his adding another crime to those which it was fully believed he had already committed, by destroying himself.

He had been remanded for further examination to Cold-Bath Fields Prison, and the police of the district had redoubled their exertions to detect and bring to justice his accomplices. Mr. Vermillee had been ordered to be set at liberty, in order that he might give evidence upon the day of the next inquiry before the magistrates, when, on the very morning on which the prisoner was to be carried before the magistrates, upon the gaoler going to call him from his cell, in order that he might prepare himself to be carried to the Police Office, he was found, heavily ironed as he was, suspended by a handkerchief from a beam in the apartment in which he was confined. He was instantly cut down, but upon his body being examined, it was found that he was quite dead and cold, and that he had evidently been hanging during several hours.

The excitement produced by this termination of the investigation would be difficult to describe, but all persons now expressed their full belief that the deceased prisoner was the author of the crimes which had attracted such universal attention. An inquest was held upon his body, and a verdict of *felo de se* was returned by the jury ; but it now became a question, how the public indignation could be best satisfied? The rule in such cases was, that the deceased should be buried in the nearest cross road ; but a conference was held with the Home Secretary by Mr. Capper, the magistrate, with the view of ascertaining how far this regulation might be departed from, at which it was determined that a public exhibition of the body should be made through the neighbourhood which had been the scene of the monster's crimes. In conformity with this decision, on the 31st of December, the body of the deceased was privately removed from the prison at eleven o'clock at night, and conveyed to St. George's watch-house, near the London docks, and on the following (Tuesday) morning, at half-past ten o'clock, a procession was formed in the following order :—

Several hundred constables, with their staves, clearing the way.

The newly-formed patrole, with drawn cutlasses.

Another body of constables.

Parish officers of St. George's, St. Paul's, and Shadwell, on horseback.

Peace-officers, on horseback.

Constables.

The high constable of the county of Middlesex, on horseback.

The Body of Williams,

Extended at full length on an inclined platform erected on the cart, about four feet high at the head, and gradually sloping towards the horse, giving a full view of the body, which was dressed in blue trowsers and a white-and-blue-striped waistcoat, but without a coat, as when found in the cell. On the left side of the head the fatal maul, and on the right the ripping-chisel, with which the murders were perpetrated, were exposed to view. The countenance of Williams was ghastly in the extreme, and the whole had an appearance too horrible for description.

A strong body of constables brought up the rear.

The procession advanced slowly up Ratcliffe Highway, accompanied by an immense concourse of persons, eager to get a sight of the murderer's remains. When the cart came opposite to the late Mr. Marr's house, a halt was made for near a quarter of an hour. The procession then moved down Old Gravel-lane, along Wapping, up New Crane-lane, and into New Gravel-lane. When the platform arrived at Mr. Williamson's late house, a second halt took place. It then proceeded up the hill, and again entered Ratcliffe Highway, down which it moved into Cannon-street, and advanced to St. George's turnpike, where the New Road is intersected by Cannon-street. There a grave, about six feet deep, had been prepared, immediately over which the main water-pipe runs. Between twelve and one o'clock the body was taken from the platform, and lowered into the grave, after which a stake was driven through it; and, the pit being covered, the ceremony concluded.

During the last half-hour the crowd had increased immensely—they poured in from all parts, but their demeanour was perfectly quiet. All the shops in the neighbourhood were shut, and the windows and tops of the houses were crowded with spectators. On every side, mingled with execrations of the murderer, were heard fervent prayers for the speedy detection of his accomplices.

A conclusive evidence of the guilt of this wretched suicide was afterwards found, in the discovery of a knife, which he always carried with him, concealed in a hole in the room which he occupied, encrusted with blood.

Fearful as were the horrid crimes committed by this blood-thirsty assassin, they were not without their good effect in the metropolis. The sensation produced by the murders awakened the apprehension of all persons for their own safety; and local meetings were held in the various parishes of the metropolis, at which resolutions were passed, in pursuance of which a system of police was established far more complete than that which before existed, although still infinitely inferior in point of regularity and competence to that which has since been adopted.

WILLIAM KING,

IMPRISONED FOR ROBBERY.

THE offence of which this man was convicted was attended by a frau-dulent assumption of character, which we should have imagined would have made him a fit object of severe punishment.

At the time of his conviction he was fifty-two years of age, and ap-peared to be a person of some respectability. He, however, declined giving any account of himself.

He was indicted at the Bridgewater assizes, on the 7th of August, 1831, for assaulting Elias Cashin upon the king's highway, putting him in fear, and taking from his person and against his will a box containing twenty-four gold seals, forty-five brooches, and a variety of other articles of jewellery.

The robbery was alleged to have been committed at Huntspill, on the 10th of March; and Cashin, who was a member of the Jewish persuasion, stated, that on that day he was offering his wares for sale at Huntspill, when the prisoner came up to him, and representing himself to be an inspector of pedlars' licences, demanded to see his licence. He admitted that he had none, upon which the prisoner seized his box containing his jewellery, and took him by the collar, saying, that he must accompany him to a magistrate's. They went together to the house of a Mr. Rockett, where the prisoner behaved with much violence, in consequence of which Cashin rung the bell. Young Mr. Rockett appeared, who said that his father was not at home; and the prisoner then desired the Jew to meet him on the next day, at the house of a Mr. Phippen, another magistrate, residing a short distance off. Cashin begged for his box, but the supposed inspector refused to give it up, and the poor Jew was at length compelled to go away, leaving his property in the hands of the prisoner.

On the next day he was faithful to his appointment, but neither the prisoner nor his box was to be seen; and Cashin added, that he could never meet him afterwards, until a short time before the trial, when he accidentally ran against him in Bristol. He now, in turn, became the assailant, and seizing the prisoner by the collar, demanded his box. He at first denied all knowledge of him, but then finding that the Jew was determined to take decisive steps against him, said that he had been robbed of it himself. Cashin, however, called in the aid of the police, and, upon the prisoner being searched, a pair of spectacles was found upon him, which had been in the box when he had carried it off.

The jury at once declared the prisoner guilty, but of the mitigated offence of larceny only, negativing the capital charge; and he was sen-tenced to twelve months' imprisonment.

ABDUCTION OF MISS GOOLD.

DANIEL AND WILLIAM DOODY, JOHN CUSSEN (*alias* WALSH), JAMES, MAURICE, & DAVID LEAHY, DANIEL RIEDY, WILLIAM COSTELLO, AND WALTER FITZ-MAURICE (*alias* CAPTAIN ROCK),

CONVICTED OF ABDUCTION.

IT was the opinion of Dr. Johnson, that many of the romantic tales of the middle ages had their origin in truth, and that the absolute distress of females might, in all probability, have called for the institution of " knight errantry." To protect the defenceless is a natural impulse, having its foundation in the sympathies of our nature; but when a female—young, beautiful, and innocent—is the victim of oppression, there is no man, with common feelings, who would not risk his life to snatch her from despair and misery. In this happy country there are few instances of abduction; but in Ireland this unmanly crime is too prevalent. The disturbed state of certain parts of the country gives aid to the schemes of unprincipled ruffians, who act on the presumption that injured females, when degraded and dishonoured, will, of necessity, save the violators of their innocence from ignominy by marriage—the only means, they suppose, left them to escape from unmerited shame. The persons thus forcibly carried away are generally the daughters of opulent farmers—a fact which clearly shows the mercenary views of those who commit so base and cowardly an outrage.

Among the numerous outrages of this nature was one on the person of Miss Honora Goold, a young lady remarkable for her personal beauty. She lived in the house of her mother at Glangurt, in the county of Cork, and had two sisters older than herself, she being scarcely sixteen, and a brother.   On the 4th of March, 1822, about twelve o'clock at night, their dwelling was attacked by an armed banditti, who, on threatening to burn the house, were admitted.   One of the ferocious ruffians burst into Miss Honora's apartment, and asked if she was the eldest Miss Goold. She replied in the negative, and said that her sister was on a visit in Cork.   The inquirer then withdrew, and having searched several other apartments, returned, followed by five or six others, and repeated his interrogations, but on this occasion answered them himself in the affirmative, and then ordered her to rise and dress herself, and to accompany them.   At the suggestion of one of the party, they withdrew from the room ; but Miss Goold was scarcely dressed when they returned, and one of them seizing her round the waist, carried her screaming to the outside of the house, where she was received by a stranger on horseback. She was placed in front of the horseman, and then the party, in spite of her cries and entreaties, set off in the direction of the Galties, a range of hills between the counties of Cork and Limerick.   At the distance of several miles they halted, and there, having procured a pillion, their captive was compelled to ride behind the leader of this atrocious band. In her eagerness to escape she fell several times during their progress ; and having continued her screams all the time, one of the ruffians threatened to murder her unless she desisted.

By daylight they had entered the recesses of the Galties ; and several of the party having occasionally dropped off, she was conducted by the few that remained to the house of David Leahy, a substantial farmer.

The leader of this outrage was a young man named Brown, of a respectable family, and who had received an education which should have rendered him incapable of such base and unmanly conduct.   The elder Miss Goold was entitled, on her marriage, to a large fortune ; and Brown, hoping to possess himself of it, resolved to carry off the young lady. Being disappointed by the precipitancy and mistake of his assistants, he determined to make sure of the lovely victim who had fallen into his power, knowing that the opulence of her family could make him independent, provided he could insure the consent of the astonished girl whom he had forcibly carried off.   With virtuous indignation, however, she repulsed his advances, and begged the protection of Mrs. Leahy, in whose parlour she now was ; but, strange to say, this woman, who was herself a mother, connived at the ruin of her unprotected guest.

Foiled in his direct attack, Brown had recourse to an expedient which, for the honour of human nature, we would wish never to record, did not impartial justice demand an honest discharge of our duty as faithful narrators of criminal occurrences.   It was proposed, immediately after breakfast, that Miss Goold should take some rest.   A bed was in the parlour, and she was directed to repose upon it.   This, indeed, after the fatigue of the night, was most desirable ; but, to her utter astonishment, the family, in which were two females, left the room, at the same time locking the door upon herself and Brown. The reader need not be told the rest—in spite of her screams and entreaties, the purity of female innocence was grossly violated; and her destroyer arose from his bed of lust, the polluter of one whose peace of mind neither the world's sympathy nor the world's wealth could restore.

The friends of Miss Goold, who comprised the wealth and respectability of the county of Cork, instantly set about recovering the injured lady. The pursuit was continued from day to day for three weeks; and the vigilance of her friends was only evaded by her being removed from house to house, and from cabin to cabin; and even once, by her being exposed for a whole day and night to the inclemency of the weather on a bleak mountain, when she had the agony of seeing her friends at a distance, but was prevented from calling to them, or flying to join them, by a ruffian, who stood sentinel over her with a loaded pistol. At length, however, her sufferings were to be terminated. Though weak and almost exhausted by opposition to her foul abuser, she still remained firm in her virtuous resolve to be no consenting party to the violence offered to her, and at the conclusion of three weeks she was placed by her ferocious guards in a poor cabin on the roadside, where her friends might find her. When discovered, she was in a condition of the greatest misery, being so weak as to be unable to walk, stand, or sit. Seventeen hours were occupied in removing her thirteen miles, to her mother's house; but when once restored to home and its enjoyments, her recovery was rapid, and in a short time her health was re-established, as far as it was possible under all the frightful circumstances of her affecting case. From the description which she gave of the perpetrators of this act of violence, several of the party were apprehended. Brown, the guilty contriver of the plan, escaped from the country; and Fitzmaurice, alias Captain Rock, evaded the pursuit of justice for a considerable time, but at last surrendered to a magistrate. The men whose names head this article, except Fitzmaurice and Costello, were brought to trial on the 29th of July, 1822, at Limerick. Miss Goold appeared to give evidence, and her narrative, which she delivered with modest dignity, procured her the willing sympathy of a crowded court. The prisoners were found Guilty—Death; but the three Leahys and Cussen were subsequently discharged, on a point of law operating in their favour.

On the 23rd of August following, Walter Fitzmaurice, better known at the time as Captain Rock, pleaded guilty at the Cork assizes; and, along with Costello, who was found guilty on the solitary evidence of Miss Goold's brother, who swore to his having seen him on the night of the abduction, received sentence of death.

On the ensuing Saturday, Costello underwent the awful sentence of the law; but Fitzmaurice was respited, something having arisen in his favour, principally on the ground of his having pleaded guilty in consequence of the judge refusing to put off his trial in the absence of a material witness. Costello, to the last, declared his innocence, not only of the crime for which he was convicted, but of any connexion whatever with the White Boys.

WILLIAM JOURDAN (*alias* LEARY), THOMAS SULLIVAN, HENRY MOTT, AND WILLIAM SEALE.

TRANSPORTED FOR A ROBBERY AT THE CUSTOM-HOUSE.

THE extraordinary robbery, for their participation in which these men were convicted, was committed on the 25th of November, 1834, and Bank-notes and money to the amount of £4824 were then carried off. The whole of the particulars of this most daring burglary were revealed, at the trial of the offenders whose names are above-mentioned, by one of the men who were concerned in it; and they exhibit, probably more plainly than any case which ever came before the public, the system to which modern thieves have reduced their plans of depredation, while at the same time they show the success which but too frequently attends their enterprising attempts at robbery.

The extensive depredation for which these men were convicted and transported, was committed in the office of Mr. Frederick Thomas Walsh, the receiver of fines and forfeitures. The office, on the evening before the robbery, was left securely fastened in the ordinary manner; but on the next morning it was ascertained that the iron safe had been broken open, and property to the value of £4824, carried off. The consternation produced in the establishment by such an event, it may be easily conceived, was of an extraordinary description, and upon its discovery instant information was conveyed to the various police-offices in the metropolis of the circumstance, as well as of the numbers and dates of such of the notes as, by memoranda made of their particulars, could be identified. More than a year elapsed, however, before any of the perpetrators of this daring outrage were apprehended. Lea, an officer of Lambeth-street police-office, was the person to whom the duty of making inquiries into the case was deputed; and, after the most arduous investigation, carried on with praiseworthy perseverance, he was at length enabled to bring the principal parties to this burglary to punishment.

On Wednesday, the 2nd of December 1835, Jourdan and Sullivan were taken into custody, and the circumstances of their apprehension deserve to be narrated. Lea, it seems, had been long convinced of their participation in the robbery, and had striven hard to obtain evidence confirmatory of his suspicions, and at the same time to procure such a knowledge of the " whereabouts " of the objects of his investigation, as to enable him, when a fitting opportunity should present itself, to secure them, and to bring them to account for the long list of evil deeds of which he knew they had been guilty. Keeping them in his eye, he at the same time was anxiously engaged in procuring testimony of their criminality; but, at the moment when this evidence came to his knowledge, he found that his birds had suddenly flown. For two months all his exertions to discover their retreat were useless; but at length chance threw him again upon their track. An assistant to the officer watched a well-known associate of theirs to the Red Lion, in King-street, Holborn, and in that house they were captured on the morning of the 2nd of December. Upon inquiry it was ascertained that they had been staying there during a short time only, and that they passed as mercantile men. They occupied an upper room, where they kept their trunks; and they appeared to be possessed of plenty of money, an excellent wardrobe, and, indeed, they seemed to lack nothing to render their appearance highly respectable. Upon the introduction of Lea to the " gentlemen," they appeared astonished to find that he had discovered them, and, without hesitation, consented to accompany him; but Sullivan declared, that if he had been armed, nothing should have induced him to surrender himself alive. They were instantly taken to Lambeth-street, and Lea then commenced a search through the apartment which they had occupied. In their trunks he found a great variety of house-breaking implements, of the most ingenious construction. Files, centre-bits, spring saws, and every sort of tool used by " cracksmen," were among those which were discovered, while a pair of scales, calculated for ascertaining the precise weight of metals and precious stones, was also discovered to be in their possession. These, of course, were instantly seized by the officer, who, having further examined the room, and satisfied himself that nothing was concealed, retired from the house. A gold watch and a £10 note were taken from the person of Jourdan, as being calculated to lead to the discovery of further evidence against him; and the circumstances of the apprehension of the two prisoners having been detailed to the magistrates, they were ordered to be remanded.

In the course of the subsequent investigation of the case, information was obtained with respect to the two prisoners, which exhibited them to be most determined and successful thieves. They were both Irishmen, and many years had not elapsed since they were known as common pickpockets in Whitechapel, associating with the very lowest class of vagabonds in that notorious vicinity. With regard to Jourdan, whose real name was Leary, it was ascertained that four years before he had introduced himself to a Mr. Brace, a baker in Goodman's-yard, Minories, one of the committee of management of an Irish free-school in the neighbourhood, and placing £12 in his hands, had requested him to appropriate a weekly sum of five shillings towards the support of his mother (Mrs. Hart) and his half-sister, Mary Hart, who was then a pupil in the school. Mr. Brace at once consented to this, and Leary went away, saying that he was about to sail for America, but that he would send more money for the use of his mother, and to carry her and her daughter to meet him at New York. Some time elapsed before anything more was heard of him, but then a letter was received from him, containing a sum of money which Mr. Brace was requested to forward to Mrs. Hart, in order that she and Mary Hart might at once proceed to join him. The amount was amply sufficient to carry them to New York in good style, and thither they proceeded. From that time up to the year 1834 Mr. Brace had neither seen nor heard anything of them, but in that year Leary called to inquire whether there were any letters lying there for him from his mother. He came on

horseback, was well dressed, and appeared to be in a respectable position in life; and he accounted for this change in his appearance by
saying, that a Spanish gentleman, in whose service he had been, had
died and left him a large sum of money; that he had taken the name of
Jourdan, and had then just arrived from Virginia, having left his mother
at New York. No letters had then arrived for him, and he went away;
but shortly afterwards a letter was brought by the post from the landlord of an hotel in New York, announcing the death of Mrs. Hart. This
letter was given to Jourdan upon a subsequent visit, and then he expressed his intention to send for his half-sister. Subsequently to this,
Jourdan's wife called upon Mr. Brace, and saying that her husband
was gone to Birmingham on a journey in pursuance of his trade as a
travelling jeweller, requested to be permitted to leave with him a box
of valuable papers, which she was afraid of having stolen from her house.
They lived then in White-Hart-row, Kennington, at a house which they
had hired upon the representations of Mr. Brace as to their respectability, and Mrs. Jourdan declared that an attempt had been made to
break into it. Mr. Brace expressed his willingness to take charge of
the trunk, and it was sent to him; and, in the month of September
1835, Jourdan called upon him and deposited with him £100 in £10
bank notes, which he requested him to take care of for him until he
should call for it, promising to give him six months' notice of his desire
to have the money refunded. The box with its contents was given up
to Lea, the officer; and the papers which he found in it, consisting of
letters, memoranda, bills of parcels, and other documents, afforded him
material assistance in tracing the notes which had formed a part of the
booty in the Custom-house robbery, while, at the same time, they
bore upon the face of them conclusive testimony of the fact of both
Jourdan and Sullivan having for years carried on a system of plunder
together, both in England and America, in which they had been highly
successful, and by means of which they had amassed a very large sum
of money.

Sullivan, it appeared, had been already indicted for a robbery at
Macclesfield four years before, from the consequences of which he had
escaped by breaking out of jail. He was apprehended in company with
a man named Wilson, upon suspicion of having been concerned in a
robbery upon the person of a Mr. Stephens, an Irish gentleman residing
in Cork, in Vauxhall-gardens. The produce of the robbery, which consisted of notes and bills to the amount of £238, was found in the pockets
of Sullivan, and he was committed for trial for the offence. He managed, however, before many days had passed, to escape from the prison
in which he was confined, and subsequently to America, where he joined
Jourdan. Wilson, his fellow-prisoner, was tried for the robbery, but
acquitted; but the indictment still remained in operation against Sullivan at the time of his apprehension on this charge.

Since the prisoner had been in custody at that office, infinite pains
had been taken by their friends to procure admission to the room which
they had occupied at the Red Lion. Persons, apparently recently
arrived from a journey, would drive up in a coach and demand to be

supplied with lodgings; but although this and many other *ruses* were resorted to, evidently with an object, the precise nature of which could not be discovered, all was in vain, and Mr. Proctor, the landlord, refused to admit any strange person to reside in his house. On Monday, the 28th of December, a Mr. Hanson, an old customer at the Red Lion, arrived in town, and, upon his presenting himself to the landlord, he was immediately shown to the long vacant apartment. A fire was kindled by the servant, and, in the course of the evening, the attention of Mr. Hanson was attracted to some brilliant substance which he perceived amidst the flames. With the tongs he drew it forth, and he perceived it to be a brooch, set with splendid pearls, which, however, was much injured by the fire. Further search presented to his view other articles of a similar description; and, in the course of a short time, he picked from the embers two other brooches, seven large brilliants, seven emeralds, one or two of which were of very great value, and about four dozen small diamonds. This discovery, it may be supposed, excited great astonishment; but, upon its being communicated to the landlord of the house, the mystery was at once solved by his recollection of the former inmates of the apartment. Lea was instantly sent for; and, on his instituting a further examination, he found in a bag, suspended in the chimney, three massive gold chains of foreign manufacture, which he immediately recognised as answering the description of some chains which had been stolen from the warehouses of Messrs. Hall and Co., on the Custom-house Quay, in the previous month of February, when property of the value of nearly £8000 was carried off. A renewed investigation brought other articles to light, and the anxiety of the strange visitors to the house was at once accounted for, while, at the same time, strong grounds of suspicion were excited that Jourdan and Sullivan had been parties to that robbery, and had secreted the produce of their depredation during their stay at the Red Lion, lest any accidental circumstance should reveal their possession of it.

During the investigation a great variety of minute facts were proved, which traced the possession of some of the stolen notes to them; but all doubts which might have existed were at length satisfied by the confession of Mr. William Huey, a landing-waiter of the Custom-house, to whom also some notes had been traced. This statement was at first confined to a declaration on the part of Huey, that he had received the notes which he was proved to possess at a gambling-house, No. 1, Leicester-square. Subsequently, however, he gave a full account of all the proceedings antecedent to and attendant upon the burglary. This confession led to the apprehension of Mr. Henry Mott and Mr. William Seale, both holding situations in the Custom-house; and, after repeated examinations, in the course of which an enormous mass of evidence was collected, all four prisoners were fully committed for trial, which took place at the Central Criminal Court, on Wednesday 2nd March, when Huey was examined at length as to the circumstances of the robbery.

He said, that he was a landing-waiter at the Custom-house, and had held that situation since the year 1827. Soon after his appointment he became acquainted with the prisoner Seale, whose office was similar to

his own. After about six months, however, they quarrelled, and it was
not until June 1834 that their difference was made up. They were then
stationed at the London Docks; and after business they were in the
habit of frequenting various public-houses, and, among others, the Three
Kingdoms, near the Custom-house. Shortly after their reconciliation,
Seale mentioned to him a design which existed to "crack" the Custom-
house; and on the same afternoon they met the prisoner Mott at the
Three Kingdoms; he was a clerk in the king's warehouse. Mott spoke
of the subject as if it were a familiar one, and advised delaying the robbery until an opportunity presented itself of obtaining a larger booty
than at present, which was agreed to by all parties. In the following
August, the witness went to see his father at Drogheda. He had previously been introduced to Jourdan and Sullivan, and he knew that the
object of their introduction was, that they might assist in the project
which they had in view. He met them in Dublin, and they inquired
whether he had any means of assisting them in robbing the Custom-
houses at Drogheda and at Dublin. He answered in the negative, and
returned to London the same day; and on the 4th of September he
resumed his occupation. He soon after met Mott and Seale at the
London Docks, and the discussion of the subject of the robbery was
resumed. After a short time they proceeded to Jourdan's lodgings, at
No. 3, East-street, Walworth, and acquainted him with their plans. He
made various inquiries with regard to the contents of the strong box in
the office of the Receiver of Fines, upon which it had been determined
their attack should be made, and on the next day went with Sullivan to
inspect the place. At a subsequent meeting they declared that it would
be easy to commit the robbery; and Sullivan suggested that the best
means of effecting their purpose would be to fit the locks with false keys.
Mott said he could procure impressions of one of the keys,—that of the
outer door; and at a meeting which they afterwards held, he produced
the key of which he had spoken, saying that he had taken it from the
desk of Mr. Billing, in the king's warehouse, who was out on leave. An
impression of it was taken in wax by Sullivan, from which subsequently
a skeleton key was made. The assistance of a fifth person was now
spoken of, and Seale introduced a man named William May, or Morgan,
(a thief, and the former companion of Jourdan and Sullivan). At the
next meeting Sullivan produced the skeleton key, and said, that he and
Jourdan had tried it and found that it would fit, but it was not strong
enough, and a new and firmer key was ordered to be prepared. Seale
then also showed them some padlock keys, one of which he suggested
would open the padlock with which the door was fastened; but after
impressions of them had been taken, and trials made with skeleton keys
made from the model, it was found that none of them belonged to the
lock which they desired to open. A suggestion was then made, that the
best way to commit the robbery would be by "stowing away," by which
was meant, hiding one of the party in the house, who could, undisturbed,
secure the booty and then make his escape. May volunteered to conceal himself, and a proposal was made that they should again inspect
the place in order to ascertain whether this could be done. The king's

sale was now approaching, and Jourdan said that he should like to know what would be the probable amount of the contents of the box. This, it was observed, might be easily ascertained. One of the party could buy a lot at the sale, and going to pay for it, he could see what money was in the chest, by presenting a note of such an amount as that Mr. Walsh would not be likely to be able to give change without going to the safe. This was agreed to; and a lot of rum having been purchased for £11, Jourdan took a £50 note to pay for it. On the 26th of November he informed his associates of his success in the project which he had undertaken. He said, that on his presenting the £50 note, Mr. Walsh felt his pockets, and looked into his drawers, but finding that he had not got sufficient change, he went to the iron-chest. Having only one key, he was obliged to wait until the person who kept the other came down stairs; (it is the custom to have a double lock to the iron safes of public institutions, so that they cannot be opened except with the concurrence of two persons, each of whom has a key). He then took out a large cash-box, which he could only move with both his hands, and on its being opened there appeared to be about £5000, in it at least. Jourdan gave his own name and address to be indorsed on the note which he paid; and, having received the change, he went away satisfied with the observation he had made. Mott censured him for giving his own name, and observing that all the particulars were written in a book, it was agreed that when the robbery was effected, the book should be destroyed, by the leaves being cut out and burned. The final plans were then arranged, and it was decided that May should go to the Custom-house at a little before four o'clock, accompanied by Jourdan and Sullivan, and that in the confusion which usually prevailed at the time of shutting the offices, the former should enter the Receiver's Office and conceal himself behind the door. On the next morning at nine o'clock, Jourdan and Sullivan were to be again in waiting, and having seen all safe, they were to give a signal to May, so that he might quit the place when the watchmen had opened the doors. Mott was also to assist in this design by keeping the clerks in his office, where they went to sign the appearance-sheet. If May got clear off, they were all to meet at Seale's house at Peckham on the same morning, to divide the booty. These arrangements being completed, they separated, and the witness remained away from business next day, on the pretended ground of ill-health. In the afternoon, Seale, and subsequently Jourdan and Sullivan, called on him and told him, that May had been safely " lodged;" that they had all walked into the passage together, and in the confusion had " flashed" an umbrella, under cover of which May entered the office. They afterwards waited on the esplanade for ten minutes to see that all was right, when seeing the doors locked, they went away. On the next morning, the 28th, witness went to Peckham, and meeting Seale, they went together to the Watermen's Arms, which commanded a view of the road by which Jourdan and the others must go to them. They remained there until they saw them coming, and then they went and met them, and they all proceeded to Seale's house together; Mott was not present. May then produced the money from his pocket, and it was divided into six equal parcels: it consisted of £4700 in notes, £122 in gold, and about 50s. in silver. May detailed to them the manner in which he had committed the robbery. He said, that as soon as he was locked in, he set to work: he found the key which opened the Receiver's lock to the chest, and employed it; but he was compelled to break open the other lock. Having done so, he took out the money and put it into his pockets. He next tore out the leaves from the book, and he now produced them. One of them bore the name "Leary, East-lane, Walworth," and that with the rest was burned. The whole party then tossed for choice of the lots of money, because some contained more gold than others; and the selection having been made, Jourdan and Sullivan claimed something for expenses. A £20 note and some silver were paid them, as well as the £50 note marked "Leary;" and they, with May, went away. Seale then took the three remaining shares up stairs, saying, that he should send them out of town; and on the same evening he said that they were sixty or seventy miles off. In about a month afterwards, however, he told the witness that they were at Leicester, and he went and fetched them. The lots were then counted over, and the share of each was £745 in notes. The witness further stated, that he disposed of all the notes under £20 in amount to Jourdan at £20 per cent. discount, and subsequently all under £100 in value upon the same terms; and that having done so, he concealed the remainder in Camberwell churchyard, where they remained for several months. Seale then introduced a person who undertook to dispose of some of those which were left, on the Continent; and a portion of the notes were given to him, and he brought back cash. Seale took away what was left of his money, and the witness retained £900, in three notes of the value of £300 each. These he concealed in the panneling of one of the doors of his house, by boring a hole with a centre-bit, and then having introduced the notes, filled up the remaining space with a cork; and on his apprehension he disclosed the place of their concealment, and they were seized by the officers.

On his cross-examination, the witness declared that he had no object in making this disclosure, but that of saving his friends from disgrace. He did not desire to screen himself from punishment; but, having committed so heinous a crime, he felt called upon to repair the mischief he had done so far as he was able.

The prisoners declared that Huey's story was untrue, and had been invented by him to screen himself; and attempts were made to show that at various periods of the transaction Jourdan and Sullivan had been at places which forbade their implication in the robbery. Other witnesses gave Mott and Seale a good character'. The jury, on Thursday night, found all the prisoners "Guilty," but recommended Mott and Seale to mercy.

On Tuesday, the 8th of March, the prisoners received sentence of transportation for life; Jourdan and Sullivan being informed that they would be sent to a penal settlement, where they would be compelled to undergo the most severe and painful labour; while Mott and Seale were told that, upon their arrival in the colony to which they were about to be sent, they also would be severely punished, by their being worked in road-gangs.

The convicts were subsequently conveyed to the penal settlements, where they were immediately placed in the positions of painful punishment which had been described to them by the learned judge at the time sentence was passed upon them. Reports afterwards reached England, that Sullivan had escaped from custody immediately upon his arrival in Sydney. It appears that he secreted himself on board a Dutch vessel bound for England. But the period during which he retained his freedom was short; for the captain discovering him, put back to Hobart Town, and he was conducted to a place called Goat Island, from which no subsequent effort enabled him to retreat.

JAMES PAGE,

TRANSPORTED FOR MALICIOUSLY WOUNDING CATTLE.

As yet we have presented our readers with no instance of the conviction of a prisoner for the offence of maiming cattle. The case of James Page is worthy of observation.

He was indicted at the Bedford assizes, on Wednesday, the 16th of July, 1834, for maliciously and feloniously wounding three cows and a mare, the property of Mr. William George, a farmer at Houghton Conquest, on the previous 1st of May. The prisoner was a pauper of the parish of which the prosecutor was overseer; and, having applied for relief, was set to break stones on the roads. This employment seemed to produce an ill feeling in his mind towards Mr. George, and he was heard to express his dissatisfaction. On the night of the 30th of April, Mr. George's cattle were placed in a particular field in his farm in good health and condition, but in the morning, at four o'clock, three fine cows and a mare were found to have been hamstrung, and so severely injured as to render it necessary that they should all be killed. The evidence by which this offence was brought home to the prisoner consisted of the repetition of observations made by him, subsequent to the 1st of May, in reference to the act, and the testimony of one Chappell, to whom the prisoner had proposed that he should accompany him to execute his base purpose.

The prisoner was found " Guilty," and sentenced to be transported for life.

HENRY WILLIAMS,

TRANSPORTED FOR BURGLARY.

THIS man had been tried at the Central Criminal Court Sessions, in the month of July, 1836, for a burglary at Islington, and being convicted was sentenced to death, according to the then existing law.

The prisoner, it appears, had been brought up to the trade of a sweep; but, naturally disinclined to follow a steady and honest course of life, he quitted the business to which he had been educated, and made his aptitude for it subservient to a new avocation. He joined with a gang of fellows of bad character, who pursued a system of plunder to gain a livelihood, and with them he adopted a means of effecting robberies, as remarkable as it was novel. Procuring access to the roof of an empty house, they would fix upon some other house in the row, from which they might hope to obtain a good booty, and one of them descending the chimney, would generally succeed in carrying off such a prize as well repaid his daring. The burglary for which Williams was committed, however, was one of an ordinary character; but while in gaol he still found his climbing powers of use to him. It appears that he was confined in the condemned yard, with two other prisoners; and on the 26th of July, the day of his escape, while his companions were reading in the room appropriated to their use, he managed to work his way to the roof of the gaol by means of his hand, back, and knees, sweep-like, up the angular corner of the building. The ascent, to a person of his accomplishment in this particular line, was comparatively easy, by reason of the roughness of the face of the wall, and he soon gained the top of the building, in spite of all the obstacles, in the shape of chevaux-de-frise and iron spikes, which presented themselves. To traverse the roof of the prison and gain the houses in Warwick-lane, was the work of a very few minutes; and availing himself of an open skylight, he dropped through it. To his astonishment, he found himself confronted with a woman who was at work in the room into which he had fallen; but, speedily taking advantage of her alarm, he slipped past her, and had reached the open street before she had time to recover her scattered senses, or to give any intimation of her fright to the other occupants of the house.

His want of means of support, or his unfortunate disinclination for an honest life, soon again placed him in the custody of his late keeper, Mr. Cope, the governor of Newgate. Within a fortnight after his escape, Mr. Cope received an intimation that he was in Winchester gaol, upon a new charge of burglary, committed since he had gained his liberty in the extraordinary manner which we have described. He, in consequence, proceeded to that place to receive his prisoner back into his custody, and in a few days Williams was once again lodged in his old quarters.

A humane consideration of his case subsequently procured for him a commutation of his punishment to transportation for life.

JOHN TOMS, *alias* SIR WILLIAM COURTENAY,

AND

𝕿𝖍𝖊 𝕮𝖆𝖓𝖙𝖊𝖗𝖇𝖚𝖗𝖞 𝕴𝖓𝖘𝖚𝖗𝖗𝖊𝖈𝖙𝖎𝖔𝖓.

THIS extraordinary person, whose evident insanity led to a most lamentable effusion of blood, first appeared at Canterbury about Michaelmas of the year 1832. The first rumour of him was, that an eccentric character was living at the Rose Inn, who passed under the name of Count Rothschild, but had who been recently known in London by the name of Thompson. His countenance and costume denoted foreign extraction, while his language and conversation showed that he was well acquainted with almost every part of the kingdom. About the period of his first attracting notice, a large political dinner was given to the poorer classes of Reformers, in a field near the Dane John; and here he first betrayed symptoms of a most violent and outrageous disposition. As the general election approached, in December of the same year, he became highly attractive to the lower orders, by assuming costumes of a most extravagant character— by theatrical displays of himself from the balcony in front of the Rose Inn—and by riding through the streets on horseback and in carriages, generally attended by two young men of the names of Robinson and Denne. From the latter gentleman, whose friends were very respectable and resided in the neighbourhood, he succeeded in obtaining considerable sums of money. He continued to harangue the populace daily with novel and ludicrous addresses, encased in a superb dress of crimson velvet, richly ornamented with gold lacings, tassels, and gold epaulets, and armed with a valuable sword and dagger, with which he occasionally used to menace any person who interrupted him. His dress was stated to have cost upwards of £200, and to have been made for him while he was at the Clarendon Hotel, in London, a short time before he made his appearance at Canterbury. At the election of knights of the shire for the eastern division of Kent, he offered himself as a candidate, under the appellation of Sir William Honeywood Courtenay, Knight of Malta, &c., and was proposed by Mr. Denne, and seconded by Mr. Chapman, a baker of Canterbury. At the nomination on Barham Downs, he acted in the most extravagant manner, and upon this occasion he polled but two or three votes. He then immediately offered himself a candidate for the city of Canterbury, and succeeded so well, that he obtained upwards of 400 votes during the contest. His promises and addresses were of the most absurd description; yet, from the fineness of his figure and person, his richness of costume, and broad assertions of intimate acquaintance with royalty and persons of distinction, he succeeded in duping numbers even of respectable people. It was the Tory and agricultural party that supported him. The whole affair would be extremely amusing, if it were not for the melancholy reflection, that in the 19th century 400 individuals could be found, in one of the oldest and largest cities in England, weak enough to place serious trust in such a man as Toms at any period must have appeared to thinking or educated persons.

After striving to possess himself of a seat in parliament, or at least a return as having been elected for one, he appears to have studied with much more ardour and vigilance than before to captivate the affections of the lower orders of the people. He made it known that his condescension was as great as his rank and wealth, and he should be willing to accept of invitations to visit the humblest families—to eat and drink at the peasant's and labourer's table—to make one of a larger or smaller party at the lowest public-house—to enrol his name in the meanest society, and to have it published abroad that Sir William Courtenay preferred being the companion of the cottager and the friend of the poor. It is easy to conclude that such intelligence charmed many hearts, and obtained entreaties for his company from every quarter. So numerous were his engagements, that he was obliged to run or ride from house to house, taking a slight repast at each, and generally concluding the day at a banquet prepared by a number of his new friends in some obscure club-room. The condescension of Sir William did not stop here: it is now known to have been his practice to dispatch the husband to the beer shop, whilst he occupied his place at home, and it is even said that there was scarcely a woman in a village wherein he passed much of his time, who had not sacrificed her honour to the prevailing infatuation for Courtenay.

After his defeat at Canterbury he published, for several weeks, a newspaper, called *The Lion of England*, full of wild declamation, asserting in the boldest terms the rights of the poor; and he continued to act in this way, assisted by people whose hearts he had won with loans of money from time to time, until the period when he was arraigned at Maidstone assizes for the crime of perjury, arising out of the following circumstances:—In the month of February an action took place between her Majesty's sloop Lively, a revenue cruiser, and a smuggling boat called the Admiral Hood, near the Goodwin Sands, which ended in the capture of the latter, which, with the crew, was taken to Rochester for adjudication. On boarding the smuggler no contraband goods were found; but, during the chase, she had been distinctly seen by the Lively throwing tubs overboard, and some of them were marked and picked up by the crew of the cruiser. On the examination of the smugglers before the magistrates at Rochester, Sir William Courtenay made his appearance, attired in a grotesque costume, and having a small scymitar suspended from his neck by a massive gold chain. On one of the men being examined, Sir William became his advocate; but the man being convicted, a professional gentleman from London defended the next, and Sir William presented himself as a witness; when he swore that he saw the whole transaction between the Lively and the Admiral Hood, and was positive that the tubs, stated to have come from the Admiral Hood, had been floating about in the sea all the morning, and were not thrown overboard from that vessel. The object of this statement was evidently to prove that the Admiral Hood was not a smuggler, and consequently to procure the liberation of the men. The solicitor for the Customs, having undoubted evidence that this testimony was false, determined to proceed against an individual who had been guilty of such a daring act of perjury. The trial came on at Maidstone before Mr. Justice Parke, on the 25th of July, 1833, when he was found guilty of wilful and corrupt perjury, and sentenced to imprisonment in gaol for three calendar months, and at the expiration of that term to be transported to such place beyond the seas as his Majesty by the advice of his Privy Council should direct, for the term of seven years. Before, however, the three months' imprisonment had expired, it was found that Sir William was completely out of his senses; the sentence appears to have been annulled; and he was sent to the Kent Lunatic Asylum, at Barming, where he was confined until a few months previous to the catastrophe we are about to narrate.

He subsequently resided with Mr. Francis, a farmer at Boughton, nearly adjoining the London road, and for some time was apparently in a very tranquil state. From the house of this gentleman he removed to the cottage of a rustic named Wills, and then to a lone farm-house on the left-hand top of Boughton-hill, rented by Culver, about five miles from Canterbury. Here he declaimed, among the rustics in the adjoining villages, against the operation of the poor-laws, and the grievances under which they laboured, until at length he led them into the lawless and horrible scene of bloodshed which we are about to narrate.

On Monday, May 28, 1838, he met several of them at Boughton, and, after purchasing bread, they went to Fairbrook, increasing in numbers. Parading a loaf on a pole, with flags and a lion (his old device) exhibited in front of the procession, they continued to go on to the village of Goodnestone, near Faversham, increasing in numbers and excitement, having made one attempt to put a match to a bean-stack, talking and threatening in the most dreadful language of bloody work, and Courtenay saying repeatedly, he would himself ' strike the bloody blow.' They then went to Herne-hill, and obtained some refreshment, and thence to Dargate-common, a straggling hamlet of labourers' cottages, where Toms divested himself of his shoes. At this place he and his poor followers went on their knees, while he prayed for half an hour; and night coming on, he and a great number of them went to Bossenden-farm and had supper, and many of them slept in a barn. At daylight on Tuesday morning they mustered, and went to Sittingbourne, nine miles distant, to breakfast, Sir William paying £1. 5s. for breakfast. They then marched to the villages of Newnham, Eastling, Throwley, Seldwich, Lees, and Selling, occasionally getting refreshment, and progressively increasing in numbers, the leader at times addressing their poor deluded creatures, and holding out inducements to create a riot. At night they retreated to a chalk-pit; and after parading through this district the following day (Wednesday), in the evening they returned to Culver's farm, at Bossenden, close to the scene of the dreadful tragedy.

A farmer under the hill, Mr. Curling, having had his men seduced from their employment, made an application for their apprehension; and a constable of the name of Mears, assisted by two others, one a relation, proceeded on Thursday morning to Bossenden, to execute

his mission.   After a litttle parley, Courtenay, while they were
arguing, inquired which was the constable, and, on the young man
replying he was, he immediately produced a pistol and shot him.   The
two other constables, seeing that it would be madness for them to
interfere against so large a gang, immediately rode back to the magistrates, and narrated the facts, when expresses were sent to Canterbury,
and to Dr. Poore, an active magistrate of the neighbourhood.   The
country was now in a state of great alarm and excitement, and it was
deemed expedient by the magistrates to call in the military, who were
first sent for from Maidstone ; but the party bearing only the verbal
message of the magistrates, the commanding officer did not feel himself
at liberty to act without more formal orders.   Ultimately, a party of
100 soldiers was procured at Canterbury, who were immediately sent off
in coaches and vans, under the command of Lieutenant Bennett, of the
45th regiment.

On their arrival at the scene of bloodshed, the magistrates entreated
the people to disperse; and, on their positive refusal, the Riot Act was
read.   By this time the whole party had retreated to a deep and seques-
tered part of the wood, known as the Osier-bed ; and here Sir William
shouted and encouraged his adherents to behave like men, and excited
them to desperate fury, he having, in the interim between the first
murder and the arrival of the military, shot at the Rev. Charles Hand-
ley, of Herne Hill, who, with his brother, was assisting to take him into
custody.   Sir William, on perceiving his opponents, advanced with the
greatest *sang froid*, and deliberately shot Lieutenant Bennett, who
was in advance of his party, and who fell dead upon the spot.   Courtenay
and the party round him were immediately fired upon by the military,
and Sir William was one of the first killed, almost at the point of the
bayonets.   Several of his misguided followers also fell dead at the
discharge, and others were wounded ; the principals were immediately
secured, and those not hurt were marched under escort to St. Augus-
tine's gaol.   The excitement at the fall of the two principals, and the
short struggle that followed, was savagely dreadful ; the labourers being
all armed, principally with huge bludgeons.   Thus, in a few moments,
ten lives were sacrificed, and several rendered cripples for the remainder
of their days.

After the inquest on the bodies, and a lengthened inquiry before the
magistrates, the prisoners were brought to trial at the Maidstone assizes,
on Thursday, August 9th, 1838.   As might have been expected, the
trial excited immense interest, and the court-house was crowded.

William Price, aged thirty, and Thomas Mears, alias Tyler, aged
twenty-nine, were first put to the bar, charged with the murder of
Nicholas Mears, the officer.   The indictment contained two counts—the
first charging the deceased Toms as principal in the murder in the first
degree, and the prisoners as principals in the second degree ; the second
charged all parties as equally principals.   Mr. Shee made an ingenious
address to the jury on behalf of the prisoners, in which he laid down
the doctrine, acquiesced in by Lord Denman, who presided, that no
second person could be responsible for the act of a madman ; and that

therefore, to make out the charge contained in the first count, of being accessary with Courtenay, it was essential to show that Toms was a person capable of distinguishing between right and wrong. Upon the second count, however, the learned judge repeated the established axiom, that where parties are banded together for a common and illegal object, and murder ensues, they are all principals; and upon this count the prisoners were found guilty.

On the following day, the 10th, Mears was arraigned for the murder of Lieutenant Bennett, in conjunction with William Wills, aged forty-six; Edward Wraight, jun., thirty-three; Alexander Foad, forty-two; Edward Curling, thirty-three; Thomas Griggs, thirty; Richard Foreman, thirty; Charles Hills, forty-seven; and William Foad. Under the advice of their counsel, they severally pleaded guilty; and, after numerous testimonials to their general good character from the clergyman of Herne Hill, and other persons of high respectability residing in the neighbourhood, Lord Denman passed sentence of death on them, but followed it immediately with an intimation that the sentence would not be carried into effect. " I have, however," said his lordship, " had very great difficulty in coming to this conclusion. The offence of which you have been guilty is so enormous, and, along with the fanaticism that has marked it, there has been so much of bad feeling, so much of recklessness and disregard of the quiet and happiness of your fellow creatures, that I have felt the extension of mercy to be a very strong act on my part. Two circumstances have weighed with me very considerably in the conclusion I have come to. One is, that some of the principal delinquents in this gross outrage have already met their punishment in their death—a very considerable number of your misguided fellow-men having actually fallen under the execution of those who were called on to protect and support the law. Another circumstance is, that the relations and friends of the unfortunate young man, the officer who was shot by the leader whom you thought proper to maintain in the violation of the law, have stated, that it would be the greatest aggravation of their sufferings if any more blood should be spilled in consequence of this unhappy affair; and I do feel that there is much respect due to the feelings of those unfortunate persons. Nevertheless, while I have thus determined that the last punishment of the law shall not take effect upon you, it is absolutely necessary that the next example, in point of severity, should be made on some of those who now appear before me. Thomas Mears, otherwise Thomas Tyler, was not only extremely active in exposing the unfortunate man, his near relation, to the shot by which he lost his life, but remained for one whole day afterwards in the company of his fanatic leader, encouraging him in all the violence which he knew him to be so capable of committing. He cannot, therefore, be allowed to remain longer among that society where he has made himself so unfavourably known. In the case of Wills, also, from circumstances that have transpired—from his being better educated, and from his moving in a sphere somewhat higher in society, it will be impossible not to come to the same conclusion."— The other prisoners were subjected to various periods of imprisonment.

It is an extraordinary fact connected with this strange drama, that even up to the period of the trial, and when the grave absolutely yawned beneath them, some of the prisoners were still understood to cling to the fanaticism that had led them into crime; and the evidence of a female relative of one of them was given in a way that bespoke the faith strong within her.

We cannot better bring to a close our somewhat lengthened narative of these memorable Canterbury riots than by quoting a few passages from the address of the Lord Chief Justice to the grand jury, on directing their attention to the case :—

" If it is the credulity arising from extreme ignorance which has made these unfortunate men the dupes of one himself not under the guidance of reason, it is urgently necessary that the country should apply itself to the discovery of some remedy for an evil so great and alarming. Should it appear that ignorance has been the cause of these unfortunate men being so easily led astray, I trust that we shall all admit the necessity there exists for the most strenuous efforts on our parts to secure a better state of things, and thereby lay a foundation for a better observance and obedience of the laws. If the minds of these poor men had been properly directed, or if they had enjoyed a higher degree of intelligence, it would, to a considerable extent, if not entirely, have tended to the defeat of the strange delusions under which they appear at the time to have been labouring. If this prove to be the case—if the mischiefs which have taken place have arisen from the absence of a proper cultivation of the mind,—there is no one who will not readily join in attempting the improvement which might materially be effected by inculcating the great truths of religious morality, and teaching them to understand and reason on the occurrences passing around them. In my opinion, too, opportunities may arise of introducing into the pastimes of the people such a spirit of cheerfulness and interest, as may have the effect of laying the foundation for weaning them from the dangerous and delusive inclinations they seem to have existing among them."

JAMES HILLS, WILLIAM HARLEY, AND WILLIAM FISHER (*alias* CURLEY BILL),

TRIED FOR BURGLARY.

THIS burglary was marked by circumstances of very considerable peculiarity.

The men whose names appear at the head of this article were indicted at the Kingston Assizes, on Thursday the 31st of March, 1836, for a burglary in the house of Mrs. Mary Anne Long, at Chipstead, in Surrey, on the night of the 2nd of September, 1835, and for stealing therefrom various articles of property.

The circumstances attending the robbery were well described by Mrs. Long at the trial. She said, " I am sixty-six years of age, a widow, and reside, with my sister, Mrs. Scholefield, at Mint House, Chipstead, which is a lone house, situate between Gatton and Reigate. On the night of the 2nd of September last, I, Mrs. Scholefield, my son (Mr. Rankin), and a female servant, were the only inmates. We retired to bed, after having seen that all the premises were properly fastened. I slept with my sister; and about ten minutes past one in the morning I was awoke by hearing the dog, which was kept in the yard, barking violently. I got up, and opened the bed-room window, and thinking that some persons were about the premises, I hallooed out that they had better keep out of the way, or I would put a bullet into their stomach, which was not a pleasant thing. I did so to intimidate them, and then retired to bed. Shortly after I heard a noise, and again got up. On going to the window, I saw a man trying to get in; he had smashed the pane, and was armed with a stake. I seized hold of the stake, and tried to wrest it from him; but he was too strong for me, and struck me a violent blow on the head, inflicting a wound of an inch and a half in length; he also struck me on the shoulder and hand, of which I lost the use for some time. I then called to my nephew, Mr. Rankin, and he came armed with a cutlass; he made a cut at the man; but the night being very dark, and there being railings at the window, he missed him, and he got down the ladder and went away. I then lit three or four candles, and went down stairs for my nephew's gun. I brought it up; but recollecting that I had left the powder and ammunition, I again went down for it, and locked the pantry-door after me. I returned up stairs, and my nephew loaded the gun. About a half or three-quarters of an hour afterwards we heard a great noise outside the house, and the panel of the south door looking out upon a meadow was smashed in. We heard the voices of six or seven men, who entered the house; they remained down stairs three-quarters of an hour. I slept in a room at the end of a passage, and my nephew's bed-room was opposite; there is a door at the top of the passage leading down the stairs. We placed ourselves in the passage; we then heard one of the men say, ' Now we will go up stairs,' and I heard what I supposed to be a man crawling on his hands and knees—I judged so from the scraping his toes made along the floor-cloth. Mrs. Scholefield was very much alarmed, and cried out for mercy; the men said, ' Give us £50, or £30, or £20 ;' I told them that all my money was in the bank, and my plate at my banker's; one of the men said, ' I will murder you ;' and another man said, ' We will murder you all.' They then forced in the panel of the door, and a man at the bottom of the stairs said, ' Go it, my boys.' Mr. Rankin dropped on his knee, and presented the gun through the panel; I could only see the rim of the hat of a man who appeared to be stooping down. Mr. Rankin fired, and the men fell back, and the candle went out. They all then went away. We waited for some time, and the dog having ceased barking, I and my nephew proceeded down stairs, he armed with a gun, and I carrying the cutlass; we fastened up the door as well as we could, and then went into the parlour, and found that the men had drunk two bottles of wine; we also found the cores of fourteen apples; they had taken away a watch, some cruet-frames, and other articles."

This statement of facts was corroborated by the testimony of Mrs. Scholefield and Mr. Rankin, who added their positive declaration as to the identity of the prisoners Hills and Harley. The former was the man who had been shot; and on his being taken into custody, shot of the same description as that which had been fired from the gun by Mr. Rankin were found in his breast. Fisher had been apprehended at the same time, and in company with the other prisoners; but there appeared to be considerable doubt whether he had been personally concerned in the burglary.

The jury found Hills and Harley " Guilty," but acquitted Fisher.

Mr. Justice Vaughan, in passing sentence of death upon the prisoners, remarked upon the great courage which had been displayed by Mrs. Long and Mr. Rankin, and directed that they should receive a reward as a mark of the high estimation in which he held their conduct.

After their conviction the prisoners were removed to Horsemonger-lane Gaol, where they paid the most assiduous attention to the spiritual consolation offered to them by the Rev. Mr. Mann, the chaplain.

On Monday, the 11th of April, the last sentence of the law was carried into execution upon the person of the convict Harley, a respite during pleasure having been granted on the previous day in the case of his fellow-convict Hills. The convict maintained a deportment of great firmness, unmixed, however, with any symptoms of bravado, or unnatural courage. He appeared sincerely penitent, and met his fate with becoming resignation.

The sentence of Hills was eventually commuted to transportation for life, in consequence of some favourable circumstances which transpired.

Both convicts were men of an inferior station, but there was good reason to believe that in the course of their lives they had been guilty of more than one offence of considerable enormity.

CHARLES SAMUEL BARTLETT,

EXECUTED FOR MURDER.

AT the Gloucester Assizes, on Thursday the 6th of April, 1837, Charles Samuel Bartlett was indicted for the wilful murder of Mary Lewis, his mother-in-law, on the 10th of September in the previous year, at Stapleton, near Bristol.

The circumstances, which were detailed by a great number of witnesses, were these:—The prisoner was a young man of decent parentage and education, but of a somewhat dissipated disposition; and he had followed a wandering life as a member of a strolling company of players, called Ingleby's Company, frequenting fairs, race-courses, and other such places of entertainment. In the month of August, 1836, he visited Monmouth with his troop; and having become acquainted with the daughter of a shoemaker named Lewis, he was married to her. He received £45 as her wedding portion, with the promise of a further sum upon the death of her father; and, after a short sojourn with his wife's friends, he proceeded to join his party. On the 5th of September, hearing that her daughter and son-in-law were at Bristol, Mrs. Lewis went to see them, and she visited them there repeatedly, the prisoner being engaged in the usual manner in attending the fair. On the 9th of September, Bartlett was seen in the possession of a horse-pistol; and he sent a boy to purchase powder and percussion caps, and the boy saw him roll up a piece of lead in the form of a bullet. Previously to this he and his mother-in-law had had some difference; but on Saturday, the 10th of September, they quitted his lodgings together, and were seen walking on the Stapleton-road. They entered the Mason's Arms, and partook of some refreshment; and, while there, Bartlett borrowed a knife from the landlady, saying that he wanted to cut a piece of wood. He went out to the back yard with it where the firewood was kept; and, on his return to the house, he was observed to be agitated, and he strove to conceal his features. Having then paid for the liquor which they had had, he and Mrs. Lewis went away, and they were seen to turn down a place called Tebbutt's-lane, leading towards the river Frome. Soon afterwards a shot was heard; and within an hour the murdered body of Mrs. Lewis was discovered stretched on the ground. Her dress was disordered, her bonnet and shawl had been torn from her person, and one of her legs was found doubled under her, as if in the agonies of death. She was instantly conveyed to the Mason's Arms; and, upon an examination of her person, she was found to have been shot through the back part of her head, the ball having passed through her bonnet. Bartlett went to the Mason's Arms to see the body; and, on being introduced to the room where it lay, he exclaimed, with affected surprise, " Good God! it is my mother-in-law!" Suspicion had already attached to him, and he was now taken into custody; and, upon his lodgings being searched, a pistol was found which had been recently discharged, together with a piece of wood newly cut into the form of a ramrod. The evidence extended to the most minute particulars in reference to the transaction; and the chain of proof appeared to leave no possible doubt of the guilt of the prisoner.

The defence which was set up was, that Bartlett had left his mother-in-law immediately on his quitting the Mason's Arms, and that the pistol which had been found at his lodgings was one which he had been in the habit of discharging at the fairs, in order to attract attention to his employer's booth.

The trial lasted during the whole of two days, and then a verdict of " Guilty " was returned. Upon the unhappy man being called up for judgment, he threw himself into a theatrical attitude, and delivered a set speech of some length, which was distinguished by great force and vehemence both of style and manner, and produced an extremely strong and painful sensation throughout the court. He stated, in sub-stance, that he should meet his death with firmness and resignation, protesting his innocence even in his dying moments, and calling upon God to visit with his awful retribution the murderer of his mother-in-law. Sentence of death was then passed, and the prisoner was removed from the bar.

On Saturday, the 15th of April, the sentence of the law was carried into effect upon the wretched criminal. He had been visited by the clergymen of the gaol, but they could not succeed in making any im-pression on him; and although in his demeanour he was serious and respectful, he remained firm and prompt in his denial of the existence of any circumstances from which an inference of his guilt or even guilty knowledge could be drawn.

Throughout the whole of the preparations for his execution he main-tained his characteristic steadiness. Before, however, he paid the last penalty of the law, he spoke to the assembled crowd in a calm and im-pressive manner as follows :—

" Englishmen and fellow-countrymen,—I have a few words to say to you—and they shall be but very few. Yet let me entreat you, one and all, that the few words that I shall utter may strike deep into your hearts. Bear them in your mind, not only now while you are witnessing this sad scene, but take them to your homes—take them and repeat them to your children and friends—I implore you, as a dying man, one for whom the instrument of death is even now prepared; and these words are, that you may loose yourselves from the love of this deceitful world, and its vain pleasures. Think less of it, and more of your God. Do this; repent! repent! for be assured that without deep and true repentance, without turning to your heavenly Father, you will never attain, or can hold the slightest hope of ever reaching, those bowers of bliss and that land of peace to which I trust I am now fast advancing.— I will say a few more words. All good Christians and repentant men, that behold my disgrace here, shall—at least I trust they will—behold my glory hereafter; and my last words are—I am an injured man!"

The cap was then drawn over his face, and in a few moments the drop fell from under his feet, and he ceased to exist.

GEORGE DARWELL,

CONVICTED OF EMBEZZLEMENT.

THE scene of this very extraordinary case was Liverpool, where Darwell had for a considerable time occupied the situation of confidential clerk to Mr. Wolstenholme, a cotton-broker of that city. On Saturday the 14th of October, 1837, he was taken, in the custody of Whitty, a police-officer, before Mr. Hall, the chief magistrate of Liverpool, charged with having embezzled sums of money amounting to £8264, the property of his employer; and at the same time a fat and somewhat vulgar woman, named Frances M'Lean (*alias* Flood, *alias* Butler), and Richard M'Lean, were charged with having participated in the proceeds of the robbery.

The circumstances of the case were remarkable, and afford a striking instance of the extent of delinquency which may be produced by the commission of one error. Darwell was about fifty years of age, and it appeared that some years before his apprehension he had formed an intimacy with Mrs. M'Lean, the result of which was the birth of an infant. Alarmed for the effects which a public knowledge of this circumstance might produce upon his character, he was induced to hand over to her various sums of money, to secure her silence as to the paternity of her child; and, his own means being exhausted, he at length gave her money which was the property of his employer. Having thus taken one false step, every month served to increase his difficulties; and the constant demands which were made upon him, accompanied by threats of exposure if they were not complied with, in the course of time, drew from him sums of money to a very considerable amount, until at length he had appropriated money to the extent of upwards of £8000 of his master's property. The abstraction of so large an amount, it may be presumed, could not long remain undiscovered; and at length Whitty, having received certain information upon the subject, took the prisoner into custody. Darwell at once candidly confessed to him his criminality, and explained to him the manner in which he had disposed of the money; informing him at the same time that he would find Mrs. M'Lean residing in Junction-street, Manchester. Whitty, in consequence, proceeded thither, and finding the male prisoner M'Lean, he demanded to know whether he was acquainted with a person named Darwell? He answered in the negative: but the officer having searched the house, found a great number of documents in the handwriting of Darwell, which appeared to be letters in which money had been transmitted to the female prisoner. M'Lean, it was ascertained, had been recently married to the woman, and it was also found that he had engaged largely in the business of brick-making, and had a stock valued at between £2000 and £3000. Mrs. M'Lean was not then in the house; and, upon his return to Liverpool, Whitty found that she had just before arrived there, having started upon another expedition to procure **money** from Darwell. Upon his finding her, he acquainted her with the fact of the apprehension of Darwell, when she declared her regret for what had occurred, and admitted that she had received about £8000 from him; but assured the officer, that she had always believed that the money belonged to Darwell himself, whom she took to be a person of property. She expressed her willingness to give up all that she retained, but asserted her innocence of any felonious intention. The officer added, in his evidence, that he had found books in the possession of the female prisoner, in which the amounts which she had received from Darwell were regularly entered and posted up; and he ascertained from them, that since the preceding Christmas he had paid her no less than £2273.

These were the main facts of the case; and a legal gentleman, who attended for the two M'Leans, contended that there was nothing in the evidence to implicate them in the felonious charge. The prisoners were all remanded; but, after another examination, the M'Leans were set at liberty, and Darwell was committed for trial.

Between the period of the inquiry before the magistrates and the final investigation of the case before the jury, upwards of £5000 was given up by the M'Leans to Mr. Wolstenholme; and a singular circumstance in the transaction was elicited, in the fact that Mrs. M'Lean, at the very time at which she was so unscrupulously receiving such large sums from Darwell, was in the possession of a handsome annuity, granted to her by a merchant resident in America, in respect of the same child, which had been the cause of the unfortunate Darwell's crime.

At the Liverpool sessions, on Friday the 27th of October, Darwell was put upon his trial. The facts of the case were clear and uncontradicted, and a verdict of " Guilty " was returned. Mr. Wolstenholme recommended the convict to the mercy of the court; and in consideration of the atonement which he had made, by his confession and interference to procure the return of the money, he was sentenced to twelve months imprisonment only.

INDEX.

———

THE END.

PRINTED BY R. MACDONALD, 30, GREAT SUTTON STREET, CLERKENWELL.

www.ingramcontent.com/pod-product-compliance
Lightning Source LLC
Chambersburg PA
CBHW080857020726
47502CB00008B/2268